At the Back
of the North Wind

The Princess and the Goblin

The Princess and Curdie

George MacDonald

At the Back
of the North Wind

Page 5

The Princess
and the Goblin

Page 295

The Princess
and Curdie

Page 461

George MacDonald

George MacDonald, poet and novelist, was born in 1824 in Aberdeenshire, Scotland, and was educated in Aberdeen and later in London. He spent a few years as a Congregational Minister until his health prevented him from continuing and he turned to writing full time. He was happily married and had eleven children; Lewis Carroll and other literary figures of the time were among his friends.

George MacDonald wrote over fifty books and collections of poems, most of which dealt with the mystical and philosophical and are now hardly remembered although two of his tales for adults, *Phantastes* and *Lilith* are still well known.

He is principally remembered for his children's books; the most famous of which are included in this volume. *The Light Princess and Other Stories* was published in 1867 in *Dealings with Fairies*; *At the Back of the North Wind* and *The Princess and the Goblin* first appeared in the magazine 'Good Words for the Young' of which MacDonald was the sole editor for a time, and were then published in 1870 and 1871 respectively. *The Princess and Curdie* did not appear in book form until 1882.

George MacDonald died in 1905.

This edition first published in Great Britain in 1979 by
Octopus Books Limited
59 Grosvenor Street London W1

ISBN 0 7064 1054 8

Filmset in Great Britain by
Northumberland Press Ltd, Gateshead, Tyne and Wear
Printed in Czechoslovakia
50376

At the Back
of the North Wind

At the Back of the North Wind

With the original illustrations by

Arthur Hughes

after Dalziel

George MacDonald

Contents

1 The Hay-Loft

I have been asked to tell you about the back of the North Wind. An old Greek writer mentions a people who lived there, and were so comfortable that they could not bear it any longer, and drowned themselves. My story is not the same as his. I do not think Herodotus had got the right account of the place. I am going to tell you how it fared with a boy who went there.

He lived in a low room over a coach-house; and that was not by any means at the back of the North Wind, as his mother very well knew. For one side of the room was built only of boards, and the boards were so old that you might run a penknife through into the north wind. And then let them settle between them which was the sharper! I know that when you pulled it out again the wind would be after it like a cat after a mouse, and you would know soon enough you were *not* at the back of the North Wind. Still, this room was not very cold, except when the north wind blew stronger than usual: the room I have to do with now was always cold, except in summer, when the sun took the matter into his own hands. Indeed, I am not sure whether I ought to call it a room at all; for it was just a loft where they kept hay and straw and oats for the horses. And when little Diamond—— but stop: I must tell you that his father, who was a coachman, had named him after a favourite horse, and his mother had had no objection:– when little Diamond then lay there in bed, he could hear the horses under him munching away in the dark, or moving sleepily in their dreams. For Diamond's father had built him a bed in the loft with boards all round it, because they had so little room in their own end over the coach-house; and Diamond's father put old Diamond in the stall under the bed, because he was a quiet horse, and did not go to sleep standing, but lay down like a reasonable creature. But, although he was a surprisingly reasonable

creature, yet, when young Diamond woke in the middle of the night, and felt the bed shaking in the blasts of the north wind, he could not help wondering whether, if the wind should blow the house down, and he were to fall through into the manger, old Diamond mightn't eat him up before he knew him in his night-gown. And although old Diamond was very quiet all night long, yet when he woke he got up like an earthquake, and then young Diamond knew what o'clock it was, or at least what was to be done next, which was – to go to sleep again as fast as he could.

There was hay at his feet and hay at his head, piled up in great trusses to the very roof. Indeed it was sometimes only through a little lane with several turnings, which looked as if it had been sawn out for him, that the could reach his bed at all. For the stock of hay was, of course, always in a state of slow ebb or of sudden flow. Sometimes the whole space of the loft, with the little panes in the roof for the stars to look in, would lie open before his open eyes as he lay in bed; sometimes a yellow wall of sweet-smelling fibres closed up his view at the distance of half a yard. Sometimes, when his mother had undressed him in her room, and told him to trot away to bed by himself, he would creep into the heart of the hay, and lie there thinking how cold it was outside in the wind, and how warm it was inside there in his bed, and how he could go to it when he pleased, only he wouldn't just yet; he would get a little colder first. And ever as he grew colder, his bed would grow warmer, till at last he would scramble out of the hay, shoot like an arrow into his bed, cover himself up, and snuggle down, thinking what a happy boy he was. He had not the least idea that the wind got in at a chink in the wall, and blew about him all night. For the back of his bed was only of boards an inch thick, and on the other side of them was the north wind.

Now, as I have already said, these boards were soft and crumbly. To be sure, they were tarred on the outside, yet in many places they were more like tinder than timber. Hence it happened that the soft part having worn away from about it, little Diamond found one night, after he lay down, that a knot had come out of one of them, and that the wind was blowing in upon him in a cold and rather imperious fashion. Now he had no fancy for leaving things wrong that might be set right; so he jumped out of bed again, got a little strike of hay, twisted it up, folded it in the middle, and, having thus made it into a cork, stuck it into the hole in the wall. But the wind began to blow loud and angrily, and, as Diamond was falling asleep, out blew his cork and hit him on the nose, just hard enough to wake him up quite, and let him hear the wind whistling shrill in the hole. He searched for his hay-cork, found it, stuck it in harder, and was just dropping off once more, when, pop! with an angry whistle behind it, the cork struck him again, this time on the cheek. Up he rose once more, made a fresh stopple of hay, and corked the hole severely. But he was hardly down again before – pop! it came on his forehead. He gave it up, drew the clothes above his head, and was soon fast asleep.

Although the next day was very stormy, Diamond forgot all about the hole, for he was busy making a cave by the side of his mother's fire with a broken chair, a three-legged stool, and a blanket, and then sitting in it. His mother, however, discovered it, and pasted a bit of brown paper over it, so that, when Diamond had snuggled down the next night, he had no occasion to think of it.

Presently, however, he lifted his head and listened. Who could that be talking to him? The wind was rising again, and getting very loud, and full of rushes and whistles. He was sure some one was talking – and

very near him too it was. But he was not frightened, for he had not yet learned how to be; so he sat up and hearkened. At last the voice, which, though quite gentle, sounded a little angry, appeared to come from the back of the bed. He crept nearer to it, and laid his ear against the wall. Then he heard nothing but the wind, which sounded very loud indeed. The moment, however, that he moved his head from the wall, he heard the voice again, close to his ear. He felt about with his hand, and came upon the piece of paper his mother had pasted over the hole. Against this he laid his ear, and then he heard the voice quite distinctly. There was, in fact, a little corner of the paper loose, and through that, as from a mouth in the wall, the voice came.

'What do you mean, little boy, closing up my window?'

'What window?' asked Diamond.

'You stuffed hay into it three times last night. I had to blow it out again three times.'

'You can't mean this little hole! It isn't a window; it's a hole in my bed.'

'I did not say it was *a* window: I said it was *my* window.'

'But it can't be a window, because windows are holes to see out of.'

'Well, that's just what I made this window for.'

'But you are outside: you can't want a window.'

'You are quite mistaken. Windows are to see out of, you say. Well, I'm in my house, and I want windows to see out of it.'

'But you've made a window into my bed.'

'Well, your mother has got three windows into my dancing-room, and you have three into my garret.'

'But I heard father say, when my mother wanted him to make a window through the wall, that it was against the law, for it would look into Mr. Dyves's garden.'

The voice laughed.

'The law would have some trouble to catch me!' it said.

'But if it's not right, you know,' said Diamond, 'that's no matter. You shouldn't do it.'

'I am so tall I am above *that* law,' said the voice.

'You must have a tall house, then,' said Diamond.

'Yes; a tall house: the clouds are inside it.'

'Dear me!' said Diamond, and thought a minute. 'I think, then, you can hardly expect me to keep a window in my bed for you. Why

don't you make a window into Mr. Dyves's bed?'

'Nobody makes a window into an ash-pit,' said the voice, rather sadly. 'I like to see nice things out of my windows.'

'But he must have a nicer bed than I have, though mine is *very* nice – so nice that I couldn't wish a better.'

'It's not the bed I care about: it's what is in it. – But you just open that window.'

'Well, mother says I shouldn't be disobliging; but it's rather hard. You see the north wind will blow right in my face if I do.'

'I am the North Wind.'

'O-o-oh!' said Diamond, thoughtfully. 'Then will you promise not to blow on my face if I open your window?'

'I can't promise that.'

'But you'll give me the toothache. Mother's got it already.'

'But what's to become of me without a window?'

'I'm sure I don't know. All I say is, it will be worse for me than for you.'

'No; it will not. You shall not be the worse for it – I promise you that. You will be much the better for it. Just you believe what I say, and do as I tell you.'

'Well, I *can* pull the clothes over my head,' said Diamond, and feeling with his little sharp nails, he got hold of the open edge of the paper and tore it off at once.

In came a long whistling spear of cold, and struck his little naked chest. He scrambled and tumbled in under the bed-clothes, and covered himself up: there was no paper now between him and the voice, and he felt a little – not frightened exactly – I told you he had not learned that yet – but rather queer; for what a strange person this North Wind must be that lived in the great house – 'called Out-of-Doors, I suppose,' thought Diamond – and made windows into people's beds! But the voice began again; and he could hear it quite plainly, even with his head under the bed clothes. It was a still more gentle voice now, although six times as large and loud as it had been, and he thought it sounded a little like his mother's.

'What is your name little boy?' it asked.

'Diamond,' answered Diamond, under the bed-clothes.

'What a funny name!'

'It's a very nice name,' returned its owner.

'I don't know that,' said the voice.

'Well, I do,' retorted Diamond, a little rudely.

'Do you know to whom you are speaking?'

'No,' said Diamond.

And indeed he did not. For to know a person's name is not always to know the person's self.

'Then I must not be angry with you. — You had better look and see, though.'

'Diamond is a very pretty name,' persisted the boy, vexed that it should not give satisfaction.

'Diamond is a useless thing rather,' said the voice.

'That's not true. Diamond is very nice — as big as two — and so quiet all night! And doesn't he make a jolly row in the morning, getting up on his four great legs! It's like thunder.'

'You don't seem to know what a diamond is.'

'Oh, don't I just! Diamond is a great and good horse; and he sleeps right under me. He is Old Diamond, and I am Young Diamond; or, if you like it better, for you're very particular, Mr. North Wind, he's Big Diamond, and I'm Little Diamond; and I don't know which of us my father likes best.'

A beautiful laugh, large but very soft and musical, sounded somewhere beside him, but Diamond kept his head under the clothes.

'I'm not Mr. North Wind,' said the voice.

'You told me that you were the North Wind,' insisted Diamond.

'I did not say *Mister* North Wind,' said the voice.

'Well, then, I do; for mother tells me I ought to be polite.'

'Then let me tell you I don't think it at all polite of you to say *Mister* to me.'

'Well, I didn't know better. I'm very sorry.'

'But you ought to know better.'

'I don't know that.'

'I do. You can't say it's polite to lie there talking — with your head under the bed-clothes, and never look up to see what kind of person you are talking to. — I want you to come out with me.'

'I want to to go to sleep,' said Diamond, very nearly crying, for he did not like to be scolded, even when he deserved it.

'You shall sleep all the better to-morrow night.'

'Besides,' said Diamond, 'you are out in Mr. Dyves's garden, and I

can't get there. I can only get into our own yard.'

'Will you take your head out of the bed-clothes?' said the voice, just a little angrily.

'No!' answered Diamond, half peevish, half frightened.

The instant he said the word, a tremendous blast of wind crashed in a board of the wall, and swept the clothes off Diamond. He started up in terror. Leaning over him was the large beautiful pale face of a woman. Her dark eyes looked a little angry, for they had just begun to flash; but a quivering in her sweet upper lip made her look as if she were going to cry. What was most strange was that away from her head streamed out her black hair in every direction, so that the darkness in the hay-loft looked as if it were made of her hair; but as Diamond gazed at her in speechless amazement, mingled with confidence – for the boy was entranced with her mighty beauty – her hair began to gather itself out of the darkness, and fell down all about her again, till her face looked out of the midst of it like a moon out of a cloud. From her eyes came all the light by which Diamond saw her face and her hair; and that was all he did see of her yet. The wind was over and gone.

'Will you go with me now, you little Diamond? I am sorry I was forced to be so rough with you, said the lady.

'I will; yes, I will,' answered Diamond, holding out both his arms. 'But,' he added, dropping them, 'how shall I get my clothes? They are in mother's room, and the door is locked.'

'Oh, never mind your clothes. You will not be cold. I shall take care of that. Nobody is cold with the North Wind.'

'I thought everybody was,' said Diamond.

'That is a great mistake. Most people make it, however. They are cold because they are not with the North Wind, but without it.'

If Diamond had been a little older, and had supposed himself a good deal wiser, he would have thought the lady was joking. But he was not older, and did not fancy himself wiser, and therefore understood her well enough. Again he stretched out his arms. The lady's face drew back a little.

'Follow me, Diamond,' she said.

'Yes,' said Diamond, only a little ruefully.

'You're not afraid?' said the North Wind.

'No, ma'am; but mother never would let me go without shoes: she never said anything about clothes, so I dare say she wouldn't mind that.'

'I know your mother very well,' said the lady. 'She is a good woman. I have visited her often. I was with her when you were born. I saw her laugh and cry both at once. I love your mother, Diamond.'

'How was it you did not know my name, then, ma'am? Please am I to say *ma'am* to you, ma'am?'

'One question at a time, dear boy. I knew your name quite well, but I wanted to hear what you would say for it. Don't you remember that day when the man was finding fault with your name – how I blew the window in?'

'Yes, yes,' answered Diamond, eagerly. 'Our window opens like a door, right over the coach-house door. And the wind – you, ma'am – came in, and blew the bible out of the man's hands, and the leaves went all flutter flutter on the floor, and my mother picked it up and gave it back to him open, and there——'

'Was your name in the bible, – the sixth stone in the high-priest's breast-plate.'

'Oh! – a stone, was it?' said Diamond. 'I thought it had been a horse – I did.'

'Never mind. A horse is better than a stone any day. Well, you see, I know all about you and your mother.'

'Yes. I will go with you.'

'Now for the next question: you're not to call me *ma'am*. You must call me just my own name – respectfully, you know – just North Wind.'

'Well, please, North Wind, you are so beautiful, I am quite ready to go with you.'

'You must not be ready to go with everything beautiful all at once, Diamond.'

'But what's beautiful can't be bad. You're not bad, North Wind?'

'No; I'm not bad. But sometimes beautiful things grow bad by doing bad, and it takes some time for their badness to spoil their beauty. So little boys may be mistaken if they go after things because they are beautiful.'

'Well, I will go with you because you are beautiful and good too.'

'Ah, but there's another thing, Diamond:– What if I should look ugly without being bad – look ugly myself because I am making ugly things beautiful? – What then?'

'I don't quite understand you, North Wind. You tell me what then.'

'Well, I will tell you. If you see me with my face all black, don't be frightened. If you see me flapping wings like a bat's, as big as the whole sky, don't be frightened. If you hear me raging ten times worse than Mrs. Bill, the blacksmith's wife – even if you see me looking in at people's windows like Mrs. Eve Dropper, the gardener's wife – you must believe that I am doing my work. Nay, Diamond, if I change into a serpent or a tiger, you must not let go your hold of me, for my hand will never change in yours if you keep a good hold. If you keep hold, you will know who I am all the time, even when you look at me and can't see me the least like the North Wind. I may look something very awful. Do you understand?'

'Quite well,' said little Diamond.

'Come along, then,' said North Wind, and disappeared behind the mountain of hay.

Diamond crept out of bed and followed her.

2   The Lawn

When Diamond got round the corner of the hay, for a moment he
hesitated. The stair by which he would naturally have gone down to
the door was at the other side of the loft, and looked very black indeed;
for it was full of North Wind's hair, as she descended before him. And
just beside him was the ladder going straight down into the stable, up
which his father always came to fetch the hay for Diamond's dinner.
Through the opening in the floor the faint gleam of the stable lantern
was enticing, and Diamond thought he would run down that way.

The stair went close past the loose-box in which Diamond the
horse lived. When Diamond the boy was half-way down, he remembered that it was of no use to go this way, for the stable-door was
locked. But at the same moment there was horse Diamond's great head
poked out of his box on to the ladder, for he knew boy Diamond
although he was in his night-gown, and wanted him to pull his ears for
him. This Diamond did very gently for a minute or so, and patted and
stroked his neck too, and kissed the big horse, and had begun to take
the bits of straw and hay out of his mane, when all at once he
recollected that the Lady North Wind was waiting for him in the yard.

'Good night, Diamond,' he said, and darted up the ladder, across
the loft, and down the stair to the door. But when he got out into the
yard, there was no lady.

Now it is always a dreadful thing to think there is somebody and
find nobody. Children in particular have not made up their minds to it;
they generally cry at nobody, especially when they wake up at night. But
it was an especial disappointment to Diamond, for his little heart had
been beating with joy: the face of the North Wind was so grand! To
have a lady like that for a friend – with such long hair, too! Why, it was
longer than twenty Diamonds' tails! She was gone. And there he stood,

with his bare feet on the stones of the paved yard.

It was a clear night overhead, and the stars were shining. Orion in particular was making the most of his bright belt and golden sword. But the moon was only a poor thin crescent. There was just one great, jagged, black and grey cloud in the sky, with a steep side to it like a precipice; and the moon was against this side, and looked as if she had tumbled off the top of the cloud-hill, and broken herself in rolling down the precipice. She did not seem comfortable, for she was looking down into the deep pit waiting for her. At least that was what Diamond thought as he stood for a moment staring at her. But he was quite wrong, for the moon was not afraid, and there was no pit she was going going down into, for there were no sides to it, and a pit without sides to it is not a pit at all. Diamond, however, had not been out so late before in all his life, and things looked so strange about him! – just as if he had got into Fairyland, of which he knew quite as much as anybody; for his mother had no money to buy books to set him wrong on the subject. I have seen this world – only sometimes, just now and then, you know – look as strange as ever I saw Fairyland. But I confess that I have not yet seen Fairyland at its best. I am always *going* to see it so some time. But if you had been out in the face and not at the back of the North

Wind, on a cold *rather* frosty night, and in your night-gown, you would
have felt it all quite as strange as Diamond did. He cried a little, just a
little, he was so disappointed to lose the lady: of course, you, little man,
wouldn't have done that! But for my part, I don't mind people crying,
so much as I mind what they cry about, and how they cry – whether
they cry quietly like ladies and gentlemen, or go shrieking like vulgar
emperors, or ill-natured cooks; for all emperors are not gentlemen, and
all cooks are not ladies – nor all queens and princesses for that matter,
either.

But it can't be denied that a little gentle crying does one good. It
did Diamond good; for as soon as it was over he was a brave boy again.

'She shan't say it was my fault anyhow!' said Diamond. 'I daresay
she is hiding somewhere to see what I will do. I will look for her.'

So he went round the end of the stable towards the kitchen-garden.
But the moment he was clear of the shelter of the stable, sharp as a
knife came the wind against his little chest and his bare legs. Still he
would look into the kitchen-garden, and went on. But when he got
round the weeping-ash that stood in the corner, the wind blew much
stronger, and it grew stronger and stronger till he could hardly fight
against it. And it was so cold! All the flashy spikes of the stars seemed
to have got somehow into the wind. Then he thought of what the lady
had said about people being cold because they were not *with* the North
Wind. How it was that he should have guessed what she meant at that
very moment I cannot tell, but I have observed that the most wonderful thing in the world is how people come to understand anything. He
turned his back to the wind, and trotted again towards the yard;
whereupon, strange to say, it blew so much more gently against his
calves than it had blown against his shins, that he began to feel almost
warm by contrast.

You must not think it was cowardly of Diamond to turn his back to
the wind: he did so only because he thought Lady North Wind had said
something like telling him to do so. If she had said to him that he must
hold his face to it, Diamond would have held his face to it. But the
most foolish thing is to fight for no good, and to please nobody.

Well, it was just as if the wind was pushing Diamond along. If he
turned round, it grew very sharp on his legs especially, and so he
thought the wind might really be Lady North Wind, though he could
not see her, and he had better let her blow him wherever she pleased.

So she blew and blew, and he went and went, until he found himself standing at a door in a wall, which door led from the yard into a little belt of shrubbery, flanking Mr. Coleman's house. Mr. Coleman was his father's master, and the owner of Diamond. He opened the door, and went through the shrubbery, and out into the middle of the lawn, still hoping to find North Wind. The soft grass was very pleasant to his bare feet, and felt warm after the stones of the yard; but the lady was nowhere to be seen. Then he began to think that after all he must have done wrong, and she was offended with him for not following close after her, but staying to talk to the horse, which certainly was neither wise nor polite.

There he stood in the middle of the lawn, the wind blowing his night-gown till it flapped like a loose sail. The stars were very shiny over his head; but they did not give light enough to show that the grass was green; and Diamond stood alone in the strange night, which looked half solid all about him. He began to wonder whether he was in a dream or not. It was important to determine this; 'for,' thought Diamond, 'if I am in a dream, I am safe in my bed, and I needn't cry. But if I'm not in a dream, I'm out here, and perhaps I had better cry, or, at least, I'm not sure whether I can help it.' He came to the conclusion, however, that, whether he was in a dream or not, there could be no harm in not crying for a little while longer: he could begin whenever he liked.

The back of Mr. Coleman's house was to the lawn, and one of the drawing-room windows looked out upon it. The ladies had not gone to bed; for the light was still shining in that window. But they had no idea that a little boy was standing on the lawn in his night-gown, or they would have run out in a moment. And as long as he saw that light, Diamond could not feel quite lonely. He stood staring, not at the great warrior Orion in the sky, nor yet at the disconsolate, neglected moon going down in the west, but at the drawing-room window with the light shining through its green curtains. He had been in that room once or twice that he could remember at Christmas times; for the Colemans were kind people, though they did not care much about children.

All at once the light went nearly out: he could only see a glimmer of the shape of the window. Then, indeed, he felt that he was left alone. It was so dreadful to be out in the night after *everybody* was gone to bed! That was more than he *could* bear. He burst out crying in good earnest, beginning with a wail like that of the wind when it is waking up.

Perhaps you think this was very foolish; for could he not go home to his own bed again when he liked? Yes; but it looked dreadful to him to creep up that stair again and lie down in his bed again, and know that North Wind's window was open beside him, and she gone, and he might never see her again. He would be just as lonely there as here. Nay, it would be much worse if he had to think that the window was nothing but a hole in the wall.

At the very moment when he burst out crying, the old nurse, who had grown to be one of the family, for she had not gone away when Miss Coleman did not want any more nursing, came to the back-door, which was of glass, to close the shutters. She thought she heard a cry, and, peering out with a hand on each side of her eyes like Diamond's blinkers, she saw something white on the lawn. Too old and too wise to be frightened, she opened the door, and went straight towards the white thing to see what it was. And when Diamond saw her coming he was not frightened either, though Mrs. Crump was a little cross sometimes; for there is a good kind of crossness that is only disagreeable, and there is a bad kind of crossness that is very nasty

indeed. So she came up with her neck stretched out, and her head at the end of it, and her eyes foremost of all, like a snail's, peering into the night to see what it could be that went on glimmering white before her. When she did see, she made a great exclamation, and threw up her hands. Then without a word, for she thought Diamond was walking in his sleep, she caught hold of him, and led him towards the house. He made no objection, for he was just in the mood to be grateful for notice of any sort, and Mrs. Crump led him straight into the drawing-room.

Now, from the neglect of the new housemaid, the fire in Miss Coleman's bed-room had gone out, and her mother had told her to brush her hair by the drawing-room fire – a disorderly proceeding which a mother's wish could justify. The young lady was very lovely, though not nearly so beautiful as North Wind; and her hair was extremely long, for it came down to her knees – though that was nothing at all to North Wind's hair. Yet when she looked round, with her hair all about her, as Diamond entered, he thought for one moment that it was North Wind, and, pulling his hand from Mrs. Crump's, he stretched out his arms and ran towards Miss Coleman. She was so pleased that she threw down her brush, and almost knelt on the floor to

receive him in her arms. He saw the next moment that she was not Lady North Wind, but she looked so like her he could not help running into her arms and bursting into tears afresh. Mrs. Crump said the poor child had walked out in his sleep, and Diamond thought she ought to know, and did not contradict her: for anything he knew, it might be so indeed. He let them talk on about him, and said nothing; and when, after their astonishment was over, and Miss Coleman had given him a sponge-cake, it was decreed that Mrs. Crump should take him to his mother, he was quite satisfied.

His mother had to get out of bed to open the door when Mrs. Crump knocked. She was indeed surprised to see her boy; and having taken him in her arms and carried him to his bed, returned and had a long confabulation with Mrs. Crump, for they were still talking when Diamond fell fast asleep, and could hear them no longer.

3   Old Diamond

Diamond woke very early in the morning, and thought what a curious dream he had had. But the memory grew brighter and brighter in his head, until it did not look altogether like a dream, and he began to doubt whether he had not really been abroad in the wind last night. He came to the conclusion that, if he had really been brought home to his mother by Mrs. Crump, she would say something to him about it, and that would settle the matter. Then he got up and dressed himself, but, finding that his father and mother were not yet stirring, he went down the ladder to the stable. There he found that even old Diamond was not awake yet, for he, as well as young Diamond, always got up the moment he woke, and now he was lying as flat as a horse could lie upon his nice trim bed of straw.

'I'll give old Diamond a surprise,' thought the boy; and creeping up very softly, before the horse knew, he was astride of his back. Then it was young Diamond's turn to have more of a surprise than he had expected; for as with an earthquake, with a rumbling and a rocking hither and thither, a sprawling of legs and heaving as of many backs, young Diamond found himself hoisted up in the air, with both hands twisted in the horse's mane. The next instant old Diamond lashed out with both his hind legs, and giving one cry of terror young Diamond found himself lying on his neck, with his arms as far round it as they would go. But then the horse stood as still as a stone, except that he lifted his head gently up, to let the boy slip down to his back. For when he heard young Diamond's cry he knew that there was nothing to kick about; for young Diamond was a good boy, and old Diamond was a good horse, and the one was all right on the back of the other.

As soon as Diamond had got himself comfortable on the saddle place, the horse began pulling at the hay, and the boy began thinking.

He had never mounted Diamond himself before, and he had never got off him without being lifted down. So he sat, while the horse ate, wondering how he was to reach the ground.

But while he meditated, his mother woke, and her first thought was to see her boy. She had visited him twice during the night, and found him sleeping quietly. Now his bed was empty, and she was frightened.

'Diamond! Diamond! Where are you, Diamond?' she called out.

Diamond turned his head where he sat like a knight on his steed in enchanted stall, and cried aloud, –

'Here, mother!'

'Where, Diamond?' she returned.

'Here, mother, on Diamond's back.'

She came running to the ladder, and peeping down, saw him aloft on the great horse.

'Come down, Diamond,' she said.

'I can't,' answered Diamond.

'How did you get up?' asked his mother.

'Quite easily,' answered he; 'but when I got up, Diamond would

get up too, and so here I am.'

His mother thought he had been walking in his sleep again, and hurried down the ladder. She did not much like going up to the horse, for she had not been used to horses; but she would have gone into a lion's den, not to say a horse's stall, to help her boy. So she went and lifted him off Diamond's back, and felt braver all her life after. She carried him in her arms up to her room; but, afraid of frightening him at his own sleep-walking, as she supposed it, said nothing about last night. Before the next day was over, Diamond had almost concluded the whole adventure a dream.

For a week his mother watched him very carefully – going into the loft several times a night, – as often, in fact, as she woke. Every time she found him fast asleep.

All that week it was hard weather. The grass showed white in the morning with the hoar-frost which clung like tiny comfits to every blade. And as Diamond's shoes were not good, and mother had not quite saved up enough money to get him the new pair she so much wanted for him, she would not let him run out. He played all his games over and over indoors, especially that of driving two chairs harnessed

to the baby's cradle; and if they did not go very fast, they went as fast as could be expected of the best chairs in the world, although one of them had only three legs, and the other only half a back.

At length his mother brought home his new shoes, and no sooner did she find they fitted him than she told him he might run out in the yard and amuse himself for an hour.

The sun was going down when he flew from the door like a bird from its cage. All the world was new to him. A great fire of sunset burned on the top of the gate that led from the stables to the house; above the fire in the sky lay a large lake of green light, above that a golden cloud, and over that the blue of the wintry heavens. And Diamond thought that, next to his own home, he had never seen any place he would like so much to live in as that sky. For it is not fine things that make home a nice place, but your mother and your father.

As he was yet looking at the lovely colours, the gates were thrown open, and there was old Diamond and his friend in the carriage, dancing with impatience to get at their stalls and their oats. And in they came. Diamond was not in the least afraid of his father driving over him, but, careful not to spoil the grand show he made with his fine horses and his multitudinous cape, with a red edge to every fold, he slipped out of the way and let him dash right on to the stables. To be quite safe he had to step into the recess of the door that led from the yard to the shrubbery.

As he stood there he remembered how the wind had driven him to this same spot on the night of his dream. And once more he was almost sure that it was no dream. At all events, he would go in and see whether things looked at all now as they did then. He opened the door, and passed through the little belt of shrubbery. Not a flower was to be seen in the beds on the lawn. Even the brave old chrysanthemums and Christmas roses had passed away before the frost. What? Yes! There was one! He ran and knelt down to look at it.

It was a primrose – a dwarfish thing, but perfect in shape – a baby-wonder. As he stooped his face to see it close, a little wind began to blow, and two or three long leaves that stood up behind the flower shook and waved and quivered, but the primrose lay still in the green hollow, looking up at the sky, and not seeming to know that the wind was blowing at all. It was just a one eye that the dull black wintry earth had opened to look at the sky with. All at once Diamond thought it was saying its prayers, and he ought not to be staring at it so. He ran to the stable to see his father make Diamond's bed. Then his father took him in his arms, carried him up the ladder, and set him down at the table where they were going to have their tea.

'Miss is very poorly,' said Diamond's father; 'Mis'ess has been to the doctor with her to-day, and she looked very glum when she came out again. I was a-watching of them to see what the doctor had said.'

'And didn't Miss look glum too?' asked his mother.

'Not half as glum as Mis'ess,' returned the coachman. 'You see——'

But he lowered his voice, and Diamond could not make out more than a word here and there. For Diamond's father was not only one of the finest of coachmen to look at, and one the best of drivers, but one of the most discreet of servants as well. Therefore he did not talk about family affairs to any one but his wife, whom he had proved better than himself long ago, and was careful that even Diamond should hear nothing he could repeat again concerning master and his family.

It was bed-time soon, and Diamond went to bed and fell fast asleep.

He awoke all at once, in the dark.

'Open the window, Diamond,' said a voice.

Now Diamond's mother had once more pasted up North Wind's window.

'Are you North Wind?' said Diamond: 'I don't hear you blowing.'

'No; but you hear me talking. Open the window, for I haven't overmuch time.'

'Yes,' returned Diamond. 'But please, North Wind, where's the use? You left me all alone last time.'

He had got up on his knees, and was busy with his nails once more at the paper over the hole in the wall. For now that North Wind spoke again, he remembered all that had taken place before as distinctly as if it had happened only last night.

'Yes, but that was your fault,' returned North Wind. 'I had work to do; and, besides, a gentleman should never keep a lady waiting.'

'But I'm not a gentleman,' said Diamond, scratching away at the paper.

'I hope you won't say so ten years after this.'

'I'm going to be a coachman, and a coachman is not a gentleman,' persisted Diamond.

'We call your father a gentleman in our house,' said North Wind.

'He doesn't call himself one,' said Diamond.

'That's of no consequence: every man ought to be a gentleman, and your father is one.'

Diamond was so pleased to hear this that he scratched at the paper like ten mice, and getting hold of the edge of it, tore it off. The next instant a young girl glided across the bed, and stood upon the floor.

'Oh dear!' said Diamond, quite dismayed; 'I didn't know – who are you, please?'

'I'm North Wind.'

'Are you really?'

'Yes. Make haste.'

'But you're no bigger than me.'

'Do you think I care about how big or how little I am? Didn't you see me this evening. I was less then.'

'No. Where was you?'

'Behind the leaves of the primrose. Didn't you see them blowing?'

'Yes.'

'Make haste, then, if you want to go with me.'

'But you are not big enough to take care of me. I think you are only Miss North Wind.'

'I am big enough to show you the way, anyhow. But if you won't come, why, you must stay.'

'I must dress myself. I didn't mind with a grown lady, but I couldn't go with a little girl in my night-gown.'

'Very well. I'm not in such a hurry as I was the other night. Dress as fast as you can, and I'll go and shake the primrose leaves till you come.'

'Don't hurt it,' said Diamond.

North Wind broke out in a little laugh like the breaking of silver bubbles, and was gone in a moment. Diamond saw – for it was a starlit night, and the mass of hay was at a low ebb now – the gleam of something vanishing down the stair, and, springing out of bed, dressed himself as fast as ever he could. Then he crept out into the yard, through the door in the wall, and away to the primrose. Behind it stood North Wind, leaning over it, and looking at the flower as if she had been its mother.

'Come along,' she said, jumping up and holding out her hand.

Diamond took her hand. It was cold, but so pleasant and full of life, it was better than warm. She led him across the garden. With one bound she was on the top of the wall. Diamond was left at the foot.

'Stop, stop!' he cried. 'Please, I can't jump like that.'

'You don't try,' said North Wind, who from the top looked down a foot taller than before.

'Give me your hand again, and I will try,' said Diamond.

She reached down, Diamond laid hold of her hand, gave a great spring, and stood beside her.

'This *is* nice!' he said.

Another bound, and they stood in the road by the river. It was full tide, and the stars were shining clear in its depths, for it lay still, waiting for the turn to run down again to the sea. They walked along its side. But they had not walked far before its surface was covered with ripples, and the stars had vanished from its bosom.

And North Wind was now tall as a full-grown girl. Her hair was flying about her head, and the wind was blowing a breeze down the

river. But she turned aside and went up a narrow lane, and as she went her hair fell down around her.

'I have some rather disagreeable work to do to-night,' she said, 'before I get out to sea, and I must set about it at once. The disagreeable work must be looked after first.'

So saying, she laid hold of Diamond and began to run, gliding along faster and faster. Diamond kept up with her as well as he could. She made many turnings and windings, apparently because it was not quite easy to get him over walls and houses. Once they ran through a hall where they found back and front doors open. At the foot of the stair North Wind stood still, and Diamond, hearing a great growl, started in terror, and there, instead of North Wind, was a huge wolf by his side. He let go his hold in dismay, and the wolf bounded up the stair. The windows of the house rattled and shook as if guns were firing, and the sound of a great fall came from above. Diamond stood with white face staring up at the landing.

'Surely,' he thought, 'North Wind can't be eating one of the children!' Coming to himself all at once, he rushed after her with his little fist clenched. There were ladies in long trains going up and down the stairs, and gentlemen in white neckties attending on them, who stared at him, but none of the people of the house, and they said nothing. Before he reached the head of the stair, however, North Wind met him, took him by the hand, and hurried down and out of the house.

'I hope you haven't eaten a baby, North Wind!' said Diamond, very solemnly.

North Wind laughed merrily, and went tripping on faster. Her grassy robe swept and swirled about her steps, and wherever it passed over withered leaves, they went fleeing and whirling in spirals, and running on their edges like wheels, all about her feet.

'No,' she said at last, 'I did not eat a baby. You would not have had to ask that foolish question if you had not let go your hold of me. You would have seen how I served a nurse that was calling a child bad names, and telling her she was wicked. She had been drinking. I saw an ugly gin bottle in a cupboard.'

'And you frightened her?' said Diamond.

'I believe so!' answered North Wind, laughing merrily. 'I flew at her throat, and she tumbled over on the floor with such a crash that

they ran in. She'll be turned away to-morrow – and quite time, if they knew as much as I do.'

'But didn't you frighten the little one?'

'She never saw me. The woman would not have seen me either if she had not been wicked.'

'Oh!' said Diamond, dubiously.

'Why should you see things,' returned North Wind, 'that you wouldn't understand or know what to do with? Good people see good things; bad people, bad things.'

'Then are you a bad thing?'

'No. For *you* see me, Diamond, dear,' said the girl, and she looked down at him, and Diamond saw the loving eyes of the great lady beaming from the depths of her falling hair.

'I had to make myself look like a bad thing before she could see me. If I had put on any other shape than a wolf's she would not have seen me, for that is what is growing to be her own shape inside of her.'

'I don't know what you mean,' said Diamond, 'but I suppose it's all right.'

They were now climbing the slope of a grassy ascent. It was

Primrose Hill, in fact, although Diamond had never heard of it. The moment they reached the top, North Wind stood and turned her face towards London. The stars were still shining clear and cold overhead. There was not a cloud to be seen. The air was sharp, but Diamond did not find it cold.

'Now,' said the lady, 'whatever you do, do not let my hand go. I might have lost you the last time, only I was not in a hurry then: now I am in a hurry.'

Yet she stood still for a moment.

4 North Wind

And as she stood looking towards London, Diamond saw that she was trembling.

'Are you cold, North Wind?' he asked.

'No, Diamond,' she answered, looking down upon him with a smile; 'I am only getting ready to sweep one of my rooms. Those careless, greedy, untidy children make it in such a mess.'

As she spoke he could have told by her voice, if he had not seen with his eyes, that she was growing larger and larger. Her head went up and up towards the stars; and as she grew, still trembling through all her body, her hair also grew – longer and longer, and lifted itself from her head, and went out in black waves. The next moment, however, it fell back around her, and she grew less and less till she was only a tall woman. Then she put her hands behind her head, and gathered some of her hair, and began weaving and knotting it together. When she had done, she bent down her beautiful face close to his, and said –

'Diamond, I am afraid you would not keep hold of me, and if I were to drop you, I don't know what might happen; so I have been making a place for you in my hair. Come.'

Diamond held out his arms, for with that grand face looking at him, he believed like a baby. She took him in her hands, threw him over her shoulder, and said, 'Get in, Diamond.'

And Diamond parted her hair with his hands, crept between, and feeling about soon found the woven nest. It was just like a pocket, or like the shawl in which gipsy women carry their children. North Wind put her hands to her back, felt all about the nest, and finding it safe, said, –

'Are you comfortable, Diamond?'

'Yes, indeed,' answered Diamond.

The next moment he was rising in the air. North Wind grew towering up to the place of the clouds. Her hair went streaming out from her, till it spread like a mist over the stars. She flung herself abroad in space.

Diamond held on by two of the twisted ropes which, parted and interwoven, formed his shelter, for he could not help being afraid. As soon as he had come to himself, he peeped through the woven meshes, for he did not dare to look over the top of the nest. The earth was rushing past like a river or a sea below him. Trees, and water, and green grass hurried away beneath. A great roar of wild animals rose as they rushed over the Zoological Gardens, mixed with a chattering of monkeys and a screaming of birds; but it died away in a moment behind them. And now there was nothing but the roofs of houses, sweeping along like a great torrent of stones and rocks. Chimney-pots fell, and tiles flew from the roofs; but it looked to him as if they were left behind by the roofs and the chimneys as they scudded away. There was a great roaring, for the wind was dashing against London like a sea; but at North Wind's back, Diamond, of course, felt nothing of it all.

He was in a perfect calm. He could hear the sound of it, that was all.

By and by he raised himself and looked over the edge of his nest. There were the houses rushing up and shooting away below him, like a fierce torrent of rocks instead of water. Then he looked up to the sky, but could see no stars; the were hidden by the blinding masses of the lady's hair which swept between. He began to wonder whether she would hear him if he spoke. He would try.

'Please, North Wind,' he said, 'what is that noise?'

From high over his head came the voice of North Wind, answering him gently, −

'The noise of my besom. I am the old woman that sweeps the cobwebs from the sky; only I'm busy with the floor now.'

'What makes the houses look as if they were running away?'

'I am sweeping so fast over them.'

'But, please, North Wind, I knew London was very big, but I didn't know it was so big as this. It seems as if we should never get away from it.'

'We are going round and round, else we should have left it long ago.'

'Is this the way you sweep, North Wind?'

'Yes; I go round and round with my great besom.'

'Please, would you mind going a little slower, for I want to see the streets?'

'You won't see much now.'

'Why?'

'Because I have nearly swept all the people home.'

'Oh! I forgot,' said Diamond, and was quiet after that, for he did not want to be troublesome.

But she dropped a little towards the roofs of the houses, and Diamond could see down into the streets. There were very few people about, though. The lamps flickered and flared again, but nobody seemed to want them.

Suddenly Diamond espied a little girl coming along a street. She was dreadfully blown by the wind, and a broom she was trailing behind her was very troublesome. It seemed as if the wind had a spite at her − it kept worrying her like a wild beast, and tearing at her rags. She was so lonely there!

'Oh! please, North Wind,' he cried, 'won't you help that little girl?'

'No, Diamond; I mustn't leave my work.'

'But why shouldn't you be kind to her?'

'I am kind to her: I am sweeping the wicked smells away.'

'But you're kinder to me, dear North Wind. Why shouldn't you be as kind to her as you are to me?'

'There are reasons, Diamond. Everybody can't be done to all the same. Everybody is not ready for the same thing.'

'But I don't see why I should be kinder used than she.'

'Do you think nothing's to be done but what you can see, Diamond, You silly! It's all right. Of course you can help her if you like. You've got nothing particular to do at this moment; I have.'

'Oh! do let me help her, then. But you won't be able to wait perhaps?'

'No, I can't wait; you must do it yourself. And, mind, the wind will get a hold of you too.'

'Don't you want to help her, North Wind?'

'Not without having some idea what will happen. If you break down and cry, that won't be much of a help to her, and it will make a goose of little Diamond.'

'I want to go,' said Diamond. 'Only there's just one thing – how am I to get home?'

'If you're anxious about that, perhaps you had better go with me. I am bound to take you home again, if you do.'

'There!' cried Diamond, who was still looking after the little girl; 'I'm sure the wind will blow her over, and perhaps kill her. Do let me go.'

They had been sweeping more slowly along the line of the street. There was a lull in the roaring.

'Well, though I cannot promise to take you home,' said North Wind, as she sank nearer and nearer to the tops of the houses, 'I can promise you it will be all right in the end. You will get home somehow. Have you made up your mind what to do?'

'Yes; to help the little girl,' said Diamond firmly.

The same moment North Wind dropt into the street and stood, only a tall lady, but with her hair flying up over the housetops. She put her hands to her back, took Diamond, and set him down in the street. The same moment he was caught in the fierce coils of the blast, and all but blown away. North wind stepped back a pace, and at once towered in stature to the height of the houses. A chimney-pot clashed at Diamond's feet. He turned in terror, but it was to look for the little girl, and when he turned again the lady had vanished, and the wind was roaring along the street as if it had been the bed of an invisible torrent. The little girl was scudding before the blast, her hair flying too, and behind her she dragged her broom. Her little legs were going as fast as ever they could to keep her from falling. Diamond crept into the shelter of a doorway, thinking to stop her; but she passed him like a bird, crying gently and pitifully.

'Stop! stop! little girl,' shouted Diamond, starting in pursuit.

'I can't,' wailed the girl; 'the wind won't leave go of me.'

Diamond could run faster than she, and he had no broom. In a few moments he had caught her by the frock. But it tore in his hand, and away went the little girl. So he had to run again, and this time he ran so fast that he got before her, and turning round caught her in his arms, when down they went both together, which made the little girl laugh in the midst of her crying.

'Where are you going?' asked Diamond, rubbing the elbow that had stuck farthest out. The arm it belonged to was twined round a lamp-post as he stood between the little girl and the wind.

'Home,' she said, gasping for breath.

'Then I will go with you,' said Diamond.

And then they were silent for a while, for the wind blew worse than ever, and they had both to hold on to the lamp-post.

'Where is your crossing?' asked the girl at length.

'I don't sweep,' answered Diamond.

'What *do* you do, then?' asked she. 'You ain't big enough for most things.'

'I don't know what I do do,' answered he, feeling rather ashamed. 'Nothing, I suppose. My father's Mr. Coleman's coachman.'

'Have you a father?' she said, staring at him as if a boy with a father was a natural curiosity.

'Yes. Haven't *you?*' returned Diamond.

'No; nor mother neither. Old Sal's all I've got.'

And she began to cry again.

'I wouldn't go to her if she wasn't good to me,' said Diamond.

'But you must go somewheres.'

'Move on,' said the voice of a policeman behind them.

'I told you so,' said the girl. 'You must go somewheres. They're always at it.'

'But Old Sal doesn't beat you, does she?'

'I wish she would.'

'What do you mean?' asked Diamond, quite bewildered.

'She would if she was my mother. But she wouldn't lie abed a-cuddlin' of her ugly old bones, and laugh to hear me crying at the door.'

'You don't mean she won't let you in to-night?'

'It'll be a good chance if she does.'

'Why are you out so late, then?' asked Diamond.

'My crossing's a long way off at the West End, and I had been indulgin' in door-steps and mewses.'

'We'd better have a try anyhow,' said Diamond. 'Come along.'

As he spoke Diamond thought he caught a glimpse of North Wind turning a corner in front of them; and when they turned the corner too, they found it quite quiet there, but he saw nothing of the lady.

'Now you lead me,' he said, taking her hand, 'and I'll take care of you.'

The girl withdrew her hand, but only to dry her eyes with her frock, for the other had enough to do with her broom. She put it in his again, and led him, turning after turning, until they stopped at a cellar-door in a very dirty lane. There she knocked.

'I shouldn't like to live here,' said Diamond.

'Oh yes, you would, if you had nowheres else to go to,' answered the girl. 'I only wish we may get in.'

'I don't want to go in,' said Diamond.

'Where do you mean to go, then?'

'Home to my home.'

'Where's that?'

'I don't exactly know.'

'Then you're worse off than I am.'

'Oh no, for North Wind –' began Diamond, and stopped he hardly knew why.

'*What?*' said the girl, as she held her ear to the door listening.

But Diamond did not reply. Neither did Old Sal.

'I told you so,' said the girl. 'She is wide awake hearkening. But we don't get in.'

'What will you do, then?' asked Diamond.

'Move on,' she answered.

'Where?'

'Oh, anywheres. Bless you, I'm used to it.'

'Hadn't you better come home with me, then?'

'That's a good joke, when you don't know where it is. Come on.'

'But where?'

'Oh, nowheres in particular. Come on.'

Diamond obeyed. The wind had now fallen considerably. They wandered on and on, turning in this direction and that, without any reason for one way more than another, until they had got out of the thick of the houses into a waste kind of place. By this time they were both very tired. Diamond felt a good deal inclined to cry, and thought he had been very silly to get down from the back of the North Wind; not that he would have minded it if he had done the girl any good; but he thought he had been of no use to her. He was mistaken there, for she was far happier for having Diamond with her than if she had been wandering about alone. She did not seem so tired as he was.

'Do let us rest a bit,' said Diamond.

'Let's see,' she answered. 'There's something like a railway there. Perhaps there's an open arch.'

They went towards it and found one, and, better still, there was an empty barrel lying under the arch.

'Hillo! here we are!' said the girl. 'A barrel's the jolliest bed going – on the tramp, I mean.

'We'll have forty winks, and then go on again.'

She crept in, and Diamond crept in beside her. They put their arms round each other, and when he began to grow warm, Diamond's courage began to come.

'This *is* jolly!' he said. 'I'm *so* glad!'

'I don't think so much of it,' said the girl. 'I'm used to it, I suppose. But I can't think how a kid like you comes to be out all alone this time o' the night.'

She called him a *kid*, but she was not really a month older than he was; only she had had to work for her bread, and that so soon makes people older.

'But I shouldn't have been out so late if I hadn't got down to help you,' said Diamond. 'North Wind is gone home long ago.'

'I think you must ha' got out o' one o' them Hidget Asylms,' said the girl. 'You said something about the north wind afore that I couldn't get the rights of.'

So now, for the sake of his character, Diamond had to tell her the whole story.

She did not believe a word of it. She said she wasn't such a flat as to believe all that bosh. But as she spoke there came a great blast of wind through the arch, and set the barrel rolling. So they made haste to get out of it, for they had no notion of being rolled over and over as if they had been packed tight and wouldn't hurt, like a barrel of herrings.

'I thought we should have had a sleep,' said Diamond; 'but I can't say I'm very sleepy after all. Come, let's go on again.'

They wandered on and on, sometimes sitting on a door-step, but always turning into lanes or fields when they had a chance.

They found themselves at last on a rising ground that sloped rather steeply on the other side. It was a waste kind of spot below, bounded by an irregular wall, with a few doors in it. Outside lay broken things in general, from garden-rollers to flower-pots and wine-bottles. But the moment they reached the brow of the rising ground a gust of wind seized them and blew them down hill as fast as they could run. Nor could Diamond stop before he went bang against one of the doors in the wall. To his dismay it burst open. When they came to themselves they peeped in. It was the back-door of a garden.

'Ah, ah!' cried Diamond, after staring for a few moments, 'I thought so! North Wind takes nobody in! Here I am in master's garden! I tell you what, little girl, you just bore a hole in old Sal's wall, and put you mouth to it, and say, 'Please, North Wind, mayn't I go out with you?' and then you'll see what'll come.'

'I daresay I shall. But I'm out in the wind too often already to want more of it.'

'I said *with* the North Wind, not *in* it.'

'It's all one.'

'It's *not* all one.'

'It *is* all one.'

'But I know best.'

'And I know better. I'll box your ears,' said the girl.

Diamond got very angry. But he remembered that even if she did box his ears, he mustn't box hers again, for she was a girl, and all that boys must do, if girls are rude, is to go away and leave them. So he went in at the door.

'Good-bye, mister,' said the girl.

This brought Diamond to his senses.

'I'm sorry I was cross,' he said. 'Come in, and my mother will give you some breakfast.'

'No, thank you. I must be off to my crossing. It's morning now.'

'I'm very sorry for you,' said Diamond.

'Well, it *is* a life to be tired of – what with old Sal, and so many holes in my shoes.'

'I wonder you're so good. I should kill myself.'

'Oh no, you wouldn't! When I think of it, I always want to see what's coming next, and so I always wait till next is over. Well! I suppose there's somebody happy somewheres. But it ain't in them carriages. Oh my! *how* they *do* look sometimes – fit to bite your head off! Good-bye!'

She ran up the hill and disappeared behind it. Then Diamond shut the door as he best could, and ran through the kitchen-garden to the stable. And wasn't he glad to get into his own blessed bed again!

5 The Summer-House

Diamond said nothing to his mother about his adventures. He had half a notion that North Wind was a friend of his mother, and that, if she did not know *all* about it, at least she did not mind his going anywhere with the lady of the wind. At the same time he doubted whether he might not appear to be telling stories if he told all, especially as he could hardly believe it himself when he thought about it in the middle of the day, although when the twilight was once half-way on to night he had no doubt about it, at least for the first few days after he had been with her. The girl that swept the crossing had certainly refused to believe him. Besides, he felt sure that North Wind would tell him if he ought to speak.

It was some time before he saw the lady of the wind again. Indeed nothing remarkable took place in Diamond's history until the following week. This was what happened then. Diamond the horse wanted new shoes, and Diamond's father took him out of the stable, and was just getting on his back to ride him to the forge, when he saw his little boy standing by the pump, and looking at him wistfully. Then the coachman took his foot out of the stirrup, left his hold of the mane and bridle, came across to his boy, lifted him up, and setting him on the horse's back, told him to sit up like a man. He then led away both Diamonds together.

The boy atop felt not a little tremulous as the great muscles that lifted the legs of the horse knotted and relaxed against his legs, and he cowered towards the withers, grasping with his hands the bit of mane worn short by the collar; but when his father looked back at him, saying once more, 'Sit up, Diamond,' he let the mane go and sat up, notwithstanding that the horse, thinking, I suppose, that his master had said to him, '*Come* up, Diamond,' stepped out faster. For both the

Diamonds were just grandly obedient. And Diamond soon found that, as he was obedient to his father, so the horse was obedient to him. For he had not ridden far before he found courage to reach forward and catch hold of the bridle, and when his father, whose hand was upon it, felt the boy pull it towards him, he looked up and smiled, and, well pleased, let go his hold, and left Diamond to guide Diamond; and the boy soon found that he could do so perfectly. It was a grand thing to be able to guide a great beast like that. And another discovery he made was that, in order to guide the horse, he had in a measure to obey the horse first. If he did not yield his body to the motions of the horse's body, he could not guide him; he must fall off.

The blacksmith lived at some distance, deeper into London. As they crossed the angle of a square, Diamond, who was now quite comfortable on his living throne, was glancing this way and that in a gentle pride, when he saw a girl sweeping a crossing scuddingly before a lady. The lady was his father's mistress, Mrs. Coleman, and the little girl was she for whose sake he had got off North Wind's back. He drew Diamond's bridle in eager anxiety to see whether her outstreched hand

would gather a penny from Mrs. Coleman. But she had given one at the last crossing, and the hand returned only to grasp its broom. Diamond could not bear it. He had a penny in his pocket, the gift of the same lady the day before, and he tumbled off his horse to give it to the girl. He tumbled off, I say, for he did tumble when he reached the ground. But he got up in an instant, and ran, searching his pocket as he ran. She made him a pretty courtesy when he offered his treasure, but with a bewildered stare. She thought first: 'Then he *was* on the back of the North Wind after all!' but, looking up at the sound of the horse's feet on the paved crossing, she changed her idea, saying to herself, 'North Wind is his father's horse! That's the secret of it! Why couldn't he say so?' And she had a mind to refuse the penny. But his smile put it all right, and she not only took his penny but put it in her mouth with a 'Thank you, mister. Did they wollop you then?'

'Oh no!' answered Diamond. 'They never wollops me.'

'Lor!' said the little girl, and was speechless.

Meantime his father, looking up, and seeing the horse's back bare, suffered a pang of awful dread, but the next moment catching sight of him, took him up and put him on, saying –

'Don't get off again, Diamond. The horse might have put his foot on you.'

'No, father,' answered the boy, and rode on in majestic safety.

The summer drew near, warm and splendid. Miss Coleman was a little better in health, and sat a good deal in the garden. One day she saw Diamond peeping through the shrubbery, and called him. He talked to her so frankly that she often sent for him after that, and by degrees it came about that he had leave to run in the garden as he pleased. He never touched any of the flowers or blossoms, for he was not like some boys who cannot enjoy a thing without pulling it to pieces, and so preventing every one from enjoying it after them.

A week even makes such a long time in a child's life, that Diamond had begun once more to feel as if North Wind were a dream of some far-off year.

One hot evening, he had been sitting with the young mistress, as they called her, in a little summer-house at the bottom of the lawn – a wonderful thing for beauty, the boy thought, for a little window in the side of it was made of coloured glass. It grew dusky, and the lady began to feel chill, and went in, leaving the boy in the summer-house. He sat

there gazing out at a bed of tulips, which, although they had closed for
the night, could not go quite asleep for the wind that kept waving them
about. All at once he saw a great humble-bee fly out of one of the
tulips.

'There! that is something done,' said a voice – a gentle, merry,
childish voice, but *so* tiny. 'At last it was. I thought he would have had
to stay there all night, poor fellow! I did.'

Diamond could not tell whether the voice was near or far away, it
was so small and yet so clear. He had never seen a fairy, but he had
heard of such, and he began to look all about for one. And there was the
tiniest creature sliding down the stem of the tulip!

'Are you the fairy that herds the bees?' he asked, going out of the
summer-house, and down on his knees on the green shore of the tulip-
bed.

'I'm not a fairy,' answered the little creature.

'How do you know that?'

'It would become you better to ask how *you* are to know it.'

'You've just told me.'

'Yes. But what's the use of knowing a thing only because you're told it?'

'Well, how *am* I to know you are not a fairy? You do look very like one.'

'In the first place, fairies are much bigger than you see me.'

'Oh!' said Diamond reflectively; 'I thought they were very little.'

'But they might be tremendously bigger than I am, and yet not *very* big. Why, *I* could be six times the size I am, and not be very huge. Besides, a fairy can't grow big and little at will, though the nursery-tales do say so: they don't know better. You stupid Diamond! have you never seen me before?'

And, as she spoke, a moan of wind bent the tulips almost to the ground, and the creature laid her hand on Diamonds shoulder. In a moment he knew that it was North Wind.

'I *am* very stupid,' he said; 'but I never saw you so small before, not even when you were nursing the primrose.'

'Must you see me every size that can be measured before you know me, Diamond?'

'But how could I think it was you taking care of a great stupid humble-bee?'

'The more stupid he was the more need he had to be taken care of. What with sucking honey and trying to open the door, he was nearly dazed; and when it opened in the morning to let the sun see the tulip's heart, what would the sun have thought to find such a stupid thing lying there – with wings too?'

'But how do you have time to look after bees?'

'I don't look after bees. I had this one to look after. It was hard work, though.'

'Hard work! Why, you could blow a chimney down, or – or – a boy's cap off,' said Diamond.

'Both are easier than blow a tulip open. But I scarcely know the difference between hard and easy. I am always able for what I have to do. When I see my work, I just rush at it – and it is done. But I mustn't chatter. I have got to sink a ship to-night.'

'Sink a ship! What! with men in it?'

'Yes, and women too.'

'How dreadful! I wish you wouldn't talk so.'

'It is rather dreadful. But it is my work. I must do it.'

'I hope you won't ask me to go with you.'

'No, I won't ask you. But you must come for all that.'

'I won't, then.'

'Won't you?'

And North Wind grew a tall lady, and looked him in the eyes, and Diamond said –

'Please take me. You cannot be cruel.'

'No; I could not be cruel if I would. I can do nothing cruel, although I often do what looks like cruel to those who do not know what I really am doing. The people they say I drown, I only carry away to – to – to – well, the back of the North Wind – that is what they used to call it long ago, only *I* never saw the place.'

'How can you carry them there if you never saw it?'

'I know the way.'

'But how is it you never saw it?'

'Because it is behind me.'

'But you can look round.'

'Not far enough to see my own back. No; I always look before me. In fact, I grow quite blind and deaf when I try to see my back. I only mind my work.'

'But how does it be your work?'

'Ah, that I can't tell you. I only know it is, because when I do it I feel all right, and when I don't I feel all wrong. East Wind says – only one does not exactly know how much to believe of what she says, for she is very naughty sometimes – she says it is all managed by a baby; but whether she is good or naughty when she says that, I don't know. I just stick to my work. It is all one to me to let a bee out of a tulip, or to sweep the cobwebs from the sky. You would like to go with me to-night?'

'I don't want to see a ship sunk.'

'But suppose I had to take you?'

'Why, then, of course I must go.'

'There's a good Diamond. – I think I had better be growing a bit. Only you must go to bed first. I can't take you till you're in bed. That's the law about the children. So I had better go and do something else first.'

'Very well, North Wind,' said Diamond. 'What are you going to do first, if you please?'

'I think I may tell you. Jump up on the top of the wall, there.'
'I can't.'

'Ah! and I can't help you – you haven't been to bed yet, you see. Come out to the road with me, just in front of the coach-house, and I will show you.'

North Wind grew very small indeed, so small that she could not have blown the dust off a dusty miller, as the Scotch children call a yellow auricula. Diamond could not even see the blades of grass move as she flitted along by his foot. They left the lawn, went out by the wicket in the coach-house gates, and then crossed the road to the low wall that separated it from the river.

'You can get up on this wall, Diamond,' said North Wind.

'Yes; but my mother has forbidden me.'

'Then don't,' said North Wind.

'But I can see over,' said Diamond.

'Ah! to be sure. I can't.'

So saying, North Wind gave a little bound, and stood on the top of the wall. She was just about the height a dragon-fly would be, if it stood on end.

'You darling!' said Diamond, seeing what a lovely little toy-woman she was.

'Don't be impertinent, Master Diamond,' said North Wind. 'If there's one thing makes me more angry than another, it is the way you humans judge things by their size. I am quite as respectable now as I shall be six hours after this, when I take an East Indiaman by the royals, twist her round, and push her under. You have no right to address me in such a fashion.'

But as she spoke, the tiny face wore the smile of a great grand woman. She was only having her own beautiful fun out of Diamond, and true woman's fun never hurts.

'But look there!' she resumed. 'Do you see a boat with one man in it – a green and white boat?'

'Yes; quite well.'

'That's a poet.'

'I thought you said it was a bo-at.'

'Stupid pet! Don't you know what a poet is?'

'Why, a thing to sail on the the water in.'

'Well, perhaps you're not so far wrong. Some poets do carry

people over the sea. But I have no business to talk so much. The man is a poet.'

'The boat is a boat,' said Diamond.

'Can't you spell?' asked North Wind.

'Not very well.'

'So I see. A poet is not a bo-at, as you call it. A poet is a man who is glad of something, and tries to make other people glad of it too.'

'Ah! now I know. Like the man in the sweety-shop.'

'Not very. But I see it is no use. I wasn't sent to tell you, and so I can't tell you. I must be off. Only first just look at the man.'

'He's not much of a rower,' said Diamond – 'paddling first with one fin and then with the other.'

'Now look here!' said North Wind.

And she flashed like a dragon-fly across the water, whose surface rippled and puckered as she passed. The next moment the man in the boat glanced about him, and bent to his oars. The boat flew over the rippling water. Man and boat and river were awake. The same instant almost, North Wind perched again upon the river wall.

'How did you do that?' asked Diamond.

'I blew in his face,' answered North Wind.

'I don't see how that could do it,' said Diamond.

'I daresay not. And therefore you will say you don't believe it could.'

'No, no, dear North Wind. I know you too well not to believe you.'

'Well, I blew in his face, and that woke him up.'

'But what was the good of it?'

'Why! don't you see? Look at him – how he is pulling. I blew the mist out of him.'

'How was that?'

'That is just what I cannot tell you.'

'But you did it.'

'Yes. I have to do ten thousand things without being able to tell how.'

'I don't like that,' said Diamond.

He was staring after the boat. Hearing no answer, he looked down to the wall.

North Wind was gone. Away across the river went a long ripple – what sailors call a cat's paw. The man in the boat was putting up a sail. The moon was coming to herself on the edge of a great cloud, and the sail began to shine white. Diamond rubbed his eyes, and wondered what it was all about. Things seemed going on around him, and all to understand each other; but he could make nothing of it. So he put his hands in his pockets, and went in to have his tea. The night was very hot, for the wind had fallen again.

'You don't seem very well to-night, Diamond,' said his mother.

'I am quite well, mother,' returned Diamond, who was only puzzled.

'I think you had better go to bed,' she added.

'Very well, mother,' he answered.

He stopped for one moment to look out of the window. Above the moon the clouds were going different ways. Somehow or other this troubled him, but, notwithstanding, he was soon fast asleep.

He woke in the middle of the night and the darkness. A terrible noise was rumbling overhead, like the rolling beat of great drums echoing through a brazen vault. The roof of the loft in which he lay had no ceiling; only the tiles were between him and the sky. For a while he could not come quite awake, for the noise kept beating him down, so

that his heart was troubled and fluttered painfully. A second peal of thunder burst over his head, and almost choked him with fear. Nor did he recover until the great blast that followed, having torn some tiles off the roof, sent a spout of wind down into his bed and over his face, which brought him wide awake, and gave him back his courage. The same moment he heard a mighty yet musical voice calling him.

'Come up, Diamond,' it said. 'It's all ready. I'm waiting for you.'

He looked out of the bed, and saw a gigantic, powerful, but most lovely arm – with a hand whose fingers were nothing the less ladylike that they could have strangled a boa-constrictor, or choked a tigress off its prey – stretched down through a big hole in the roof. Without a moment's hesitation he reached out his tiny one, and laid it in the grand palm before him.

6 Out in the Storm

The hand felt its way up his arm, and, grasping it gently and strongly above the elbow, lifted Diamond from the bed. The moment he was through the hole in the roof, all the winds of heaven seemed to lay hold upon him, and buffet him hither and thither. His hair blew one way, his night-gown another, his legs threatened to float from under him, and his head to grow dizzy with the swiftness of the invisible assailant. Cowering he clung with the other hand to the huge hand which held his arm, and fear invaded his heart.

'Oh, North Wind!' he murmured, but the words vanished from his lips as he had seen the soap-bubbles that burst too soon vanish from the mouth of his pipe. The wind caught them, and they were nowhere. They couldn't get out at all, but were torn away and strangled. And yet North Wind heard them, and in her answer it seemed to Diamond that just because she was so big and could not help it, and just because her ear and her mouth must seem to him so dreadfully far away, she spoke to him more tenderly and graciously than ever before. Her voice was like the bass of a deep organ, without the groan in it; like the most delicate of violin tones without the wail in it; like the most glorious of trumpet-ejaculations without the defiance in it; like the sound of falling water without the clatter and clash in it: it was like all of them and neither of them – all of them without their faults, each of them without its peculiarity: after all, it was more like his mother's voice than anything else in the world.

'Diamond, dear,' she said, 'be a man. What is fearful to you is not the least fearful to me.'

'But it can't hurt you,' murmured Diamond, 'for you're *it*.'

'Then if I'm *it*, and have you in my arms, how can it hurt you?'

'Oh yes! I see,' whispered Diamond. 'But it looks so dreadful, and it pushes me about so.'

'Yes, it does, my dear. That is what it was sent for.'

At the same moment, a peal of thunder which shook Diamond's heart against the sides of his bosom hurtled out of the heavens: I cannot say out of the sky, for there was no sky. Diamond had not seen the lightning, for he had been intent on finding the face of North Wind. Every moment the folds of her garment would sweep across his eyes and blind him, but between, he could just persuade himself that he saw great glories of woman's eyes looking down through rifts in the mountainous clouds over his head.

He trembled so at the thunder, that his knees failed him, and he sunk down at North Wind's feet, and clasped her round the column of her ankle. She instantly stooped and lifted him from the roof – up – up into her bosom, and helf him there, saying, as if to an inconsolable child –

'Diamond, dear, this will never do.'

'Oh yes, it will,' answered Diamond. 'I am all right now – quite comfortable, I assure you, dear North Wind. If you will only let me stay here, I shall be all right indeed.'

'But you will feel the wind here, Diamond.'

'I don't mind that a bit, so long as I feel your arms through it,' answered Diamond, nestling closer to her grand bosom.

'Brave boy!' returned North Wind, pressing him closer.

'No,' said Diamond, 'I don't see that. It's not courage at all, so long as I feel you there.'

'But hadn't you better get into my hair? Then you would not feel the wind; you will here.'

'Ah, but, dear North Wind, you don't know how nice it is to feel your arms about me. It is a thousand times better to have them and the wind together, than to have only your hair and the back of your neck and no wind at all.

'But it is surely more comfortable there?'

'Well, perhaps; but I begin to think there are better things than being comfortable.'

'Yes, indeed there are. Well, I will keep you in front of me. You will feel the wind, but not too much. I shall only want one arm to take care of you; the other will be quite enough to sink the ship.'

'Oh, dear North Wind! how can you talk so?'

'My dear boy, I never talk; I always mean what I say.'

'Then you do mean to sink the ship with the other hand?'

'Yes.'

'It's not like you.'

'How do you know that?'

'Quite easily. Here you are taking care of a poor little boy with one arm, and there you are sinking a ship with the other. It can't be like you.'

'Ah! but which is me? I can't be two mes, you know.'

'No. Nobody can be two mes.'

'Well, which me is me?'

'Now I must think. There looks to be two.'

'Yes. That's the very point. – You can't be knowing the thing you don't know, can you?'

'No.'

'Which me do you know?'

'The kindest, goodest, best me in the world,' answered Diamond, clinging to North Wind.

'Why am I good to you?'

'I don't know.'

'Have you ever done anything for me?'

'No.'

'Then I must be good to you because I choose to be good to you.'

'Yes.'

'Why should I choose?'

'Because – because – because you like.'

'Why should I like to be good to you?'

'I don't know, except it be because it's good to be good to me.'

'That's just it, I am good to you because I like to be good.'

'Then why shouldn't you be good to other people as well as to me?'

'That's just what I don't know. Why shouldn't I?'

'I don't know either. Then why shouldn't you?'

'Because I am.'

'There it is again,' said Diamond. 'I don't see that you are. It looks quite the other thing.'

'Well, but listen to me, Diamond. You know the one *me*, you say, and that is good.'

'Yes.'

'Do you know the other *me* as well?'

'No. I can't. I shouldn't like to.'

'There it is. You don't know the other me. You are sure of one of them?'

'Yes.'

'And you are sure there can't be two mes?'

'Yes.'

'Then the me you don't know must be the same as the me you do know, – else there would be two mes?'

'Yes.'

'Then the other me you don't know must be as kind as the me you do know?'

'Yes.'

'Besides, *I* tell you that it is so, only it doesn't look like it. That I confess freely. Have you anything more to object?'

'No, no, dear North Wind; I am quite satisfied.'

'Then I will tell you something you might object. You might say that the me you know is like the other me, and that I am cruel all through.'

'I know that can't be, because you are so kind.'

'But that kindness might be only a pretence for the sake of being more cruel afterwards.'

'Diamond clung to her tighter than ever, crying –

'No, no, dear North Wind; I can't believe that. I don't believe it. I won't believe it. That would kill me. I love you, and you must love me, else how did I come to love you? How could you know how to put on such a beautiful face if you did not love me and the rest? No. You may sink as many ships as you like, and I won't say another word. I can't say I shall like to see it, you know.'

'That's quite another thing,' said North Wind; and as she spoke she gave one spring from the roof of the hay-loft, and rushed up into the clouds, with Diamond on her left arm close to her heart. And as if the clouds knew she had come, they burst into a fresh jubilation of thunderous light. For a few moments, Diamond seemed to be borne up through the depths of an ocean of dazzling flame; the next, the winds were writhing around him like a storm of serpents. For they were in the midst of the clouds and mists, and they of course took the

shapes of the wind, eddying and wreathing and whirling and shooting
and dashing about like grey and black water, so that it was as if the
wind itself had taken shape, and he saw the grey and black wind tossing
and raving most madly all about him. Now it blinded him by smiting
him upon the eyes; now it deafened him by bellowing in his ears; for
even when the thunder came he knew now that it was the billows of the
great ocean of the air dashing against each other in their haste to fill the
hollow scooped out by the lightning; now it took his breath quite away
by sucking it from his body with the speed of its rush. But he did not
mind it. He only gasped first and then laughed, for the arm of North
Wind was about him, and he was leaning against her bosom. It is quite
impossible for me to describe what he saw. Did you ever watch a great
wave shoot into a winding passage amongst rocks? If you ever did, you
would see that the water rushed every way at once, some of it even
turning back and opposing the rest; greater confusion you might see
nowhere except in a crowd of frightened people. Well, the wind was
like that, except that it went much faster, and therefore was much
wilder, and twisted and shot and curled and dodged and clashed and
raved ten times more madly than anything else in creation except

human passions. Diamond saw the threads of the lady's hair streaking it all. In parts indeed he could not tell which was hair and which was black storm and vapour. It seemed sometimes that all the great billows of mist-muddy wind were woven out of the crossing lines of North Wind's infinite hair, sweeping in endless intertwistings. And Diamond felt as the wind seized on his hair, which his mother kept rather long, as if he too was a part of the storm, and some of its life went out from him. But so sheltered was he by North Wind's arm and bosom that only at times, in the fiercer onslaught of some curl-billowed eddy, did he recognize for a moment how wild was the storm in which he was carried, nestling in its very core and formative centre.

It seemed to Diamond likewise that they were motionless in this centre, and that all the confusion and fighting went on around them. Flash after flash illuminated the fierce chaos, revealing in varied yellow and blue and grey and dusky red the vaporous contention; peal after peal of thunder tore the infinite waste; but it seemed to Diamond that North Wind and he were motionless, all but the hair. It was not so. They were sweeping with the speed of the wind itself towards the sea.

7 The Cathedral

I must not go on describing what cannot be described, for nothing is more wearisome.

Before they reached the sea, Diamond felt North Wind's hair beginning to fall about him.

'Is the storm over, North Wind?' he called out.

'No, Diamond. I am only waiting a moment to set you down. You would not like to see the ship sunk, and I am going to give you a place to stop in till I come back for you.'

'Oh! thank you,' said Diamond. 'I shall be sorry to leave you, North Wind, but I would rather not see the ship go down. And I'm afraid the poor people will cry, and I should hear them. Oh, dear!'

'There are a good many passengers on board; and to tell the truth, Diamond, I don't care about your hearing the cry you speak of. I am afraid you would not get it out of your little head again for a long time.'

'But how can you bear it then, North Wind? For I am sure you are kind. I shall never doubt that again.'

'I will tell you how I am able to bear it, Diamond: I am always hearing, through every noise, through all the noise I am making myself even, the sound of a far-off song. I do not exactly know where it is, or what it means; and I don't hear much of it, only the odour of its music, as it were, flitting across the great billows of the ocean outside this air in which I make such a storm; but what I do hear, is quite enough to make me able to bear the cry from the drowning ship. So it would you if you could hear it.'

'No, it wouldn't,' said Diamond, stoutly. 'For *they* wouldn't hear the music of the far-away song; and if they did, it wouldn't do them any good. You see you and I are not going to be drowned, and so *we* might enjoy it.'

'But you have never heard the psalm, and you don't know what it is like. Somehow, I can't say how, it tells me that all is right; that it is coming to swallow up all cries.'

'But that won't do them any good – the people, I mean,' persisted Diamond.

'It must. It must,' said North Wind, hurriedly. 'It wouldn't be the song it seems to be if it did not swallow up all their fear and pain too, and set them singing it themselves with the rest. I am sure it will. And do you know, ever since I knew I had hair, that is, ever since it began to go out and away, that song has been coming nearer and nearer. Only I must say it was some thousand years before I heard it.'

'But how can you say it was coming nearer when you did not hear it?' asked doubting little Diamond.

'Since I began to hear it, I know it is growing louder, therefore I judge it was coming nearer and nearer until I did hear it first. I'm not so very old, you know – a few thousand years only – and I was quite a baby when I heard the noise first, but I knew it must come from the voices of people ever so much older and wiser than I was. I can't sing at all, except now and then, and I can never tell what my song is going to be; I only know what it is after I have sung it. – But this will never do. Will you stop here?'

'I can't see anywhere to stop,' said Diamond. 'Your hair is all down like a darkness, and I can't see through it if I knock my eyes into it ever so much.'

'Look then,' said North Wind; and, with one sweep of her great white arm, she swept yards deep of darkness like a great curtain from before the face of the boy.

And lo! it was a blue night, lit up with stars. Where it did not shine with stars it shimmered with the milk of the stars, except where, just opposite to Diamond's face, the grey towers of a cathedral blotted out each its own shape of sky and stars.

'Oh! what's that?' cried Diamond, struck with a kind of terror, for he had never seen a cathedral, and it rose before him with awful reality in the midst of the wide spaces, conquering emptiness with grandeur.

'A very good place for you to wait in,' said North Wind. 'But we shall go in, and you shall judge for yourself.'

There was an open door in the middle of one of the towers leading out upon the roof, and through it they passed. Then North Wind set

Diamond on his feet, and he found himself at the top of a stone stair, which went twisting away down into the darkness. For only a little light came in at the door. It was enough, however, to allow Diamond to see that North Wind stood beside him. He looked up to find her face, and saw that she was no longer a beautiful giantess, but the tall gracious lady he liked best to see. She took his hand, and, giving him the broad part of the spiral stair to walk on, led him down a good way; then, opening another little door, led him out upon a narrow gallery that ran all round the central part of the church, on the ledges of the windows of the clerestory, and through openings in the parts of the wall that divided the windows from each other. It was very narrow, and except when they were passing through the wall, Diamond saw nothing to keep him from falling into the church. It lay below him like a great silent gulf hollowed in stone, and he held his breath for fear as he looked down.

'What are trembling for, little Diamond?' said the lady, as she walked gently along, with her hand held out behind her leading him, for there was not breadth enough for them to walk side by side.

'I am afraid of falling down there,' answered Diamond. 'It is so deep down.'

'Yes, rather,' answered North Wind; 'but you were a hundred times higher a few minutes ago.'

'Ah, yes, but somebody's arm was about me then,' said Diamond, putting his little mouth to the beautiful cold hand that had a hold of his.

'What a dear little warm mouth you've got!' said North Wind. 'It is a pity you should talk nonsense with it. Don't you know I have a hold of you?'

'Yes; but I'm walking on my own legs, and they might slip. I can't trust myself so well as your arms.'

'But I have a hold of you, I tell you, foolish child.'

'Yes, but somehow I can't feel comfortable.'

'If you were to fall, and my hold of you were to give way, I should be down after you in a less moment than a lady's watch can tick, and catch you before you had reached the ground.'

'I don't like it, though,' said Diamond.

'*Oh! oh! oh!*' he screamed the next moment, bent double with terror, for North Wind had let go her hold of his hand, and had vanished, leaving him standing as if rooted to the gallery.

She left the words, 'Come after me,' sounding in his ears.

But move he dared not. In a moment more he would from very terror have fallen into the church, but suddenly there came a gentle breath of cool wind upon his face, and it kept blowing upon him in little puffs, and at every puff Diamond felt his faintness going away, and his fear with it. Courage was reviving in his little heart, and still the cool wafts of the soft wind breathed upon him, and the soft wind was so mighty and strong within its gentleness, that in a minute more Diamond was marching along the narrow ledge as fearless for the time as North Wind herself.

He walked on and on, with the windows all in a row on one side of him, and the great empty nave of the church echoing to every one of his brave strides on the other, until at last he came to a little open door, from which a broader stair led him down and down and down, till at last all at once he found himself in the arms of North Wind, who held him close to her, and kissed him on the forehead. Diamond nestled to her, and murmured in her bosom, –

'Why did you leave me, dear North Wind?'

'Because I wanted you to walk alone,' she answered.

'But it is so much nicer here!' said Diamond.

'I daresay; but I couldn't hold a little coward to my heart. It would make me so cold!'

'But I wasn't brave of myself,' said Diamond, whom my older readers will have already discovered to be a true child in this, that he was given to metaphysics. 'It was the wind that blew in my face that made me brave. Wasn't it now, North Wind?'

'Yes: I know that. You had to be taught what courage was. And you couldn't know what it was without feeling it: therefore it was given you. But don't you feel as if you would try to be brave yourself next time?'

'Yes, I do. But trying is not much.'

'Yes, it is – a very great deal, for it is a beginning. And a beginning is the greatest thing of all. To try to be brave is to be brave. The coward who tries to be brave is before the man who is brave because he is made so, and never had to try.'

'How kind you are, North Wind!'

'I am only just. All kindness is but justice. We owe it.'

'I don't quite understand that.'

'Never mind; you will some day. There is no hurry about understanding it now.'

'Who blew the wind on me that made me brave?'

'I did.'

'I didn't see you.'

'Therefore you can believe me.'

'Yes, yes; of course. But how was it that such a little breath could be so strong?'

'That I don't know.'

'But you made it strong?'

'No: I only blew it. I knew it would make you strong, just as it did the man in the boat, you remember. But how my breath has that power I cannot tell. It was put into it when I was made. That is all I know. But really I must be going about my work.'

'Ah! the poor ship! I wish you would stop here, and let the poor ship go.'

'That I dare not do. Will you stop here till I come back?'

'Yes. You won't be long?'

'Not longer than I can help. Trust me, you shall get home before the morning.'

In a moment North Wind was gone, and the next Diamond heard a moaning about the church, which grew and grew to a roaring. The storm was up again, and he knew that North Wind's hair was flying.

The church was dark. Only a little light came through the windows, which were almost all of that precious old stained glass which is so much lovelier than the new. But Diamond could not see how beautiful they were, for there was not enough of light in the stars to show the colours of them. He could only just distinguish them from the walls. He looked up, but could not see the gallery along which he had passed. He could only tell where it was far up by the faint glimmer of the windows of the clerestory, whose sills made part of it. The church grew very lonely about him, and he began to feel like a child whose mother has forsaken it. Only he knew that to be left alone is not always to be forsaken.

He began to feel his way about the place, and for a while went wandering up and down. His little footsteps waked little answering echoes in the great house. It wasn't too big to mind him. It was as if the church knew he was there, and meant to make itself his house. So it went on giving back an answer to every step, until at length Diamond thought he should like to say something out loud, and see what the church would answer. But he found he was afraid to speak. He could not utter a word for fear of the loneliness. Perhaps it was as well that he did not, for the sound of a spoken word would have made him feel the place yet more deserted and empty. But he thought he could sing. He was fond of singing, and at home he used to sing, to tunes of his own, all the nursery rhymes he knew. So he began to try *Hey diddle diddle*, but it wouldn't do. Then he tried *Little Boy Blue*, but it was no better. Neither would *Sing a Song of Sixpence* sing itself at all. Then he tried *Poor old Cockytoo*, but he wouldn't do. They all sounded so silly! and he had never thought them silly before. So he was quiet, and listened to the echoes that came out of the dark corners in answer to his footsteps.

At last he gave a great sigh, and said, 'I'm so tired'. But he did not hear the gentle echo that answered from far away over his head, for at the same moment he came against the lowest of a few steps that stretched across the church, and fell down and hurt his arm. He cried a little first, and then crawled up the steps on his hands and knees. At the top he came to a little bit of carpet, on which he lay down; and there he lay staring at the dull window that rose nearly a hundred feet above his head.

Now this was the eastern window of the church, and the moon was at that moment just on the edge of the horizon. The next, she was peeping over it. And lo! with the moon, St. John and St. Paul, and the rest of them, began to dawn in the window in their lovely garments. Diamond did not know that the wonder-working moon was behind, and he thought all the light was coming out of the window itself, and that the good old men were appearing to help him, growing out of the night and the darkness, because he had hurt his arm, and was very tired and lonely, and North Wind was so long in coming. So he lay and looked at them backwards over his head, wondering when they would come down or what they would do next. They were very dim, for the moonlight was not strong enough for the colours, and he had enough to do with his eyes trying to make out their shapes. So his eyes grew tired, and more and more tired, and his eyelids grew so heavy that they would keep tumbling down over his eyes. He kept lifting them and lifting them, but every time they were heavier than the last. It was no use: they were too much for him. Sometimes before he had got them half up, down they were again; and at length he gave it up quite, and the moment he gave it up, he was fast asleep.

8 The East Window

That Diamond had fallen fast asleep is very evident from the strange things he now fancied as taking place. For he thought he heard a sound as of whispering up in the great window. He tried to open his eyes, but he could not. And the whispering went on and grew louder and louder, until he could hear every word that was said. He thought it was the Apostles talking about him. But he could not open his eyes.

'And how comes he to be lying there, St. Peter?' said one.

'I think I saw him a while ago up in the gallery, under the Nicodemus window. Perhaps he has fallen down. What do you think, St. Matthew?'

'I don't think he could have crept here after falling from such a height. He must have been killed.'

'What are we to do with him? We can't leave him lying there. And we could not make him comfortable up here in the window: it's rather crowded already. What do you say, St. Thomas?'

'Let's go down and look at him.'

There came a rustling, and a chinking, for some time, and then there was a silence, and Diamond felt somehow that all the Apostles were standing round him and looking down on him. And still he could not open his eyes.

'What is the matter with him, St. Luke?' asked one.

'There's nothing the matter with him,' answered St. Luke, who must have joined the company of the Apostles from the next window, one would think. 'He's in a sound sleep.'

'I have it,' cried another. 'This is one of North Wind's tricks. She has caught him up and dropped him at our door, like a withered leaf or a foundling baby. I don't understand that woman's conduct, I must say. As if we hadn't enough to do with our money, without going taking care of other people's children! That's not what our forefathers built cathedrals for.'

Now Diamond could not bear to hear such things against North Wind, who, he knew, never played anybody a trick. She was far too busy with her own work for that. He struggled hard to open his eyes, but without success.

'She should consider that a church is not a place for pranks, not to mention that *we* live in it,' said another.

'It certainly is disrespectful of her. But she always is disrespectful. What right has she to bang at our windows as she has been doing the whole of this night? I daresay there is glass broken somewhere. I know my blue robe is in a dreadful mess with the rain first and the dust after. It will cost me shillings to clean it.'

Then Diamond knew that they could not be Apostles, talking like this. They could only be the sextons and vergers, and such-like, who got up at night, and put on the robes of deans and bishops, and called each other grand names, as the foolish servants he had heard his father tell of call themselves lords and ladies, after their masters and mistresses. And he was so angry at their daring to abuse North Wind, that he jumped up, crying –

'North Wind knows best what she is about. She has a good right to blow the cobwebs from your windows, for she was sent to do it. She sweeps them away from grander places, I can tell you, for I've been with her at it.'

This was what he began to say, but as he spoke his eyes came wide open, and behold, there were neither Apostles nor vergers there – not even a window with the effigies of holy men in it, but a dark heap of hay all about him, and the little panes in the roof of his loft glimmering blue in the light of the morning. Old Diamond was coming awake down below in the stable. In a moment more he was on his feet, and shaking himself so that young Diamond's bed trembled under him.

'He's grand at shaking himself,' said Diamond. 'I wish I could shake myself like that. But then I can wash myself, and he can't. What fun it would be so see Old Diamond washing his face with his hoofs and iron shoes! Wouldn't it be a picture?'

So saying, he got up and dressed himself. Then he went out into the garden. There must have been a tremendous wind in the night, for although all was quiet now, there lay the little summer-house crushed to the ground, and over it the great elm-tree, which the wind had broken across, being much decayed in the middle. Diamond almost cried to see the wilderness of green leaves, which used to be so far up in the blue air, tossing about in the breeze, and liking it best when the wind blew it most, now lying so near the ground, and without any hope of ever getting up into the deep air again.

'I wonder how old the tree is!' thought Diamond. 'It must take a long time to get so near the sky as that poor tree was.'

'Yes, indeed,' said a voice beside him, for Diamond had spoken the last words aloud.

Diamond started, and looking round saw a clergyman, a brother of Mrs. Coleman, who happened to be visiting her. He was a great scholar, and was in the habit of rising early.

'Who are you, my man?' he added.

'Little Diamond,' answered the boy.

'Oh! I have heard of you. How do you come to be up so early?'

'Because the sham Apostles talked such nonsense, they waked me up.'

The clergyman stared. Diamond saw that he had better have held his tongue, for he could not explain things.

'You must have been dreaming, my little man,' said he. 'Dear! dear!' he went on, looking at the tree, 'there has been terrible work here. This is the north wind's doing. What a pity! I wish we lived at the back of it, I'm sure.'

'What is that, sir?' asked Diamond.

'Away in the Hyperborean regions,' answered the clergyman, smiling.

'I never heard of the place,' returned Diamond.

'I daresay not,' answered the clergyman; 'but if this tree had been there now, it would not have been blown down, for there is no wind there.'

'But, please, sir, if it had been there,' said Diamond, 'we should not have had to be sorry for it.'

'Certainly not.'

'Then we shouldn't have had to be glad for it either.'

'You're quite right, my boy,' said the clergyman, looking at him very kindly, as he turned away to the house, with his eyes bent towards the earth. But Diamond thought within himself, 'I will ask North Wind next time I see her to take me to that country. I think she did speak about it once before.'

9 How Diamond got to the Back of the North Wind

When Diamond went home to breakfast, he found his father and mother already seated at the table. They were both busy with their bread and butter, and Diamond sat himself down in his usual place. His mother looked up at him, and, after watching him for a moment, said:

'I don't think the boy is looking well, husband.'

'Don't you? Well, I don't know. I think he looks pretty bobbish. How do you feel yourself, Diamond, my boy?'

'Quite well, thank you, father; at least, I think I've got a little headache.'

'There! I told you,' said his father and mother both at once.

'The child's very poorly,' added his mother.

'The child's quite well,' added his father.

And then they both laughed.

'You see,' said his mother, 'I've had a letter from my sister at Sandwich.'

'Sleepy old hole!' said his father.

'Don't abuse the place; there's good people in it,' said his mother.

'Right, old lady,' returned his father; 'only I don't believe there are more than two pair of carriage-horses in the whole blessed place.'

'Well, people can get to heaven without carriages – or coachmen either husband. Not that I should like to go without *my* coachman, you know. But about the boy?'

'What boy?'

'That boy, there, staring at you with his goggle-eyes.'

'Have I got goggle-eyes, mother?' asked Diamond, a little dismayed.

'Not too goggle,' said his mother, who was quite proud of her boy's

eyes, only did not want to make him vain. 'Not too goggle; only you need not stare so.'

'Well, what about him?' said his father.

'I told you I had got a letter.'

'Yes, from your sister; not from Diamond.'

'La, husband! you've got out of bed the wrong leg first this morning, I do believe.'

'I always get out with both at once,' said his father, laughing.

'Well, listen then. His aunt wants the the boy to go down and see her.'

'And that's why you want to make out that he ain't looking well.'

'No more he is. I think he had better go.'

'Well, I don't care, if you can find the money,' said his father.

'I'll manage that,' said his mother; and so it was agreed that Diamond should go to Sandwich.

I will not describe the preparations Diamond made. You would have thought he had been going on a three months' voyage. Nor will I describe the journey, for our business is now at the place. He was met at the station by his aunt, a cheerful middle-aged woman, and conveyed in safety to the sleepy old town, as his father had called it. And no wonder that it was sleepy, for it was nearly dead of old age.

Diamond went about staring with his beautiful goggle-eyes, at the quaint old streets, and the shops, and the houses. Everything looked very strange, indeed; for here was a town abandoned by its nurse, the sea, like an old oyster left on the shore till it gaped for weariness. It used to be one of the five chief seaports in England, but it began to hold itself too high, and the consequence was the sea grew less and less intimate with it, gradually drew back, and kept more to itself, till at length it left it high and dry: Sandwich was a seaport no more; the sea went on with its own tide-business a long way off, and forgot it. Of course it went to sleep, and had no more to do with ships. That's what comes to cities and nations, and boys and girls, who say, 'I can do without *your* help. I'm enough for myself.'

Diamond soon made great friends with an old woman who kept a toyshop, for his mother had given him twopence for pocket-money before he left, and he had gone into her shop to spend it, and she got

talking to him. She looked very funny, because she had not got any teeth, but Diamond liked her, and went often to her shop, although he had nothing to spend there after the twopence was gone.

One afternoon he had been wandering rather wearily about the streets for some time. It was a hot day, and he felt tired. As he passed the toyshop, he stepped in.

'Please may I sit down for a minute on this box?' he said, thinking the old woman was somewhere in the shop. But he got no answer, and sat down without one. Around him were a great many toys of all prices, from a penny up to shillings. All at once he heard a gentle whirring somewhere amongst them. It made him start and look behind him. There were the sails of a windmill going round and round almost close to his ear. He thought at first it must be one of those toys which are wound up and go with clockwork; but no, it was a common penny toy, with the windmill at the end of a whistle, and when the whistle blows the windmill goes. But the wonder was that there was no one at the whistle end blowing, and yet the sails were turning round and round – now faster, now slower, now faster again.

'What can it mean?' said Diamond, aloud.

'It means me,' said the tiniest voice he had ever heard.

'Who are you, please?' asked Diamond.

'Well, really, I begin to be ashamed of you,' said the voice. 'I wonder how long it will be before you know me; or how often I might take you in before you got sharp enough to suspect me. You are as bad as a baby that doesn't know his mother in a new bonnet.'

'Not quite so bad as that, dear North Wind,' said Diamond, 'for I didn't see you at all, and indeed, I don't see you yet, although I recognize your voice. Do grow a little, please.'

'Not a hair's-breadth,' said the voice, and it was the smallest voice that ever spoke. 'What are you doing here?'

'I am come to see my aunt. But, please, North Wind, why didn't you come back for me in the church that night?'

'I did. I carried you safe home. All the time you were dreaming about the glass apostles, you were lying in my arms.'

'I'm so glad,' said Diamond. 'I thought that must be it, only I wanted to hear you say so. Did you sink the ship, then?'

'Yes.'

'And drown everybody?'

'Not quite. One boat got away with six or seven men in it.'

'How could the boat swim when the ship couldn't?'

'Of course I had some trouble with it. I had to contrive a bit, and manage the waves a little. When they're once thoroughly waked up, I have a good deal of trouble with them sometimes. They're apt to get stupid with tumbling over each other's heads. That's when they're fairly at it. However, the boat got to a desert island before noon the next day.'

'And what good will come of that?'

'I don't know. I obeyed orders. Good-bye.'

'Oh! stay, North Wind, *do* stay!' cried Diamond, dismayed to see the windmill get slower and slower.

'What is it, my dear child?' said North Wind, and the windmill began turning again so swiftly that Diamond could scarcely see it. 'What a big voice you've got! and what a noise you do make with it! What is it you want? I have little to do, but that little must be done.'

'I want you to take me to the country at the back of the north wind.'

'That's not so easy,' said North Wind, and was silent for so long that Diamond thought she was gone indeed. But after he had quite given her up, the voice began again.

'I almost wish old Herodotus had held his tongue about it. Much he knew of it!'

'Why do you wish that, North Wind?'

'Because then that clergyman would never have heard of it, and set you wanting to go. But we shall see. We shall see. You must go home now, my dear, for you don't seem very well, and I'll see what can be done for you. Don't wait for me. I've got to break a few of old Goody's toys: she's thinking too much of her new stock. Two or three will do. There! go now.'

Diamond rose, quite sorry, and without a word left the shop, and went home.

It soon appeared that his mother had been right about him, for that same afternoon his head began to ache very much, and he had to go to bed.

He awoke in the middle of the night. The lattice window of his room had blown open, and the curtains of his little bed were swinging about in the wind.

'If that should be North Wind now!' thought Diamond.

But the next moment he heard some one closing the window, and his aunt came to the bedside. She put her hand on his face, and said –

'How's your head, dear?'

'Better, auntie, I think.'

'Would you like something to drink?'

'Oh, yes! I should, please.'

So his aunt gave him some lemonade, for she had been used to nursing sick people, and Diamond felt very much refreshed, and laid his head down again to go very fast asleep, as he thought. And so he did, but only to come awake again, as a fresh burst of wind blew the lattice open a second time. The same moment he found himself in a cloud of North Wind's hair, with her beautiful face, set in it like a moon, bending over him.

'Quick, Diamond!' she said. 'I have found such a chance!'

'But I'm not well,' said Diamond.

'I know that, but you will be better for a little fresh air. You shall have plenty of that.'

'You want me to go, then?'

'Yes, I do. It won't hurt you.'

'Very well,' said Diamond; and getting out of the bed-clothes, he jumped into North Wind's arms.

'We must make haste before your aunt comes,' said she, as she glided out of the open lattice and left it swinging.

The moment Diamond felt her arms fold around him he began to feel better. It was a moonless night, and very dark, with glimpses of stars when the clouds parted.

'I used to dash the waves about here,' said North Wind, 'where cows and sheep are feeding now; but we shall soon get to them. There they are.'

And Diamond, looking down, saw the white glimmer of breaking water far below him.

'You see, Diamond,' said North Wind, 'it is very difficult for me to get you to the back of the north wind, for that country lies in the very north itself, and of course I can't blow northwards.'

'Why not?' asked Diamond.

'You little silly!' said North Wind. 'Don't you see that if I were to blow northwards I should be South Wind, and that is as much as to say that one person could be two persons?'

'But how can you ever get home at all, then?'

'You are quite right – that is my home, though I never get farther than the outer door. I sit on the doorsteps, and hear the voices inside. I am nobody there, Diamond.'

'I'm very sorry.'

'Why?'

'That you should be nobody.'

'Oh, I don't mind it. Dear little man! you will be very glad some day to be nobody yourself. But you can't understand that now, and you had better not try; for if you do, you will be certain to go fancying some egregious nonsense, and making yourself miserable about it.'

'Then I won't,' said Diamond.

'There's a good boy. It will all come in good time.'

'But you haven't told me how you get to the doorstep, you know.'

'It is easy enough for me. I have only to consent to be nobody, and there I am. I draw into myself, and there I am on the doorstep. But you can easily see, or you have less sense than I think, that to drag you, you heavy thing, along with me, would take centuries, and I could not give the time to it.'

'Oh, I'm so sorry!' said Diamond.

'What for now, pet?'

'That I'm so heavy for you. I would be lighter if I could, but I don't know how.'

'You silly darling! Why, I could toss you a hundred miles from me if I liked. It is only when I am going home that I shall find you heavy.'

'Then you are going home with me?'

'Of course. Did I not come to fetch you just for that?'

'But all this time you must be going southwards.'

'Yes. Of course I am.'

'How can you be taking me northwards, then?'

'A very sensible question. But you shall see. I will get rid of a few of these clouds – only they do come up so fast! It's like trying to blow a brook dry. There! What do you see now?'

'I think I see a little boat, away there, down below.'

'A little boat, indeed! Well! She's a yacht of two hundred tons; and the captain of it is a friend of mine; for he is a man of good sense, and can sail his craft well. I've helped him many a time when he little thought it. I've heard him grumbling at me, when I was doing the very best I could for him. Why, I've carried him eighty miles a day, again and again, right north.'

'He must have dodged for that,' said Diamond, who had been watching the vessels, and had seen that they went other ways than the wind blew.

'Of course he must. But don't you see, it was the best I could do? I couldn't be South Wind. And besides it gave him a share in the business. It is not good at all – mind that, Diamond – to do everything for those you love, and not give them a share in the doing. It's not kind. It's making too much of yourself, my child. If I had been South Wind, he would only have smoked his pipe all day, and made himself stupid.'

'But how could he be a man of sense and grumble at you when you were doing your best for him?'

'Oh! you must make allowances,' said North Wind, 'or you will never do justice to anybody. – You do understand, then, that a captain may sail north——'

'In spite of a north wind – yes,' supplemented Diamond.

'Now, I do think you must be stupid, my dear,' said North Wind. 'Suppose the north wind did not blow, where would he be then?'

'Why then the south wind would carry him.'

'So you think that when the north wind stops the south wind blows. Nonsense. If I didn't blow, the captain couldn't sail his eighty miles a day. No doubt South Wind would carry him faster, but South Wind is sitting on her doorstep then, and if I stopped there would be a dead calm. So you are all wrong to say he can sail north in spite of me; he sails north by my help, and my help alone. You see that, Diamond?'

'Yes, I do, North Wind. I am stupid, but I don't want to be stupid.'

'Good boy! I am going to blow you north in that little craft, one of the finest that ever sailed the sea. Here we are, right over it. I shall be blowing against you; you will be sailing against me; and all will be just as we want it. The captain won't get on so fast as he would like, but he will get on, and so shall we. I'm just going to put you on board. Do you see in front of the tiller – that thing the man is working, now to one side, now to the other – a round thing like the top of a drum?'

'Yes,' said Diamond.

'Below that is where they keep their spare sails, and some stores of that sort. I am going to blow that cover off. The same moment I will drop you on deck, and you must tumble in. Don't be afraid, it is of no depth, and you will fall on a roll of sail-cloth. You will find it nice and warm and dry – only dark; and you will know I am near you by every roll and pitch of the vessel. Coil yourself up and go to sleep. The yacht shall be my cradle, and you shall be my baby.'

'Thank you, dear North Wind. I am not a bit afraid,' said Diamond.

In a moment they were on a level with the bulwarks, and North Wind sent the hatch of the after-store rattling away over the deck to leeward. The next, Diamond found himself in the dark, for he had tumbled through the hole as North Wind had told him, and the cover was replaced over his head. Away he went rolling to leeward, for the wind began all at once to blow hard. He heard the call of the captain, and the loud trampling of the men over his head, as they hauled at the main sheet to get the boom on board that they might take in a reef in the mainsail. Diamond felt about until he had found what seemed the most comfortable place, and there he snuggled down and lay.

Hours after hours, a great many of them, went by; and still Diamond lay there. He never felt in the least tired or impatient, for a strange pleasure filled his heart. The straining of the masts, the creaking of the boom, the singing of the ropes, the banging of the blocks as they put the vessel about, all fell in with the roaring of the wind above, the surge of the waves past her sides, and the thud with which every now and then one would strike her; while through it all Diamond could hear the gurgling, rippling, talking flow of the water against her planks, as she slipped through it, lying now on this side, now on that – like a subdued air running through the grand music his North Wind was making about him to keep him from tiring as they sped on towards the country at the back of her doorstep.

How long this lasted Diamond had no idea. He seemed to fall asleep sometimes, only through the sleep he heard the sounds going on. At length the weather seemed to get worse. The confusion and trampling of feet grew more frequent over his head; the vessel lay over more and more on her side, and went roaring through the waves, which banged and thumped at her as if in anger. All at once arose a terrible uproar. The hatch was blown off; a cold fierce wind swept in upon him; and a long arm came with it which laid hold of him and lifted him out. The same moment he saw the little vessel far below him righting herself. She had taken in all her sails and lay now tossing on the waves like a sea-bird with folded wings. A short distance to the south lay a much larger vessel, with two or three sails set, and towards it North Wind was carrying Diamond. It was a German ship, on its way to the North Pole.

'That vessel down there will give us a lift now,' said North Wind; 'and after that I must do the best I can.'

She managed to hide him amongst the flags of the big ship, which were all snugly stowed away, and on and on they sped towards the north. At length one night she whispered in his ear, 'Come on deck, Diamond;' and he got up at once and crept on deck. Everything looked very strange. Here and there on all sides were huge masses of floating ice, looking like cathedrals, and castles, and crags, while away beyond was a blue sea.

'Is the sun rising or setting?' asked Diamond.

'Neither or both, which you please. I can hardly tell which myself. If he is setting now, he will be rising the next moment.'

'What a strange light it is!' said Diamond. 'I have heard that the sun doesn't go to bed all the summer in these parts. Miss Coleman told me that. I suppose he feels very sleepy, and that is why the light he sends out looks so like a dream.'

'That will account for it well enough for all practical purposes,' said North Wind.

Some of the icebergs were drifting northward: one was passing very near the ship. North Wind seized Diamond, and with a single bound lighted on one of them – a huge thing, with sharp pinnacles and great clefts. The same instant a wind began to blow from the south. North Wind hurried Diamond down the north side of the iceberg, stepping by its jags and splintering; for this berg had never got far enough south to be melted and smoothed by the summer sun. She brought him to a cave near the water, where she entered, and, letting Diamond go, sat down as if weary on a ledge of ice.

Diamond seated himself on the other side, and for a while was enraptured with the colour of the air inside the cave. It was a deep, dazzling, lovely blue, deeper than the deepest blue of the sky. The blue seemed to be in constant motion, like the blackness when you press your eyeballs with your fingers, boiling and sparkling. But when he looked across to North Wind he was frightened; her face was worn and livid.

'What is the matter with you, dear North Wind?' he said.

'Nothing much. I feel very faint. But you mustn't mind it, for I can bear it quite well. South Wind always blows me faint. If it were not for the cool of the thick ice between me and her, I should faint altogether. Indeed, as it is, I fear I must vanish.'

Diamond stared at her in terror, for he saw that her form and face were growing, not small, but transparent, like something dissolving, not in water, but in light. He could see the side of the blue cave through her very heart. And she melted away till all that was left was a pale face, like the moon in the morning, with two great lucid eyes in it.

'I am going, Diamond,' she said.

'Does it hurt you?' asked Diamond.

'It's very uncomfortable,' she answered; 'but I don't mind it, for I shall come all right again before long. I thought I should be able to go with you all the way, but I cannot. You must not be frightened though. Just go straight on, and you will come all right. You'll find me on the doorstep.'

As she spoke, her face too faded quite away, only Diamond thought he could still see her eyes shining through the blue. When he went closer, however, he found that what he thought her eyes were only two hollows in the ice. North Wind was quite gone; and Diamond would have cried, if he had not trusted her so thoroughly. So he sat still in the blue air of the cavern listening to the wash and ripple of the water all about the base of the iceberg, as it sped on and on into the open sea northwards. It was an excellent craft to go with a current, for there was twice as much of it below water as above. But a light south wind was blowing too, and so it went fast.

After a little while Diamond went out and sat on the edge of his floating island, and looked down into the ocean beneath him. The white sides of the berg reflected so much light below the water, that he could see far down into the green abyss. Sometimes he fancied he saw the eyes of North Wind looking up at him from below, but the fancy never lasted beyond the moment of its birth. And the time passed he did not know how, for he felt as if he were in a dream. When he got tired of the green water, he went into the blue cave; and when he got tired of the blue cave he went out and gazed all about him on the blue sea, ever sparkling in the sun, which kept wheeling about the sky, never going below the horizon. But he chiefly gazed northwards, to see whether any land were appearing. All this time he never wanted to eat. He broke off little bits of the berg now and then and sucked them, and he thought them very nice.

At length, one time he came out of his cave, he spied, far off upon the horizon, a shining peak that rose into the sky like the top of some tremendous iceberg; and his vessel was bearing him straight towards it. As it went on the peak rose and rose higher and higher above the horizon; and other peaks rose after it, with sharp edges and jagged ridges connecting them. Diamond thought this must be the place he was going to; and he was right; for the mountains rose and rose, till he saw the line of the coast at their feet, and at length the iceberg drove into a little bay, all round which were lofty precipices with snow on their tops, and streaks of ice down their sides. The berg floated slowly up to a projecting rock. Diamond stepped on shore, and without looking behind him began to follow a natural path which led windingly towards the top of the precipice.

When he reached it, he found himself on a broad table of ice, along which he could walk without much difficulty. Before him, at a considerable distance, rose a lofty ridge of ice, which shot up into fantastic pinnacles and towers and battlements. The air was very cold, and seemed somehow dead, for there was not the slightest breath of wind.

In the centre of the ridge before him appeared a gap like the opening of a valley. But as he walked towards it, gazing, and wondering whether that could be the way he had to take, he saw that what had appeared a gap was the form of a woman seated against the ice front of the ridge, leaning forward with her hands in her lap, and her hair hanging down to the ground.

'It is North Wind on her doorstep,' said Diamond joyfully, and hurried on.

He soon came up to the place, and there the form sat, like one of the great figures at the door of an Egyptian temple, motionless, with drooping arms and head. Then Diamond grew frightened, because she did not move nor speak. He was sure it was North Wind, but he thought she must be dead at last. Her face was white as the snow, her eyes were blue as the air in the ice-cave, and her hair hung down straight, like icicles. She had on a greenish robe, like the colour in the hollows of a glacier seen from far off.

He stood up before her, and gazed fearfully into her face for a few minutes before he ventured to speak. At length, with a great effort and a trembling voice, he faltered out –

'North Wind!'

'Well, child?' said the form, without lifting its head.

'Are you ill, dear North Wind?'

'No. I am waiting.'

'What for?'

'Till I'm wanted.'

'You don't care for me any more,' said Diamond, almost crying now.

'Yes, I do. Only I can't show it. All my love is down at the bottom of my heart. But I feel it bubbling there.'

'What do you want me to do next, dear North Wind?' said Diamond, wishing to show his love by being obedient.

'What do you want to do yourself?'

'I want to go into the country at your back.'

'Then you must go through me.'

'I don't know what you mean.'

'I mean just what I say. You must walk on as if I were an open door, and go right through me.'

'But that will hurt you.'

'Not in the least. It will hurt you, though.'

'I don't mind that, if you tell me to do it.'

'Do it,' said North Wind.

Diamond walked towards her instantly. When he reached her knees, he put out his hand to lay it on her, but nothing was there save an intense cold. He walked on. Then all grew white about him; and the cold stung him like fire. He walked on still, groping through the whiteness. It thickened about him. At last, it got into his heart, and he lost all sense. I would say that he fainted – only whereas in common faints all grows black about you, he felt swallowed up in whiteness. It was when he reached North Wind's heart that he fainted and fell. But as he fell, he rolled over the threshold, and it was thus that Diamond got to the back of the north wind.

I have now come to the most difficult part of my story. And why?
Because I do not know enough about it. And why should I not know as
much about this part as about any other part? for of course I could
know nothing about the story except Diamond had told it; and why
should not Diamond tell about the country at the back of the north
wind, as well as about his adventures in getting there? Because, when
he came back, he had forgotten a great deal, and what he did remember
was very hard to tell. Things there are so different from things here!
The people there do not speak the same language for one thing.
Indeed, Diamond insisted that there they do not speak at all. I do not
think he was right, but it may well have appeared so to Diamond. The
fact is, we have different reports of the place from the most
trustworthy people. Therefore we are bound to believe that it appears
somewhat different to different people. All, however, agree in a
general way about it.

I will tell you something of what two very different people have
reported, both of whom knew more about it, I believe, than
Herodotus. One of them speaks from his experience, for he visited the
country; the other from the testimony of a young peasant girl who
came back from it for a month's visit to her friends. The former was a
great Italian of noble family, who died more than five hundred years
ago; the latter a Scotch shepherd who died not forty years ago.

The Italian, then, informs us that he had to enter that country
through a fire so hot that he would have thrown himself into boiling
glass to cool himself. This was not Diamond's experience, but then
Durante – that was the name of the Italian, and it means Lasting, for
his books will last as long as there are enough men in the world worthy
of having them – Durante was an elderly man, and Diamond was a

little boy, and so their experience must be a little different. The peasant girl, on the other hand, fell fast asleep in a wood, and woke in the same country.

In describing it, Durante says that the ground everywhere smelt sweetly, and that a gentle, even-tempered wind, which never blew faster or slower, breathed in his face as he went, making all the leaves point one way, not so as to disturb the birds in the tops of the trees, but, on the contrary, sounding a bass to their song. He describes also a little river which was so full that its little waves, as it hurried along, bent the grass, full of red and yellow flowers, through which it flowed. He says that the purest stream in the world beside this one would look as if it were mixed with something that did not belong to it, even although it was flowing ever in the brown shadow of the trees, and neither sun nor moon could shine upon it. He seems to imply that it is always the month of May in that country. It would be out of place to describe here the wonderful sights he saw, for the music of them is in another key from that of this story, and I shall therefore only add from the account of this traveller, that the people there are so free and so just and so healthy, that every one of them has a crown like a king and a mitre like a priest.

The peasant girl – Kilmeny was her name – could not report such grand things as Durante, for, as the shepherd says, telling her story as I tell Diamond's –

> 'Kilmeny had been she knew not where,
> And Kilmeny had seen what she could not declare;
> Kilmeny had been where the cock never crew,
> Where the rain never fell, and the wind never blew;
> But it seemed as the harp of the sky had rung,
> And the airs of heaven played round her tongue,
> When she spoke of the lovely forms she had seen,
> And a land where sin had never been;
> A land of love and a land of light,
> Withouten sun, or moon, or night;
> Where the river swayed a living stream,
> And the light a pure and cloudless beam:
> The land of vision it would seem,
> And still an everlasting dream.'

The last two lines are the shepherd's own remark, and a matter of opinion. But it is clear, I think, that Kilmeny must have described the same country as Durante saw, though, not having his experience, she could neither understand nor describe it so well.

Now I must give you such fragments of recollection as Diamond was able to bring back with him.

When he came to himself after he fell, he found himself at the back of the north wind. North Wind herself was nowhere to be seen. Neither was there a vestige of snow or of ice within sight. The sun too had vanished; but that was no matter, for there was plenty of a certain still rayless light. Where it came from he never found out; but he thought it belonged to the country itself. Sometimes he thought it came out of the flowers, which were very bright, but had no strong colour. He said the river – for all agree that there is a river there – flowed not only through, but over grass: its channel, instead of being rock, stones, pebbles, sand, or anything else, was of pure meadow grass, not over long. He insisted that if it did not sing tunes in people's ears, it sung tunes in their heads, in proof of which I may mention, that, in the troubles which followed, Diamond was often heard singing; and when asked what he was singing, would answer, 'One of the tunes the river at the back of the north wind sung.' And I may as well say at once that Diamond never told these things to any one but – no, I had better not say who it was; but whoever it was told me, and I thought it would be well to write them for my child-readers.

He could not say he was very happy there, for he had neither his father nor mother with him, but he felt so still and quiet and patient and contented, that, as far as the mere feeling went, it was something better than mere happiness. Nothing went wrong at the back of the north wind. Neither was anything quite right, he thought. Only everything was going to be right some day. His account disagreed with that of Durante, and agreed with that of Kilmeny, in this, that he protested there was no wind there at all. I fancy he missed it. At all events *we* could not do without wind. It all depends on how big our lungs are whether the wind is too strong for us or not.

When the person he told about it asked him whether he saw anybody he knew there, he answered, 'Only a little girl belonging to the gardener, who thought he had lost her, but was quite mistaken, for there she was safe enough, and was to come back some day, as I came back, if they would only wait.'

'Did you talk to her, Diamond?'

'No. Nobody talks there. They only look at each other and understand everything.'

'Is it cold there?'

'No.'

'Is it hot?'

'No.'

'What is it then?'

'You never think about such things there.'

'What a queer place it must be!'

'It's a very good place.'

'Do you want to go back again?'

'No: I don't think I have ever left it; I feel it here, somewhere.'

'Did the people there look pleased?'

'Yes – quite pleased, only a little sad.'

'Then they didn't look glad?'

'They looked as if they were waiting to be gladder some day.'

This was how Diamond used to answer questions about that country. And now I will take up the story again, and tell you how he got back to this country.

11 How Diamond Got Home Again

When one at the back of the north wind wanted to know how things were going with any one he loved, he had to go to a certain tree, climb the stem, and sit down in the branches. In a few minutes, if he kept very still, he would see something at least of what was going on with the people he loved.

One day when Diamond was sitting in this tree, he began to long very much to get home again, and no wonder, for he saw his mother crying. Durante says that the people there may always follow their wishes, because they never wish but what is good. Diamond's wish was to get home, and he would fain follow his wish.

But how was he to set about it? If he could only see North Wind! But the moment he had got to her back, she was gone altogether from his sight. He had never seen her back. She might be sitting on her doorstep still, looking southwards, and waiting, white and thin and blue-eyed, until she was wanted. Or she might have again become a mighty creature, with power to do that which was demanded of her, and gone far away upon many missions. She must be somewhere, however. He could not go home without her, and therefore he must find her. She could never have intended to leave him always away from his mother. If there had been any danger of that, she would have told him, and given him his choice about going. For North Wind was right honest. How to find North Wind, therefore, occupied all his thoughts.

In his anxiety about his mother, he used to climb the tree every day, and sit in its branches. However many of the dwellers there did so, they never incommoded one another; for the moment one got into the tree, he became invisible to every one else; and it was such a wide-spreading tree that there was room for every one of the people of the country in it, without the least interference with each other.

Sometimes, on getting down, two of them would meet at the root, and then they would smile to each other more sweetly than at any other time, as much as to say, 'Ah, you've been up there too!'

One day he was sitting on one of the outer branches of the tree, looking southwards after his home. Far away was a blue shining sea, dotted with gleaming and sparkling specks of white. Those were the icebergs. Nearer he saw a great range of snow-capped mountains, and down below him the lovely meadow-grass of the country, with the stream flowing and flowing through it, away towards the sea. As he looked he began to wonder, for the whole country lay beneath him like a map, and that which was near him looked just as small as that which he knew to be miles away. The ridge of ice which encircled it appeared but a few yards off, and no larger than the row of pebbles with which a child will mark out the boundaries of the kingdom he has appropriated on the sea-shore. He thought he could distinguish the vapoury form of North Wind, seated as he had left her, on the other side. Hastily he descended the tree, and to his amazement found that the map or model of the country still lay at his feet. He stood in it. With one stride he had crossed the river; with another he had reached the ridge of ice; with the third he stepped over its peaks, and sank wearily down at North Wind's knees. For there she sat on her doorstep. The peaks of the great ridge of ice were as lofty as ever behind her, and the country at her back had vanished from Diamond's view.

North Wind was as still as Diamond had left her. Her pale face was white as the snow, and her motionless eyes were as blue as the caverns in the ice. But the instant Diamond touched her, her face began to change like that of one waking from sleep. Light began to glimmer from the blue of her eyes. A moment more, and she laid her hand on Diamond's head, and began playing with his hair. Diamond took hold of her hand, and laid his face to it. She gave a little start.

'How very alive you are, child!' she murmured. 'Come nearer to me.'

By the help of the stones all around he clambered up beside her, and laid himself against her bosom. She gave a great sight, slowly lifted her arms, and slowly folded them about him, until she clasped him close. Yet a moment, and she roused herself, and came quite awake; and the cold of her bosom, which had pierced Diamond's bones, vanished.

'Have you been sitting here ever since I went through you, dear North Wind?' asked Diamond, stroking her hand.

'Yes,' she answered, looking at him with her old kindness.

'Ain't you very tired?'

'No; I've often had to sit longer. Do you know how long you have been?'

'Oh! years and years,' answered Diamond.

'You have just been seven days,' returned North Wind.

'I thought I had been a hundred years!' exclaimed Diamond.

'Yes, I dare say,' replied North Wind. 'You've been away from here seven days; but how long you may have been in there is quite another thing. Behind my back and before my face things are so different! They don't go at all by the same rule.'

'I'm very glad,' said Diamond, after thinking a while.

'Why?' asked North Wind.

'Because I've been such a long time there, and such a little while away from mother. Why, she won't be expecting me home from Sandwich yet!'

'No. But we mustn't talk any longer. I've got my orders now, and we must be off in a few minutes.'

Next moment Diamond found himself sitting alone on the rock. North Wind had vanished. A creature like a great humble-bee or cockchafer flew past his face; but it could be neither, for there were no insects amongst the ice. It passed him again and again, flying in circles around him, and he concluded that it must be North Wind herself, no bigger than Tom Thumb when his mother put him in the nutshell lined with flannel. But she was no longer vapoury and thin. She was solid, although tiny. A moment more, and she perched on his shoulder.

'Come along, Diamond,' she said in his ear, in the smallest and highest of treble voices; 'it is time we were setting out for Sandwich.'

Diamond could just see her, by turning his head towards his shoulder as far as he could, but only with one eye, for his nose came between her and the other.

'Won't you take me in your arms and carry me?' he said in a whisper, for he knew she did not like a loud voice when she was small.

'Ah! you ungrateful boy,' returned North Wind, smiling, 'how dare you make game of me? Yes, I will carry you, but you shall walk a bit for your impertinence first. Come along.'

She jumped from his shoulder, but when Desmond looked for her upon the ground, he could see nothing but a little spider with long legs that made its way over the ice towards the south. It ran very fast indeed for a spider, but Diamond ran a long way before it, and then waited for it. It was up with him sooner than he had expected, however, and it had grown a good deal. And the spider grew and grew and went faster and faster, till all at once Diamond discovered that it was not a spider, but a weasel; and away glided the weasel, and away went Diamond after it, and it took all the run there was in him to keep up with the weasel. And the weasel grew, and grew, and grew, till all at once Diamond saw that the weasel was not a weasel but a cat. And away went the cat, and Diamond after it. And when he had run half a mile, he found the cat waiting for him, sitting up and washing her face not to lose time. And away went the cat again, and Diamond after it. But the next time he came up with the cat, the cat was not a cat, but a hunting-leopard. And the hunting-leopard grew to a jaguar, all covered with spots like eyes. And the jaguar grew to a Bengal tiger. And at none of them was Diamond afraid, for he had been at North Wind's back, and he could be afraid of her no longer whatever she did or grew. And the tiger flew over the snow in a straight line for the south, growing less and less to Diamond's eyes till it was only a black speck upon the whiteness; and then it vanished altogether. And now Diamond felt that he would rather not run any farther, and that the ice had got very rough. Besides, he was near the precipices that bounded the sea, so he slackened his pace to a walk, saying aloud to himself:

'When North Wind has punished me enough for making game of her, she will come back to me; I know she will, for I can't go much farther without her.'

'You dear boy! It was only in fun. Here I am!' said North Wind's voice behind him.

Diamond turned, and saw her as he best liked to see her, standing beside him, a tall lady.

'Where's the tiger?' he asked, for he knew all the creatures from a picture book that Miss Coleman had given him. 'But, of course,' he added, 'you were the tiger. I was puzzled and forgot. I saw it such a long way off before me, and there you were behind me. It's so odd, you know.'

'It must look very odd to you, Diamond: I see that. But it's no more odd to me than to break an old pine in two.'

'Well, that's odd enough,' remarked Diamond.

'So it is! I forgot. Well, none of these things are odder to me than it is to you to eat bread and butter.'

'Well, that's odd too, when I think of it,' persisted Diamond. 'I should just like a slice of bread and butter! I'm afraid to say how long it is – how long it seems to me, that is – since I had anything to eat.'

'Come then,' said North Wind, stooping and holding out her arms. 'You shall have some bread and butter very soon. I am glad to find you want some.'

Diamond held up his arms to meet hers, and was safe upon her bosom. North Wind bounded into the air. Her tresses began to lift and rise and spread and stream and flow and flutter; and with a roar from her hair and an answering roar from one of the great glaciers beside them, whose slow torrent tumbled two or three icebergs at once into the waves at their feet, North Wind and Diamond went flying southwards.

12 Who Met Diamond at Sandwich

As they flew, so fast they went that the sea slid away from under them like a great web of shot silk, blue shot with grey, and green shot with purple. They went so fast that the stars themselves appeared to sail away past them overhead, 'like golden boats', on a blue sea turned upside down. And they went so fast that Diamond himself went the other way as fast – I mean he went fast asleep in North Wind's arms.

When he woke, a face was bending over him; but it was not North Wind's; it was his mother's. He put out his arms to her, and she clasped him to her bosom and burst out crying. Diamond kissed her again and again to make her stop. Perhaps kissing is the best thing for crying, but it will not always stop it.

'What is the matter, mother?' he said.

'Oh, Diamond, my darling! you have been so ill!' she sobbed.

'No, mother dear. I've only been at the back of the north wind,' returned Diamond.

'I thought you were dead,' said his mother.

But that moment the doctor came in.

'Oh! there!' said the doctor with gentle cheerfulness; 'we're better to-day, I see.'

Then he drew the mother aside, and told her not to talk to Diamond, or to mind what he might say; for he must be kept as quiet as possible. And indeed Diamond was not much inclined to talk, for he felt very strange and weak, which was little wonder, seeing that all the time he had been away he had only sucked a few lumps of ice, and there could not be much nourishment in them.

Now while he is lying there, getting strong again with chicken broth and other nice things, I will tell my readers what had been taking place at his home, for they ought to be told it.

They may have forgotten that Miss Coleman was in a poor state of health. Now there were three reasons for this. In the first place, her lungs were not strong. In the second place, there was a gentleman somewhere who had not behaved very well to her. In the third place, she had not anything particular to do. These three *nots* together are enough to make a lady very ill indeed. Of course she could not help the first cause; but if the other two causes had not existed, that would have been of little consequence; she would only have had to be a little careful. The second she could not help quite; but if she had had anything to do, and had done it well, it would have been very difficult for any man to behave badly to her. And for this third cause of her illness, if she had had anything to do that was worth doing, she might have borne his bad behaviour so that even that would not have made her ill. It is not always easy, I confess, to find something to do that is worth doing, but the most difficult things are constantly being done, and she might have found something if she had tried. Her fault lay in this, that she had not tried. But, to be sure, her father and mother were to blame that they had never set her going. Only then again, nobody had told her father and mother that they ought to set her going in that direction. So as none of them would find it out of themselves, North Wind had to teach them.

We know that North Wind was very busy that night on which she left Diamond in the cathedral. She had in a sense been blowing through and through the Colemans' house the whole of the night. First, Miss Coleman's maid had left a chink of her mistress's window open, thinking she had shut it, and North Wind had wound a few of her hairs round the lady's throat. She was considerably worse the next morning. Again, the ship which North Wind had sunk that very night belonged to Mr. Coleman. Nor will my readers understand what a heavy loss this was to him until I have informed them that he had been getting poorer and poorer for some time. He was not so successful in his speculations as he had been, for he speculated a great deal more than was right, and it was time he should be pulled up. It is a hard thing for a rich man to grow poor; but it is an awful thing for him to grow dishonest, and some kinds of speculation lead a man deep into dishonesty before he thinks what he is about. Poverty will not make a man worthless – he may be worth a great deal more when he is poor than he was when he was rich; but dishonesty goes very far indeed to make a man of no value – a thing to be thrown out in the dust-hole of the creation, like a bit of a broken basin, or a dirty rag. So North Wind had to look after Mr. Coleman, and try to make an honest man of him. So she sank the ship which was his last venture, and he was what himself and his wife and the world called ruined.

Nor was this all yet. For on board that vessel Miss Coleman's lover was a passenger; and when the news came that the vessel had gone down, and that all on board had perished, we may be sure she did not think the loss of their fine house and garden and furniture the greatest misfortune in the world.

Of course, the trouble did not end with Mr. Coleman and his family. Nobody can suffer alone. When the cause of suffering is most deeply hidden in the heart, and nobody knows anything about it but the man himself, he must be a great and a good man indeed, such as few of us have known, if the pain inside him does not make him behave so as to cause all about him to be more or less uncomfortable. But when a man brings money-troubles on himself by making haste to be rich, then most of the people he has to do with must suffer in the same way with himself. The elm-tree which North Wind blew down that very

night, as if small and great trials were to be gathered in one heap, crushed Miss Coleman's pretty summer-house: just so the fall of Mr. Coleman crushed the little family that lived over his coach-house and stable. Before Diamond was well enough to be taken home, there was no home for him to go to. Mr. Coleman – or his creditors, for I do not know the particulars – had sold house, carriage, horses, furniture, and everything. He and his wife and daughter and Mrs. Crump had gone to live in a small house in Hoxton, where he would be unknown, and whence he could walk to his place of business in the City. For he was not an old man, and hoped yet to retrieve his fortunes. Let us hope that he lived to retrieve his honesty, the tail of which had slipped through his fingers to the very last joint, if not beyond it.

Of course, Diamond's father had nothing to do for a time, but it was not so hard for him to have nothing to do as it was for Miss Coleman. He wrote to his wife that, if her sister would keep her there till he got a place, it would be better for them, and he would be greatly obliged to her. Meantime, the gentleman who had bought the house had allowed his furniture to remain where it was for a little while.

Diamond's aunt was quite willing to keep them as long as she could. And indeed Diamond was not yet well enough to be moved with safety.

When he had recovered so far as to be able to go out, one day his mother got her sister's husband, who had a little pony-cart, to carry them down to the sea-shore, and leave them there for a few hours. He had some business to do farther on at Ramsgate, and would pick them up as he returned. A whiff of the sea-air would do them both good, she said, and she thought besides she could best tell Diamond what had happened if she had him quite to herself.

13   The Seaside

Diamond and his mother sat down upon the edge of the rough grass that bordered the sand. The sun was just far enough past its highest not to shine in their eyes when they looked eastward. A sweet little wind blew on their left side, and comforted the mother without letting her know what it was that comforted her. Away before them stretched the sparkling waters of the ocean, every wave of which flashed out its own delight back in the face of the great sun, which looked down from the stillness of its blue house with gloriously silent face upon its flashing children. On each hand the shore rounded outwards, forming a little bay. There were no white cliffs here, as farther north and south, and the place was rather dreary, but the sky got at them so much the better. Not a house, not a creature was within sight. Dry sand was about their feet, and under them thin wiry grass, that just managed to grow out of the poverty-stricken shore.

'Oh dear!' said Diamond's mother, with a deep sigh, 'it's a sad world!'

'Is it?' said Diamond; 'I didn't know.'

'How should you know, child? You've been too well taken care of, I trust.'

'Oh yes, I have,' returned Diamond. 'I'm so sorry! I thought you were taken care of too. I thought my father took care of you. I will ask him about it. I think he must have forgotten.'

'Dear boy!' said his mother; 'your father's the best man in the world.'

'So I thought!' returned Diamond with triumph. 'I was sure of it! – Well, doesn't he take very good care of you?'

'Yes, yes, he does,' answered his mother, bursting into tears. 'But who's to take care of him? And how is he to take care of us if he's got nothing to eat himself?'

'Oh dear!' said Diamond with a gasp; 'hasn't he got anything to eat? Oh! I must go home to him.'

'No, no, child. He's not come to that yet. But what's to become of us, I don't know.'

'Are you very hungry, mother? There's the basket. I thought you put something to eat in it.'

'Oh you darling stupid! I didn't say I was hungry,' returned his mother, smiling through her tears.

'Then I don't understand you at all,' said Diamond. 'Do tell me what's the matter.'

'There *are* people in the world who have nothing to eat, Diamond.'

'Then I suppose they don't stop in it any longer. They – they – what you call – die – don't they?'

'Yes, they do. How would you like that?'

'I don't know. I never tried. But I suppose they go where they get something to eat.'

'Like enough they don't want it,' said his mother, petulantly.

'That's all right then,' said Diamond, thinking I daresay more than he chose to put in words.

'Is it though? Poor boy! how little *you* know about things! Mr.
Coleman's lost all his money, and your father has nothing to do, and
we shall have nothing to eat by and by.'

'Are you sure, mother?'

'Sure of what?'

'Sure that we shall have nothing to eat.'

'No, thank Heaven! I'm not sure of it. I hope not.'

'Then I *can't* understand it, mother. There's a piece of gingerbread
in the basket, I know.'

'O you little bird! You have no more sense than a sparrow that
picks what it wants, and never thinks of the winter and the frost and
the snow.'

'Ah – yes – I see. But the birds get through the winter, don't they?'

'Some of them fall dead on the ground.'

'They must die some time. They wouldn't like to be birds always.
Would you, mother?'

'What a child it is!' thought his mother, but she said nothing.

'Oh! now I remember,' Diamond went on. 'Father told me that
day I went to Epping Forest with him, that the rose-bushes, and the
may-bushes, and the holly-bushes were the birds' barns, for there
were the hips, and the haws, and the holly-berries, all ready for the
winter.'

'Yes; that's all very true. So you see the birds are provided for. But
there are no such barns for you and me, Diamond.'

'Ain't there?'

'No. We've got to work for our bread.'

'Then let's go and work,' said Diamond, getting up.

'It's no use. We've not got anything to do.'

'Then let's wait.'

'Then we shall starve.'

'No. There's the basket. Do you know, mother, I think I shall call
that basket the barn.'

'It's not a very big one. And when it's empty – where are we then?'

'At auntie's cupboard,' returned Diamond promptly.

'But we can't eat auntie's things all up and leave her to starve.'

'No, no. We'll go back to father before that. He'll have found a
cupboard somewhere by that time.'

'How do you know that?'

'I don't know it. But *I* haven't got even a cupboard, and I've always had plenty to eat. I've heard you say I had too much, sometimes.'

'But I tell you that's because I've had a cupboard for you, child.'

'And when yours was empty, auntie opened hers.'

'But that can't go on.'

'How do you know? I think there must be a big cupboard somewhere, out of which the little cupboards are filled, you know, mother.'

'Well, I wish I could find the door of that cupboard,' said his mother. But the same moment she stopped, and was silent for a good while. I cannot tell whether Diamond knew what she was thinking, but I think I know. She had heard something at church the day before, which came back upon her – something like this, that she hadn't to eat for to-morrow as well as for to-day; and that what was not wanted couldn't be missed. So, instead of saying anything more, she stretched out her hand for the basket, and she and Diamond had their dinner.

And Diamond did enjoy it. For the drive and the fresh air had made him quite hungry; and he did not, like his mother, trouble himself about what they should dine off that day week. The fact was he had lived so long without any food at all at the back of the north wind, that he knew quite well, that food was not essential to existence; that in fact, under certain circumstances, people could live without it well enough.

His mother did not speak much during their dinner. After it was over she helped him to walk about a little, but he was not able for much and soon got tired. He did not get fretful, though. He was too glad of having the sun and the wind again, to fret because he could not run about. He lay down on the dry sand, and his mother covered him with a shawl. She then sat by his side, and took a bit of work from her pocket. But Diamond felt rather sleepy, and turned on his side, and gazed sleepily over the sand. A few yards off he saw something fluttering.

'What is that, mother?' he said.

'Only a bit of paper,' she answered.

'It flutters more than a bit of paper would, I think,' said Diamond.

'I'll go and see if you like,' said his mother. 'My eyes are none of the best.'

So she rose and went and found that they were both right, for it was a little book, partly buried in the sand. But several of its leaves were clear of the sand, and these the wind kept blowing about in a very flutterful manner. She took it up and brought it to Diamond.

'What is it, mother?' he asked.

'Some nursery rhymes, I think,' she answered.

'I'm too sleepy,' said Diamond. 'Do read some of them to me,'

'Yes, I will,' she said, and began one. – 'But this is such nonsense!' she said again. 'I will try to find a better one.'

She turned the leaves searching, but three times, with sudden puffs, the wind blew the leaves rustling back to the same verses.

'Do read that one,' said Diamond, who seemed to be of the same mind as the wind. 'It sounded very nice. I am sure it is a good one.'

So his mother thought it might amuse him, though she couldn't find any sense in it. She never thought he might understand it, although she could not.

Now I do not exactly know what the mother read, but this is what Diamond heard, or thought afterwards that he had heard. He was, however, as I have said, very sleepy, and when he thought he understood the verses he may have been only dreaming better ones. This is how they went –

> I know a river
> whose waters run asleep
> run run ever
> singing in the shallows
> dumb in the hollows
> sleeping so deep
> and all the swallows
> that dip their feathers
> in the hollows
> or in the shallows
> are the merriest swallows of all
> for the nests they bake
> with the clay they cake
> with the water they shake
> from their wings that rake

the water out of the shallows
or the hollows
will hold together
in any weather and so the swallows
are the merriest fellows
and have the merriest children
and are built so narrow
like the head of an arrow
to cut the air
and go just where
the nicest water is flowing
and the nicest dust is blowing
for each so narrow
like head of an arrow
is only a barrow
to carry the mud he makes
from the nicest water flowing
and the nicest dust that is blowing
to build his nest
for her he loves best
with the nicest cakes
which the sunshine bakes
all for their merry children
all so callow
with beaks that follow
gaping and hollow
wider and wider
after their father
or after their mother
the food-provider
who brings them a spider
or a worm the poor hider
down in the earth
so there's no dearth
for their beaks as yellow
as the buttercups growing
beside the flowing
of the singing river

always and ever
growing and blowing
for fast as the sheep
awake or asleep
crop them and crop them
they cannot stop them
but up they creep
and on they go blowing
and so with the daisies
the little white praises
they grow and they blow
and they spread out their crown
and they praise the sun
and when he goes down
their praising his done
and they fold up their crown
and they sleep every one
till over the plain
he's shining amain
and they're at it again
praising and praising
such low songs raising
that no one hears them
but the sun who rears them
and the sheep that bite them
are the quietest sheep
awake or asleep
with the merriest bleat
and the little lambs
they forget to eat
for the frolic in their feet
and the lambs and their dams
are the whitest sheep
with the woolliest wool
and the longest wool
and the trailingest tails
and they shine like snow
in the grasses that grow

by the singing river
that sings for ever
and the sheep and the lambs
are merry for ever
because the river
sings and they drink it
and the lambs and their dams
are quiet
and white
because of their diet
for what they bite
is buttercups yellow
and daisies white
and grass as green
as the river can make it
with wind as mellow
to kiss it and shake it
as never was seen
but here in the hollows
beside the river
where all the swallows
are merriest of fellows
for the nests they make
with the clay they cake
in the sunshine bake
till they are like bone
as dry in the wind
as a marble stone
so firm they bind
the grass in the clay
that dries in the wind
the sweetest wind
that blows by the river
flowing for ever
but never you find
whence comes the wind
that blows on the hollows
and over the shallows

where dip the swallows
alive it blows
the life as it goes
awake or asleep
into the river
that sings as it flows
and the life it blows
into the sheep
awake or asleep
with the woolliest wool
and the trailingest tails
and it never fails
gentle and cool
to wave the wool
and to toss the grass
as the lambs and the sheep
over it pass
and tug and bite
with their teeth so white
and then with the sweep
of their trailing tails
smooth it again
and it grows amain
and amain it grows
and the wind as it blows
tosses the swallows
over the hollows
and down on the shallows
till every feather
doth shake and quiver
and all their feathers
go all together
blowing the life
and the joy so rife
into the swallows
that skim the shallows
and have the yellowest children
for the wind that blows

is the life of the river
flowing for ever
that washes the grasses
still as it passes
and feeds the daisies
the little white praises
and buttercups bonny
so golden and sunny
with butter and honey
that whiten the sheep
awake or asleep
that nibble and bite
and grow whiter than white
and merry and quiet
on the sweet diet
fed by the river
and tossed for ever
by the wind that tosses
the swallow that crosses
over the shallows
dipping his wings
to gather the water
and bake the cake
that the wind shall make
as hard as a bone
as dry as a stone
it's all in the wind
that blows from behind
and all in the river
that flows for ever
and all in the grasses
and the white daisies
and the merry sheep
awake or asleep
and the happy swallows
skimming the shallows
and it's all in the wind
that blows from behind

Here Diamond became aware that his mother had stopped reading.

'Why don't you go on, mother dear?' he asked.

'It's such nonsense!' said his mother. 'I believe it would go on for ever.'

'That's just what it did,' said Diamond.

'What did?' she asked.

'Why, the river. That's almost the very tune it used to sing.'

His mother was frightened, for she thought the fever was coming on again. So she did not contradict him.

'Who made that poem?' asked Diamond.

'I don't know,' she answered. 'Some silly woman for her children, I suppose – and then thought it good enough to print.'

'She must have been at the back of the north wind some time or other, anyhow,' said Diamond. 'She couldn't have got a hold of it anywhere else. That's just how it went.' And he began to chant bits of it here and there; but his mother said nothing for fear of making him worse; and she was very glad indeed when she saw her brother-in-law jogging along in his little cart. They lifted Diamond in, and got up themselves, and away they went, 'home again, home again, home again,' as Diamond sang. But he soon grew quiet, and before they reached Sandwich he was fast asleep and dreaming of the country at the back of the north wind.

14 Old Diamond

After this Diamond recovered so fast, that in a few days he was quite able to go home as soon as his father had a place for them to go to. Now his father having saved a little money, and finding that no situation offered itself, had been thinking over a new plan. A strange occurrence it was which turned his thoughts in that direction. He had a friend in the Bloomsbury region, who lived by letting out cabs and horses to the cabmen. This man, happening to meet him one day as he was returning from an unsuccessful application, said to him:

'Why don't you set up for yourself now – in the cab line, I mean?'

'I haven't enough for that,' answered Diamond's father.

'You must have saved a goodish bit, I should think. Just come home with me now and look at a horse I can let you have cheap. I bought him only a few weeks ago, thinking he'd do for a Hansom, but I was wrong. He's got bone enough for a wagon, but a wagon ain't a Hansom. He ain't got enough go for a Hansom. You see parties as takes Hansoms wants to go like the wind, and he ain't got wind enough, for he ain't so young as he once was. But for a four-wheeler as takes families and their luggages, he's the very horse. He'd carry a small house any day. I bought him cheap, and I'll sell him cheap.'

'Oh, I don't want him,' said Diamond's father. 'A body must have time to think over an affair of so much importance. And there's the cab too. That would come to a deal of money.'

'I could fit you there, I daresay,' said his friend. 'But come and look at the animal, anyhow.'

Since I lost my own old pair, as was Mr. Coleman's,' said Diamond's father, turning to accompany the cab-master, 'I ain't almost got the heart to look a horse in the face. It's a thousand pities to part man and horse.'

'So it is,' said his friend sympathetically.

But what was the ex-coachman's delight, when, on going into the stable where his friend led him, he found the horse he wanted him to buy was no other than his own old Diamond, grown very thin and bony and long-legged, as if they had been doing what they could to fit him for Hansom work!

'*He* ain't a Hansom horse,' said Diamond's father indignantly.

'Well, you're right. He ain't handsome, but he's a good un,' said his owner.

'Who says he ain't handsome? He's one of the handsomest horses a gentleman's coachman ever druv,' said Diamond's father; remarking to himself under his breath – 'thought I says it as shouldn't' – for he did not feel inclined all at once to confess that his own old horse could have sunk so low.

'Well,' said his friend, 'all I say is – There's a animal for you, as strong as a church; an' 'll go like a train, leastways a parly,' he added, correcting himself.

But the coachman had a lump in his throat and tears in his eyes. For the old horse, hearing his voice, had turned his long neck, and

when his old friend went up to him and laid his hand on his side, he whinnied for joy, and laid his big head on his master's breast. This settled the matter. The coachman's arms were round the horse's neck in a moment, and he fairly broke down and cried. The cab-master had never been so fond of a horse himself as to hug him like that, but he saw in a moment how it was. And he must have been good-hearted fellow, for I never heard of such an idea coming into the head of any other man with a horse to sell: instead of putting something on to the price because he was now pretty sure of selling him, he actually took a pound off what he had meant to ask for him, saying to himself it was a shame to part old friends.

Diamond's father, as soon as he came to himself, turned and asked how much he wanted for the horse.

'I see you're old friends,' said the owner.

'It's my own old Diamond. I liked him far the best of the pair, though the other was good. You ain't got him too, have you?'

'No; nothing in the stable to match *him* there.'

'I believe you,' said the coachman. 'But you'll be wanting a long price for *him*, *I* know.'

'No, not so much. I bought him cheap, and as I say, he ain't for my work.'

The end of it was that Diamond's father bought old Diamond again, along with a four-wheeled cab. And as there were some rooms to be had over the stable, he took them, wrote to his wife and to come home, and set up as a cabman.

15   The Mews

It was late in the afternoon when Diamond and his mother and the baby reached London. I was so full of Diamond that I forgot to tell you a baby had arrived in the meantime. His father was waiting for them with his own cab, but they had not told Diamond who the horse was; for his father wanted to enjoy the pleasure of his surprise when he found it out. He got in with his mother without looking at the horse, and his father having put up Diamond's carpet-bag and his mother's little trunk, got upon the box himself and drove off; and Diamond was quite proud of riding home in his father's own carriage. But when he got to the mews, he could not help being a little dismayed at first; and if he had never been to the back of the north wind, I am afraid he would have cried a little. But instead of that, he said to himself it was a fine thing all the old furniture was there. And instead of helping his mother to be miserable at the change, he began to find out all the advantages of the place; for every place has some advantages, and they are always better worth knowing than the disadvantages. Certainly the weather was depressing, for a thick dull persistent rain was falling by the time they reached home. But happily the weather is very changeable; and besides, there was a good fire burning in the room, which their neighbour with the drunken husband had attended to for them; and the tea-things were put out, and the kettle was boiling on the fire. And with a good fire, and tea and bread and butter, things cannot be said to be miserable.

Diamond's father and mother were, notwithstanding, *rather* miserable, and Diamond began to feel a kind of darkness beginning to spread over his own mind. But the same moment he said to himself, 'This will never do. I can't give in to this. I've been to the back of the north wind. Things go right there, and so I must try to get things to go right here. I've got to fight the miserable things. They shan't make me miserable if I can help it.' I do not mean that he thought these very words. They are perhaps too grown-up for him to have thought, but they represent the kind of thing that was in his heart and his head. And when heart and head go together, nothing can stand before them.

'What nice bread and butter this is!' said Diamond.

'I'm glad you like it, my dear,' said his father. 'I bought the butter myself at the little shop round the corner.'

'It's very nice, thank you, father. Oh, there's baby waking! I'll take him.'

'Sit still, Diamond,' said his mother. 'Go on with your bread and butter. You're not strong enough to lift him yet.'

So she took the baby herself, and set him on her knee. Then Diamond began to amuse him, and went on till the little fellow was shrieking with laughter. For the baby's world was his mother's arms; and the drizzling rain, and the dreary mews, and even his father's troubled face could not touch him. What cared baby for the loss of a hundred situations? Yet neither father nor mother thought him hard-hearted because he crowed and laughed in the middle of their troubles.

On the contrary, his crowing and laughing were infectious. His little heart was so full of merriment that it could not hold it all, and it ran over into theirs. Father and mother began to laugh too, and Diamond laughed till he had a fit of coughing which frightened his mother, and made them all stop. His father took the baby, and his mother put him to bed.

But it was indeed a change to them all, not only from Sandwich, but from their old place. Instead of the great river where the huge barges with their mighty brown and yellow sails went tacking from side to side like little pleasure-skiffs, and where the long thin boats shot past with eight and sometimes twelve rowers, their windows now looked out upon a dirty paved yard. And there was no garden more for Diamond to run into when he pleased, with gay flowers about his feet, and solemn sun-filled trees over his head. Neither was there a wooden wall at the back of his bed with a hole in it for North Wind to come in at when she liked. Indeed, there was such a high wall, and there were so many houses about the mews, that North Wind seldom got into the place at all, except when something *must* be done, and she had a grand cleaning out like other housewives; while the partition at the head of

Diamond's new bed only divided it from the room occupied by a cabman who drank too much beer, and came home chiefly to quarrel with his wife and pinch his children. It was dreadful to Diamond to hear the scolding and the crying. But it could not make him miserable, because he had been at the back of the north wind.

If my reader find it hard to believe that Diamond should be so good, he must remember that he had been to the back of the north wind. If he never knew a boy so good, did he ever know a boy that had been to the back of the north wind? It was not in the least strange to Diamond to behave as he did; on the contrary, it was thoroughly sensible of him.

We shall see how he got on.

16 Diamond Makes a Beginning

The wind blew loud, but Diamond slept a deep sleep and never heard it. My own impression is that every time when Diamond slept well and remembered nothing about it in the morning, he had been all that night at the back of the north wind. I am almost sure that was how he woke so refreshed, and felt so quiet and hopeful all the day. Indeed he said this much, though not to me, – that always when he woke from such a sleep there was a something in his mind, he could not tell what – could not tell whether it was the last far-off sounds of the river dying away in the distance, or some of the words of the endless song his mother had read to him on the seashore. Sometimes he thought it must have been the twittering of the swallows – over the shallows, you know; but it *may* have been the chirping of the dingy sparrows picking up their breakfast in the yard – how can I tell? I don't know what I know, I only know what I think; and to tell the truth, I am more for the swallows than the sparrows. When he knew he was coming awake, he would sometimes try hard to keep hold of the words of what seemed a new song, one he had not heard before – a song in which the words and the music somehow appeared to be all one; but even when he thought he had got them well fixed in his mind, ever as he came *awaker* – as he would say – one line faded away out of it, and then another, and then another, till at last there was nothing left but some lovely picture of water or grass or daises, or something else very common, but with all the commonness polished off it, and the lovely soul of it, which people so seldom see, and, alas! yet seldomer believe in, shining out. But after that he would sing the oddest, loveliest little songs to the baby – of his own making, his mother said; but Diamond said he did not make them; they were made somewhere inside of him, and he knew nothing about them till they were coming out.

When he woke that first morning he got up at once, saying to himself, 'I've been ill long enough, and have given a great deal of trouble; I must try and be of use now, and help my mother.' When he went into her room he found her lighting the fire, and his father just getting out of bed. They had only the one room, besides the little one, not much more than a closest, in which Diamond slept. He began at once to set things to rights, but the baby waking up, he took him, and nursed him till his mother had got the breakfast ready. She was looking gloomy, and his father was silent; and indeed except Diamond had done all he possibly could to keep out of the misery that was trying to get in at doors and windows, he too would have grown miserable, and then they would have been all miserable together. But to try to make others comfortable is the only way to get right comfortable ourselves, and that comes partly of not being able to think so much about ourselves when we are helping other people. For our Selves will always do pretty well if we don't pay them too much attention. Our Selves are like some little children who will be happy enough so long as they are left to their own games, but when we begin to interfere with them, and make them presents of too nice playthings, or too many sweet things, they begin at once to fret and spoil.

'Why, Diamond, child!' said his mother at last, 'you're as good to your mother as if you were a girl – nursing the baby, and toasting the bread, and sweeping up the hearth! I declare a body would think you had been among the fairies.'

Could Diamond have had greater praise or greater pleasure? You see when he forgot his Self his mother took care of his Self, and loved and praised his Self. Our own praises poison our Selves, and puff and swell them up, till they lose all shape and beauty, and become like great toadstools. But the praises of father or mother do our Selves good, and comfort them and make them beautiful. *They* never do them any harm. If they do any harm, it comes of our mixing some of our own praises with them, and that turns them nasty and slimy and poisonous.

When his father had finished his breakfast, which he did rather in a hurry, he got up and went down into the yard to get out his horse and put him to the cab.

'Won't you come and see the cab, Diamond?' he said.

'Yes, *please*, father – if mother can spare me a minute,' answered Diamond.

'Bless the child! I don't want him,' said his mother cheerfully.

But as he was following his father out of the door, she called him back.

'Diamond, just hold the baby one minute. I have something to say to your father.'

So Diamond sat down again, took the baby in his lap, and began poking his face into its little body, laughing and singing all the while, so that the baby crowed like a little bantam. And what he sang was something like this – such nonsense to those that couldn't understand it! but not to the baby, who got all the good in the world out of it:

> baby's a-sleeping
> wake up baby
> for all the swallows
> are the merriest fellows
> and have the yellowest children
> who would go sleeping

and snore like a baby
disturbing his mother
and father and brother
and all a-boring
their ears with his snoring
snoring snoring
for himself and no other
for himself in particular
wake up baby
sit up perpendicular
hark to the gushing
hark to the rushing
where the sheep are the woolliest
and the lambs the unruliest
and their tails the whitest
and their eyes the brightest
and baby's the bonniest
and baby's the funniest
and baby's the shiniest
and baby's the tiniest
and baby's the merriest
and baby's the worriest
of all the lambs
that plague their dams
and mother's the whitest
of all the dams
that feed the lambs
that go crop-cropping
without stop-stopping
and father's the best
of all the swallows
that build their nest
out of the shining shallows
and he has the merriest children
that's baby and Diamond
and Diamond and baby
and baby and Diamond
and Diamond and baby

Here Diamond's knees went off in a wild dance which tossed the baby about and shook the laughter out of him in immoderate peals. His mother had been listening at the door to the last few lines of his song, and came in with the tears in her eyes. She took the baby from him, gave him a kiss, and told him to run to his father.

By the time Diamond got into the yard, the horse was between the shafts, and his father was looping the traces on. Diamond went round to look at the horse. The sight of him made him feel very queer. He did not know much about different horses, and all other horses than their own were very much the same to him. But he could not make it out. This was Diamond and it wasn't Diamond. Diamond didn't hang his head like that; yet the head that was hanging was very like the one that Diamond used to hold so high. Diamond's bones didn't show through his skin like that; but the skin they pushed out of shape so was very like Diamond's skin; and the bones might be Diamond's bones, for he had never seen the shape of *them*. But when he came round in front of the old horse, and he put out his long neck, and began sniffing at him and rubbing his upper lip and his nose on him, then Diamond saw it *could* be no other than old Diamond, and he did just as his father had done before – put his arms round his neck and cried – but not much.

'Ain't it jolly, father?' he said. 'Was there ever anybody so lucky as me? Dear old Diamond!'

And he hugged the horse again, and kissed both his big hairy cheeks. He could only manage one at a time however – the other cheek was so far off on the other side of his big head.

His father mounted the box with just the same air, as Diamond thought, with which he had used to get upon the coach-box, and Diamond said to himself, 'Father's as grand as ever anyhow.' He had kept his brown livery-coat, only his wife had taken the silver buttons off and put brass ones instead, because they did not think it polite to Mr. Coleman in his fallen fortunes to let his crest be seen upon the box of a cab. Old Diamond had kept just his collar; and that had the silver crest upon it still, for his master thought nobody would notice that, and so let it remain for a memorial of the better days of which it reminded him – not unpleasantly, seeing it had been by no fault either of his or of the old horse's that they had come down in the world together.

'Oh, father, do let me drive a bit,' said Diamond, jumping up on the box beside him.

His father changed places with him at once, putting the reins into his heads. Diamond gathered them up eagerly.

'Don't pull at his mouth,' said his father; 'just feel at it gently to let him know you're there and attending to him. That's what I call talking to him through the reins.'

'Yes, father, I understand,' said Diamond. Then to the horse he said, 'Go on, Diamond.' And old Diamond's ponderous bulk began at once to move to the voice of the little boy.

But before they had reached the entrance of the mews, another voice called after young Diamond, which, in his turn, he had to obey, for it was that of his mother. 'Diamond! Diamond!' it cried; and Diamond pulled the reins, and the horse stood still as a stone.

'Husband,' said his mother, coming up, 'you're never going to trust *him* with the reins – a baby like that?'

'He must learn some day, and he can't begin too soon. I see already he's a born coachman,' said his father proudly. 'And I don't see well how he could escape it, for my father and my grandfather, that's his great-grandfather, was all coachmen, I'm told; so it must come natural to him, any one would think. Besides, you see, old Diamond's as proud of him as we are our own selves, wife. Don't you see how he's turning round his ears, with the mouths of them open, for the first word he speaks to tumble in? He's too well bred to turn his head, you know.'

'Well, but, husband, I can't do without him to-day. Everything's got to be done, you know. It's my first day here. And there's that baby!'

'Bless you, wife! I never meant to take him away – only to the bottom of Endell Street. He can watch his way back.'

No, thank you, father; not to-day,' said Diamond. 'Mother wants me. Perhaps she'll let me go another day.'

'Very well, my man,' said his father, and took the reins which Diamond was holding out to him.

Diamond got down, a little disappointed of course, and went in with his mother, who was too pleased to speak. She only took hold of his hand as tight as if she had been afraid of his running away instead of glad that he would not leave her.

Now, although they did not know it, the owner of the stables, the same man who had sold the horse to his father, had been standing just inside one of the stable-doors, with his hands in his pockets, and had heard and seen all that passed; and from that day John Stonecrop took a great fancy to the little boy. And this was the beginning of what came of it.

That same evening, just as Diamond was feeling tired of the day's work, and wishing his father would come home, Mr. Stonecrop knocked at the door. His mother went and opened it.

'Good evening, ma'am,' said he. 'Is little master in?'

'Yes, to be sure he is – at your service, I'm sure, Mr. Stonecrop,' said his mother.

'No, no, ma'am; it's I'm at his service. I'm just a-going out with my own cab, and if he likes to come with me, he shall drive my old horse till he's tired.'

'It's getting rather late for him,' said his mother thoughtfully. 'You see he's been an invalid.'

Diamond thought, what a funny thing! How could he have been an invalid when he did not even know what the word meant? But, of course, his mother was right.

'Oh, well,' said Mr Stonecrop, 'I can just let him drive through Bloomsbury Square, and then he shall run home again.'

'Very good, sir. And I'm much obliged to you,' said his mother. And Diamond, dancing with delight, got his cap, put his hand in Mr. Stonecrop's, and went with him to the yard where the cab was waiting. He did not think the horse looked nearly so nice as Diamond, nor Mr. Stonecrop nearly so grand as his father; but he was none the less pleased. He got up on the box, and his new friend got up beside him.

'What's the horse's name?' whispered Diamond, as he took the reins from the man.

'It's not a nice name,' said Mr. Stonecrop. 'You needn't call him by it. I didn't give it him. He'll go well enough without it. Give the boy a whip, Jack. I never carries one when I drives old——'

He didn't finish the sentence. Jack handed Diamond a whip, with which, by holding it half down the stick, he managed just to flack the haunches of the horse; and away he went.

'Mind the gate,' said Mr. Stonecrop; and Diamond did mind the gate, and guided the nameless horse through it in safety, pulling him this way and that according as was necessary. Diamond learned to drive all the sooner that he had been accustomed to do what he was told, and could obey the smallest hint in a moment. Nothing helps one to get on like that. Some people don't know how to do what they are told; they have not been used to it, and they neither understand quickly nor are able to turn what they do understand into action quickly. With an obedient mind one learns the rights of things fast enough; for it is the law of the universe, and to obey is to understand.

'Look out!' cried Mr. Stonecrop, as they were turning the corner into Bloomsbury Square.

It was getting dusky now. A cab was approaching rather rapidly from the opposite direction, and Diamond pulling aside, and the other driver pulling up, they only just escaped a collision. Then they knew each other.

'Why, Diamond, it's a bad beginning to run into your own father,' cried the driver.

'But, father, wouldn't it have been a bad ending to run into your own son?' said Diamond in return; and the two men laughed heartily.

'This is very kind of you, I'm sure, Stonecrop,' said his father.

'Not a bit. He's a brave fellow, and'll be fit to drive on his own hook in a week or two. But I think you'd better let him drive you home now, for his mother don't like his having over much of the night air, and I promised not to take him farther than the square.'

'Come along then, Diamond,' said his father, as he brought his cab up to the other, and moved off the box to the seat beside it. Diamond jumped across, caught at the reins, said 'Good night, and thank you, Mr. Stonecrop,' and drove away home, feeling more of a man than he had ever yet had a chance of feeling in all his life. Nor did his father find it necessary to give him a single hint as to his driving. Only I suspect the fact that it was old Diamond, and old Diamond on his way to his stable, may have had something to do with young Diamond's success.

'Well, child,' said his mother, when he entered the room, 'you've not been long gone.'

'No, mother; here I am. Give me the baby.'

'The baby's asleep,' said his mother.

'Then give him to me, and I'll lay him down.'

But as Diamond took him, he woke up and began to laugh. For he was indeed one of the merriest children. And no wonder, for he was as

plump as a plum-pudding, and had never had an ache or a pain that
lasted more than five minutes at a time. Diamond sat down with him
and began to sing to him.

> baby baby babbing
> your father's gone a-cabbing
> to catch a shilling for its pence
> to make the baby babbing dance
> for old Diamond's a duck
> they say he can swim
> but the duck of diamonds
> is baby that's him
> and of all the swallows
> the merriest fellows
> that bake their cake
> with the water they shake
> out of the river
> flowing for ever
> and make dust into clay
> on the shiniest day
> to build their nest
> father's the best
> and mother's the whitest
> and her eyes are the brightest
> of all the dams
> that watch their lambs
> cropping the grass
> where the waters pass
> singing for ever
> and of all the lambs
> with the shakingest tails
> and the jumpingest feet
> baby's the funniest
> baby's the bonniest
> and he never wails
> and he's always sweet
> and Diamond's his nurse
> and Diamond's his nurse
> and Diamond's his nurse

When Diamond's rhymes grew scarce, he always began dancing the baby. Some people wondered that such a child could rhyme as he did, but his rhymes were not very good, for he was only trying to remember what he had heard the river sing at the back of the north wind.

17 Diamond Goes On

Diamond became a great favourite with all the men about the mews. Some may think it was not the best place in the world for him to be brought up in; but it must have been, for there he was. At first, he heard a good many rough and bad words; but he did not like them, and so they did him little harm. He did not know in the least what they meant, but there was something in the very sound of them, and in the tone of voice in which they were said, which Diamond felt to be ugly. So they did not even stick to him, not to say get inside him. He never took any notice of them, and his face shone pure and good in the middle of them, like a primrose in a hailstorm. At first, because his face was so quiet and sweet, with a smile always either awake or asleep in his eyes, and because he never heeded their ugly words and rough jokes, they said he wasn't all there, meaning that he was half an idiot, whereas he was a great deal more there than they had the sense to see. And before long the bad words found themselves ashamed to come out of the men's mouths when Diamond was near. The one would nudge the other to remind him that the boy was within hearing, and the words choked themselves before they got any farther. When they talked to him nicely he had always a good answer, sometimes a smart one, ready, and that helped much to make them change their minds about him.

One day Jack gave him a curry-comb and a brush to try his hand upon old Diamond's coat. He used them so deftly, so gently, and yet so thoroughly, as far as he could reach, that the man could not help admiring him.

'You must make haste and grow,' he said. 'It won't do to have a horse's belly clean and his back dirty, you know.'

'Give me a leg,' said Diamond, and in a moment he was on the old horse's back with the comb and brush. He sat on his withers, and reaching forward as he ate his hay, he curried and he brushed, first at one side of his neck, and then at the other. When that was done he asked for a dressing-comb, and combed his mane thoroughly. Then he pushed himself on to his back, and did his shoulders as far down as he could reach. Then he sat on his croup, and did his back and sides; then he turned round like a monkey, and attacked his hind-quarters, and combed his tail. This last was not so easy to manage, for he had to lift it up, and every now and then old Diamond would whisk it out of his hands, and once he sent the comb flying out of the stable-door, to the great amusement of the men. But Jack fetched it again, and Diamond began once more, and did not leave off till he had done the whole business fairly well, if not in a first-rate, experienced fashion. All the time the old horse went on eating his hay, and, but with an occasional whisk of his tail when Diamond tickled or scratched him, took no notice of the proceeding. But that was all a pretence, for he knew very well who it was that was perched on his back, and rubbing away at him with the comb and the brush. So he was quite pleased and proud,

and perhaps said to himself something like this, –

'I'm a stupid old horse, who can't brush his own coat; but there's my young godson on my back, cleaning me like an angel.'

I won't vouch for what the old horse was thinking, for it is very difficult to find out what any old horse is thinking.

'Oh dear!' said Diamond when he had done, 'I'm so tired!'

And he laid himself down at full length on old Diamond's back.

By this time all the men in the stable were gathered about the two Diamonds, and all much amused. One of them lifted him down, and from that time he was a greater favourite than before. And if ever there was a boy who had a chance of being a prodigy at cab-driving, Diamond was that boy, for the strife came to be who should have him out with him on the box.

His mother, however, was a little shy of the company for him, and besides she could not always spare him. Also his father liked to have him himself when he could; so that he was more desired than enjoyed among the cabmen.

But one way and another he did learn to drive all sorts of horses, and to drive them well, and that through the most crowded streets in London city. Of course there was the man always on the box-seat beside him, but before long there was seldom the least occasion to take the reins out of his hands. For one thing he never got frightened, and consequently was never in too great a hurry. Yet when the moment came for doing something sharp, he was always ready for it. I must once more remind my readers that he had been to the back of the north wind.

One day, which was neither washing-day nor cleaning-day, nor marketing-day, nor Saturday, nor Monday – upon which consequently Diamond could be spared from the baby – his father took him on his own cab. After a stray job or two by the way, they drew up in the row upon the stand between Cockspur Street and Pall Mall. They waited a long time, but nobody seemed to want to be carried anywhere. By and by ladies would be going home from the Academy exhibition, and there would be a chance of a job.

'Though, to be sure,' said Diamond's father – with what truth I cannot say, but he believed what he said – 'some ladies is very hard, and keeps you to the bare sixpence a mile, when every one knows that ain't enough to keep a family *and* a cab upon. To be sure it's the law;

but mayhap they may get more law than they like some day themselves.'

As it was very hot, Diamond's father got down to have a glass of beer himself, and give another to the old waterman. He left Diamond on the box.

A sudden noise got up, and Diamond looked round to see what was the matter.

There was a crossing near the cab-stand, where a girl was sweeping. Some rough young imps had picked a quarrel with her, and were now hauling at her broom to get it away from her. But as they did not pull all together, she was holding it against them, scolding and entreating alternately.

Diamond was off his box in a moment, and running to the help of the girl. He got hold of the broom at her end and pulled along with her. But the boys proceeded to rougher measures, and one of them hit Diamond on the nose, and made it bleed; and as he could not let go the broom to mind his nose, he was soon a dreadful figure. But presently his father came back, and missing Diamond, looked about. He had to look twice, however, before he could be sure that that was his boy in the middle of the tumult. He rushed in, and sent the assailants flying in all directions. The girl thanked Diamond, and began sweeping as if nothing had happened, while his father led him away. With the help of old Tom, the waterman, he was soon washed into decency, and his father set him on the box again, perfectly satisfied with the account he gave of the cause of his being in a fray.

'I couldn't let them behave so to a poor girl – could I, father?' he said.

'Certainly not, Diamond,' said his father, quite pleased, for Diamond's father was a gentleman.

A moment after, up came the girl, running, with her broom over her shoulder, and calling, 'Cab, there! cab!'

Diamond's father turned instantly, for he was the foremost in the rank, and followed the girl. One or two other passing cabs heard the cry, and made for the place, but the girl had taken care not to call till she was near enough to give her friends the first chance. When they reached the curbstone – who should it be waiting for the cab but Mrs. and Miss Coleman! They did not look at the cabman, however. The girl opened the door for them; they gave her the address, and a penny; she told the cabman, and away they drove.

When they reached the house, Diamond's father got down and rang the bell. As he opened the door of the cab, he touched his hat as he had been wont to do. The ladies both stared for a moment, and then exclaimed together:

'Why, Joseph! can it be you?'

'Yes, ma'am; yes, miss;' answered he, again touching his hat, with all the respect he could possibly put into the action. 'It's a lucky day which I see you once more upon it.'

'Who would have thought it?' said Mrs. Coleman. 'It's changed times for both of us, Joseph, and it's not very often we can have a cab even; but you see my daughter is still very poorly, and she can't bear the motion of the omnibuses. Indeed we meant to walk a bit first before we took a cab, but just at the corner, for as hot as the sun was, a cold wind came down the street, and I saw that Miss Coleman must not face it. But to think that we should have fallen upon you, of all the cabmen in London! I didn't know you had got a cab.'

'Well, you see, ma'am, I had a chance of buying the old horse, and

I couldn't resist *him*. There he is, looking at you, ma'am. Nobody knows the sense in that head of his.'

The two ladies went near to pat the horse, and then they noticed Diamond on the box.

'Why, you've got both Diamonds with you,' said Miss Coleman. 'How do you do, Diamond?'

Diamond lifted his cap, and answered politely.

'He'll be fit to drive himself before long,' said his father, proudly. 'The old horse is a-teaching of him.'

'Well, he must come and see us, now you've found us out. Where do you live?'

Diamond's father gave the ladies a ticket with his name and address printed on it; and then Mrs. Coleman took out her purse, saying:

'And what's your fare, Joseph?'

'No, thank you, ma'am,' said Joseph. 'It was your own old horse as took you; and me you paid long ago.'

He jumped on his box before she could say another word, and with a parting salute drove off, leaving them on the pavement, with the maid holding the door for them.

It was a long time now since Diamond had seen North Wind, or even thought much about her. And as his father drove along, he was thinking not about her, but about the crossing-sweeper, and was wondering what made him feel as if he knew her quite well, when he could not remember anything of her. But a picture arose in his mind of a little girl running before the wind and dragging her broom after her; and from that, by degrees, he recalled the whole adventure of the night when he got down from North Wind's back in a London street. But he could not quite satisfy himself whether the whole affair was not a dream which he had dreamed when he was a very little boy. Only he had been to the back of the north wind since – there could be no doubt of that; for when he woke every morning, he always knew that he had been there again. And as he thought and thought, he recalled another thing that had happened that morning, which, although it seemed a mere accident, might have something to do with what had happened since. His father had intended going on the stand at King's Cross that morning, and had turned into Gray's Inn Lane to drive there, when they found the way blocked up, and upon inquiry were informed that a stack of chimneys had been blown down in the night, and had fallen across the road. They were just clearing the rubbish away. Diamond's father turned, and made for Charing Cross.

That night the father and mother had a great deal to talk about.

'Poor things!' said the mother; 'it's worse for them than it is for us. You see they've been used to such grand things, and for them to come down to a little poky house like that – it breaks my heart to think of it.'

'I don't know,' said Diamond thoughtfully, 'whether Mrs. Coleman had bells on her toes.'

'What do you mean, child?' said his mother.

'She had rings on her fingers, anyhow,' returned Diamond.

'Of course she had, as any lady would. What has that to do with it?'

'When we were down at Sandwich,' said Diamond, 'you said you would have to part with your mother's ring, now we were poor.'

'Bless the child! he forgets nothing,' said his mother. 'Really, Diamond, a body would need to mind what they say to you.'

'Why?' said Diamond. 'I only think about it.'

'That's just why,' said the mother.

'Why is that why?' persisted Diamond, for he had not yet learned that grown-up people are not often so much grown up that they never talk like children – and spoilt ones too.

'Mrs. Coleman is none so poor as all that yet. No, thank Heaven! she's not come to that.'

'Is it a *great* disgrace to be poor?' asked Diamond, because of the tone in which his mother had spoken.

But his mother, whether conscience-stricken I do not know, hurried him away to bed, where after various attempts to understand her, resumed and resumed again in spite of invading sleep, he was conquered at last, and gave in, murmuring over and over to himself, 'Why is why?' but getting no answer to the question.

18 The Drunken Cabman

A few nights after this, Diamond woke up suddenly, believing he heard the North Wind thundering along. But it was something quite different. South Wind was moaning round the chimneys, to be sure, for she was not very happy that night, but it was not her voice that had wakened Diamond. Her voice would only have lulled him the deeper asleep. It was a loud, angry voice, now growling like that of a beast, now raving like that of a madman; and when Diamond came a little wider awake, he knew that it was the voice of the drunken cabman, the wall of whose room was at the head of his bed. It was anything but pleasant to hear, but he could not help hearing it. At length there came a cry from the woman, and then a scream from the baby. Thereupon Diamond thought it time that somebody did something, and as himself was the only somebody at hand, he must go and see whether he could not do the something. So he got up and put on part of his clothes, and went down the stair, for the cabman's room did not open upon their stair, and he had to go out into the yard, and in at the next door. This, fortunately, the cabman, being drunk, had left open. By the time he reached their stair, all was still except the voice of the crying baby, which guided him to the right door. He opened it softly and peeped in. There, leaning back in a chair, with his arms hanging down by his sides, and his legs stretched out before him and supported on his heels, sat the drunken cabman. His wife lay in her clothes upon the bed, sobbing, and the baby was wailing in the cradle. It was very miserable altogether.

Now the way most people do when they see anything very miserable is to turn away from the sight, and try to forget it. But Diamond began as usual to try to destroy the misery. The little boy was just as much one of God's messengers as if he had been an angel with a flaming sword, going out to fight the devil. The devil he had to fight just then was Misery. And the way he fought him was the very best. Like a wise soldier, he attacked him first in his weakest point – that was the baby; for Misery can never get such a hold of a baby as of a grown person. Diamond was knowing in babies, and he knew he could do something to make the baby happy; for although he had only known one baby as yet, and although not one baby is the same as another, yet they are so very much alike in some things, and he knew that one baby so thoroughly, that he had good reason to believe he could do something for any other. I have known people who would have begun to fight the devil in a very different and a very stupid way. They would have begun by scolding the idiotic cabman; and next they would make his wife angry by saying it must be her fault as well as his, and by leaving ill-bred though well-meant shabby little books for them to read, which they were sure to hate the sight of; while all the time they would not have put out a finger to touch the wailing baby. But Diamond had him out of the cradle in a moment, set him up on his knee, and told him to look at the light. Now all the light there was came only from a lamp in the yard, and it was a very dingy and yellow light,

for the glass of the lamp was dirty, and the gas was bad; but the light that came from it was, notwithstanding, as certainly light as if it had come from the sun itself, and the baby knew that, and smiled to it; and although it was indeed a wretched room which that lamp lighted – so dreary, and dirty, and empty, and hopeless! – there in the middle of it sat Diamond on a stool, smiling to the baby, and the baby on his knees smiling to the lamp. The father of him sat staring at nothing, neither asleep nor awake, not quite lost in stupidity either, for through it all he was dimly angry with himself, he did not know why. It was that he had struck his wife. He had forgotten it, but was miserable about it, notwithstanding. And this misery was the voice of the great Love that had made him and his wife and the baby and Diamond, speaking in his heart, and telling him to be good. For that great Love speaks in the most wretched and dirty hearts; only the tone of its voice depends on the echoes of the place in which it sounds. On Mount Sinai, it was thunder; in the cabman's heart it was *misery*; in the soul of St. John it was perfect blessedness.

By and by he became aware that there was a voice of singing in the room. This, of course, was the voice of Diamond singing to the baby – song after song, every one as foolish as another to the cabman, for he was too tipsy to part one word from another: all the words mixed up in his ear in a gurgle without division or stop; for such was the way he spoke himself, when he was in this horrid condition. But the baby was more than content with Diamond's songs, and Diamond himself was so contented with what the songs were all about, that he did not care a bit about the songs themselves, if only baby liked them. But they did the cabman good as well as the baby and Diamond, for they put him to sleep, and the sleep was busy all the time it lasted, smoothing the wrinkles out of his temper.

At length Diamond grew tired of singing, and began to talk to the baby instead. And as soon as he stopped singing, the cabman began to wake up. His brain was a little clearer now, his temper a little smoother, and his heart not quite so dirty. He began to listen and he went on listening, and heard Diamond saying to the baby something like this, for he thought the cabman was asleep:

'Poor daddy! Baby's daddy takes too much beer and gin, and that makes him somebody else, and not his own self at all. Baby's daddy would never hit baby's mammy if he didn't take too much beer. He's

very fond of baby's mammy, and works from morning to night to
get her breakfast and dinner and supper, only at night he forgets, and
pays the money away for beer. And they put nasty stuff in the beer,
I've heard my daddy say, that drives all the good out, and lets all the
bad in. Daddy says when a man takes to drink there's a thirsty devil
creeps into his inside, because he knows he will always get enough
there. And the devil is always crying out for more drink, and that
makes the man thirsty, and so he drinks more and more, till he kills
himself with it. And then the ugly devil creeps out of him, and crawls
about on his belly, looking for some other cabman to get into, that he
may drink, drink, drink. That's what *my* daddy says, baby. And he
says, too, the only way to make the devil come out, is to give him plenty
of cold water and tea and coffee, and nothing at all that comes from the
public-house; for the devil can't abide that kind of stuff, and creeps out
pretty soon, for fear of being drowned in it. But your daddy *will* drink
the nasty stuff, poor man! I wish he wouldn't, for it makes mammy
cross with him, and no wonder! and then when mammy's cross, he's
crosser, and there's nobody in the house to take care of them but baby;
and you *do* take care of them, baby – don't you, baby? I know you do.

Babies always take care of their fathers and mothers – don't they, baby? That's what they come for – isn't it, baby? And when daddy stops drinking beer and nasty gin with turpentine in it, father says, then mammy *will* be so happy, and look so pretty! and daddy will be so good to baby! and baby will be as happy as a swallow, which is the merriest fellow! And Diamond will be so happy too! And when Diamond's a man, he'll take baby out with him on the box, and teach him to drive a cab.'

He went on with chatter like this till baby was asleep, by which time he was tired, and father and mother were both wide awake, – only rather confused – the one from the beer, the other from the blow – and staring, the one from his chair, the other from her bed, at Diamond. But he was quite unaware of their notice, for he sat half-asleep, with his eyes wide open, staring in his turn, though without knowing it, at the cabman, while the cabman could not withdraw his gaze from Diamond's white face and big eyes. For Diamond's face was always rather pale, and now it was paler than usual with sleeplessness, and the light of the street-lamp upon it. At length he found himself nodding, and he knew then it was time to put the baby down, lest he should let him fall. So he rose from the little three-legged stool, and laid the baby in the cradle, and covered him up – it was well it was a warm night, and he did not want much covering – and then he all but staggered out of the door, he was so tipsy himself with sleep.

'Wife,' said the cabman, turning towards the bed, 'I do somehow believe that wur a angel just gone. Did you see him, wife? He warn't wery big, and he hadn't got none o' them wingses, you know. It wur one o' them baby-angels you sees on the gravestones, you know.'

'Nonsense, hubby!' said his wife; 'but it's just as good. I might say better, for you can ketch hold of *him* when you like. That's little Diamond as everybody knows, and a duck o' diamonds he is! No woman could wish for a better child than he be.'

'I ha' heerd on him in the stable, but I never see the brat afore. Come, old girl, let bygones be bygones, and gie us a kiss, and we'll go to bed.'

The cabman kept his cab in another yard, although he had his room in this. He was often late in coming home, and was not one to take notice of children, especially when he was tipsy, which was oftener than not. Hence, if he had ever seen Diamond, he did not know him. But his wife knew him well enough, as did every one else who lived all day in the yard. She was a good-natured woman. It was she who had got the fire lighted and the tea ready for them when Diamond and his mother came home from Sandwich. And her husband was not an ill-natured man either, and when in the morning he recalled not only Diamond's visit, but how he himself had behaved to his wife, he was very vexed with himself, and gladdened his poor wife's heart by telling her how sorry he was. And for a whole week after, he did not go near the public-house, hard as it was to avoid it, seeing a certain rich brewer had built one, like a trap to catch souls and bodies in, at almost every corner he had to pass on his way home. Indeed, he was never quite so bad after that, though it was some time before he began really to reform.

19   Diamond's Friends

One day when old Diamond was standing with his nose in his bag between Pall Mall and Cockspur Street, and his master was reading the newspaper on the box of his cab, which was the last of a good many in the row, little Diamond got down for a run, for his legs were getting cramped with sitting. And first of all he strolled with his hands in his pockets up to the crossing, where the girl and her broom were to be found in all weathers. Just as he was going to speak to her, a tall gentleman stepped upon the crossing. He was pleased to find it so clean, for the streets were muddy, and he had nice boots on; so he put his hand in his pocket, and gave the girl a penny. But when she gave him a sweet smile in return, and made him a pretty courtesy, he looked at her again, and said:

'Where do you live, my child?'

'Paradise Row,' she answered; 'next door to the Adam and Eve – down the area.'

'Whom do you live with?' he asked.

'My wicked old grannie,' she replied.

'You shouldn't call your grannie wicked,' said the gentleman.

'But she is,' said the girl, looking up confidently in his face. 'If you don't believe me, you can come and take a look at her.'

The words sounded rude, but the girl's face looked so simple that the gentleman saw that she did not mean to be rude, and became still more interested in her.

'Still you shouldn't say so,' he insisted.

'Shouldn't I? Everbody calls her wicked old grannie – even them that's as wicked as her. You should hear her swear. There's nothing like it in the Row. Indeed, I assure you, sir, there's ne'er a one of them can shut my grannie up once she begins and gets right a-going. You must put her in a passion first, you know. It's no good till you do that – she's so old now. How she *do* make them laugh, to be sure!'

Although she called her wicked, the child spoke so as plainly to indicate pride in her grannie's pre-eminence in swearing.

The gentleman looked very grave to hear her, for he was sorry that such a nice little girl should be in such bad keeping. But he did not know what to say next, and stood for a moment with his eyes on the ground. When he lifted them, he saw the face of Diamond looking up in his.

'Please, sir,' said Diamond, 'her grannie's very cruel to her sometimes, and shuts her out in the streets at night, if she happens to be late.'

'Is this your brother?' asked the gentleman of the girl.

'No, sir.'

'How does he know your grandmother, then? He does not look like one of her sort.'

'Oh no, sir! He's a good boy – quite.'

Here she tapped her forehead with her finger in a significant manner.

'What do you mean by that?' asked the gentleman, while Diamond looked on smiling.

'The cabbies call him God's baby,' she whispered. 'He's not right in the head, you know. A tile loose.'

Still Diamond, though he heard every word, and understood it too, kept on smiling. What could it matter what people called him, so long as he did nothing that he ought not to do? And, besides, *God's baby* was surely the best of names!

'Well, my little man, and what can you do?' asked the gentleman, turning towards him – just for the sake of saying something.

'Drive a cab,' said Diamond.

'Good; and what else?' he continued; for, accepting what the girl had said, he regarded the still sweetness of Diamond's face as a sign of silliness, and wished to be kind to the poor little fellow.

'Nurse a baby,' said Diamond.

'Well – and what else?'

'Clean father's boots, and make him a bit of toast for his tea.'

'You're a useful little man,' said the gentleman. 'What else can you do?'

'Not much that I know of,' said Diamond. 'I can't curry a horse, except somebody puts me on his back. So I don't count that.'

'Can you read?'

'No; but mother can and father can, and they're going to teach me some day soon.'

'Well, here's a penny for you.'

'Thank you, sir.'

'And when you have learned to read, come to me, and I'll give you sixpence and a book with fine pictures in it.'

'Please, sir, where am I to come?' asked Diamond, who was too much a man of the world not to know that he must have the gentleman's address before he could go and see him.

'You're no such silly!' thought he, as he put his hand in his pocket, and brought out a card. 'There,' he said, 'your father will be able to read that, and tell you where to go.'

'Yes, sir. Thank you, sir,' said Diamond, and put the card in his pocket.

The gentlemand walked away, but turning round a few paces off, saw Diamond give his penny to the girl, and, walking slower, heard him say:

'I've got a father, and mother, and little brother, and you've got noting but a wicked old grannie. You may have my penny.'

The girl put it beside the other in her pocket, the only trustworthy article of dress she wore. Her grandmother always took care that she had a stout pocket.

'Is she as cruel as ever?' asked Diamond.

'Much the same. But I gets more coppers now than I used to, and I can get summats to eat, and take browns enough home besides to keep her from grumbling. It's a good thing she's so blind, though.'

'Why?' asked Diamond.

''Cause if she was as sharp in the eyes as she used to be, she would find out I never eats her broken wittles, and then she'd know as I must get something somewheres.'

'Doesn't she watch you, then?'

'O' course she do. Don't she just! But I make believe and drop it in my lap, and then hitch it into my pocket.'

'What would she do if she found you out?'

'She'd never give me no more.'

'But you don't want it!'

'Yes, I do want it.'

'What do you do with it, then?'

'Give it to cripple Jim.'

'Who's cripple Jim?'

'A boy in the Row. His mother broke his leg when he wur a kid, so he's never come to much; but he's a good boy, is Jim, and I love Jim dearly. I always keeps off a penny for Jim – leastways as often as I can. – But there, I must sweep again, for them busses makes no end o' dirt.'

'Diamond! Diamond!' cried his father, who was afraid he might get no good by talking to the girl; and Diamond obeyed, and got up again upon the box. He told his father about the gentleman, and what he had promised him if he would learn to read, and showed him the gentleman's card.

'Why, it's not many doors from the Mews!' said his father, giving him back the card. 'Take care of it, my boy, for it may lead to something. God knows, in these hard times a man wants as many friends as he's ever likely to get.'

'Haven't you got friends enough, father?' asked Diamond.

'Well, I have no right to complain; but the more the better, you know.'

'Just let me count,' said Diamond.

And he took his hands from his pockets, and spreading out the fingers of his left hand, began to count, beginning at the thumb.

'There's mother first; and then baby, and then me. Next there's old Diamond – and the cab – no, I won't count the cab, for it never looks at you, and when Diamond's out of the shafts, it's nobody. Then there's the man that drinks next door, and his wife, and his baby.'

'They're no friends of mine,' said his father.

'Well, they're friends of mine,' said Diamond.

His father laughed.

'Much good they'll do you!' he said.

'How do you know they won't?' returned Diamond.

'Well, go on,' said his father.

'Then there's Jack and Mr. Stonecrop, and, deary me! not to have mentioned Mr. Coleman and Mrs. Coleman, and Miss Coleman, and Mrs. Crump. And then there's the clergyman that spoke to me in the garden that day the tree was blown down.'

'What's his name?'

'I don't know his name.'

'Where does he live?'

'I don't know.'

'How can you count him, then?'

'He did talk to me, and very kindlike too.'

His father laughed again.

'Why, child, you're just counting everybody you know. That don't make 'em friends.'

'Don't it? I thought it did. Well, but they shall be my friends. I shall make 'em.'

'How will you do that?'

'They can't help themselves then, if they would. If I choose to be their friend, you know, they can't prevent me. Then there's that girl at the crossing.'

'A fine set of friends you do have, to be sure, Diamond!'

'Surely *she's* a friend anyhow, father. If it hadn't been for her, you would never have got Mrs. Coleman and Miss Coleman to carry home.'

His father was silent, for he saw that Diamond was right, and was ashamed to find himself more ungrateful than he had thought.

'Then there's the new gentleman,' Diamond went on.

'If he do as he say,' interposed his father.

'And why shouldn't he? I daresay sixpence ain't too much for him to spare. But I don't quite understand, father: is nobody your friend but the one that does something for you?'

'No, I won't say that, my boy. You would have to leave out baby, then.'

'Oh no, I shouldn't. Baby can laugh in your face, and crow in your ears, and make you feel so happy. Call you that nothing, father?'

The father's heart was fairly touched now. He made no answer to this last appeal, and Diamond ended off with saying:

'And there's the best of mine to come yet – and that's you, daddy – except it be mother, you know. You're my friend, daddy, ain't you? And I'm your friend, ain't I?'

'And God for us all,' said his father, and then they were both silent, for that was very solemn.

The question of the tall gentleman as to whether Diamond could read or not, set his father thinking it was high time he could; and as soon as old Diamond was suppered and bedded, he began the task that very night. But it was not much of a task to Diamond, for his father took for his lesson-book those very rhymes his mother had picked up on the sea-shore; and as Diamond was not beginning too soon, he learned very fast indeed. Within a month he could spell out most of the verses for himself.

But he had never come upon the poem he thought he had heard his mother read from it that day. He had looked through and through the book several times after he knew the letters and a few words, fancying he could tell the look of it, but had always failed to find one more like it than another. So he wisely gave up the search till he could really read. Then he resolved to begin at the beginning, and read them all straight through. This took him nearly a fortnight. When he had almost reached the end, he came upon the following verses, which took his fancy much, although they were certainly not very like those he was in search of.

LITTLE BOY BLUE

Little Boy Blue lost his way in a wood.
    Sing apples and cherries, roses and honey;
He said, 'I would not go back if I could,
    It's all so jolly and funny.'

He sang, 'This wood is all my own,
    Apples and cherries, roses and honey;

So here I'll sit, like a king on my throne,
  All so jolly and funny.'

A little snake crept out of the tree,
  Apples and cherries, roses and honey;
'Lie down at my feet, little snake,' said he,
  All so jolly and funny.

A little bird sang in the tree overhead,
  Apples and cherries, roses and honey,
'Come and sing your song on my finger instead,
  All so jolly and funny.'

The snake coiled up; and the bird flew down,
And sang him the song of Birdie Brown.

Little Boy Blue found it tiresome to sit,
And he thought he had better walk on a bit.

So up he got, his way to take,
And he said, 'Come along, little bird and snake.'

And waves of snake o'er the damp leaves passed,
And the snake went first and Birdie Brown last;

By Boy Blue's head, with a flutter and dart,
Flew Birdie Brown with its song in its heart.

He came where the apples grew red and sweet:
'Tree, drop me an apple down at my feet.'

He came where the cherries hung plump and red:
'Come to my mouth, sweet kisses,' he said.

And the boughs bow down, and the apples they dapple
The grass, too many for him to grapple.

And the cheeriest cherries, with never a miss,
Fall to his mouth, each a full-grown kiss.

He met a little brook singing a song.
He said, 'Little brook, you are going wrong.

'You must follow me, follow me, follow, I say,
Do as I tell you, and come this way.'

And the song-singing, sing-songing forest brook
Leaped from its bed and after him took,

Followed him, followed. And pale and wan,
The dead leaves rustled as the water ran.

And every bird high up on the bough,
And every creature low down below,

He called, and the creatures obeyed the call,
Took their legs and their wings and followed him all;

Squirrels that carried their tails like a sack,
Each on his own little humpy brown back;

Householder snails, and slugs all tails,
And butterflies, flutterbies, ships all sails;

And weasels, and ousels, and mice, and larks,
And owls, and rere-mice, and harkydarks,

All went running, and creeping, and flowing,
After the merry boy fluttering and going;

The dappled fawns fawning, the fallow-deer following,
The swallows and flies, flying and swallowing;

Cockchafers, henchafers, cockioli-birds,
Cockroaches, henroaches, cuckoos in herds.

The spider forgot and followed him spinning,
And lost all his thread from end to beginning.

The gay wasp forgot his rings and his waist,
He never had made such undignified haste.

The dragon-flies melted to mist with their hurrying.
The mole in his moleskins left his barrowing burrowing.

The bees went buzzing, so busy and beesy,
And the midges in columns so upright and easy.

But Little Boy Blue was not content,
Calling for followers still as he went,

Blowing his horn, and beating his drum,
And crying aloud, 'Come all of you, come!'

He said to the shadows, 'Come after me;'
And the shadows began to flicker and flee,

And they flew through the wood all flattering and fluttering,
Over the dead leaves flickering and muttering.

And he said to the wind, 'Come, follow; come, follow,
With whistle and pipe, and rustle and hollo.'

And the wind wound round at his desire,
As if he had been the gold cock on the spire.

And the cock itself flew down from the church
And left the farmers all in the lurch.

They run and they fly, they creep and they come,
Everything, everything, all and some.

The very trees they tugged at their roots,
Only their feet were too fast in their boots.

After him leaning and straining and bending,
As on through their boles he kept walking and wending,

Till out of the wood he burst on a lea,
Shouting and calling, 'Come after me!'

And then they rose up with a leafy hiss,
And stood as if nothing had been amiss.

Little Boy Blue sat down on a stone,
And the creatures came round him every one.

And he said to the clouds, 'I want you there;'
And down they sank through the thin blue air.

And he said to the sunset far in the west,
'Come here; I want you; I know best.'

And the sunset came and stood up on the wold,
And burned and glowed in purple and gold.

Then Little Boy Blue began to ponder:
'What's to be done with them all, I wonder.'

Then Little Boy Blue, he said, quite low,
'What to do with you all I am sure I don't know.'

Then the clouds clodded down till dismal it grew;
The snake sneaked close; round Birdie Brown flew;

The brook sat up like a snake on its tail;
And the wind came up with a *what-will-you* wail;

And all the creatures sat and stared;
The mole opened his very eyes and glared;

And for rats and bats and the world and his wife,
Little Boy Blue was afraid of his life.

Then Birdie Brown began to sing,
And what he sang was the very thing:

'You have brought us all hither, Little Boy Blue,
Pray what do you want us all to do?'

'Go away! go away!' said Little Boy Blue;
'I'm sure I don't want you – get away – do.'

'No, no; no, no; no, yes, and no, no,'
Sang Birdie Brown, 'it mustn't be so.

'We cannot for nothing come here, and away.
Gives us some work, or else we stay.'

'Oh dear! and oh dear!' with sob and with sigh,
Said Little Boy Blue, and began to cry.

But before he got far, he thought of a thing;
And up he stood, and spoke like a king.

'Why do you hustle and jostle and bother?
Off with you all! Take me back to my mother.'

The sunset stood at the gates of the west.
'Follow *me*, follow *me*,' came from Birdie Brown's breast.

'I am going that way as fast as I can,'
Said the brook, as it sank and turned and ran.

Back to the woods fled the shadows like ghosts:
'If we stay, we shall all be missed from our posts.'

Said the wind with a voice that had changed its cheer,
'I was just going there, when you brought me here.'

'That's where I live,' said the sack-backed squirrel,
And he turned his sack with a swing and a swirl.

Said the cock of the spire, 'His father's churchwarden.'
Said the brook running faster, 'I run through his garden.'

Said the mole, 'Two hundred worms – there I caught 'em
Last year, and I'm going again next autumn.'

Said they all, 'If that's where you want us to steer for,
What in earth or in water did you bring us here for?'

'Never you mind,' said Little Boy Blue;
'That's what I tell you. If that you won't do,

'I'll get up at once, and go home without you.
I think I will; I begin to doubt you.'

He rose; and up rose the snake on its tail,
And hissed three times, half a hiss, half a wail.

Little Boy Blue he tried to go past him;
But wherever he turned, sat the snake and faced him.

'If you don't get out of my way,' he said,
'I tell you, snake, I will break your head.'

The snake he neither would go nor come;
So he hit him hard with the stick of his drum.

The snake fell down as if he were dead,
And Little Boy Blue set his foot on his head.

And all the creatures they marched before him,
And marshalled him home with a high cockolorum.

And Birdie Brown sang Twirrrr twitter twirrrr twee –
    Apples and cherries, roses and honey;
Little Boy Blue has listened to me –
    All so jolly and funny.

21   Sal's Nanny

Diamond managed with many blunders to read this rhyme to his mother.

'Isn't it nice, mother?' he said.

'Yes, it's pretty,' she answered.

'I think it means something,' returned Diamond.

'I'm sure I don't know what,' she said.

'I wonder if it's the same boy – yes, it must be the same – Little Boy Blue, you know. Let me see – how does that rhyme go?

> Little Boy Blue, come blow me your horn –

Yes, of course it is – for this one went 'blowing his horn and beating his drum.' He had a drum too.

> Little Boy Blue, come blow me your horn;
> The sheep's in the meadow, the cow's in the corn.

He had to keep them out, you know. But he wasn't minding his work. It goes –

> Where's the little boy that looks after the sheep?
> He's under the haystack, fast asleep.

There, you see, mother! And then, let me see –

> Who'll go and wake him? No, not I;
> For if I do he'll be sure to cry.

So I suppose nobody did wake him. He was a rather cross little boy, I daresay, when woke up. And when he did wake of himself, and saw the mischief the cow had done to the corn, instead of running home to his mother, he ran away into the wood and lost himself. Don't you think that's very likely, mother?'

'I shouldn't wonder,' she answered.

'So you see he was naughty; for even when he lost himself he did not want to go home. Any of the creatures would have shown him the way if he had asked it – all but the snake. He followed the snake, you know, and he took him farther away. I suppose it was a young one of the same serpent that tempted Adam and Eve. Father was telling us about it last Sunday, you remember.'

'Bless the child!' said his mother to herself; and then added aloud, finding that Diamond did not go on, 'Well, what next?'

'I don't know, mother. I'm sure there's a great deal more, but what it is I can't say. I only know that he killed the snake. I suppose that's what he had a drumstick for. He couldn't do it with his horn.'

'But surely you're not such a silly as to take it all for true, Diamond?'

'I think it must be. It looks true. That killing of the snake looks true. It's what *I*'ve got to do so often.'

His mother looked uneasy. Diamond smiled full in her face, and added –

'When baby cries and won't be happy, and when father and you talk about your troubles, I mean.'

This did little to reassure his mother; and lest my reader should have his qualms about it too, I venture to remind him once more that Diamond had been to the back of the north wind.

Finding she made no reply, Diamond went on –

'In a week or so, I shall be able to go to the tall gentleman and tell him I can read. And I'll ask him if he can help me to understand the rhyme.'

But before the week was out, he had another reason for going to Mr. Raymond.

For three days, on each of which, at one time or other, Diamond's father was on the same stand near the National Gallery, the girl was not at her crossing, and Diamond got quite anxious about her, fearing she must be ill. On the fourth day, not seeing her yet, he said to his father, who had that moment shut the door of his cab upon a fare –

'Father, I want to go and look after the girl. She can't be well.'
'All right,' said his father. 'Only take care of yourself, Diamond.'
So saying he climbed on his box and drove off.

He had great confidence in his boy, you see, and would trust him
anywhere. But if he had known the kind of place in which the girl
lived, he would perhaps have thought twice before he allowed him to
go alone. Diamond, who did know something of it, had not, however,
any fear. From talking to the girl he had a good notion of where about
it was, and he remembered the address well enough; so by asking his
way some twenty times, mostly of policemen, he came at length pretty
near the place. The last policeman he questioned looked down upon
him from the summit of six feet two inches, and replied with another
question, but kindly:

'What do you want there, my small kid? It ain't where you was
bred, I guess.'

'No, sir,' answered Diamond. 'I live in Bloomsbury.'

'That's a long way off,' said the policeman.

'Yes, it's a good distance,' answered Diamond; 'but I find my way about pretty well. Policemen are always kind to me.'

'But what on earth do you want here?'

Diamond told him plainly what he was about, and of course the man believed him, for nobody ever disbelieved Diamond. People might think he was mistaken, but they never thought he was telling a story.

'It's an ugly place,' said the policeman.

'Is it far off?' asked Diamond.

'No. It's next door almost. But it's not safe.'

'Nobody hurts me,' said Diamond.

'I must go with you, I suppose.'

'Oh, no! please not,' said Diamond. 'They might think I was going to meddle with them, and I ain't, you know.'

'Well, do as you please,' said the man, and gave him full directions.

Diamond set off, never suspecting that the policeman, who was a kind-hearted man, with children of his own, was following him close, and watching him round every corner. As he went on, all at once he thought he remembered the place, and whether it really was so, or only that he had laid up the policeman's instructions well in his mind, he went straight for the cellar of old Sal.

'He's a sharp little kid, anyhow, for as simple as he looks,' said the man to himself. 'Not a wrong turn does he take! But old Sal's a rum un for such a child to pay a morning visit to. She's worse when she's sober than when she's half drunk. I've seen her when she'd have torn him in pieces.'

Happily then for Diamond, old Sal had gone out to get some gin. When he came to her door at the bottom of the area-stair and knocked, he received no answer. He laid his ear to the door, and thought he heard a moaning within. So he tried the door, and found it was not locked. It was a dreary place indeed, – and very dark, for the window was below the level of the street, and covered with mud, while over the grating which kept people from falling into the area, stood a chest of drawers, placed there by a dealer in second-hand furniture, which shut out almost all the light. And the smell in the place was dreadful. Diamond stood still for a while, for he could see next to nothing, but he heard the moaning plainly enough now. When he got used to the

darkness, he discovered his friend lying with closed eyes and a white suffering face on a heap of little better than rags in a corner of the den. He went up to her and spoke; but she made him no answer. Indeed, she was not in the least aware of his presence, and Diamond saw that he could do nothing for her without help. So taking a lump of barley-sugar from his pocket, which he had bought for her as he came along, and laying it beside her, he left the place, having already made up his mind to go and see the tall gentleman, Mr. Raymond, and ask him to do something for Sal's Nanny, as the girl was called.

By the time he got up the area-steps, three or four women who had seen him go down were standing together at the top waiting for him. They wanted his clothes for their children; but they did not follow him down lest Sal should find them there. The moment he appeared, they laid their hands on him, and all began talking at once, for each wanted to get some advantage over her neighbours. He told them quite quietly, for he was not frightened, that he had come to see what was the matter with Nanny.

'What do you know about Nanny?' said one of them fiercely. 'Wait till old Sal comes home, and you'll catch it, for going prying into her house when she's out. If you don't give me your jacket directly, I'll go and fetch her.'

'I can't give you my jacket,' said Diamond. 'It belongs to my father and mother, you know. It's not mine to give. Is it now? You would not think it right to give away what wasn't yours – would you now?'

'Give it away! No, that I wouldn't; I'd keep it,' she said, with a rough laugh. 'But if the jacket ain't yours, what right have you to keep it? Here, Cherry, make haste. It'll be one go apiece.'

They all began to tug at the jacket, while Diamond stooped and kept his arms bent to resist them. Before they had done him or the jacket any harm, however, suddenly they all scampered away; and Diamond, looking in the opposite direction, saw the tall policeman coming towards him.

'You had better have let me come with you, little man,' he said, looking down in Diamond's face, which was flushed with his resistance.

'You came just in the right time, thank you,' returned Diamond. 'They've done me no harm.'

'They would have if I hadn't been at hand, though.'

'Yes; but you were at hand, you know, so they couldn't.'

Perhaps the answer was deeper in purport than either Diamond or the policeman knew. They walked away together, Diamond telling his new friend how ill poor Nanny was, and that he was going to let the tall gentleman know. The policeman put him in the nearest way for Bloomsbury, and stepping out in good earnest, Diamond reached Mr. Raymond's door in less than an hour. When he asked if he was at home, the servant, in return, asked what he wanted.

'I want to tell him something.'

'But I can't go and trouble him with such a message as that.'

'He told me to come to him – that is, when I could read – and I can.'

'How am I to know that?'

Diamond stared with astonishment for one moment, then answered:

'Why, I've just told you. That's how you know it.'

But this man was made of coarser grain than the policeman, and, instead of seeing that Diamond could not tell a lie, he put his answer down as impudence, and saying, 'Do you think I'm going to take your word for it?' shut the door in his face.

Diamond turned and sat down on the doorstep, thinking with himself that the tall gentleman must either come in or come out, and he was therefore in the best possible position for finding him. He had not waited long before the door opened again; but when he looked round, it was only the servant once more.

'Get away,' he said. 'What are you doing on the doorstep?'

'Waiting for Mr. Raymond,' answered Diamond, getting up.

'He's not at home.'

'Then I'll wait till he comes,' returned Diamond, sitting down again with a smile.

What the man would have done next I do not know, but a step sounded from the hall, and when Diamond looked round yet again, there was the tall gentleman.

'Who's this, John?' he asked.

'I don't know, sir. An imperent little boy as will sit on the doorstep.'

'Please, sir,' said Diamond, 'he told me you weren't at home, and I sat down to wait for you.'

'Eh, what!' said Mr. Raymond. 'John! John! This won't do. Is it a håbit of yours to turn away my visitors? There'll be some one else to turn away, I'm afraid, if I find any more of this kind of thing. Come in, my little man. I suppose you've come to claim your sixpence?'

'No, sir, not that.'

'What! can't you read yet?'

'Yes, I can now, a little. But I'll come for that next time. I came to tell you about Sal's Nanny.'

'Who's Sal's Nanny?'

'The girl at the crossing you talked to the same day.'

'Oh, yes; I remember. What's the matter? Has she got run over?'

Then Diamond told him all.

Now Mr. Raymond was one of the kindest men in London. He sent at once to have the horse put to the brougham, took Diamond with him, and drove to the Children's Hospital. There he was well known to everybody, for he was not only a large subscriber, but he used to go and tell the children stories of an afternoon. One of the doctors promised to go and find Nanny, and do what could be done – have her brought to the hospital, if possible.

That same night they sent a litter for her, and as she could be of no use to old Sal until she was better, she did not object to having her removed. So she was soon lying in the fever ward – for the first time in her life in a nice clean bed. But she knew nothing of the whole affair. She was too ill to know anything.

22   Mr. Raymond's Riddle

Mr. Raymond took Diamond home with him, stopping at the mews to tell his mother that he would send him back soon. Diamond ran in with the message himself, and when he reappeared he had in his hand the torn and crumpled book which North Wind had given him.

'Ah! I see,' said Mr. Raymond: 'you are going to claim your sixpence now.'

'I wasn't thinking of that so much as of another thing,' said Diamond. 'There's a rhyme in this book I can't quite understand. I want you to tell me what it means, if you please.'

'I will if I can,' answered Mr. Raymond. 'You shall read it to me when we get home, and then I shall see.'

Still with a good many blunders, Diamond did read it after a fashion. Mr. Raymond took the little book and read it over again.

Now Mr. Raymond was a poet himself, and so, although he had never been at the back of the north wind, he was able to understand the poem pretty well. But before saying anything about it, he read it over aloud, and Diamond thought he understood it much better already.

'I'll tell you what I think it means,' he then said. 'It means that people may have their way for a while, if they like, but it will get them into such troubles they'll wish they hadn't had it.'

'I know, I know!' said Diamond. 'Like the poor cabman next door. He drinks too much.'

'Just so,' returned Mr. Raymond. 'But when people want to do right, things about them will try to help them. Only they must kill the snake, you know.'

'I was sure the snake had something to do with it,' cried Diamond triumphantly.

A good deal more talk followed, and Mr. Raymond gave Diamond his sixpence.

'What will you do with it?' he asked.

'Take it home to my mother,' he answered. 'She has a teapot – such a black one! – with a broken spout, and she keeps all her money in it. It ain't much; but she saves it up to buy shoes for me. And there's baby coming on famously, and he'll want shoes soon. And every sixpence is something – ain't it, sir?'

'To be sure, my man. I hope you'll always make as good a use of your money.'

'I hope so, sir,' said Diamond.

'And here's a book for you, full of pictures and stories and poems. I wrote it myself, chiefly for the children of the hospital where I hope Nanny is going. I don't mean I printed it, you know. I made it,' added Mr. Raymond, wishing Diamond to understand that he was the author of the book.

'I know what you mean. I make songs myself. They're awfully silly, but they please baby, and that's all they're meant for.'

'Couldn't you let me hear one of them now?' said Mr. Raymond.

'No, sir, I couldn't. I forget them as soon as I've done with them. Besides, I couldn't make a line without baby on my knee. We make them together, you know. They're just as much baby's as mine. It's he that pulls them out of me.'

'I suspect the child's a genius,' said the poet to himself, 'and that's what makes people think him silly.'

Now if any of my child readers want to know what a genius is – shall I try to tell them or shall I not? I will give them one very short answer: it means one who understands things without any other body telling him what they mean. God makes a few such now and then to teach the rest of us.

'Do you like riddles?' asked Mr. Raymond, turning over the leaves of his own book.

'I don't know what a riddle is,' said Diamond.

'It's something that means something else, and you've got to find out what the something else is.'

Mr. Raymond liked the old-fashioned riddle best, and had written a few – one of which he now read.

I have only one foot, but thousands of toes;

My one foot stands, but never goes.
I have many arms, and they're mighty all;
And hundreds of fingers, large and small.
From the ends of my fingers my beauty grows.
I breathe with my hair, and I drink with my toes.
I grow bigger and bigger about the waist,
And yet I am always very tight laced.
None e'er saw me eat – I've no mouth to bite;
Yet I eat all day in the full sunlight.
In the summer with song I shake and quiver,
But in winter I fast and groan and shiver.

'Do you know what that means, Diamond?' he asked, when he had finished.

'No, indeed, I don't,' answered Diamond.

'Then you can read it for yourself, and think over it, and see if you can find it out,' said Mr. Raymond, giving him the book. 'And now you had better go home to your mother. When you've found the riddle, you can come again.'

If Diamond had had to find out the riddle in order to see Mr. Raymond again, I doubt if he would ever have seen him.

'Oh then,' I think I hear some little reader say, 'he could not have been a genius, for a genius finds out things without being told.'

I answer, 'Genius finds out truths, not tricks'. And if you do not understand that, I am afraid you must be content to wait till you grow older and know more.

23   The Early Bird

When Diamond got home he found his father at home already, sitting by the fire and looking rather miserable, for his head ached and he felt sick. He had been doing night work of late, and it had not agreed with him, so he had given it up, but not in time, for he had taken some kind of fever. The next day he was forced to keep his bed, and his wife nursed him, and Diamond attended to the baby. If he had not been ill, it would have been delightful to have him at home; and the first day Diamond sang more songs than ever to the baby, and his father listened with some pleasure. But the next he could not bear even Diamond's sweet voice, and was very ill indeed; so Diamond took the baby into his own room, and had no end of quiet games with him there. If he did pull all his bedding on the floor, it did not matter, for he kept baby very quiet, and made the bed himself again, and slept in it with baby all the next night, and many nights after.

But long before his father got well, his mother's savings were all but gone. She did not say a word about it in the hearing of her husband, lest she should distress him; and one night, when she could not help crying, she came into Diamond's room that his father might not hear her. She thought Diamond was asleep, but he was not. When he heard her sobbing, he was frightened, and said –

'Is father worse, mother?'

'No, Diamond,' she answered, as well as she could; 'he's a good bit better.'

'Then what are you crying for, mother?'

'Because my money is almost all gone,' she replied.

'O mammy, you make me think of a little poem baby and I learned out of North Wind's book to-day. Don't you remember how I bothered you about some of the words?'

'Yes, child,' said his mother heedlessly, thinking only of what she should do after to-morrow.

Diamond began and repeated the poem, for he had a wonderful memory.

A little bird sat on the edge of her nest;
   Her yellow-beaks slept as sound as tops;
That day she had done her very best,
   And had filled every one of their little crops.
She had filled her own just over-full,
And hence she was feeling a little dull.

'Oh dear!' she sighed, as she sat with her head
   Sunk in her chest, and no neck at all,
While her crop stuck out like a feather bed
   Turned inside out, and rather small;
'What shall I do if things don't reform?
I don't know where there's a single worm.

'I've had twenty to-day, and the children five each,
   Besides a few flies, and some very fat spiders:
No one will say I don't do as I preach –
   I'm one of the best of bird-providers;
But where's the use? We want a storm –
I don't know where there's a single worm.'

'There's five in my crop,' said a wee, wee bird,
   Which woke at the voice of his mother's pain;
'I know where there's five.' And with the word
   He tucked in his head, and went off again.
'The folly of childhood,' sighed his mother,
'Has always been my especial bother.'

The yellow-beaks they slept on and on –
   They never had heard of the bogy To-morrow;
But the mother sat outside, making her moan –
   She'll soon have to beg, or steal, or borrow;

For she never can tell the night before
Where she shall find one red worm more.

The fact, as I say, was, she'd had too many;
   She couldn't sleep, and she called it virtue,
Motherly foresight, affection, any
   Name you may call it that will not hurt you;
So it was late ere she tucked her head in,
And she slept so late it was almost a sin.

But the little fellow who knew of five,
   Nor troubled his head about any more,
Woke very early, felt quite alive,
   And wanted a sixth to add to his store:
He pushed his mother, the greedy elf,
Then thought he had better try for himself.

When his mother awoke and had rubbed her eyes
   Feeling less like a bird, and more like a mole,
She saw him – fancy with what surprise –
   Dragging a huge worm out of a hole!
'T was of this same hero the proverb took form:
'T is the early bird that catches the worm.

'There, mother!' said Diamond, as he finished; 'ain't it funny?'
'I wish you were like that little bird, Diamond, and could catch worms for yourself,' said his mother, as she rose to go and look after her husband.

Diamond lay awake for a few minutes, thinking what he could do to catch worms. It was very little trouble to make up his mind, however, and still less to go to sleep after it.

24 Another Early Bird

He got up in the morning as soon as he heard the men moving in the yard. He tucked in his little brother so that he could not tumble out of bed, and then went out, leaving the door open, so that if he should cry his mother might hear him at once. When he got into the yard he found the stable-door just opened.

'I'm the early bird, I think,' he said to himself. 'I hope I shall catch the worm.'

He would not ask any one to help him, fearing his project might meet with disapproval and opposition. With great difficulty, but with the help of a broken chair he brought down from his bedroom, he managed to put the harness on Diamond. If the old horse had had the least objection to the proceeding, of course he could not have done it; but even when it came to the bridle, he opened his mouth for the bit, just as if he had been taking the apple which Diamond sometimes gave him. He fastened the cheek-strap very carefully, just in the usual hole, for fear of choking his friend, or else letting the bit get amongst his teeth. It was a job to get the saddle on; but with the chair he managed it. If old Diamond had had an education in physics to equal that of the camel, he would have knelt down to let him put it on his back, but that was more than could be expected of him, and then Diamond had to creep quite under him to get hold of the girth. The collar was almost the worst part of the business; but there Diamond could help Diamond. He held his head very low till his little master had got it over and turned it round, and then he lifted his head, and shook it on to his shoulders. The yoke was rather difficult; but when he had laid the traces over the horse's neck, the weight was not too much for him. He got him right at last, and led him out of the stable.

By this time there were several of the men watching him, but they

would not interfere, they were so anxious to see how he would get over the various difficulties. They followed him as far as the stable-door, and there stood watching him again as he put the horse between the shafts, got them up one after the other into the loops, fastened the traces, the belly-band, the breeching, and the reins.

Then he got his whip. The moment he mounted the box, the men broke into a hearty cheer of delight at his success. But they would not let him go without a general inspection of the harness; and although they found it right, for not a buckle had to be shifted, they never allowed him to do it for himself again all the time his father was ill.

The cheer brought his mother to the window, and there she saw her little boy setting out alone with the cab in the grey of the morning. She tugged at the window, but it was stiff; and before she could open it, Diamond, who was in a great hurry, was out of the mews, and almost out of the street. She called 'Diamond! Diamond!' but there was no answer except from Jack.

'Never fear for him, ma'am,' said Jack. 'It 'ud be only a devil as would hurt him, and there ain't so many o' them as some folk 'ud have you believe. A boy o' Diamond's size as can 'arness a 'oss o' t'other Diamond's size, and put him to, right as a trivet – if he do upset the keb – 'll fall on *his* feet, ma'am.'

'But he won't upset the cab, will he, Jack?'

'Not he, ma'am. Leastways he won't go for to do it.'

'I know as much as that myself. What do you mean?'

'I mean he's as little likely to do it as the oldest man in the stable. How's the guv'nor to-day, ma'am?'

'A good deal better, thank you,' she answered, closing the window in some fear lest her husband should have been made anxious by the news of Diamond's expedition. He knew pretty well, however, what his boy was capable of, and although not quite easy was less anxious than his mother. But as the evening drew, the anxiety of both of them increased, and every sound of wheels made his father raise himself in his bed, and his mother peep out of the window.

Diamond had resolved to go straight to the cabstand where he was best known, and never to crawl for fear of getting annoyed by idlers. Before he got across Oxford Street, however, he was hailed by a man who wanted to catch a train, and was in too great a hurry to think about the driver. Having carried him to King's Cross in good time, and got a good fare in return, he set off again in great spirits, and reached the stand in safety. He was the first there after all.

As the men arrived they all greeted him kindly, and inquired after his father.

'Ain't you afraid of the old 'oss running away with you?' asked one.

'No, he wouldn't run away with *me*,' answered Diamond. 'He knows I'm getting the shillings for father. Or if he did he would only run home.'

'Well, you're a plucky one, for all your girl's looks!' said the man; 'and I wish ye luck.'

'Thank you, sir,' said Diamond. 'I'll do what I can. I came to the old place, you see, because I knew you would let me have my turn here.'

In the course of the day one man did try to cut him out, but he was a stranger; and the shout the rest of them raised let him see it would not do, and made him so far ashamed besides, that he went away crawling.

Once, in a block, a policeman came up to him, and asked him for his number. Diamond showed him his father's badge, saying with a smile:

'Father's ill at home, and so I came out with the cab. There's no fear of me. I can drive. Besides, the old horse could go alone.'

'Just as well, I daresay. You're a pair of 'em. But you *are* a rum 'un for a cabby – ain't you now?' said the policeman. 'I don't know as I ought to let you go.'

'I ain't done nothing,' said Diamond. 'It's not my fault I'm no bigger. I'm big enough for my age.'

'That's where it is,' said the man. 'You ain't fit.'

'How do you know that?' asked Diamond, with his usual smile, and turning his head like a little bird.

'Why, how are you to get out of this ruck now, when it begins to move?'

'Just you get up on the box,' said Diamond, 'and I'll show you. There, that van's a-moving now. Jump up.'

The policeman did as Diamond told him, and was soon satisfied that the little fellow could drive.

'Well,' he said, as he got down again, 'I don't know as I should be right to interfere. Good luck to you, my little man!'

'Thank you, sir,' said Diamond, and drove away.

In a few minutes a gentleman hailed him.

'Are you the driver of this cab?' he asked.

'Yes, sir,' said Diamond, showing his badge, of which he was proud.

'You're the youngest cabman I ever saw. How am I to know you won't break all my bones?'

'I would rather break all my own,' said Diamond. 'But if you're afraid, never mind me; I shall soon get another fare.'

'I'll risk it,' said the gentleman; and, opening the door himself, he jumped in.

He was going a good distance, and soon found that Diamond got him over the ground well. Now when Diamond had only to go straight ahead, and had not to mind so much what he was about, his thoughts always turned to the riddle Mr. Raymond had set him; and this gentleman looked so clever that he fancied he must be able to read it for him. He had given up all hope of finding it out for himself, and he could not plague his father about it when he was ill. He had thought of the answer himself, but fancied it could not be the right one, for to see how it all fitted required some knowledge of physiology. So, when he reached the end of his journey, he got down very quickly, and with his head just looking in at the window, said, as the gentleman gathered his gloves and newspapers:

'Please, sir, can you tell me the meaning of a riddle?'

'You must tell me the riddle first,' answered the gentleman, amused.

Diamond repeated the riddle.

'Oh! that's easy enough,' he returned. 'It's a tree.'

'Well, it ain't got no mouth, sure enough; but how then does it eat all day long?'

'It sucks in its food through the tiniest holes in its leaves,' he answered. 'Its breath is its food. And it can't do it except in the daylight.'

'Thank you, sir, thank you,' returned Diamond. 'I'm sorry I couldn't find it out myself; Mr. Raymond would have been better pleased with me.'

'But you needn't tell him any one told you.'

Diamond gave him a stare which came from the back of the north wind, where that kind of thing is unknown.

'That would be cheating,' he said at last.

'Ain't you a cabby, then?'

'Cabbies don't cheat.'

'Don't they? I am of a different opinion.'

'I'm sure my father don't.'

'What's your fare, young innocent?'

'Well, I think the distance is a good deal over three miles – that's two shillings. Only father says sixpence a mile is too little, though we can't ask for more.'

'You're a deep one. But I think you're wrong. It's over four miles – not much, but it is.'

'Then that's half-a-crown,' said Diamond.

'Well, here's three shillings. Will that do?'

'Thank you kindly, sir. I'll tell my father how good you were to me – first to tell me my riddle, then to put me right about the distance, and then to give me sixpence over. It'll help father to get well again, it will.'

'I hope it may, my man. I shouldn't wonder if you're as good as you look, after all.'

As Diamond returned, he drew up at a stand he had never been on before: it was time to give Diamond his bag of chopped beans and oats. The men got about him, and began to chaff him. He took it all good-humouredly, until one of them, who was an ill-conditioned fellow, began to tease old Diamond by poking him roughly in the ribs, and making general game of him. That he could not bear, and the tears came in his eyes. He undid the nose-bag, put it in the boot, and was just going to mount and drive away, when the fellow interfered, and would not let him get up. Diamond endeavoured to persuade him, and was very civil, but he would have his fun out of him, as he said. In a few minutes a group of idle boys had assembled, and Diamond found himself in a very uncomfortable position. Another cab drew up at the stand, and the driver got off and approached the assemblage.

'What's up here?' he asked, and Diamond knew the voice. It was that of the drunken cabman.

'Do you see this young oyster? He pretends to drive a cab,' said his enemy.

'Yes, I do see him. And I sees you too. You'd better leave him alone. He ain't no oyster. He's a angel come down on his own business. You be off, or I'll be nearer you than quite agreeable.'

The drunken cabman was a tall, stout man, who did not look one to take liberties with.

'Oh! if he's a friend of yours,' said the other, drawing back.

Diamond got out the nose-bag again. Old Diamond should have his feed out now.

'Yes, he is a friend o' mine. One o' the best I ever had. It's a pity he ain't a friend o' yourn. You'd be the better for it, but it ain't no fault of hisn.'

When Diamond went home at night, he carried with him one pound one shilling and sixpence, besides a few coppers extra, which had followed some of the fares.

His mother had got very anxious indeed – so much so that she was almost afraid, when she did hear the sound of his cab, to go and look, lest she should be yet again disappointed, and should break down before her husband. But there was the old horse, and there was the cab all right, and there was Diamond on the box, his pale face looking triumphant as a full moon in the twilight.

When he drew up at the stable-door, Jack came out, and after a good many friendly questions and congratulations said:

'You go in to your mother, Diamond. I'll put up the old 'oss. I'll take care on him. He do deserve some small attention, he do.'

'Thank you, Jack,' said Diamond, and bounded into the house, and into the arms of his mother, who was waiting him at the top of the stair.

The poor, anxious woman led him into his own room, sat down on his bed, took him on her lap as if he had been a baby, and cried.

'How's father?' asked Diamond, almost afraid to ask.

'Better, my child,' she answered, 'but uneasy about you, my dear.'

'Didn't you tell him I was the early bird gone out to catch the worm?'

'*That* was what put it into your head, was it, you monkey?' said his mother, beginning to get better.

'That or something else,' answered Diamond, so very quietly that his mother held his head back and stared in his face.

'Well! of all the children!' she said, and said no more.

'And here's my worm,' resumed Diamond.

But to see her face as he poured the shillings and sixpences and

pence into her lap! She burst out crying a second time, and ran with the money to her husband.

And how pleased he was! It did him no end of good. But while he was counting the coins, Diamond turned to baby, who was lying awake in his cradle, sucking his precious thumb, and took him up, saying:

'Baby, baby! I haven't seen you for a whole year.'

And then he began to sing to him as usual. And what he sang was this, for he was too happy either to make a song of his own or to sing sense. It was one out of Mr. Raymond's book.

THE TRUE HISTORY OF THE CAT AND THE FIDDLE

Hey, diddle, diddle!
The cat and the fiddle!
He played such a merry tune,
That the cow went mad
With the pleasure she had,
And jumped right over the moon.
But then, don't you see?
Before that could be,
The moon had come down and listened.
The little dog hearkened,
So loud that he barkened,
'There's nothing like it, there isn't.'

Hey, diddle, diddle!
Went the cat and the fiddle,
Hey diddle, diddle, dee, dee!
The dog laughed at the sport
Till his cough cut him short,
It was hey diddle, diddle, oh me!
And back came the cow
With a merry, merry low,
For she'd humbled the man in the moon.
The dish got excited,
The spoon was delighted,
And the dish waltzed away with the spoon.

But the man in the moon,
Coming back too soon
From the famous town of Norwich,
Caught up the dish,
Said, 'It's just what I wish
To hold my cold plum-porridge!'
Gave the cow a rat-tat,
Flung water on the cat,
And sent him away like a rocket.
Said, 'O Moon there you are!'
Got into her car,
And went off with the spoon in his pocket.

Hey ho! diddle, diddle!
The wet cat and wet fiddle,
They made such a caterwauling,
That the cow in a fright
Stood bolt upright
Bellowing now, and bawling;
And the dog on his tail,
Stretched his neck with a wail.
But 'Ho! ho!' said the man in the moon –
'No more in the South
Shall I burn my mouth,
For I've found a dish and a spoon.'

25 Diamond's Dream

'There, baby!' said Diamond; 'I'm so happy that I can only sing nonsense. Oh, father, think if you had been a poor man, and hadn't had a cab and old Diamond! What should I have done?'

'I don't know indeed what you could have done,' said his father from the bed.

'We should have all starved, my precious Diamond,' said his mother, whose pride in her boy was even greater than her joy in the shillings. Both of them together made her heart ache, for pleasure can do that as well as pain.

'Oh, no! we shouldn't,' said Diamond. 'I could have taken Nanny's crossing till she came back; and then the money, instead of going for Old Sal's gin, would have gone for father's beef-tea. I wonder what Nanny will do when she gets well again. Somebody else will be sure to have taken the crossing by that time. I wonder if she will fight for it, and whether I shall have to help her. I won't bother my head about that. Time enough yet! Hey diddle! hey diddle! hey diddle diddle! I wonder whether Mr. Raymond would take me to see Nanny. Hey diddle! hey diddle! hey diddle diddle! The baby and fiddle! O, mother, I'm such a silly! But I can't help it. I wish I could think of something else, but there's nothing will come into my head but *hey diddle diddle! the cat and the fiddle*! I wonder what the angels do – when they're extra happy, you know – when they've been driving cabs all day and taking home the money to their mothers. Do you think they ever sing nonsense, mother?'

'I daresay they've got their own sort of it,' answered his mother, 'else they wouldn't be like other people.'

She was thinking more of her twenty-one shillings and sixpence, and of the nice dinner she would get for her sick husband next day, than of the angels and their nonsense, when she said it. But Diamond found her answer all right.

'Yes, to be sure,' he replied. 'They wouldn't be like other people if they hadn't their nonsense sometimes. But it must be very pretty nonsense, and not like that silly hey diddle diddle! the cat and the fiddle! I wish I could get it out of my head. I wonder what the angels' nonsense is like. Nonsense is a very good thing, ain't it, mother? – a little of it now and then; more of it for baby, and not so much for grown people like cabmen and their mothers? It's like the pepper and salt that goes in the soup – that's it – isn't it, mother? There's baby fast alseep! Oh, what a nonsense baby it is – to sleep so much! Shall I put him down, mother?'

Diamond chattered away. What rose in his happy little heart ran out of his mouth, and did his father and mother good. When he went to bed, which he did early, being more tired, as you may suppose, than usual, he was still thinking what the nonsense could be like which the angels sang when they were too happy to sing sense. But before coming to any conclusion he fell fast asleep. And no wonder, for it must be acknowledged a difficult question.

That night he had a very curious dream which I think my readers would like to have told them. They would, at least, if they are as fond of nice dreams as I am, and don't have enough of them of their own.

He dreamed that he was running about in the twilight in the old garden. He thought he was waiting for North Wind, but she did not come. So he would run down to the back gate, and see if she were there. He ran and ran. It was a good long garden out of his dream, but in his dream it had grown so long and spread out so wide that the gate he wanted was nowhere. He ran and ran, but instead of coming to the gate found himself in a beautiful country, not like any country he had ever been in before. There were no trees of any size; nothing bigger in fact than hawthorns, which were full of may-blossom. The place in which they grew was wild and dry, mostly covered with grass, but having patches of heath. It extended on every side as far as he could see. But although it was so wild, yet wherever in an ordinary heath you might have expected furze bushes, or holly, or broom, there grew roses – wild and rare – all kinds. On every side, far and near, roses were glowing. There too was the gum–cistus, whose flowers fall every night and come again the next morning, lilacs and syringas and laburnums,

and many shrubs besides, of which he did not know the names; but the roses were everywhere. He wandered on and on, wondering when it would come to an end. It was of no use going back, for there was no house to be seen anywhere. But he was not frightened, for you know Diamond was used to things that were rather out of the way. He threw himself down under a rose-bush, and fell asleep.

He woke, not out of his dream, but into it, thinking he heard a child's voice, calling 'Diamond, Diamond!' He jumped up, but all was still about him. The rose-bushes were pouring out their odours in clouds. He could see the scent like mists of the same colour as the rose, issuing like a slow fountain and spreading in the air till it joined the thin rosy vapour which hung over all the wilderness. But again came the voice calling him, and it seemed to come from over his head. He looked up, but saw only the deep blue sky full of stars – more brilliant, however, than he had seen them before; and both sky and stars looked nearer to the earth.

While he gazed up, again he heard the cry. At the same moment he saw one of the biggest stars over his head give a kind of twinkle and jump, as if it went out and came in again. He threw himself on his back, and fixed his eyes upon it. Nor had he gazed long before it went out, leaving something like a scar in the blue. But as he went on gazing he saw a face where the star had been – a merry face, with bright eyes. The eyes appeared not only to see Diamond, but to know that Diamond had caught sight of them, for the face withdrew the same moment. Again came the voice, calling 'Diamond, Diamond'; and in jumped the star to its place.

Diamond called as loud as he could, right up into the sky:

'Here's Diamond, down below you. What do you want him to do?'

The next instant many of the stars round about that one went out, and many voices shouted from the sky, –

'Come up; come up. We're so jolly! Diamond! Diamond!'

This was followed by a peal of the merriest, kindliest laughter, and all the stars jumped into their places again.

'How am I to come up?' shouted Diamond.

'Go round the rose-bush. It's got its foot in it,' said the first voice.

Diamond got up at once, and walked to the other side of the rose-bush.

There he found what seemed the very opposite of what he wanted – a stair down into the earth. It was of turf and moss. It did not seem to promise well for getting into the sky, but Diamond had learned to look through the look of things. The voice must have meant that he was to go down this stair; and down this stair Diamond went, without waiting to think more about it.

It was such a nice stair, so cool and soft – all the sides as well as the steps grown with moss and grass and ferns! Down and down Diamond went – a long way, until at last he heard the gurgling and plashing of a little stream; nor had he gone much farther before he met it – yes, met it coming up the stairs to meet him, running up just as naturally as if it had been doing the other thing. Neither was Diamond in the least surprised to see it pitching itself from one step to another as it climbed towards him: he never thought it was odd – and no more it was, there. It would have been odd here. It made a merry tune as it came, and its voice was like the laughter he had heard from the sky. This appeared promising; and he went on, down and down the stair, and up and up the stream, till at last he came where it hurried out from under a stone, and the stair stopped altogether. And as the stream bubbled up, the

stone shook and swayed with its force; and Diamond thought he would try to lift it. Lightly it rose to his hand, forced up by the stream from below; and, by what would have seemed an unaccountable perversion of things had he been awake, threatened to come tumbling upon his head. But he avoided it, and when it fell, got upon it. He now saw that the opening through which the water came pouring in was over his head, and with the help of the stone he scrambled out by it, and found himself on the side of a grassy hill which rounded away from him in every direction, and down which came the brook which vanished in the hole. But scarcely had he noticed so much as this before a merry shouting and laughter burst upon him, and a number of naked little boys came running, every one eager to get to him first. At the shoulders of each fluttered two little wings, which were of no use for flying, as they were mere buds; only being made for it they could not help fluttering as if they were flying. Just as the foremost of the troop reached him, one or two of them fell, and the rest with shouts of laughter came tumbling over them till they heaped up a mound of struggling merriment. One after another they extricated themselves, and each as he got free threw his arms round Diamond and kissed him. Diamond's heart was ready to melt within him from clear delight. When they had all embraced him, –

'Now let us have some fun,' cried one, and with a shout they all scampered hither and thither, and played the wildest gambols on the grassy slopes. They kept constantly coming back to Diamond, however, as the centre of their enjoyment, rejoicing over him as if they had found a lost playmate.

There was a wind on the hillside which blew like the very embodiment of living gladness. It blew into Diamond's heart, and made him so happy that he was forced to sit down and cry.

'Now let's go and dig for stars,' said one who seemed to be the captain of the troop.

They all scurried away, but soon returned one after another, each with a pickaxe on his shoulder and a spade in his hand. As soon as they were gathered, the captain led them in a straight line to another part of the hill. Diamond rose and followed.

'Here is where we begin our lesson for to-night,' he said. 'Scatter and dig.'

There was no more fun. Each went by himself, walking slowly with bent shoulders and his eyes fixed on the ground. Every now and then one would stop, kneel down, and look intently, feeling with his hands and parting the grass. One would get up and walk on again, another spring to his feet, catch eagerly at his pickaxe and strike it into the ground once and again, then throw it aside, snatch up his spade, and commence digging at the loosened earth. Now one would sorrowfully shovel the earth into the hole again, trample it down with his little bare white feet, and walk on. But another would give a joyful shout, and after much tugging and loosening would draw from the hole a lump as big as his head, or no bigger than his fist; when the under side of it would pour such a blaze of golden or bluish light into Diamond's eyes that he was quite dazzled. Gold and blue were the commoner colours: the jubilation was greater over red or green or purple. And every time a star was dug up all the little angels dropped their tools and crowded about it, shouting and dancing and fluttering their wing-buds.

When they had examined it well, they would kneel down one after the other and peep through the hole; but they always stood back to give Diamond the first look. All that Diamond could report, however, was, that through the star-holes he saw a great many things and places and people he knew quite well, only somehow they were different – there was something marvellous about them – he could not tell what. Every time he rose from looking through a star-hole, he felt as if his heart would break for joy; and he said that if he had not cried, he did not know what would have become of him.

As soon as all had looked, the star was carefully fitted in again, a little mould was strewn over it, and the rest of the heap left as a sign that that star had been discovered.

At length one dug up a small star of a most lovely colour – a colour Diamond had never seen before. The moment the angel saw what it was, instead of showing it about, he handed it to one his neighbours, and seated himself on the edge of the hole, saying:

'This will do for me. Good-bye. I'm off.'

They crowded about him, hugging and kissing him; then stood back with a solemn stillness, their wings lying close to their shoulders. The little fellow looked round on them once with a smile, and then shot himself headlong through the star-hole. Diamond, as privileged, threw himself on the ground to peep after him, but he saw nothing.

'It's no use,' said the captain. 'I never saw anything more of one that went that way.'

'His wings can't be much use,' said Diamond, concerned and fearful, yet comforted by the calm looks of the rest.

'That's true,' said the captain. 'He's lost them by this time. They all do that go that way. You haven't got any, you see.'

'No,' said Diamond. 'I never did have any.'

'Oh! didn't you?' said the captain.

'Some people say,' he added, after a pause, 'that they come again. I don't know. I've never found the colour I care about myself. I suppose I shall some day.'

Then they looked again at the star, put it carefully into its hole, danced round it and over it – but solemnly, and called it by the name of the finder.

'Will you know it again?' asked Diamond.

'Oh yes. We never forget a star that's been made a door of.'

Then they went on with their searching and digging.

Diamond having neither pickaxe nor spade, had the more time to think.

'I don't see any little girls,' he said at last.

The captain stopped his shovelling, leaned on his spade, rubbed his forehead thoughtfully with his left hand – the little angels were all left-handed – repeated the words 'little girls', and then, as if a thought had struck him, resumed his work, saying –

'I think I know what you mean. I've never seen any of them, of course; but I suppose that's the sort you mean. I'm told – but mind I don't say it is so, for I don't know – that when we fall asleep, a troop of angel very like ourselves, only quite different, goes round to all the stars we have discovered, and discovers them after us. I suppose with our shovelling and handling we spoil them a bit; and I daresay the clouds that come up from below make them smoky and dull sometimes. They say – mind, I say *they say* – these other angels take them out one by one, and pass each round as we do, and breathe over it, and rub it with their white hands, which are softer than ours, because they don't do any pick-and-spade work, and smile at it, and put it in again; and that is what keeps them from growing dark.'

'How jolly!' thought Diamond. 'I should like to see *them* at their work too. – When do you go to sleep?' he asked the captain.

'When we grow sleepy,' answered the captain. 'They do say – but mind I say *they say* – that it is when those others – what do you call them? I don't know if that is their name; I am only guessing that may be the sort you mean – when they are on their rounds and come near any troop of us we fall asleep. They live on the west side of the hill. None of *us* have ever been to the top of it yet.'

Even as he spoke, he dropped his spade. He tumbled down beside it, and lay fast asleep. One after the other each of the troop dropped his pickaxe or shovel from his listless hands, and lay fast asleep by his work.

'Ah!' thought Diamond to himself, with delight, 'now the girl-angels are coming, and I, not being an angel, shall not fall asleep like the rest, and I shall see the girl-angels.'

But the same moment he felt himself growing sleepy. He struggled hard with the invading power. He put up his fingers to his eyelids and pulled them open. But it was of no use. He thought he saw a glimmer of pale rosy light far up the green hill, and ceased to know.

When he awoke, all the angel were starting up wide awake too. He expected to see them lift their tools, but no, the time for play had come.

They looked happier than ever, and each began to sing where he stood. He had not heard them sing before.

'Now,' he thought, 'I shall know what kind of nonsense the angels sing when they are merry. They don't drive cabs, I see, but they dig for stars, and they work hard enough to be merry after it.'

And he did hear some of the angels' nonsense; for if it was all sense to them, it had only just as much sense to Diamond as made good nonsense of it. He tried hard to set it down in his mind, listening as closely as he could, now to one, now to another, and now to all together. But while they were yet singing he began, to his dismay, to find that he was coming awake – faster and faster. And as he came awake, he found that, for all the goodness of his memory, verse after verse of the angels' nonsense vanished from it. He always thought he could keep the last, but as the next began he lost the one before it, and at length awoke, struggling to keep hold of the last verse of all. He felt as if the effort to keep from forgetting that one verse of the vanishing song nearly killed him. And yet by the time he was wide awake he could not be sure of that even. It was something like this:

> White hands of whiteness
> Wash the stars' faces,
> Till glitter, glitter, glit, goes their brightness
> Down to poor places.

This, however, was so near sense that he thought it could not be really what they did sing.

26   Diamond Takes a Fare the Wrong Way Right

The next morning Diamond was up almost as early as before. He had nothing to fear from his mother now, and made no secret of what he was about. By the time he reached the stable, several of the men were there. They asked him a good many questions as to his luck the day before, and he told them all they wanted to know. But when he proceeded to harness the old horse, they pushed him aside with rough kindness, called him a baby, and began to do it all for him. So Diamond ran in and had another mouthful of tea and bread and butter; and although he had never been so tired as he was the night before, he started quite fresh this morning. It was a cloudy day, and the wind blew hard from the north – so hard sometimes that, perched on the box with just his toes touching the ground, Diamond wished that he had some kind of strap to fasten himself down with lest he should be blown away. But he did not really mind it.

His head was full of the dream he had dreamed; but it did not make him neglect his work, for his work was not to dig stars but to drive old Diamond and pick up fares. There are not many people who can think about beautiful things and do common work at the same time. But then there are not many people who have been to the back of the north wind.

There was not much business doing. And Diamond felt rather cold, notwithstanding his mother had herself put on his comforter and helped him with his greatcoat. But he was too well aware of his dignity to get inside his cab as some do. A cabman ought to be above minding the weather – at least so Diamond thought. At length he was called to a neighbouring house, where a young woman with a heavy box had to be taken to Wapping for a coast-steamer.

He did not find it at all pleasant, so far east and so near the river; for the roughs were in great force. However, there being no block, not even in Nightingale Lane, he reached the entrance of the wharf, and set down his passenger without annoyance. But as he tuned to go back, some idlers, not content with chaffing him, showed a mind to the fare the young woman had given him. They were just pulling him off the box, and Diamond was shouting for the police, when a pale-faced man, in very shabby clothes, but with the look of a gentleman somewhere about him, came up, and making good use of his stick, drove them off.

'Now, my little man,' he said; 'get on while you can. Don't lose any time. This is not a place for you.'

But Diamond was not in the habit of thinking only of himself. He saw that his new friend looked weary, if not ill, and very poor.

'Won't you jump in, sir?' he said. 'I will take you wherever you like.'

'Thank you, my man; but I have no money; so I can't.'

'Oh! I don't want any money. I shall be much happier if you will get in. You have saved me all I had. I owe you a lift, sir.'

'Which way are you going?'

'To Charing Cross; but I don't mind where I go.'

'Well, I am very tired. If you will take me to Charing Cross, I shall be greatly obliged to you. I have walked from Gravesend, and had hardly a penny left to get through the tunnel.'

So saying, he opened the door and got in, and Diamond drove away.

But as he drove, he could not help fancying he had seen the gentleman – for Diamond knew he was a gentleman – before. Do all he could, however, he could not recall where or when. Meantime his fare, if we may call him such, seeing he was to pay nothing, whom the relief of being carried had made less and less inclined to carry himself, had been turning over things in his mind, and, as they passed the Mint, called to Diamond, who stopped his horse, got down, and went to the window.

'If you didn't mind taking me to Chiswick, I should be able to pay you when we got there. It's a long way, but you shall have the whole fare from the Docks – and something over.'

'Very well, sir,' said Diamond. 'I shall be most happy.'

He was just clambering up again, when the gentleman put his head out of the window and said –

'It's The Wilderness – Mr. Coleman's place; but I'll direct you when we come into the neighbourhood.'

It flashed upon Diamond who he was. But he got upon his box to arrange his thoughts before making any reply.

The gentleman was Mr. Evans, to whom Miss Coleman was to have been married, and Diamond had seen him several times with her in the garden. I have said that he had not behaved very well to Miss Coleman. He had put off their marriage more than once in a cowardly fashion, merely because he was ashamed to marry upon a small income, and live in a humble way. When a man thinks of what people will say in such a case, he may love, but his love is but a poor affair. Mr. Coleman took him into the firm as a junior partner, and it was in a measure through his influence that he entered upon those speculations which ruined him. So his love had not been a blessing. The ship which North Wind had sunk was their last venture, and Mr. Evans had gone out with it in the hope of turning its cargo to the best advantage. He was one of the single boat-load which managed to reach a desert island, and he had gone through a great many hardships and sufferings since then. But he was not past being taught, and his troubles had done him no end of good, for they had made him doubt himself, and begin to think, so that he had come to see that he had been foolish as well as wicked. For, if he had had Miss Coleman with him in the desert island, to build her a hut, and hunt for her food, and make clothes for her, he would have thought himself the most fortunate of men; and when he was at home, he would not marry till he could afford a man-servant. Before he got home again, he had even begun to understand that no man can make haste to be rich without going against the will of God, in which case it is the one frightful thing to be successful. So he had come back a more humble man, and longing to ask Miss Coleman to forgive him. But he had no idea what ruin had fallen upon them, for he had never made himself thoroughly acquainted with the firm's affairs. Few speculative people do know their own affairs. Hence he never doubted he should find matters much as he left them, and expected to see them all at The Wilderness as before. But if he had not fallen in with Diamond, he would not have thought of going there first.

What was Diamond to do? He had heard his father and mother drop some remarks concerning Mr. Evans which made him doubtful of him. He understood that he had not been so considerate as he might have been. So he went rather slowly till he should make up his mind. It was, of course, of no use to drive Mr. Evans to Chiswick. But if he should tell him what had befallen them, and where they lived now, he might put off going to see them, and he was certain that Miss Coleman, at least, must want very much to see Mr. Evans. He was pretty sure also that the best thing in any case was to bring them together, and let them set matter right for themselves.

The moment he came to this conclusion, he changed his course from westward to northward, and went straight for Mr. Coleman's poor little house in Hoxton. Mr. Evans was too tired and too much occupied with his thoughts to take the least notice of the streets they passed through, and had no suspicion, therefore, of the change of direction.

By this time the wind had increased almost to a hurricane, and as they had often to head it, it was no joke for either of the Diamonds. The distance, however, was not great. Before they reached the street where Mr. Coleman lived it blew so tremendously, that when Miss

Coleman, who was going out a little way, opened the door, it dashed against the wall with such a bang, that she was afraid to venture, and went in again. In five minutes after, Diamond drew up at the door. As soon as he had entered the street, however, the wind blew right behind them, and when he pulled up, old Diamond had so much ado to stop the cab against it, that the breeching broke. Young Diamond jumped off his box, knocked loudly at the door, then turned to the cab and said – before Mr. Evans had quite begun to think something must be amiss:

'Please, sir, my harness has given way. Would you mind stepping in here for a few minutes? They're friends of mine. I'll take you where you like after I've got it mended. I shan't be many minutes, but you can't stand in this wind.'

Half stupid with fatigue and want of food, Mr. Evans yielded to the boy's suggestion, and walked in at the door which the maid held with difficulty against the wind. She took Mr. Evans for a visitor, as indeed he was, and showed him into the room on the ground-floor. Diamond, who had followed into the hall, whispered to her as she closed the door –

'Tell Miss Coleman. It's Miss Coleman he wants to see.'

'I don't know,' said the maid. – 'He don't look much like a gentleman.'

'He is, though; and I know him, and so does Miss Coleman.'

The maid could not but remember Diamond, having seen him when he and his father brought the ladies home. So she believed him, and went to do what he told her.

What passed in the little parlour when Miss Coleman came down does not belong to my story, which is all about Diamond. If he had known that Miss Coleman thought Mr. Evans was dead, perhaps he would have managed it differently. There was a cry and a running to and fro in the house, and then all was quiet again.

Almost as soon as Mr. Evans went in, the wind began to cease, and was now still. Diamond found that by making the breeching just a little tighter than was quite comfortable for the old horse he could do very well for the present; and, thinking it better to let him have his bag in this quiet place, he sat on the box till the old horse should have eaten his dinner. In a little while Mr. Evans came out, and asked him to come in. Diamond obeyed, and to his delight Miss Coleman put her arms round him and kissed him, and there was payment for him! not to

mention the five precious shillings she gave him, which he could not
refuse because his mother wanted them so much at home for his father.
He left them nearly as happy as they were themselves.

The rest of the day he did better, and, although he had not so much
to take home as the day before, yet on the whole the result was
satisfactory. And what a story he had to tell his father and mother
about his adventures, and how he had done, and what was the result!
They asked him such a multitude of questions! some of which he could
answer, and some of which he could not answer; and his father seemed
ever so much better from finding that his boy was already not only
useful to his family but useful to other people, and quite taking his
place as a man who judged what was wise, and did work worth doing.

For a fortnight Diamond went on driving his cab, and keeping his
family. He had begun to be known about some parts of London, and
people would prefer taking his cab because they liked what they heard
of him. One gentleman who lived near the mews, engaged him to carry
him to the City every morning at a certain hour; and Diamond was
punctual as clockwork – though to effect that, required a good deal of

care, for his father's watch was not much to be depended on, and had to be watched itself by the clock of St. George's church. Between the two, however, he did make a success of it.

After that fortnight, his father was able to go out again. Then Diamond went to make inquiries about Nanny, and this led to something else.

27 The Children's Hospital

The first day his father resumed his work, Diamond went with him as usual. In the afternoon, however, his father, having taken a fare to the neighbourhood, went home, and Diamond drove the cab the rest of the day. It was hard for old Diamond to do all the work, but they could not afford to have another horse. They contrived to save him as much as possible, and fed him well, and he did bravely.

The next morning his father was so much stronger that Diamond thought he might go and ask Mr. Raymond to take him to see Nanny. He found him at home. His servant had grown friendly by this time, and showed him in without any cross-questioning. Mr. Raymond received him with his usual kindness, consented at once, and walked with him to the Hospital, which was close at hand. It was a comfortable old-fashioned house, built in the reign of Queen Anne, and in her day, no doubt, inhabited by rich and fashionable people: now it was a home for poor sick children, who were carefully tended for love's sake. There are regions in London where a hospital in every other street might be full of such children, whose fathers and mothers are dead, or unable to take care of them.

When Diamond followed Mr. Raymond into the room where those children who had got over the worst of their illness and were growing better lay, he saw a number of little iron bedsteads, with their heads to the walls, and in every one of them a child, whose face was a story in itself. In some health had begun to appear in a tinge upon the cheeks, and a doubtful brightness in the eyes, just as out of the cold dreary winter the spring comes in blushing buds and bright crocuses. In others there were more of the signs of winter left. Their faces reminded you of snow and keen cutting winds, more than of sunshine and soft breezes and butterflies; but even in them the signs of suffering told that the suffering was less, and that if the spring-time had but arrived, it had yet arrived.

Diamond looked all round, but could see no Nanny. He turned to Mr. Raymond with a question in his eyes.

'Well?' said Mr. Raymond.

'Nanny's not here,' said Diamond.

'Oh, yes, she is.'

'I don't see her.'

'I do, though. There she is.'

He pointed to a bed right in front of where Diamond was standing.

'That's not Nanny,' he said.

'It *is* Nanny. I have seen her many times since you have. Illness makes a great difference.'

'Why, that girl must have been to the back of the north wind!' thought Diamond, but he said nothing, only stared; and as he stared, something of the old Nanny began to dawn through the face of the new Nanny. The old Nanny, though a good girl, and a friendly girl, had been rough, blunt in her speech, and dirty in her person. Her face would always have reminded one who had already been to the back of the north wind of something he had seen in the best of company, but it had been coarse notwithstanding, partly from the weather, partly from her living amongst low people, and partly from having to defend herself: now it was so sweet, and gentle, and refined, that she might have had a lady and a gentleman for a father and mother. And Diamond could not help thinking of words which he had heard in the church the day before: 'Surely it is good to be afflicted;' or something like that. North Wind, somehow or other, must have had to do with her! She had grown from a rough girl into a gentle maiden.

Mr. Raymond, however, was not surprised, for he was used to see such lovely changes – something like the change which passes upon the crawling, many-footed creature, when it turns sick and ill, and revives a butterfly, with two wings instead of many feet. Instead of her having to take care of herself, kind hands ministered to her, making her comfortable and sweet and clean, soothing her aching head, and giving her cooling drink when she was thirsty; and kind eyes, the stars of the kingdom of heaven, had shone upon her; so that, what with the fire of the fever and the dew of tenderness, that which was coarse in her had melted away, and her whole face had grown so refined and sweet that

Diamond did not know her. But as he gazed, the best of the old face, all the true and good part of it, that which was Nanny herself, dawned upon him, like the moon coming out of a cloud, until at length, instead of only believing Mr. Raymond that this was she, he saw for himself that it was Nanny indeed – very worn, but grown beautiful.

He went up to her. She smiled. He had heard her laugh, but had never seen her smile before.

'Nanny, do you know me?' said Diamond.

She only smiled again, as if the question was amusing.

She was not likely to forget him; for although she did not yet know it was he who had got her there, she had dreamed of him often, and had talked much about him when delirious. Nor was it much wonder, for he was the only boy except Joe who had ever shown her kindness.

Meantime Mr. Raymond was going from bed to bed, talking to the little people. Every one knew him, and every one was eager to have a look, and a smile, and a kind word from him. Diamond sat down on a stool at the head of Nanny's bed. She laid her hand in his. No one else of her old acquaintance had been near her.

Suddenly a little voice called out –

'Won't Mr. Raymond tell us a story?'

'Oh, yes, please do! please do!' cried several little voices which also were stronger than the rest. For Mr. Raymond was in the habit of telling them a story when he went to see them, and they enjoyed it far more than the other nice things which the doctor permitted him to give them.

'Very well,' said Mr. Raymond, 'I will. What sort of a story shall it be?'

'A true story,' said one little girl.

'A fairy tale,' said a little boy.

'Well,' said Mr. Raymond, 'I suppose, as there is a difference, I may choose. I can't think of any true story just at this moment, so I well tell you a sort of a fairy one.'

'Oh, jolly!' exclaimed the little boy who had called out for a fairy tale.

'It came into my head this morning as I got out of bed,' continued Mr. Raymond; 'and if it turns out pretty well, I will write it down, and get somebody to print it for me, and then you shall read it when you like.'

'Then nobody ever heard it before?' asked one older child.

'No, nobody.'

'Oh!' exclaimed several, thinking it very grand to have the first telling; and I daresay there might be a peculiar freshness about it, because everything would be nearly as new to the story-teller himself as to the listeners.

Some were only sitting up and some were lying down, so there could not be the same busy gathering, and bustling, and shifting to and fro with which children generally prepare themselves to hear a story; but their faces, and the turning of their heads, and many feeble exclamations of expected pleasure, showed that all such preparations were making within them.

Mr. Raymond stood in the middle of the room, that he might turn from side to side, and give each a share of seeing him. Diamond kept his place by Nanny's side, with her hand in his. I do not know how much of Mr. Raymond's story the smaller children understood; indeed, I don't quite know how much there was in it to be understood, for in such a story every one has just to take what he can get. But they all listened with apparent satisfaction, and certainly with great attention. Mr. Raymond wrote it down afterwards, and here it is –

somewhat altered no doubt, for a good story-teller tries to make his stories better every time he tells them. I cannot myself help thinking that he was somewhat indebted for this one to the old story of The Sleeping Beauty.

28   Little Daylight

No house of any pretension to be called a palace is in the least worthy of the name, except it has a wood near it – very near it – and the nearer the better. Not all round it – I don't mean that, for a palace ought to be open to the sun and wind, and stand high and brave, with weather-cocks glittering and flags flying; but on one side of every palace there must be a wood. And there was a very grand wood indeed beside the palace of the king who was going to be Daylight's father; such a grand wood, that nobody yet had ever got to the other end of it. Near the house it was kept very trim and nice, and it was free of brushwood for a long way in; but by degrees it got wild, and it grew wilder, and wilder, and wilder, until some said wild beasts at last did what they liked in it. The king and his courtiers often hunted, however, and this kept the wild beasts far away from the palace.

One glorious summer morning, when the wind and sun were out together, when the vanes were flashing and the flags frolicking against the blue sky, little Daylight made her appearance from somewhere – nobody could tell where – a beautiful baby, with such bright eyes that she might have come from the sun, only by and by she might equally well have come out of the wind. There was great jubilation in the palace, for this was the first baby the queen had had, and there is as much happiness over a new baby in a palace as in a cottage.

But there is one disadvantage of living near a wood: you do not know quite who your neighbours may be. Everybody knew there were in it several fairies, living within a few miles of the palace, who always had had something to do with each new baby that came; for fairies live so much longer than we, that they can have business with a good many generations of human mortals. The curious houses they lived in were well known also, – one, a hollow oak; another, a birch-tree, though

nobody could ever find how that fairy made a house of it; another, a hut of growing trees intertwined, and patched up with turf and moss. But there was another fairy who had lately come to the place, and nobody even knew she was a fairy except the other fairies. A wicked old thing she was, always concealing her power, and being as disagreeable as she could, in order to tempt people to give her offence, that she might have the pleasure of taking vengeance upon them. The people about thought she was a witch, and those who knew her by sight were careful to avoid offending her. She lived in a mud house, in a swampy part of the forest.

In all history we find that fairies give their remarkable gifts to prince or princess, or any child of sufficient importance in their eyes, always at the christening. Now this we can understand, because it is an ancient custom among human beings as well; and it is not hard to explain why wicked fairies should choose the same time to do unkind things; but it is difficult to understand how they should be able to do them, for you would fancy all wicked creatures would be powerless on such an occasion. But I never knew of any interference on the part of a wicked fairy that did not turn out a good thing in the end.

What a good thing, for instance, it was that one princess should sleep for a hundred years! Was she not saved from all the plague of young men who were not worthy of her? And did she not come awake exactly at the right moment when the right prince kissed her? For my part, I cannot help wishing a good many girls would sleep till just the same fate overtook them. It would be happier for them, and more agreeable to their friends.

Of course all the known fairies were invited to the christening. But the king and queen never thought of inviting an old witch. For the power of the fairies they have by nature; whereas a witch gets her power by wickedness. The other fairies, however, knowing the danger thus run, provided as well as they could against accidents from her quarter. But they could neither render her powerless, nor could they arrange their gifts in reference to hers beforehand, for they could not tell what those might be.

Of course the old hag was there without being asked. Not to be asked was just what she wanted, that she might have a sort of a reason for doing what she wished to do. For somehow even the wickedest of creatures likes a pretext for doing the wrong thing.

Five fairies had one after the other given the child such gifts as

each counted best, and the fifth had just stepped back to her place in the surrounding splendour of ladies and gentlemen, when, mumbling a laugh between her toothless gums, the wicked fairy hobbled out into the middle of the circle, and at the moment when the archbishop was handing the baby to the lady at the head of the nursery department of state affairs, addressed him thus, giving a bite or two to every word before she could part with it:

'Please your Grace, I'm very deaf: would your Grace mind repeating the prince's name?'

'With pleasure, my good woman,' said the archbishop, stooping to shout in her ear: 'the infant's name is little Daylight.'

'And little daylight it shall be,' cried the fairy, in the tone of a dry axle, 'and little good shall any of her gifts do her. For I bestow upon her the gift of sleeping all day long, whether she will or not. Ha, ha! He, he! Hi, hi!'

Then out started the sixth fairy, who, of course, the others had arranged should come after the wicked one, in order to undo as much as she might.

'If she sleep all day,' she said mournfully, 'she shall, at least, wake all night.'

'A nice prospect for her mother and me!' thought the poor king; for they loved her far too much to give her up to nurses, especially at night, as most kings and queens do – and are sorry for it afterwards.

'You spoke before I had done,' said the wicked fairy. 'That's against the law. It gives me another chance.'

'I beg you pardon,' said the other fairies, all together.

'She did. I hadn't done laughing,' said the crone. 'I had only got to Hi, hi! and I had to go through Ho, ho! and Hu, hu! So I decree that if she wakes all night she shall wax and wane with its mistress the moon. And what that may mean I hope her royal parents will live to see. Ho, ho! Hu, hu!'

But out stepped another fairy, for they had been wise enough to keep two in reserve, because every fairy knew the trick of one.

'Until,' said the seventh fairy, 'a prince comes who shall kiss her without knowing it.'

The wicked fairy made a horrid noise like an angry cat, and hobbled away. She could not pretend that she had not finished her speech this time, for she had laughed Ho, ho! and Hu, hu!

'I don't know what that means,' said the poor king to the seventh fairy.

'Don't be afraid. The meaning will come with the thing itself,' said she.

The assembly broke up, miserable enough – the queen, at least, prepared for a good many sleepless nights, and the lady at the head of the nursery department anything but comfortable in the prospect before her, for of course the queen could not do it all. As for the king, he made up his mind, with what courage he could summon, to meet the demands of the case, but wondered whether he could with any propriety require the First Lord of the Treasury to take a share in the burden laid upon him.

I will not attempt to describe what they had to go through for some time. But at last the household settled into a regular system – a very irregular one in some respects. For at certain seasons the palace rang all night with bursts of laughter from little Daylight, whose heart the old fairy's curse could not reach; she was Daylight still, only a little in the wrong place, for she always dropped asleep at the first hint of dawn in the east. But her merriment was of short duration. When the moon was at the full, she was in glorious spirits, and as beautiful as it was possible for a child of her age to be. But as the moon waned, she faded, until at last she was wan and withered like the poorest, sickliest child you might come upon in the streets of a great city in the arms of a homeless mother. Then the night was quiet as the day, for the little creature lay in her gorgeous cradle night and day with hardly a motion, and indeed at last without even a moan, like one dead. At first they often thought she was dead, but at last they got used to it, and only consulted the almanac to find the moment when she would begin to revive, which, of course, was with the first appearance of the silver thread of the crescent moon. Then she would move her lips, and they would give her a little nourishment; and she would grow better and better and better, until for a few days she was splendidly well. When well, she was always merriest out in the moonlight; but even when near her worst, she seemed better when, in warm summer nights, they carried her cradle out into the light of the waning moon. Then in her sleep she would smile the faintest, most pitiful smile.

For a long time few people ever saw her awake. As she grew older she became such a favourite, however, that about the palace there were always some who would contrive to keep awake at night, in order to be near her. But she soon began to take every chance of getting away from her nurses and enjoying her moonlight alone. And thus things went on until she was nearly seventeen years of age. Her father and mother had by that time got so used to the odd state of things that they had ceased to wonder at them. All their arrangements had reference to the state of the Princess Daylight, and it is amazing how things contrive to accommodate themselves. But how any prince was ever to find and deliver her, appeared inconceivable.

As she grew older she had grown more and more beautiful, with the sunniest hair and the loveliest eyes of heavenly blue, brilliant and profound as the sky of a June day. But so much more painful and sad was the change as her bad time came on. The more beautiful she was in the full moon, the more withered and worn did she become as the moon waned. At the time at which my story has now arrived, she looked, when the moon was small or gone, like an old woman exhausted with suffering. This was the more painful that her appearance was unnatural; for her hair and eyes did not change. Her wan face was both drawn and wrinkled, and had an eager hungry look. Her skinny hands moved as if wishing, but unable, to lay hold of something. Her shoulders were bent forward, her chest went in, and she stooped as if she were eighty years old. At last she had to be put to bed, and there await the flow of the tide of life. But she grew to dislike being seen, still more being touched by any hands, during this season. One lovely summer evening, when the moon lay all but gone upon the verge of the horizon, she vanished from her attendants, and it was only after searching for her a long time in great terror, that they found her fast asleep in the forest, at the foot of a silver birch, and carried her home.

A little way from the palace there was a great open glade, covered with the greenest and softest grass. This was her favourite haunt; for here the full moon shone free and glorious, while through a vista in the trees she could generally see more or less of the dying moon as it crossed the opening. Here she had a little rustic house built for her, and here she mostly resided. None of the court might go there without leave, and her own attendants had learned by this time not to be officious in waiting upon her, so that she was very much at liberty. Whether the good fairies had anything to do with it or not I cannot tell, but at last she got into the way of retreating further into the wood every night as the moon waned, so that sometimes they had great trouble in finding her; but as she was always very angry if she discovered they were watching her, they scarcely dared to do so. At length one night they thought they had lost her altogether. It was morning before they found her. Feeble as she was, she had wandered into a thicket a long way from the glade, and there she lay – fast asleep, of course.

Although the fame of her beauty and sweetness had gone abroad, yet as everybody knew she was under a bad spell, no king in the neighbourhood had any desire to have her for a daughter-in-law. There were serious objections to such a relation.

About this time in a neighbouring kingdom, in consequence of the wickedness of the nobles, an insurrection took place upon the death of the old king, the greater part of the nobility was massacred, and the young prince was compelled to flee for his life, disguised like a peasant. For some time, until he got out of the country, he suffered much from hunger and fatigue; but when he got into that ruled by the princess's father, and had no longer any fear of being recognized, he fared better, for the people were kind. He did not abandon his disguise, however. One tolerable reason was that he had no other clothes to put on, and another that he had very little money, and did not know where to get any more. There was no good in telling everbody he met that he was a prince, for he felt that a prince ought to be able to get on like other people, else his rank only made a fool of him. He had read of princes setting out upon adventure; and here he was out in similar case, only without having had a choice in the matter. He would go on, and see what would come of it.

For a day or two he had been walking through the palace-wood, and had had next to nothing to eat, when he came upon the strangest little house, inhabited by a very nice tidy motherly old woman. This was one of the good fairies. The moment she saw him she knew quite well who he was and what was going to come of it; but she was not at liberty to interfere with the orderly march of events. She received him with the kindness she would have shown to any other traveller, and gave him bread and milk, which he thought the most delicious food he had ever tasted, wondering that they did not have it for dinner at the palace sometimes. The old woman pressed him to stay all night. When he awoke he was amazed to find how well and strong he felt. She would not take any of the money he offered, but begged him, if he found occasion of continuing in the neighbourhood, to return and occupy the same quarters.

'Thank you much, good mother,' answered the prince; 'but there is little chance of that. The sooner I get out of this wood the better.'

'I don't know that,' said the fairy.

'What do you mean?' asked the prince.

'Why how *should* I know?' returned she.

'I can't tell,' said the prince.

'Very well,' said the fairy.

'How strangely you talk!' said the prince.

'Do I?' said the fairy.

'Yes, you do,' said the prince.

'Very well,' said the fairy.

The prince was not used to be spoken to in this fashion, so he felt a little angry, and turned and walked away. But this did not offend the fairy. She stood at the door of her little house looking after him till the trees hid him quite. Then she said 'At last!' and went in.

The prince wandered and wandered, and got nowhere. The sun sank and sank and went out of sight, and he seemed no nearer the end of the wood than ever. He sat down on a fallen tree, ate a bit of bread the old woman had given him, and waited for the moon; for, although he was not much of an astronomer, he knew the moon would rise some time, because she had risen the night before. Up she came, slow and slow, but of a good size, pretty nearly round indeed; whereupon, greatly refreshed with his piece of bread, he got up and went – he knew not whither.

After walking a considerable distance, he thought he was coming to the outside of the forest; but when he reached what he thought the last of it, he found himself only upon the edge of a great open space in it, covered with grass. The moon shone very bright, and he thought he had never seen a more lovely spot. Still it looked dreary because of its loneliness, for he could not see the house at the other side. He sat down weary again, and gazed into the glade. He had not seen so much room for several days.

All at once he spied something in the middle of the grass. What could it be? It moved; it came nearer. Was it a human creature, gliding across – a girl dressed in white, gleaming in the moonshine? She came nearer and nearer. He crept behind a tree and watched, wondering. It must be some strange being of the wood – a nymph whom the moonlight and the warm dusky air had enticed from her tree. But when she came close to where he stood, he no longer doubted she was human – for he hâd caught sight of her sunny hair, and her clear blue eyes, and the loveliest face and form that he had ever seen. All at once she began singing like a nightingale, and dancing to her own music, with her eyes ever turned towards the moon. She passed close to where he stood, dancing on by the edge of the trees and away in a great circle towards the other side, until he could see but a spot of white in the yellowish green of the moonlit grass. But when he feared once more it would vanish quite, the spot grew, and became a figure once more. She approached him again, singing and dancing and waving her arms over her head, until she had completed the circle. Just opposite his tree she stood, ceased her song, dropped her arms, and broke out into a long clear laugh, musical as a brook. Then, as if tired, she threw herself on the grass, and lay gazing at the moon. The prince was almost afraid to breathe lest he should startle her, and she should vanish from his sight. As to venturing near her, that never came into his head.

She had lain for a long hour or longer, when the prince began again to doubt concerning her. Perhaps she was but a vision of his own fancy. Or was she a spirit of the wood, after all? If so, he too would haunt the wood, glad to have lost kingdom and everything for the hope of being near her. He would build him a hut in the forest, and there he would live for the pure chance of seeing her again. Upon nights like this at least she would come out and bask in the moonlight, and make his soul blessed. But while he thus dreamed she sprang to her feet, turned her face full to the moon, and began singing as if she would draw her down from the sky by the power of her entrancing voice. She looked more beautiful than ever. Again she began dancing to her own music, and danced away into the distance. Once more she returned in a similar manner; but although he was watching as eagerly as before, what with fatigue and what with gazing, he fell fast asleep before she came near him. When he awoke it was broad daylight, and the princess was nowhere.

He could not leave the place. What if she should come the next night! He would gladly endure a day's hunger to see her yet again: he would buckle his belt quite tight. He walked round the glade to see if he could discover any prints of her feet. But the grass was so short, and her steps had been so light, that she had not left a single trace behind her.

He walked half-way round the wood without seeing anything to account for her presence. Then he spied a lovely little house, with thatched roof and low eaves, surrounded by an exquisite garden, with doves and peacocks walking in it. Of course this must be where the gracious lady who loved the moonlight lived. Forgetting his appearance, he walked towards the door, determined to make inquiries, but as he passed a little pond full of gold and silver fishes, he caught sight of himself and turned to find the door to the kitchen. There he knocked, and asked for a piece of bread. The good-natured cook brought him in, and gave him an excellent breakfast, which the prince found nothing the worse for being served in the kitchen. While he ate, he talked with his entertainer, and learned that this was the favourite retreat of the Princess Daylight. But he learned nothing more, both because he was afraid of seeming inquisitive, and because the cook did not choose to be heard talking about her mistress to a peasant lad who had begged for his breakfast.

As he rose to take his leave, it occurred to him that he might not be so far from the old woman's cottage as he had thought, and he asked the cook whether she knew anything of such a place, describing it as well as he could. She said she knew it well enough, adding with a smile –

'It's there you're going, is it?'

'Yes, if it's not far off.'

'It's not more than three miles. But mind what you are about, you know.'

'Why do you say that?'

'If you're after any mischief, she'll make you repent it.'

'The best thing that could happen under the circumstances,' remarked the prince.

'What do you mean by that?' asked the cook.

'Why, it stands to reason,' answered the prince, 'that if you wish to do anything wrong, the best thing for you is to be made to repent of it.'

'I see,' said the cook. 'Well, I think you may venture. She's a good old soul.'

'Which way does it lie from here?' asked the prince.

She gave him full instructions; and he left her with many thanks.

Being now refreshed, however, the prince did not go back to the cottage that day: he remained in the forest, amusing himself as best he could, but waiting anxiously for the night, in the hope that the princess would again appear. Nor was he disappointed, for, directly the moon rose, he spied a glimmering shape far across the glade. As it drew nearer, he saw it was she indeed – not dressed in white as before: in a pale blue like the sky, she looked lovelier still. He thought it was that the blue suited her yet better than the white; he did not know that she was really more beautiful because the moon was nearer the full. In fact the next night was full moon, and the princess would then be at the zenith of her loveliness.

The prince feared for some time that she was not coming near his hiding-place that night; but the circles in her dance ever widened as the moon rose, until at last they embraced the whole glade, and she came still closer to the trees where he was hiding than she had come the night before. He was entranced with her loveliness, for it was indeed a marvellous thing. All night long he watched her, but dared not go near her. He would have been ashamed of watching her too, had he not become almost incapable of thinking of anything but how beautiful she was. He watched the whole night long, and saw that as the moon went down she retreated in smaller and smaller circles, until at last he could see her no more.

Weary as he was, he set out for the old woman's cottage, where he arrived just in time for her breakfast, which she shared with him. He then went to bed, and slept for many hours. When he awoke, the sun was down, and he departed in great anxiety lest he should lose a glimpse of the lovely vision. But whether it was by the machinations of the swamp-fairy, or merely that it is one thing to go and another to return by the same road, he lost his way. I shall not attempt to describe his misery when the moon rose, and he saw nothing but trees, trees, trees. She was high in the heavens before he reached the glade. Then indeed his troubles vanished, for there was the princess coming dancing towards him, in a dress that shone like gold, and with shoes that glimmered through the grass like fire-flies. She was of course still more beautiful than before. Like an embodied sunbeam she passed him, and danced away into the distance.

Before she returned in her circle, clouds had begun to gather about the moon. The wind rose, the trees moaned, and their lighter branches leaned all one way before it. The prince feared that the princess would go in, and he should see her no more that night. But she came dancing on more jubilant than ever, her golden dress and her sunny hair streaming out upon the blast, waving her arms towards the moon, and in the exuberance of her delight ordering the clouds away from off her face. The prince could hardly believe she was not a creature of the elements, after all.

By the time she had completed another circle, the clouds had gathered deep, and there were growlings of distant thunder. Just as she passed the tree where he stood, a flash of lightning blinded him for a moment, and when he saw again, to his horror, the princess lay on the ground. He darted to her, thinking she had been struck; but when she heard him coming, she was on her feet in a moment.

'What do you want?' she asked.

'I beg your pardon. I thought – the lightning——' said the prince, hesitating.

'There is nothing the matter,' said the princess, waving him off rather haughtily.

The poor prince turned and walked towards the wood.

'Come back,' said Daylight: 'I like you. You do what you are told. Are you good?'

'Not so good as I should like to be,' said the prince.

'Then go and grow better,' said the princess.

Again the disappointed prince turned and went.

'Come back,' said the princess.

He obeyed, and stood before her waiting.

'Can you tell me what the sun is like?' she asked.

'No,' he answered. 'But where's the good of asking what you know?'

'But I don't know,' she rejoined.

'Why, everybody knows.'

'That's the very thing: I'm not everybody. I've never seen the sun.'

'Then you can't know what it's like till you do see it.'

'I think you must be a prince,' said the princess.

'Do I look like one?' said the prince.

'I can't quite say that.'

'Then why do you think so?'

'Because you both do what you are told and speak the truth. – Is the sun so very bright?'

'As bright as the lightning.'

'But it doesn't go out like that, does it?'

'Oh no. It shines like the moon, rises and sets like the moon, is much the same shape as the moon, only so bright that you can't look at it for a moment.'

'But I *would* look at it,' said the princess.

'But you couldn't,' said the prince.

'But I could,' said the princess.

'Why don't you, then?'

'Because I can't.'

'Why can't you?'

'Because I can't wake. And I never shall wake until——'

Here she hid her face in her hands, turned away, and walked in the slowest, stateliest manner towards the house. The prince ventured to follow her at a little distance, but she turned and made a repellent gesture, which, like a true gentleman-prince, he obeyed at once. He waited a long time, but as she did not come near him again, and as the night had now cleared, he set off at last for the old woman's cottage.

It was long past midnight when he reached it, but, to his surprise, the old woman was paring potatoes at the door. Fairies are fond of doing odd things. Indeed, however they may dissemble, the night is always their day. And so it is with all who have fairy blood in them.

'Why, what are you doing there, this time of the night, mother?' said the prince; for that was the kind way in which any young man in his country would address a woman who was much older than himself.

'Getting your supper ready, my son,' she answered.

'Oh! I don't want any supper,' said the prince.

'Ah! you've seen Daylight,' said she.

'I've seen a princess who never saw it,' said the prince.

'Do you like her?' asked the fairy.

'Oh! don't I?' said the prince. 'More than you would believe, mother.'

'A fairy can believe anything that ever was or ever could be,' said the old woman.

'Then are you a fairy?' asked the prince.

'Yes,' said she.

'Then what do you do for things not to believe?' asked the prince.

'There's plenty of them – everything that never was nor ever could be.'

'Plenty, I grant you,' said the prince. 'But do you believe there could be a princess who never saw the daylight? Do you believe that, now?'

This the prince said, not that he doubted the princess, but that he wanted the fairy to tell him more. She was too old a fairy, however, to be caught so easily.

'Of all people, fairies must not tell secrets. Besides, she's a princess.'

'Well, I'll tell *you* a secret. I'm a prince.'

'I know that.'

'How do you know it?'

'By the curl of the third eyelash on your left eyelid.'

'Which corner do you count from?'

'That's a secret.'

'Another secret? Well, at least, if I am a prince, there can be no harm in telling me about a princess.'

'It's just princes I can't tell.'

'There ain't any more of them – are there?' said the prince.

'What! you don't think you're the only prince in the world, do you?'

'Oh, dear, no! not at all. But I know there's one too many just at present, except the princess——'

'Yes, yes, that's it,' said the fairy.

'What's *it*?' asked the prince.

But he could get nothing more out of the fairy, and had to go to bed unanswered, which was something of a trial.

Now wicked fairies will not be bound by the laws which the good fairies obey, and this always seems to give the bad the advantage over the good, for they use means to gain their ends which the others will not. But it is all of no consequence, for what they do never succeeds; nay, in the end it brings about the very thing they are trying to prevent. So you see that somehow, for all their cleverness, wicked fairies are dreadfully stupid, for, although from the beginning of the world they have really helped instead of thwarting the good fairies, not one of them is a bit the wiser for it. She will try the bad thing just as they all did before her; and succeeds no better of course.

The prince had so far stolen a march upon the swamp-fairy that she did not know he was in the neighbourhood until after he had seen the princess those three times. When she knew it, she consoled herself by thinking that the princess must be far too proud and too modest for any young man to venture even to speak to her before he had seen her six times at least. But there was even less danger than the wicked fairy thought; for, however much the princess might desire to be set free, she was dreadfully afraid of the wrong prince. Now, however, the fairy was going to do all she could.

She so contrived it by her deceitful spells, that the next night the prince could not by any endeavour find his way to the glade. It would take me too long to tell her tricks. They would be amusing to us, who know that they could not do any harm, but they were something other than amusing to the poor prince. He wandered about the forest till daylight, and then fell fast asleep. The same thing occurred for seven following days, during which neither could he find the good fairy's cottage. After the third quarter of the moon, however, the bad fairy thought she might be at ease about the affair for a fortnight at least, for there was no chance of the prince wishing to kiss the princess during that period. So the first day of the fourth quarter he did find the cottage, and the next day he found the glade. For nearly another week he haunted it. But the princess never came. I have little doubt she was on the farther edge of it some part of every night, but at this period she always wore black, and, there being little or no light, the prince never saw her. Nor would he have known her if he had seen her. How could he have taken the worn decrepit creature she was now, for the glorious Princess Daylight?

At last, one night when there was no moon at all, he ventured near the house. There he heard voices talking, although it was past midnight; for her women were in considerable uneasiness, because the one whose turn it was to watch her had fallen asleep, and had not seen which way she went, and this was a night when she would probably wander very far, describing a circle which did not touch the open glade at all, but stretched away from the back of the house, deep into that side of the forest – a part of which the prince knew nothing. When he understood from what they said that she had disappeared, and that she must have gone somewhere in the said direction, he plunged at once into the wood to see if he could find her. For hours he roamed with nothing to guide him but the vague notion of a circle which on one side bordered on the house, for so much had he picked up from the talk he had overheard.

It was getting towards the dawn, but as yet there was no streak of light in the sky, when he came to a great birch-tree, and sat down weary at the foot of it. While he sat – very miserable, you may be sure – full of fear for the princess, and wondering how her attendants could take it so quietly, he bethought himself that it would not be a bad plan to light a fire, which, if she were anywhere near, would attract her. This he managed with a tinder-box, which the good fairy had given him. It was just beginning to blaze up, when he heard a moan, which seemed to come from the other side of the tree. He sprung to his feet, but his heart throbbed so that he had to lean for a moment against the tree before he could move. When he got round, there lay a human form in a little dark heap on the earth. There was light enough from his fire to show that it was not the princess. He lifted it in his arms, hardly heavier than a child, and carried it to the flame. The countenance was that of an old woman, but it had a fearfully strange look. A black hood concealed her hair, and her eyes were closed. He laid her down as comfortably as he could, chafed her hands, put a little cordial from a bottle, also the gift of the fairy, into her mouth; took off his coat and wrapped it about her, and in short did the best he could. In a little while she opened her eyes and looked at him – so pitifully! The tears rose and flowed down her grey wrinkled cheeks, but she said never a word. She closed her eyes again, but the tears kept on flowing, and her whole appearance was so utterly pitiful that the prince was very near crying too. He begged her to tell him what was the matter, promising to do all he could to help her; but still she did not speak. He thought she was dying, and took her in his arms again to carry her to the princess's house, where he thought the good-natured cook might be able to do something for her. When he lifted her, the tears flowed yet faster, and she gave such a sad moan that it went to his very heart.

'Mother, mother!' he said – 'Poor mother!' and kissed her on the withered lips.

She started; and what eyes they were that opened upon him! But he did not see them, for it was still very dark, and he had enough to do to make his way through the trees towards the house.

Just as he approached the door, feeling more tired than he could have imagined possible – she was such a little thin old thing – she began to move, and became so restless that, unable to carry her a moment longer, he thought to lay her on the grass. But she stood upright on her feet. Her hood had dropped, and her hair fell about her. The first gleam of the morning was caught on her face: that face was bright as the never-ageing Dawn, and her eyes were lovely as the sky of darkest blue. The prince recoiled in over-mastering wonder. It was Daylight herself whom he had brought from the forest! He fell at her feet, nor dared look up until she laid her hand upon his head. He rose then.

'You kissed me when I was an old woman: there! I kiss you when I am a young princess,' murmured Daylight. – 'Is that the sun coming?'

29　Ruby

The children were delighted with the story, and made many amusing remarks upon it. Mr. Raymond promised to search his brain for another, and when he found one promised to bring it to them. Diamond having taken leave of Nanny, and promised to go and see her again soon, went away with him.

Now Mr. Raymond had been turning over in his mind what he could do both for Diamond and for Nanny. He had therefore made some acquaintance with Diamond's father, and had been greatly pleased with him. But he had come to the resolution, before he did anything so good as he would like to do for them, to put them all to a certain test. So as they walked away together, he began to talk with Diamond as follows:—

'Nanny must leave the hospital soon, Diamond.'

'I'm glad of that, sir.'

'Why? Don't you think it's a nice place?'

'Yes, very. But it's better to be well and doing something, you know, even if it's not quite so comfortable.'

'But they can't keep Nanny so long as they would like. They can't keep her till she's *quite* strong. There are always so many sick children they want to take in and make better. And the question is, What will she do when they send her out again?'

'That's just what I can't tell, though I've been thinking of it over and over, sir. Her crossing was taken long ago, and I couldn't bear to see Nanny fighting for it, especially with such a poor fellow as has taken it. He's quite lame, sir.'

'She doesn't look much like fighting now, does she, Diamond?'

'No, sir. She looks too like an angel. Angels don't fight – do they, sir?'

'Not to get things for themselves, at least,' said Mr. Raymond.

'Besides,' added Diamond, 'I don't quite see that she would have any better right to the crossing then the boy who has got it. Nobody gave it to her; she only took it. And now he has taken it.'

'If she were to sweep a crossing – soon at least – after the illness she has had, she would be laid up again the very first wet day,' said Mr. Raymond.

'And there's hardly any money to be got except on the wet days,' remarked Diamond reflectively. 'Is there nothing else she could do, sir?'

'Not without being taught, I'm afraid.'

'Well, couldn't somebody teach her something?'

'Couldn't you teach her, Diamond?'

'I don't know anything myself, sir. I *could* teach her to dress the baby; but nobody would give her anything for doings things like that: they are so easy. There wouldn't be much good in teaching her to drive a cab, for where would she get the cab to drive? There ain't fathers and old Diamonds everywhere. At least poor Nanny can't find any of them, I doubt.'

'Perhaps if she were taught to be nice and clean, and only speak gentle words——'

'Mother could teach her that,' interrupted Diamond.

'And to dress babies, and feed them, and take care of them,' Mr. Raymond proceeded, 'she might get a place as a nurse somewhere, you know. People do give money for that.'

'Then I'll ask mother,' said Diamond.

'But you'll have to give her her food then; and your father, not being strong, has enough to do already without that.'

'But here's me,' said Diamond: 'I help him out with it. When he's tired of driving, up I get. It don't make any difference to old Diamond. I don't mean he likes me as well as my father – of course he can't, you know – nobody could; but he does his duty all the same. It's got to be done, you know, sir; and Diamond's a good horse – isn't he, sir?'

'From your description I should say certainly; but I have not the pleasure of his acquaintance myself.'

'Don't you think he will go to heaven, sir?'

'That I don't know anything about,' said Mr. Raymond. 'I confess I should be glad to think so,' he added, smiling thoughtfully.

'I'm sure he'll get to the back of the north wind, anyhow,' said Diamond to himself; but he had learned to be very careful of saying such things aloud.

'Isn't it rather too much for him to go in the cab all day and every day?' resumed Mr. Raymond.

'So father says, when he feels his ribs of a morning. But then he says the old horse *do* eat well, and the moment, he's had his supper, down he goes, and never gets up till he's called; and, for the legs of him, father says that makes no end of a differ. Some horses, sir! they won't lie down all night long, but go to sleep on their four pins, like a haystack, father says. *I* think it's very stupid of them, and so does old Diamond. But then I suppose they don't know better, and so they can't help it. We mustn't be too hard upon them, father says.'

'Your father must be a good man, Diamond.'

Diamond looked up in Mr. Raymond's face, wondering what he could mean.

'I said your father must be a good man, Diamond.'

'Of course,' said Diamond. 'How could he drive a cab if he wasn't?'

'There are some men who drive cabs who are not very good,' objected Mr. Raymond.

Diamond remembered the drunken cabman, and saw that his friend was right.

'Ah! but,' he returned, 'he *must* be, you know, with such a horse as old Diamond.'

'That does make a difference,' said Mr. Raymond. 'But it is quite enough that he *is* a good man, without our trying to account for it. Now, if you like, I will give you a proof that *I* think him a good man. I am going away on the Continent for a while – for three months, I believe – and I am going to let my house to a gentleman who does not want the use of my brougham. My horse is nearly as old, I fancy, as your Diamond, but I don't want to part with him, and I don't want him to be idle; for nobody, as you say, ought to be idle; but neither do I want him to be worked very hard. Now, it has come into my head that perhaps your father would take charge of him, and work him under certain conditions.'

'My father will do what's right,' said Diamond. 'I'm sure of that.'

'Well, so I think. Will you ask him when he comes home to call and have a little chat with me – to-day, some time?'

'He must have his dinner first,' said Diamond. 'No, he's got his dinner with him to-day. It must be after he's had his tea.'

'Of course, of course. Any time will do. I shall be at home all day.'

'Very well, sir. I will tell him. You may be sure he will come. My father thinks you a very kind gentleman, and I know he is right, for I know your very own self, sir.'

Mr. Raymond smiled, and as they had now reached his door, they parted, and Diamond went home. As soon as his father entered the house, Diamond gave him Mr. Raymond's message, and recounted the conversation that had preceded it. His father said little, but took thought-sauce to his bread and butter, and as soon as he had finished his meal, rose, saying:

'I will go to your friend directly, Diamond. It would be a grand thing to get a little more money. We do want it.

Diamond accompanied his father to Mr. Raymond's door, and there left him.

He was shown at once into Mr. Raymond's study, where he gazed with some wonder at the multitude of books on the walls, and thought what a learned man Mr. Raymond must be.

Presently Mr. Raymond entered, and after saying much the same about his old horse, made the following distinct proposal – one not over-advantageous to Diamond's father, but for which he had reasons – namely, that Joseph should have the use of Mr. Raymond's horse while he was away, on condition that he never worked him more than six hours a day, and fed him well, and that, besides, he should take Nanny home as soon as she was able to leave the hospital, and provide for her as for one of his own children – neither better nor worse – so long, that is, as he had the horse.

Diamond's father could not help thinking it a pretty close bargain. He should have both the girl and the horse to feed, and only six hours' work out of the horse.

'It will save your own horse,' said Mr. Raymond.

'That is true,' answered Joseph; 'but all I can get by my own horse is only enough to keep us, and if I save him and feed your horse and the girl – don't you see, sir?'

'Well, you can go home and think about it, and let me know by the end of the week. I am in no hurry before then.'

So Joseph went home and recounted the proposal to his wife, adding that he did not think there was much advantage to be got out of it.

'Not much that way, husband,' said Diamond's mother; 'but there would be an advantage, and what matter who gets it!'

'I don't see it,' answered her husband. 'Mr. Raymond is a gentleman of property, and I don't discover any much good in helping him to save a little more. He won't easily get one to make such a bargain, and I don't mean he shall get me. It would be a loss rather than a gain – I do think – at least, if I took less work out of our own horse.'

'One hour would make a difference to old Diamond. But that's not the main point. You must think what an advantage it would be to the poor girl that hasn't a home to go to!'

'She *is* one of Diamond's friends,' though his father.

'I could be kind to her, you know,' the mother went on, 'and teach her housework, and how to handle a baby; and, besides, she would help me, and I should be the stronger for it, and able to do an odd bit of charing now and then, when I got the chance.'

'I won't hear of that,' said her husband. 'Have the girl by all

means. I'm ashamed I did not think of both sides of the thing at once. I wonder if the horse is a great eater. To be sure, if I gave Diamond two hours' additional rest, it would be all the better for the old bones of him, and there would be four hours extra out of the other horse. That would give Diamond something to do every day. He could drive old Diamond after dinner, and I could take the other horse out for six hours after tea, or in the morning, as I found best. It might pay for the keep of both of them, – that is, if I had good luck. I should like to oblige Mr. Raymond, though he be rather hard, for he has been very kind to our Diamond, wife. Hasn't he, now?'

'He has indeed, Joseph,' said his wife, and there the conversation ended.

Diamond's father went the very next day to Mr. Raymond, and accepted his proposal; so that the week after, having got another stall in the same stable, he had two horses instead of one. Oddly enough, the name of the new horse was Ruby, for he was a very red chestnut. Diamond's name came from a white lozenge on his forehead. Young Diamond said they *were* rich no.. with such a big diamond and such a big ruby.

30   Nanny's Dream

Nanny was not fit to be removed for some time yet, and Diamond went
to see her as often as he could. But being more regularly engaged now,
seeing he went out every day for a few hours with old Diamond, and
had his baby to mind, and one of the horses to attend to, he could not
go so often as he would have liked.

One evening, as he sat by her bedside, she said to him:

'I've had such a beautiful dream, Diamond! I should like to tell it
you.'

'Oh! do,' said Diamond; 'I am so fond of dreams!'

'She must have been to the back of the north wind,' he said to
himself.

'It was a very foolish dream, you know. But somehow it was so
pleasant! What a good thing it is that you believe the dream all the time
you are in it!'

My readers must not suppose that poor Nanny was able to say
what she meant so well as I put it down here. She had never been to
school, and had heard very little else than vulgar speech until she came
to the hospital. But I have been to school, and although that could
never make me able to dream so well as Nanny, it has made me able to
tell her dream better than she could herself. And I am the more
desirous of doing this for her that I have already done the best I could
for Diamond's dream, and it would be a shame to give the boy all the
advantage.

'I will tell you all I know about it,' said Nanny. 'The day before
yesterday a lady came to see us – a very beautiful lady, and very
beautifully dressed. I heard the matron say to her that it was very kind
of her to come in blue and gold; and she answered that she knew we
didn't like dull colours. She had such a lovely shawl on, just like

redness dipped in milk, and all worked over with flowers of the same colour. It didn't shine much; it *was* silk, but it kept in the shine. When she came to my bedside, she sat down, just where you are sitting, Diamond, and laid her hand on the counterpane. I was sitting up with my table before me, ready for my tea. Her hand looked so pretty in its blue glove, that I was tempted to stroke it. I thought she wouldn't be angry, for everybody that comes to the hospital is kind. It's only in the streets they ain't kind. But she drew her hand away, and I almost cried, for I thought I had been rude. Instead of that, however, it was only that she didn't like giving me her glove to stroke, for she drew it off, and then laid her hand where it was before. I wasn't sure, but I ventured to put out my ugly hand.

'Your hand ain't ugly, Nanny,' said Diamond; but Nanny went on –

'And I stroked it again, and then she stroked mine, – think of that! And there was a ring on her finger, and I looked down to see what it was like. And she drew it off, and put it upon one of my fingers. It was a red stone, and she told me they called it a ruby.'

'Oh, that is funny!' said Diamond. 'Our new horse is called Ruby. We've got another horse – a red one – such a beauty!'

But Nanny went on with her story.

'I looked at the ruby all the time the lady was talking to me, – it was so beautiful! And as she talked I kept seeing deeper and deeper into the stone. At last she rose to go away, and I began to pull the ring off my finger; and what do you think she said? – "Wear it all night, if you like. Only you must take care of it. I can't give it you, for some one gave it to me; but you may keep it till to-morrow." Wasn't it kind of her? I could hardly take my tea, I was so delighted to hear it; and I do think it was the ring that set me dreaming; for, after I had taken my tea, I leaned back, half lying and half sitting, and looked at the ring on my finger. By degrees I began to dream. The ring grew larger and larger, until at last I found that I was not looking at a red stone, but at a red sunset, which shone in at the end of a long street near where Grannie lives. I was dressed in rags as I used to be, and I had great holes in my shoes, at which the nasty mud came through to my feet. I didn't use to mind it before, but now I thought it horrid. And there was the great red sunset, with streaks of green and gold between, standing looking at me. Why couldn't I live in the sunset instead of in that dirt? Why was it so far away always? Why did it never come into our wretched street? It faded away, as the sunsets always do, and at last went out altogether. Then a cold wind began to blow, and flutter all my rags about————'

'That was North Wind herself,' said Diamond.

'Eh?' said Nanny, and went on with her story.

'I turned my back to it, and wandered away. I did not know where I was going, only it was warmer to go that way. I don't think it was a north wind, for I found myself somewhere in the west end at last. But it doesn't matter in a dream which wind it was.'

'I don't know that,' said Diamond. 'I believe North Wind can get into our dreams – yes, and blow in them. Sometimes she has blown me out of a dream altogether.'

'I don't know what you mean, Diamond,' said Nanny.

'Never mind,' answered Diamond. 'Two people can't always understand each other. They'd both be at the back of the north wind directly, and what would become of the other places without them?'

'You do talk so oddly!' said Nanny. 'I sometimes think they must have been right about you.'

'What did they say about me?' asked Diamond.

'They called you God's baby.'

'How kind of them! But I knew that.'

'Did you know what it meant though? It meant that you were not right in the head.'

'I feel all right,' said Diamond, putting both his hands to his head, as if it had been a globe he could take off and set on again.

'Well, as long as you are pleased I am pleased,' said Nanny.

'Thank you, Nanny. Do go on with your story. I think I like dreams even better than fairy tales. But they must be nice ones, like yours, you know.'

'Well, I went on, keeping my back to the wind, until I came to a fine street on the top of a hill. How it happened I don't know, but the front door of one of the houses was open, and not only the front door, but the back door as well, so that I could see right through the house – and what do you think I saw? A garden place with green grass, and the moon shining upon it! Think of that! There was no moon in the street, but through the house there was the moon. I looked and there was nobody near: I would not do any harm, and the grass was so much nicer than the mud! But I couldn't think of going on the grass with such dirty shoes: I kicked them off in the gutter, and ran in on my bare feet, up the steps, and through the house, and on to the grass; and the moment I came into the moonlight, I began to feel better.'

'That's why North Wind blew you there,' said Diamond.

'It came of Mr. Raymond's story about the Princess Daylight,' returned Nanny. 'Well, I lay down upon the grass in the moonlight without thinking how I was to get out again. Somehow the moon suited me exactly. There was not a breath of the north wind you talk about; it was quite gone.'

'You didn't want her any more, just then. She never goes where she's not wanted,' said Diamond. 'But she blew you into the moonlight, anyhow.'

'Well, we won't dispute about it,' said Nanny: 'you've got a tile loose, you know.'

'Suppose I have,' returned Diamond, 'don't you see it may let in the moonlight, or the sunlight for that matter?'

'Perhaps yes, perhaps no,' said Nanny.

'And you've got your dreams, too, Nanny.'

'Yes, but I know they're dreams.'

'So do I. But I know besides they are something more as well.'

'Oh! do you?' rejoined Nanny. 'I don't.'

'All right,' said Diamond. 'Perhaps you will some day.'

'Perhaps I won't,' said Nanny.

Diamond held his peace, and Nanny resumed her story.

'I lay a long time, and the moonlight got in at every tear in my clothes, and made me feel so happy——'

'There, I tell you!' said Diamond.

'What do you tell me?' returned Nanny.

'North Wind——'

'It was the moonlight, I tell you,' persisted Nanny, and again Diamond held his peace.

'All at once I felt that the moon was not shining so strong. I looked up, and there was a cloud, all crapey and fluffy, trying to drown the beautiful creature. But the moon was so round, just like a whole plate, that the cloud couldn't stick to her; she shook it off, and said *there*, and shone out clearer and brighter than ever. But up came a thicker cloud, – and "You sha'n't" said the moon; and "I will" said the cloud, – but it couldn't: out shone the moon, quite laughing at its impudence. I knew her ways, for I've always been used to watch her. She's the only thing worth looking at in our street at night.'

'Don't call it *your* street,' said Diamond. 'You're not going back to it. You're coming to us, you know.'

'That's too good to be true,' said Nanny.

'There are very few things good enough to be true,' said Diamond; 'but I hope this is. Too good to be true it can't be. Isn't *true* good? and isn't *good* true? And how, then, can anything be too good to be true? That's like old Sal – to say that.'

'Don't abuse Grannie, Diamond. She's a horrid old thing, she and her gin bottle; but she'll repent some day, and then you'll be glad not to have said anything against her.'

'Why?' said Diamond.

'Because you'll be sorry for her.'

'I'm sorry for her now.'

'Very well. That's right. She'll be sorry too. And there'll be an end of it.'

'All right. You come to us,' said Diamond.

'Where was I?' said Nanny.

'Telling me how the moon served the clouds.'

'Yes, but it couldn't do, all of it. Up came the clouds and the clouds, and they came faster and faster, until the moon was covered up. You couldn't expect her to throw off a hundred of them at once – could you?'

'Certainly not,' said Diamond.

'So it grew very dark; and a dog began to yelp in the house. I looked and saw that the door to the garden was shut. Presently it was opened – not to let me out, but to let the dog in – yelping and bounding. I thought if he caught sight of me, I was in for a biting first, and the police after. So I jumped up, and ran for a little summer-house in the corner of the garden. The dog came after me, but I shut the door in his face. It was well it had a door – wasn't it?'

'You dreamed of the door because you wanted it,' said Diamond.

'No, I didn't; it came of itself. It was there, in the true dream.'

'There – I've caught you!' said Diamond. 'I knew you believed in the dream as much as I do.'

'Oh, well, if you will lay traps for a body!' said Nanny. 'Anyhow, I was safe inside the summer-house. And what do you think? – There was the moon beginning to shine again – but only through one of the panes – and that one was just the colour of the ruby. Wasn't it funny?'

'No, not a bit funny,' said Diamond.

'If you will be contrary!' said Nanny.

'No, no,' said Diamond; 'I only meant that was the very pane I should have expected her to shine through.'

'Oh, very well!' returned Nanny.

What Diamond meant, I do not pretend to say. He had curious notions about things.

'And now,' said Nanny, 'I didn't know what to do, for the dog kept barking at the door, and I couldn't get out. But the moon was so beautiful that I couldn't keep from looking at it through the red pane. And as I looked it got larger and larger till it filled the whole pane and outgrew it, so that I could see it through the other panes; and it grew till it filled them too and the whole window, so that the summer-house was nearly as bright as day.

'The dog stopped barking, and I heard a gentle tapping at the door, like the wind blowing a little branch against it.'

'Just like her,' said Diamond, who thought everything strange and

beautiful must be done by North Wind.

'So I turned from the window and opened the door; and what do you think I saw?'

'A beautiful lady,' said Diamond.

'No – the moon itself, as big as a little house, and as round as a ball, shining like yellow silver. It stood on the grass – down on the very grass: I could see nothing else for the brightness of it. And as I stared and wondered, a door opened in the side of it, near the ground, and a curious little old man, with a crooked thing over his shoulder, looked out, and said: "Come along, Nanny, my lady wants you. We're come to fetch you." I wasn't a bit frightened. I went up to the beautiful bright thing, and the old man held down his hand, and I took hold of it, and gave a jump, and he gave me a lift, and I was inside the moon. And what do you think it was like? It was such a pretty little house, with blue windows and white curtains! At one of the windows sat a beautiful lady, with her head leaning on her hand, looking out. She seemed rather sad, and I was sorry for her, and stood staring at her.

'"You didn't think I had such a beautiful mistress as that!" said the queer little man. "No, indeed!" I answered: "who would have thought it?" "Ah! who indeed? But you see you don't know everything." The little man closed the door, and began to pull at a rope which hung behind it with a weight at the end. After he had pulled a while, he said – "There, that will do; we're all right now." then he took me by the hand and opened a little trap door in the floor, and let me down two or three steps, and I saw like a great hole below me. "Don't be frightened," said the little man. "It's not a hole. It's only a window. Put your face down and look through." I did as he told me, and there was the garden and the summer-house, far away, lying at the bottom of the moonlight. "There!" said the little man; "we've brought you off! Do you see the little dog barking at us down there in the garden?" I told him I couldn't see anything so far. "Can *you* see anything so small and so far off?" I said. "Bless you, child!" said the little man; "I could pick up a needle out of the grass if I had only a long enough arm. There's one lying by the door of the summer-house now." I looked at his eyes. They were very small, but so bright that I think he saw by the light that went out of them. Then he took me up, and up again by a little stair in a corner of the room, and through another trap-door, and there was one great round window above us, and I saw the blue sky and

the clouds, and such lots of stars, all so big, and shining as hard as ever they could!'

'The little girl-angels had been polishing them,' said Diamond.

'What nonsense you do talk!' said Nanny.

'But my nonsense is just as good as yours, Nanny. When you have done, I'll tell you my dream. The stars are in it – not the moon, though. She was away somewhere. Perhaps she was gone to fetch you then. I don't think that, though, for my dream was longer ago than yours. She might have been to fetch some one else, though; for we can't fancy it's only us that get such fine things done for them. But do tell me what came next.'

Perhaps one of my child-readers may remember whether the moon came down to fetch him or her the same night that Diamond had his dream. I cannot tell, of course. I know she did not come to fetch me, though I did think I could make her follow me when I was a boy – not a very tiny one either.

'The little man took me all round the house, and make me look out of every window. Oh, it was beautiful! There we were, all up in the air, in such a nice clean little house! "Your work will be to keep the windows bright," said the little man. "You won't find it very difficult, for there ain't much dust up here. Only, the frost settles on them sometimes, and the drops of rain leave marks on them." "I can easily clean them inside," I said; "but how am I to get the frost and rain off the outside of them?" "Oh!" he said, "it's quite easy. There are ladders all about. You've only got to go out at the door, and climb about. There are a great many windows you haven't seen yet, and some of them look into places you don't know anything about. I used to clean them myself, but I'm getting rather old, you see. Ain't I now?" "I can't tell," I answered. "You see I never saw you when you were younger." "Never saw the man in the moon?" said he. "Not very near," I answered – "not to tell you how young or how old he looked. I have seen the bundle of sticks on his back." For Jim had pointed that out to me. Jim was very fond of looking at the man in the moon. Poor Jim! I wonder he hasn't been to see me. I'm afraid he's ill too.'

'I'll try to find out,' said Diamond, 'and let you know.'

'Thank you,' said Nanny. 'You and Jim ought to be friends.'

'But what did the man in the moon say, when you told him you had seen him with the bundle of sticks on his back?'

'He laughed. But I thought he looked offended too. His little nose turned up sharper, and he drew the corners of his mouth down from the tips of his ears into his neck. But he didn't look cross, you know.'

'Didn't he say anything?'

'Oh, yes! He said: "That's all nonsense. What you saw was my bundle of dusters. I was going to clean the windows. It takes a good many, you know. Really, what they do say of their superiors down there!" "It's only because they don't know better," I ventured to say. "Of course, of course," said the little man. "Nobody ever does know better. Well, I forgive them, and *that* sets it all right, I hope." "It's very good of you," I said. "No!" said he, "it's not in the least good of me. I couldn't be comfortable otherwise." After this he said nothing for a while, and I laid myself on the floor of his garret, and stared up and around at the great blue beautifulness. I had forgotten him almost, when at last he said: "Ain't you done yet?" "Done what?" I asked. "Done saying your prayers," says he. "I wasn't saying my prayers," I answered. "Oh yes, you were," said he, "though you didn't know it! And now I must show you something else."

'He took my hand and led me down the stair again, and through a narrow passage, and through another, and another, and another. I don't know how there could be room for so many passages in such a little house. The heart of it must be ever so much farther from the sides than they are from each other. How could it have an inside that was so independent of its outside? There's the point. It was funny – wasn't it, Diamond?'

'No,' said Diamond. He was going to say that that was very much the sort of thing at the back of the north wind; but he checked himself and only added, 'All right. I don't see it. I don't see why the inside should depend on the outside. It ain't so with the crabs. They creep out of their outsides and make new ones. Mr. Raymond told me so.'

'I don't see what that has got to do with it,' said Nanny.

'Then go on with your story, please,' said Diamond. 'What did you come to, after going through all those winding passages into the heart of the moon?'

'I didn't say they were winding passages. I said they were long and narrow. They didn't wind. They went by corners.'

'That's worth knowing,' remarked Diamond. 'For who knows how soon he may have to go there? But the main thing is, what did you come to at last?'

'We came to a small box against the wall of a tiny room. The little man told me to put my ear against it. I did so, and heard a noise something like the purring of a cat, only not so loud, and much sweeter. "What is it?" I asked. "Don't you know the sound?" returned the little man. "No," I answered. "Don't you know the sound of bees?" he said. I had never heard bees, and could not know the sound of them. "Those are my lady's bees," he went on. I had heard that bees gather honey from the flowers. "But where are the flowers for them?" I asked. "My lady's bees gather their honey from the sun and the stars," said the little man. "Do let me see them," I said. "No. I daren't do that," he answered. "I have no business with them. I don't understand them. Besides, they are so bright that if one were to fly into your eye, it would blind you altogether." "Then you have seen them?" "Oh, yes! Once or twice, I think. But I don't quite know: they are so very bright – like buttons of lightning. Now I've showed you all I can to-night, and we'll go back to the room." I followed him, and he made me sit down under a lamp that hung from the roof, and gave me some bread and honey.

'The lady had never moved. She sat with her forehead leaning on her hand, gazing out of the little window, hung like the rest with white cloudy curtains. From where I was sitting I looked out of it too, but I could see nothing. Her face was very beautiful, and very white, and very still, and her hand was as white as the forehead that leaned on it. I did not see her whole face – only the side of it, for she never moved to turn it full upon me, or even to look at me.

'How long I sat after I had eaten my bread and honey, I don't know. The little man was busy about the room, pulling a string here, and a string there, but chiefly the string at the back of the door. I was thinking with some uneasiness that he would soon be wanting me to go out and clean the windows, and I didn't fancy the job. At last he came up to me with a great armful of dusters. "It's time you set about the windows," he said; "for there's rain coming, and if they're quite clean before, then the rain can't spoil them." I got up at once. "You needn't be afraid," he said. "You won't tumble off. Only you must be careful. Always hold on with one hand while you rub with the other." As he spoke, he opened the door. I started back in a terrible fright, for there was nothing but blue air to be seen under me, like a great water without a bottom at all. But what must be must, and to live up here was so much nicer than down in the mud with holes in my shoes, that I never thought of not doing as I was told. The little man showed me how and where to lay hold while I put my foot round the edge of the door on to the first round of a ladder. "Once you're up," he said, "you'll see how you have to go well enough." I did as he told me, and crept out very carefully. Then the little man handed me the bundle of dusters, saying, "I always carry them on my reaping hook, but I don't think you could manage it properly. You shall have it if you like." I wouldn't take it, however, for it looked dangerous.

'I did the best I could with the dusters, and crawled up to the top of the moon. But what a grand sight it was! The stars were all over my head, so bright and so near that I could almost have laid hold of them. The round ball to which I clung went bobbing and floating away through the dark blue above and below and on every side. It was so beautiful that all fear left me, and I set to work diligently. I cleaned window after window. At length I came to a very little one, in at which I peeped. There was the room with the box of bees in it! I laid my ear to the window, and heard the musical hum quite distinctly. A great longing to see them came upon me, and I opened the window and crept in. The little box had a door like a closet. I opened it – the tiniest crack – when out came the light with such a sting that I closed it again in terror – not, however, before three bees had shot out into the room, where they darted about like flashes of lightning. Terribly frightened, I tried to get out of the window again, but I could not: there was no way to the outside of the moon but through the door; and that was in the room where the lady sat. No sooner had I reached the room, than the three bees, which had followed me, flew at once to the lady, and settled upon her hair. Then first I saw her move. She started, put up her hand, and caught them; then rose and, having held them into the flame of the lamp one after the other, turned to me. Her face was not so sad now as stern. It frightened me much. "Nanny, you have got me into trouble," she said. "You have been letting out my bees, which it is all I can do to manage. You have forced me to burn them. It is a great loss, and there will be a storm." As she spoke, the clouds had gathered all about us. I could see them come crowding up white about the windows. "I am sorry to find," said the lady, "that you are not to be trusted. You must go home again – you won't do for us." Then came a great clap of thunder, and the moon rocked and swayed. All grew dark about me, and I fell on the floor, and lay half-stunned. I could hear everything but could see nothing. "Shall I throw her out of the door, my lady?" said the little man. "No," she answered; "she's not quite bad enough for that. I don't think there's much harm in her; only she'll never do for us. She would make dreadful mischief up here. She's only fit for the mud. It's a great pity. I am sorry for her. Just take that ring off her finger. I am sadly afraid she has stolen it." The little man caught hold of my hand, and I felt him tugging at the ring. I tried to speak what was true about it, but, after a terrible effort, only gave a groan. Other things began to come into my head. Somebody else had a hold of me. The little man wasn't there. I opened my eyes at last, and saw the nurse. I had cried out in my sleep, and she had come and waked me. But, Diamond, for all it was only a dream, I cannot help being ashamed of myself yet for opening the lady's box of bees.'

'You wouldn't do it again – would you – if she were to take you back?' said Diamond.

'No. I don't think anything would ever make me do it again. But where's the good? I shall never have the chance.'

'I don't know that,' said Diamond.

'You silly baby! It was only a dream,' said Nanny.

'I know that, Nanny, dear. But how can you tell you mayn't dream again?'

'That's not a bit likely.'

'I don't know that,' said Diamond.

'You're always saying that,' said Nanny. 'I don't like it.'

'Then I won't say it again – if I don't forget,' said Diamond. 'But it was such a beautiful dream! – wasn't it, Nanny? What a pity you opened that door and let the bees out! You might have had such a long dream, and such nice talks with the moon-lady! Do try to go again, Nanny. I do so want to hear more.'

But now the nurse came and told him it was time to go; and Diamond went, saying to himself, 'I can't help thinking that North Wind had something to do with that dream. It would be tiresome to lie there all day and night too – without dreaming. Perhaps if she hadn't done that, the moon might have carried her to the back of the north wind – who knows?'

31　The North Wind Doth Blow

It was a great delight to Diamond when at length Nanny was well enough to leave the hospital and go home to their house. She was not very strong yet, but Diamond's mother was very considerate of her, and took care that she should have nothing to do she was not quite fit for. If Nanny had been taken straight from the street, it is very probable she would not have been so pleasant in a decent household, or so easy to teach; but after the refining influences of her illness and the kind treatment she had had in the hospital, she moved about the house just like some rather sad pleasure haunting the mind. As she got better, and the colour came back to her cheeks, her step grew lighter and quicker, her smile shone out more readily, and it became certain that she would soon be a treasure of help. It was great fun to see Diamond teaching her how to hold the baby, and wash and dress him, and often they laughed together over her awkwardness. But she had not many such lessons before she was able to perform those duties quite as well as Diamond himself.

Things however did not go well with Joseph from the very arrival of Ruby. It almost seemed as if the red beast had brought ill luck with him. The fares were fewer, and the pay less. Ruby's services did indeed make the week's income at first a little beyond what it used to be, but then there were two more to feed. After the first month he fell lame, and for the whole of the next, Joseph dared not attempt to work him. I cannot say that he never grumbled, for his own health was far from what it had been; but I can say that he tried to do his best. During all that month, they lived on very short commons indeed, seldom tasting meat except on Sundays, and poor old Diamond, who worked hardest of all, not even then – so that at the end of it he was as thin as a clothes-horse, while Ruby was as plump and sleek as a bishop's cob.

Nor was it much better after Ruby was able to work again, for it was a season of great depression in business, and that is very soon felt amongst the cabmen. City men look more after their shillings, and their wives and daughters have less to spend. It was besides a wet autumn, and bread rose greatly in price. When I add to this that Diamond's mother was but poorly, for a new baby was coming, you will see that these were not very jolly times for our friends in the mews.

Notwithstanding the depressing influences around him, however, Joseph was able to keep a little hope alive in his heart; and when he came home at night, would get Diamond to read to him, and would also make Nanny produce her book that he might see how she was getting on. For Diamond had taken her education in hand, and as she was a clever child, she was very soon able to put letters and words together.

Thus the three months passed away, but Mr. Raymond did not return. Joseph had been looking anxiously for him, chiefly with the desire of getting rid of Ruby — not that he was absolutely of no use to him, but that he was a constant weight upon his mind. Indeed, as far as provision went, he was rather worse off with Ruby and Nanny than he had been before, but on the other hand. Nanny was a great help in the house, and it was a comfort to him to think that when the new baby did come, Nanny would be with his wife.

Of God's gifts a baby is one of the greatest; therefore it is no wonder that when this one came, she was as heartily welcomed by the little household as if she had brought plenty with her. Of course she made a great difference in the work to be done – far more difference than her size warranted, but Nanny was no end of help, and Diamond was as much of a sunbeam as ever, and began to sing to the new baby the first moment he got her in his arms. But he did not sing the same songs to her that he had sung to his brother; for, he said, she was a new baby and must have new songs; and besides, she was a sister-baby and not a brother-baby, and of course would not like the same kind of songs. Where the difference in his songs lay, however, I do not pretend to be able to point out. One thing I am sure of, that they not only had no small share in the education of the little girl, but helped the whole family a great deal more than they were aware.

How they managed to get through the long dreary expensive winter, I can hardly say. Sometimes things were better, sometimes

worse. But at last the spring came, and the winter was over and gone, and that was much. Still Mr. Raymond did not return, and although the mother would have been able to manage without Nanny now, they could not look for a place for her so long as they had Ruby; and they were not altogether sorry for this.

One week at last was worse than they had yet had. They were almost without bread before it was over. But the sadder he saw his father and mother looking, the more Diamond set himself to sing to the two babies.

One thing which had increased their expenses was, that they had been forced to hire another little room for Nanny. When the second baby came, Diamond gave up his room that Nanny might be at hand to help his mother, and went to hers, which, although a fine place to what she had been accustomed to, was not very nice in his eyes. He did not mind the change though, for was not his mother the more comfortable for it? And was not Nanny more comfortable too? And indeed was not Diamond himself more comfortable that other people were more comfortable? And if there was more comfort every way, the change was a happy one.

32 Diamond and Ruby

It was Friday night, and Diamond, like the rest of the household, had had very little to eat that day. The mother would always pay the week's rent before she laid out anything even on food. His father had been very gloomy – so gloomy that he had actually been cross to his wife. It is a strange thing how the pain of seeing the suffering of those we love will sometimes make us add to their suffering by being cross with them. This comes of not having faith enough in God, and shows how necessary this faith is, for when we lose it, we lose even the kindness which alone can soothe the suffering. Diamond in consequence had gone to bed very quiet and thoughtful – a little troubled indeed.

It had been a very stormy winter; and even now that the spring had come, the north wind often blew. When Diamond went to his bed, which was in a tiny room in the roof, he heard it like the sea moaning; and when he fell asleep he still heard the moaning. All at once he said to himself, 'Am I awake, or am I asleep?' But he had no time to answer the question, for there was North Wind calling him. His heart beat very fast, it was such a long time since he had heard that voice. He jumped out of bed, and looked everywhere, but could not see her. 'Diamond, come here,' she said again and again; but where the *here* was he could not tell. To be sure the room was all but quite dark, and she might be close beside him.

'Dear North Wind,' said Diamond, 'I want so much to go to you, but I can't tell where.'

'Come here, Diamond,' was all her answer.

Diamond opened the door, and went out of the room, and down the stair and into the yard. His little heart was in a flutter, for he had long given up all thought of seeing her again. Neither now was he to see her. When he got out, a great puff of wind came against him, and in obedience to it he turned his back, and went as it blew. It blew him right up to the stable-door, and went on blowing.

'She wants me to go into the stable,' said Diamond, to himself; 'but the door is locked.'

He knew where the key was, in a certain hole in the wall – far too high for him to get at. He ran to the place, however: just as he reached it there came a wild blast, and down fell the key clanging on the stones at his feet. He picked it up, and ran back and opened the stable-door, and went in. And what do you think he saw?

A little light came through the dusty window from a gas lamp, sufficient to show him Diamond and Ruby with their two heads up, looking at each other across the partition of their stalls. The light showed the white mark on Diamond's forehead, but Ruby's eye shone so bright, that he thought more light came out of it than went in. This is what he saw.

But what do you think he heard?

He heard the two horses talking to each other – in a strange language, which yet, somehow or other, he could understand, and turn over in his mind in English. The first words he heard were from

Diamond, who apparently had been already quarrelling with Ruby.

'Look how fat you are, Ruby!' said old Diamond. 'You are so plump and your skin shines so, you ought to be ashamed of yourself.'

'There's no harm in being fat,' said Ruby in a deprecating tone. 'No, nor in being sleek. I may as well shine as not.'

'No harm?' retorted Diamond. 'Is it no harm to go eating up all poor master's oats, and taking up so much of his time grooming you, when you only work six hours – no, not six hours a day, and, as I hear, get along no faster than big dray-horse with two tons behind him? – So they tell me.'

'Your master's not mine,' said Ruby. 'I must attend to my own master's interests, and eat all that is given me, and be as sleek and fat as I can, and go no faster than I need.'

'Now really if the rest of the horses weren't all asleep, poor things – *they* work till they're tired – I do believe they would get up and kick you out of the stable. You make me ashamed of being a horse. You dare to say my master ain't your master! That's your gratitude for the way he feeds you and spares you! Pray where would your carcass be if it weren't for him?'

'He doesn't do it for my sake. If I were his own horse, he would work me as hard as he does you.'

'And I'm proud to be so worked. I wouldn't be as fat as you – not for all you're worth. You're a disgrace to the stable. Look at the horse next you. *He's* something like a horse – all skin and bone. And his master ain't over kind to him either. He put a stinging lash on his whip last week. But that old horse knows he's got the wife and children to keep – as well as his drunken master – and he works *like* a horse. I daresay he grudges his master the beer he drinks, but I don't believe he grudges anything else.'

'Well, I don't grudge yours what he gets by me,' said Ruby.

'Gets!' retorted Diamond. 'What he gets isn't worth grudging. It comes to next to nothing – what with your fat and your shine.'

'Well, at least you ought to be thankful you're the better for it. You get a two hours' rest a day out of it.'

'I thank my master for that – not you, you lazy fellow! You go along like a buttock of beef upon castors – you do.'

'Ain't you afraid I'll kick, if you go on like that, Diamond?'

'Kick! You couldn't kick if you tried. You might heave your rump up half a foot, but for lashing out – oho! If you did, you'd be down on your belly before you could get your legs under you again. It's my belief, once out, they'd stick out for ever. Talk of kicking! Why don't you put one foot before the other now and then when you're in the cab? The abuse master gets for your sake is quite shameful. No decent horse would bring it on him. Depend upon it, Ruby, no cabman likes to be abused any more than his fare. But *his* fares, at least when you are between the shafts, are very much to be excused. Indeed they are.'

'Well, you see, Diamond, I don't want to go lame again.'

'I don't believe you were so very lame, after all, – there!'

'Oh, but I was.'

'Then I believe it was all your own fault. I'm not lame. I never was lame in all my life. You don't take care of your legs. You never lay them down at night. There you are with your huge carcass crushing down your poor legs all night long. You don't even care for your own legs – so long as you can eat, eat, and sleep, sleep. You a horse indeed!'

'But I tell you I *was* lame.'

'I'm not denying there was a puffy look about your off-pastern. But my belief is, it wasn't even grease – it was fat.'

'I tell you I put my foot on one of those horrid stones they make the roads with, and it gave my ankle such a twist.'

'Ankle indeed! Why should you ape your betters? Horses ain't got any ankles: they're only pasterns. And so long as you don't lift your feet better, but fall asleep between every step, you'll run a good chance of laming all your *ankles* as you call them, one after another. It's not your lively horse that comes to grief in that way. I tell you I believe it wasn't much, and if it was it was your own fault. There! I've done. I'm going to sleep. I'll try to think as well of you as I can. If you would but step out a bit and run off a little of your fat!'

Here Diamond began to double up his knees; but Ruby spoke again, and, as young Diamond thought, in a rather different tone.

'I say, Diamond, I can't bear to have an honest old horse like you, think of me like that. I will tell you the truth: it was my own fault that I fell lame.'

'I told you so,' returned the other, tumbling against the partition as he rolled over on his side to give his legs every possible privilege in their narrow circumstances.

'I meant to do it, Diamond.'

At the words, the old horse arose with a scramble like thunder, shot his angry head and glaring eye over into Ruby's stall, and said –

'Keep out of my way, you unworthy wretch, or I'll bite you. You a horse! Why did you do that?'

'Because I wanted to grow fat.'

'You grease-tub! Oh! my teeth and tail! I thought you were a humbug! Why did you want to get fat? There's no truth to be got out of you but by cross-questioning. You ain't fit to be a horse.'

'Because once I *am* fat, my nature is to keep fat for a long time; and I didn't know when master might come home and want to see me.'

'You conceited, good-for-nothing brute! You're only fit for the knacker's yard. You wanted to look handsome, did you? Hold your tongue, or I'll break my halter and be at you – with your handsome fat!'

'Never mind, Diamond. You're a good horse. You can't hurt me.'

'Can't hurt you! Just let me once try.'

'No, you can't.'

'Why then?'

'Because I'm an angel.'

'What's that?'

'Of course you don't know.'

'Indeed I don't.'

'I know you don't. An ignorant, rude old human horse, like you, couldn't know it. But there's young Diamond listening to all we're saying; and he knows well enough there are horses in heaven for angels to ride upon, as well as other animals, lions and eagles and bulls, in more important situations. The horses the angels ride, must be angel-horses, else the angels couldn't ride upon them. Well, I'm one of them.'

'You ain't.'

'Did you ever know a horse tell a lie?'

'Never before. But you've confessed to shamming lame.'

'Nothing of the sort. It was necessary I should grow fat, and necessary that good Joseph, your master, should grow lean. I could have pretended to be lame, but that no horse, least of all an angel-horse, would do. So I must *be* lame, and so I sprained my ankle – for the angel-horses *have* ankles – they don't talk horse-slang up there – and it hurt me very much, I assure you, Diamond, though you mayn't be good enough to be able to believe it.'

Old Diamond made no reply. He had lain down again, and a sleepy snort, very like a snore, revealed that, if he was not already asleep, he was past understanding a word that Ruby was saying. When young Diamond found this, he thought he might venture to take up the dropt shuttlecock of the conversation.

'I'm good enough to believe it, Ruby,' he said.

But Ruby never turned his head, or took any notice of him. I suppose he did not understand more of English than just what the coachmen and stablemen were in the habit of addressing him with. Finding, however, that his companion made no reply, he shot his head over the partition and looking down at him said –

'You just wait until to-morrow, and you'll see whether I'm speaking the truth or not. – I declare the old horse is fast asleep! – Diamond! – No I won't.'

Ruby turned away, and began pulling at his hay-rack in silence.

Diamond gave a shiver, and looking round saw that the door of the stable was open. He began to feel as if he had been dreaming, and after a glance about the stable to see if North Wind was anywhere visible he thought he had better go back to bed.

33 The Prospect Brightens

The next morning, Diamond's mother said to his father, 'I'm not quite comfortable about that child again.'

'Which child, Martha?' asked Joseph. 'You've got a choice now.'

'Well, Diamond I mean. I'm afraid he's getting into his queer ways again. He's been at his old trick of walking in his sleep. I saw him run up the stair in the middle of the night.'

'Didn't you go after him, wife?'

'Of course I did – and found him fast asleep in his bed. It's because he's had so little meat for the last six weeks, I'm afraid.'

'It may be that. I'm very sorry. But if it don't please God to send us enough, what *am* I to do, wife?'

'You can't help it, I know, my dear good man,' returned Martha. 'And after all I don't know. I don't see why he shouldn't get on as well as the rest of us. There I'm nursing baby all this time, and I get along pretty well. I'm sure to hear the little man singing, you wouldn't think there was much amiss with him.'

For at that moment Diamond was singing like a lark in the clouds. He had the new baby in his arms, while his mother was dressing herself. Joseph was sitting at his breakfast – a little weak tea, dry bread, and very dubious butter – which Nanny had set for him, and which he was enjoying because he was hungry. He had groomed both horses, and had got old Diamond ready to put to.

'Think of a fat angel, Dulcimer!' said Diamond.

The baby had not been christened yet, but Diamond, in reading his bible, had come upon the word *dulcimer*, and thought it so pretty that ever after he called his sister Dulcimer.

'Think of a red fat angel, Dulcimer!' he repeated; 'for Ruby's an angel of a horse, Dulcimer. He sprained his ankle and got fat on purpose.'

'What purpose, Diamond?' asked his father.

'Ah! that I can't tell. I suppose to look handsome when his master comes,' answered Diamond. – 'What do *you* think, Dulcimer? It must be for some good, for Ruby's an angel.'

'I wish I were rid of him, anyhow,' said his father; 'for he weighs heavy on my mind.'

'No wonder, father: he's so fat,' said Diamond. 'But you needn't be afraid, for everybody says he's in better condition than when you had him.'

'Yes, but he may be as thin as a tin horse before his owner comes. It was too bad to leave him on my hands this way.'

'Perhaps he couldn't help it,' suggested Diamond. 'I daresay he has some good reason for it.'

'So I should have said,' returned his father, 'if he had not driven such a hard bargain with me at first.'

'But we don't know what may come of it yet, husband,' said his wife. 'Mr. Raymond may give a little to boot, seeing you've had more of the bargain than you wanted or reckoned upon.'

'I'm afraid not: he's a hard man,' said Joseph, as he rose and went to get his cab out.

Diamond resumed his singing. For some time he carolled snatches of everything or anything; but at last it settled down into something like what follows. I cannot tell where or how he got it.

> Where did you come from, baby dear?
> Out of the everywhere into here.
>
> Where did you get your eyes so blue?
> Out of the sky as I came through.
>
> What makes the light in them sparkle and spin?
> Some of the starry spikes left in.
>
> Where did you get that little tear?
> I found it waiting when I got here.
>
> What makes your forehead so smooth and high?
> A soft hand stroked it as I went by.

What makes your cheek like a warm white rose?
I saw something better then any one knows.

Whence that three-cornered smile of bliss?
Three angels gave me at once a kiss.

Where did you get this pearly ear?
God spoke, and it came out to hear.

Where did you get those arms and hands?
Love made itself into hooks and bands.

Feet, whence did you come, you darling things?
From the same box as the cherubs' wings.

How did they all just come to be you?
God thought about me, and so I grew.

But how did you come to us, you dear?
God thought about you, and so I am here.

'*You* never made that song, Diamond,' said his mother.

'No, mother. I wish I had. No, I don't. That would be to take it from somebody else. But it's mine for all that.'

'What makes it yours?'

'I love it so.'

'Does loving a thing make it yours?'

'I think so, mother – at least more than anything else can. If I didn't love baby (which couldn't be, you know), she wouldn't be mine a bit. But I do love baby, and baby is my very own Dulcimer.'

'The baby's mine, Diamond.'

'That makes her the more mine, mother.'

'How do you make that out?'

'Because you're mine, mother.'

'Is that because you love me?'

'Yes, just because. Love makes the only myness,' said Diamond.

When his father came home to have his dinner, and change Diamond for Ruby, they saw him look very sad, and he told them he had not had a fare worth mentioning the whole morning.

'We shall all have to go to the workhouse, wife,' he said.

'It would be better to go to the back of the north wind,' said

Diamond, dreamily, not intending to say it aloud.

'So it would,' answered his father. 'But how are we to get there, Diamond?'

'We must wait till we're taken,' returned Diamond.

Before his father could speak again, a knock came to the door, and in walked Mr. Raymond with a smile on his face. Joseph got up and received him respectfully, but not very cordially. Martha set a chair for him, but he would not sit down.

'You are not very glad to see me,' he said to Joseph. 'You don't want to part with the old horse.'

'Indeed, sir, you *are* mistaken there. What with anxiety about him, and bad luck, I've wished I were rid of him a thousand times. It was only to be for three months, and here it's eight or nine.'

'I'm sorry to hear such a statement,' said Mr. Raymond. 'Hasn't he been of service to you?'

'Not much, not with his lameness——'

'Ah!' said Mr. Raymond, hastily – 'you've been laming him – have you? That accounts for it. I see, I see.'

'It wasn't my fault, and he's all right now. I don't know how it happened, but——'

'He did it on purpose,' said Diamond. 'He put his foot on a stone just to twist his ankle.'

'How do you know that, Diamond?' said his father, turning to him. 'I never said so, for I could not think how it came.'

'I heard it – in the stable,' said Diamond.

'Let's have a look at him,' said Mr. Raymond.

'If you'll step out into the yard,' said Joseph, 'I'll bring him out.'

They went, and Joseph, having first taken off his harness, walked Ruby into the middle of the yard.

'Why,' said Mr. Raymond, 'you've not been using him well.'

'I don't know what you mean by that, sir. I didn't expect to hear that from you. He's sound in wind and limb – as sound as a barrel.'

'And as big, you might add. Why, he's as fat as a pig! You don't call that good usage!'

Joseph was too angry to make any answer.

'You've not worked him enough, I say. That's not making a good use of him. That's not doing as you'd be done by.'

'I shouldn't be sorry if I was served the same, sir.'

'He's too fat, I say.'

'There was a whole month I couldn't work him at all, and he did nothing but eat his head off. He's an awful eater. I've taken the best part of six hours a day out of him since, but I'm always afraid of his coming to grief again, and so I couldn't make the most even of that. I declare to you, sir, when he's between the shafts, I sit on the box as miserable as if I'd stolen him. He looks all the time as if he was a-bottling up of complaints to make of me the minute he sets eyes on you again. There! look at him now, squinting round at me with one eye! I declare to you, on my word, I haven't laid the whip on him more than three times.'

'I'm glad to hear it. He never did want the whip.'

'I didn't say that, sir. If ever a horse wanted the whip, he do. He's brought me to beggary almost with his snail's pace. I'm very glad you've come to rid me of him.'

'I don't know that,' said Mr. Raymond. 'Suppose I were to ask you to buy him of me – cheap.'

'I wouldn't have him in a present, sir. I don't like him. And I wouldn't drive a horse that I didn't like – no, not for gold. It can't come to good where there's no love between 'em.'

'Just bring out your own horse, and let me see what sort of a pair they'd make.'

Joseph laughed rather bitterly as he went to fetch Diamond.

When the two were placed side by side, Mr. Raymond could hardly keep his countenance, but from a mingling of feelings. Beside the great red round barrel Ruby, all body and no legs, Diamond looked like a clothes-horse with a skin thrown over it. There was hardly a spot of him where you could not descry some sign of a bone underneath. Gaunt and grim and weary he stood, kissing his master, and heeding no one else.

'You haven't been using him well,' said Mr. Raymond.

'I must say,' returned Joseph, throwing an arm round his horse's neck, 'that the remark had better have been spared, sir. The horse is worth three of the other now.'

'I don't think so. I think they make a very nice pair. If the one's too fat, the other's too lean – so that's all right. And if you won't buy my Ruby, I must buy your Diamond.'

'Thank you, sir,' said Joseph, in a tone implying anything but thanks.

'You don't seem to like the proposal,' said Mr. Raymond.

'I don't,' returned Joseph. 'I wouldn't part with my old Diamond for his skin as full of nuggets as it is of bones.'

'Who said anything about parting with him?'

'You did now, sir.'

'No; I didn't. I only spoke of buying him to make a pair with Ruby. We could pare Ruby and patch Diamond a bit. And for height, they are as near a match as I care about. Of course you would be the coachman – if only you would consent to be reconciled to Ruby.'

Joseph stood bewildered, unable to answer.

'I've bought a small place in Kent,' continued Mr. Raymond, 'and I must have a pair to my carriage, for the roads are hilly thereabouts. I don't want to make a show with a pair of high-steppers. I think these will just do. Suppose for a week or two, you set yourself to take Ruby down and bring Diamond up. If we could only lay a pipe from Ruby's sides into Diamond's, it would be the work of a moment. But I fear that wouldn't answer.'

A strong inclination to laugh intruded upon Joseph's inclination to cry, and made speech still harder than before.

'I beg your pardon, sir,' he said at length. 'I've been so miserable, and for so long, that I never thought you was only a-chaffing of me when you said I hadn't used the horses well. I did grumble at you, sir, many's the time in my trouble; but whenever I said anything, my little Diamond would look at me with a smile, as much as to say: "I know him better than you, father;" and upon my word, I always thought the boy must be right.'

'Will you sell me old Diamond then?'

'I will, sir, on one condition – that if ever you want to part with him or me, you give me the option of buying him. I could *not* part with him, sir. As to who calls him his, that's nothing; for, as Diamond says, it's only loving a thing that can make it yours – and I love old Diamond, sir, dearly.'

'Well, there's a cheque for twenty pounds, which I wrote to offer you for him, in case I should find you had done the handsome thing by Ruby. Will that be enough?'

'It's too much, sir. His body ain't worth it – shoes and all. It's only his heart, sir – that's worth millions – but his heart'll be mine all the same – so, it's too much, sir.'

'I don't think so. It won't be, at least, by the time we've got him fed up again. You take it and welcome. Just go on with your cabbing for another month, only take it out of Ruby and let Diamond rest; and by that time I shall be ready for you to go down into the country.'

'Thank you, sir; thank you. Diamond set you down for a friend, sir, the moment he saw you. I do believe that child of mine knows more than other people.'

'I think so too,' said Mr. Raymond as walked away.

He had meant to test Joseph when he made the bargain about Ruby, but had no intention of so greatly prolonging the trial. He had been taken ill in Switzerland, and had been quite unable to return sooner. He went away now highly gratified at finding that he had stood the test, and was a true man.

Joseph rushed in to his wife who had been standing at the window anxiously waiting the result of the long colloquy. When she heard that the horses were to go together in double harness, she burst forth into an immoderate fit of laughter. Diamond came up with the baby in his arms and made big anxious eyes at her, saying:

'What is the matter with you, mother dear? Do cry a little. It will do you good. When father takes ever so small a drop of spirits, he puts water to it.'

'You silly darling!" said his mother; "how could I but laugh at the notion of that great fat Ruby going side by side with our poor old Diamond?'

'But why not, mother? With a month's oats, and nothing to do, Diamond'll be nearer Ruby's size than you will father's. I think it's very good for different sorts to go together. Now Ruby will have a chance of teaching Diamond better manners.'

'How dare you say such a thing, Diamond?' said his father, angrily. 'To compare the two for manners, there's no comparison possible. Our Diamond's a gentleman.'

'I don't mean to say he isn't, father; for I daresay some gentlemen judge their neighbours unjustly. That's all I mean. Diamond shouldn't have thought such bad things of Ruby. He didn't try to make the best of him.'

'How do you know that, pray?'

'I heard them talking about it one night.'

'Who?'

'Why, Diamond and Ruby. Ruby's an angel.'

Joseph stared and said no more. For all his new gladness, he was very gloomy as he re-harnessed the angel, for he thought his darling Diamond was going out of his mind.

He could not help thinking rather differently, however, when he found the change that had come over Ruby. Considering his fat, he exerted himself amazingly, and got over the ground with incredible speed. So willing, even anxious, was he to go now, that Joseph had to hold him quite tight.

Then, as he laughed at his own fancies, a new fear came upon him lest the horse should break his wind, and Mr. Raymond have good cause to think he had not been using him well. He might even suppose that he had taken advantage of his new instructions, to let out upon the horse some of his pent-up dislike; whereas in truth, it had so utterly vanished that he felt as if Ruby too had been his friend all the time.

34   In the Country

Before the end of the month Ruby had got respectably thin, and Diamond respectably stout. They really began to look fit for double harness.

Joseph and his wife had got their affairs in order, and everything ready for migrating at the shortest notice; and they felt so peaceful and happy that they judged all the trouble they had gone through well worth enduring. As for Nanny, she had been so happy ever since she left the hospital, that she expected nothing better, and saw nothing attractive in the notion of the country. At the same time, she had not the least idea of what the word *country* meant, for she had never seen anything about her but streets and gas-lamps. Besides, she was more attached to Jim than to Diamond: Jim was a reasonable being, Diamond in her eyes at best only an amiable, over-grown baby, whom no amount of expostulation would ever bring to talk sense, not to say think it. Now that she could manage the baby as well as he, she judged herself altogether his superior. Towards his father and mother, she was all they could wish.

Diamond had taken a great deal of pains and trouble to find Jim, and had at last succeeded through the help of the tall policeman, who was glad to renew his acquaintance with the strange child. Jim had moved his quarters, and had not heard of Nanny's illness till some time after she was taken to the hospital, where he was too shy to go and inquire about her. But when at length she went to live with Diamond's family, Jim was willing enough to go and see her. It was after one of his visits, during which they had been talking of her new prospects, that Nanny expressed to Diamond her opinion of the country.

'There ain't nothing in it but the sun and moon, Diamond.'

'There's trees and flowers,' said Diamond.

'Well, they ain't no count,' returned Nanny.

'Ain't they? They're so beautiful, they make you happy to look at them.'

'That's because you're such a silly.'

Diamond smiled with a far-away look, as if he were gazing through clouds of green leaves and the vision contented him. But he was thinking with himself what more he could do for Nanny; and that same evening he went to find Mr. Raymond, for he had heard that he had returned to town.

'Ah! how do you do, Diamond?' said Mr. Raymond; 'I am glad to see you.'

And he was indeed, for he had grown very fond of him. His opinion of him was very different from Nanny's.

'What do you want now, my child?' he asked.

'I'm always wanting something, sir,' answered Diamond.

'Well, that's quite right, so long as what you want is right. Everybody is always wanting something; only we don't mention it in the right place often enough. What is it now?'

'There's a friend of Nanny's, a lame boy called Jim.'

'I've heard of him,' said Mr. Raymond. 'Well?'

'Nanny doesn't care much about going to the country, sir.'

'Well, what has that to do with Jim?'

'You couldn't find a corner for Jim to work in – could you, sir?'

'I don't know that I couldn't. That is if you could show good reason for it.'

'He's a good boy, sir.'

'Well, so much the better for him.'

'I know he can shine boots, sir.'

'So much the better for us.'

'You want your boots shined in the country – don't you, sir?'

'Yes, to be sure.'

'It wouldn't be nice to walk over the flowers with dirty boots – would it, sir?'

'No, indeed.'

'They wouldn't like it – would they?'

'No, they wouldn't.'

'Then Nanny would be better pleased to go, sir.'

'If the flowers didn't like dirty boots to walk over them, Nanny wouldn't mind going to the country? Is that it? I don't quite see it.'

'No, sir; I didn't mean that. I meant, if you would take Jim with you to clean your boots, and do odd jobs, you know, sir, then Nanny would like it better. She's so fond of Jim!'

'Now you come to the point, Diamond. I see what you mean, exactly. I will turn it over in my mind. Could you bring Jim to see me?'

'I'll try, sir. But they don't mind me much. – They think I'm silly,' added Diamond, with one of his sweetest smiles.

What Mr. Raymond thought, I dare hardly attempt to put down here. But one part of it was, that the highest wisdom must ever appear folly to those who do not possess it.

'I think he would come though – after dark, you know,' Diamond continued. 'He does well at shining boots. People's kind to lame boys, you know, sir. But after dark, there ain't so much doing.'

Diamond succeeded in bringing Jim to Mr. Raymond, and the consequence was that he resolved to give the boy a chance. He provided new clothes for both him and Nanny; and upon a certain day, Joseph took his wife and three children, and Nanny and Jim, by train to a certain station in the county of Kent, where they found a cart waiting to carry them and their luggage to The Mound, which was the name of Mr. Raymond's new residence. I will not describe the varied feelings of the party as they went, or when they arrived. All I will say is, that Diamond, who is my only care, was full of quiet delight – a gladness too deep to talk about.

Joseph returned to town the same night, and the next morning drove Ruby and Diamond down, with the carriage behind them, and Mr. Raymond and a lady in the carriage. For Mr. Raymond was an old bachelor no longer: he was bringing his wife with him to live at The Mound. The moment Nanny saw her she recognized her as the lady who had lent her the ruby-ring. That ring had been given her by Mr. Raymond.

The weather was very hot, and the woods very shadowy. There were not a great many wild flowers, for it was getting well towards autumn, and the most of the wild flowers rise early to be before the leaves, because if they did not, they would never get a glimpse of the sun for them. So they have their fun over, and are ready to go to bed again by the time the trees are dressed. But there was plenty of the loveliest grass and daisies about the house, and Diamond's chief

pleasure seemed to be to lie amongst them, and breathe the pure air. But all the time, he was dreaming of the country at the back of the north wind, and trying to recall the songs the river used to sing. For this was more like being at the back of the north wind than anything he had known since he left it. Sometimes he would have his little brother, sometimes his little sister, and sometimes both of them in the grass with him, and then he felt just like a cat with her first kittens, he said, only he couldn't purr – all he could do was to sing.

These were very different times from those when he used to drive the cab, but you must not suppose that Diamond was idle. He did not do so much for his mother now, because Nanny occupied his former place; but he helped his father still, both in the stable and the harness-room, and generally went with him on the box that he might learn to drive a pair, and be ready to open the carriage-door. Mr. Raymond advised his father to give him plenty of liberty.

'A boy like that,' he said, 'ought not to be pushed.'

Joseph assented heartily, smiling to himself at the idea of pushing Diamond. After doing everything that fell to his share, the boy had a wealth of time at his disposal. And a happy, sometimes a merry time it was. Only for two months or so, he neither saw nor heard anything of North Wind.

35   I Make Diamond's Acquaintance

Mr. Raymond's house was called The Mound, because it stood upon a little steep knoll, so smooth and symmetrical that it showed itself at once to be artificial. It had, beyond doubt, been built for Queen Elizabeth as a hunting-tower – a place, namely, from the top of which you could see the country for miles on all sides, and so be able to follow with your eyes the flying deer and the pursuing hounds and horsemen. The mound had been cast up to give a good basement-advantage over the neighbouring heights and woods. There was a great quarry-hole not far off, brimful of water, from which, as the current legend stated, the materials forming the heart of the mound – a kind of stone unfit for building – had been dug. The house itself was of brick, and they said the foundations were first laid in the natural level, and then the stones and earth of the mound heaped about and between them, so that its great height should be well buttressed.

Joseph and his wife lived in a little cottage a short way from the house. It was real cottage, with a roof of thick thatch, which, in June and July, the wind sprinkled with the red and white petals it shook from the loose topmost sprays of the rose-trees climbing the walls. At first Diamond had a nest under this thatch – a pretty little room with white muslin curtains; but afterwards Mr. and Mrs. Raymond wanted to have him for a page in the house, and his father and mother were quite pleased to have him employed without his leaving them. So he was dressed in a suit of blue, from which his pale face and fair hair came out like the loveliest blossom, and took up his abode in the house.

'Would you be afraid to sleep alone, Diamond?' asked his mistress.

'I don't know what you mean, ma'am,' said Diamond. 'I never was afraid of anything that I can recollect – not much, at least.'

'There's a little room at the top of the house – all alone,' she returned: 'perhaps you would not mind sleeping there?'

'I can sleep anywhere, and I like best to be high up. Should I be able to see out?'

'I will show you the place,' she answered; and taking him by the hand, she led him up and up the oval-winding stair in one of the two towers.

Near the top they entered a tiny little room, with two windows from which you could see over the whole country. Diamond clapped his hands with delight.

'You would like this room, then, Diamond?' said his mistress.

'It's the grandest room in the house,' he answered. 'I shall be near the stars, and yet not far from the tops of the trees. That's just what I like.'

I daresay he thought also, that it would be a nice place for North Wind to call at in passing; but he said nothing of that sort. Below him spread a lake of green leaves, with glimpses of grass here and there at the bottom of it. As he looked down, he saw a squirrel appear suddenly, and as suddenly vanish amongst the topmost branches.

'Aha! little squirrel,' he cried, 'my nest is built higher than yours.'

'You can be up here with your books as much as you like,' said his mistress. 'I will have a little bell hung at the door, which I can ring when I want you. Half-way down the stair is the drawing-room.'

So Diamond was installed as page, and his new room got ready for him.

It was very soon after this that I came to know Diamond. I was then a tutor in a family whose estate adjoined the little property belonging The Mound. I had made the acquaintance of Mr. Raymond in London some time before, and was walking up the drive towards the house to call upon him one fine warm evening, when I saw Diamond for the first time. He was sitting at the foot of a great beech-tree, a few yards from the road, with a book on his knees. He did not see me. I walked up behind the tree, and peeping over his shoulder, saw that he was reading a fairy-book.

'What are you reading?' I said, and spoke suddenly, with the hope of seeing a startled little face look round at me. Diamond turned his head as quietly as if he were only obeying his mother's voice, and the calmness of his face rebuked my unkind desire and made me ashamed of it.

'I am reading the story of the Little Lady and the Goblin Prince,' said Diamond.

'I am sorry I don't know the story,' I returned. 'Who is it by?'

'Mr. Raymond made it.'

'Is he your uncle?' I asked at a guess.

'No. He's my master.'

'What do you do for him?' I asked respectfully.

'Anything he wishes me to do,' he answered. 'I am busy for him now. He gave me this story to read. He wants my opinion upon it.'

'Don't you find it rather hard to make up your mind?'

'Oh dear no! Any story always tells me itself what I'm to think about it. Mr. Raymond doesn't want me to say whether it is a clever story or not, but whether I like it, and why I like it. I never can tell what they call clever from what they call silly, but I always know whether I like a story or not.'

'And can you always tell why you like it or not?'

'No. Very often I can't at all. Sometimes I can. I always know, but I can't always tell why. Mr. Raymond writes the stories, and then tries them on me. Mother does the same when she makes jam. She's made such a lot of jam since we came here! And she always makes me taste it to see if it'll do. Mother knows by the face I make whether it will or not.'

At this moment I caught sight of two more children approaching. One was a handsome girl, the other a pale-faced, awkward-looking boy, who limped much on one leg. I withdrew a little, to see what would follow, for they seemed in some consternation. After a few hurried words, they went off together, and I pursued my way to the house, where I was as kindly received by Mr. and Mrs. Raymond as I could have desired. From them I learned something of Diamond, and was in consequence the more glad to find him, when I returned, seated in the same place as before.

'What did the boy and girl want with you, Diamond?' I asked.

'They had seen a creature that frightened them.'

'And they came to tell you about it?'

'They couldn't get water out of the well for it. So they wanted me to go with them.'

'They're both bigger than you.'

'Yes, but they were frightened at it.'

'And weren't you frightened at it?'

'No.'

'Why?'

'Because I'm silly. I'm never frightened at things.'

I could not help thinking of the old meaning of the word *silly*.

'And what was it?' I asked.

'I think it was a kind of an angel – a very little one. It had a long body and great wings, which it drove about it so fast that they grew a thin cloud all round it. It flew backwards and forwards over the well, or hung right in the middle, making a mist of its wings, as if its business was to take care of the water.'

'And what did you do to drive it away?'

'I didn't drive it away. I knew, whatever the creature was, the well was to get water out of. So I took the jug, dipped it in, and drew the water.'

'And what did the creature do?'

'Flew about.'

'And it didn't hurt you?'

'No. Why should it? I wasn't doing anything wrong.'

'What did your companions say then?'

'They said – "Thank you, Diamond. What a dear silly you are!"'

'And weren't you angry with them?'

'No! Why should I? I should like if they would play with me a little; but they always like better to go away together when their work is over. They never heed me. I don't mind it much, though. The other creatures are friendly. They don't run away from me. Only they're all so busy with their own work, they don't mind me much.'

'Do you feel lonely, then?'

'Oh, no! When nobody minds me, I get into my nest, and look up. And then the sky does mind me, and thinks about me.'

'Where is your nest?'

He rose, saying 'I will show you,' and led me to the other side of the tree.

There hung a little rope-ladder from one of the lower boughs. The boy climbed up the ladder and got upon the bough. Then he climbed farther into the leafy branches, and went out of sight.

After a little while, I heard his voice coming down out of the tree.

'I am in my nest now,' said the voice.

'I can't see you,' I returned.

'I can't see you either, but I can see the first star peeping out of the sky. I should like to get up into the sky. Don't you think I shall, some day?'

'Yes, I do. Tell me what more you see up there.'

'I don't see anything more, except a few leaves, and the big sky over me. It goes swinging about. The earth is all behind my back. There comes another star! The wind is like kisses from a big lady. When I get up here I feel as if I were in North Wind's arms.'

This was the first I heard of North Wind.

The whole ways and looks of the child, so full of quiet wisdom, yet so ready to accept the judgment of others in his own dispraise, took hold of my heart, and I felt myself wonderfully drawn towards him. It seemed to me, somehow, as if little Diamond possessed the secret of life, and was himself what he was so ready to think the lowest thing living – an angel of God with something special to say or do. A gush of reverence came over me, and with a single *good night*, I turned and left him in his nest.

I saw him often after this, and gained so much of his confidence that he told me all I have told you. I cannot pretend to account for it. I leave that for each philosophical reader to do after his own fashion. The easiest way is that of Nanny and Jim, who said often to each other that Diamond had a tile loose. But Mr. Raymond was much of my opinion concerning the boy; while Mrs. Raymond confessed that she often rang her bell just to have once more the pleasure of seeing the lovely stillness of the boy's face, with those blue eyes which seemed rather made for other people to look into than for himself to look out of.

It was plainer to others than to himself that he felt the desertion of Nanny and Jim. They appeared to regard him as a mere toy, except when they found he could minister to the increase of their privileges or indulgences, when they made no scruple of using him – generally with success. They were however well-behaved to a wonderful degree; while I have little doubt that much of their good behaviour was owing to the unconscious influence of the boy they called God's baby.

One very strange thing is, that I could never find out where he got some of his many songs. At times they would be but bubbles blown out of a nursery rhyme, as was the following, which I heard him sing one

evening to his little Dulcimer. There were about a score of sheep feeding in a paddock near him, their white wool dyed a pale rose in the light of the setting sun. Those in the long shadows from the trees were dead white; those in the sunlight were half glorified with pale rose.

Little Bo Peep, she lost her sheep,
    And didn't know where to find them;
They were over the height and out of sight,
    Trailing their tails behind them.

Little Bo Peep woke out of her sleep,
    Jump'd up and set out to find them:
'The silly things, they've got no wings,
    And they've left their trails behind them:

'They've taken their tails, but they've left their trails,
    And so I shall follow and find them;'
For wherever a tail dragged a trail,
    The long grass grew behind them.

And day's eyes and butter-cups, cow's lips and crow's feet
   Were glittering in the sun.
She threw down her book, and caught up her crook,
   And after her sheep did run.

She ran, and she ran, and ever as she ran,
   The grass grew higher and higher;
Till over the hill the sun began
   To set in a flame of fire.

She ran on still – up the grassy hill,
   And the grass grew higher and higher;
When she reached its crown, the sun was down,
   And she left a trail of fire.

The sheep and their tails were gone, all gone –
   And no more trail behind them!
Yes, yes! they were there – long-tailed and fair,
   But, alas! she could not find them.

Purple and gold, and rosy and blue,
   With their tails all white behind them,
Her sheep they did run in the trail of the sun;
   She saw them, but could not find them.

After the sun, like clouds they did run,
   But she knew they were her sheep;
She sat down to cry, and look up at the sky,
   But she cried herself asleep.

And as she slept the dew fell fast,
   And the wind blew from the sky;
And strange things took place that shun the day's face,
   Because they are sweet and shy.

Nibble, nibble, crop! she heard as she woke:
   A hundred little lambs
Did pluck and eat the grass so sweet
   That grew in the trails of their dams.

Little Bo Peep caught up her crook,
  And wiped the tears that did blind her;
And nibble nibble crop! without a stop,
  The lambs came eating behind her.

Home, home she came, both tired and lame,
  With three times as many sheep.
In a month or more, they'll be as big as before,
  And then she'll laugh in her sleep.

But what would you say, if one fine day,
  When they've got their bushiest tails,
Their grown up game should be just the same,
  And she have to follow their trails?

Never weep, Bo Peep, though you lose your sheep,
  And do not know where to find them;
'Tis after the sun the mothers have run,
  And there are their lambs behind them.

I confess again to having touched up a little, but it loses far more in
Diamond's sweet voice singing it than it gains by a rhyme here and
there.

Some of them were out of books Mr. Raymond had given him.
These he always knew, but about the others he could seldom tell.
Sometimes he would say, 'I made that one;' but generally he would say,
'I don't know; I found it somewhere;' or 'I got it at the back of the
north wind.'

One evening I found him sitting on the grassy slope under the
house, with his Dulcimer in his arms and his little brother rolling on
the grass beside them. He was chanting in his usual way, more like the
sound of a brook than anything else I can think of. When I went up to
them he ceased his chant.

'Do go on, Diamond. Don't mind me,' I said.

He began again at once. While he sang, Nanny and Jim sat a little
way off, one hemming a pocket-handkerchief, and the other reading a
story to her, but they never heeded Diamond. This is as near what he
sang as I can recollect, or reproduce rather.

What would you see if I took you up
  To my little nest in the air?
You would see the sky like a clear blue cup
  Turned upside downwards there.

What would you do if I took you there
  To my little nest in the tree?
My child with cries would trouble the air,
  To get what she could but see.

What would you get in the top of the tree
  For all your crying and grief?
Not a star would you clutch of all you see –
  You could only gather a leaf.

But when you lost your greedy grief,
  Content to see from afar,
You would find in your hand a withering leaf,
  In your heart a shining star.

As Diamond went on singing, it grew very dark, and just as he ceased, there came a great flash of lightning, that blinded us all for a moment. Dulcimer crowed with pleasure; but when the roar of thunder came after it, the little brother gave a loud cry of terror. Nanny and Jim came running up to us, pale with fear. Diamond's face too was paler than usual, but with delight. Some of the glory seemed to have clung to it, and remained shining.

'You're not frightened – are you, Diamond?' I said.

'No. Why should I be?' he answered with his usual question, looking up in my face with calm shining eyes.

'He ain't got sense to be frightened,' said Nanny, going up to him and giving him a pitying hug.

'Perhaps there's more sense in not being frightened, Nanny,' I returned. 'Do you think the lightning can do as it likes?'

'It might kill you,' said Jim.

'Oh no, it mightn't!' said Diamond.

As he spoke there came another great flash, and a tearing crack.

'There's a tree struck!' I said; and when we looked round, after the

blinding of the flash had left out eyes, we saw a hugh bough of the
beech-tree in which was Diamond's nest, hanging to the ground like
the broken wing of a bird.

'There!' cried Nanny; 'I told you so. If you had been up there you
see what would have happened, you little silly!'

'No, I don't,' said Diamond, and began to sing to Dulcimer. All I
could hear of the song, for the other children were going on with their
chatter, was –

> The clock struck one,
> And the mouse came down.
> Dickery, dickery, dock!

Then there came a blast of wind, and the rain followed in straight-
pouring lines, as if out of a watering-pot. Diamond jumped up with his
little Dulcimer in his arms, and Nanny caught up the little boy, and
they ran for the cottage. Jim vanished with a double shuffle, and I went
into the house.

When I came out again to return home, the clouds were gone, and
the evening sky glimmered through the trees, blue, and pale-green

towards the west, I turned my steps a little aside to look at the stricken beech. I saw the bough torn from the stem, and that was all the twilight would allow me to see. While I stood gazing, down from the sky came a sound of singing, but the voice was neither of lark nor of nightingale: it was sweeter than either: it was the voice of Diamond, up in his airy nest:—

> The lightning and thunder,
>   They go and they come;
> But the stars and the stillness
>   Are always at home.

And then the voice ceased.
  'Good night, Diamond,' I said.
  'Good night, sir,' answered Diamond.
  As I walked away pondering, I saw the great black top of the beech swaying against the sky in an upper wind, and heard the murmur as of many dim half-articulate voices filling the solitude around Diamond's nest.

36 Diamond Questions North Wind

My readers will not wonder that, after this, I did my very best to gain the friendship of Diamond. Nor did I find this at all difficult, the child was so ready to trust. Upon one subject alone was he reticent – the story of his relations with North Wind. I fancy he could not quite make up his mind what to think of them. At all events it was some little time before he trusted me with this, only then he told me everything. If I could not regard it all in exactly the same light as he did, I was, while guiltless of the least pretence, fully sympathetic, and he was satisfied without demanding of me any theory of difficult points involved. I let him see plainly enough, that whatever might be the explanation of the marvellous experience, I would have given much for a similar one myself.

On an evening soon after the thunderstorm, in a late twilight, with a half-moon high in the heavens, I came upon Diamond in the act of climbing by his little ladder into the beech-tree.

'What are you always going up there for, Diamond?' I heard Nanny ask, rather rudely, I thought.

'Sometimes for one thing, sometimes for another, Nanny,' answered Diamond, looking skywards as he climbed.

'You'll break your neck some day,' she said.

'I'm going up to look at the moon to-night,' he added, without heeding her remark.

'You'll see the moon just as well down here,' she returned.

'I don't think so.'

'You'll be no nearer to her up there.'

'Oh, yes! I shall. I must be nearer her, you know. I wish I could dream as pretty dreams about her as you can, Nanny.'

'You silly! you never have done about that dream. I never dreamed but that one, and it was nonsense enough, I'm sure.'

'It wasn't nonsense. It was a beautiful dream – and a funny one too, both in one.'

'But what's the good of talking about it that way, when you know it was only a dream? Dreams ain't true.'

'That one was true, Nanny. You know it was. Didn't you come to grief for doing what you were told not to? And isn't that true?'

'I can't get any sense into him,' exclaimed Nanny, with an expression of mild despair. 'Do you really believe, Diamond, that there's a house in the moon, with a beautiful lady, and a crooked old man and dusters in it?'

'If there isn't, there's something better,' he answered, and vanished in the leaves over our heads.

I went into the house, where I visited often in the evenings. When I came out, there was a little wind blowing, very pleasant after the heat of the day, for although it was late summer now it was still hot. The tree-tops were swinging about in it. I took my way past the beech, and called up to see if Diamond were still in his nest in its rocking head.

'Are you there, Diamond?' I said.

'Yes, sir,' came his clear voice in reply.

'Isn't it growing too dark for you to get down safely?'

'Oh, no, sir – if I take time to it. I know my way so well, and never let go with one hand till I've a good hold with the other.'

'Do be careful,' I insisted – foolishly, seeing the boy was as careful as he could be already.

'I'm coming,' he returned. 'I've got all the moon I want to-night.'

I heard a rustling and a rustling drawing nearer and nearer. Three or four minutes elapsed, and he appeared at length creeping down his little ladder. I took him in my arms, and set him on the ground.

'Thank you, sir,' he said. 'That's the north wind blowing, isn't it, sir?'

'I can't tell,' I answered. 'It feels cool and kind, and I think it may be. But I couldn't be sure except it were stronger, for a gentle wind might turn any way amongst the trunks of the trees.'

'I shall know when I get up to my own room,' said Diamond. 'I think I hear my mistress's bell. Good night, sir.'

He ran to the house, and I went home.

His mistress had rung for him only to send him to bed, for she was very careful over him, and I daresay thought he was not looking well.

When he reached his own room, he opened both his windows, one of which looked to the north and the other to the east, to find how the wind blew. It blew right in at the northern window. Diamond was very glad, for he thought perhaps North Wind herself would come now: a real north wind had never blown all the time since he left London. But, as she always came of herself, and never when he was looking for her, and indeed almost never when he was thinking of her, he shut the east window, and went to bed. Perhaps some of my readers may wonder that he could go to sleep with such an expectation; and, indeed, if I had not known him, I should have wondered at it myself; but it was one of his pecularities, and seemed nothing strange in him. He was so full of quietness that he could go to sleep almost at any time, if he only composed himself and let the sleep come. This time he went fast asleep as usual.

But he woke in the dim blue night. The moon had vanished. He thought he had heard a knocking at his door.

'Somebody wants me,' he said to himself, and jumping out of bed, ran to open it.

But there was no one there. He closed it again, and, the noise still continuing, found that another door was rattling. It belonged to a closet, he thought, but he had never been able to open it. The wind blowing in at the window must be shaking it. He would go and see if it was so.

The door now opened quite easily, but to his surprise, instead of a closet he found a long narrow room. The moon, which was sinking in the west, shone in at an open window at the further end. The room was low with a coved ceiling, and occupied the whole top of the house, immediately under the roof. It was quite empty. The yellow light of the half-moon streamed over the dark floor. He was so delighted at the discovery of the strange desolate moonlit place close to his own snug little room, that he began to dance and skip about the floor. The wind came in through the door he had left open, and blew about him as he danced, and he kept turning towards it that it might blow in his face. He kept picturing to himself the many places, lovely and desolate, the hill-sides and farm-yards and tree-tops and meadows, over which it had blown on its way to the Mound. And as he danced he grew more and more delighted with the motion and the wind; his feet grew stronger, and his body lighter, until at length it seemed as if he were borne up on the air, and could almost fly. So strong did his feeling become that at last he began to doubt whether he was not in one of those precious dreams he had so often had, in which he floated about on the air at will. But something made him look up, and to his unspeakable delight, he found his uplifted hands lying in those of North Wind, who was dancing with him, round and round the long bare room, her hair now falling to the floor, now filling the arched ceiling, her eyes shining on him like thinking stars, and the sweetest of grand smiles playing breezily about her beautiful mouth. She was, as so often before, of the height of a rather tall lady. She did not stoop in order to dance with him, but held his hands high in hers. When he saw her, he gave one spring, and his arms were about her neck, and her arms holding him to her bosom. The same moment she swept with him through the open window in at which the moon was shining, made a circuit like a bird about to alight, and settled with him in his nest on the top of the great beech-tree. There she placed him on her lap and began to hush him as if he were her own baby, and Diamond was so entirely happy that he did not care to speak a word. At length, however, he found that he was going to sleep, and that would be to lose so much, that, pleasant as it was, he could not consent.

'Please, dear North Wind,' he said, 'I am so happy that I'm afraid it's a dream. How am I to know that it's not a dream?'

'What does it matter?' returned North Wind.

'I should cry,' said Diamond.

'But why should you cry? The dream, if it is a dream, is a pleasant one – is it not?'

'That's just why I want it to be true.'

'Have you forgotten what you said to Nanny about her dream?'

'It's not for the dream itself – I mean, it's not for the pleasure of it,' answered Diamond, 'for I have that, whether it be a dream or not; it's for you, North Wind: I can't bear to find it a dream, because then I should lose you. You would be nobody then, and I could not bear that. You ain't a dream, are you, dear North Wind? Do say *No*, else I shall cry, and come awake, and you'll be gone for ever. I daren't dream about you once again if you ain't anybody.'

'I'm either not a dream, or there's something better that's not a dream, Diamond,' said North Wind, in a rather sorrowful tone, he thought.

'But it's not something better – it's you I want, North Wind,' he persisted, already beginning to cry a little.

She made no answer, but rose with him in her arms and sailed away over the tree-tops till they came to a meadow, where a flock of sheep was feeding.

'Do you remember what the song you were singing a week ago says about Bo Peep – how she lost her sheep, but got twice as many lambs?' asked North Wind, sitting down on the grass, and placing him in her lap as before.

'Oh yes, I do, well enough,' answered Diamond; 'but I never just quite liked that rhyme.'

'Why not, child?'

'Because it seems to say one's as good as another, or two new ones are better than one that's lost. I've been thinking about it a great deal, and it seems to me that although any one sixpence is as good as any other sixpence, not twenty lambs would do instead of one sheep whose face you knew. Somehow, when once you've looked into anybody's eyes, right deep down into them, I mean, nobody will do for that one any more. Nobody, ever so beautiful or so good, will make up for that one going out of sight. So you see, North Wind, I can't help being frightened to think that perhaps I am only dreaming, and you are nowhere at all. Do tell me that you are my own real beautiful North Wind.'

Again she rose, and shot herself into the air, as if uneasy because she could not answer him; and Diamond lay quiet in her arms, waiting for what she would say. He tried to see up into her face, for he was dreadfully afraid she was not answering him because she could not say that she was not a dream; but she had let her hair fall all over her face so he could not see it. This frightened him still more.

'Do speak, North Wind,' he said at last.

'I never speak when I have nothing to say,' she replied.

'Then I do think you must be a real North Wind, and no dream,' said Diamond.

'But I'm looking for something to say all the time.'

'But I don't want you to say what's hard to find. If you were to say one word to comfort me that wasn't true, then I should know you must be a dream, for a great beautiful lady like you could never tell a lie.'

'But she mightn't know how to say what she had to say, so that a little boy like you would understand it,' said North Wind. 'Here, let us get down again, and I will try to tell you what I think. You mustn't suppose I am able to answer all your questions, though. There are a great many things I don't understand more than you do.'

She descended on a grassy hillock, in the midst of a wild furzy common. There was a rabbit-warren underneath, and some of the rabbits came out of their holes, in the moonlight, looking very sober and wise, just like patriarchs standing in their tent-doors, and looking about them before going to bed. When they saw North Wind, instead of turning round and vanishing again with a thump of their heels, they cantered slowly up to her and snuffed all about her with their long upper lips, which moved every way at once. That was their way of kissing her; and, as she talked to Diamond, she would every now and then stroke down their furry backs, or lift and play with their long ears. They would, Diamond thought, have leaped upon her lap, but that he was there already.

'I think,' said she, after they have been sitting silent for a while, 'that if I were only a dream, you would not have been able to love me so. You love me when you are not with me, don't you?'

'Indeed I do,' answered Diamond, stroking her hand. 'I see! I see! How could I be able to love you as I do if you weren't there at all, you know? Besides, I couldn't be able to dream anything half so beautiful out of my own head; or if I did, I couldn't love a fancy of my own like that, could I?'

'I think not. You might have loved me in a dream, dreamily, and forgotten me when you woke, I daresay, but not loved me like a real being as you love me. Even then, I don't think you could dream anything that hadn't something real like it somewhere. But you've seen me in many shapes, Diamond: you remember I was a wolf once – don't you?'

'Oh yes – a good wolf that frightened a naughty drunken nurse.'

'Well, suppose I were to turn ugly, would you rather I weren't a dream then?'

'Yes; for I should know that you were beautiful inside all the same. You would love me, and I should love you all the same. I shouldn't like you to look ugly, you know. But I shouldn't believe it a bit.'

'Not if you saw it?'

'No, not if I saw it ever so plain.'

'There's my Diamond! I will tell you all I know about it then. I don't think I am just what you fancy me to be. I have to shape myself various ways to various people. But the heart of me is true. People call me by dreadful names, and think they know all about me. But they don't. Sometimes they call me Bad Fortune, sometimes Evil Chance, sometimes Ruin; and they have another name for me which they think the most dreadful of all.'

'What is that?' asked Diamond, smiling up in her face.

'I won't tell you that name. Do you remember having to go through me to get into the country at my back?'

'Oh yes, I do. How cold you were, North Wind! and so white, all but your lovely eyes! My heart grew like a lump of ice, and then I forgot for a while.'

'You were very near knowing what they call me then. Would you be afraid of me if you had to go through me again?'

'No. Why should I? Indeed I should be glad enough, if it was only to get another peep of the country at your back.'

'You've never seen it yet.'

'Haven't I, North Wind? Oh! I'm so sorry! I thought I had. What did I see then?'

'Only a picture of it. The real country at my real back is ever so much more beautiful than that. You shall see it one day – perhaps before very long.'

'Do they sing songs there?'

'Don't you remember the dream you had about the little boys that dug for the stars?'

'Yes, that I do. I thought you must have had something to do with that dream, it was so beautiful.'

'Yes; I gave you that dream.'

'Oh! thank you. Did you give Nanny her dream too – about the moon and the bees?'

'Yes. I was the lady that sat at the window of the moon.'

'Oh, thank you. I was almost sure you had something to do with that too. And did you tell Mr. Raymond the story about the Princess Daylight?'

'I believe I had something to do with it. At all events he thought about it one night when he couldn't sleep. But I want to ask you whether you remember the song the boy-angels sang in that dream of yours.'

'No. I couldn't keep it, do what I would, and I did try.'

'That was my fault.'

'How could that be, North Wind?'

'Because I didn't know it properly myself, and so I couldn't teach it to you. I could only make a rough guess at something like what it would be, and so I wasn't able to make you dream it hard enough to remember it. Nor would I have done so if I could, for it was not correct. I made you dream pictures of it, though. But you will hear the very song itself when you get to the back of——'

'My own dear North Wind,' said Diamond, finishing the sentence for her, and kissing the arm that held him leaning against her.

'And now we've settled all this – for the time, at least,' said North Wind.

'But I can't feel quite sure yet,' said Diamond.

'You must wait a while for that. Meantime you may be hopeful, and content not to be quite sure. Come now, I will take you home again, for it won't do to tire you too much.'

'Oh! no, no. I'm not the least tired,' pleaded Diamond.

'It is better, though.'

'Very well; if you wish it,' yielded Diamond with a sigh.

'You are a dear good boy,' said North Wind. 'I will come for you again to-morrow night and take you out for a longer time. We shall make a little journey together, in fact. We shall start earlier; and as the moon will be later, we shall have a little moonlight all the way.'

She rose, and swept over the meadow and the trees. In a few moments the Mound appeared below them. She sank a little, and floated in at the window of Diamond's room. There she laid him on his bed, covered him over, and in a moment he was lapt in a dreamless sleep.

37   Once More

The next night Diamond was seated by his open window, with his head on his hand, rather tired, but so eagerly waiting for the promised visit that he was afraid he could not sleep. But he started suddenly, and found that he had been already asleep. He rose, and looking out of the window saw something white against his beech-tree. It was North Wind. She was holding by one hand to a top branch. Her hair and her garments went floating away behind her over the tree, whose top was swaying about while the others were still.

'Are you ready, Diamond?' she asked.

'Yes,' answered Diamond, 'quite ready.'

In a moment she was at the window, and her arms came in and took him. She sailed away so swiftly that he could at first mark nothing but the speed with which the clouds above and the dim earth below went rushing past. But soon he began to see that the sky was very lovely, with mottled clouds all about the moon, on which she threw faint colours like those of mother-of-pearl, or an opal. The night was warm, and in the lady's arms he did not feel the wind which down below was making waves in the ripe corn, and ripples on the rivers and lakes. At length they descended on the side of an open earthy hill, just where, from beneath a stone, a spring came bubbling out.

'I am going to take you along this little brook,' said North Wind. 'I am not wanted for anything else to-night, so I can give you a treat.'

She stooped over the stream, and holding Diamond down close to the surface of it, glided along level with its flow as it ran down the hill. And the song of the brook came up into Diamond's ears, and grew and grew and changed with every turn. It seemed to Diamond to be singing the story of its life to him. And so it was. It began with a musical tinkle which changed to a babble and then to a gentle rushing.

Sometimes its song would almost cease, and then break out again, tinkle, and babble, and rush, all at once. At the bottom of the hill they came to a small river, into which the brook flowed with a muffled but merry sound. Along the surface of the river, darkly clear below them in the moonlight, they floated; now, where it widened out into a little lake, they would hover for a moment over a bed of water-lilies, and watch then swing about, folded in sleep, as the water on which they leaned swayed in the presence of North Wind; and now they would watch the fishes asleep among the roots below. Sometimes she would hold Diamond over a deep hollow curving into the bank, that he might look far into the cool stillness. Sometimes she would leave the river and sweep across a clover-field. The bees were all at home, and the clover was asleep. Then she would return and follow the river. It grew wider and wider as it went. Now the armies of wheat and of oats would hang over its rush from the opposite banks; now the willows would dip low branches in its still waters; and now it would lead them through stately trees and grassy banks into a lovely garden, where the roses and lilies were asleep, the tender flowers quite folded up, and only a few wide-awake and sending out their life in sweet strong odours. Wider and

wider grew the stream, until they came upon boats lying along its banks, which rocked a little in the flutter of North Wind's garments. then came houses on the banks, each standing in a lovely lawn, with grand trees; and in parts the river was so high that some of the grass and the roots of some of the trees were under water, and Diamond, as they glided through between the stems, could see the grass at the bottom of the water. Then they would leave the river and float about and over the houses, one after another – beautiful rich houses, which, like fine trees, had taken centuries to grow. There was scarcely a light to be seen, and not a movement to be heard: all the people in them lay fast asleep.

'What a lot of dreams they must be dreaming!' said Diamond.

'Yes,' returned North Wind. 'They can't surely be all lies – can they?'

'I should think it depends a little on who dreams them,' suggested Diamond.

'Yes,' said North Wind. 'The people who think lies, and do lies, are very likely to dream lies. But the people who love what is true will surely now and then dream true things. But then something depends on whether the dreams are home-grown, or whether the seed of them is blown over somebody else's garden-wall. Ah! there's some one awake in this house!'

They were floating past a window in which a light was burning. Diamond heard a moan, and looked up anxiously in North Wind's face.

'It's a lady,' said North Wind. 'She can't sleep for pain.'

'Couldn't you do something for her?' said Diamond.

'No, I can't. But you could.'

'What could I do?'

'Sing a little song to her.'

'She wouldn't hear me.'

'I will take you in, and then she will hear you.'

'But that would be rude, wouldn't it? You can go where you please, of course, but I should have no business in her room.'

'You may trust me, Diamond. I shall take as good care of the lady as of you. The window is open. Come.'

By a shaded lamp, a lady was seated in a white wrapper, trying to read, but moaning every minute. North Wind floated behind her chair, set Diamond down, and told him to sing something. He was a little frightened, but he thought a while, and then sang –

> The sun is gone down,
>   And the moon's in the sky:
> But the sun will come up,
>   And the moon be laid by.
>
> The flower is asleep
>   But it is not dead,
> When the morning shines,
>   It will lift its head.
>
> When winter comes,
>   It will die – no, no;
> It will only hide
>   From the frost and the snow.
>
> Sure is the summer,
>   Sure is the sun;
> The night and the winter
>   Are shadows that run.

The lady never lifted her eyes from her book, or her head from her hand.

As soon as Diamond had finished, North Wind lifted him and carried him away.

'Didn't the lady hear me?' asked Diamond, when they were once more floating down with the river.

'Oh, yes, she heard you,' answered North Wind.

'Was she frightened then?'

'Oh, no.'

'Why didn't she look to see who it was?'

'She didn't know you were there.'

'How could she hear me then?'

'She didn't hear you with her ears.'

'What did she hear me with?'

'With her heart.'

'Where did she think the words came from?'

'She thought they came out of the book she was reading. She will search all through to-morrow to find them, and won't be able to understand it at all.'

'Oh, what fun!' said Diamond. 'What *will* she do?'

'I can tell you what she won't do: she'll never forget the meaning of them; and she'll never be able to remember the words of them.'

'If she sees them in Mr. Raymond's book, it will puzzle her, won't it?'

'Yes, that it will. She will never be able to understand it.'

'Until she gets to the back of the north wind,' suggested Diamond.

'Until she gets to the back of the north wind,' assented the lady.

'Oh!' cried Diamond, 'I know now where we are. Oh! do let me go into the old garden, and into mother's room, and Diamond's stall. I wonder if the hole is at the back of my bed still. I should like to stay there all the rest of the night. It won't take you long to get me home from here, will it, North Wind?'

'No,' she answered; 'you shall stay as long as you like.'

'Oh, how jolly!' cried Diamond, as North Wind sailed over the house with him, and set him down on the lawn at the back.

Diamond ran about the lawn for a little while in the moonlight. He found part of it cut up into flower-beds, and the little summer-house with the coloured glass and the great elm-tree gone. He did not like this, and ran into the stable. There were no horses there at all. He ran upstairs. The rooms were empty. The only thing left that he cared about was the hole in the wall where his little bed had stood; and that was not enough to make him wish to stop. He ran down the stair again, and out upon the lawn. There he threw himself down and began to cry. It was all so dreary and lost!

'I thought I liked the place so much,' said Diamond to himself, 'but I find I don't care about it. I suppose it's only the people in it that make you like a place, and when they're gone, it's dead, and you don't care a bit about it. North Wind told me I might stop as long as I liked, and I've stopped longer already. – North Wind!' he cried aloud, turning his face towards the sky.

The moon was under a cloud, and all was looking dull and dismal. A star shot from the sky, and fell in the grass beside him. The moment it lighted, there stood North Wind.

'Oh!' cried Diamond, joyfully, 'were you the shooting star?'

'Yes, my child.'

'Did you hear me call you then?'

'Yes.'

'So high up as that?'

'Yes; I heard you quite well.'

'Do take me home.'

'Have you had enough of your old home already?'

'Yes, more than enough. It isn't a home at all now.'

'I thought that would be it,' said North Wind. 'Everything, dreaming and all, has got a soul in it, or else it's worth nothing, and we don't care a bit about it. Some of our thoughts are worth nothing, because they've got no soul in them. The brain puts them into the mind, not the mind into the brain.'

'But how can you know about that, North Wind? You haven't got a body.'

'If I hadn't, you wouldn't know anything about me.' No creature can know another without the help of a body. But I don't care to talk about that. It is time for you to go home.'

So saying, North Wind lifted Diamond and bore him away.

38　At the Back of the North Wind

I did not see Diamond for a week or so after this, and then he told me
what I have now told you. I should have been astonished at his being
able even to report such conversations as he said he had had with
North Wind, had I not known already that some children are profound
in metaphysics. But a fear crosses me, lest, by telling so much about
my friend, I should lead people to mistake him for one of those
consequential, priggish little monsters, who are always trying to say
clever things, and looking to see whether people appreciate them.
When a child like that dies, instead of having a silly book written about
him, he should be stuffed like one of those awful big-headed fishes you
see in museums. But Diamond never troubled his head about what
people thought of him. He never set up for knowing better than others.
The wisest things he said came out when he wanted one to help him
with some difficulty he was in. He was not even offended with Nanny
and Jim for calling him a silly. He supposed there was something in it,
though he could not quite understand what. I suspect however that the
other name they gave him, *God's Baby*, had some share in reconciling
him to it.

Happily for me, I was as much interested in metaphysics as
Diamond himself, and therefore, while he recounted his conversations
with North Wind, I did not find myself at all in a strange sea, although
certainly I could not always feel the bottom, being indeed convinced
that the bottom was miles away.

'*Could* it be all dreaming, do you think, sir?' he asked anxiously.

'I daren't say, Diamond,' I answered. 'But at least there is one
thing you may be sure of, that there is a still better love than that of the
wonderful being you call North Wind. Even if she be a dream, the
dream of such a beautiful creature could not come to you by chance.'

'Yes, I know,' returned Diamond; 'I know.'

Then he was silent, but, I confess, appeared more thoughtful than satisfied.

The next time I saw him, he looked paler than usual.

'Have you seen your friend again?' I asked him.

'Yes,' he answered, solemnly.

'Did she take you out with her?'

'No. She did not speak to me. I woke all at once, as I generally do when I am going to see her, and there she was against the door into the big room, sitting just as I saw her sit on her own door-step, as white as snow, and her eyes as blue as the heart of an iceberg. She looked at me, but never moved or spoke.'

'Weren't you afraid?' I asked.

'No. Why should I?' he answered. 'I only felt a little cold.'

'Did she stay long?'

'I don't know. I fell asleep again. I think I have been rather cold ever since though,' he added with a smile.

I did not quite like this, but I said nothing.

Four days after, I called again at the Mound. The maid who

opened to door looked grave, but I suspected nothing. When I reached the drawing-room, I saw Mrs. Raymond had been crying.

'Haven't you heard?' she said, seeing my questioning looks.

'I've heard nothing,' I answered.

'This morning we found our dear little Diamond lying on the floor of the big attic-room, just outside his own door -- fast asleep, as we thought. But when we took him up, we did not think he was asleep. We saw that——'

Here the kind-hearted lady broke out crying afresh.

'May I go and see him?' I asked.

'Yes,' she sobbed. 'You know your way to the top of the tower.'

I walked up the winding stair, and entered his room. A lovely figure, as white and almost as clear as alabaster, was lying on the bed. I saw at once how it was. They thought he was dead. I knew that he had gone to the back of the north wind.

The Princess and the Goblin
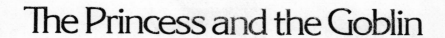

The Princess and the Goblin

With the original illustrations by
Arthur Hughes
after Dalziel

George MacDonald

Contents

1 Why the Princess has a Story about Her

There was once a little princess whose father was king over a great country full of mountains and valleys. His palace was built upon one of the mountains, and was very grand and beautiful. The princess, whose name was Irene, was born there, but she was sent soon after her birth, because her mother was not very strong, to be brought up by country people in a large house, half castle, half farmhouse, on the side of another mountain, about half-way between its base and its peak.

The princess was a sweet little creature, and at the time my story begins, was about eight years old, I think, but she got older very fast. Her face was fair and pretty, with eyes like two bits of night-sky, each with a star dissolved in the blue. Those eyes you would have thought must have known they came from there, so often were they turned up in that direction. The ceiling of her nursery was blue, with stars in it, as like the sky as they could make it. But I doubt if ever she saw the real sky with the stars in it, for a reason which I had better mention at once.

These mountains were full of hollow places underneath; huge caverns, and winding ways, some with water running through them, and some shining with all colours of the rainbow when a light was taken in. There would not have been much known about them, had there not been mines there, great deep pits, with long galleries and passages running off from them, which had been dug to get at the ore of which the mountains were full. In the course of digging, the miners came upon many of these natural caverns. A few of them had far-off openings out on the side of a mountain, or into a ravine.

Now in these subterranean caverns lived a strange race of beings, called by some gnomes, by some kobolds, by some goblins. There was a legend current in the country, that at one time they lived above ground, and were very like other people. But for some reason or other,

concerning which there were different legendary theories, the king
had laid what they thought too severe taxes upon them, or had
required observances of them they did not like, or had begun to treat
them with more severity, in some way or other, and impose stricter
laws; and the consequence was that they had all disappeared from the
face of the country. According to the legend, however, instead of going
to some other country, they had all taken refuge in the suberranean
caverns, whence they never came out but at night, and then seldom
showed themselves in any numbers, and never to many people at once.
It was only in the least frequented and most difficult parts of the
mountains that they were said to gather even at night in the open air.
Those who had caught sight of any of them said that they had greatly
altered in the course of generations; and no wonder, seeing they lived
away from the sun, in cold and wet and dark places. They were now,
not ordinarily ugly, but either absolutely hideous, or ludicrously
grotesque both in face and form. There was no invention, they said, of
the most lawless imagination expressed by pen or pencil, that could
surpass the extravagance of their appearance. But I suspect those who

said so, had mistaken some of their animal companions for the goblins themselves – of which more by and by. The goblins themselves were not so far removed from the human as such a description would imply. And as they grew misshapen in body, they had grown in knowledge and cleverness, and now were able to do things no mortal could see the possibility of. But as they grew in cunning, they grew in mischief, and their great delight was in every way they could think of to annoy the people who lived in the open-air-storey above them. They had enough of affection left for each other, to preserve them from being absolutely cruel for cruelty's sake to those that came in their way; but still they so heartily cherished the ancestral grudge against those who occupied their former possessions, and especially against the descendants of the king who had caused their expulsion, that they sought every opportunity of tormenting them in ways that were as odd as their inventors; and although dwarfed and misshapen, they had strength equal to their cunning. In the process of time they had got a king and a government of their own, whose chief business, beyond their own simple affairs, was to devise trouble for their neighbours. It will now be pretty

evident why the little princess had never seen the sky at night. They were much too afraid of the goblins to let her out of the house then, even in company with ever so many attendants; and they had good reason, as we shall see by and by.

2　The Princess loses Herself

I have said the Princess Irene was about eight years old when my story begins. And this is how it begins.

One very wet day, when the mountain was covered with mist which was constantly gathering itself together into raindrops, and pouring down on the roofs of the great old house, whence it fell in a fringe of water from the eaves all round about it, the princess could not of course go out. She got very tired, so tired that even her toys could no longer amuse her. You would wonder at that if I had time to describe to you one half of the toys she had. But then you wouldn't have the toys themselves, and that makes all the difference: you can't get tired of a thing before you have it. It was a picture, though, worth seeing – the princess sitting in the nursery with the sky ceiling over her head, at a great table covered with her toys. If the artist would like to draw this, I should advise him not to meddle with the toys. I am afraid of attempting to describe them, and I think he had better not try to draw them. He had better not. He can do a thousand things I can't, but I don't think he could draw those toys. No man could better make the princess herself than he could, though – leaning with her back bowed into the back of the chair, her head hanging down, and her hands in her lap, very miserable as she would say herself, not even knowing what she would like, except it were to go out and get thoroughly wet, and catch a particularly nice cold, and have to go to bed and take gruel. The next moment after you see her sitting there, her nurse goes out of the room.

Even that is a change, and the princess wakes up a little, and looks about her. Then she tumbles off her chair, and runs out of the door, not the same door the nurse went out of, but one which opened at the foot of a curious old stair of worm-eaten oak, which looked as if never

anyone had set foot upon it. She had once before been up six steps, and that was sufficient reason, in such a day, for trying to find out what was at the top of it.

Up and up she ran – such a long way it seemed to her! until she came to the top of the third flight. There she found the landing was the end of a long passage. Into this she ran. It was full of doors on each side. There were so many that she did not care to open any, but ran on to the end, where she turned into another passage, also full of doors. When she had turned twice more, and still saw doors and only doors about her, she began to get frightened. It was so silent! And all those doors must hide rooms with nobody in them! That was dreadful. Also the rain made a great trampling noise on the roof. She turned and started at full speed, her little footsteps echoing through the sounds of the rain – back for the stairs and her safe nursery. So she thought, but she had lost herself long ago. It doesn't follow that she *was* lost, because she had lost herself, though.

She ran for some distance, turned several times, and then began to be afraid. Very soon she was sure that she had lost the way back. Rooms everywhere, and no stair! Her little heart beat as fast as her little feet ran, and a lump of tears was growing in her throat. But she was too eager and perhaps too frightened to cry for some time. At last her hope failed her. Nothing but passages and doors everywhere! She threw herself on the floor, and burst into a wailing cry broken by sobs.

She did not cry long, however, for she was as brave as could be expected of a princess of her age. After a good cry, she got up, and brushed the dust from her frock. Oh what old dust it was! Then she wiped her eyes with her hands, for princesses don't always have their handkerchiefs in their pockets, any more than some other little girls I know of. Next, like a true princess, she resolved on going wisely to work to find her way back: she would walk through the passages, and look in every direction for the stair. This she did, but without success. She went over the same ground again and again without knowing it, for the passages and doors were all alike. At last, in a corner, through a half-open door, she did see a stair. But alas! it went the wrong way: instead of going down, it went up. Frightened as she was, however, she could not help wishing to see where yet further the stair could lead. It was very narrow, and so steep that she went on like a four-legged creature on her hands and feet.

3   The Princess and – we shall see who

When she came to the top, she found herself in a little square place, with three doors, two opposite each other, and one opposite the top of the stair. She stood for a moment, without an idea in her little head what to do next. But as she stood, she began to hear a curious humming sound. Could it be the rain? No. It was much more gentle, and even monotonous than the sound of the rain, which now she scarcely heard. The low sweet humming sound went on, sometimes stopping for a little while and then beginning again. It was more like the hum of a very happy bee that had found a rich well of honey in some globular flower, than anything else I can think of at this moment. Where could it come from? She laid her ear first to one of the doors to hearken if it was there – then to another. When she laid her ear against the third door, there could be no doubt where it came from: it must be from something in that room. What could it be? She was rather afraid, but her curiosity was stronger than her fear, and she opened the door very gently and peeped in. What do you think she saw? A very old lady who sat spinning.

Perhaps you will wonder how the princess could tell that the old lady was an old lady, when I inform you that not only was she beautiful, but her skin was smooth and white. I will tell you more. Her hair was combed back from her forehead and face, and hung loose far down and all over her back. That is not much like an old lady – is it? Ah! but it was white almost as snow. And although her face was so smooth, her eyes looked so wise that you could not have helped seeing she must be old. The princess, though she could not have told you why, did think her very old indeed – quite fifty – she said to herself. But she was rather older than that, as you shall hear.

While the princess stared bewildered, with her head just inside the door, the old lady lifted hers, and said, in a sweet, but old and rather shaky voice, which mingled very pleasantly with the continued hum of her wheel: 'Come in, my dear; come in. I am glad to see you.'

That the princess was a real princess, you might see now quite plainly; for she didn't hang on to the handle of the door, and stare without moving, as I have known some do who ought to have been princesses but were only rather vulgar little girls. She did as she was told, stepped inside the door at once, and shut it gently behind her.

'Come to me, my dear,' said the old lady.

And again the princess did as she was told. She approached the old lady – rather slowly, I confess, but did not stop until she stood by her side, and looked up in her face with her blue eyes and the two melted stars in them.

'Why, what have you been doing with your eyes, child?' asked the old lady.

'Crying,' answered the princess.

'Why, child?'

'Because I couldn't find my way down again.'

'But you could find your way up.'

'Not at first – not for a long time.'

'But your face is streaked like the back of a zebra. Hadn't you a handkerchief to wipe your eyes with?'

'No.'

'Then why didn't you come to me to wipe them for you?'

'Please, I didn't know you were here. I will next time.'

'There's a good child!' said the old lady.

Then she stopped her wheel, and rose, and, going out of the room, returned with a little silver basin and a soft white towel, with which she washed and wiped the bright little face. And the princess thought her hands were so smooth and nice!

When she carried away the basin and towel, the little princess wondered to see how straight and tall she was, for, although she was so old, she didn't stoop a bit. She was dressed in black velvet with thick white heavy-looking lace about it; and on the black dress, her hair shone like silver. There was hardly any more furniture in the room than there might have been in that of the poorest old woman who made her bread by her spinning. There was no carpet on the floor – no table anywhere – nothing but the spinning-wheel and the chair beside it. When she came back, she sat down again, and without a word began her spinning once more, while Irene, who had never seen a spinning-wheel, stood by her side and looked on. When the old lady had got her thread fairly going again, she said to the princess, but without looking at her:

'Do you know my name, child?'

'No, I don't know it,' answered the princess.

'My name is Irene.'

'That's *my* name!' cried the princess.

'I know that. I let you have mine. I haven't got your name. You've got mine.'

'How can that be?' asked the princess, bewildered. 'I've always had my name.'

'Your papa, the king, asked me if I had any objection to your having it; and of course I hadn't. I let you have it with pleasure.'

'It was very kind of you to give me your name – and such a pretty one,' said the princess.

'Oh, not so *very* kind!' said the old lady. 'A name is one of those things one can give away and keep all the same. I have a good many such things. Wouldn't you like to know who I am, child?'

'Yes, that I should – very much.'

'I'm your great-great-grandmother,' said the lady.

'What's that?' asked the princess.

'I'm your father's mother's father's mother.'

'Oh dear! I can't understand that,' said the princess.

'I dare say not. I didn't expect you would. But that's no reason why I shouldn't say it.'

'Oh, no!' answered the princess.

'I will explain it all to you when you are older,' the lady went on. 'But you will be able to understand this much now: I came here to take care of you.'

'Is it long since you came? Was it yesterday? Or was it to-day, because it was so wet that I couldn't get out?'

'I've been here ever since you came yourself.'

'What a long time!' said the princess. 'I don't remember it at all.'

'No. I suppose not.'

'But I never saw you before.'

'No. But you shall see me again.'

'Do you live in this room always?'

'I don't sleep in it. I sleep on the opposite side of the landing. I sit here most of the day.'

'I shouldn't like it. My nursery is much prettier. You must be a queen too, if you are my great big grandmother.'

'Yes, I am a queen.'

'Where is your crown then?'

'In my bedroom.'

'I *should* like to see it.'

'You shall some day – not to-day.'

'I wonder why nursie never told me.'

'Nursie doesn't know. She never saw me.'

'But somebody knows that you are in the house?'

'No; nobody.'

'How do you get your dinner then?'

'I keep poultry – of a sort.'

'Where do you keep them?'

'I will show you.'

'And who makes the chicken broth for you?'

'I never kill any of my chickens.'

'Then I can't understand.'

'What did you have for breakfast this morning?' asked the lady.

'Oh! I had bread and milk, and an egg. – I dare say you eat their eggs.'

'Yes, that's it. I eat their eggs.'

'Is that what makes your hair so white?'

'No, my dear. It's old age. I am very old.'

'I thought so. Are you fifty?'

'Yes – more than that.'

'Are you a hundred?'

'Yes – more than that. I am too old for you to guess. Come and see my chickens.'

Again she stopped her spinning. She rose, took the princess by the hand, led her out of the room and opened the door opposite the stair. The princess expected to see a lot of hens and chickens, but instead of that, she saw the blue sky first, and then the roofs of the house, with a multitude of the loveliest pigeons, mostly white, but of all colours, walking about, making bows to each other, and talking a language she could not understand. She clapped her hands with delight, and up rose such a flapping of wings, that she in her turn was startled.

'You've frightened my poultry,' said the old lady, smiling.

'And they've frightened me,' said the princess, smiling too. 'But what very nice poultry! Are the eggs nice?'

'Yes, very nice.'

'What a small egg-spoon you must have! Wouldn't it be better to keep hens, and get bigger eggs?'

'How should I feed them, though?'

'I see,' said the princess. 'The pigeons feed themselves. They've got wings.'

'Just so. If they couldn't fly, I couldn't eat their eggs.'

'But how do you get at the eggs? Where are their nests?'

The lady took hold of a little loop of string in the wall at the side of the door, and lifting a shutter, showed a great many pigeonholes with nests, some with young ones and some with eggs in them. The birds came in at the other side, and she took out the eggs on this side. She closed it again quickly, lest the young ones should be frightened.

'Oh what a nice way!' cried the princess. 'Will you give me an egg to eat, I'm rather hungry.'

'I will some day, but now you must go back, or nursie will be miserable about you. I dare say she's looking for you everywhere.'

'Except here,' answered the princess. 'Oh how surprised she *will* be when I tell her about my great big grand-grandmother!'

'Yes, that she will!' said the old lady with a curious smile. 'Mind you tell her all about it exactly.'

'That I will. Please will you take me back to her?'

'I can't go all the way, but I will take you to the top of the stair, and then you must run down quite fast into your own room.'

The little princess put her hand in the old lady's, who, looking this way and that, brought her to the top of the first stair, and thence to the bottom of the second, and did not leave her till she saw her half-way down the third. When she heard the cry of her nurse's pleasure at finding her, she turned and walked up the stairs again, very fast indeed for such a very great grandmother, and sat down to her spinning with another strange smile on her sweet old face.

About this spinning of hers I will tell you more another time.

Guess what she was spinning.

4 What the Nurse thought of it

'Why, where can you have been, princess?' asked the nurse, taking her in her arms. 'It's very unkind of you to hide away so long. I began to be afraid——'

Here she checked herself.

'What were you afraid of, nursie?' asked the princess.

'Never mind,' she answered. 'Perhaps I will tell you another day. Now tell me where you have been?'

'I've been up a long way to see my very great, huge, old grandmother,' said the princess.

'What do you mean by that?' asked the nurse, who thought she was making fun.

'I mean that I've been a long way up and up to see my GREAT grandmother. Ah, nursie, you don't know what a beautiful mother of grandmothers I've got upstairs. She is *such* an old lady! with such lovely white hair! – as white as my silver cup. Now, when I think of it, I think her hair must be silver.'

'What nonsense you are talking, princess!' said the nurse.

'I'm not talking nonsense,' returned Irene, rather offended. 'I will tell you all about her. She's much taller than you, and much prettier.'

'Oh, I dare say!' remarked the nurse.

'And she lives upon pigeons' eggs.'

'Most likely,' said the nurse.

'And she sits in an empty room, spin-spinning all day long.'

'Not a doubt of it,' said the nurse.

'And she keeps her crown in her bedroom.'

'Of course – quite the proper place to keep her crown in. She wears it in bed, I'll be bound.'

'She didn't say that. And I don't think she does. That wouldn't be

comfortable – would it? I don't think my papa wears his crown for a
nightcap. Does he, nursie?'

'I never asked him. I dare say he does.'

'And she's been there ever since I came here – ever so many years.'

'Anybody could have told you that,' said the nurse, who did not
believe a word Irene was saying.

'Why didn't you tell me then?'

'There was no necessity. You could make it all up for yourself.'

'You don't believe me then!' exclaimed the princess, astonished
and angry, as she well might be.

'Did you expect me to believe you, princess?' asked the nurse
coldly. 'I know princesses are in the habit of telling make-believes, but
you are the first I ever heard of who expected to have them believed,'
she added, seeing that the child was strangely in earnest.

The princess burst into tears.

'Well, I must say,' remarked the nurse, now thoroughly vexed
with her for crying, 'it is not at all becoming in a princess to tell stories
and expect to be believed just because she is a princess.'

'But it's quite true, I tell you.'

'You've dreamt it, then, child.'

'No, I didn't dream it. I went upstairs, and I lost myself, and if I
hadn't found the beautiful lady, I should never have found myself.'

'Oh, I dare say!'

'Well, you just come up with me, and see if I'm not telling the
truth.'

'Indeed I have other work to do. It's your dinner-time, and I won't
have any more such nonsense.'

The princess wiped her eyes, and her face grew so hot that they
were soon quite dry. She sat down to her dinner, but ate next to
nothing. Not to be believed does not at all agree with princesses; for a
real princess cannot tell a lie. So all the afternoon she did not speak a
word. Only when the nurse spoke to her, she answered her, for a real
princess is never rude – even when she does well to be offended.

Of course the nurse was not comfortable in her mind – not that she
suspected the least truth in Irene's story, but that she loved her dearly,
and was vexed with herself for having been cross to her. She thought
her crossness was the cause of the princess's unhappiness, and had no
idea that she was really and deeply hurt at not being believed. But, as it

became more and more plain during the evening in her every motion and look, that, although she tried to amuse herself with her toys, her heart was too vexed and troubled to enjoy them, her nurse's discomfort grew and grew. When bedtime came, she undressed and laid her down, but the child, instead of holding up her little mouth to be kissed, turned away from her and lay still. Then nursie's heart gave way altogether, and she began to cry. At the sound of her first sob, the princess turned again, and held her face to kiss her as usual. But the nurse had her handkerchief to her eyes, and did not see the movement.

'Nursie,' said the princess, 'why won't you believe me?'

'Because I can't believe you,' said the nurse, getting angry again.

'Ah! then, you can't help it,' said Irene, 'and I will not be vexed with you any more. I will give you a kiss and go to sleep.'

'You little angel!' cried the nurse, and caught her out of bed, and walked about the room with her in her arms, kissing and hugging her.

'You *will* let me take you to see my dear old great big grandmother? won't you?' said the princess, as she laid her down again.

'And *you* won't say I'm ugly, any more – will you, princess?'

'Nursie, I never said you were ugly. What can you mean?'

'Well, if you didn't say it, you meant it.'

'Indeed, I never did.'

'You said I wasn't so pretty as that――'

'As my beautiful grandmother – yes, I did say that; and I say it again, for it's quite true.'

'Then I *do* think you *are* unkind!' said the nurse, and put her handkerchief to her eyes again.

'Nursie, dear, everybody can't be as beautiful as every other body, you know. You are *very* nice-looking, but if you had been as beautiful as my grandmother――'

'Bother your grandmother!' said the nurse.

'Nurse, that's very rude. You are not fit to be spoken to – till you behave better.'

The princess turned away once more, and again the nurse was ashamed of herself.

'I'm sure I beg your pardon, princess,' she said, though still in an offended tone. But the princess let the tone pass, and heeded only the words.

'You won't say it again, I am sure,' she answered, once more turning towards her nurse. 'I was only going to say that if you had been twice as nice-looking as you are, some king or other would have married you, and then what would have become of me?'

'You are an angel!' repeated the nurse, again embracing her.

'Now,' insisted Irene, 'you *will* come and see my grandmother – won't you?'

'I will go with you anywhere you like, my cherub,' she answered; and in two minutes the weary little princess was fast asleep.

5   The Princess lets well alone

When she woke the next morning, the first thing she heard was the rain still falling. Indeed, this day was so like the last, that it would have been difficult to tell where was the use of it. The first thing she thought of, however, was not the rain, but the lady in the tower; and the first question that occupied her thoughts was whether she should not ask the nurse to fulfil her promise this very morning, and go with her to find her grandmother as soon as she had had her breakfast. But she came to the conclusion that perhaps the lady would not be pleased if she took anyone to see her without first asking leave; especially as it was pretty evident, seeing she lived on pigeons' eggs, and cooked them herself, that she did not want the household to know she was there. So the princess resolved to take the first opportunity of running up alone and asking whether she might bring her nurse. She believed the fact that she could not otherwise convince her she was telling the truth, would have much weight with her grandmother.

The princess and her nurse were the best of friends all dressing time, and the princess in consequence ate an enormous little breakfast.

'I wonder, Lootie' – that was her pet name for her nurse –'what pigeons' eggs taste like?' she said, as she was eating her egg – not quite a common one, for they always picked out the pinky ones for her.

'We'll get you a pigeon's egg, and you shall judge for yourself,' said the nurse.

'Oh, no, no!' returned Irene, suddenly reflecting they might disturb the old lady in getting it, and that even if they did not, she would have one less in consequence.

'What a strange creature you are,' said the nurse – 'first to want a thing and then to refuse it!'

But she did not say it crossly, and the princess never minded any remarks that were not unfriendly.

'Well, you see, Lootie, there are reasons,' she returned, and said no more, for she did not want to bring up the subject of their former strife, lest her nurse should offer to go before she had had her grandmother's permission to bring her. Of course she could refuse to take her, but then she would believe her less than ever.

Now the nurse, as she said herself afterwards, could not be every moment in the room, and as never before yesterday had the princess given her the smallest reason for anxiety, it had not yet come into her head to watch her more closely. So she soon gave her a chance, and, the very first that offered, Irene was off and up the stairs again.

This day's adventure, however, did not turn out like yesterday's, although it began like it; and indeed to-day is very seldom like yesterday, if people would note the differences – even when it rains. The princess ran through passage after passage, and could not find the stair of the tower. My own suspicion is that she had not gone up high enough, and was searching on the second instead of the third floor. When she turned to go back, she failed equally in her search after the stair. She was lost once more.

Something made it even worse to bear this time, and it was no wonder that she cried again. Suddenly it occurred to her that it was after having cried before that she had found her grandmother's stair. She got up at once, wiped her eyes, and started upon a fresh quest. This time, although she did not find what she hoped, she found what was next best: she did not come on a stair that went up, but she came upon one that went down. It was evidently not the stair she had come up, yet it was a good deal better than none; so down she went, and was singing merrily before she reached the bottom. There, to her surprise, she found herself in the kitchen. Although she was not allowed to go there alone, her nurse had often taken her, and she was a great favourite with the servants. So there was a general rush at her the moment she appeared, for everyone wanted to have her; and the report of where she was soon reached the nurse's ears. She came at once to fetch her; but she never suspected how she had got there, and the princess kept her own counsel.

Her failure to find the old lady not only disappointed her, but made her very thoughtful. Sometimes she came almost to the nurse's opinion that she had dreamed all about her; but that fancy never lasted very long. She wondered much whether she should ever see her again, and thought it very sad not to have been able to find her when she particularly wanted her. She resolved to say nothing more to her nurse on the subject, seeing it was so little in her power to prove her words.

6   The Little Miner

The next day the great cloud still hung over the mountain, and the rain poured like water from a full sponge. The princess was very fond of being out-of-doors, and she nearly cried when she saw that the weather was no better. But the mist was not of such a dark dingy grey; there was light in it; and as the hours went on, it grew brighter and brighter, until it was almost too brilliant to look at; and late in the afternoon, the sun broke out so gloriously that Irene clapped her hands, crying,

'See, see, Lootie! The sun has had his face washed. Look how bright he is! Do get my hat, and let us go out for a walk. Oh dear! oh dear! how happy I am!'

Lootie was very glad to please the princess. She got her hat and cloak, and they set out together for a walk up the mountain; for the road was so hard and steep that the water could not rest upon it, and it was always dry enough for walking a few minutes after the rain ceased. The clouds were rolling away in broken pieces, like great, overwoolly sheep, whose wool the sun had bleached till it was almost too white for the eyes to bear. Between them the sky shone with a deeper and purer blue, because of the rain. The trees on the roadside were hung all over with drops, which sparkled in the sun like jewels. The only things that were no brighter for the rain, were the brooks that ran down the mountain; they had changed from the clearness of crystal to a muddy brown; but what they lost in colour they gained in sound – or at least in noise, for a brook when it is swollen is not so musical as before. But Irene was in raptures with the great brown streams tumbling down everywhere; and Lootie shared in her delight, for she too had been confined to the house for three days. At length she observed that the sun was getting low, and said it was time to be going back. She made the remark again and again, but, every time, the princess begged her to go on just a little farther and a little farther; reminding her that it was much easier to go downhill, and saying that when they did turn, they would be at home in a moment. So on and on they did go, now to look at a group of ferns over whose tops a stream was pouring in a watery arch, now to pick a shining stone from a rock by the wayside, now to watch the flight of some bird. Suddenly the shadow of a great mountain peak came up from behind, and shot in front of them. When the nurse saw it, she started and shook, and catching hold of the princess's hand turned and began to run down the hill.

'What's all the haste, nursie?' asked Irene, running alongside of her.

'We must not be out a moment longer.'

'But we can't help being out a good many moments longer.'

It was too true. The nurse almost cried. They were much too far from home. It was against express orders to be out with the princess one moment after the sun was down; and they were nearly a mile up the mountain! If his majesty, Irene's papa, were to hear of it, Lootie would certainly be dismissed; and to leave the princess would break

her heart. It was no wonder she ran. But Irene was not in the least frightened, not knowing anything to be frightened at. She kept on chattering as well as she could, but it was not easy.

'Lootie! Lootie! why do you run so fast? It shakes my teeth when I talk.'

'Then don't talk,' said Lootie.

But the princess went on talking. She was always saying, 'Look, look, Lootie!' but Lootie paid no more heed to anything she said, only ran on.

'Look, look, Lootie! Don't you see that funny man peeping over the rock?'

Lootie only ran the faster. They had to pass the rock, and when they came nearer, the princess saw it was only a lump of the rock itself that she had taken for a man.

'Look, look, Lootie! There's *such* a curious creature at the foot of that old tree. Look at it, Lootie! It's making faces at us, I do think.'

Lootie gave a stifled cry, and ran faster still – so fast, that Irene's little legs could not keep up with her, and she fell with a clash. It was a hard downhill road, and she had been running very fast – so it was no wonder she began to cry. This put the nurse nearly beside herself; but all she could do was to run on, the moment she got the princess on her feet again.

'Who's that laughing at me?' said the princess, trying to keep in her sobs, and running too fast for her grazed knees.

'Nobody, child,' said the nurse, almost angrily.

But that instant there came a burst of coarse tittering from somewhere near, and a hoarse indistinct voice that seemed to say, 'Lies! lies! lies!'

'Oh!' cried the nurse with a sigh that was almost a scream, and ran on faster than ever.

'Nursie! Lootie! I can't run any more. Do let us walk a bit.'

'What *am* I to do?' said the nurse. 'Here I will carry you.'

She caught her up; but found her much too heavy to run with, and had to set her down again. Then she looked wildly about her, gave a great cry, and said –

'We've taken the wrong turning somewhere, and I don't know where we are. We are lost, lost!'

The terror she was in had quite bewildered her. It was true enough

they had lost the way. They had been running down into a little valley in which there was no house to be seen.

Now Irene did not know what good reason there was for her nurse's terror, for the servants had all strict orders never to mention the goblins to her, but it was very discomposing to see her nurse in such a fright. Before, however, she had time to grow thoroughly alarmed like her, she heard the sound of whistling, and that revived her. Presently she saw a boy coming up the road from the valley to meet them. He was the whistler; but before they met, his whistling changed to singing. And this is something like what he sang.

> 'Ring! dod! bang!
> Go the hammers' clang!
> Hit and turn and bore!
> Whizz and puff and roar!
> Thus we rive the rocks,
> Force the goblin locks. –
> See the shining ore!
> One, two, three –

Bright as gold can be!
Four, five, six –
Shovels, mattocks, picks!
Seven, eight, nine –
Light your lamp at mine.
Ten, eleven, twelve –
Loosely hold the helve.
We're the merry miner-boys,
Make the goblins hold their noise.'

'I wish you would hold *your* noise,' said the nurse rudely, for the very word goblin at such a time and in such a place made her tremble. It would bring the goblins upon them to a certainty, she thought, to defy them in that way. But whether the boy heard her or not, he did not stop his singing.

'Thirteen, fourteeen, fifteen –
This is worth the siftin';
Sixteen, seventeen, eighteen –
There's the match, and lay't in.
Nineteen, twenty –
Goblins in a plenty.'

'Do be quiet,' cried the nurse, in a whispered shriek. But the boy, who was now close at hand, still went on.

'Hush! scush! scurry!
There you go in a hurry!
Gobble! gobble! goblin!
There you go a wobblin';
Hobble, hobble, hobblin';
Cobble! cobble! cobblin'!
Hob-bob-goblin!——Huuuuuh!'

'There!' said the boy, as he stood still opposite them. 'There! that'll do for them. They can't bear singing, and they can't stand that song. They can't sing themselves, for they have no more voice than a crow; and they don't like other people to sing.'

The boy was dressed in a miner's dress, with a curious cap on his head. He was a very nice-looking boy, with eyes as dark as the mines in which he worked, and as sparkling as the crystals in their rocks. He was about twelve years old. His face was almost too pale for beauty, which came of his being so little in the open air and the sunlight – for even vegetables grown in the dark are white; but he looked happy, merry indeed – perhaps at the thought of having routed the goblins; and his bearing as he stood before them had nothing clownish or rude about it.

'I saw them,' he went on, 'as I came up; and I'm very glad I did. I knew they were after somebody, but I couldn't see who it was. They won't touch you so long as I'm with you.'

'Why, who are you?' asked the nurse, offended at the freedom with which he spoke to them.

'I'm Peter's son.'

'Who's Peter?'

'Peter the miner.'

'I don't know him.'

'I'm his son, though.'

'And why should the goblins mind *you*, pray?'

'Because I don't mind them. I'm used to them.

'What difference does that make?'

'If you're not afraid of them, they're afraid of you. I'm not afraid of them. That's all. But it's all that's wanted – up here, that is. It's a different thing down there. They won't always mind that song even, down there. And if anyone sings it, they stand grinning at him awfully; and if he gets frightened, and misses a word, or says a wrong one, they – oh! don't they give it him!'

'What do they do to him?' asked Irene, with a trembling voice.

'Don't go frightening the princess,' said the nurse.

'The princess!' repeated the little miner, taking off his curious cap. 'I beg your pardon; but you oughtn't to be out so late. Everybody knows that's against the law.'

'Yes, indeed it is!' said the nurse, beginning to cry again. 'And I shall have to suffer for it.'

'What does that matter?' said the boy. 'It must be your fault. It is the princess who will suffer for it. I hope they didn't hear you call her the princess. If they did, they're sure to know her again: they're awfully sharp.'

'Lootie! Lootie!' cried the princess. 'Take me home.'

'Don't go on like that,' said the nurse to the boy, almost fiercely. 'How could I help it? I lost my way.'

'You shouldn't have been out so late. You wouldn't have lost your way if you hadn't been frightened,' said the boy. 'Come along. I'll soon set you right again. Shall I carry your little highness?'

'Impertinence!' murmured the nurse, but she did not say it aloud, for she thought if she made him angry, he might take his revenge by telling someone belonging to the house, and then it would be sure to come to the king's ears.

'No, thank you,' said Irene. 'I can walk very well, though I can't run so fast as nursie. If you will give me one hand, Lootie will give me another, and then I shall get on famously.'

They soon had her between them, holding a hand of each.

'Now let's run,' said the nurse.

'No, no,' said the little miner. 'That's the worst thing you can do. If you hadn't run before, you would not have lost your way. And if you run now, they will be after you in a moment.'

'I don't want to run,' said Irene.

'You don't think of *me*,' said the nurse.

'Yes, I do, Lootie. The boy says they won't touch us if we don't run.'

'Yes, but if they know at the house that I've kept you out so late, I shall be turned away, and that would break my heart.'

'Turned away, Lootie! Who would turn you away?'

'Your papa, child.'

'But I'll tell him it was all my fault. And you know it was, Lootie.'

'He won't mind that. I'm sure he won't.'

'Then I'll cry, and go down on my knees to him, and beg him not to take away my own dear Lootie.'

The nurse was comforted at hearing this, and said no more. They went on, walking pretty fast, but taking care not to run a step.

'I want to talk to you,' said Irene to the little miner; 'but it's so awkward! I don't know your name.'

'My name's Curdie, little princess.'

'What a funny name! Curdie! What more?'

'Curdie Peterson. What's your name, please?'

'Irene.'

'What more?'

'I don't know what more. – What more is my name, Lootie?'

'Princesses haven't got more than one name. They don't want it.'

'Oh then, Curdie, you must call me just Irene and no more.'

'No, indeed,' said the nurse indignantly. 'He shall do no such thing.'

'What shall he call me, then, Lootie?'

'Your royal Highness.'

'My royal Highness! What's that? No, no, Lootie. I won't be called names. I don't like them. You told me once yourself it's only rude children that call names; and I'm sure Curdie wouldn't be rude. – Curdie, my name's Irene.'

'Well, Irene,' said Curdie, with a glance at the nurse which showed he enjoyed teasing her, 'it is very kind of you to let me call you anything. I like your name very much.'

He expected the nurse to interfere again; but he soon saw that she was too frightened to speak. She was staring at something a few yards before them, in the middle of the path, where it narrowed between rocks so that only one could pass at a time.

'It is very much kinder of you to go out of your way to take us home,' said Irene.

'I'm not going out of my way yet,' said Curdie. 'It's on the other side of those rocks the path turns off to my father's.'

'You wouldn't think of leaving us till we're safe home, I'm sure,' gasped the nurse.

'Of course not,' said Curdie.

'You dear, good, kind Curdie! I'll give you a kiss when we get home,' said the princess.

The nurse gave her a great pull by the hand she held. But at that instant the something in the middle of the way, which had looked like a great lump of earth brough down by the rain, began to move. One after another it shot out four long things, like two arms and two legs, but it was now too dark to tell what they were. The nurse began to tremble from head to foot. Irene clasped Curdie's hand yet faster, and Curdie began to sing again.

'One, two –
Hit and hew!

Three, four –
Blast and bore!
Five, six –
There's a fix!
Seven, eight,
Hold it straight.
Nine, ten –
Hit again!
Hurry! scurry!
Bother! smother!
There's a toad
In the road!
Smash it!
Squash it!
Fry it!
Dry it!
You're another!
Up and off!
There's enough! – Huuuuh!'

As he uttered the last words, Curdie let go his hold of his companion, and rushed at the thing in the road, as if he would trample it under his feet. It gave a great spring, and ran straight up one of the rocks like a huge spider. Curdie turned back laughing, and took Irene's hand again. She grasped his very tight, but said nothing till they had passed the rocks. A few yards more and she found herself on a part of the road she knew, and was able to speak again.

'Do you know, Curdie, I don't quite like your song: it sounds to me rather rude,' she said.

'Well, perhaps it is,' answered Curdie. 'I never thought of that; it's a way we have. We do it because they don't like it.'

'Who don't like it?'

'The cobs, as we call them.'

'Don't !' said the nurse.

'Why not?' said Curdie.

'I beg you won't. Please don't.'

'Oh! if you ask me that way, of course I won't; though I don't a bit know why. – Look! there are the lights of your great house down

below. You'll be at home in five minutes now.'

Nothing more happened. They reached home in safety. Nobody had missed them, or even known they had gone out; and they arrived at the door belonging to their part of the house without anyone seeing them. The nurse was rushing in with a hurried and not over-gracious good-night to Curdie; but the princess pulled her hand from hers, and was just throwing her arms round Curdie's neck, when she caught her again and dragged her away.

'Lootie! Lootie! I promised Curdie a kiss,' cried Irene.

'A princess mustn't give kisses. It's not at all proper,' said Lootie.

'But I promised,' said the princess.

'There's no occasion; he's only a miner-boy.'

'He's a good boy, and a brave boy, and he has been very kind to us. Lootie! Lootie! I *promised*.'

'Then you shouldn't have promised.'

'Lootie, I promised him a kiss.'

'Your royal Highness,' said Lootie, suddenly grown very respectful, 'must come in directly.'

'Nurse, a princess must *not* break her word,' said Irene, drawing herself up and standing stockstill.

Lootie did not know which the king might count the worst – to let the princess be out after sunset, or to let her kiss a miner-boy. She did not know that, being a gentleman, as many kings have been, he would have counted neither of them the worse. However much he might have disliked his daughter to kiss the miner-boy, he would not have had her break her word for all the goblins in creation. But, as I say, the nurse was not lady enough to understand this, and so she was in a great difficulty, for, if she insisted, someone might hear the princess cry and run to see, and then all would come out. But here Curdie came again to the rescue.

'Never mind, Princess Irene,' he said. 'You mustn't kiss me to-night. But you sha'n't break your word. I will come another time. You may be sure I will.'

'Oh, thank you, Curdie!' said the princess, and stopped crying.

'Good-night, Irene; good-night, Lootie,' said Curdie, and turned and was out of sight in a moment.

'I should like to see him!' muttered the nurse, as she carried the princess to the nursery.

'You *will* see him,' said Irene. 'You may be sure Curdie will keep his word. He's *sure* to come again.'

'I should like to see him!' repeated the nurse, and said no more. She did not want to open a new cause of strife with the princess by saying more plainly what she meant. Glad enough that she had succeeded both in getting home unseen, and in keeping the princess from kissing the miner's boy, she resolved to watch her far better in future. Her carelessness had already doubled the danger she was in. Formerly the goblins were her only fear: now she had to protect her charge from Curdie as well.

7   The Mines

Curdie went home whistling. He resolved to say nothing about the princess for fear of getting the nurse into trouble, for while he enjoyed teasing her because of her absurdity, he was careful not to do her any harm. He saw no more of the goblins, and was soon fast asleep in his bed.

He woke in the middle of the night, and thought he heard curious noises outside. He sat up and listened; then got up, and, opening the door very quietly, went out. When he peeped round the corner, he saw, under his own window, a group of stumpy creatures, whom he at once recognized by their shape. Hardly, however, had he begun his 'One, two, three!' when they broke asunder, scurried away, and were out of sight. He returned laughing, got into bed again, and was fast asleep in a moment.

Reflecting a little over the matter in the morning, he came to the conclusion that, as nothing of the kind had ever happened before, they must be annoyed with him for interfering to protect the princess. By the time he was dressed, however, he was thinking of something quite different, for he did not value the enmity of the goblins in the least.

As soon as they had had breakfast, he set off with his father for the mine.

They entered the hill by a natural opening under a huge rock, where a little stream rushed out. They followed its course for a few yards, when the passage took a turn, and sloped steeply into the heart of the hill. With many angles and windings and branchings off, and sometimes with steps where it came upon a natural gulf, it led them deep into the hill before they arrived at the place where they were at present digging out the precious ore. This was of various kinds, for the mountain was very rich in the better sorts of metals. With flint and steel, and tinder-box, they lighted their lamps, then fixed them on their heads, and were soon hard at work with their pickaxes and shovels and hammers. Father and son were at work near each other, but not in the same *gang* – the passages out of which the ore was dug, they called *gangs* – for when the *lode*, or vein of ore, was small, one miner would have to dig away alone in a passage no bigger than gave him just room to work – sometimes in uncomfortable cramped positions. If they stopped for a moment they could hear everywhere around them, some nearer, some farther off, the sounds of their companions burrowing away in all directions in the inside of the great mountain – some boring holes in the rock in order to blow it up with gunpowder, others shovelling the broken ore into baskets to be carried to the mouth of the mine, others hitting away with their pickaxes. Sometimes, if the miner was in a very lonely part, he would hear only a tap-tapping, no louder than that of a woodpecker, for the sound would come from a great distance off through the solid mountain-rock.

The work was hard at best, for it is very warm underground; but it was not particularly unpleasant, and some of the miners, when they

wanted to earn a little more money for a particular purpose, would stop behind the rest and work all night. But you could not tell night from day down there, except from feeling tired and sleepy; for no light of the sun ever came into those gloomy regions. Some who had thus remained behind during the night, although certain there were none of their companions at work, would declare the next morning that they heard, every time they halted for a moment to take breath, a tap-tapping all about them, as if the mountain were then more full of miners than ever it was during the day; and some in consequence would never stay over night, for all knew those were the sounds of the goblins. They worked only at night, for the miners' night was the goblins' day. Indeed, the greater number of the miners were afraid of the goblins; for there were strange stories well known amongst them of the treatment some had received whom the goblins had surprised at their work during the night. The more courageous of them, however, amongst them Peter Peterson and Curdie, who in this took after his father, had stayed in the mine all night again and again, and although they had several times encountered a few stray goblins, had never yet failed in driving them away. As I have indicated already, the chief defence against them was verse, for they hated verse of every kind, and some kinds they could not endure at all. I suspect they could not make any themselves, and that was why they disliked it so much. At all events, those who were most afraid of them were those who could neither make verses themselves, nor remember the verses that other people made for them; while those who were never afraid were those who could make verses for themselves; for although there were certain old rhymes which were very effectual, yet it was well known that a new rhyme, if of the right sort, was even more distasteful to them, and therefore more effectual in putting them to flight.

Perhaps my readers may be wondering what the goblins could be about, working all night long, seeing they never carried up the ore and sold it; but when I have informed them concerning what Curdie learned the very next night, they will be able to understand.

For Curdie had determined, if his father would permit him, to remain there alone this night – and that for two reasons: first, he wanted to get extra wages that he might buy a very warm red petticoat for his mother, who had begun to complain of the cold of the mountain air sooner than usual this autumn; and second, he had just a faint hope of finding out what the goblins were about under his window the night before.

When he told his father, he made no objection, for he had great confidence in his boy's courage and resources.

'I'm sorry I can't stay with you,' said Peter; 'but I want to go and pay the parson a visit this evening, and besides I've had a bit of a headache all day.'

'I'm sorry for that, father,' said Curdie.

'Oh! it's not much. You'll be sure to take care of yourself, won't you?'

'Yes, father; I will. I'll keep a sharp lookout, I promise you.'

Curdie was the only one who remained in the mine. About six o'clock the rest went away, everyone bidding him good-night, and telling him to take care of himself; for he was a great favourite with them all.

'Don't forget your rhymes,' said one.

'No, no,' answered Curdie.

'It's no matter if he does,' said another, 'for he'll only have to make a new one.'

'Yes; but he mightn't be able to make it fast enough,' said another; 'and while it was cooking in his head, they might take a mean advantage and set upon him.'

'I'll do my best,' said Curdie. 'I'm not afraid.'

'We all know that,' they returned and left him.

8   The Goblins

For some time Curdie worked away briskly, throwing all the ore he had disengaged on one side behind him, to be ready for carrying out in the morning. He heard a good deal of goblin-tapping, but it all sounded far away in the hill, and he paid it little heed. Towards midnight he began to feel rather hungry; so he dropped his pickaxe, got out a lump of bread which in the morning he had laid in a damp hole in the rock, sat down on a heap of ore and ate his supper. Then he leaned back for five minutes' rest before beginning his work again, and laid his head against the rock. He had not kept the position for one minute before he heard something which made him sharpen his ears. It sounded like a voice inside the rock. After a while he heard it again. It was a goblin-voice – there could be no doubt about that – and this time he could make out the words.

'Hadn't we better be moving?' it said.

A rougher and deeper voice replied –

'There's no hurry. That wretched little mole won't be through to-night, if he work ever so hard. He's not by any means at the thinnest place.'

'But you still think the lode does come through into our house?' said the first voice.

'Yes, but a good bit farther on than he has got to yet. If he had struck a stroke more to the side just here,' said the goblin, tapping the very stone, as it seemed to Curdie, against which his head lay, 'he would have been through; but he's a couple of yards past it now, and if he follow the lode it will be a week before it leads him in. You see it back there – a long way. Still, perhaps, in case of accident, it would be as well to be getting out of this. Helfer, you'll take the great chest. That's your business, you know.'

'Yes, dad,' said a third voice. 'But you must help me to get it on my back. It's awfully heavy, you know.'

'Well, it isn't just a bag of smoke, I admit. But you're as strong as a mountain, Helfer.'

'You say so, dad. I think myself I'm all right. But I could carry ten times as much if it wasn't for my feet.'

'That *is* your weak point, I confess, my boy.'

'Ain't it yours too, father?'

'Well, to be honest, it is a goblin-weakness. Why *they* come so soft, I declare I haven't an idea.'

'Specially when your head's so hard, you know, father.'

'Yes, my boy. The goblin's glory is his head. To think how the fellows up above there have to put on helmets and things when they go fighting! Ha! ha!'

'But why don't we wear shoes like them, father? I should like it – especially when I've got a chest like that on my head.'

'Well, you see, it's not the fashion. The king never wears shoes.'

'The queen does.'

'Yes; but that's for distinction. The first queen, you see – I mean

the king's first wife – wore shoes of course, because she came from upstairs; and so, when she died, the next queen would not be inferior to her as she called it, and would wear shoes too. It was all pride. She is the hardest in forbidding them to the rest of the women.'

'I'm sure I wouldn't wear them – no, not for – that I wouldn't!' said the first voice, which was evidently that of the mother of the family. 'I can't think why either of them should.'

'Didn't I tell you the first was from upstairs?' said the other. 'That was the only silly thing I ever knew his majesty guilty of. Why should he marry an outlandish woman like that – one of our natural enemies too?'

'I suppose he fell in love with her.'

'Pooh! pooh! He's just as happy now with one of his own people.'

'Did she die *very* soon? They didn't tease her to death, did they?'

'Oh dear no! The king worshipped her very footmarks.'

'What made her die, then? Didn't the air agree with her?'

'She died when the young prince was born.'

'How silly of her! *We* never do that. It must have been because she wore shoes.'

'I don't know that.'

'Why do they wear shoes up there?'

'Ah! now that's a sensible question, and I will answer it. But in order to do so, I must first tell you a secret. I once saw the queen's feet.'

'Without her shoes?'

'Yes – without her shoes.'

'No! Did you? How was it?'

'Never you mind how it was. *She* didn't know I saw them. And what do you think! – they had *toes*!'

'Toes! What's that?'

'You may well ask! I should never have known if I had not seen the queen's feet. Just imagine! the ends of her feet were split up into five or six thin pieces!'

'Oh, horrid! How *could* the king have fallen in love with her?'

'You forget that she wore shoes. That is just why she wore them. That is why all the men, and women too, upstairs wear shoes. They can't bear the sight of their own feet without them.'

'Ah! now I understand. If ever you wish for shoes again, Helfer, I'll hit your feet – I will.'

'No, no, mother; pray don't.'

'Then don't you.'

'But with such a big box on my head——'

A horrid scream followed, which Curdie interpreted as in reply to a blow from his mother upon the feet of her eldest goblin.

'Well, I never knew so much before!' remarked a fourth voice.

'Your knowledge is not universal quite yet,' said the father. 'You were only fifty last month. Mind you see to the bed and bedding. As soon as we've finished our supper, we'll be up and going. Ha! ha! ha!'

'What are you laughing at, husband?'

'I'm laughing to think what a mess the miners will find themselves in – somewhere before this day ten years.'

'Why, what do you mean?'

'Oh, nothing.'

'Oh yes, you do mean something. You always do mean something.'

'It's more than you do, then, wife.'

'That may be; but it's not more than I find out, you know.'

'Ha! ha! You're a sharp one. What a mother you've got, Helfer!'

'Yes, father.'

'Well, I suppose I must tell you. They're all at the palace consulting about it to-night; and as soon as we've got away from this thin place, I'm going there to hear what night they fix upon. I should like to see that young ruffian there on the other side, struggling in the agonies of——'

He dropped his voice so low that Curdie could hear only a growl. The growl went on in the low bass for a good while, as inarticulate as if the goblin's tongue had been a sausage; and it was not until his wife spoke again that it rose to its former pitch.

'But what shall we do when you are at the palace?' she asked.

'I will see you safe in the new house I've been digging for you for the last two months. Podge, you mind the table and chairs. I commit them to your care. The table has seven legs – each chair three. I shall require them all at your hands.'

After this arose a confused conversation about the various household goods and their transport; and Curdie heard nothing more that was of any importance.

He now knew at least one of the reasons for the constant sound of the goblin hammers and pickaxes at night. They were making new houses for themselves, to which they might retreat when the miners should threaten to break into their dwellings. But he had learned two things of far greater importance. The first was, that some grievous calamity was preparing, and almost ready to fall upon the heads of the miners; the second was – the one weak point of a goblin's body: he had not known that their feet were so tender as he had now reason to suspect. He had heard it said that they had no toes: he had never had opportunity of inspecting them closely enough in the dusk in which they always appeared, to satisfy himself whether it was a correct report. Indeed, he had not been able even to satisfy himself as to whether they had no fingers, although that also was commonly said to be the fact. One of the miners, indeed, who had had more schooling than the rest, was wont to argue that such must have been the primordial condition of humanity, and that education and handicraft had developed both toes and fingers – with which proposition Curdie had once heard his father sarcastically agree, alleging in support of it the probability that babies' gloves were a traditional remnant of the old state of things; while the stockings of all ages, no regard being paid in them to the toes, pointed in the same direction. But what was of importance was the fact concerning the softness of the goblin-feet, which he foresaw might be useful to all miners. What he had to do in the meantime, however, was to discover, if possible, the special evil design the goblins had now in their heads.

Although he knew all the gangs and all the natural galleries with which they communicated in the mined part of the mountain, he had not the least idea where the palace of the king of the gnomes was; otherwise he would have set out at once on the enterprise of discovering what the said design was. He judged, and rightly, that it must lie in a farther part of the mountain, between which and the mine there was as yet no communication. There must be one nearly completed, however; for it could be but a thin partition which now separated them. If only he could get through in time to follow the goblins as they retreated! A few blows would doubtless be sufficient – just where his ear now lay; but if he attempted to strike there with his pickaxe, he would only hasten the departure of the family, put them on their guard, and perhaps lose their involuntary guidance. He therefore began to feel the wall with his hands, and soon found that some of the stones were loose enough to be drawn out with little noise.

Laying hold of a large one with both his hands, he drew it gently out, and let it down softly.

'What was that noise?' said the goblin-father.

Curdie blew out his light, lest it should shine through.

'It must be that one miner that stayed behind the rest,' said the mother.

'No; he's been gone a good while. I haven't heard a blow for an hour. Besides, it wasn't like that.'

'Then I suppose it must have been a stone carried down the brook inside.'

'Perhaps. It will have more room by and by.'

Curdie kept quite still. After a little while, hearing nothing but the sounds of their preparations for departure, mingled with an occasional word of direction, and anxious to know whether the removal of the stone had made an opening into the goblins' house, he put in his hand to feel. It went in a good way, and then came in contact with something soft. He had but a moment to feel it over, it was so quickly withdrawn: it was one of the toeless goblin-feet. The owner of it gave a cry of fright.

'What's the matter, Helfer?' asked his mother.

'A beast came out of the wall and licked my foot.'

'Nonsense! There are no wild beasts in our country,' said his father.

'But it was, father. I felt it.'

'Nonsense, I say. Will you malign your native realms and reduce them to a level with the country upstairs? That is swarming with wild beasts of every description.'

'But I did feel it, father.'

'I tell you to hold your tongue. You are no patriot.'

Curdie suppressed his laughter, and lay still as a mouse – but no stiller, for every moment he kept nibbling away with his fingers at the edges of the hole. He was slowly making it bigger, for here the rock had been very much shattered with the blasting.

There seemed to be a good many in the family, to judge from the mass of confused talk which now and then came through the hole; but when all were speaking together, and just as if they had bottle-brushes – each at least one – in their throats, it was not easy to make out much that was said. At length he heard once more what the father-goblin was saying.

'Now then,' he said, 'get your bundles on your backs. Here, Helfer, I'll help you up with your chest.'

'I wish it *was* my chest, father.'

'Your turn will come in good time enough! Make haste. I *must* go to the meeting at the palace to-night. When that's over, we can come back and clear out the last of the things before our enemies return in the morning. Now light your torches, and come along. What a distinction it is to provide our own light, instead of being dependent on a thing hung up in the air – a most disagreeable contrivance – intended no doubt to blind us when we venture out under its baleful influence! Quite glaring and vulgar, I call it, though no doubt useful to poor creatures who haven't the wit to make light for themselves!'

Curdie could hardly keep himself from calling through to know whether they made the fire to light their torches by. But a moment's reflection showed him that they would have said they did, inasmuch as they struck two stones together, and the fire came.

9   The Hall of the Goblin Palace

A sound of many soft feet followed, but soon ceased. Then Curdie flew at the hole like a tiger, and tore and pulled. The sides gave way, and it was soon large enough for him to crawl through. He would not betray himself by rekindling his lamp, but the torches of the retreating company, which he found departing in a straight line up a long avenue from the door of their cave, threw back light enough to afford him a glance round the deserted home of the goblins. To his surprise, he could discover nothing to distinguish it from an ordinary natural cave in the rock, upon many of which he had come with the rest of the miners in the progress of their excavations. The goblins had talked of coming back for the rest of their household gear: he saw nothing that would have made him suspect a family had taken shelter there for a single night. The floor was rough and stony; the walls full of projecting corners; the roof in one place twenty feet high, in another endangering his forehead; while on one side a stream, no thicker than a needle, it is true, but still sufficient to spread a wide dampness over the wall, flowed down the face of the rock. But the troop in front of him was toiling under heavy burthens. He could distinguish Helfer now and then, in the flickering light and shade, with his heavy chest on his bending shoulders; while the second brother was almost buried in what looked like a great feather bed. 'Where do they get the feathers?' thought Curdie; but in a moment the troop disappeared at a turn of the way, and it was now both safe and necessary for Curdie to follow them, lest they should be round the next turning before he saw them again, for so he might lose them altogether. He darted after them like a greyhound. When he reached the corner and looked cautiously round, he saw them again at some distance down another long passage. None of the galleries he saw that night bore signs of the work of man – or of

goblin either. Stalactites far older than the mines, hung from their roofs; and their floors were rough with boulders and large round stones, showing that there water must have once run. He waited again at this corner till they had disappeared round the next, and so followed them a long way through one passage after another. The passages grew more and more lofty, and were more and more covered in the roof with shining stalactites.

It was a strange enough procession which he followed. But the strangest part of it was the household animals which crowded amongst the feet of the goblins. It was true they had no wild animals down there – at least they did not know of any; but they had a wonderful number of tame ones. I must, however, reserve any contributions towards the natural history of these for a later position in my story.

At length, turning a corner too abruptly, he had almost rushed into the middle of the goblin family; for there they had already set down all their burthens on the floor of a cave considerably larger than that which they had left. They were as yet too breathless to speak, else he would have had warning of their arrest. He started back, however, before anyone saw him, and retreating a good way, stood watching till

the father should come out to go to the palace. Before very long, both
he and his son Helfer appeared and kept on in the same direction as
before, while Curdie followed them again with renewed precaution.
For a long time he heard no sound except something like the rush of a
river inside the rock; but at length what seemed the far-off noise of a
great shouting reached his ears, which however presently ceased. After
advancing a good way farther, he thought he heard a single voice. It
sounded clearer and clearer as he went on, until at last he could almost
distinguish the words. In a moment or two, keeping after the goblins
round another corner, he once more started back – this time in
amazement.

He was at the entrance of a magnificent cavern, of an oval shape,
once probably a huge natural reservoir of water, now the great palace
hall of the goblins. It rose to a tremendous height, but the roof was
composed of such shining materials, and the multitude of torches
carried by the goblins who crowded the floor lighted up the place so
brilliantly, that Curdie could see to the top quite well. But he had no
idea how immense the place was, until his eyes had got accustomed to
it, which was not for a good many minutes. The rough projections on
the walls, and the shadows thrown upwards from them by the torches,
made the sides of the chamber look as if they were crowded with
statues upon brackets and pedestals, reaching in irregular tiers from
floor to roof. The walls themselves were, in many parts, of gloriously
shining substances, some of them gorgeously coloured besides, which
powerfully contrasted with the shadows. Curdie could not help
wondering whether his rhymes would be of any use against such a
multitude of goblins as filled the floor of the hall, and indeed felt
considerably tempted to begin his shout of *One, two, three!* but as there
was no reason for routing them, and much for endeavouring to
discover their designs, he kept himself perfectly quiet, and peeping
round the edge of the doorway, listened with both his sharp ears.

At the other end of the hall, high above the heads of the multitude,
was a terrace-like ledge of considerable height, caused by the receding
of the upper part of the cavern wall. Upon this sat the king and his
court, the king on a throne hollowed out of a huge block of green
copper ore, and his court upon lower seats around it. The king had
been making them a speech, and the applause which followed it was
what Curdie had heard. One of the court was now addressing the

multitude. What he heard him say was to the following effect:–

'Hence it appears that two plans have been for some time together working in the strong head of his majesty for the deliverance of his people. Regardless of the fact that we were the first possessors of the regions they now inhabit, regardless equally of the fact that we abandoned that region from the loftiest motives; regardless also of the self-evident fact that we excel them so far in mental ability as they excel us in stature, they look upon us as a degraded race, and make a mockery of all our finer feelings. But that time has almost arrived when – thanks to his majesty's inventive genius – it will be in our power to take a thorough revenge upon them once and for all, in respect of their unfriendly behaviour.'

'May it please your majesty –' cried a voice close by the door, which Curdie recognized as that of the goblin he had followed.

'Who is he that interrupts the Chancellor?' cried another from near the throne.

'Glump,' answered several voices.

'He is our trusty subject,' said the king himself, in a slow and stately voice: 'let him come forward and speak.'

A lane was parted through the crowd, and Glump having ascended the platform and bowed to the king, spoke as follows:–

'Sire, I would have held my peace, had I not known that I only knew how near was the moment to which the Chancellor had just referred. In all probability, before another day is past, the enemy will have broken through into my house – the partition between being even now not more than a foot in thickness.'

'Not quite so much,' thought Curdie to himself.

'This very evening I have had to remove my household effects; therefore the sooner we are ready to carry out the plan, for the execution of which his majesty has been making such magnificent preparations, the better. I may just add, that within the last few days I have perceived a small outbreak in my dining-room, which, combined with observations upon the course of the river escaping where the evil men enter, has convinced me that close to the spot must lie a deep gulf in its channel. This discovery will, I trust, add considerably to the otherwise immense forces at his majesty's disposal.'

He ceased, and the king graciously acknowledged his speech with a bend of his head; whereupon, Glump, after a bow to his majesty, slid down amongst the rest of the undistinguished multitude. Then the Chancellor rose and resumed.

'The information which the worthy Glump has given us,' he said, 'might have been of considerable import at the present moment, but for that other design already referred to, which naturally takes precedence. His majesty, unwilling to proceed to extremities, and well aware that such measures sooner or later result in violent reactions, has excogitated a more fundamental and comprehensive measure, of which I need say no more. Should his majesty be successful – as who dares to doubt? – then a peace, all to the advantage of the goblin kingdom, will be established for a generation at least, rendered absolutely secure by the pledge which his royal highness the prince will have and hold for the good behaviour of her relatives. Should his majesty fail – which who shall dare even to imagine in his most secret thoughts? – then will be the time for carrying out with rigour the design to which Glump referred, and for which our preparations are even now all but completed. The failure of the former will render the latter imperative.'

Curdie perceiving that the assembly was drawing to a close, and that there was little chance of either plan being more fully discovered, now thought it prudent to make his escape before the goblins began to disperse, and slipped quietly away.

There was not much danger of meeting any goblins, for all the men at least were left behind him in the palace; but there was considerable danger of his taking a wrong turning, for he had now no light, and had therefore to depend upon his memory and his hands. After he had left behind him the glow that issued from the door of Glump's new abode, he was utterly without guide, so far as his eyes were concerned.

He was most anxious to get back through the hole before the goblins should return to fetch the remains of their furniture. It was not that he was in the least afraid of them, but, as it was of the utmost importance that he should thoroughly discover what the plans they were cherishing were, he must not occasion the slightest suspicion that they were watched by a miner.

He hurried on, feeling his way along the walls of rock. Had he not been very courageous, he must have been very anxious, for he could not but know that if he lost his way it would be the most difficult thing in the world to find it again. Morning would bring no light into these regions; and towards him least of all, who was known as a special rhymster and persecutor, could goblins be expected to exercise courtesy. Well might he wish that he had brought his lamp and tinder-box with him, of which he had not thought when he crept so eagerly after the goblins! He wished it all the more when, after a while, he found his way blocked up, and could get no farther. It was of no use to turn back for he had not the least idea where he had begun to go wrong. Mechanically, however, he kept feeling about the walls that hemmed him in. His hand came upon a place where a tiny stream of water was running down the face of the rock. 'What a stupid I am!' he said to himself. 'I am actually at the end of my journey! – And there are the goblins coming back to fetch their things!' he added, as the red glimmer of their torches appeared at the end of the long avenue that led up to the cave. In a moment he had thrown himself on the floor, and wriggled backwards through the hole. The floor on the other side was several feet lower, which made it easier to get back. It was all he could do to lift the largest stone he had taken out of the hole, but he did manage to shove it in again. He sat down on the ore-heap and thought.

He was pretty sure that the latter plan of the goblins was to inundate the mine by breaking outlets for the water accumulated in the natural reservoirs of the mountain, as well as running through portions of it. While the part hollowed by the miners remained shut off from that inhabited by the goblins, they had had no opportunity of injuring them thus; but now that a passage was broken through, and the goblins' part proved the higher in the mountain, it was clear to Curdie that the mine could be destroyed in an hour. Water was always the chief danger to which the miners were exposed. They met with a little chokedamp sometimes, but never with the explosive firedamp so common in coal mines. Hence they were careful as soon as they saw any appearance of water.

As the result of his reflections while the goblins were busy in their old home, it seemed to Curdie that it would be best to build up the whole of this gang, filling it with stone, and clay or lime, so that there should be no smallest channel for the water to get into. There was not, however, any immediate danger, for the execution of the goblins' plan was contingent upon the failure of that unknown design which was to take precedence of it; and he was most anxious to keep the door of communication open, that he might if possible discover what that former plan was. At the same time they could not resume their intermitted labours for the inundation without his finding it out; when by putting all hands to the work, the one existing outlet might in a single night be rendered impenetrable to any weight of water; for by filling the gang entirely up, their embankment would be buttressed by the sides of the mountain itself.

As soon as he found that the goblins had again retired, he lighted his lamp, and proceeded to fill the hole he had made, with such stones as he could withdraw when he pleased. He then thought it better, as he might have occasion to be up a good many nights after this, to go home and have some sleep.

How pleasant the night air felt upon the outside of the mountain after what he had gone through in the inside of it! He hurried up the hill, without meeting a single goblin on the way, and called and tapped at the window until he woke his father, who soon rose and let him in. He told him the whole story, and, just as he had expected, his father thought it best to work that lode no farther, but at the same time to pretend occasionally to be at work there still, in order that the goblins might have no suspicions. Both father and son went then to bed, and slept soundly until the morning.

10 The Princess's King-Papa

The weather continued fine for weeks, and the little princess went out every day. So long a period of fine weather had indeed never been known upon that mountain. The only uncomfortable thing was that her nurse was so nervous and particular about being in before the sun was down, that often she would take to her heels when nothing worse than a fleecy cloud crossing the sun threw a shadow on the hillside; and many an evening they were home a full hour before the sunlight had left the weathercock on the stables. If it had not been for such odd behaviour, Irene would by this time have almost forgotten the goblins. She never forgot Curdie, but him she remembered for his own sake, and indeed would have remembered him if only because a princess never forgets her debts until they are paid.

One splendid sunshiny day, about an hour after noon, Irene, who was playing on a lawn in the garden, heard the distant blast of a bugle. She jumped up with a cry of joy, for she knew by that particular blast that her father was on his way to see her. This part of the garden lay on the slope of the hill, and allowed a full view of the country below. So she shaded her eyes with her hand, and looked far away to catch the first glimpse of shining armour. In a few moments a little troop came glittering round the shoulder of a hill. Spears and helmets were sparkling and gleaming, banners were flying, horses prancing, and again came the bugle-blast, which was to her like the voice of her father calling across the distance, 'Irene, I'm coming'. On and on they came, until she could clearly distinguish the king. He rode a white horse, and was taller than any of the men with him. He wore a narrow circle of gold set with jewels around his helmet, and as he came still nearer, Irene could discern the flashing of the stones in the sun. It was a long time since he had been to see her, and her little heart beat faster and faster as the shining troop approached, for she loved her king-papa very dearly, and was nowhere so happy as in his arms. When they reached a certain point, after which she could see them no more from the garden, she ran to the gate, and there stood till up they came clanging and stamping, with one more bright bugle-blast which said 'Irene, I am come'.

By this time the people of the house were all gathered at the gate, but Irene stood alone in front of them. When the horsemen pulled up, she ran to the side of the white horse, and held up her arms. The king stooped, and took her hands. In an instant she was on the saddle, and clasped in his great strong arms. I wish I could describe the king so that you could see him in your mind. He had gentle blue eyes, but a nose that made him look like an eagle. A long dark beard, streaked with silvery lines, flowed from his mouth almost to his waist, and as Irene sat on the saddle and hid her glad face upon his bosom, it mingled with the golden hair which her mother had given her, and the two together were like a cloud with streaks of the sun woven through it. After he had held her to his heart for a minute, he spoke to his white horse, and the

great beautiful creature, which had been prancing so proudly a little
while before, walked as gently as a lady – for he knew he had a little
lady on his back – through the gate and up to the door of the house.
Then the king set her on the ground, and dismounting, took her hand
and walked with her into the great hall, which was hardly ever entered
except when he came to see his little princess. There he sat down with
two of his councillors who had accompanied him, to have some
refreshment, and Irene sat on his right hand, and drank her milk out of
a wooden bowl, curiously carved.

After the king had eaten and drunk, he turned to the princess and
said, stroking her hair –

'Now, my child, what shall we do next?'

This was the question he almost always put to her first after their
meal together; and Irene had been waiting for it with some impatience,
for now, she thought, she should be able to settle a question which
constantly perplexed her.

'I should like you to take me to see my great old grandmother.'

The king looked grave, and said –

'What does my little daughter mean?'

'I mean the Queen Irene that lives up in the tower – the very old lady, you know, with the long hair of silver.'

The king only gazed at his little princess with a look which she could not understand.

'She's got her crown in her bedroom,' she went on; 'but I've not been in there yet. You know she's here, don't you?'

'No,' said the king, very quietly.

'Then it must be all a dream,' said Irene. 'I half thought it was; but I couldn't be sure. Now I *am* sure of it. Besides, I couldn't find her the next time I went up.'

At that moment a snow-white pigeon flew in at an open window and settled upon Irene's head. She broke into a merry laugh, cowered a little, and put up her hands to her head, saying –

'Dear dovey, don't peck me. You'll pull out my hair with your long claws if you don't mind.'

The king stretched out his hand to take the pigeon, but it spread its wings and flew again through the open window, when its whiteness made one flash in the sun and vanished. The king laid his hand on his princess's head, held it back a little, gazed in her face, smiled half a smile, and sighed half a sigh.

'Come, my child; we'll have a walk in the garden together,' he said.

'You won't come up and see my huge, great beautiful grand-mother, then, king-papa?' said the princess.

'Not this time,' said the king very gently. 'She has not invited me, you know, and great old ladies like her do not choose to be visited without leave asked and given.'

The garden was a very lovely place. Being upon a mountain side there were parts in it where the rocks came through in great masses, and all immediately about them remained quite wild. Tufts of heather grew upon them, and other hardy mountain plants and flowers, while near them would be lovely roses and lilies, and all pleasant garden flowers. This mingling of the wild mountain with the civilized garden was very quaint, and it was impossible for any number of gardeners to make such a garden look formal and stiff.

Against one of these rocks was a garden-seat, shadowed from the afternoon sun by the overhanging of the rock itself. There was a little winding path up to the top of the rock, and on the top another seat; but they sat on the seat at its foot, because the sun was hot; and there they talked together of many things. At length the king said –

'You were out late one evening, Irene.'

'Yes, papa. It was my fault; and Lootie was very sorry,'

'I must talk to Lootie about it,' said the king.

'Don't speak loud to her, please, papa,' said Irene. 'She's been so afraid of being late ever since! Indeed she has not been naughty. It was only a mistake for once.'

'Once might be too often,' murmured the king to himself, as he stroked his child's head.

I cannot tell you how he had come to know. I am sure Curdie had not told him. Someone about the palace must have seen them, after all. He sat for a good while thinking. There was no sound to be heard except that of a little stream which ran merrily out of an opening in the rock by where they sat, and sped away down the hill through the garden. Then he rose, and leaving Irene where she was, went into the house and sent for Lootie, with whom he had a talk that made her cry.

When in the evening he rode away upon his great white horse, he left six of his attendants behind him, with orders that three of them should watch outside the house every night, walking round and round it from sunset to sunrise. It was clear he was not quite comfortable about the princess.

11   The Old Lady's Bedroom

Nothing more happened worth telling for some time. The autumn came and went by. There were no more flowers in the garden. The wind blew strong, and howled among the rocks. The rain fell, and drenched the few yellow and red leaves that could not get off the bare branches. Again and again there would be a glorious morning followed by a pouring afternoon, and sometimes, for a week together, there would be rain, nothing but rain, all day, and then the most lovely cloudless night, with the sky all out in full-blown stars – not one missing. But the princess could not see much of them, for she went to bed early. The winter drew on, and she found things growing dreary. When it was too stormy to go out, and she had got tired of her toys, Lootie would take her about the house, sometimes to the housekeeper's room, where the housekeeper, who was a good, kind old woman, made much of her – sometimes to the servants' hall or the kitchen, where she was not princess merely, but absolute queen, and ran a great risk of being spoiled. Sometimes she would run off herself to the room where the men-at-arms whom the king had left, sat, and they showed her their arms and accoutrements, and did what they could to amuse her. Still at times she found it very dreary, and often and often wished that her huge great grandmother had not been a dream.

One morning the nurse left her with the housekeeper for a while. To amuse her, she turned out the contents of an old cabinet upon the table. The little princess found her treasures, queer ancient orna- ments, and many things the uses of which she could not imagine, far more interesting than her own toys, and sat playing with them for two hours or more. But at length, in handling a curious old-fashioned brooch, she ran the pin of it into her thumb, and gave a little scream with the sharpness of the pain, but would have thought little more of it, had not the pain increased and her thumb begun to swell. This alarmed the housekeeper greatly. The nurse was fetched; the doctor was sent for; her hand was poulticed, and long before her usual time she was put to bed. The pain still continued, and although she fell asleep and dreamed a good many dreams, there was the pain always in every dream. At last it woke her up.

The moon was shining brightly into the room. The poultice had fallen off her hand, and it was burning hot. She fancied if she could hold it into the moonlight, that would cool it. So she got out of bed, without waking the nurse who lay at the other end of the room, and went to the window. When she looked out, she saw one of the men-at-arms walking in the garden, with the moonlight glancing on his armour. She was just going to tap on the window and call him, for she wanted to tell him all about it, when she bethought herself that that might wake Lootie, and she would put her into her bed again. So she resolved to go to the window of another room, and call him from there. It was so much nicer to have somebody to talk to than to lie awake in bed with the burning pain in her hand. She opened the door very gently and went through the nursery, which did not look into the garden, to go to the other window. But when she came to the foot of the old staircase, there was the moon shining down from some window high up, and making the worm-eaten oak look very strange and delicate and lovely. In a moment she was putting her little feet one after the other in the silvery path up the stair, looking behind as she went, to see the shadow they made in the middle of the silver. Some little girls would have been afraid to find themselves thus alone in the middle of the night, but Irene was a princess.

As she went slowly up the stair, not quite sure that she was not dreaming, suddenly a great longing woke up in her heart to try once more whether she could not find the old lady with the silvery hair.

'If she is a dream,' she said to herself, 'then I am the likelier to find her, if I am dreaming.'

So up and up she went, stair after stair, until she came to the many rooms – all just as she had seen them before. Through passage after passage she softly sped, comforting herself that if she should lose her way it would not matter much, because when she woke she would find herself in her own bed, with Lootie not far off. But as if she had known

every step of the way, she walked straight to the door at the foot of the narrow stair that led to the tower.

'What if I should realliality-really find my beautiful old grand-mother up there!' she said to herself, as she crept up the steep steps.

When she reached the top, she stood a moment listening in the dark, for there was no moon there. Yes! it was! it was the hum of the spinning-wheel! What a diligent grandmother to work both day and night!

She tapped gently at the door.

'Come in, Irene,' said the sweet voice.

The princess opened the door, and entered. There was the moonlight streaming in at the window, and in the middle of the moonlight sat the old lady in her black dress with the white lace, and her silvery hair mingling with the moonlight, so that you could not have told which was which.

'Come in, Irene,' she said again. 'Can you tell me what I am spinning?'

'She speaks,' thought Irene, 'just as if she had seen me five minutes ago, or yesterday at the farthest. – No,' she answered; 'I don't know what you are spinning. Please, I thought you were a dream. Why couldn't I find you before great-great-grandmother?'

'That you are hardly old enough to understand. But you would have found me sooner if you hadn't come to think I was a dream. I will give you one reason though why you couldn't find me. I didn't want you to find me.'

'Why, please?'

'Because I did not want Lootie to know I was here.'

'But you told me to tell Lootie.'

'Yes. But I knew Lootie would not believe you. If she were to see me sitting spinning here, she wouldn't believe me either.'

'Why?'

'Because she couldn't. She would rub her eyes, and go away and say she felt queer, and forget half of it and more, and then say it had been all a dream.'

'Just like me,' said Irene, feeling very much ashamed of herself.

'Yes, a good deal like you, but not just like you; for you've come again; and Lootie wouldn't have come again. She would have said, No, no – she had had enough of such nonsense.'

'Is it naughty of Lootie then?'

'It would be naughty of you. I've never done anything for Lootie.'

'And you did wash my face and hands for me,' said Irene, beginning to cry.

The old lady smiled a sweet smile and said –

'I'm not vexed with you, my child – nor with Lootie either. But I don't want you to say anything more to Lootie about me. If she should ask you, you must just be silent. But I do not think she will ask you.'

All the time they talked, the old lady kept on spinning.

'You haven't told me yet what I am spinning,' she said.

'Because I don't know. It's very pretty stuff.'

It was indeed very pretty stuff. There was a good bunch of it on the distaff attached to the spinning-wheel, and in the moonlight it shone like – what shall I say it was like? It was not white enough for silver – yes, it was like silver, but shone grey rather than white, and glittered only a little. And the thread the old lady drew out from it was so fine that Irene could hardly see it.

'I am spinning this for you, my child.'

'For me! What am I to do with it, please?'

'I will tell you by and by. But first I will tell you what it is. It is spider-webs – of a particular kind. My pigeons bring it me from over the great sea. There is only one forest where the spiders live who make this particular kind – the finest and strongest of any. I have nearly finished my present job. What is on the rock now will be enough. I have a week's work there yet, though,' she added, looking at the bunch.

'Do you work all day and all night too, great-great-great-great-grandmother?' said the princess, thinking to be very polite with so many *greats*.

'I am not quite so great as all that,' she answered, smiling almost merrily. 'If you call me grandmother, that will do. – No, I don't work every night – only moonlit nights, and then no longer than the moon shines upon my wheel. I sha'n't work much longer to-night.'

'And what will you do next, grandmother?'

'Go to bed. Would you like to see my bedroom?'

'Yes, that I should.'

'Then I think I won't work any longer to-night. I shall be in good time.'

The old lady rose, and left her wheel standing just as it was. You see there was no good in putting it away, for where there was not any furniture, there was no danger of being untidy.

Then she took Irene by the hand, but it was her bad hand, and Irene gave a little cry of pain.

'My child!' said her grandmother, 'what is the matter?'

Irene held her hand into the moonlight, that the old lady might see it, and told her all about it, at which she looked grave. But she only said – 'Give me your other hand;' and, having led her out upon the little dark landing, opened the door on the opposite side of it. What was Irene's surprise to see the loveliest room she had ever seen in her life! It was large and lofty, and dome-shaped. From the centre hung a lamp as round as a ball, shining as if with the brightest moonlight, which made everything visible in the room, though not so clearly that the princess could tell what many of the things were. A large oval bed stood in the middle, with a cover-lid of rose-colour, and velvet curtains all round it of a lovely pale blue. The walls were also blue – spangled all over with what looked like stars of silver.

The old lady left her, and going to a strange-looking cabinet, opened it and took out a curious silver casket. Then she sat down on a low chair, and calling Irene, made her kneel before her, while she looked at her hand. Having examined it, she opened the casket, and took from it a little ointment. The sweetest odour filled the room, like that of roses and lilies – as she rubbed the ointment gently all over the hot swollen hand. Her touch was so pleasant and cool, that it seemed to drive away the pain and heat wherever it came.

'Oh, grandmother! it is *so* nice!' said Irene. 'Thank you; thank you.'

Then the old lady went to a chest of drawers, and took out a large handkerchief of gossamer-like cambric, which she tied round her hand.

'I don't think I can let you go away to-night,' she said. 'Would you like to sleep with me?'

'Oh, yes, yes, dear grandmother!' said Irene, and would have clapped her hands, forgetting that she could not.

'You won't be afraid then to go to bed with such an old woman?'

'No. You are so beautiful, grandmother.'

'But I am *very* old.'

'And I suppose I am very young. You won't mind sleeping with such a *very* young woman, grandmother?'

'You sweet little pertness!' said the old lady, and drew her towards her, and kissed her on the forehead and the cheek and the mouth.

Then she got a large silver basin, and having poured some water into it, made Irene sit on the chair, and washed her feet. This done, she was ready for bed. And oh, what a delicious bed it was into which her grandmother laid her! She hardly could have told she was lying upon anything: she felt nothing but the softness. The old lady having undressed herself lay down beside her.

'Why don't you put out your moon?' asked the princess.

'That never goes out, night or day,' she answered. 'In the darkest night, if any of my pigeons are out on a message, they always see my moon, and know where to fly to.'

'But if somebody besides the pigeons were to see it – somebody about the house, I mean – they would come to look what it was, and find you.'

'The better for them then,' said the old lady. 'But it does not happen above five times in a hundred years that anyone does see it. The greater part of those who do, take it for a meteor, wink their eyes and forget it again. Besides, nobody could find the room except I pleased. Besides again – I will tell you a secret – if that light were to go out, you would fancy yourself lying in a bare garret, on a heap of old straw, and would not see one of the pleasant things round about you all the time.'

'I hope it will never go out,' said the princess.

'I hope not. But it is time we both went to sleep. Shall I take you in my arms?'

The little princess nestled close up to the old lady, who took her in both her arms, and held her close to her bosom.

'Oh dear! this is so nice!' said the princess. 'I didn't know anything in the whole world could be so comfortable. I should like to lie here for ever.'

'You may if you will,' said the old lady. 'But I must put you to one trial – not a *very* hard one, I hope. – This night week you must come back to me. If you don't, I do not know when you may find me again, and you will soon want me very much.'

'Oh! please, don't let me forget.'

'You shall not forget. The only question is whether you will believe I am anywhere – whether you will believe I am anything but a dream. You may be sure I will do all I can to help you to come. But it will rest with yourself after all. On the night of next Friday, you must come to me. Mind now.'

'I *will* try,' said the princess.

'Then good-night,' said the old lady, and kissed the forehead which lay in her bosom.

In a moment more the little princess was dreaming in the midst of the loveliest dreams – of summer seas and moonlight and mossy springs and great murmuring trees, and beds of wild flowers with such odours as she had never smelled before. But after all, no dream could be more lovely than what she had left behind when she fell asleep.

In the morning she found herself in her own bed. There was no handkerchief or anything else on her hand, only a sweet odour lingered about it. The swelling had all gone down; the prick of the brooch had vanished; – in fact her hand was perfectly well.

12   A Short Chapter about Curdie

Curdie spent many nights in the mine. His father and he had taken Mrs. Peterson into the secret, for they knew mother could hold her tongue, which was more than could be said of all the miners' wives. But Curdie did not tell her that every night he spent in the mine, part of it went in earning a new red petticoat for her.

Mrs. Peterson was such a nice good mother! All mothers are nice and good more or less, but Mrs. Peterson was nice and good all *more* and no *less*. She made and kept a little heaven in that poor cottage on the high hillside – for her husband and son to go home to out of the low and rather dreary earth in which they worked. I doubt if the princess was very much happier even in the arms of her huge great-grandmother than Peter and Curdie were in the arms of Mrs. Peterson. True, her hands were hard and chapped and large, but it was with work for them; and therefore in the sight of the angels, her hands were so much the more beautiful. And if Curdie worked hard to get her a petticoat, she worked hard every day to get him comforts which he would have missed much more than she would a new petticoat even in winter. Not that she and Curdie ever thought of how much they worked for each other: that would have spoiled everything.

When left alone in the mine, Curdie always worked on for an hour or two at first, following the lode which, according to Glump, would lead at last into the deserted habitation. After that, he would set out on a reconnoitring expedition. In order to manage this, or rather the return from it, better than the first time, he had bought a huge ball of fine string, having learned the trick from Hop-o'-my-Thumb, whose history his mother had often told him. Not that Hop-o'-my-Thumb had ever used a ball of string – I should be sorry to be supposed so far out in my classics – but the principle was the same as that of the pebbles. The end of this string he fastened to his pickaxe, which figured no bad anchor, and then, with the ball in his hand, unrolling it as he went, set out in the dark through the natural gangs of the goblins' territory. The first night or two he came upon nothing worth remembering; saw only a little of the home-life of the *cobs* in the various caves they called houses; failed in coming upon anything to cast light upon the foregoing design which kept the inundation for the present in the background. But at length, I think on the third or fourth night, he found, partly guided by the noise of their implements, a company of evidently the best sappers and miners amongst them, hard at work. What were they about? It could not well be the inundation, seeing that had in the meantime been postponed to something else. Then what was it? He lurked and watched, every now and then in the greatest risk of being detected, but without success. He had again and again to retreat in haste, a proceeding rendered the more difficult that he had to gather up his string as he returned upon its course. It was not that he was afraid of the goblins, but that he was afraid of their finding out that they were watched, which might have prevented the discovery at which he aimed. Sometimes his haste had to be such that, when he reached home towards morning, his string, for lack of time to wind it up as he 'dodged the cobs', would be in what seemed the most hopeless entanglement; but after a good sleep though a short one, he always found his mother had got it right again. There it was, wound in a most respectable ball, ready for use the moment he should want it!

'I can't think how you do it, mother,' he would say.

'I follow the thread,' she would answer – 'just as you do in the mine.'

She never had more to say about it; but the less clever she was with her words, the more clever she was with her hands; and the less his mother said, the more Curdie believed she had to say.

But still he had made no discovery as to what the goblin miners were about.

13 The Cobs' Creatures

About this time, the gentlemen whom the king had left behind him to watch over the princess, had each occasion to doubt the testimony of his own eyes, for more than strange were the objects to which they would bear witness. They were of one sort – creatures – but so grotesque and misshapen as to be more like a child's drawings upon his slate than anything natural. They saw them only at night, while on guard about the house. The testimony of the man who first reported having seen one of them was that, as he was walking slowly round the house, while yet in the shadow, he caught sight of a creature standing on its hind legs in the moonlight, with its fore feet upon a window ledge, staring in at the window. Its body might have been that of a dog or wolf – he thought, but he declared on his honour that its head was twice the size it ought to have been for the size of its body, and as round as a ball, while the face, which it turned upon him as it fled, was more like one carved upon the turnip inside which he is going to put a candle, than anything else he could think of. It rushed into the garden. He sent an arrow after it, and thought he must have struck it; for it gave an unearthly howl, and he could not find his arrow any more than the beast, although he searched all about the place where it vanished. They laughed at him until he was driven to hold his tongue; and said he must have taken too long a pull at the ale-jug. But before two nights were over, he had one to side with him; for he too had seen something strange, only quite different from that reported by the other. The description the second man gave of the creature he had seen, was yet more grotesque and unlikely. They were both laughed at by the rest; but night after night another came over to their side, until at last there was only one left to laugh at all his companions. Two nights more passed, and he saw nothing; but on the third, he came rushing from the

garden to the other two before the house, in such an agitation that they declared – for it was their turn now – that the band of his helmet was cracking under his chin with the rising of his hair inside it. Running with him into that part of the garden which I have already described, they saw a score of creatures, to not one of which they could give a name, and not one of which was like another, hideous and ludicrous at once, gambolling on the lawn in the moonlight. The supernatural or rather subnatural ugliness of their faces, the length of legs and necks in some, the apparent absence of both or either in others, made the spectators, although in one consent as to what they saw, yet doubtful, as I have said, of the evidence of their own eyes – and ears as well; for the noises they made, although not loud, were as uncouth and varied as their forms, and could be described neither as grunts nor squeaks nor roars nor howls nor barks nor yells nor screams nor croaks nor hisses nor mews nor shrieks, but only as something like all of them mingled in one horrible dissonance. Keeping in the shade, the watchers had a few moments to recover themselves before the hideous assembly suspected their presence; but all at once, as if by common consent, they

scampered off in the direction of a great rock, and vanished before the men had come to themselves sufficiently to think of following them.

My readers will suspect what these were; but I will now give them full information concerning them. They were of course household animals belonging to the goblins, whose ancestors had taken their ancestors many centuries before from the upper regions of light into the lower regions of darkness. The original stocks of these horrible creatures were very much the same as the animals now seen about farms and homes in the country, with the exception of a few of them, which had been wild creatures, such as foxes, and indeed wolves and small bears, which the goblins, from their proclivity towards the animal creation, had caught when cubs and tamed. But in the course of time, all had undergone even greater changes than had passed upon their owners. They had altered – that is, their descendants had altered – into such creatures as I have not attempted to describe except in the vaguest manner – the various parts of their bodies assuming, in an apparently arbitrary and self-willed manner, the most abnormal developments. Indeed, so little did any distinct type predominate in some of the bewildering results, that you could only have guessed at any known animal as the original, and even then, what likeness remained would be more one of general expression than of definable conformation. But what increased the gruesomeness tenfold, was that, from constant domestic, or indeed rather family association with the goblins, their countenances had grown in grotesque resemblance to the human. No one understands animals who does not see that every one of them, even amongst the fishes, it may be with a dimness and vagueness infinitely remote, yet shadows the human: in the case of these the human resemblance had greatly increased: while their owners had sunk towards them, they had risen towards their owners. But the conditions of subterranean life being equally unnatural for both, while the goblins were worse, the creatures had not improved by the approximation, and its result would have appeared far more ludicrous than consoling to the warmest lover of animal nature. I shall now explain how it was that just then these animals began to show themselves about the king's country house.

The goblins, as Curdie had discovered, were mining on – at work both day and night, in divisions, urging the scheme after which he lay in wait. In the course of their tunnelling, they had broken into the channel of a small stream, but the break being in the top of it, no water had escaped to interfere with their work. Some of the creatures, hovering as they often did about their masters, had found the hole, and had, with the curiosity which had grown to a passion from the restraints of their unnatural circumstances, proceeded to explore the channel. The stream was the same which ran out by the seat on which Irene and her king-papa had sat as I have told, and the goblin-creatures found it jolly fun to get out for a romp on a smooth lawn such as they had never seen in all their poor miserable lives. But although they had partaken enough of the nature of their owners to delight in annoying and alarming any of the people whom they met on the mountain, they were of course incapable of designs of their own, or of intentionally furthering those of their masters.

For several nights after the men-at-arms were at length of one mind as to the fact of the visits of some horrible creatures, whether bodily or spectral they could not yet say, they watched with special attention that part of the garden where they had last seen them. Perhaps indeed they gave in consequence too little attention to the house. But the creatures were too cunning to be easily caught; nor were the watchers quick-eyed enough to descry the head, or the keen eyes in it, which, from the opening whence the stream issued, would watch them in turn, ready, the moment they should leave the lawn, to report the place clear.

14   That Night Week

During the whole of the week, Irene had been thinking every other moment of her promise to the old lady, although even now she could not feel quite sure that she had not been dreaming. Could it really be that an old lady lived up in the top of the house, with pigeons and a spinning-wheel, and a lamp that never went out? She was, however, none the less determined, on the coming Friday, to ascend the three stairs, walk through the passages with the many doors, and try to find the tower in which she had either seen or dreamed her grandmother.

Her nurse could not help wondering what had come to the child – she would sit so thoughtfully silent, and even in the midst of a game with her, would so suddenly fall into a dreamy mood. But Irene took care to betray nothing, whatever efforts Lootie might make to get at her thoughts. And Lootie had to say to herself, 'What an odd child she is!' and give it up.

At length the longed-for Friday arrived, and lest Lootie should be moved to watch her, Irene endeavoured to keep herself as quiet as possible. In the afternoon she asked for her doll's house, and went on arranging and re-arranging the various rooms and their inhabitants for a whole hour. Then she gave a sigh and threw herself back in her chair. One of the dolls would not sit, and another would not stand, and they were all very tiresome. Indeed there was one would not even lie down, which was too bad. But it was now getting dark, and the darker it got the more excited Irene became, and the more she felt it necessary to be composed.

'I see you want your tea, princess,' said the nurse: 'I will go and get it. The room feels close: I will open the window a little. The evening is mild: it won't hurt you.'

'There's no fear of that, Lootie,' said Irene, wishing she had put off going for the tea till it was darker, when she might have made her attempt with every advantage.

I fancy Lootie was longer in returning than she had intended; for when Irene, who had been lost in thought, looked up, she saw it was nearly dark, and at the same moment caught sight of a pair of eyes, bright with a green light, glowering at her through the open window. The next instant, something leaped into the room. It was like a cat, with legs as long as a horse's, Irene said, but its body no bigger and its legs no thicker than those of a cat. She was too frightened to cry out, but not too frightened to jump from her chair and run from the room.

It is plain enough to every one of my readers what she ought to have done – and indeed Irene thought of it herself; but when she came to the foot of the old stair, just outside the nursery door, she imagined the creature running up those long ascents after her, and pursuing her through the dark passages – *which, after all, might lead to no tower!* That thought was too much. Her heart failed her, and turning from the stair, she rushed along to the hall, whence, finding the front-door open, she darted into the court, pursued – at least she thought so – by the creature. No one happening to see her, on she ran, unable to think for fear, and ready to run anywhere to elude the awful creature with the stilt-legs. Not daring to look behind her, she rushed straight out of the gate, and up the mountain. It was foolish indeed – thus to run farther and farther from all who could help her, as if she had been seeking a fit spot for the goblin-creature to eat her in at his leisure; but that is the way fear serves us: it always sides with the thing we are afraid of.

The princess was soon out of breath with running uphill; but she ran on, for she fancied the horrible creature just behind her, forgetting that, had it been after her, such legs as those must have overtaken her long ago. At last she could run no longer, and fell, unable even to scream, by the roadside, where she lay for some time, half-dead with terror. But finding nothing lay hold of her, and her breath beginning to come back, she ventured at length to get half up, and peer anxiously about her. It was now so dark that she could see nothing. Not a single star was out. She could not even tell in what direction the house lay, and between her and home she fancied the dreadful creature lying ready to pounce upon her. She saw now that she ought to have run up the stairs at once. It was well she did not scream; for, although very few of the goblins had come out for weeks, a stray idler or two might have heard her. She sat down upon a stone, and nobody but one who had done something wrong could have been more miserable. She had quite forgotten her promise to visit her grandmother. A raindrop fell on her face. She looked up, and for a moment her terror was lost in astonishment. At first she thought the rising moon had left her place, and drawn nigh to see what could be the matter with the little girl, sitting alone, without hat or cloak, on the dark bare mountain; but she soon saw she was mistaken, for there was no light on the ground at her feet, and no shadow anywhere. But a great silvery globe was hanging in the air; and as she gazed at the lovely thing, her courage revived. If she were but indoors again, she would fear nothing, not even the terrible creature with the long legs! But how was she to find her way back? What could that light be? Could it be——? No, it couldn't. But what if it should be – yes – it must be – her great-great-grandmother's lamp, which guided her pigeons home through the darkest night! She jumped up: she had but to keep that light in view, and she must find the house.

Her heart grew strong. Speedily, yet softly, she walked down the

hill, hoping to pass the watching creature unseen. Dark as it was, there was little danger now of choosing the wrong road. And – which was most strange – the light that filled her eyes from the lamp, instead of blinding them for a moment to the object upon which they next fell, enabled her for a moment to see it, despite the darkness. By looking at the lamp and then dropping her eyes, she could see the road for a yard or two in front of her, and this saved her from several falls, for the road was very rough. But all at once, to her dismay, it vanished, and the terror of the beast, which had left her the moment she began to return, again laid hold of her heart. The same instant, however, she caught the light of the windows, and knew exactly where she was. It was too dark to run, but she made what haste she could, and reached the gate in safety. She found the house-door still open, ran through the hall, and, without even looking into the nursery, bounded straight up the stair, and the next, and the next; then turning to the right, ran through the long avenue of silent rooms, and found her way at once to the door at the foot of the tower stair.

When first the nurse missed her, she fancied she was playing her a trick, and for some time took no trouble about her; but at last, getting frightened, she had begun to search; and when the princess entered, the whole household was hither and thither over the house, hunting for her. A few seconds after she reached the stair of the tower, they had even begun to search the neglected rooms, in which they would never have thought of looking had they not already searched every other place they could think of in vain. But by this time she was knocking at the old lady's door.

15 Woven and then Spun

'Come in, Irene,' said the silvery voice of her grandmother.

The princess opened the door, and peeped in. But the room was quite dark, and there was no sound of the spinning-wheel. She grew frightened once more, thinking that, although the room was there, the old lady might be a dream after all. Every little girl knows how dreadful it is to find a room empty where she thought somebody was; but Irene had to fancy for a moment that the person she came to find was nowhere at all. She remembered however that at night she spun only in the moonlight, and concluded that must be why there was no sweet, bee-like humming: the old lady might be somewhere in the darkness. Before she had time to think another thought, she heard her voice again, saying as before –

'Come in, Irene.'

From the sound, she understood at once that she was not in the room beside her. Perhaps she was in her bedroom. She turned across the passage, feeling her way to the other door. When her hand fell on the lock, again the old lady spoke –

'Shut the other door behind you, Irene. I always close the door of my workroom when I go to my chamber.'

Irene wondered to hear her voice so plainly through the door: having shut the other, she opened it and went in. Oh, what a lovely haven to reach from the darkness and fear through which she had come! The soft light made her feel as if she were going into the heart of the milkiest pearl; while the blue walls and their silver stars for a moment perplexed her with the fancy that they were in reality the sky which she had left outside a minute ago covered with rainclouds.

'I've lighted a fire for you, Irene: you're cold and wet,' said her grandmother.

Then Irene looked again, and saw that what she had taken for a huge bouquet of red roses on a low stand against the wall, was in fact a fire which burned in the shapes of the loveliest and reddest roses, glowing gorgeously between the heads and wings of two cherubs of shining silver. And when she came nearer, she found that the smell of roses with which the room was filled, came from the fire-roses on the hearth. Her grandmother was dressed in the loveliest pale-blue velvet, over which her hair, no longer white, but of a rich golden colour, streamed like a cataract, here falling in dull gathered heaps, there rushing away in smooth shining falls. And ever as she looked, the hair seemed pouring down from her head, and vanishing in a golden mist ere it reached the floor. It flowed from under the edge of a circle of shining silver, set with alternated pearls and opals. On her dress was no ornament whatever, neither was there a ring on her hand, or a necklace or carcanet about her neck. But her slippers glimmered with the light of the milky way, for they were covered with seed-pearls and opals in one mass. Her face was that of a woman of three-and-twenty.

The princess was so bewildered with astonishment and admiration that she could hardly thank her, and drew nigh with timidity, feeling dirty and uncomfortable. The lady was seated on a low chair by the side of the fire, with hands outstretched to take her, but the princess hung back with a troubled smile.

'Why, what's the matter?' asked her grandmother. 'You haven't been doing anything wrong – I know that by your face, though it *is* rather miserable. What's the matter, my dear?'

And she still held out her arms.

'Dear grandmother,' said Irene, 'I'm not so sure that I haven't done something wrong. I ought to have run up to you at once when the long-legged cat came in at the window, instead of running out on the mountain, and making myself such a fright.'

'You were taken by surprise, my child, and are not so likely to do it again. It is when people do wrong things wilfully that they are the more likely to do them again. Come.'

And still she held out her arms.

'But, grandmother, you're so beautiful and grand with your crown on! and I am so dirty with mud and rain ! – I should quite spoil your beautiful blue dress.'

With a merry little laugh, the lady sprung from her chair, more

lightly far than Irene herself could, caught the child to her bosom, and kissing the tear-stained face over and over, sat down with her in her lap.

'Oh, grandmother! you'll make yourself such a mess!' cried Irene, clinging to her.

'You darling! do you think I care more for my dress than for my little girl? Besides – look here.'

As she spoke she set her down, and Irene saw to her dismay that the lovely dress was covered with the mud of her fall on the mountain road. But the lady stooped to the fire, and taking from it, by the stalk in her fingers, one of the burning roses, passed it once and again and a third time over the front of her dress; and when Irene looked, not a single stain was to be discovered.

'There!' said her grandmother, 'you won't mind coming to me now?'

But Irene again hung back, eyeing the flaming rose which the lady held in her hand.

'You're not afraid of the rose – are you?' she said, about to throw it on the hearth again.

'Oh! don't, please!' cried Irene. 'Won't you hold it to my frock and my hands and my face? And I'm afraid my feet and my knees want it too!'

'No,' answered her grandmother, smiling a little sadly, as she threw the rose from her; 'it is too hot for you yet. It would set *your* frock in a flame. Besides, I don't want to make you clean to-night. I want your nurse and the rest of the people to see you as you are, for you will have to tell them how you ran away for fear of the long-legged cat. I should like to wash you, but they would not believe you then. Do you see that bath behind you?'

The princess looked, and saw a large oval tub of silver, shining brilliantly in the light of the wonderful lamp.

'Go and look into it,' said the lady.

Irene went, and came back very silent, with her eyes shining.

'What did you see?' asked her grandmother.

'The sky and the moon and the stars,' she answered. 'It looked as if there was no bottom to it.'

The lady smiled a pleased satisfied smile, and was silent also for a few moments. Then she said –

'Any time you want a bath, come to me. I know you have a bath every morning, but sometimes you want one at night too.'

'Thank you, grandmother; I will – I will indeed,' answered Irene, and was again silent for some moments thinking. Then she said, 'How was it, grandmother, that I saw your beautiful lamp – not the light of it only – but the great round silvery lamp itself, hanging alone in the great open air high up? It was your lamp I saw – wasn't it?'

'Yes, my child; it was my lamp.'

'Then how was it? I don't see a window all round.'

'When I please, I can make the lamp shine through the walls – shine so strong that it melts them away from before the sight, and shows itself as you saw it. But, as I told you, it is not everybody can see it.'

'How is it that I can then? I'm sure I don't know.'

'It is a gift born with you. And one day I hope everybody will have it.'

'But how do you make it shine through the walls?'

'Ah! that you would not understand if I were to try ever so much to make you – not yet – not yet. But,' added the lady rising, 'you must sit in my chair while I get you the present I have been preparing for you. I told you my spinning was for you. It is finished now, and I am going to fetch it. I have been keeping it warm under one of my brooding pigeons.'

Irene sat down in the low chair, and her grandmother left her, shutting the door behind her. The child sat gazing, now at the rose-fire, now at the starry walls, now at the silvery light; and a great quietness grew in her heart. If all the long-legged cats in the world had come rushing at her then, she would not have been afraid of them for a moment. How this was she could not tell; – she only knew there was no fear in her, and everything was so right and safe that it could not get in.

She had been gazing at the lovely lamp for some minutes fixedly: turning her eyes, she found the wall had vanished, for she was looking out on the dark cloudy night. But though she heard the wind blowing, none of it blew upon her. In a moment more, the clouds themselves parted, or rather vanished like the wall, and she looked straight into the starry herds, flashing gloriously in the dark blue. It was but for a moment. The clouds gathered again and shut out the stars; the wall gathered again and shut out the clouds; and there stood the lady beside her with the loveliest smile on her face, and a shimmering ball in her hand, about the size of a pigeon's egg.

'There, Irene; there is my work for you!' she said, holding out the ball to the princess.

She took it in her hand, and looked at it all over. It sparkled a little, and shone here and shone there, but not much. It was of a sort of grey whiteness, something like spun glass.

'Is this *all* your spinning, grandmother?' she asked.

'All since you came to the house. There is more there than you think.'

'How pretty it is! What am I to do with it, please?'

'That I will now explain to you,' answered the lady, turning from her, and going to her cabinet.

She came back with a small ring in her hand. Then she took the ball from Irene's, and did something with the two – Irene could not tell what.

'Give me your hand,' she said.

Irene held up her right hand.

'Yes, that is the hand I want,' said the lady, and put the ring on the forefinger of it.

'What a beautiful ring!' said Irene. 'What is the stone called?'

'It is a fire-opal.'

'Please, am I to keep it?'

'Always.'

'Oh, thank you, grandmother! It's prettier than anything I ever saw, except those – of all colours – in your – Please, is that your crown?'

'Yes, it is my crown. The stone in your ring is of the same sort – only not so good. It has only red, but mine have all colours, you see.'

'Yes, grandmother. I will take such care of it! – But——' she added, hesitating.

'But what?' asked her grandmother.

'What am I to say when Lootie asks me where I got it?'

'*You* will ask *her* where you got it,' answered the lady smiling.

'I don't see how I can do that.'

'You will though.'

'Of course I will if you say so. But you know I can't pretend not to know.'

'Of course not. But don't trouble yourself about it. You will see when the time comes.'

So saying, the lady turned, and threw the little ball into the rose-fire.

'Oh, grandmother!' exclaimed Irene; 'I thought you had spun it for me.'

'So I did, my child. And you've got it.'

'No; it's burnt in the fire!'

The lady put her hand in the fire, brought out the ball, glimmering as before, and held it towards her. Irene stretched out her hand to take it, but the lady turned, and going to her cabinet, opened a drawer, and laid the ball in it.

'Have I done anything to vex you, grandmother?' said Irene pitifully.

'No, my darling. But you must understand that no one ever gives anything to another properly and really without keeping it. That ball is yours.'

'Oh! I'm not to take it with me! You are going to keep it for me!'

'You are to take it with you. I've fastened the end of it to the ring on your finger.'

Irene looked at the ring.

'I can't see it there, grandmother,' she said.

'Feel – a little way from the ring – towards the cabinet,' said the lady.

'Oh! I do feel it!' exclaimed the princess. 'But I can't see it,' she added, looking close to her outstretched hand.

'No. The thread is too fine for you to see it. You can only feel it. Now you can fancy how much spinning that took, although it does seem such a little ball.'

'But what use can I make of it, if it lies in your cabinet?'

'That is what I will explain to you. It would be of no use to you – it wouldn't be yours at all if it did not lie in my cabinet. – Now listen. – If ever you find yourself in any danger – such, for example, as you were in this same evening – you must take off your ring and put it under the pillow of your bed. Then you must lay your forefinger, the same that wore the ring, upon the thread, and follow the thread wherever it leads you.'

'Oh, how delightful! It will lead me to you, grandmother, I know!'

'Yes. But, remember, it may seem to you a very roundabout way indeed, and you must not doubt the thread. Of one thing you may be sure, that while you hold it, I hold it too.'

'It is very wonderful!' said Irene thoughtfully. Then suddenly becoming aware, she jumped up, crying – 'Oh, grandmother! here have I been sitting all this time in your chair, and you standing! I *beg* your pardon.'

The lady laid her hand on her shoulder, and said –

'Sit down again, Irene. Nothing pleases me better than to see anyone sit in my chair. I am only too glad to stand so long as anyone will sit in it.'

'How kind of you!' said the princess, and sat down again.

'It makes me happy,' said the lady.

'But,' said Irene, still puzzled, 'won't the thread get in somebody's way and be broken, if the one end is fast to my ring, and the other laid in your cabinet?'

'You will find all that arrange itself. – I am afraid it is time for you to go.'

'Mightn't I stay and sleep with you to-night, grandmother?'

'No, not to-night. If I had meant you to stay to-night, I should have given you a bath; but you know everybody in the house is miserable about you, and it would be cruel to keep them so all night. You must go downstairs.'

'I'm so glad, grandmother, you didn't say – *go home* – for this is my home. Mayn't I call this my home?'

'You may, my child. And I trust you will always think it your home. Now come. I must take you back without anyone seeing you.'

'Please, I want to ask you one question more,' said Irene. 'Is it because you have your crown on that you look so young?'

'No, child,' answered her grandmother; 'it is because I felt so young this evening, that I put my crown on. And I thought you would like to see your old grandmother in her best.'

'Why do you call yourself old? You're not old, grandmother.'

'I am very old indeed. It is so silly of people – I don't mean you, for you are such a tiny, and couldn't know better – but it *is* so silly of people to fancy that old age means crookedness and witheredness and feebleness and sticks and spectacles and rheumatism and forgetfulness! It is so silly! Old age has nothing whatever to do with all that. The right old age means strength and beauty and mirth and courage and clear eyes and strong painless limbs. I am older than you are able to think, and——'

'And look at you, grandmother!' cried Irene, jumping up and flinging her arms about her neck. 'I won't be so silly again, I promise you. At least – I'm rather afraid to promise – but if I am, I promise to be sorry for it – I do. – I wish I were as old as you, grandmother. I don't think you are ever afraid of anything.'

'Not for long, at least, my child. Perhaps by the time I am two thousand years of age, I shall, indeed, never be afraid of anything. But I confess I have sometimes been afraid about my children – sometimes about you, Irene.'

'Oh, I'm *so* sorry, grandmother! – To-night, I suppose, you mean.'

'Yes – a little to-night; but a good deal when you had all but made up your mind that I was a dream, and no real great-great-grandmother. – You must not suppose I am blaming you for that. I dare say you could not help it.'

'I don't know, grandmother,' said the princess, beginning to cry. 'I can't always do myself as I should like. And I don't always try. – I'm very sorry anyhow.'

The lady stooped, lifted her in her arms, and sat down with her in her chair, holding her close to her bosom. In a few minutes the princess had sobbed herself to sleep. How long she slept, I do not know. When she came to herself she was sitting in her own high chair at the nursery table, with her doll's house before her.

16   The Ring

The same moment her nurse came into the room, sobbing. When she saw her sitting there, she started back with a loud cry of amazement and joy. Then running to her, she caught her in her arms and covered her with kisses.

'My precious darling princess! where have you been? What has happened to you? We've all been crying our eyes out, and searching the house from top to bottom for you.'

'Not quite from the top,' thought Irene to herself; and she might have added – 'not quite to the bottom,' perhaps, if she had known all. But the one she would not, and the other she could not say.

'Oh, Lootie! I've had such a dreadful adventure!' she replied, and told her all about the cat with the long legs, and how she ran out upon the mountain, and came back again. But she said nothing of her grandmother or her lamp.

'And there we've been searching for you all over the house for more than an hour and a half!' exclaimed the nurse. 'But that's no matter, now we've got you! Only, princess, I must say,' she added, her mood changing, 'what you ought to have done was to call for your own Lootie to come and help you, instead of running out of the house, and up the mountain, in that wild – I must say, foolish fashion.'

'Well, Lootie,' said Irene quietly, 'perhaps if you had a big cat, all legs, running at you, you mightn't exactly know which was the wisest thing to do at the moment.'

'I wouldn't run up the mountain, anyhow,' returned Lootie.

'Not if you had time to think about it. But when those creatures came at you that night on the mountain, you were so frightened yourself that you lost your way home.'

This put a stop to Lootie's reproaches. She had been on the point of saying that the long-legged cat must have been a twilight fancy of the princess's, but the memory of the horrors of that night, and of the talking-to which the king had given her in consequence, prevented her from saying what after all she did not half believe – having a strong suspicion that the cat was a goblin; for she knew nothing of the difference between the goblins and their creatures: she counted them all just goblins.

Without another word she went and got some fresh tea and bread and butter for the princess. Before she returned, the whole household, headed by the housekeeper, burst into the nursery to exult over their darling. The gentlemen-at-arms followed, and were ready enough to believe all she told them about the long-legged cat. Indeed, though wise enough to say nothing about it, they remembered, with no little horror, just such a creature amongst those they had surprised at their gambols upon the princess's lawn. In their own hearts they blamed themselves for not having kept better watch. And their captain gave order that from this night the front door and all the windows on the ground floor, should be locked immediately the sun set, and opened after upon no pretence whatever. The men-at-arms redoubled their vigilance, and for some time there was no further cause of alarm.

When the princess woke the next morning, her nurse was bending over her.

'How your ring does glow this morning, princess! – just like a fiery rose!' she said.

'Does it, Lootie!' returned Irene. 'Who gave me the ring, Lootie? I know I've had it a long time, but where did I get it? I don't remember.'

'I think it must have been your mother gave it you, princess; but really, for as long as you have worn it, I don't remember that ever I heard,' answered her nurse.

'I will ask my king-papa the next time he comes,' said Irene.

17 Spring-time

The spring so dear to all creatures, young and old, came at last, and before the first few days of it had gone, the king rode through its budding valleys to see his little daughter. He had been in a distant part of his dominions all the winter, for he was not in the habit of stopping in one great city, or of visiting only his favourite country houses, but he moved from place to place, that all his people might know him. Wherever he journeyed, he kept a constant lookout for the ablest and best men to put into office; and wherever he found himself mistaken, and those he had appointed incapable or unjust, he removed them at once. Hence you see it was his care of the people that kept him from seeing his princess so often as he would have liked. You may wonder why he did not take her about with him; but there were several reasons against his doing so, and I suspect her great-great-grandmother had had a principal hand in preventing it. Once more, Irene heard the bugle-blast, and once more she was at the gate to meet her father as he rode up on his great white horse.

After they had been alone for a little while, she thought of what she had resolved to ask him.

'Please, king-papa,' she said, 'will you tell me where I got this pretty ring? I can't remember.'

The king looked at it. A strange beautiful smile spread like sunshine over his face, and an answering smile, but at the same time a questioning one, spread like moonlight over Irene's.

'It was your queen-mamma's once,' he said.

'And why isn't it hers now?' asked Irene.

'She does not want it now,' said the king, looking grave.

'Why doesn't she want it now?'

'Because she's gone where all those rings are made.'

'And when shall I see her?' asked the princess.

'Not for some time yet,' answered the king, and the tears came into his eyes.

Irene did not remember her mother, and did not know why her father looked so, and why the tears came in his eyes; but she put her arms round his neck and kissed him, and asked no more questions.

The king was much disturbed on hearing the report of the gentlemen-at-arms concerning the creatures they had seen; and I presume would have taken Irene with him that very day, but for what the presence of the ring on her finger assured him of. About an hour before he left, Irene saw him go up the old stair; and he did not come down again till they were just ready to start; and she thought with herself that he had been up to see the old lady. When he went away, he left other six gentlemen behind him, that there might be six of them always on guard.

And now, in the lovely spring weather, Irene was out on the mountain the greater part of the day. In the warmer hollows there were lovely primroses, and not so many that she ever got tired of them. As often as she saw a new one opening an eye of light in the blind earth, she would clap her hands with gladness, and unlike some children I

know, instead of pulling it, would touch it as tenderly, as if it had been a new baby, and, having made its acquaintance, would leave it as happy as she found it. She treated the plants on which they grew like birds nests; every fresh flower was like a new little bird to her. She would pay visits to all the flower-nests she knew, remembering each by itself. She would go down on her hands and knees beside one and say 'Good-morning! Are you all smelling very sweet this morning? Good-bye!' and then she would go to another nest, and say the same. It was a favourite amusement with her. There were many flowers up and down, and she loved them all, but the primroses were her favourites.

'They're not too shy, and they're not a bit forward,' she would say to Lootie.

There were goats too about, over the mountain, and when the little kids came, she was as pleased with them as with the flowers. The goats belonged to the miners mostly – a few of them to Curdie's mother; but there were a good many wild ones that seemed to belong to nobody. These the goblins counted theirs, and it was upon them partly that they lived. They set snares and dug pits for them; and did not scruple to take what tame ones happened to be caught; but they did not try to steal them in any other manner, because they were afraid of the dogs the hill-people kept to watch them, for the knowing dogs always tried to bite their feet. But the goblins had a kind of sheep of their own – very queer creatures, which they drove out to feed at night, and the other goblin-creatures were wise enough to keep good watch over them, for they knew they should have their bones by and by.

18 Curdie's Clue

Curdie was as watchful as ever, but was almost getting tired of his ill success. Every other night or so, he followed the goblins about, as they went on digging and boring, and getting as near them as he could, watched them from behind stones and rocks; but as yet he seemed no nearer finding out what they had in view. As at first, he always kept hold of the end of his string, while his pickaxe, left just outside the hole by which he entered the goblins' country from the mine, continued to serve as an anchor and hold fast the other end. The goblins hearing no more noise in that quarter, had ceased to apprehend an immediate invasion, and kept no watch.

One night, after dodging about and listening till he was nearly falling asleep with weariness, he began to roll up his ball, for he had resolved to go home to bed. It was not long, however, before he began to feel bewildered. One after another he passed goblin-houses, caves that is, occupied by goblin families, and at length was sure they were many more than he had passed as he came. He had to use great caution to pass unseen – they lay so close together. Could his string have led him wrong? He still followed winding it, and still it led him into more thickly populated quarters, until he became quite uneasy, and indeed apprehensive; for although he was not afraid of the *cobs*, he was afraid of not finding his way out. But what could he do? It was of no use to sit down, and wait for the morning – the morning made no difference here. It was all dark, and always dark; and if his string failed him, he was helpless. He might even arrive within a yard of the mine, and never know it. Seeing he could do nothing better he would at least find where the end of his string was, and if possible how it had come to play him such a trick. He knew by the size of the ball, that he was getting pretty near the last of it, when he began to feel a tugging and pulling at it. What could it mean? Turning a sharp corner, he thought he heard strange sounds. These grew, as he went on, to a scuffling and growling and squeaking; and the noise increased, until, turning a second sharp corner, he found himself in the midst of it, and the same moment tumbled over a wallowing mass, which he knew must be a knot of the cobs' creatures. Before he could recover his feet, he had caught some great scratches on his face, and several severe bites on his legs and arms. But as he scrambled to get up, his hand fell upon his pickaxe, and before the horrid beasts could do him any serious harm, he was laying about with it right and left in the dark. The hideous cries which followed gave him the satisfaction of knowing that he had punished some of them pretty smartly for their rudeness, and by their scampering and their retreating howls, he perceived that he had routed them. He stood for a little, weighing his battleaxe in his hand as if it had been the most precious lump of metal – but indeed no lump of gold itself could have been so precious at the time as that common tool – then untied the end of the string from it, put the ball in his pocket, and still stood thinking. It was clear that the cobs' creatures had found his axe, had between them carried it off, and had so led him he knew not where. But for all his thinking he could not tell what he ought to do, until

suddenly he became aware of a glimmer of light in the distance. Without a moment's hesitation he set out for it, as fast as the unknown and rugged way would permit. Yet again turning a corner, led by the dim light, he spied something quite new in his experience of the underground regions – a small irregular shape of something shining. Going up to it, he found it was a piece of mica, or Muscovy glass, called sheep-silver in Scotland, and the light flickered as if from a fire behind it. After trying in vain for some time to discover an entrance to the place where it was burning, he came at length to a small chamber in which an opening high in the wall, revealed a glow beyond. To this opening he managed to scramble up, and then he saw a strange sight.

Below sat a little group of goblins around a fire, the smoke of which vanished in the darkness far aloft. The sides of the cave were full of shining minerals like those of the palace-hall; and the company was evidently of a superior order, for everyone wore stones about head, or arms, or waist, shining dull gorgeous colours in the light of the fire. Nor had Curdie looked long before he recognized the king himself, and found that he had made his way into the inner apartment of the royal family. He had never had such a good chance of hearing something! He crept through the hole as softly as he could, scrambled a good way down the wall towards them without attracting attention, and then sat down and listened. The king, evidently the queen, and probably the crown-prince and the Prime Minister were talking together. He was sure of the queen by her shoes, for as she warmed her feet at the fire, he saw them quite plainly.

'That *will* be fun!' said the one he took for the crown-prince.

It was the first whole sentence he heard.

'I don't see why you should think it such a grand affair!' said his stepmother, tossing her head backward.

'You must remember, my spouse,' interposed his majesty, as if making excuse for his son, 'he has got the same blood in him. His mother——'

'Don't talk to me of his mother! You positively encourage his unnatural fancies. Whatever belongs to *that* mother, ought to be cut out of him.'

'You forget yourself, my dear!' said the king.

'I don't,' said the queen, 'nor you either. If you expect *me* to approve of such coarse tastes, you will find yourself mistaken. *I* don't wear shoes for nothing.'

'You must acknowledge, however,' the king said, with a little groan, 'that this at least is no whim of Harelip's, but a matter of state-policy. You are well aware that his gratification comes purely from the pleasure of sacrificing himself to the public good. Does it not, Harelip?'

'Yes, father; of course it does. Only it *will* be nice to make her cry. I'll have the skin taken off between her toes, and tie them up till they grow together. Then her feet will be like other people's, and there will be no occasion for her to wear shoes.'

'Do you mean to insinuate *I*'ve got toes, you unnatural wretch?' cried the queen; and she moved angrily towards Harelip. The councillor, however, who was betwixt them, leaned forward so as to prevent her touching him, but only as if to address the prince.

'Your royal highness,' he said, 'possibly requires to be reminded that you have got three toes yourself – one on one foot, two on the other.'

'Ha! ha! ha!' shouted the queen triumphantly.

The councillor, encouraged by this mark of favour, went on.

'It seems to me, your royal highness, it would greatly endear you to your future people, proving to them that you are not the less one of themselves that you had the misfortune to be born of a sun-mother, if you were to command upon yourself the comparatively slight operation which, in a more extended form, you so wisely meditate with regard to your future princess.'

'Ha! ha! ha!' laughed the queen, louder than before, and the king and the minister joined in the laugh. Harelip growled, and for a few moments the others continued to express their enjoyment of his discomfiture.

The queeen was the only one Curdie could see with any distinctness. She sat sideways to him, and the light of the fire shone full upon her face. He could not consider her handsome. Her nose was certainly broader at the end than its extreme length, and her eyes, instead of being horizontal, were set up like two perpendicular eggs, one on the broad, the other on the small end. Her mouth was no bigger than a small buttonhole until she laughed, when it stretched from ear to ear – only to be sure her ears were very nearly in the middle of her cheeks.

Anxious to hear everything they might say, Curdie ventured to

slide down a smooth part of the rock just under him, to a projection below, upon which he thought to rest. But whether he was not careful enough, or the projection gave way, down he came with a rush on the floor of the cavern, bringing with him a great rumbling shower of stones.

The goblins jumped from their seats in more anger than consternation, for they had never yet seen anything to be afraid of in the palace. But when they saw Curdie with his pick in his hand, their rage was mingled with fear, for they took him for the first of an invasion of miners. The king notwithstanding drew himself up to his full height of four feet, spread himself to his full breadth of three and a half, for he was the handsomest and squarest of all the goblins, and strutting up to Curdie, planted himself with out-spread feet before him, and said with dignity –

'Pray what right have you in my palace?'

'The right of necessity, your majesty,' answered Curdie. 'I lost my way, and did not know where I was wandering to.'

'How did you get in?'

'By a hole in the mountain.'

'But you are a miner! Look at your pickaxe!'

Curdie did look at it, answering,

'I came upon it, lying on the ground, a little way from here. I tumbled over some wild beasts who were playing with it. Look, your majesty.' And Curdie showed him how he was scratched and bitten.

The king was pleased to find him behave more politely than he had expected from what his people had told him concerning the miners, for he attributed it to the power of his own presence; but he did not therefore feel friendly to the intruder.

'You will oblige me by walking out of my dominions at once,' he said, well knowing what a mockery lay in the words.

'With pleasure, if your majesty will give me a guide,' said Curdie.

'I will give you a thousand,' said the king with a scoffing air of magnificent liberality.

'One will be quite sufficient,' said Curdie.

But the king uttered a strange shout, half-halloo, half-roar, and in rushed goblins till the cave was swarming. He said something to the first of them which Curdie could not hear, and it was passed from one to another till in a moment the farthest in the crowd had evidently heard and understood it. They began to gather about him in a way he did not relish, and he retreated towards the wall. They pressed upon him.

'Stand back,' said Curdie, grasping his pickaxe tighter by his knee.

They only grinned and pressed closer. Curdie bethought himself, and began to rhyme.

'Ten, twenty, thirty –
You're all so very dirty!
Twenty, thirty, forty –
You're all so thick and snorty!

'Thirty, forty, fifty –
You're all so puff-and-snifty!
Forty, fifty, sixty –
Beast and man so mixty!

'Fifty, sixty, seventy –
Mixty, maxty, leaventy!
Sixty, seventy, eighty –
All your cheeks so slaty!

'Seventy, eighty, ninety,
All your hands so flinty!
Eighty, ninety, hundred,
Altogether dundred!'

The goblins fell back a little when he began, and made horrible grimaces all through the rhyme, as if eating something so disagreeable that it set their teeth on edge and gave them the creeps; but whether it was that the rhyming words were most of them no words at all, for, a new rhyme being considered the more efficacious, Curdie had made it on the spur of the moment, or whether it was that the presence of the king and queen gave them courage, I cannot tell; but the moment the rhyme was over, they crowded on him again, and out shot a hundred long arms, with a multitude of thick nailless fingers at the ends of them, to lay hold upon him. Then Curdie heaved up his axe. But being as gentle as courageous and not wishing to kill any of them, he turned the end which was square and blunt like a hammer, and with that came down a great blow on the head of the goblin nearest him. Hard as the heads of all goblins are, he thought he must feel that. And so he did, no doubt; but he only gave a horrible cry, and sprung at Curdie's throat. Curdie however drew back in time, and just at that critical moment, remembered the vulnerable part of the goblin-body. He made a sudden rush at the king, and stamped with all his might on his majesty's feet. The king gave a most unkingly howl, and almost fell into the fire. Curdie then rushed into the crowd, stamping right and left. The goblins drew back, howling on every side as he approached, but they were so crowded that few of those he attacked could escape his tread; and the shrieking and roaring that filled the cave would have appalled Curdie, but for the good hope it gave him. They were tumbling over each other in heaps in their eagerness to rush from the cave, when a new assailant suddenly faced him: – the queen, with flaming eyes and expanded nostrils, her hair standing half up from her head, rushed at him. She trusted in her shoes: they were of granite – hollowed like French *sabots*. Curdie would have endured much rather than hurt a woman, even if she was a goblin; but here was an affair of life and death: forgetting her shoes, he made a great stamp on one of her feet. But she instantly returned it with very different effect, causing him frightful pain, and almost disabling him. His only chance with her would have been to attack the granite shoes with his pickaxe, but before he could think of that, she had caught him up in her arms, and was rushing with him across the cave. She dashed him into a hole in the wall, with a force that almost stunned him. But although he could not move, he was not too far gone to hear her great cry, and the rush of multitudes of soft feet, followed by the sounds of something heaved up against the rock; after which came a multitudinous patter of stones falling near him. The last had not ceased when he grew very faint, for his head had been badly cut, and at last insensible.

When he came to himself, there was perfect silence about him, and utter darkness, but for the merest glimmer in one tiny spot. He crawled to it, and found that they had heaved a slab against the mouth of the hole, past the edge of which a poor little gleam found its way from the fire. He could not move it a hair's breadth, for they had piled a great heap of stones against it. He crawled back to where he had been lying, in the faint hope of finding his pickaxe. But after a vain search, he was at last compelled to acknowledge himself in an evil plight. He sat down and tried to think, but soon fell fast asleep.

19   Goblin Counsels

He must have slept a long time, for when he awoke, he felt wonderfully restored – indeed almost well, and very hungry. There were voices in the outer cave.

Once more then, it was night; for the goblins slept during the day, and went about their affairs during the night.

In the universal and constant darkness of their dwelling, they had no reason to prefer the one arrangement to the other; but from aversion to the sun-people, they chose to be busy when there was least chance of their being met either by the miners below, when they were burrowing, or by the people of the mountain above, when they were feeding their sheep or catching their goats. And indeed it was only when the sun was away that the outside of the mountain was sufficiently like their own dismal regions to be endurable to their mole-eyes, so thoroughly had they become disused to any light beyond that of their own fires and torches.

Curdie listened, and soon found that they were talking of himself.

'How long will it take?' asked Harelip.

'Not many days, I should think,' answered the king. 'They are poor feeble creatures, those sun-people, and want to be always eating. *We* can go a week at a time without food, and be all the better for it; but I've been told *they* eat two or three times every day! Can you believe it? – They must be quite hollow inside – not at all like us, nine-tenths of whose bulk is solid flesh and bone. Yes – I judge a week of starvation will do for him.'

'If *I* may be allowed a word,' interposed the queen, '– and I think I ought to have some voice in the matter——'

'The wretch is entirely at your disposal, my spouse,' interrupted the king. 'He is your property. You caught him yourself. We should never have done it.'

The queen laughed. She seemed in far better humour than the night before.

'I was about to say,' she resumed, 'that it does seem a pity to waste so much fresh meat.'

'What are you thinking of, my love?' said the king. 'The very notion of starving him implies that we are not going to give him any meat, either salt or fresh.'

'I'm not such a stupid as that comes to,' returned her majesty. 'What I mean is, that by the time he is starved, there will hardly be a picking upon his bones.'

The king gave a great laugh.

'Well, my spouse, you may have him when you like,' he said. 'I don't fancy him for my part. I am pretty sure he is tough eating.'

'That would be to honour instead of punish his insolence,' returned the queen. 'But why should our poor creatures be deprived of so much nourishment? Our little dogs and cats and pigs and small bears would enjoy him very much.'

'You are the best of housekeepers, my lovely queen!' said her husband. 'Let it be so by all means. Let us have our people in, and get him out and kill him at once. He deserves it. The mischief he might have brought upon us, now that he had penetrated so far as our most retired citadel, is incalculable. Or rather let us tie him hand and foot, and have the pleasure of seeing him torn to pieces by full torchlight in the great hall.'

'Better and better!' cried the queen and the prince together, both of them clapping their hands. And the prince made an ugly noise with his harelip, just as if he had intended to be one at the feast.

'But,' added the queen, bethinking herself, 'he is so troublesome. For as poor creatures as they are, there is something about those sun-people that is *very* troublesome. I cannot imagine how it is that with such superior strength and skill and understanding as ours, we permit them to exist at all. Why do we not destroy them entirely, and use their cattle and grazing lands at our pleasure? Of course, we don't want to live in their horrid country! It is far too glaring for our quieter and more refined tastes. But we might use it as a sort of outhouse, you know. Even our creatures' eyes might get used to it, and if they did grow blind, that would be of no consequence, provided they grew fat as well. But we might even keep their great cows and other creatures, and then we should have a few more luxuries, such as cream and cheese, which at present we only taste occasionally, when our brave men have succeeded in carrying some off from their farms.'

'It is worth thinking of,' said the king; 'and I don't know why *you* should be the first to suggest it, except that you have a positive genius for conquest. But still, as you say, there is something very troublesome about them; and it would be better, as I understand you to suggest, that we should starve him for a day or two first, so that he may be a little less frisky when we take him out.'

> 'One there was a goblin
> Living in a hole;
> Busy he was cobblin'
> A shoe without a sole.

> 'By came a birdie:
> "Goblin, what do you do?"
> "Cobble at a sturdie
> Upper leather shoe."

> ' "What's the good o' that, sir?"
> Said the little bird,
> "Why it's very pat, sir –
> Plain without a word.

> ' "Where 'tis all a hole, sir,
> Never can be holes:
> Why should their shoes have soles, sir,
> When *they*'ve got no souls?" '

'What's that horrible noise?' cried the queen, shuddering from pot-metal head to granite shoes.

'I declare,' said the king with solemn indignation, 'it's the sun-creature in the hole!'

'Stop that disgusting noise!' cried the crown-prince valiantly, getting up and standing in front of the heap of stones, with his face towards Curdie's prison. – 'Do now, or I'll break your head.'

'Break away,' shouted Curdie, and began singing again –

> 'Once there was a goblin,
> Living in a hole –'

'I really can*not* bear it,' said the queen. 'If I could only get at his horrid toes with my slippers again!'

'I think we had better go to bed,' said the king.

'It's not time to go to bed,' said the queen.

'I would if I was you,' said Curdie.

'Impertinent wretch!' said the queen, with the utmost scorn in her voice.

'An impossible *if*,' said his majesty with dignity.

'Quite,' returned Curdie, and began singing again –

> 'Go to bed,
> Goblin, do.
> Help the queen
> Take off her shoe.

> 'If you do,
> It will disclose
> A horid set
> Of sprouting toes.'

'What a lie!' roared the queen in a rage.

'By the way, that reminds me,' said the king, 'that, for as long as we have been married, I have never seen your feet, queen. I think you might take off your shoes when you go to bed! They positively hurt me sometimes.'

'I will do as I like,' retorted the queen sulkily.

'You ought to do as your own hubby wishes you,' said the king.

'I will not,' said the queen.

'Then I insist upon it,' said the king.

Apparently his majesty approached the queen for the purpose of following the advice given by Curdie, for the latter heard a scuffle, and then a great roar from the king.

'Will you be quiet then?' said the queen wickedly.

'Yes, yes, queen. I only meant to coax you.'

'Hands off!' cried the queen triumphantly. 'I'm going to bed. You may come when you like. But as long as I am queen, I will sleep in my shoes. It is my royal privilege. Harelip, go to bed.'

'I'm going,' said Harelip sleepily.

'So am I,' said the king.

'Come along then,' said the queen; 'and mind you are good, or I'll——'

'Oh, no, no, no!' screamed the king, in the most supplicating of tones.

Curdie heard only a muttered reply in the distance; and then the cave was quite still.

They had left the fire burning, and the light came through brighter than before. Curdie thought it was time to try again if anything could be done. But he found he could not get even a finger through the chink between the slab and the rock. He gave a great rush with his shoulder against the slab, but it yielded no more than if it had been part of the rock. All he could do, was to sit down and think again.

By and by he came to the resolution to pretend to be dying, in the hope they might take him out before his strength was too much exhausted to let him have a chance. Then, for the creatures, if he could but find his axe again, he would have no fear of them; and if it were not for the queen's horrid shoes, he would have no fear at all.

Meantime, until they should come again at night, there was nothing for him to do but forge new rhymes, now his only weapons. He had no intention of using them at present, of course; but it was well to have a stock, for he might live to want them, and the manufacture of them would help to while away the time.

That same morning early, the princess woke in a terrible fright. There was a hideous noise in her room – of creatures snarling and hissing and racketing about as if they were fighting. The moment she came to herself, she remembered something she had never thought of again – what her grandmother told her to do when she was frightened. She immediately took off her ring and put it under her pillow. As she did so, she fancied she felt a finger and thumb take it gently from under her palm. 'It must be my grandmother!' she said to herself, and the thought gave her such courage that she stopped to put on her dainty little slippers before running from the room. While doing this, she caught sight of a long cloak of sky-blue, thrown over the back of a chair by the bedside. She had never seen it before, but it was evidently waiting for her. She put it on, and then, feeling with the forefinger of her right hand, soon found her grandmother's thread, which she proceeded at once to follow, expecting it would lead her straight up the old stair. When she reached the door, she found it went down and ran along the floor, so that she had almost to crawl in order to keep a hold of it. Then, to her surprise, and somewhat to her dismay, she found that instead of leading her towards the stair it turned in quite the opposite direction. It led her through certain narrow passages towards the kitchen, turning aside ere she reached it, and guiding her to a door which communicated with a small backyard. Some of the maids were already up, and this door was standing open. Across the yard the thread still ran along the ground, until it brought her to a door in the wall which opened upon the mountain-side. When she had passed through, the thread rose to about half her height, and she could hold it with ease as she walked. It led her straight up the mountain.

The cause of her alarm was less frightful than she supposed. The cook's great black cat, pursued by the housekeeper's terrier, had bounced against her bedroom door, which had not been properly fastened, and the two had burst into the room together and commenced a battle royal. How the nurse came to sleep through it, was a mystery, but I suspect the old lady had something to do with it.

It was a clear warm morning. The wind blew deliciously over the mountain-side. Here and there she saw a late primrose, but she did not stop to call upon them. The sky was mottled with small clouds. The sun was not yet up, but some of their fluffy edges had caught his light, and hung out orange and gold-coloured fringes upon the air. The dew lay in round drops upon the leaves, and hung like tiny diamond earrings from the blades of grass about her path.

'How lovely that bit of gossamer is!' thought the princess, looking at a long undulating line that shone at some distance from her up the hill. It was not the time for gossamers though; and Irene soon discovered that it was her own thread she saw shining on before her in the light of the morning. It was leading her she knew not whither; but she had never in her life been out before sunrise, and everything was so fresh and cool and lively and full of something coming, that she felt too happy to be afraid of anything.

After leading her up a good distance, the thread turned to the left, and down the path upon which she and Lootie had met Curdie. But she never thought of that, for now in the morning light, with its far outlook over the country, no path could have been more open and airy and cheerful. She could see the road almost to the horizon, along which she had so often watched her king-papa and his troop come shining, with the bugle-blast cleaving the air before them; and it was like a companion to her. Down and down the path went, then up, and then down and then up again, getting rugged and more rugged as it went; and still along the path went the silvery thread, and still along the thread went Irene's little rosy-tipped forefinger. By and by she came to a little stream that jabbered and prattled down the hill, and up the side of the stream went both path and thread. And still the path grew rougher and steeper, and the mountain grew wilder, till Irene began to think she was going a very long way from home; and when she turned to look back, she saw that the level country had vanished and the rough bare mountain had closed in about her. But still on went the thread, and on went the princess. Everything around her was getting brighter and brighter as the sun came nearer; till at length his first rays all at once alighted on the top of a rock before her, like some golden creature fresh from the sky. Then she saw that the little stream ran out of a hole in that rock, that the path did not go past the rock, and that the thread was leading her straight up to it. A shudder ran through her from head to foot when she found that the thread was actually taking her into the hole out of which the stream ran. It ran out babbling joyously, but she had to go in.

She did not hesitate. Right into the hole she went, which was high enough to let her walk without stooping. For a little way there was a brown glimmer, but at the first turn it all but ceased, and before she had gone many paces she was in total darkness. Then she began to be frightened indeed. Every moment she kept feeling the thread backwards and forwards, and as she went farther and farther into the darkness of the great hollow mountain, she kept thinking more and more about her grandmother, and all that she had said to her, and how kind she had been, and how beautiful she was, and all about her lovely room, and the fire of roses, and the great lamp that sent its light through stone walls. And she became more and more sure that the thread could not have gone there of itself, and that her grandmother

must have sent it. But it tried her dreadfully when the path went down very steep, and especially when she came to places where she had to go down rough stairs, and even sometimes a ladder. Through one narrow passage after another, over lumps of rock and sand and clay, the thread guided her, until she came to a small hole through which she had to creep. Finding no change on the other side – 'Shall I ever get back?' she thought, over and over again, wondering at herself that she was not ten times more frightened, and often feeling as if she were only walking in the story of a dream. Sometimes she heard the noise of water, a dull gurgling inside the rock. By and by she heard the sounds of blows, which came nearer and nearer; but again they grew duller, and almost died away. In a hundred directions she turned, obedient to the guiding thread.

At last she spied a dull red shine, and came up to the mica-window, and thence away and round about, and right into a cavern, where glowed the red embers of a fire. Here the thread began to rise. It rose as high as her head, and higher still. What *should* she do if she lost her hold? She was pulling it down! She might break it! She could see it far up, glowing as red as her fire-opal in the light of the embers.

But presently she came to a huge heap of stones, piled in a slope against the wall of the cavern. On these she climbed, and soon recovered the level of the thread – only however to find, the next moment, that it vanished through the heap of stones, and left her standing on it, with her face to the solid rock. For one terrible moment, she felt as if her grandmother had forsaken her. The thread which the spiders had spun far over the seas, which her grandmother had sat in the moonlight and spun again for her, which she had tempered in the rose-fire, and tied to her opal ring, had left her – had gone where she could no longer follow it – had brought her into a horrible cavern, and there left her! She was forsaken indeed!

'When *shall* I wake?' she said to herself in an agony, but the same moment knew that it was no dream. She threw herself upon the heap, and began to cry. It was well she did not know what creatures, one of them with stone shoes on her feet, were lying in the next cave. But neither did she know who was on the other side of the slab.

At length the thought struck her, that at least she could follow the thread backwards, and thus get out of the mountain, and home. She rose at once, and found the thread. But the instant she tried to feel it backwards, it vanished from her touch. Forwards, it led her hand up to the heap of stones – backwards it seemed nowhere. Neither could she see it as before in the light of the fire. She burst into a wailing cry, and again threw herself down on the stones.

21　The Escape

As the princess lay and sobbed, she kept feeling the thread mechanically, following it with her finger many times up to the stones in which it disappeared. By and by she began, still mechanically, to poke her finger in after it between the stones as far as she could. All at once it came into her head that she might remove some of the stones and see where the thread went next. Almost laughing at herself for never having thought of this before, she jumped to her feet. Her fear vanished; once more she was certain her grandmother's thread could not have brought her there just to leave her there; and she began to throw away the stones from the top as fast as she could, sometimes two or three at a handful, sometimes taking both hands to lift one. After clearing them away a little, she found that the thread turned and went straight downwards. Hence, as the heap sloped a good deal, growing of course wider towards its base, she had to throw away a multitude of stones to follow the thread. But this was not all, for she soon found that the thread, after going straight down for a little way, turned first sideways in one direction, then sideways in another, and then shot, at various angles, hither and thither inside the heap, so that she began to be afraid that to clear the thread, she must remove the whole huge gathering. She was dismayed at the very idea, but, losing no time, set to work with a will; and with aching back, and bleeding fingers and hands, she worked on, sustained by the pleasure of seeing the heap slowly diminish, and begin to show itself on the opposite side of the fire. Another thing which helped to keep up her courage was, that as often as she uncovered a turn of the thread, instead of lying loose upon the stones, it tightened up: this made her sure that her grandmother was at the end of it somewhere.

She had got about halfway down when she started, and nearly fell with fright. Close to her ear as it seemed, a voice broke out singing –

> 'Jabber, bother, smash!
> You'll have it all in a crash.
> Jabber, smash, bother!
> You'll have the worst of the pother.
> Smash, bother, jabber! –'

Here Curdie stopped, either because he could not find a rhyme to *jabber*, or because he remembered what he had forgotten when he woke up at the sound of Irene's labours, that his plan was to make the goblins think he was getting weak. But he had uttered enough to let Irene know who he was.

'It's Curdie!' she cried joyfully.

'Hush! hush!' came Curdie's voice again from somewhere. 'Speak softly.'

'Why, you were singing loud!' said Irene.

'Yes. But they know I am here, and they don't know you are. Who are you?'

'I'm Irene,' answered the princess. 'I know who you are quite well.

You're Curdie.'

'Why, however did you come here, Irene?'

'My great-great-grandmother sent me; and I think I've found out why. You can't get out, I suppose?'

'No, I can't. What are you doing?'

'Clearing away a huge heap of stones.'

'There's a princess!' exclaimed Curdie, in a tone of delight, but still speaking in little more than a whisper. 'I can't think how you got here though.'

'My grandmother sent me after her thread.'

'I don't know what you mean,' said Curdie; 'but so you're there, it doesn't much matter.'

'Oh, yes it does!' returned Irene. 'I should never have been here but for her.'

'You can tell me all about it when we get out, then. There's no time to lose now,' said Curdie.

And Irene went to work, as fresh as when she began.

'There's such a lot of stones!' she said. 'It will take me a long time to get them all away.'

'How far on have you got?' asked Curdie.

'I've got about the half away, but the other half is ever so much bigger.'

'I don't think you will have to move the lower half. Do you see a slab laid up against the wall?'

Irene looked, and felt about with her hands, and soon perceived the outlines of the slab.

'Yes,' she answered, 'I do.'

'Then, I think,' rejoined Curdie, 'when you have cleared the slab about half-way down, or a little more, I shall be able to push it over.'

'I must follow my thread,' returned Irene, 'whatever I do.'

'What *do* you mean?' exclaimed Curdie.

'You will see when you get out,' answered the princess, and went on harder than ever.

But she was soon satisfied that what Curdie wanted done, and what the thread wanted done, were one and the same thing. For she not only saw that by following the turns of the thread she had been clearing the face of the slab, but that, a little more than half-way down, the thread went through the chink between the slab and the wall into the place where Curdie was confined, so that she could not follow it any farther until the slab was out of her way. As soon as she found this, she said in a right joyous whisper –

'Now, Curdie! I think if you were to give a great push, the slab would tumble over.'

'Stand quite clear of it then,' said Curdie, 'and let me know when you are ready.'

Irene got off the heap, and stood on one side of it.

'Now, Curdie!' she cried.

Curdie gave a great rush with his shoulder against it. Out tumbled the slab on the heap, and out crept Curdie over the top of it.

'You've saved my life, Irene!' he whispered.

'Oh, Curdie! I'm so glad! Let's get out of this horrid place as fast as we can.'

'That's easier said than done,' returned he.

'Oh, no! it's quite easy,' said Irene, 'We have only to follow my thread. I am sure that it's going to take us out now.'

She had already begun to follow it over the fallen slab into the hole, while Curdie was searching the floor of the cavern for his pickaxe.

'Here it is!' he cried. 'No, it is not!' he added, in a disappointed tone. 'What can it be then? – I declare it's a torch. That *is* jolly! It's better almost than my pickaxe. Much better if it weren't for those stone shoes!' he went on, as he lighted the torch by blowing the last embers of the expiring fire.

When he looked up, with the lighted torch casting a glare into the great darkness of the huge cavern, he caught sight of Irene disappearing in the hole out of which he had himself just come.

'Where are you going there?' he cried. 'That's not the way out. That's where I couldn't get out.'

'I know that,' whispered Irene. 'But this is the way my thread goes, and I must follow it.'

'What nonsense the child talks!' said Curdie to himself. 'I must follow her, though, and see that she comes to no harm. She will soon find she can't get out that way, and then she will come with me.'

So he crept over the slab once more into the hole with his torch in his hand. But when he looked about in it, he could see her nowhere. And now he discovered that although the hole was narrow, it was much longer than he had supposed; for in one direction the roof came down very low, and the hole went off in a narrow passage, of which he could not see the end. The princess must have crept in there. He got on his knees and one hand, holding the torch with the other, and crept after her. The hole twisted about, in some parts so low that he could hardly get through, in others so high that he could not see the roof, but everywhere it was narrow – far too narrow for a goblin to get through, and so I presume they never thought that Curdie might. He was beginning to feel very uncomfortable lest something should have befallen the princess, when he heard her voice almost close to his ear, whispering –

'Aren't you coming, Curdie?'

And when he turned the next corner, there she stood waiting for him.

'I knew you couldn't go wrong in that narrow hole, but now you must keep by me, for here is a great wide place,' she said.

'I can't understand it,' said Curdie, half to himself, half to Irene.

'Never mind,' she returned. 'Wait till we get out.'

Curdie, utterly astonished that she had already got so far, and by a path he had known nothing of, thought it better to let her do as she pleased.

'At all events,' he said again to himself, 'I know nothing about the way, miner as I am; and she seems to think she does know something about it, though how she should, passes my comprehension. So she's just as likely to find her way as I am, and as she insists on taking the lead, I must follow. We can't be much worse off than we are, anyhow.'

Reasoning thus, he followed her a few steps, and came out in another great cavern, across which Irene walked in a straight line, as confidently as if she knew every step of the way. Curdie went on after her, flashing his torch about, and trying to see something of what lay around them. Suddenly he started back a pace as the light fell upon something close by which Irene was passing. It was a platform of rock raised a few feet from the floor and covered with sheepskins, upon which lay two horrible figures asleep, at once recognized by Curdie as the king and queen of the goblins. He lowered his torch instantly lest the light should awake them. As he did so, it flashed upon his pickaxe, lying by the side of the queen, whose hand lay close by the handle of it.

'Stop one moment,' he whispered. 'Hold my torch, and don't let the light on their faces.'

Irene shuddered when she saw the frightful creatures, whom she had passed without observing them, but she did as he requested, and turning her back, held the torch low in front of her. Curdie drew his pickaxe carefully away, and as he did so, spied one of her feet, projecting from under the skins. The great clumsy granite shoe, exposed thus to his hand, was a temptation not to be resisted. He laid hold of it, and, with cautious efforts, drew it off. The moment he succeeded, he saw to his astonishment that what he had sung in ignorance, to annoy the queen, was actually true: she had six horrible toes. Overjoyed at his success, and seeing by the huge bump in the sheepskins where the other foot was, he proceeded to lift them gently, for, if he could only succeed in carrying away the other shoe as well, he would be no more afraid of the goblins than of so many flies. But as he pulled at the second shoe, the queen gave a growl and sat up in bed. The same instant the king awoke also, and sat up beside her.

'Run, Irene!' cried Curdie, for though he was not now in the least afraid for himself, he was for the princess.

Irene looked once round, saw the fearful creatures awake, and like the wise princess she was, dashed the torch on the ground and extinguished it, crying out –

'Here, Curdie, take my hand.'

He darted to her side, forgetting neither the queen's shoe nor his pickaxe, and caught hold of her hand, as she sped fearlessly where her thread guided her. They heard the queen give a great bellow; but they had a good start, for it would be some time before they could get torches lighted to pursue them. Just as they thought they saw a gleam behind them, the thread brought them to a very narrow opening, through which Irene crept easily, and Curdie with difficulty.

'Now,' said Curdie; 'I think we shall be safe.'

'Of course we shall,' returned Irene.

'Why do you think so?' asked Curdie.

'Because my grandmother is taking care of us.'

'That's all nonsense,' said Curdie. 'I don't know what you mean.'

'Then if you don't know what I mean, what right have you to call it nonsense?' asked the princess, a little offended.

'I beg your pardon, Irene,' said Curdie; 'I did not mean to vex you.'

'Of course not,' returned the princess. 'But why do *you* think we shall be safe?'

'Because the king and queen are far too stout to get through that hole.'

'There might be ways round,' said the princess.

'To be sure there might: we are not out of it yet,' acknowledged Curdie.

'But what do you mean by the king and queen?' asked the princess. 'I should never call such creatures as those a king and a queen.'

'Their own people do, though,' answered Curdie.

The princess asked more questions, and Curdie, as they walked leisurely along, gave her a full account, not only of the character and habits of the goblins, so far as he knew them, but of his own adventures with them, beginning from the very night after that in which he had met her and Lootie upon the mountain. When he had finished, he begged Irene to tell him how it was that she had come to his rescue. So Irene too had to tell a long story, which she did in rather a roundabout manner, interrupted by many questions concerning things she had not explained. But her tale, as he did not believe more than half of it, left everything as unaccountable to him as before, and he was nearly as much perplexed as to what he must think of the princess. He could not

believe that she was deliberately telling stories, and the only conclusion he could come to was that Lootie had been playing the child
tricks, inventing no end of lies to frighten her for her own purposes.

'But how ever did Lootie come to let you go into the mountains
alone?' he asked.

'Lootie knows nothing about it. I left her fast asleep – at least I
think so. I hope my grandmother won't let her get into trouble, for it
wasn't her fault at all, as my grandmother very well knows.'

'But how *did* you find your way to me?' persisted Curdie.

'I told you already,' answered Irene; – 'by keeping my finger upon
my grandmother's thread, as I am doing now.'

'You don't mean you've got the thread there?'

'Of course I do. I have told you so ten times already. I have hardly
– except when I was removing the stones – taken my finger off it.
There!' she added, guiding Curdie's hand to the thread, 'you feel it
yourself – don't you?'

'I feel nothing at all,' replied Curdie.

'Then what *can* be the matter with your finger? *I* feel it perfectly.
To be sure it is very thin, and in the sunlight looks just like the thread
of a spider, though there are many of them twisted together to make it
– but for all that I can't think why you shouldn't feel it as well as I do.'

Curdie was too polite to say he did not believe there was any thread
there at all. What he did say was –

'Well, I can make nothing of it.'

'I can though, and you must be glad of that, for it will do for both
of us.'

'We're not out yet,' said Curdie.

'We soon shall be,' returned Irene confidently.

And now the thread went downwards, and led Irene's hand to a
hole in the floor of the cavern, whence came a sound of running water
which they had been hearing for some time.

'It goes into the ground now, Curdie,' she said, stopping.

He had been listening to another sound, which his practised ear
had caught long ago, and which also had been growing louder. It was
the noise the goblin miners made at their work, and they seemed to be
at no great distance now. Irene heard it the moment she stopped.

'What is that noise?' she asked. 'Do you know, Curdie?'

'Yes. It is the goblins digging and burrowing,' he answered.

'And you don't know what they do it for?'

'No; I haven't the least idea. Would you like to see them?' he asked, wishing to have another try after their secret.

'If my thread took me there, I shouldn't much mind; but I don't want to see them, and I can't leave my thread. It leads me down into the hole, and we had better go at once.'

'Very well. Shall I go in first?' said Curdie.

'No; better not. You can't feel the thread,' she answered, stepping down through a narrow break in the floor of the cavern. 'Oh!' she cried, 'I am in the water. It is running strong – but it is not deep, and there is just room to walk. Make haste, Curdie.'

He tried, but the hole was too small for him to get in.

'Go on a little bit,' he said, shouldering his pickaxe.

In a few moments he had cleared a larger opening and followed her. They went on, down and down with the running water, Curdie getting more and more afraid it was leading them to some terrible gulf in the heart of the mountain. In one or two places he had to break away the rock to make room before even Irene could get through – at least without hurting herself. But at length they spied a glimmer of light, and in a minute more, they were almost blinded by the full sunlight, into which they emerged. It was some little time before the princess could see well enough to discover that they stood in her own garden, close by the seat on which she and her king-papa had sat that afternoon. They had come out by the channel of the little stream. She danced and clapped her hands with delight.

'Now, Curdie!' she cried, 'won't you believe what I told you about my grandmother and her thread?'

For she had felt all the time that Curdie was not believing what she told him.

'There! – don't you see it shining on before us?' she added.

'I don't see anything,' persisted Curdie.

'Then you must believe without seeing,' said the princess; 'for you can't deny it has brought us out of the mountain.'

'I can't deny we *are* out of the mountain, and I should be very ungrateful indeed to deny that *you* had brought *me* out of it.'

'I couldn't have done it but for the thread,' persisted Irene.

'That's the part I don't understand.'

'Well, come along, and Lootie will get you something to eat. I am sure you must want it very much.'

'Indeed I do. But my father and mother will be so anxious about me, I must make haste – first up the mountain to tell my mother, and then down into the mine again to let my father know.'

'Very well, Curdie; but you can't get out without coming this way, and I will take you through the house, for that is nearest.'

They met no one by the way, for indeed, as before, the people were here and there and everywhere searching for the princess. When they got in, Irene found that the thread, as she had half expected, went up the old staircase, and a new thought struck her. She turned to Curdie and said –

'My grandmother wants me. Do come up with me, and see her. Then you will know that I have been telling you the truth. Do come – to please me, Curdie. I can't bear you should think what I say is not true.'

'I never doubted you believed what you said,' returned Curdie. 'I only thought you had some fancy in your head that was not correct.'

'But do come, dear Curdie.'

The little miner could not withstand this appeal, and though he felt shy in what seemed to him a huge grand house, he yielded, and followed her up the stair.

Up the stair then they went, and the next and the next, and through the long rows of empty rooms, and up the little tower stair, Irene growing happier and happier as she ascended. There was no answer when she knocked at length at the door of the workroom, nor could she hear any sound of the spinning-wheel, and once more her heart sank within her – but only for one moment, as she turned and knocked at the other door.

'Come in,' answered the sweet voice of her grandmother, and Irene opened the door and entered, followed by Curdie.

'You darling!' cried the lady, who was seated by a fire of red roses mingled with white – 'I've been waiting for you, and indeed getting a little anxious about you, and beginning to think whether I had not better go and fetch you myself.'

As she spoke she took the little princess in her arms and placed her upon her lap. She was dressed in white now, and looking if possible more lovely than ever.

'I've brought Curdie, grandmother. He wouldn't believe what I told him, and so I've brought him.'

'Yes – I see him. He is a good boy, Curdie, and a brave boy. Aren't you glad you've got him out?'

'Yes, grandmother. But it wasn't very good of him not to believe me when I was telling him the truth.'

'People must believe what they can, and those who believe more must not be hard upon those who believe less. I doubt if you would have believed it all yourself if you hadn't seen some of it.'

'Ah! yes, grandmother, I dare say. I'm sure you are right. But he'll believe now.'

'I don't know that,' replied her grandmother.

'Won't you, Curdie?' said Irene, looking round at him as she asked the question.

He was standing in the middle of the floor, staring, and looking strangely bewildered. This she thought came of his astonishment at the beauty of the lady.

'Make a bow to my grandmother, Curdie,' she said.

'I don't see any grandmother,' answered Curdie rather gruffly.

'Don't see my grandmother, when I'm sitting in her lap!' exclaimed the princess.

'No, I don't,' reiterated Curdie, in an offended tone.

'Don't you see the lovely fire of roses – white ones amongst them this time?' asked Irene, almost as bewildered as he.

'No, I don't,' answered Curdie, almost sulkily.

'Nor the blue bed? Nor the rose-coloured counterpane? Nor the beautiful light, like the moon, hanging from the roof?'

'You're making game of me, your royal highness; and after what we have come through together this day, I don't think it is kind of you,' said Curdie, feeling very much hurt.

'Then what *do* you see?' asked Irene, who perceived at once that for her not to believe him was at least as bad as for him not to believe her.

'I see a big, bare, garret-room – like the one in mother's cottage, only big enough to take the cottage itself in, and leave a good margin all round,' answered Curdie.

'And what more do you see?'

'I see a tub, and a heap of musty straw, and a withered apple, and a ray of sunlight coming through a hole in the middle of the roof, and shining on your head, and making all the place look a curious dusky brown. I think you had better drop it, princess, and go down to the nursery, like a good girl.'

'But don't you hear my grandmother talking to me?' asked Irene, almost crying.

'No. I hear the cooing of a lot of pigeons. If you won't come down, I will go without you. I think that will be better anyhow, for I'm sure nobody who met us would believe a word we said to them. They would think we made it all up. I don't expect anybody but my own father and mother to believe me. They *know* I wouldn't tell a story.'

'And yet *you* won't believe *me*, Curdie?' expostulated the princess, now fairly crying with vexation and sorrow at the gulf between her and Curdie.

'No. I *can't*, and I can't help it,' said Curdie, turning to leave the room.

'What *shall* I do, grandmother?' sobbed the princess, turning her face round upon the lady's bosom, and shaking with suppressed sobs.

'You must give him time,' said her grandmother; 'and you must be content not to be believed for a while. It is very hard to bear; but I have had to bear it, and shall have to bear it many a time yet. I will take care of what Curdie thinks of you in the end. You must let him go now.'

'You're not coming, are you?' asked Curdie.

'No, Curdie; my grandmother says I must let you go. Turn to the right when you get to the bottom of all the stairs, and that will take you to the hall where the great door is.'

'Oh! I don't doubt I can find my way – without you, princess, or your old grannie's thread either,' said Curdie quite rudely.

'Oh! Curdie! Curdie!'

'I wish I had gone home at once. I'm very much obliged to you, Irene, for getting me out of that hole, but I wish you hadn't made a fool of me afterwards.'

He said this as he opened the door, which he left open, and, without another word, went down the stair. Irene listened with dismay to his departing footsteps. Then turning again to the lady –

'What does it all mean, grandmother?' she sobbed, and burst into fresh tears.

'It means, my love, that I did not mean to show myself. Curdie is not yet able to believe some things. Seeing is not believing – it is only seeing. You remember I told you that if Lootie were to see me, she would rub her eyes, forget the half she saw, and call the other half nonsense.'

'Yes; but I should have thought Curdie——'

'You are right. Curdie is much farther on than Lootie, and you will see what will come of it. But in the meantime, you must be content, I say, to be misunderstood for a while. We are all very anxious to be understood, and it is very hard not to be. But there is one thing much more necessary.'

'What is that, grandmother?'

'To understand other people.'

'Yes, grandmother. I must be fair – for if I'm not fair to other people, I'm not worth being understood myself. I see. So as Curdie can't help it, I will not be vexed with him, but just wait.'

'There's my own dear child,' said her grandmother, and pressed her close to her bosom.

'Why weren't you in your workroom, when we came up, grandmother?' asked Irene, after a few moments' silence.

'If I had been there, Curdie would have seen me well enough. But why should I be there rather than in this beautiful room?'

'I thought you would be spinning.'

'I've nobody to spin for just at present. I never spin without knowing for whom I am spinning.'

'That reminds me – there is one thing that puzzles me,' said the princess: 'how are you to get the thread out of the mountain again? Surely you won't have to make another for *me*? That would be such a trouble!'

The lady set her down, and rose, and went to the fire. Putting in her hand, she drew it out again, and held up the shining ball between her finger and thumb.

'I've got it now, you see,' she said, coming back to the princess, 'all ready for you when you want it.'

Going to her cabinet, she laid it in the same drawer as before.

'And here is your ring,' she added, taking it from the little finger of her left hand, and putting it on the forefinger of Irene's right hand.

'Oh! thank you, grandmother. I feel so safe now!'

'You are very tired, my child,' the lady went on. 'Your hands are hurt with the stones, and I have counted nine bruises on you. Just look what you are like.'

And she held up to her a little mirror which she had brought from the cabinet. The princess burst into a merry laugh at the sight. She was so draggled with the stream, and dirty with creeping through narrow places, that if she had seen the reflection without knowing it was a reflection, she would have taken herself for some gipsy child whose face was washed and hair combed about once in a month. The lady laughed too, and lifting her again upon her knee, took off her cloak and nightgown. Then she carried her to the side of the room. Irene wondered what she was going to do with her, but asked no questions –

only starting a little when she found that she was going to lay her in the large silver bath; for as she looked into it, again she saw no bottom, but the stars shining miles away, as it seemed, in a great blue gulf. Her hands closed involuntarily on the beautiful arms that held her, and that was all.

The lady pressed her once more to her bosom, saying – 'Do not be afraid, my child.'

'No, grandmother,' answered the princess, with a little gasp; and the next instant she sank in the clear cool water.

When she opened her eyes, she saw nothing but a strange lovely blue over and beneath and all about her. The lady and the beautiful room had vanished from her sight, and she seemed utterly alone. But instead of being afraid, she felt more than happy – perfectly blissful. And from somewhere came the voice of the lady, singing a strange sweet song, of which she could distinguish every word; but of the sense she had only a feeling – no understanding. Nor could she remember a single line after it was gone. It vanished, like the poetry in a dream, as fast as it came. In after years, however, she would sometimes fancy that snatches of melody suddenly rising in her brain, must be little phrases and fragments of the air of that song; and the very fancy would make her happier, and abler to do her duty.

How long she lay in the water, she did not know. It seemed a long time – not from weariness, but from pleasure. But at last she felt the beautiful hands lay hold of her, and through the gurgling water she was lifted out into the lovely room. The lady carried her to the fire, and sat down with her in her lap, and dried her tenderly with the softest towel. It was so different from Lootie's drying! When the lady had done, she stooped to the fire, and drew from it her nightgown, as white as snow.

'How delicious!' exclaimed the princess. 'It smells of all the roses in the world, I think.'

When she stood up on the floor, she felt as if she had been made over again. Every bruise and all weariness were gone, and her hands were soft and whole as ever.

'Now I am going to put you to bed for a good sleep,' said her grandmother.

'But what will Lootie be thinking? And what am I to say to her when she asks me where I have been?'

'Don't trouble yourself about it. You will find it all come right,' said her grandmother, and laid her into the blue bed, under the rosy counterpane.

'There is just one thing more,' said Irene. 'I am a little anxious about Curdie. As I brought him into the house, I ought to have seen him safe on his way home.'

'I took care of all that,' answered the lady. 'I told you to let him go, and therefore I was bound to look after him. Nobody saw him, and he is now eating a good dinner in his mother's cottage, far up the mountain.'

'Then I will go to sleep,' said Irene, and in a few minutes, she was fast asleep.

23   Curdie and his Mother

Curdie went up the mountain neither whistling nor singing, for he was vexed with Irene for taking him in, as he called it; and he was vexed with himself for having spoken to her so angrily. His mother gave a cry of joy when she saw him, and at once set about getting him something to eat, asking him questions all the time, which he did not answer so cheerfully as usual. When his meal was ready, she left him to eat it, and hurried to the mine to let his father know he was safe. When she came back, she found him fast asleep upon her bed; nor did he wake until his father came home in the evening.

'Now, Curdie,' his mother said, as they sat at supper, 'tell us the whole story from beginning to end, just as it all happened.'

Curdie obeyed, and told everything to the point where they came out upon the lawn in the garden of the king's house.

'And what happened after that?' asked his mother. 'You haven't told us all. You ought to be very happy at having got away from those demons, and instead of that, I never saw you so gloomy. There must be something more. Besides, you do not speak of that lovely child as I should like to hear you. She saved your life at the risk of her own, and yet somehow you don't seem to think much of it.'

'She talked such nonsense!' answered Curdie, 'and told me a pack of things that weren't a bit true; and I can't get over it.'

'What were they?' asked his father. 'Your mother may be able to throw some light upon them.'

Then Curdie made a clean breast of it, and told them everything.

They all sat silent for some time, pondering the strange tale. At last Curdie's mother spoke.

'You confess, my boy,' she said, 'there is something about the whole affair you do not understand?'

'Yes, of course, mother,' he answered. 'I cannot understand how a child knowing nothing about the mountain, or even that I was shut up in it, should come all that way alone, straight to where I was; and then, after getting me out of the hole, lead me out of the mountain too, where I should not have known a step of the way if it had been as light as in the open air.'

'Then you have no right to say that what she told you was not true. She did take you out, and she must have had something to guide her: why not a thread as well as a rope, or anything else? There is something you cannot explain, and her explanation may be the right one.'

'It's no explanation at all, mother; and I can't believe it.'

'That may be only because you do not understand it. If you did, you would probably find it was an explanation, and believe it thoroughly. I don't blame you for not being able to believe it, but I do blame you for fancying such a child would try to deceive you. Why should she? Depend upon it, she told you all she knew. Until you had found a better way of accounting for it all, you might at least have been more sparing of your judgment.'

'That is what something inside me has been saying all the time,' said Curdie, hanging down his head. 'But what do you make of the grandmother? That is what I can't get over. To take me up to an old garret, and try to persuade me against the sight of my own eyes that it was a beautiful room, with blue walls and silver stars, and no end of things in it, when there was nothing there but an old tub and a withered apple and a heap of straw and a sunbeam! It was too bad! She *might* have had some old woman there at least to pass for her precious grandmother!'

'Didn't she speak as if she saw those other things herself, Curdie?'

'Yes. That's what bothers me. You would have thought she really meant and believed that she saw every one of the things she talked about. And not one of them there! It was too bad, I say.'

'Perhaps some people can see things other people can't see, Curdie,' said his mother very gravely. 'I think I will tell you something I saw myself once – only perhaps you won't believe me either!'

'Oh, mother, mother!' cried Curdie, bursting into tears; 'I don't deserve that, surely!'

'But what I am going to tell you is very strange,' persisted his mother; 'and if having heard it you were to say I must have been dreaming, I don't know that I should have any right to be vexed with you, though I know at least that I was not asleep.'

'Do tell me, mother. Perhaps it will help me to think better of the princess.'

'That's why I am tempted to tell you,' replied his mother. 'But first, I may as well mention, that according to old whispers, there is something more than common about the king's family; and the queen was of the same blood, for they were cousins of some degree. There were strange stories told concerning them – all good stories – but strange, very strange. What they were I cannot tell, for I only remember the faces of my grandmother and my mother as they talked together about them. There was wonder and awe – not fear, in their eyes, and they whispered, and never spoke aloud. But what I saw myself, was this: Your father was going to work in the mine, one night, and I had been down with his supper. It was soon after we were married, and not very long before you were born. He came with me to the mouth of the mine, and left me to go home alone, for I knew the way almost as well as the floor of our own cottage. It was pretty dark, and in some parts of the road where the rocks overhung, nearly quite dark. But I got along perfectly well, never thinking of being afraid, until I reached a spot you know well enough, Curdie, where the path has to make a sharp turn out of the way of a great rock on the left-hand side. When I got there, I was suddenly surrounded by about half a dozen of the cobs, the first I had ever seen, although I had heard tell of them often enough. One of them blocked up the path, and they all began tormenting and teasing me in a way it makes me shudder to think of even now.'

'If I had only been with you!' cried father and son in a breath.

The mother gave a funny little smile, and went on.

'They had some of their horrible creatures with them too, and I must confess I was dreadfully frightened. They had torn my clothes very much, and I was afraid they were going to tear myself to pieces, when suddenly a great white soft light shone upon me. I looked up. A broad ray, like a shining road, came down from a large globe of silvery light, not very high up, indeed not quite so high as the horizon – so it could not have been a new star or another moon or anything of that sort. The cobs dropped persecuting me, and look dazed, and I thought they were going to run away, but presently they began again. The same moment, however, down the path from the globe of light came a bird, shining like silver in the sun. It gave a few rapid flaps first, and then, with its wings straight out, shot sliding down the slope of the light. It looked to me just like a white pigeon. But whatever it was, when the cobs caught sight of it coming straight down upon them, they took to their heels and scampered away across the mountain, leaving me safe, only much frightened. As soon as it had sent them off, the bird went gliding again up the light, and the moment it reached the globe, the light disappeared, just as if a shutter had been closed over a window, and I saw it no more. But I had no more trouble with the cobs that night, or ever after.'

'How strange!' exclaimed Curdie.

'Yes, it was strange; but I can't help believing it, whether you do or not,' said his mother.

'It's exactly as your mother told it to me the very next morning,' said his father.

'You don't think I'm doubting my own mother!' cried Curdie.

'There are other people in the world quite as well worth believing as your own mother,' said his mother. 'I don't know that she's so much the fitter to be believed that she happens to be *your* mother, Mr. Curdie. There are mothers far more likely to tell lies than the little girl I saw talking to the primroses a few weeks ago. If she were to lie I should begin to doubt my own word.'

'But princesses *have* told lies as well as other people,' said Curdie.

'Yes, but not princesses like that child. She's a good girl, I am certain, and that's more than being a princess. Depend upon it you will have to be sorry for behaving so to her, Curdie. You ought at least to have held your tongue.'

'I am sorry now,' answered Curdie.

'You ought to go and tell her so, then.'

'I don't see how I could manage that. They wouldn't let a miner boy like me have a word with her alone; and I couldn't tell her before that nurse of hers. She'd be asking ever so many questions, and I don't know how many the little princess would like me to answer. She told me that Lootie didn't know anything about her coming to get me out of the mountain. I am certain she would have prevented her somehow if she had known of it. But I may have a chance before long, and meantime I must try to do something for her. I think, father, I have got on the track at last.'

'Have you, indeed, my boy?' said Peter. 'I am sure you deserve some success; you have worked very hard for it. What have you found out?'

'It's difficult you know, father, inside the mountain, especially in the dark, and not knowing what turns you have taken, to tell the lie of things outside.'

'Impossible, my boy, without a chart, or at least a compass,' returned his father.

'Well, I think I have nearly discovered in what direction the cobs are mining. If I am right, I know something else that I can put to it, and then one and one will make three.'

'They very often do, Curdie, as we miners ought to be very well aware. Now tell us, my boy, what the two things are, and see whether we can guess at the same third as you.'

'I don't see what that has to do with the princess,' interposed his mother.

'I will soon let you see that, mother. Perhaps you may think me foolish, but until I am sure there is nothing in my present fancy, I am more determined than ever to go on with my observations. Just as we came to the channel by which we got out, I heard the miners at work somewhere near – I think down below us. Now since I began to watch them, they have mined a good half mile, in a straight line; and so far as I am aware, they are working in no other part of the mountain. But I never could tell in what direction they were going. When we came out in the king's garden, however, I thought at once whether it was possible they were working towards the king's house; and what I want to do to-night is to make sure whether they are or not. I will take a light with me——'

'Oh Curdie,' cried his mother, 'then they will see you.'

'I'm no more afraid of them now than I was before,' rejoined Curdie, '– now that I've got this precious shoe. They can't make another such in a hurry, and one bare foot will do for my purpose. Woman as she may be, I won't spare her next time. But I shall be careful with my light, for I don't want them to see me. I won't stick it in my hat.'

'Go on, then, and tell us what you mean to do.'

'I mean to take a bit of paper with me and a pencil, and go in at the mouth of the stream by which we came out. I shall mark on the paper as near as I can the angle of every turning I take until I find the cobs at work, and so get a good idea in what direction they are going. If it should prove to be nearly parallel with the stream, I shall know it is towards the king's house they are working.'

'And what if you should? How much wiser will you be then?'

'Wait a minute, mother, dear. I told you that when I came upon the royal family in the cave, they were talking of their prince – Harelip, they called him – marrying a sun-woman – that means one of us – one with toes to her feet. Now in the speech one of them made that night at their great gathering, of which I heard only a part, he said that peace would be secured for a generation at least by the pledge the prince would hold for the good behaviour of *her* relatives: that's what he said, and he must have meant the sun-woman the prince was to marry. I am quite sure the king is much too proud to wish his son to marry any but a princess, and much too knowing to fancy that his having a peasant woman for a wife would be of any great advantage to them.'

'I see what you are driving at now,' said his mother.

'But,' said his father, 'the king would dig the mountain to the plain before he would have his princess the wife of a cob, if her were ten times a prince.'

'Yes; but they think so much of themselves!' said his mother. 'Small creatures always do. The bantam is the proudest cock in my little yard.'

'And I fancy,' said Curdie, 'if they once got her, they would tell the king they would kill her except he consented to the marriage.'

'They might say so,' said his father, 'but they wouldn't kill her; they would keep her alive for the sake of the hold it gave them over our king. Whatever he did to them, they would threaten to do the same to the princess.'

'And they are bad enough to torment her just for their own amusement – I know that,' said his mother.

'Anyhow, I will keep a watch on them, and see what they are up to,' said Curdie. 'It's too horrible to think of. I daren't let myself do it. But they sha'n't have her – at least if I can help it. So, mother dear – my clue is all right – will you get me a bit of paper and a pencil and a lump of pease pudding, and I will set out at once. I saw a place where I can climb over the wall of the garden quite easily.'

'You must mind and keep out of the way of the men on the watch,' said his mother.

'That I will. I don't want them to know anything about it. They would spoil it all. The cobs would only try some other plan – they are such obstinate creatures! I shall take good care, mother. They won't kill and eat me either, if they should come upon me. So you needn't mind them.'

His mother got him what he had asked for, and Curdie set out. Close beside the door by which the princess left the garden for the mountain, stood a great rock, and by climbing it Curdie got over the wall. He tied his clue to a stone just inside the channel of the stream, and took his pickaxe with him. He had not gone far before he encountered a horrid creature coming towards the mouth. The spot was too narrow for two of almost any size or shape, and besides Curdie had no wish to let the creature pass. Not being able to use his pickaxe, however, he had a severe struggle with him, and it was only after receiving many bites, some of them bad, that he succeeded in killing him with his pocket-knife. Having dragged him out, he made haste to get in again before another should stop up the way.

I need not follow him farther in this night's adventures. He returned to his breakfast, satisfied that the goblins were mining in the direction of the palace – on so low a level that their intention must, he thought, be to burrow under the walls of the king's house, and rise up inside it – in order, he fully believed, to lay hands on the little princess, and carry her off for a wife to their horrid Harelip.

24 Irene Behaves like a Princess

When the princess awoke from the sweetest of sleeps, she found her nurse bending over her, the housekeeper looking over the nurse's shoulder, and the laundry-maid looking over the housekeeper's. The room was full of women-servants; and the gentlemen-at-arms, with a long column of servants behind them, were peeping, or trying to peep in at the door of the nursery.

'Are those horrid creatures gone?' asked the princess, remembering first what had terrified her in the morning.

'You naughty, naughty little princess!' cried Lootie.

Her face was very pale, with red streaks in it, and she looked as if she were going to shake her; but Irene said nothing – only waited to hear what should come next.

'How *could* you get under the clothes like that, and make us all fancy you were lost! And keep it up all day too! You *are* the most obstinate child! It's anything but fun to us, I can tell you!'

It was the only way the nurse could account for her disappearance.

'I didn't do that, Lootie,' said Irene, very quietly.

'Don't tell stories!' cried her nurse quite rudely.

'I shall tell you nothing at all,' said Irene.

'That's just as bad,' said the nurse.

'Just as bad to say nothing at all as to tell stories!' exclaimed the princess. 'I will ask my papa about that. He won't say so. And I don't think he will like you to say so.'

'Tell me directly what you mean by it!' screamed the nurse, half-wild with anger at the princess, and fright at the possible consequences to herself.

'When I tell you the truth, Lootie,' said the princess, who somehow did not feel at all angry, 'you say to me *Don't tell stories:* it seems I must tell stories before you will believe me.'

'You are very rude, princess,' said the nurse.

'You are so rude, Lootie, that I will not speak to you again till you are sorry. Why should I, when I know you will not believe me?' returned the princess.

For she did know perfectly well that if she were to tell Lootie what she had been about, the more she went on to tell her, the less would she believe her.

'You are the most provoking child!' cried her nurse. 'You deserve to be well punished for your wicked behaviour.'

'Please, Mrs. Housekeeper,' said the princess, 'will you take me to your room, and keep me till my king-papa comes? I will ask him to come as soon as he can.'

Everyone stared at these words. Up to this moment, they had all regarded her as little more than a baby.

But the housekeeper was afraid of the nurse, and sought to patch matters up, saying –

'I am sure, princess, nursie did not mean to be rude to you.'

'I do not think my papa would wish me to have a nurse who spoke to me as Lootie does. If she thinks I tell lies, she had better either say so to my papa, or go away. Sir Walter, will you take charge of me?'

'With the greatest of pleasure, princess,' answered the captain of the gentlemen-at-arms, walking with his great stride into the room. The crowd of servants made eager way for him, and he bowed low before the little princess's bed. 'I shall send my servant at once, on the fastest horse in the stable, to tell your king-papa that your royal highness desires his presence. When you have chosen one of these under-servants to wait upon you, I shall order the room to be cleared.'

'Thank you very much, Sir Walter,' said the princess, and her eye glanced towards a rosy-cheeked girl who had lately come to the house as a scullery-maid.

But when Lootie saw the eyes of her dear princess going in search of another instead of her, she fell upon her knees by the bedside, and burst into a great cry of distress.

'I think, Sir Walter,' said the princess, 'I will keep Lootie. But I put myself under your care; and you need not trouble my king-papa until I speak to you again. Will you all please to go away. I am quite safe and well, and I did not hide myself for the sake either of amusing myself, or of troubling my people. – Lootie, will you please to dress me.'

25 Curdie comes to Grief

Everything was for some time quiet above-ground. The king was still away in a distant part of his dominions. The men-at-arms kept watching about the house. They had been considerably astonished by finding at the foot of the rock in the garden, the hideous body of the goblin creature killed by Curdie; but they came to the conclusion that it had been slain in the mines, and had crept out there to die; and except an occasional glimpse of a live one they saw nothing to cause alarm. Curdie kept watching in the mountain, and the goblins kept burrowing deeper into the earth. As long as they went deeper, there was, Curdie judged, no immediate danger.

To Irene, the summer was as full of pleasure as ever, and for a long time, although she often thought of her grandmother during the day, and often dreamed about her at night, she did not see her. The kids and the flowers were as much her delight as ever, and she made as much friendship with the miners' children she met on the mountain as Lootie would permit; but Lootie had very foolish notions concerning the dignity of a princess, not understanding that the truest princess is just the one who loves all her brothers and sisters best, and who is most able to do them good by being humble towards them. At the same time she was considerably altered for the better in her behaviour to the princess. She could not help seeing that she was no longer a mere child, but wiser than her age would account for. She kept foolishly whispering to the servants, however – sometimes that the princess was not right in her mind, sometimes that she was too good to live, and other nonsense of the same sort.

All this time, Curdie had to be sorry, without a chance of confessing, that he had behaved so unkindly to the princess. This perhaps made him the more diligent in his endeavours to serve her. His mother and he often talked on the subject, and she comforted him, and told him she was sure he would some day have the opportunity he so much desired.

Here I should like to remark, for the sake of princes and princesses in general, that it is a low and contemptible thing to refuse to confess a fault, or even an error. If a true princess has done wrong, she is always uneasy until she has had an opportunity of throwing the wrongness away from her by saying, 'I did it; and I wish I had not; and I am sorry for having done it.' So you see there is some ground for supposing that Curdie was not a miner only, but a prince as well. Many such instances have been known in the world's history.

At length, however, he began to see signs of a change in the proceedings of the goblin excavators: they were going no deeper, but had commenced running on a level; and he watched them, therefore, more closely than ever. All at once, one night, coming to a slope of very hard rock, they began to ascend along the inclined plane of its surface. Having reached its top, they went again on a level for a night or two, after which they began to ascend once more, and kept on, at a pretty steep angle. At length Curdie judged it time to transfer his observation to another quarter, and the next night, he did not go to the mine at all; but, leaving his pickaxe and clue at home, and taking only his usual lumps of bread and pease pudding, went down the mountain to the king's house. He climbed over the wall, and remained in the garden the whole night, creeping on hands and knees from one spot to the other, and lying at full length with his ear to the ground, listening. But he heard nothing except the tread of the men-at-arms as they marched about, whose observation, as the night was cloudy and there was no moon, he had little difficulty in avoiding. For several following nights, he continued to haunt the garden and listen, but with no success.

At length, early one evening, whether it was that he had got careless of his own safety, or that the growing moon had become strong enough to expose him, his watching came to a sudden end. He was creeping from behind the rock where the stream ran out, for he had been listening all round it in the hope it might convey to his ear some indication of the whereabouts of the goblin miners, when just as he came into the moonlight on the lawn, a whizz in his ear and a blow upon his leg startled him. He instantly squatted in the hope of eluding further notice. But when he heard the sound of running feet, he jumped up to take the chance of escape by flight. He fell, however,

with a keen shoot of pain, for the bolt of a crossbow had wounded his leg, and the blood was now streaming from it. He was instantly laid hold of by two or three of the men-at-arms. It was useless to struggle, and he submitted in silence.

'It's a boy!' cried several of them together, in a tone of amazement. 'I thought it was one of those demons.'

'What are you about here?'

'Going to have a little rough usage, apparently,' said Curdie laughing, as the men shook him.

'Impertinence will do you no good. You have no business here in the king's grounds, and if you don't give a true account of yourself, you shall fare as a thief.'

'Why, what else could he be?' said one.

'He might have been after a lost kid, you know,' suggested another.

'I see no good in trying to excuse him. He has no business here, anyhow.'

'Let me go away then, if you please,' said Curdie.

'But we don't please – not except you give a good account of yourself.'

'I don't feel quite sure whether I can trust you,' said Curdie.

'We are the king's own men-at-arms,' said the captain courteously, for he was taken with Curdie's appearance and courage.

'Well, I will tell you all about it – if you will promise to listen to me and not do anything rash.'

'I call that cool!' said one of the party laughing. 'He will tell us what mischief he was about, if we promise to do as pleases him.'

'I was about no mischief,' said Curdie.

But ere he could say more he turned faint, and fell senseless on the grass. Then first they discovered that the bolt they had shot, taking him for one of the goblin creatures, had wounded him.

They carried him into the house, and laid him down in the hall. The report spread that they had caught a robber, and the servants crowded in to see the villain. Amongst the rest came the nurse. The moment she saw him she exclaimed with indignation:

'I declare it's the same young rascal of a miner that was rude to me and the princess on the mountain. He actually wanted to kiss the princess. *I* took good care of that – the wretch! And *he* was prowling about – was he? Just like his impudence!'

The princess being fast asleep, and Curdie in a faint, she could misrepresent at her pleasure.

When he heard this, the captain, although he had considerable doubt of its truth, resolved to keep Curdie a prisoner until they could search into the affair. So, after they had brought him round a little, and attended to his wound, which was rather a bad one, they laid him, still exhausted from the loss of blood, upon a mattress in a disused room – one of those already so often mentioned – and locked the door, and left him. He passed a troubled night, and in the morning they found him talking wildly. In the evening he came to himself, but felt very weak, and his leg was exceedingly painful. Wondering where he was, and seeing one of the men-at-arms in the room, he began to question him, and soon recalled the events of the preceding night. As he was himself unable to watch any more, he told the soldier all he knew about the goblins, and begged him to tell his companions, and stir them up to watch with tenfold vigilance; but whether it was that he did not talk quite coherently, or that the whole thing appeared incredible, certainly the man concluded that Curdie was only raving still, and tried to coax him into holding his tongue. This, of course, annoyed

Curdie dreadfully, who now felt in his turn what it was not to be believed, and the consequence was that his fever returned, and by the time when, at his persistent entreaties, the captain was called, there could be no doubt that he was raving. They did for him what they could, and promised everything he wanted, but with no intention of fulfilment. At last he went to sleep, and when at length his sleep grew profound and peaceful, they left him, locked the door again, and withdrew, intending to revisit him early in the morning.

26   The Goblin-Miners

That same night several of the servants were having a chat together before going to bed. 'What can that noise be?' said one of the housemaids, who had been listening for a moment or two.

'I've heard it the last two nights,' said the cook. 'If there were any about the place, I should have taken it for rats, but my Tom keeps them far enough.'

'I've heard though,' said the scullery-maid, 'that rats move about in great companies sometimes. There may be an army of them invading us. I've heard the noises yesterday and to-day too.'

'It'll be grand fun then for my Tom and Mrs. Housekeeper's Bob,' said the cook. 'They'll be friends for once in their lives, and fight on the same side. I'll engage Tom and Bob together will put to flight any number of rats.'

'It seems to me,' said the nurse, 'that the noises are much too loud for that. I have heard them all day, and my princess has asked me several times what they could be. Sometimes they sound like distant thunder, and sometimes like the noises you hear in the mountain from those horrid miners underneath.'

'I shouldn't wonder,' said the cook, 'if it was the miners after all. They may have come on some hole in the mountain through which the noises reach to us. They are always boring and blasting and breaking, you know.'

As he spoke, there came a great rolling rumble beneath them, and the house quivered. They all started up in affright, and rushing to the hall found the gentlemen-at-arms in consternation also. They had sent to wake their captain, who said from their description that it must have been an earthquake, an occurrence which, although very rare in that country, had taken place almost within the century; and then went to bed again, strange to say, and fell fast asleep without once thinking of

Curdie, or associating the noises they had heard with what he had told them. He had not believed Curdie. If he had, he would at once have thought of what he had said, and would have taken precautions. As they heard nothing more, they concluded that Sir Walter was right, and that the danger was over for perhaps another hundred years. The fact, as discovered afterwards, was that the goblins had, in working up a second sloping face of stone, arrived at a huge block which lay under the cellars of the house, within the line of the foundations. It was so round that when they succeeded, after hard work, in dislodging it without blasting, it rolled thundering down the slope with a bounding, jarring roll, which shook the foundations of the house. The goblins were themselves dismayed at the noise, for they knew, by careful spying and measuring, that they must now be very near, if not under, the king's house, and they feared giving an alarm. They, therefore, remained quiet for a while, and when they began to work again, they no doubt thought themselves very fortunate in coming upon a vein of sand which filled a winding fissure in the rock on which the house was built. By scooping this away they soon came out in the king's wine cellar.

No sooner did they find where they were, than they scurried back again, like rats into their holes, and running at full speed to the goblin palace, announced their success to the king and queen with shouts of triumph. In a moment the goblin royal family and the whole goblin people were on their way in hot haste to the king's house, each eager to have a share in the glory of carrying off that same night the Princess Irene.

The queen went stumping along in one shoe of stone and one of skin. This could not have been pleasant, and my readers may wonder that, with such skilful workmen about her, she had not yet replaced the shoe carried off by Curdie. As the king however had more than one ground of objection to her stone shoes, he no doubt took advantage of the discovery of her toes, and threatened to expose her deformity if she had another made. I presume he insisted on her being content with skin shoes, and allowed her to wear the remaining granite one on the present occasion only because she was going out to war.

They soon arrived in the king's wine cellar, and regardless of its huge vessels, of which they did not know the use, proceeded at once, but as quietly as they could, to force the door that led upwards.

27 The Goblins in the King's House

When Curdie fell asleep he began at once to dream. He thought he was ascending the mountain-side from the mouth of the mine, whistling and singing '*Ring, dod, bang!*' when he came upon a woman and child who had lost their way; and from that point he went on dreaming everything that had happened to him since he thus met the princess and Lootie; how he had watched the goblins, how he had been taken by them, how he had been rescued by the princess; everything, indeed, until he was wounded, captured, and imprisoned by the men-at-arms. And now he thought he was lying wide awake where they had laid him, when suddenly he heard a great thundering sound.

'The cobs are coming!' he said. 'They didn't believe a word I told them! The cobs 'll be carrying off the princess from under their stupid noses! But they sha'n't! that they sha'n't!'

He jumped up, as he thought, and began to dress, but, to his dismay, found that he was still lying in bed.

'Now then I will!' he said. 'Here goes! I *am* up now!'

But yet again he found himself snug in bed. Twenty times he tried, and twenty times he failed; for in fact he was not awake, only dreaming that he was. At length in an agony of despair, fancying he heard the goblins all over the house, he gave a great cry. Then there came, as he thought, a hand upon the lock of his door. It opened, and, looking up, he saw a lady with white hair, carrying a silver box in her hand, enter the room. She came to his bed, he thought, stroked his head and face with cool, soft hands, took the dressing from his leg, rubbed it with something that smelt like roses, and then waved her hands over him three times. At the last wave of her hands everything vanished, he felt himself sinking into the profoundest slumber, and remembered nothing more until he awoke in earnest.

The setting moon was throwing a feeble light through the casement, and the house was full of uproar. There was soft heavy multitudinous stamping, a clashing and clanging of weapons, the voices of men and the cries of women, mixed with a hideous bellowing, which sounded victorious. The cobs were in the house! He sprung from his bed, hurried on some of his clothes, not forgetting his shoes, which were armed with nails; then spying an old hunting-knife, or short sword, hanging on the wall, he caught it, and rushed down the stairs, guided by the sounds of strife, which grew louder and louder.

When he reached the ground floor he found the whole place swarming. All the goblins of the mountain seemed gathered there. He rushed amongst them, shouting –

> 'One, two,
> Hit and hew!
> Three, four,
> Blast and bore!'

and with every rhyme he came down a great stamp upon a foot, cutting at the same time their faces – executing, indeed, a sword dance of the wildest description. Away scattered the goblins in every direction, – into closets, up stairs, into chimneys, up on rafters, and down to the cellars. Curdie went on stamping and slashing and singing, but saw nothing of the people of the house until he came to the great hall, in which, the moment he entered it, arose a great goblin shout. The last of the men-at-arms, the captain himself was on the floor, buried beneath a wallowing crowd of goblins. For, while each knight was busy defending himself as well as he could, by stabs in the thick bodies of the goblins, for he had soon found their heads all but invulnerable, the queen had attacked his legs and feet with her horrible granite shoe, and he was soon down; but the captain had got his back to the wall and stood out longer. The goblins would have torn them all to pieces, but the king had given orders to carry them away alive, and over each of them, in twelve groups, was standing a knot of goblins, while as many as could find room were sitting upon their prostrate bodies.

Curdie burst in dancing and gyrating and stamping and singing like a small incarnate whirlwind.

'Where 't is all a hole, sir,
   Never can be holes:
Why should their shoes have soles, sir,
   When they've got no souls?

'But she upon her foot, sir,
   Has a granite shoe:
The strongest leather boot, sir,
   Six would soon be through,'

The queen gave a howl of rage and dismay; and before she recovered her presence of mind, Curdie, having begun with the group nearest him, had eleven of the knights on their legs again.

'Stamp on their feet!' he cried as each man rose, and in a few minutes the hall was nearly empty, the goblins running from it as fast as they could, howling and shrieking and limping, and cowering every now and then as they ran to cuddle their wounded feet in their hard hands, or to protect them from the frightful stamp-stamp of the armed men.

And now Curdie approached the group which, trusting in the queen and her shoe, kept their guard over the prostrate captain. The king sat on the captain's head, but the queen stood in front, like an infuriated cat, with her perpendicular eyes gleaming green, and her hair standing half up from her horrid head. Her heart was quaking however, and she kept moving about her skin-shod foot with nervous apprehension. When Curdie was within a few paces, she rushed at him, made one tremendous stamp at his opposing foot, which happily he withdrew in time, and caught him round the waist, to dash him on the marble floor. But just as she caught him, he came down with all the weight of his iron-shod shoe upon her skin-shod foot, and with a hideous howl she dropped him, squatted on the floor and took her foot in both her hands. Meanwhile the rest rushed on the king and the bodyguard, sent them flying, and lifted the prostrate captain, who was all but pressed to death. It was some moments before he recovered breath and consciousness.

'Where's the princess?' cried Curdie, again and again.

No one knew, and off they all rushed in search of her.

Through every room in the house they went, but nowhere was she

to be found. Neither was one of the servants to be seen. But Curdie, who had kept to the lower part of the house, which was now quiet enough, began to hear a confused sound as of a distant hubbub, and set out to find where it came from. The noise grew as his sharp ears guided him to a stair and so to the wine cellar. It was full of goblins, whom the butler was supplying with wine as fast as he could draw it.

While the queen and her party had encountered the men-at-arms, Harelip with another company had gone off to search the house. They captured everyone they met, and when they could find no more, they hurried away to carry them safe to the caverns below. But when the butler, who was amongst them, found that their path lay through the wine cellar, he bethought himself of persuading them to taste the wine, and, as he had hoped, they no sooner tasted than they wanted more. The routed goblins, on their way below, joined them, and when Curdie entered, they were all, with outstretched hands, in which were vessels of every description from saucepan to silver cup, pressing around the butler, who sat at the tap of a huge cask, filling and filling. Curdie cast one glance around the place before commencing his attack, and saw in the farthest corner a terrified group of the domestics unwatched, but cowering without courage to attempt their escape. Amongst them was the terror-stricken face of Lootie; but nowhere could he see the princess. Seized with the horrible conviction that Harelip had already carried her off, he rushed amongst them, unable for wrath to sing any more, but stamping and cutting with greater fury than ever.

'Stamp on their feet; stamp on their feet!' he shouted, and in a moment the goblins were disappearing through the hole in the floor like rats and mice.

They could not vanish so fast, however, but that many more goblin-feet had to go limping back over the underground ways of the mountain that morning.

Presently however they were reinforced from above by the king and his party, with the redoubtable queen at their head. Finding Curdie again busy amongst her unfortunate subjects, she rushed at him once more with the rage of despair, and this time gave him a bad bruise on the foot. Then a regular stamping fight got up between them, Curdie, with the point of his hunting-knife keeping her from clasping her mighty arms about him, as he watched his opportunity of getting once more a good stamp at her skin-shod foot. But the queen was more wary as well as more agile than hitherto.

The rest meantime, finding their adversary thus matched for the moment, paused in their headlong hurry, and turned to the shivering group of women in the corner. As if determined to emulate his father and have a sun-woman of some sort to share his future throne, Harelip rushed at them, caught up Lootie and sped with her to the hole. She gave a great shriek, and Curdie heard her, and saw the plight she was in. Gathering all his strength, he gave the queen a sudden cut across the face with his weapon, came down, as she started back, with all his weight on the proper foot, and sprung to Lootie's rescue. The prince had two defenceless feet, and on both of them Curdie stamped just as he reached the hole. He dropped his burden and rolled shrieking into the earth. Curdie made one stab at him as he disappeared, caught hold of the senseless Lootie, and having dragged her back to the corner, there mounted guard over her, preparing once more to encounter the queen. Her face streaming with blood, and her eyes flashing green lightning through it, she came on with her mouth open and her teeth grinning like a tiger's, followed by the king and her bodyguard of the thickest goblins. But the same moment in rushed the captain and his men, and ran at them stamping furiously. They dared not encounter such an onset. Away they scurried, the queen foremost. Of course the right thing would have been to take the king and queen prisoners, and hold them hostages for the princess, but they were so anxious to find her that no one thought of detaining them until it was too late.

Having thus rescued the servants, they set about searching the house once more. None of them could give the least information concerning the princess. Lootie was almost silly with terror, and although scarcely able to walk, would not leave Curdie's side for a single moment. Again he allowed the others to search the rest of the house – where, except a dismayed goblin lurking here and there, they found no one – while he requested Lootie to take him to the princess's room. She was as submissive and obedient as if he had been the king.

He found the bedclothes tossed about, and most of them on the floor, while the princess's garments were scattered all over the room, which was in the greatest confusion. It was only too evident that the goblins had been there, and Curdie had no longer any doubt that she had been carried off at the very first of the inroad. With a pang of despair he saw how wrong they had been in not securing the king and queen and prince; but he determined to find and rescue the princess as she had found and rescued him, or meet the worst fate to which the goblins could doom him.

28 Curdie's Guide

Just as the consolation of this resolve dawned upon his mind, and he was turning away for the cellar to follow the goblins into their hole, something touched his hand. It was the slightest touch, and when he looked he could see nothing. Feeling and peering about in the grey of the dawn, his fingers came upon a tight thread. He looked again, and narrowly, but still could see nothing. It flashed upon him that this must be the princess's thread. Without saying a word, for he knew no one would believe him any more than he had believed the princess, he followed the thread with his finger, contrived to give Lootie the slip, and was soon out of the house, and on the mountain-side -- surprised that, if the thread were indeed her grandmother's messenger, it should have led the princess, as he supposed it must, into the mountain, where she would be certain to meet the goblins rushing back enraged from their defeat. But he hurried on in the hope of overtaking her first. When he arrived however at the place where the path turned off for the mine, he found that the thread did not turn with it, but went straight up the mountain. Could it be that the thread was leading him home to his mother's cottage? Could the princess be there? He bounded up the mountain like one of its own goats, and before the sun was up, the thread had brought him indeed to his mother's door. There it vanished from his fingers, and he could not find it, search as he might.

The door was on the latch, and he entered. There sat his mother by the fire, and in her arms lay the princess fast asleep.

'Hush, Curdie!' said his mother. 'Do not wake her. I'm so glad you're come! I thought the cobs must have got you again!'

With a heart full of delight, Curdie sat down at a corner of the hearth, on a stool opposite his mother's chair, and gazed at the princess, who slept as peacefully as if she had been in her own bed. All at once she opened her eyes and fixed them on him.

'Oh, Curdie! you're come!' she said quietly. 'I thought you would!'

Curdie rose and stood before her with downcast eyes.

'Irene,' he said, 'I am very sorry I did not believe you.'

'Oh, never mind, Curdie!' answered the princess. 'You couldn't, you know. You do believe me now, don't you?'

'I can't help it now. I ought to have helped it before.'

'Why can't you help it now?'

'Because, just as I was going into the mountain to look for you, I got a hold of your thread, and it brought me here.'

'Then you've come from my house, have you?'·

'Yes, I have.'

'I didn't know you were there.'

'I've been there two or three days, I believe.'

'And I never knew it! – Then perhaps you can tell me why my grandmother has brought me here? I can't think. Something woke me – I didn't know what, but I was frightened, and I felt for the thread, and there it was! I was more frightened still when it brought me out on the mountain, for I thought it was going to take me into it again, and I like the outside of it best. I supposed you were in trouble again, and I had to get you out. But it brought me here instead; and, oh Curdie! your mother has been so kind to me – just like my own grandmother!'

Here Curdie's mother gave the princess a hug, and the princess turned and gave her a sweet smile, and held up her mouth to kiss her.

'Then you didn't see the cobs?' asked Curdie.

'No; I haven't been into the mountain, I told you, Curdie.'

'But the cobs have been into your house – all over it – and into your bedroom, making such a row!'

'What did they want there? It was very rude of them.'

'They wanted you – to carry you off into the mountain with them, for a wife to their Prince Harelip.'

'Oh, how dreadful!' cried the princess, shuddering.

'But you needn't be afraid, you know. Your grandmother takes care of you.'

'Ah! you do believe in my grandmother then? I'm so glad! She made me think you would some day.'

All at once Curdie remembered his dream, and was silent, thinking.

'But how did you come to be in my house, and me not know it?' asked the princess.

Then Curdie had to explain everything – how he had watched for her sake, how he had been wounded and shut up by the soldiers, how he heard the noises and could not rise, and how the beautiful old lady had come to him, and all that followed.

'Poor Curdie! to lie there hurt and ill, and me never to know it!' exclaimed the princess, stroking his rough hand. 'I would have come and nursed you, if they had told me.'

'I didn't see you were lame,' said his mother.

'Am I, mother? Oh – yes – I suppose I ought to be. I declare I've never thought of it since I got up to go down amongst the cobs!'

'Let me see the wound,' said his mother.

He pulled down his stocking – when behold, except a great scar, his leg was perfectly sound!

Curdie and his mother gazed in each other's eyes, full of wonder, but Irene called out –

'I thought so, Curdie! I was sure it wasn't a dream. I was sure my grandmother had been to see you. – Don't you smell the roses? It was my grandmother healed your leg, and sent you to help me.'

'No, Princess Irene,' said Curdie; 'I wasn't good enough to be allowed to help you: I didn't believe you. Your grandmother took care of you without me.'

'She sent you to help my people, anyhow. I wish my king-papa would come. I do want so to tell him how good you have been!'

'But,' said the mother, 'we are forgetting how frightened your people must be. – You must take the princess home at once, Curdie – or at least go and tell them where she is.'

'Yes, mother. Only I'm dreadfully hungry. Do let me have some breakfast first. They ought to have listened to me, and then they wouldn't have been taken by surprise as they were.'

'That is true, Curdie; but it is not for you to blame them much. You remember?'

'Yes, mother, I do. Only I must really have something to eat.'

'You shall, my boy – as fast as I can get it,' said his mother, rising and setting the princess on her chair.

But before his breakfast was ready, Curdie jumped up so suddenly as to startle both his companions.

'Mother, mother!' he cried, 'I was forgetting. You must take the princess home yourself. I must go and wake my father.'

Without a word of explanation, he rushed to the place where his father was sleeping. Having thoroughly roused him with what he told him, he darted out of the cottage.

29   Masonwork

He had all at once remembered the resolution of the goblins to carry out their second plan upon the failure of the first. No doubt they were already busy, and the mine was therefore in the greatest danger of being flooded and rendered useless – not to speak of the lives of the miners.

When he reached the mouth of the mine, after rousing all the miners within reach, he found his father and a good many more just entering. They all hurried to the gang by which he had found a way into the goblin country. There the foresight of Peter had already collected a great many blocks of stone, with cement, ready for building up the weak place – well enough known to the goblins. Although there was not room for more than two to be actually building at once, they managed, by setting all the rest to work in preparing the cement and passing the stones, to finish in the course of the day a huge buttress filling the whole gang, and supported everywhere by the live rock. Before the hour when they usually dropped work, they were satisfied the mine was secure.

They had heard goblin hammers and pickaxes busy all the time, and at length fancied they heard sounds of water they had never heard before. But that was otherwise accounted for when they left the mine; for they stepped out into a tremendous storm which was raging all over the mountain. The thunder was bellowing, and the lightning lancing out of a huge black cloud which lay above it, and hung down its edges of thick mist over its sides. The lightning was breaking out of the mountain, too, and flashing up into the cloud. From the state of the brooks, now swollen into raging torrents, it was evident that the storm had been storming all day.

The wind was blowing as if it would blow him off the mountain, but, anxious about his mother and the princess, Curdie darted up through the thick of the tempest. Even if they had not set out before the storm came on, he did not judge them safe, for, in such a storm even their poor little house was in danger. Indeed he soon found that but for a huge rock against which it was built, and which protected it both from the blasts and the waters, it must have been swept if it was not blown away; for the two torrents into which this rock parted the rush of water behind it united again in front of the cottage – two roaring and dangerous streams, which his mother and the princess could not possibly have passed. It was with great difficulty that he forced his way through one of them, and up to the door.

The moment his hand fell on the latch, through all the uproar of winds and waters came the joyous cry of the princess:–

'There's Curdie! Curdie! Curdie!'

She was sitting wrapped in balnkets on the bed, his mother trying for the hundredth time to light the fire which had been drowned by the rain that came down the chimney. The clay floor was one mass of mud, and the whole place looked wretched. But the faces of the mother and the princess shone as if their troubles only made them the merrier. Curdie burst out laughing at the sight of them.

'I never *had* such fun!' said the princess, her eyes twinkling and her pretty teeth shining. 'How nice it must be to live in a cottage on the mountain!'

'It all depends on what kind your inside house is,' said the mother.

'I know what you mean,' said Irene. 'That's the kind of thing my grandmother says.'

By the time Peter returned, the storm was nearly over, but the streams were so fierce and so swollen, that it was not only out of the question for the princess to go down the mountain, but most dangerous for Peter even or Curdie to make the attempt in the gathering darkness.

'They will be dreadfully frightened about you,' said Peter to the princess, 'but we cannot help it. We must wait till the morning.'

With Curdie's help, the fire was lighted at last, and the mother set about making their supper; and after supper they all told the princess stories till she grew sleepy. Then Curdie's mother laid her in Curdie's bed, which was in a tiny little garret-room. As soon as she was in bed, through a little window low down in the roof she caught sight of her grandmother's lamp shining far away beneath, and she gazed at the beautiful silvery globe until she fell fast asleep.

30   The King and the Kiss

The next morning the sun rose so bright that Irene said the rain had washed his face and let the light out clean. The torrents were still roaring down the side of the mountain, but they were so much smaller as not to be dangerous in the daylight. After an early breakfast, Peter went to his work, and Curdie and his mother set out to take the princess home. They had difficulty in getting her dry across the streams, and Curdie had again and again to carry her, but at last they got safe on the broader part of the road, and walked gently down towards the king's house. And what should they see as they turned the last corner, but the last of the king's troop riding through the gate!

'Oh, Curdie!' cried Irene, clapping her hands right joyfully, 'my king-papa is come.'

The moment Curdie heard that, he caught her up in his arms, and set off at full speed, crying –

'Come on, mother dear! The king may break his heart before he knows that she is safe.'

Irene clung round his neck, and he ran with her like a deer. When he entered the gate into the court, there sat the king on his horse, with all the people of the house about him, weeping and hanging their heads. The king was not weeping, but his face was white as a dead man's, and he looked as if the life had gone out of him. The men-at-arms he had brought with him, sat with horror-stricken faces, but eyes flashing with rage, waiting only for the word of the king to do something – they did not know what, and nobody knew what.

The day before, the men-at-arms belonging to the house, as soon as they were satisfied the princess had been carried away, rushed after the goblins into the hole, but found that they had already so skilfully blockaded the narrowest part, not many feet below the cellar, that without miners and their tools they could do nothing. Not one of them knew where the mouth of the mine lay, and some of those who had set out to find it had been overtaken by the storm and had not even yet returned. Poor Sir Walter was especially filled with shame, and almost hoped the king would order his head to be cut off, for to think of that sweet little face down amongst the goblins was unendurable.

When Curdie ran in at the gate with the princess in his arms, they were all so absorbed in their own misery and awed by the king's presence and grief, that no one observed his arrival. He went straight up to the king, where he sat on his horse.

'Papa! papa!' the princess cried, stretching out her arms to him; 'here I am!'

The king started. The colour rushed to his face. He gave an inarticulate cry. Curdie held up the princess, and the king bent down and took her from his arms. As he clasped her to his bosom, the big tears went dropping down his cheeks and his beard. And such a shout arose from all the bystanders, that the startled horses pranced and capered, and the armour rang and clattered, and the rocks of the mountain echoed back the noises. The princess greeted them all as she nestled in her father's bosom, and the king did not set her down until

she had told them all the story. But she had more to tell about Curdie than about herself, and what she did tell about herself none of them could understand except the king and Curdie, who stood by the king's knee stroking the neck of the great white horse. And still as she told what Curdie had done, Sir Walter and others added to what she told, even Lootie joining in the praises of his courage and energy.

Curdie held his peace, looking quietly up in the king's face. And his mother stood on the outskirts of the crowd listening with delight, for her son's deeds were pleasant in her ears, until the princess caught sight of her.

'And there is his mother, king-papa!' she said. 'See – there. She is such a nice mother, and has been so kind to me!'

They all parted asunder as the king made a sign to her to come forward. She obeyed, and he gave her his hand, but could not speak.

'And now, king-papa,' the princess went on, 'I must tell you another thing. One night long ago Curdie drove the goblins away and brought Lootie and me safe from the mountain. And I promised him a kiss when we got home, but Lootie wouldn't let me give it him. I don't want you to scold Lootie, but I want you to tell her that a princess *must*

do as she promises.'

'Indeed she must, my child – except it be wrong,' said the king. 'There, give Curdie a kiss.'

And as he spoke he held her towards him.

The princess reached down, threw her arms round Curdie's neck, and kissed him on the mouth, saying –

'There, Curdie! There's the kiss I promised you!'

Then they all went into the house, and the cook rushed to the kitchen, and the servants to their work. Lootie dressed Irene in her shiningest clothes, and the king put off his armour, and put on purple and gold; and a messenger was sent for Peter and all the miners, and there was a great and a grand feast, which continued long after the princess was put to bed.

31   The Subterranean Waters

The king's harper, who always formed a part of his escort, was chanting a ballad which he made as he went on playing on his instrument – about the princess and the goblins, and the prowess of Curdie, when all at once he ceased, with his eyes on one of the doors of the hall. Thereupon the eyes of the king and his guests turned thitherward also. The next moment, through the open doorway came the princess Irene. She went straight up to her father, with her right hand stretched out a little sideways, and her forefinger, as her father and Curdie understood, feeling its way along the invisible thread. The king took her on his knee, and she said in his ear –

'King-papa, do you hear that noise?'

'I hear nothing,' said the king.

'Listen,' she said, holding up her forefinger.

The king listened, and a great stillness fell upon the company. Each man, seeing that the king listened, listened also, and the harper sat with his harp between his arms, and his fingers silent upon the strings.

'I do hear a noise,' said the king at length – 'a noise as of distant thunder. It is coming nearer and nearer. What can it be?'

They all heard it now, and each seemed ready to start to his feet as he listened. Yet all sat perfectly still. The noise came rapidly nearer.

'What *can* it be?' said the king again.

'I think it must be another storm coming over the mountain,' said Sir Walter.

Then Curdie, who at the first word of the king had slipped from his seat, and laid his ear to the ground, rose up quickly, and approaching the king said, speaking very fast –

'Please your majesty, I think I know what it is. I have no time to explain, for that might make it too late for some of us. Will your majesty give orders that everybody leave the house as quickly as possible and get up the mountain.'

The king, who was the wisest man in the kingdom, knew well there was a time when things must be done, and questions left till afterwards. He had faith in Curdie, and rose instantly, with Irene in his arms.

'Every man and woman follow me,' he said, and strode out into the darkness.

Before he had reached the gate, the noise had grown to a great thundering roar, and the ground trembled beneath their feet, and before the last of them had crossed the court, out after them from the great hall-door came a huge rush of turbid water, and almost swept them away. But they got safe out of the gate and up the mountain, while the torrent went roaring down the road into the valley beneath.

Curdie had left the king and the princess to look after his mother, whom he and his father, one on each side, caught up when the stream overtook them and carried safe and dry.

When the king had got out of the way of the water, a little up the mountain, he stood with the princess in his arms, looking back with amazement on the issuing torrent, which glimmered fierce and foamy through the night. There Curdie rejoined them.

'Now, Curdie,' said the king, 'what does it mean? Is this what you expected?'

'It is, your majesty,' said Curdie; and proceeded to tell him about the second scheme of the goblins, who, fancying the miners of more importance to the upper world than they were, had resolved, if they should fail in carrying off the king's daughter, to flood the mine and drown the miners. Then he explained what the miners had done to prevent it. The goblins had, in pursuance of their design, let loose all the underground reservoirs and streams, expecting the water to run down into the mine, which was lower than their part of the mountain, for they had, as they supposed, not knowing of the solid wall close behind, broken a passage through into it. But the readiest outlet the water could find had turned out to be the tunnel they had made to the king's house, the possibility of which catastrophe had not occurred to the young miner until he had laid his ear to the floor of the hall.

What was then to be done? The house appeared in danger of falling, and every moment the torrent was increasing.

'We must set out at once,' said the king. 'But how to get at the horses!'

'Shall I see if we can manage that?' said Curdie.

'Do,' said the king.

Curdie gathered the men-at-arms, and took them over the garden wall, and so to the stables. They found their horses in terror; the water was rising fast around them, and it was quite time they were got out. But there was no way to get them out, except by riding them through the stream, which was now pouring from the lower windows as well as the door. As one horse was quite enough for any man to manage through such a torrent, Curdie got on the king's white charger, and leading the way, brought them all in safety to the rising ground.

'Look, look, Curdie!' cried Irene, the moment that, having dismounted, he led the horse up to the king.

Curdie did look, and saw, high in the air, somewhere about the top of the king's house, a great globe of light, shining like the purest silver.

'Oh!' he cried in some consternation, 'that is your grandmother's lamp! We *must* get her out. I will go and find her. The house may fall, you know.'

'My grandmother is in no danger,' said Irene, smiling.

'Here, Curdie, take the princess while I get on my horse,' said the king.

Curdie took the princess again, and both turned their eyes to the globe of light. The same moment there shot from it a white bird, which, descending with outstretched wings, made one circle round the king and Curdie and the princess, and then glided up again. The light and the pigeon vanished together.

'Now, Curdie,' said the princess, as he lifted her to her father's arms, 'you see my grandmother knows all about it, and isn't frightened. I believe she could walk through that water and it wouldn't wet her a bit.'

'But, my child,' said the king, 'you will be cold if you haven't something more on. Run, Curdie, my boy, and fetch anything you can lay your hands on, to keep the princess warm. We have a long ride before us.'

Curdie was gone in a moment, and soon returned with a great rich fur, and the news that dead goblins were tossing about in the current through the house. They had been caught in their own snare; instead of the mine they had flooded their own country, whence they were now swept up drowned. Irene shuddered, but the king held her close to his bosom. Then he turned to Sir Walter, and said –

'Bring Curdie's father and mother here.'

'I wish,' said the king, when they stood before him, 'to take your son with me. He shall enter my bodyguard at once, and wait further promotion.'

Peter and his wife, overcome, only murmured almost inaudible thanks. But Curdie spoke aloud.

'Please your majesty,' he said, 'I cannot leave my father and mother.'

'That's right, Curdie!' cried the princess. '*I* wouldn't if I was you.'

The king looked at the princess and then at Curdie with a glow of satisfaction on his countenance.

'I too think you are right, Curdie,' he said, 'and I will not ask you again. But I shall have a chance of doing something for you some time.'

'Your majesty has already allowed me to serve you,' said Curdie.

'But, Curdie,' said his mother, 'why shouldn't you go with the king? We can get on very well without you.'

'But I can't get on very well without you,' said Curdie. 'The king is very kind, but I could not be half the use to him that I am to you. Please your majesty, if you wouldn't mind giving my mother a red petticoat! I should have got her one long ago, but for the goblins.'

'As soon as we get home,' said the king, 'Irene and I will search out the warmest one to be found, and send it by one of the gentlemen.'

'Yes, that we will, Curdie!' said the princess. 'And next summer we'll come back and see you wear it, Curdie's mother,' she added. 'Sha'n't we, king-papa?'

'Yes, my love; I hope so,' said the king.

Then turning to the miners, he said –

'Will you do the best you can for my servants to-night. I hope they will be able to return to the house to-morrow.'

The miners with one voice promised their hospitality.

Then the king commanded his servants to mind whatever Curdie should say to them, and after shaking hands with him and his father and mother, the king and the princess and all their company rode away down the side of the new stream which had already devoured half the road, into the starry night.

32   The Last Chapter

All the rest went up the mountain, and separated in groups to the homes of the miners. Curdie and his father and mother took Lootie with them. And the whole way, a light, of which all but Lootie understood the origin, shone upon their path. But when they looked round they could see nothing of the silvery globe.

For days and days the water continued to rush from the doors and windows of the king's house, and a few goblin bodies were swept out into the road.

Curdie saw that something must be done. He spoke to his father and the rest of the miners, and they at once proceeded to make another outlet for the waters. By setting all hands to the work, tunnelling here and building there, they soon succeeded; and having also made a little tunnel to drain the water away from under the king's house, they were soon able to get into the wine cellar, where they found a multitude of dead goblins – among the rest the queen, with the skin-shoe gone, and the stone one fast to her ankle – for the water had swept away the barricade which prevented the men-at-arms from following the goblins, and had greatly widened the passage. They built it securely up, and then went back to their labours in the mine.

A good many of the goblins with their creatures escaped from the inundation out upon the mountain. But most of those who remained grew milder in character, and indeed became very much like the Scotch Brownies. Their skulls became softer as well as their hearts, and their feet grew harder, and by degrees they became friendly with the inhabitants of the mountain and even with the miners. But the latter were merciless to any of the *cobs' creatures* that came in their way, until at length they all but disappeared.

The rest of the history of *The Princess and Curdie* must be kept for another volume.

The Princess and Curdie

The Princess
and Curdie

Illustrated by
James Allen

George
MacDonald

Contents

List of Illustrations

1 The Mountain

Curdie was the son of Peter the miner. He lived with his father and mother in a cottage built on a mountain, and he worked with his father inside the mountain.

A mountain is a strange and awful thing. In old times, without knowing so much of their strangeness and awfulness as we do, people were yet more afraid of mountains. But then somehow they had not come to see how beautiful they are as well as awful, and they hated them – and what people hate they must fear. Now that we have learned to look at them with admiration, perhaps we do not always feel quite awe enough of them. To me they are beautiful terrors.

I will try to tell you what they are. They are portions of the heart of the earth that have escaped from the dungeon down below, and rushed up and out. For the heart of the earth is a great wallowing mass, not of blood, as in the hearts of men and animals, but of glowing hot melted metals and stones. And as our hearts keep us alive, so that great lump of heat keeps the earth alive: it is a huge power of buried sunlight – that is what it is. Now think: out of that cauldron, where all the bubbles would be as big as the Alps if it could get room for its boiling, certain bubbles have bubbled out and escaped – up and away, and there they stand in the cool, cold sky – mountains. Think of the change, and you will no more wonder that there should be something awful about the very look of a mountain: from the darkness – for where the light has nothing to shine upon, it is much the same as darkness – from the heat, from the endless tumult of boiling unrest – up, with a sudden heavenward shoot, into the wind, and the cold, and the starshine, and a cloak of snow that lies like ermine above the blue-green mail of the glaciers; and the great sun, their grandfather, up there in the sky; and their little old cold aunt, the moon, that comes wandering about the house at night; and everlasting stillness, except for the wind that turns the rocks and caverns into a roaring organ for the young archangels that are studying how to let out the pent-up praises of their hearts, and the molten music of the streams, rushing ever from the bosoms of the glaciers fresh-born. Think too of the change in their own substance – no longer molten and soft, heaving and glowing, but hard and shining and cold. Think of the creatures scampering over and burrowing in it, and the birds building their nests upon it, and the trees growing out of its sides, like hair to clothe it, and the lovely grass in the valleys, and the gracious flowers even at the very edge of its armour of ice, like the rich embroidery of the garment below, and the rivers galloping down the valleys in a tumult of white and green! And along with all these, think of the terrible precipices down which the traveller may fall and be lost, and the frightful gulfs of blue air cracked in the glaciers, and the park profound lakes, covered like little arctic oceans with floating lumps of ice. All this outside the mountain! But the inside, who shall tell what lies there? Caverns of awfullest solitude, their walls miles thick, sparkling with ores of gold or silver, copper or iron, tin or mercury, studded perhaps with precious stones – perhaps a brook, with eyeless fish in it, running ceaseless, cold and babbling, through banks crusted with carbuncles and golden topazes, or over a gravel of which some of the stones are rubies and emeralds, perhaps diamonds and sapphires – who can tell? – and whoever can't tell is free to think – all waiting to flash, waiting for millions of ages – ever since the earth flew off from the sun, a great blot of fire, and began to cool. Then there are caverns full of water, numbing cold, fiercely hot – hotter than any boiling water. From some of these the water cannot get out, and from others it runs in channels as the blood in the body: little veins bring it down from the ice above the great caverns of the mountain's heart whence the arteries let it out again, gushing in pipes and clefts and ducts of all shapes and kinds, through and through its bulk, until it springs new-born to the light, and rushes down the mountain-side in torrents, and down the valleys in rivers – down, down, rejoicing, to the mighty lungs of the world, that is the sea, where it is tossed in storms and cyclones, heaved up in billows, twisted in waterspouts, dashed to mist upon rocks, beaten by millions of tails, and breathed by millions of gills, whence at last, melted into vapour by the sun, it is lifted up pure into the air, and borne by the servant winds back to the mountain tops and the snow, the solid ice, and the molten stream.

Well, when the heart of the earth has thus come rushing up among her children, bringing with it gifts of all that she possesses, then straightway into it rush her children to see what they can find there. With pickaxe and spade and crowbar, with boring chisel and blasting powder, they force their way back: is it to search for what toys they may have left in their long-forgotten nurseries? Hence the mountains that lift their heads into the clear air, and are dotted over with the dwellings of men, are tunnelled and bored in the darkness of their bosoms by the dwellers in the houses which they hold up to the sun and air.

Curdie and his father were of these: their business was to bring to light hidden things; they sought silver in the rock and found it, and carried it out. Of the many other precious things in their mountain they knew little or nothing. Silver ore was what they were sent to find, and in darkness and danger they found it. But oh, how sweet was the air on the mountain face when they came out at sunset to go home to wife and mother! They did breathe deep then!

The mines belonged to the king of the country, and the miners were his servants, working under his overseers and officers. He was a real king – that is, one who ruled for the good of his people, and not to please himself, and he wanted the silver not to buy rich things for himself, but to help him to govern the country, and pay the armies that defended it from certain troublesome neighbours, and the judges whom he set to portion out righteousness amongst the people, so that they might learn it themselves, and come to do without judges at all. Nothing that could be got from the heart of the earth could have been put to better purposes than the silver the king's miners got for him. There were people in the country who, when it came into their hands, degraded it by locking it up in a chest, and then it grew diseased, and was called *mammon*, and bred all sorts of quarrels; but when first it left the king's hands it never made any but friends, and the air of the world kept it clean.

About a year before this story began, a series of very remarkable events had just ended. I will narrate as much of them as will serve to show the tops of the roots of my tree.

Upon the mountain, on one of its many claws, stood a grand old house, half farmhouse, half castle, belonging to the king; and there his only child, the Princess Irene, had been brought up till she was nearly nine years old, and would doubtless have continued much longer, but for the strange events to which I have referred.

At that time the hollow places of the mountain were inhabited by creatures called goblins, who for various reasons and in various ways made themselves troublesome to all, but to the little princess dangerous. Mainly by the watchful devotion and energy of Curdie, however, their designs had been utterly defeated, and made to recoil upon themselves to their own destruction, so that now there were very few of them left alive, and the miners did not believe that there was a single goblin remaining in the whole inside of the mountain.

The king had been so pleased with the boy – then approaching thirteen years of age – that when he carried away his daughter he asked him to accompany them; but he was still better pleased with him when he found that he preferred staying with his father and mother. He was a right good king, and knew that the love of a boy who would not leave his father and mother to be made a great man, was worth ten thousand offers to die for his sake, and would prove so when the right time came. For his father and mother, they would have given him up without a grumble, for they were just as good as the king, and he and they perfectly understood each other; but in this matter, not seeing that he could do anything for the king which one of his numerous attendants could not do as well, Curdie felt that it was for him to decide. So the king took a kind farewell of them all and rode away, with his daughter on his horse before him.

A gloom fell upon the mountain and the miners when he was gone, and Curdie did not whistle for a whole week. As for his verses, there was no occasion to make any now. He had made them only to drive away the goblins, and they were all gone – a good riddance – only the princess was gone too! He would rather have had things as they were, except for the princess's sake. But whoever is diligent will soon be cheerful, and though the miners missed the household of the castle, they yet managed to get on without them.

Peter and his wife, however, were troubled with the fancy that they had stood in the way of their boy's good fortune. It would have been such a fine thing for him and them too, they thought, if he had ridden with the good king's train. How beautiful he looked, they said, when he rode the king's own horse through the river that the goblins had

sent out of the hill! He might soon have been a captain, they did
believe! The good, kind people did not reflect that the road to the next
duty is the only straight one, or that, for their fancied good, we should
never wish our children or friends to do what we would not do
ourselves if we were in their position. We must accept righteous
sacrifices as well as make them.

2 The White Pigeon

When in the winter they had had their supper and sat about the fire, or
when in the summer they lay on the border of the rock-margined
stream that ran through their little meadow, close by the door of their
cottage, issuing from the far-up whiteness often folded in clouds,
Curdie's mother would not seldom lead the conversation to one
peculiar personage said and believed to have been much concerned in
the late issue of events. That personage was the great-great-
grandmother of the princess, of whom the princess had often talked,
but whom neither Curdie nor his mother had ever seen. Curdie could
indeed remember, although already it looked more like a dream that he
could account for if it had really taken place, how the princess had once
led him up many stairs to what she called a beautiful room in the top of
the tower, where she went through all the – what should he call it? –
the behaviour of presenting him to her grandmother, talking now to
her and now to him, while all the time he saw nothing but a bare garret,
a heap of musty straw, a sunbeam, and a withered apple. Lady, he
would have declared before the king himself, young or old, there was
none, except the princess herself, who was certainly vexed that he
could not see what she at least believed she saw. And for his mother,
she had once seen, long before Curdie was born, a certain mysterious
light of the same description with one Irene spoke of, calling it her
grandmother's moon; and Curdie himself had seen this same light,
shining from above the castle, just as the king and princess were taking
their leave. Since that time neither had seen or heard anything that
could be supposed connected with her. Strangely enough, however,
nobody had seen her go away. If she was such an old lady, she could
hardly be supposed to have set out alone and on foot when all the house
was asleep. Still, away she must have gone, for of course, if she was so

powerful, she always be about the princess to take care of her.

But as Curdie grew older, he doubted more and more whether Irene had not been talking of some dream she had taken for reality: he had heard it said that children could not always distinguish betwixt dreams and actual events. At the same time there was his mother's testimony: what was he to do with that? His mother, through whom he had learned everything, could hardly be imagined by her own dutiful son to have mistaken a dream for a fact of the waking world. So he rather shrunk from thinking about it, and the less he thought about it, the less he was inclined to believe it when he did think about it, and therefore, of course, the less inclined to talk about it to his father and mother; for although his father was one of those men who for one word they say think twenty thoughts, Curdie was well assured that he would rather doubt his own eyes than his wife's testimony. There were no others to whom he could have talked about it. The miners were a mingled company – some good, some not so good, some rather bad – none of them so bad or so good as they might have been; Curdie liked most of them, and was a favourite with all; but they knew very little about the upper world, and what might or might not take place there. They knew silver from copper ore; they understood the underground ways of things, and they could look very wise with their lanterns in their hands searching after this or that sign of ore, or for some marks to guide their way in the hollows of the earth; but as to great-great-grandmothers, they would have mocked him all the rest of his life for the absurdity of not being absolutely certain that the solemn belief of his father and mother was nothing but ridiculous nonsense. Why, to them the very word 'great-great-grandmother' would have been a week's laughter! I am not sure that they were able quite to believe there were such persons as great-great-grandmothers; they had never seen one. They were not companions to give the best of help towards progress, and as Curdie grew, he grew at this time faster in body than in mind – with the usual consequence, that he was getting rather stupid – one of the chief signs of which was that he believed less and less of things he had never seen. At the same time I do not think he was ever so stupid as to imagine that this was a sign of superior faculty and strength of mind. Still, he was becoming more and more a miner, and less and less a man of the upper world where the wind blew. On his way to and from the mine he took less and less notice of bees and butterflies, moths and dragon-flies, the flowers and the brooks and the clouds. He was gradually changing into a commonplace man. There is this difference between the growth of some human beings and that of others: in the one case it is a continuous dying, in the other a continuous resurrection. One of the latter sort comes at length to know at once whether a thing is true the moment it comes before him; one of the former class grows more and more afraid of being taken in, so afraid of it that he takes himself in altogether, and comes at length to believe in nothing but his dinner: to be sure of a thing with him is to have it between his teeth. Curdie was not in a very good way then at that time. His father and mother had, it is true, no fault to find with him – and yet – and yet – neither of them was ready to sing when the thought of him came up. There must be something wrong when a mother catches herself sighing over the time when her boy was in petticoats, or the father looks sad when he thinks how he used to carry him on his shoulder. The boy should enclose and keep, as his life, the old child at the heart of him, and never let it go. He must still, to be a right man, be his mother's darling, and more, his father's pride, and more. The child is not meant to die, but to be for ever fresh-born.

Curdie had made himself a bow and some arrows, and was teaching himself to shoot with them. One evening in the early summer, as he was walking home from the mine with them in his hand, a light flashed across his eyes. He looked, and there was a snow-white pigeon settling on a rock in front of him, in the red light of the level sun. There it fell at once to work with one of its wings, in which a feather or two had got some sprays twisted, causing a certain roughness unpleasant to the fastidious creature of the air. It was indeed a lovely being, and Curdie thought how happy it must be flitting through the air with a flash – a live bolt of light. For a moment he became so one with the bird that he seemed to feel both its bill and its feathers, as the one adjusted the other to fly again, and his heart swelled with the pleasure of its involuntary sympathy. Another moment and it would have been aloft in the waves of rosy light – it was just bending its little legs to spring: that moment it fell on the path broken-winged and bleeding from Curdie's cruel arrow. With a gush of pride at his skill, and pleasure at its success, he ran to pick up his prey. I must say for him he picked it up gently – perhaps it was the beginning of his repentance. But when he had the white thing in his hands – its whiteness stained with another red

That moment the pigeon fell on the path,
broken-winged and bleeding

than that of the sunset flood in which it had been revelling – ah God! who knows the joy of a bird, the ecstasy of a creature that has neither storehouse nor barn! – when he held it, I say, in his victorious hands, the winged thing looked up in his face – and with such eyes! asking what was the matter, and where the red sun had gone, and the clouds, and the wind of its flight. Then they closed, but to open again presently, with the same questions in them. And so they closed and opened several times, but always when they opened their look was fixed on his. It did not once flutter or try to get away; it only throbbed and bled and looked at him. Curdie's heart began to grow very large in his bosom. What could it mean? It was nothing but a pigeon, and why should he not kill a pigeon? But the fact was, that not till this very moment had he ever known what a pigeon was. A good many discoveries of a similar kind have to be made by most of us. Once more it opened its eyes – then closed them again, and its throbbing ceased. Curdie gave a sob: its last look reminded him of the princess – he did not know why. He remembered how hard he had laboured to set her beyond danger, and yet what dangers she had had to encounter for his sake: they had been saviours to each other – and what had he done now? He had stopped saving, and had begun killing! What had he been sent into the world for? Surely not to be a death to its joy and loveliness. He had done the thing that was contrary to gladness; he was a destroyer! He was not the Curdie he had been meant to be! Then the underground waters gushed from the boy's heart. And with the tears came the remembrance that a white pigeon, just before the princess went away with her father, came from somewhere – yes, from the grandmother's lamp, and flew round the king and Irene and himself, and then flew away: this might be that very pigeon! Horrible to think! And if it wasn't, yet it was a white pigeon, the same as it. And if she kept a great many pigeons – and white ones, as Irene had told him, then whose pigeon could he have killed but the grand old princess's? Suddenly everything round about him seemed against him. The red sunset stung him: the rocks frowned at him; the sweet wind that had been laving his face as he walked up the hill dropped – as if he wasn't fit to be kissed any more. Was the whole world going to cast him out? Would he have to stand there for ever, not knowing what to do, with the dead pigeon in his hand? Things looked bad indeed. Was the whole world going to make a work about a pigeon – a white pigeon? The sun went down. Great clouds gathered over the west, and shortened the twilight. The wind gave a howl, and then lay down again. The clouds gathered thicker. Then came a rumbling. He thought it was thunder. It was a rock that fell inside the mountain. A goat ran past him down the hill, followed by a dog sent to fetch him home. He thought they were goblin creatures and trembled. He used to despise them. And still he held the dead pigeon tenderly in his hand. It grew darker and darker. An evil something began to move in his heart. 'What a fool I am!' he said to himself. Then he grew angry, and was just going to throw the bird from him and whistle, when a brightness shone all round him. He lifted his eyes, and saw a great globe of light – like silver at the hottest heat: he had once seen silver run from the furnace. It shone from somewhere above the roofs of the castle: it must be the great old princess's moon! How could she be there? Of course she was not there! He had asked the whole household, and nobody knew anything about her or her globe either. It couldn't be! And yet what did that signify, when there was the white globe shining, and here was the dead white bird in his hand? That moment the pigeon gave a little flutter. 'It's not dead!' cried Curdie, almost with a shriek. The same instant he was running full speed towards the castle, never letting his heels down, lest he should shake the poor wounded bird.

3   The Mistress of the Silver Moon

When Curdie reached the castle, and ran into the little garden in front
of it, there stood the door wide open. This was as he had hoped, for
what could he have said if he had had to knock at it? Those whose
business it is to open doors so often mistake and shut them! But the
woman now in charge often puzzled herself greatly to account for the
strange fact that however often she shut the door, which, like the rest,
she took a great deal of unnecessary trouble to do, she was certain, the
next time she went to it, to find it open. I speak now of the great front
door, of course: the back door she as persistently kept wide: if people
could only go by that, she said, she would then know what sort they
were, and what they wanted. But she would neither have known what
sort Curdie was, nor what he wanted, and would assuredly have denied
him admittance, for she knew nothing of who was in the tower. So the
front door was left open for him, and in he walked.

But where to go next he could not tell. It was not quite dark: a dull,
shineless twilight filled the place. All he knew was that he must go up,
and that proved enough for the present, for there he saw the great
staircase rising before him. When he reached the top of it, he knew
there must be more stairs yet, for he could not be near the top of the
tower. Indeed by the situation of the stair, he must be a good way from
the tower itself. But those who work well in the depths more easily
understand the heights, for indeed in their true nature they are one and
the same: mines are in mountains; and Curdie, from knowing the ways
of the king's mines, and being able to calculate his whereabouts in
them, was now able to find his way about the king's house. He knew its
outside perfectly, and now his business was to get his notion of the
inside right with the outside. So he shut his eyes and made a picture of
the outside of it in his mind. Then he came in at the door of the picture,

and yet kept the picture before him all the time – for you can do that kind of thing in your mind – and took every turn of the stair over again, always watching to remember, every time he turned his face, how the tower lay, and then when he came to himself at the top where he stood, he knew exactly where it was, and walked at once in the right direction. On his way, however, he came to another stair, and up that he went of course, watching still at every turn how the tower must lie. At the top of this stair was yet another – they were the stairs up which the princess ran when first, without knowing it, she was on her way to find her great-great-grandmother. At the top of the second stair he could go no farther, and must therefore set out again to find the tower, which, as it rose far above the rest of the house, must have the last of its stairs inside itself. Having watched every turn to the very last, he still knew quite well in what direction he must go to find it, so he left the stair and went down a passage that led, if not exactly towards it, yet nearer it. This passage was rather dark, for it was very long, with only one window at the end, and although there were doors on both sides of it, they were all shut. At the distant window glimmered the chill east, with a few feeble stars in it, and its light was dreary and old, growing brown, and looking as if it were thinking about the day that was just gone. Presently he turned into another passage, which also had a window at the end of it; and in at that window shone all that was left of the sunset, a few ashes, with here and there a little touch of warmth: it was nearly as sad as the east, only there was one difference – it was very plainly thinking of to-morrow. But at present Curdie had nothing to do with to-day or to-morrow; his business was with the bird, and the tower where dwelt the grand old princess to whom it belonged. So he kept on his way, still eastward, and came to yet another passage, which brought him to a door. He was afraid to open it without first knocking. He knocked, but heard no answer. He was answered nevertheless; for the door gently opened, and there was a narrow stair – and so steep that, big lad as he was, he too, like the Princess Irene before him, found his hands needful for the climbing. And it was a long climb, but he reached the top at last – a little landing, with a door in front and one on each side. Which should he knock at?

As he hesitated, he heard the noise of a spinning-wheel. He knew it at once, because his mother's spinning-wheel had been his governess long ago and still taught him things. It was the spinning-wheel that first taught him to make verses, and to sing, and to think whether all was right inside him; or at least it had helped him in all these things. Hence it was no wonder he should know a spinning-wheel when he heard it sing – even although as the bird of paradise to other birds was the song of that wheel to the song of his mother's.

He stood listening so entranced that he forgot to knock, and the wheel went on and on, spinning in his brain songs and tales and rhymes, till he was almost asleep as well as dreaming, for sleep does not *always* come first. But suddenly came the thought of the poor bird, which had been lying motionless in his hand all the time, and that woke him up, and at once he knocked.

'Come in, Curdie', said a voice.

Curdie shook. It was getting rather awful. The heart that had never much heeded an army of goblins trembled at the soft word of invitation. But then there was the red-spotted white thing in his hand! He dared not hesitate, though. Gently he opened the door through which the sound came, and what did he see? Nothing at first – except indeed a great sloping shaft of moonlight, that came in at a high window, and rested on the floor. He stood and stared at it, forgetting to shut the door.

'Why don't you come in, Curdie?' said the voice. 'Did you never see moonlight before?'

'Never without a moon,' answered Curdie, in a trembling tone, but gathering courage.

'Certainly not,' returned the voice, which was thin and quavering. '*I* never saw moonlight without a moon.'

'But there's no moon outside,' said Curdie.

'Ah! but you're inside now,' said the voice.

The answer did not satisfy Curdie; but the voice went on.

'There are more moons than you know of, Curdie. Where there is one sun there are many moons – and of many sorts. Come in and look out of my window, and you will soon satisfy yourself that there is a moon looking in at it.'

The gentleness of the voice made Curdie remember his manners. He shut the door, and drew a step or two nearer to the moonlight.

All the time the sound of the spinning had been going on and on, and Curdie now caught sight of the wheel. Oh, it was such a thin, delicate thing – reminding him of a spider's web in a hedge! It stood in the middle of the moonlight, and it seemed as if the moonlight had nearly melted it away. A step nearer, he saw, with a start, two little hands at work with it. And then at last, in the shadow on the other side of the moonlight which came like a river between, he saw the form to which the hands belonged: a small, withered creature, so old that no age would have seemed too great to write under her picture, seated on a stool beyond the spinning-wheel, which looked very large beside her, but, as I said, very thin, like a long-legged spider holding up its own web, which was the round wheel itself. She sat crumpled together, a filmy thing that it seemed a puff would blow away, more like the body of a fly the big spider had sucked empty and left hanging in his web than anything else I can think of.

When Curdie saw her, he stood still again, a good deal in wonder, a very little in reverence, a little in doubt, and, I must add, a little in amusement at the odd look of the old marvel. Her grey hair mixed with the moonlight so that he could not tell where the one began and the other ended. Her crooked back bent forward over her chest, her shoulders nearly swallowed up her head between them, and her two little hands were just like the grey claws of a hen, scratching at the thread, which to Curdie was of course invisible across the moonlight. Indeed Curdie laughed within himself, just a little, at the sight; and when he thought of how the princess used to talk about her huge great old grandmother, he laughed more. But that moment the little lady leaned forward into the moonlight, and Curdie caught a glimpse of her eyes, and all the laugh went out of him.

'What do you come here for, Curdie?' she said, as gently as before.

Then Curdie remembered that he stood there as a culprit, and worst of all, as one who had his confession yet to make. There was no time to hesitate over it.

'Oh, ma'am! see here,' he said, and advanced a step or two, holding out the dead pigeon.

'What have you got there?' she asked.

Again Curdie advanced a few steps, and held out his hand with the pigeon, that she might see what it was, into the moonlight. The moment the rays fell upon it the pigeon gave a faint flutter. The old lady put out her old hands and took it, and held it to her bosom, and rocked it, murmuring over it as if it were a sick baby.

When Curdie saw how distressed she was he grew sorrier still, and said:

'I didn't mean to do any harm, ma'am. I didn't think of its being yours.'

'Ah, Curdie! if it weren't mine, what would become of it now?' she returned. 'You say you didn't mean any harm: did you mean any good, Curdie?'

'No,' answered Curdie.

'Remember, then, that whoever does not mean good is always in danger of harm. But I try to give everybody fair play; and those that are in the wrong are in far more need of it always than those who are in the right: they can afford to do without it. Therefore I say for you that when you shot that arrow you did not know what a pigeon is. Now that you do know, you are sorry. It is very dangerous to do things you don't know about.'

'But, please, ma'am – I don't mean to be rude or to contradict you,' said Curdie, 'but if a body was never to do anything but what he knew to be good, he would have to live half his time doing nothing.'

'There you are very much mistaken,' said the old quavering voice. 'How little you must have thought! Why, you don't seem even to know the good of the things you are constantly doing. Now don't mistake me. I don't mean you are good for doing them. It is a good thing to eat your breakfast, but you don't fancy it's very good of you to do it. The thing is good – not you.'

Curdie laughed.

'There are a great many more good things than bad things to do. Now tell me what bad thing you have done to-day besides this sore hurt to my little white friend.'

While she talked Curdie had sunk into a sort of reverie, in which he hardly knew whether it was the old lady or his own heart that spoke. And when she asked him that question, he was at first much inclined to consider himself a very good fellow on the whole. 'I really don't think I did anything else that was very bad all day,' he said to himself. But at the same time he could not honestly feel that he was worth standing up for. All at once a light seemed to break in upon his mind, and he woke up, and there was the withered little atomy of the old lady on the other side of the moonlight, and there was the spinning-wheel on and on in the middle of it!

'I know now, ma'am; I understand now,' he said. 'Thank you, ma'am, for spinning it into me with your wheel. I see now that I have been doing wrong the whole day, and such a many days besides! Indeed, I don't know when I ever did right, and yet it seems as if I had done right some time and had forgotten how. When I killed your bird I did not know I was doing wrong, just because I was always doing wrong, and the wrong had soaked all through me.'

'What wrong were you doing all day, Curdie? It is better to come to the point, you know,' said the old lady, and her voice was gentler even than before.

'I was doing the wrong of never wanting or trying to be better. And now I see that I have been letting things go as they would for a long time. Whatever came into my head I did, and whatever didn't come into my head I didn't do. I never sent anything away, and never looked out for anything to come. I haven't been attending to my mother – or my father either. And now I think of it, I know I have often seen them looking troubled, and I have never asked them what was the matter. And now I see too that I did not ask because I suspected it had something to do with me and my behaviour, and didn't want to hear the truth. And I know I have been grumbling at my work, and doing a hundred other things that are wrong.'

'You have got it, Curdie,' said the old lady, in a voice that sounded almost as if she had been crying. 'When people don't care to be better they must be doing everything wrong. I am so glad you shot my bird!'

'Ma'am!' exclaimed Curdie. 'How *can* you be?'

'Because it has brought you to see what sort you were when you did it, and what sort you will grow to be again, only worse, if you don't mind. Now that you are sorry, my poor bird will be better. Look up, my dovey.'

The pigeon gave a flutter, and spread out one of its red-spotted wings across the old woman's bosom.

'I will mend the little angel,' she said, 'and in a week or two it will be flying again. So you may ease your heart about the pigeon.'

'Oh, thank you! thank you!' cried Curdie. 'I don't know how to thank you.'

'Then I will tell you. There is only one way I care for. Do better, and grow better, and be better. And never kill anything without good reason for it.'

*The wounded bird now spread out both its wings
across her bosom*

'Ma'am, I will go and fetch my bow and arrows, and you shall burn them yourself.'

'I have no fire that would burn your bow and arrows, Curdie.'

'Then I promise you to burn them all under my mother's porridge-pot to-morrow morning.'

'No, no, Curdie. Keep them, and practise with them every day, and grow a good shot. There are plenty of bad things that want killing, and a day will come when they will prove useful. But I must see first whether you will do as I tell you.'

'That I will!' said Curdie. 'What is it, ma'am?'

'Only something not to do,' answered the old lady; 'if you should hear any one speak about me, never to laugh or make fun of me.'

'Oh, ma'am!' exclaimed Curdie, shocked that she should think such a request needful.

'Stop, stop,' she went on. 'People hereabout sometimes tell very odd and in fact ridiculous stories of an old woman who watches what is going on, and occasionally interferes. They mean me, though what they say is often great nonsense. Now what I want of you is not to laugh, or side with them in any way; because they will take that to mean that you don't believe there is any such a person a bit more than they do. Now that would not be the case – would it, Curdie?'

'No indeed, ma'am. I've seen you.'

The old woman smiled very oddly.

'Yes, you've seen me,' she said. 'But mind,' she continued, 'I don't want you to say anything – only to hold your tongue, and not seem to side with them.'

'That will be easy,' said Curdie, 'now that I've seen you with my very own eyes, ma'am.'

'Not so easy as you think, perhaps,' said the old lady, with another curious smile. 'I want to be your friend,' she added after a little pause, 'but I don't quite know yet whether you will let me.'

'Indeed I will, ma'am,' said Curdie.

'That is for me to find out,' she rejoined, with yet another strange smile. 'In the meantime all I can say is, come to me again when you find yourself in any trouble, and I will see what I can do for you – only the *canning* depends on yourself. I am greatly pleased with you for bringing me my pigeon, doing your best to set right what you had set wrong.'

As she spoke she held out her hand to him, and when he took it she made use of his to help herself up from her stool, and – when or how it came about, Curdie could not tell – the same instant she stood before him a tall, strong woman – plainly very old, but as grand as she was old, and only *rather* severe-looking. Every trace of the decrepitude and witheredness she showed as she hovered like a film about her wheel had vanished. Her hair was very white, but it hung about her head in great plenty, and shone like silver in the moonlight. Straight as a pillar she stood before the astonished boy, and the wounded bird had now spread out both its wings across her bosom, like some great mystical ornament of frosted silver.

'Oh, now I can never forget you!' cried Curdie. 'I see now what you really are!'

'Did I not tell you the truth when I sat at my wheel?' said the old lady.

'Yes, ma'am,' answered Curdie.

'I can do no more than tell you the truth now,' she rejoined. 'It is a bad thing indeed to forget one who has told us the truth. Now go.'

Curdie obeyed, and took a few steps towards the door.

'Please, ma'am – what am I to call you?' he was going to say; but when he turned to speak, he saw nobody. Whether she was there or not he could not tell, however, for the moonlight had vanished, and the room was utterly dark. A great fear, such as he had never before known, came upon him, and almost overwhelmed him. He groped his way to the door, and crawled down the stair – in doubt and anxiety as to how he should find his way out of the house in the dark. And the stair seemed ever so much longer than when he came up. Nor was that any wonder, for down and down he went, until at length his foot struck on a door, and when he rose and opened it he found himself under the starry, moonless sky at the foot of the tower. He soon discovered the way out of the garden, with which he had some acquaintance already, and in a few minutes was climbing the mountain with a solemn and cheerful heart. It was rather dark, but he knew the way well. As he passed the rock from which the poor pigeon fell wounded with his arrow a great joy filled his heart at the thought that he was delivered from the blood of the little bird, and he ran the next hundred yards at full speed up the hill. Some dark shadows passed him: he did not even care to think what they were, but let them run. When he reached home, he found his father and mother waiting supper for him.

4   Curdie's Father and Mother

The eyes of the fathers and mothers are quick to read their children's
looks, and when Curdie entered the cottage, his parents saw at once
that something unusual had taken place. When he said to his mother,
'I beg your pardon for being so late,' there was something in the tone
beyond the politeness that went to her heart, for it seemed to come
from the place where all lovely things were born before they began to
grow in this world. When he set his father's chair to the table, an
attention he had not shown him for a long time, Peter thanked him
with more gratitude than the boy had ever yet felt in all his life. It was a
small thing to do for the man who had been serving him since ever he
was born, but I suspect there is nothing a man can be so grateful for as
that to which he has the most right. There was a change upon Curdie,
and father and mother felt there must be something to account for it,
and therefore were pretty sure he had something to tell them. For
when a child's heart is *all* right, it is not likely he will want to keep
anything from his parents. But the story of the evening was too solemn
for Curdie to come out with all at once. He must wait until they had
had their porridge, and the affairs of this world were over for the day.
But when they were seated on the grassy bank of the brook that went so
sweetly blundering over the great stones of its rocky channel, for the
whole meadow lay on the top of a huge rock, then he felt that the right
hour had come for sharing with them the wonderful things that had
come to him. It was perhaps the loveliest of all hours in the year. The
summer was young and soft, and this was the warmest evening they
had yet had – dusky, dark even below, while above the stars were
bright and large and sharp in the blackest blue sky. The night came
close around them, clasping them in one universal arm of love, and
although it neither spoke nor smiled, seemed all eye and ear, seemed to

see and hear and know everything they said and did. It is a way the night has sometimes, and there is a reason for it. The only sound was that of the brook, for there was no wind, and no trees for it to make its music upon if there had been, for the cottage was high up on the mountain, on a great shoulder of stone where trees would not grow. There, to the accompaniment of the water, as it hurried down to the valley and the sea, talking busily of a thousand true things which it could not understand, Curdie told his tale, outside and in, to his father and mother. What a world had slipped in between the mouth of the mine and his mother's cottage! Neither of them said a word until he had ended.

'Now what am I to make of it, mother? It's so strange!' he said, and stopped.

'It's easy enough to see what Curdie has got to make of it – isn't it, Peter?' said the good woman, turning her face towards all she could see of her husband's.

'It seems so to me,' answered Peter, with a smile, which only the night saw, but his wife felt in the tone of his words. They were the happiest couple in that country, because they always understood each other, and that was because they always meant the same thing, and that was because they always loved what was fair and true and right better – not than anything else, but than everything else put together.

'Then will you tell Curdie?' said she.

'You can talk best, Joan,' said he. 'You tell him, and I will listen – and learn how to say what I think,' he added, laughing.

'*I*,' said Curdie, 'don't know what to think.'

'It does not matter so much,' said his mother. 'If only you know what to make of a thing, you'll know soon enough what to think of it. Now I needn't tell you, surely, Curdie, what you've got to do with this?'

'I suppose you mean, mother,' answered Curdie, 'that I must do as the old lady told me?'

'That is what I mean: what else could it be? Am I not right, Peter?'

'Quite right, Joan,' answered Peter, 'so far as my judgment goes. It is a very strange story, but you see the question is not about believing it, for Curdie knows what came to him.'

'And you remember, Curdie,' said his mother, 'that when the princess took you up that tower once before, and there talked to her great-great-grandmother, you came home quite angry with her, and said there was nothing in the place but an old tub, a heap of straw – oh, I remember your inventory quite well! – an old tub, a heap of straw, a withered apple, and a sunbeam. According to your eyes, that was all there was in the great old musty garret. But now you have had a glimpse of the old princess herself!'

'Yes, mother, I *did* see her – or if I didn't——' said Curdie very thoughtfully – then began again. 'The hardest thing to believe, though I saw it with my own eyes, was when the thin, filmy creature, that seemed almost to float about in the moonlight like a bit of the silver paper they put over pictures, or like a handkerchief made of spider-threads, took my hand, and rose up. She was taller and stronger than you, mother, ever so much! – at least, she looked so.'

'And most certainly was so, Curdie, if she looked so,' said Mrs Peterson.

'Well, I confess,' returned her son, 'that one thing, if there were no other, would made me doubt whether I was not dreaming after all, for as wide awake as I fancied myself to be.'

'Of course,' answered his mother, 'it is not for me to say whether you were dreaming or not if you are doubtful of it yourself; but it doesn't make me think I am dreaming when in the summer I hold in my hand the bunch of sweet peas that make my heart glad with their colour and scent, and remember the dry, withered-looking little thing I dibbled into the hole in the same spot in the spring. I only think how wonderful and lovely it all is. It seems just as full of reason as it is of wonder. How it is done I can't tell, only there it is! And there is this in it too, Curdie – of which you would not be so ready to think – that when you come home to your father and mother, and they find you behaving more like a dear good son than you have behaved for a long time, they at least are not likely to think you were only dreaming.'

'Still,' said Curdie, looking a little ashamed, 'I might have dreamed my duty.'

'Then dream often, my son; for there must then be more truth in your dreams than in your waking thoughts. But however any of these things may be, this one point remains certain: there can be no harm in doing as she told you. And, indeed, until you are sure there is no such person, you are bound to do it, for you promised.'

'It seems to me,' said his father, 'that if a lady comes to you in a dream, Curdie, and tells you not to talk about her when you wake, the least you can do is to hold your tongue.'

'True, father! – Yes, mother, I'll do it,' said Curdie.

Then they went to bed, and sleep, which is the night of the soul, next took them in its arms and made them well.

5   The Miners

It much increased Curdie's feeling of the strangeness of the whole affair, that, the next morning, when they were at work in the mine, the party of which he and his father were two, just as if they had known what had happened to him the night before, began talking about all manner of wonderful tales that were abroad in the country, chiefly of course those connected with the mines, and the mountains in which they lay. Their wives and mothers and grandmothers were their chief authorities. For when they sat by their firesides they heard their wives telling their children the self-same tales, with little differences, and here and there one they had not heard before, which they had heard their mothers and grandmothers tell in one or other of the same cottages. At length they came to speak of a certain strange being called Old Mother Wotherwop. Some said their wives had seen her. It appeared as they talked that not one had seen her more than once. Some of their mothers and grandmothers, however, had seen her also, and they all had told them tales about her when they were children. They said she could take any shape she liked, but that in reality she was a withered old woman, so old and so withered that she was as thin as a sieve with a lamp behind it; that she was never seen except at night, and when something terrible had taken place, or was going to take place – such as the falling in of the roof of a mine, or the breaking out of water in it. She had more than once been seen – it was always at night – beside some well, sitting on the brink of it, and leaning over and stirring it with her forefinger, which was six times as long as any of the rest. And whoever for months after drank of that well was sure to be ill. To this one of them, however, added that he remembered his mother saying that whoever in bad health drank of the well was sure to get better. But the majority agreed that the former was the right version of the story – for was she not a witch, an old hating witch, whose delight was to do mischief? One said he had heard that she took the shape of a young woman sometimes, as beautiful as an angel, and then was most dangerous of all, for she struck every man who looked upon her stone-blind. Peter ventured the question whether she might not as likely be an angel that took the form of an old woman, as an old woman that took the form of an angel. But nobody except Curdie, who was holding his peace with all his might, saw any sense in the question. They said an old woman might be very glad to make herself look like a young one, but who ever heard of a young and beautiful one making herself look old and ugly? Peter asked why they were so much ready to believe the bad that was said of her than the good. They answered because she was bad. He asked why they believed her to be bad, and they answered, because she did bad things. When he asked how they knew that, they said, because she was a bad creature. Even if they didn't know it, they said, a woman like that was so much more likely to be bad than good. Why did she go about at night? Why did she appear only now and then, and on such occasions? One went on to tell how one night when his grandfather had been having a jolly time of it with his friends in the market town, she had served him so upon his way home that the poor man never drank a drop of anything stronger than water after it to the day of his death. She dragged him into a bog, and tumbled him up and down in it till he was nearly dead.

'I suppose that was her way of teaching him what a good thing water was,' said Peter; but the man, who liked strong drink, did not see the joke.

'They do say,' said another, 'that she has lived in the old house over there ever since the little princess left it. They say too that the housekeeper knows all about it, and is hand and glove with the old witch. I don't doubt they have many a nice airing together on broomsticks. But I don't doubt either it's all nonsense, and there's no such person at all.'

'When our cow died,' said another, 'she was seen going round and round the cowhouse the same night. To be sure she left a fine calf behind her – I mean the cow did, not the witch. I wonder she didn't kill that too, for she'll be a far finer cow than ever her mother was.'

'My old woman came upon her one night, not long before the water broke out in the mine, sitting on a stone on the hill-side with a whole congregation of cobs about her. When they saw my wife they all scampered off as fast as they could run, and where the witch was sitting there was nothing to be seen but a withered bracken bush. I make no doubt myself she was putting them up to it.'

And so they went on with one foolish tale after another, while Peter put in a word now and then, and Curdie diligently held his peace. But his silence at last drew attention upon it, and one of them said:

'Come, young Curdie, what are you thinking of?'

'How do you know I'm thinking of anything?' asked Curdie.

'Because you're not saying anything.'

'Does it follow then that, as you are saying so much, you're not thinking at all?' said Curdie.

'I know what he's thinking,' said one who had not yet spoken; 'he's thinking what a set of fools you are to talk such rubbish; as if ever there was or could be such an old woman as you say! I'm sure Curdie knows better than all that comes to.'

'I think,' said Curdie, 'it would be better that he who says anything about her should be quite sure it is true, lest she should hear him, and not like to be slandered.'

'But would she like it any better if it were true?' said the same man. 'If she is what they say – I don't know – but I never knew a man that wouldn't go in a rage to be called the very thing he was.'

'If bad things were true of her, and I *knew* it,' said Curdie, 'I would not hesitate to say them, for I will never give in to being afraid of anything that's bad. I suspect that the things they tell, however, if we knew all about them, would turn out to have nothing but good in them; and I won't say a word more for fear I should say something that mightn't be to her mind.'

They all burst into a loud laugh.

'Hear the parson!' they cried. 'He believes in the witch! Ha! ha'

'He's afraid of her!'

'And says all she does is good!'

'He wants to make friends with her, that she may help him to find the gangue.'

'Give me my own eyes and a good dividing rod before all the witches in the world! and so I'd advise you too, Master Curdie; that is, when your eyes have grown to be worth anything, and you have learned to cut the hazel fork.'

Thus they all mocked and jeered at him, but he did his best to keep his temper and go quietly on with his work. He got as close to his father as he could, however, for that helped him to bear it. As soon as they were tired of laughing and mocking, Curdie was friendly with them, and long before their midday meal all between them was as it had been.

But when the evening came, Peter and Curdie felt that they would rather walk home together without other company, and therefore lingered behind when the rest of the men left the mine.

6   The Emerald

Father and son had seated themselves on a projecting piece of the rock at a corner where three galleries met – the one they had come along from their work, one to the right leading out of the mountain, and the other to the left leading far into a portion of it which had been long disused. Since the inundation caused by the goblins, it had indeed been rendered impassable by the settlement of a quantity of the water, forming a small but very deep lake, in a part where was a considerable descent. They had just risen and were turning to the right, when a gleam caught their eyes, and made them look along the whole gangue. Far up they saw a pale green light, whence issuing they could not tell, about half-way between floor and roof of the passage. They saw nothing but the light, which was like a large star, with a point of darker colour yet brighter radiance in the heart of it, whence the rest of the light shot out in rays that faded towards the ends until they vanished. It shed hardly any light around it, although in itself it was so bright as to sting the eyes that beheld it. Wonderful stories had from ages gone been current in the mines about certain magic gems which gave out light of themselves, and this light looked just like what might be supposed to shoot from the heart of such a gem. They went up the old gallery to find out what it could be.

To their surprise they found, however, that, after going some distance, they were no nearer to it, so far as they could judge, than when they started. It did not seem to move, and yet they moving did not approach it. Still they persevered, for it was far too wonderful a thing to lose sight of so long as they could keep it. At length they drew near the hollow where the water lay, and still were no nearer the light. Where they expected to be stopped by the water, however, water was none: something had taken place in some part of the mine that had drained it off, and the gallery lay open as in former times. And now, to their surprise, the light, instead of being in front of them, was shining at the same distance to the right, where they did not know there was any passage at all. Then they discovered, by the light of the lanterns they carried, that there the water had broken through, and made an adit to a part of the mountain of which Peter knew nothing. But they were hardly well into it, still following the light, before Curdie thought he recognized some of the passages he had so often gone through when he was watching the goblins. After they had advanced a long way, with many turnings, now to the right, now to the left, all at once their eyes seemed to come suddenly to themselves, and they became aware that the light which they had taken to be a great way from them was in reality almost within reach of their hands. The same instant it began to grow larger and thinner, the point of light grew dim as it spread, the greenness melted away, and in a moment or two, instead of the star, a dark, dark and yet luminous, face was looking at them with living eyes. And Curdie felt a great awe swell up in his heart, for he thought he had seen those eyes before.

'I see you know me, Curdie,' said a voice.

'If your eyes are you, ma'am, then I know you,' said Curdie. 'But I never saw your face before.'

'Yes, you have seen it, Curdie,' said the voice.

And with that the darkness of its complexion melted away, and down from the face dawned out the form that belonged to it, until at last Curdie and his father beheld a lady, 'beautiful exceedingly,' dressed in something pale green, like velvet, over which her hair fell in cataracts of a rich golden colour. It looked as if it were pouring down from her head, and, like the water of the Dustbrook, vanishing in a golden vapour ere it reached the floor. It came flowing from under the edge of a coronet of gold, set with alternated pearls and emeralds. In front of the crown was a great emerald, which looked somehow as if out of it had come the light they had followed. There was no ornament else about her, except on her slippers, which were one mass of gleaming emeralds, of various shades of green, all mingling lovelily like the waving of grass in the wind and sun. She looked about five-and-twenty years old. And for all the difference, Curdie knew somehow or other, he could not have told how, that the face before him was that of the old princess, Irene's great-great-grandmother.

By this time all round them had grown light, and now first they could see where they were. They stood in a great splendid cavern, which Curdie recognized as that in which the goblins held their state assemblies. But, strange to tell, the light by which they saw came streaming, sparkling, and shooting from stones of many colours in the sides and roof and floor of the cavern – stones of all the colours of the rainbow, and many more. It was a glorious sight – the whole rugged place flashing with colours – in one spot a great light of deep carbuncular red, in another of sapphirine blue, in another of topaz-yellow; while here and there were groups of stones of all hues and sizes, and again nebulous spaces of thousands of tiniest spots of brilliancy of every conceivable shade. Sometimes the colours ran together, and made a little river or lake of lambent interfusing and changing tints, which, by their variegation, seemed to imitate the flowing of water, or waves made by the wind. Curdie would have gazed entranced, but that all the beauty of the cavern, yes, of all he knew of the whole creation, seemed gathered in one centre of harmony and loveliness in the person of the ancient lady who stood before him in the very summer of beauty and strength. Turning from the first glance at the circumfulgent splendour, it dwindled into nothing as he looked again at the lady. Nothing flashed or glowed or shone about her, and yet it was with a prevision of the truth that he said:

'I was here once before, ma'am.'

'I know that, Curdie,' she replied.

'The place was full of torches, and the walls gleamed, but nothing as they do now, and there is no light in the place.'

'You want to know where the light comes from?' she said, smiling.

'Yes, ma'am.'

'Then see: I will go out of the cavern. Do not be afraid, but watch.'

She went slowly out. The moment she turned her back to go, the light began to pale and fade; the moment she was out of their sight the place was black as night, save that now the smoky yellow-red of their lamps, which they thought had gone out long ago, cast a dusky glimmer around them.

7 What *is* in a Name?

For a time that seemed to them long, the two men stood waiting, while still the Mother of Light did not return. So long was she absent that they began to grow anxious: how were they to find their way from the natural hollows of the mountain crossed by goblin paths, if their lamps should go out? To spend the night there would mean to sit and wait until an earthquake rent the mountain, or the earth herself fell back into the smelting furnace of the sun whence she had issued -- for it was all night and no faintest dawn in the bosom of the world. So long did they wait unrevisited, that, had there not been two of them, either would at length have concluded the vision a home-born product of his own seething brain. And their lamps *were* going out, for they grew redder and smokier! But they did not lose courage, for there is a kind of capillary attraction in the facing of two souls, that lifts faith quite beyond the level to which either could raise it alone: they knew that they had seen the lady of emeralds, and it was to give them their own desire that she had gone from them, and neither would yield for a moment to the half-doubts and half-dreads that awoke in his heart. And still she who with her absence darkened their air did not return. They grew weary, and sat down on the rocky floor, for wait they would – indeed, wait they must. Each set his lamp by his knee, and watched it die. Slowly it sank, dulled, looked lazy and stupid. But ever as it sank and dulled, the image in his mind of the Lady of Light grew stronger and clearer. Together the two lamps panted and shuddered. First one, then the other, went out, leaving for a moment a great red, evil-smelling snuff. Then all was the blackness of darkness up to their very hearts and everywhere around them. Was it? No. Far away – it looked miles away – shone one minute faint point of green light – where, who could tell? They only knew that it shone. It grew larger, and seemed to draw nearer, until at last, as they watched with speechless delight and expectation, it seemed once more within reach of an outstretched hand. Then it spread and melted away as before, and there were eyes – and a face – and a lovely form – and lo! the whole cavern blazing with lights innumerable, and gorgeous, yet soft and interfused – so blended, indeed, that the eye had to search and see in order to separate distinct spots of special colour.

The moment they saw the speck in the vast distance they had risen and stood on their feet. When it came nearer they bowed their heads. Yet now they looked with fearless eyes, for the woman that was old and yet young was a joy to see, and filled their hearts with reverent delight. She turned first to Peter.

'I have known you long,' she said. 'I have met you going to and from the mine, and seen you working in it for the last forty years.'

'How should it be, madam, that a grand lady like you should take notice of a poor man like me?' said Peter, humbly, but more foolishly than he could then have understood.

'I am poor as well as rich,' said she. 'I too work for my bread, and I show myself no favour when I pay myself my own wages. Last night when you sat by the brook, and Curdie told you about my pigeon, and my spinning, and wondered whether he could believe that he had actually seen me, I heard all you said to each other. I am always about, as the miners said the other night when they talked of me as Old Mother Wotherwop.'

The lovely lady laughed, and her laugh was lightning of delight in their souls.

'Yes,' she went on, 'you have got to thank me that you are so poor, Peter. I have seen to that, and it has done well for both you and me, my friend. Things come to the poor that can't get in at the door of the rich. Their money somehow blocks it up. It is a great privilege to be poor, Peter – one that no man ever coveted, and but a very few have sought to retain, but one that yet many have learned to prize. You must not mistake, however, and imagine it a virtue; it is but a privilege, and one also that, like other privileges, may be terribly misused. Hadst thou been rich, my Peter, thou wouldst not have been so good as some rich men I know. And now I am going to tell you what no one knows but myself: you, Peter, and your wife have both the blood of the royal family in your veins. I have been trying to cultivate your family tree, every branch of which is known to me, and I expect Curdie to turn out a blossom on it. Therefore I have been training him for a work that must soon be done. I was near losing him, and had to send my pigeon. Had he not shot it, that would have been better; but he repented and that shall be as good in the end.'

She turned to Curdie and smiled.

'Ma'am,' said Curdie, 'may I ask questions?'

'Why not, Curdie?'

'Because I have been told, ma'am, that nobody must ask the king questions.'

'The king never made that law,' she answered, with some displeasure. 'You may ask me as many as you please – that is, so long as they are sensible. Only I may take a few thousand years to answer some of them. But that's nothing. Of all things time is the cheapest.'

'Then would you mind telling me now, ma'am, for I feel very confused about it – are you the Lady of the Silver Moon?'

'Yes, Curdie; you may call me that if you like. What it means is true.'

'And now I see you dark, and clothed in green, and the mother of all the light that dwells in the stones of the earth! And up there they call you Old Mother Wotherwop! And the Princess Irene told me you were her great-great-grandmother! And you spin the spider-threads, and take care of a whole people of pigeons; and you are worn to a pale shadow with old age; and are as young as anybody can be, not to be too young; and as strong, I do believe, as I am.'

The lady stooped towards a large green stone bedded in the rock of the floor, and looking like a well of grassy light in it. She laid hold if it with her fingers, broke it out, and gave it to Peter.

'There!' said Curdie, 'I told you so. Twenty men could not have done that. And your fingers are white and smooth as any lady's in the land. I don't know what to make of it.'

'I could give you twenty names more to call me, Curdie, and not one of them would be a false one. What does it matter how many names if the person is one?'

'Ah? but it is not names only, ma'am. Look at what you were like last night, and what I see you now!'

'Shapes are only dresses, Curdie, and dresses are only names. That which is inside is the same all the time.'

'But then how can all the shapes speak the truth?'

'It would want thousands more to speak the truth, Curdie; and then they could not. But there is a point I must not let you mistake about. It is one thing the shape I choose to put on, and quite another the shape that foolish talk and nursery tale may please to put upon me. Also, it is one thing what you or your father may think about me, and quite another what a foolish or bad man may see in me. For instance, if a thief were to come in here just now, he would think he saw the demon of the mine, all in green flames, come to protect her treasure, and would run like a hunted wild goat. I should be all the same, but his evil eyes would see me as I was not.'

'I think I understand,' said Curdie.

'Peter,' said the lady, turning then to him, 'you will have to give up Curdie for a little while.'

'So long as he loves us, ma'am, that will not matter – much.'

'Ah! you are right there, my friend,' said the beautiful princess.

And as she said it she put out her hand, and took the hard, horny hand of the miner in it, and held it for a moment lovingly.

'I need say no more,' she added, 'for we understand each other – you and I, Peter.'

The tears came into Peter's eyes. He bowed his head in thankfulness, and his heart was much too full to speak.

Then the great old young beautiful princess turned to Curdie.

'Now, Curdie, are you ready?' she said.

'Yes, ma'am,' answered Curdie.

'You do not know what for.'

'You do, ma'am. That is enough.'

'You could not have given me a better answer, or done more to prepare yourself, Curdie,' she returned, with one of her radiant smiles. 'Do you think you will know me again?'

'I think so. But how can I tell what you may look like next?'

'Ah, that indeed! How can you tell? Or how could I expect you should? But those who know me *well*, know me whatever new dress or shape or name I may be in; and by and by you will have learned to do so too.'

'But if you want me to know you again, ma'am, for certain sure,' said Curdie, 'could you not give me some sign, or tell me something about you that never changes – or some other way to know you, or thing to know you by?'

'No, Curdie; that would be to keep you from knowing me. You must know me in quite another way from that. It would not be the least use to you or me either if I were to make you know me in that way. It would be but to know the sign of me – not to know me myself. It would be no better than if I were to take this emerald out of my crown and give it you to take home with you, and you were to call it me, and talk to it as if it heard and saw and loved you. Much good that would do you, Curdie! No; you must do what you can to know me, and if you do, you will. You shall see me again – in very different circumstances from these, and, I will tell you so much, it *may* be in a very different shape. But come now, I will lead you out of this cavern; my good Joan will be getting too anxious about you. One word more: you will allow that the men knew little what they were talking about this morning, when they told all those tales of Old Mother Wotherwop; but did it occur to you to think how it was they fell to talking about me at all? It was because I came to them; I was beside them all the time they were talking about me, though they were far enough from knowing it, and had very little besides foolishness to say.'

As she spoke she turned and led the way from the cavern, which, as if a door had been closed, sunk into absolute blackness behind them. And now they saw nothing more of the lady except the green star, which again seemed a good distance in front of them, and to which they came no nearer, although following it at a quick pace through the mountain. Such was their confidence in her guidance, however, and so fearless were they in consequence, that they felt their way neither with hand nor foot, but walked straight on through the pitch-dark galleries. When at length the night of the upper world looked in at the mouth of the mine, the green light seemed to lose its way amongst the stars, and they saw it no more.

Out they came into the cool, blessed night. It was very late, and only starlight. To their surprise, three paces away they saw, seated upon a stone, an old countrywoman, in a cloak which they took for black. When they came close up to it, they saw it was red.

'Good evening!' said Peter.

'Good evening!' returned the old woman, in a voice as old as herself.

But Curdie took off his cap and said:

'I am your servant, princess.'

The old woman replied:

'Come to me in the dove-tower to-morrow night, Curdie – alone.'

'I will, ma'am,' said Curdie.

So they parted, and father and son went home to wife and mother – two persons in one rich, happy woman.

8   Curdie's Mission

The next night Curdie went home from the mine a little earlier than usual, to make himself tidy before going to the dove-tower. The princess had not appointed an exact time for him to be there; he would go as near the time he had gone first as he could. On his way to the bottom of the hill, he met his father coming up. The sun was then down, and the warm first of the twilight filled the evening. He came rather wearily up the hill: the road, he thought, must have grown steeper in parts since he was Curdie's age. His back was to the light of the sunset, which closed him all round in a beautiful setting, and Curdie thought what a grand-looking man his father was, even when he was tired. It is greed and laziness and selfishness, not hunger or weariness or cold, that take the dignity out of a man, and make him look mean.

'Ah, Curdie! there you are!' he said, seeing his son come bounding along as if it were morning with him and not evening.

'You look tired, father,' said Curdie.

'Yes, my boy. I'm not so young as you.'

'Nor so old as the princess,' said Curdie.

'Tell me this,' said Peter. 'Why do people talk about going down-hill when they begin to get old? It seems to me that then first they begin to go up-hill.'

'You looked to me, father, when I caught sight of you, as if you had been climbing the hill all your life, and were soon to get to the top.'

'Nobody can tell when that will be,' returned Peter. 'We're so ready to think we're just at the top when it lies miles away. But I must not keep you, my boy, for you are wanted; and we shall be anxious to know what the princess says to you – that is, if she will allow you to tell us.'

'I think she will, for she knows there is nobody more to be trusted than my father and mother,' said Curdie, with pride.

And away he shot, and ran, and jumped, and seemed almost to fly down the long, winding, steep path, until he came to the gate of the king's house.

There he met an unexpected obstruction: in the open door stood the housekeeper, and she seemed to broaden herself out until she almost filled the doorway.

'So!' she said; 'it's you, is it, young man? You are the person that comes in and goes out when he pleases, and keeps running up and down my stairs, without ever saying by your leave, or even wiping his shoes, and always leaves the door open! Don't you know that this is my house?'

'No, I do not,' returned Curdie, respectfully. 'You forget, ma'am, that it is the king's house.'

'That is all the same. The king left it to me to take care of, and that you shall know!'

'Is the king dead, ma'am, that he has left it to you?' asked Curdie, half in doubt from the self-assertion of the woman.

'Insolent fellow!' exclaimed the housekeeper. 'Don't you see by my dress that I am in the king's service?'

'And am I not one of his miners?'

'Ah! that goes for nothing. I am one of his household. You are an out-of-doors labourer. You are a nobody. You carry a pickaxe. I carry the keys at my girdle. See!'

'But you must not call one a nobody to whom the king has spoken,' said Curdie.

'Go along with you!' cried the housekeeper, and would have shut the door in his face, had she not been afraid that when she stepped back he would step in ere she could get it in motion, for it was very heavy, and always seemed unwilling to shut. Curdie came a pace nearer. She lifted the great house key from her side, and threatened to strike him down with it, calling aloud on Mar and Whelk and Plout, the men-servants under her, to come and help her. Ere one of them could answer, however, she gave a great shriek and turned and fled, leaving the door wide open.

Curdie looked behind him, and saw an animal whose gruesome oddity even he, who knew so many of the strange creatures, two of which were never the same, that used to live inside the mountain with their masters the goblins, had never seen equalled. Its eyes were flaming with anger, but it seemed to be at the housekeeper, for it came cowering and creeping up, and laid its head on the ground at Curdie's feet. Curdie hardly waited to look at it, however, but ran into the house, eager to get up the stairs before any of the men should come to annoy – he had no fear of their preventing him. Without halt or hindrance, though the passages were nearly dark, he reached the door of the princess's workroom, and knocked.

'Come in,' said the voice of the princess.

Curdie opened the door – but, to his astonishment, saw no room there. Could he have opened a wrong door? There was the great sky, and the stars, and beneath he could see nothing – only darkness! But what was that in the sky, straight in front of him? A great wheel of fire, turning and turning, and flashing out blue lights!

'Come in, Curdie,' said the voice again.

'I would at once, ma'am,' said Curdie, 'if I were sure I was standing at your door.'

'Why should you doubt it, Curdie?'

'Because I see neither walls nor floor, only darkness and the great sky.'

'That is all right, Curdie. Come in.'

Curdie stepped forward at once. He was indeed, for the very crumb of a moment, tempted to feel before him with his foot; but he saw that would be to distrust the princess, and a greater rudeness he could not offer her. So he stepped straight in – I will not say without a slight tremble at the thought of finding no floor beneath his foot. But that which had need of the floor found it, and his foot was satisfied.

No sooner was he in than he saw that the great revolving wheel in the sky was the princess's spinning-wheel, near the other end of the room, turning very fast. He could so no sky or stars any more, but the wheel was flashing out blue – oh, such lovely sky-blue light! – and behind it of course sat the princess, but whether an old woman as thin as a skeleton leaf, or a glorious lady as young as perfection, he could not tell for the turning and flashing of the wheel.

'Listen to the wheel,' said the voice which had already grown dear to Curdie: its very tone was precious like a jewel, not *as* a jewel, for no jewel could compare with it in preciousness.

And Curdie listened and listened.

'Come in, Curdie,' said the voice

'What is it saying?' asked the voice.

'It is singing,' answered Curdie.

'What is it singing?'

Curdie tried to make out, but thought he could not; for no sooner had he got a hold of something than it vanished again. Yet he listened, and listened, entranced with delight.

'Thank you, Curdie,' said the voice.

'Ma'am,' said Curdie, 'I did try hard for a while, but I could not make anything of it.'

'Oh, yes, you did, and you have been telling it to me! Shall I tell you again what I told my wheel, and my wheel told you, and you have just told me without knowing it?'

'Please, ma'am.'

Then the lady began to sing, and her wheel spun an accompaniment to her song, and the music of the wheel was like the music of an Aeolian harp blown upon by the wind that bloweth where it listeth. Oh, the sweet sounds of that spinning-wheel! Now they were gold, now silver, now grass, now palm-trees, now ancient cities, now rubies, now mountain brooks, now peacock's feathers, now clouds, now snowdrops, and now mid-sea islands. But for the voice that sang through it all, about that I have no words to tell. It would make you weep if I were able to tell you what that was like, it was so beautiful and true and lovely. But this is something like the words of its song:

> The stars are spinning their threads,
>   And the clouds are the dust that flies,
> And the suns are weaving them up
>   For the time when the sleepers shall rise.
>
> The ocean in music rolls,
>   And gems are turning to eyes,
> And the trees are gathering souls
>   For the time when the sleepers shall rise.
>
> The weepers are learning to smile,
>   And laughter to glean the sighs;
> Burn and bury the care and guile,
>   For the day when the sleepers shall rise.

Oh, the dews and the moths and the daisy-red
The larks and the glimmers and flows!
The lilies and sparrows and daily bread,
And the something that nobody knows!

The princess stopped, her wheel stopped, and she laughed. And her laugh was sweeter than song and wheel; sweeter than running brook and silver bell; sweeter than joy itself, for the heart of the laugh was love.

'Come now, Curdie, to this side of my wheel, and you will find me,' she said; and her laugh seemed sounding on still in the words, as if they were made of breath that had laughed.

Curdie obeyed, and passed the wheel, and there she stood to receive him! – fairer than when he saw her last, a little younger still, and dressed not in green and emeralds, but in pale blue, with a coronet of silver set with pearls, and slippers covered with opals, that gleamed every colour of the rainbow. It was some time before Curdie could take his eyes from the marvel of her loveliness. Fearing at last that he was rude, he turned them away; and, behold, he was in a room that was for beauty marvellous! The lofty ceiling was all a golden vine, whose great clusters of carbuncles, rubies, and chrysoberyls hung down like the bosses of groined arches, and in its centre hung the most glorious lamp that human eyes ever saw – the Silver Moon itself, a globe of silver, as it seemed, with a heart of light so wondrous potent that it rendered the mass translucent, and altogether radiant.

The room was so large that, looking back, he could scarcely see the end at which he entered; but the other was only a few yards from him – and there he saw another wonder: on a huge hearth a great fire was burning, and the fire was a huge heap of roses, and yet it was fire. The smell of the roses filled the air, and the heat of the flames of them glowed upon his face. He turned an inquiring look upon the lady, and saw that she was now seated in an ancient chair, the legs of which were crusted with gems, but the upper part like a nest of daisies and moss and green grass.

'Curdie,' she said in answer to his eyes, 'you have stood more than one trial already, and have stood them well: now I am going to put you to a harder. Do you think you are prepared for it?'

'How can I tell, ma'am,' he returned, 'seeing I do not know what it

510 The Princess and Curdie

is, or what preparation it needs? Judge me yourself, ma'am.'

'It needs only trust and obedience,' answered the lady.

'I dare not say anything, ma'am. If you think me fit, command me.'

'It will hurt you terribly, Curdie, but that will be all; no real hurt, but much real good will come to you from it.'

Curdie made no answer, but stood gazing with parted lips in the lady's face.

'Go and thrust both your hands into that fire,' she said quickly, almost hurriedly.

Curdie dared not stop to think. It was much too terrible to think about. He rushed to the fire, and thrust both his hands right into the middle of the heap of flaming roses, and his arms half-way up to the elbows. And it *did* hurt! But he did not draw them back. He held the pain as if it were a thing that would kill him if he let it go – as indeed it would have done. He was in terrible fear lest it should conquer him. But when it had risen to the pitch that he thought he *could* bear it no longer, it began to fall again, and went on growing less and less until by contrast with its former severity it had become rather pleasant. At last it ceased altogether, and Curdie thought his hands must be burnt to cinders if not ashes, for he did not feel them at all. The princess told him to take them out and look at them. He did so, and found that all that was gone of them was the rough hard skin; they were white and smooth like the princess's.

'Come to me,' she said.

He obeyed, and saw, to his surprise, that her face looked as if she had been weeping.

'Oh, princess! what *is* the matter?' he cried. 'Did I make a noise and vex you?'

'No, Curdie,' she answered; 'but it was very bad.'

'Did you feel it too then?'

'Of course I did. But now it is over, and all is well. Would you like to know why I made you put your hands in the fire?'

Curdie looked at them again – then said:

'To take the marks of the work off them, and make them fit for the king's court, I suppose.'

'No, Curdie,' answered the princess, shaking her head, for she was not pleased with the answer. 'It would be a poor way of making your hands fit for the king's court to take off them all signs of his service.

There is a far greater difference on them than that. Do you feel none?'

'No, ma'am.'

'You will, though, by and by, when the time comes. But perhaps even you might not know what had been given you, therefore I will tell you. Have you ever heard what some philosophers say – that men were all animals once?'

'No, ma'am.'

'It is of no consequence. But there is another thing that is of the greatest consequence – this: that all men, if they do not take care, go down the hill to the animals' country; that many men are actually, all their lives, going to be beasts. People knew it once, but it is long since they forgot it.'

'I am not surprised to hear it, ma'am, when I think of some of our miners.'

'Ah! but you must beware, Curdie, how you say of this man or that man that he is travelling beastward. There are not nearly so many going that way as at first sight you might think. When you met your father on the hill to-night, you stood and spoke together on the same spot; and although one of you was going up and the other coming down, at a little distance no one could have told which was bound in the one direction and which in the other. Just so two people may be at the same spot in manners and behaviour, and yet one may be getting better and the other worse, which is just the greatest of all differences that could possibly exist between them.'

'But, ma'am,' said Curdie, 'where is the good of knowing that there is such a difference, if you can never know where it is?'

'Now, Curdie, you must mind exactly what words I use, because although the right words cannot do exactly what I want them to do, the wrong words will certainly do what I do not want them to do. I did not say *you can never know*. When there is a necessity for your knowing, when you have to do important business with this or that man, there is always a way of knowing enough to keep you from any great blunder. And as you will have important business to do by and by, and that with people of whom you yet know nothing, it will be necessary that you should have some better means than usual of learning the nature of them. Now listen. Since it is always what they *do*, whether in their minds or their bodies, that makes men go down to be less than men, that is, beasts, the change always comes first in their hands – and first of all in the inside hands, to which the outside ones are but as the gloves. They do not know it of course; for a beast does not know that he is a beast, and the nearer a man gets to being a beast the less he knows it. Neither can their best friends, or their worst enemies indeed, *see* any difference in their hands, for they see only the living gloves of them. But there are not a few who feel a vague something repulsive in the hand of a man who is growing a beast. Now here is what the rose-fire has done for you: it has made your hands so knowing and wise, it has brought your real hands so near the outside of your flesh-gloves, that you will henceforth be able to know at once the hand of a man who is growing into a beast; nay, more – you will at once feel the foot of the beast he is growing, just as if there were no glove made like a man's hand between you and it. Hence of course it follows that you will be able often, and with further education in zoology, will be able always to tell, not only when a man is growing a beast, but what beast he is growing to, for you will know the foot – what it is and what beast's it is. According then to your knowledge of that beast, will be your knowledge of the man you have to do with. Only there is one beautiful and awful thing about it, that if any one gifted with this perception once uses it for his own ends, it is taken from him, and then, not knowing that it is gone, he is in a far worse condition than before, for he trusts to what he has not got.'

'How dreadful!' said Curdie. 'I must mind what I am about.'

'Yes, indeed, Curdie.'

'But may not one sometimes make a mistake without being able to help it?'

'Yes. But so long as he is not after his own ends, he will never make a serious mistake.'

'I suppose you want me, ma'am, to warn every one whose hand tells me that he is growing a beast – because as you say, he does not know it himself.'

The princess smiled.

'Much good that would do, Curdie! I don't say there are no cases in which it would be of use, but they are very rare and peculiar cases, and if such come you will know them. To such a person there is in general no insult like the truth. He cannot endure it, not because he is growing a beast, but because he is ceasing to be a man. It is the dying man in him that it makes uncomfortable, and he trots, or creeps, or swims, or flutters out of its way – calls it a foolish feeling, a whim, an old wives' fable, a bit of priests' humbug, an effete superstition, and so on.'

'And is there no hope for him? Can nothing be done? It's so awful to think of going down, down, down like that!'

'Even when it is with his own will?'

'That's what seems to me to make it worst of all,' said Curdie.

'You are right,' answered the princess, nodding her head; 'but there is this amount of excuse to make for all such, remember – that they do not know what or how horrid their coming fate is. Many a lady, so delicate and nice that she can bear nothing coarser than the finest linen to touch her body, if she had a mirror that could show her the animal she is growing to, as it lies waiting within the fair skin and the fine linen and the silk and the jewels, would receive a shock that might possibly wake her up.'

'Why then, ma'am, shouldn't she have it?'

The princess held her peace.

'Come here, Lina,' she said after a long pause.

From somewhere behind Curdie crept forward the same hideous animal which had fawned at his feet at the door, and which, without his knowing it, had followed him every step up the dove-tower. She ran to the princess, and lay down at her feet, looking up at her with an expression so pitiful that in Curdie's heart it overcame all the ludicrousness of her horrible mass of incongruities. She had a very short body, and very long legs made like an elephant's, so that in lying down she kneeled with both pairs. Her tail, which dragged on the floor behind her, was twice as long and quite as thick as her body. Her head was something between that of a polar bear and a snake. Her eyes were dark green, with a yellow light in them. Her under teeth came up like a fringe of icicles, only very white, outside of her upper lip. Her throat looked as if the hair had been plucked off. It showed a skin white and smooth.

'Give Curdie a paw, Lina,' said the princess.

The creature rose, and, lifting a long fore-leg, held up a great dog-like paw to Curdie. He took it gently. But what a shudder, as of terrified delight, ran through him, when, instead of the paw of a dog, such as it seemed to his eyes, he clasped in his great mining fist the soft, neat little hand of a child! He took it in both of his, and held it as if he could not let it go. The green eyes stared at him with their yellow light, and the mouth was turned up towards him with its constant half-grin; but here *was* the child's hand! If he could but pull the child out of the beast! His eyes sought the princess. She was watching him with evident satisfaction.

'Ma'am, here is a child's hand!' said Curdie.

'Your gift does more for you than it promised. It is yet better to perceive a hidden good than a hidden evil.'

'But——' began Curdie.

'I am not going to answer any more questions this evening,' interrupted the princess. 'You have not half got to the bottom of the answers I have already given you. That paw in your hand now might almost teach you the whole science of natural history – the heavenly sort, I mean.'

'I will think,' said Curdie. 'But oh! please! one word more: may I tell my father and mother all about it!'

'Certainly – though perhaps now it may be their turn to find it a little difficult to believe that things went just as you must tell them.'

'They shall see that I believe it all this time,' said Curdie.

'Tell them that to-morrow morning you must set out for the court – not like a great man, but just as poor as you are. They had better not speak about it. Tell them also that it will be a long time before they hear of you again, but they must not lose heart. And tell your father to lay that stone I gave him last night in a safe place – not because of the greatness of its price, although it is such an emerald as no prince has in his crown, but because it will be a news-bearer between you and him. As often as he gets at all anxious about you, he must take it and lay it in the fire, and leave it there when he goes to bed. In the morning he must find it in the ashes, and if it be as green as ever, then all goes well with you; if it has lost colour, things go ill with you; but if it be very pale indeed, then you are in great danger, and he must come to me.'

'Yes, ma'am,' said Curdie. 'Please, am I to go now?'

'Yes,' answered the princess, and held out her hand to him.

Curdie took it, trembling with joy. It was a very beautiful hand – not small, very smooth, but not very soft – and just the same to his fire-taught touch that it was to his eyes. He would have stood there all night holding it if she had not gently withdrawn it.

'I will provide you a servant,' she said, 'for your journey, and to wait upon you afterwards.'

'But where am I to go, ma'am, and what am I to do? You have given me no message to carry, neither have you said what I am wanted for. I go without a notion whether I am to walk this way or that, or what I am to do when I get I don't know where.'

'Curdie!' said the princess, and there was a tone of reminder in his own name as she spoke it, 'did I not tell you to tell your father and mother that you were to set out for the court? and you *know* that lies to the north. You must learn to use far less direct directions than that. You must not be like a dull servant that needs to be told again and again before he will understand. You have orders enough to start with, and you will find, as you go on, and as you need to know, what you have to do. But I warn you that perhaps it will not look the least like what you may have been fancying I should require of you. I have one idea of you and your work, and you have another. I do not blame you for that – you cannot help it yet; but you must be ready to let my idea, which sets you working, set your idea right. Be true and honest and fearless, and all shall go well with you and your work, and all with whom your work lies, and so with your parents – and me too, Curdie,' she added after a little pause.

The young miner bowed his head low, patted the strange head that lay at the princess's feet, and turned away.

As soon as he passed the spinning-wheel, which looked, in the midst of the glorious room, just like any wheel you might find in a country cottage – old and worn and dingy and dusty – the splendour of the place vanished, and he saw but the big bare room he seemed at first to have entered, with the moon – the princess's moon no doubt – shining in at one of the windows upon the spinning-wheel.

9   Hands

Curdie went home, pondering much, and told everything to his father and mother. As the old princess had said, it was now their turn to find what they heard hard to believe. If they had not been able to trust Curdie himself, they would have refused to believe more than the half of what he reported, then they would have refused that half too, and at last would most likely for a time have disbelieved in the very existence of the princess, what evidence their own senses had given them notwithstanding. For he had nothing conclusive to show in proof of what he told them. When he held out his hands to them, his mother said they looked as if he had been washing them with soft soap, only they did smell of something nicer than that, and she must allow it was more like roses than anything else she knew. His father could not see any difference upon his hands, but then it was night, he said, and their poor little lamp was not enough for his old eyes. As to the feel of them, each of his own hands, he said, was hard and horny enough for two, and it must be the fault of the dullness of his own thick skin that he felt no change on Curdie's palms.

'Here, Curdie,' said his mother, 'try my hand, and see what beast's paw lies inside it.'

'No, mother,' answered Curdie, half beseeching, half indignant, 'I will not insult my new gift by making pretence to try it. That would be mockery. There is no hand within yours but the hand of a true woman, my mother.'

'I should like you just to take hold of my hand, though,' said his mother. 'You are my son, and may know all the bad there is in me.'

Then at once Curdie took her hand in his. And when he had it, he kept it, stroking it gently with his other hand.

'Mother,' he said at length, 'your hand feels just like that of the princess.'

'What! my horny, cracked, rheumatic old hand, with its big joints, and its short nails all worn down to the quick with hard work – like the hand of the beautiful princess! Why, my child, you will make me fancy your fingers have grown very dull indeed, instead of sharp and delicate, if you talk such nonsense. Mine is such an ugly hand I should be ashamed to show it to any but one that loved me. But love makes all safe – doesn't it, Curdie?'

'Well, mother, all I can say is that I don't feel a roughness, or a crack, or a big joint, or a short nail. Your hand feels just and exactly, as near as I can recollect, and it's not now more than two hours since I had it in mine – well, I will say, very like indeed to that of the old princess.'

'Go away, you flatterer,' said his mother, with a smile that showed how she prized the love that lay beneath what she took for its hyperbole. The praise even which one cannot accept is sweet from a true mouth. 'If that is all your new gift can do, it won't make a warlock of you,' she added.

'Mother, it tells me nothing but the truth,' insisted Curdie, 'however unlike the truth it may seem. It wants no gift to tell what anybody's outside hands are like. But by it I *know* your inside hands are like the princess's.'

'And I am sure the boy speaks true,' said Peter. 'He only says about your hand what I have known ever so long about yourself, Joan. Curdie, your mother's foot is as pretty a foot as any lady's in the land, and where her hand is not so pretty it comes of killing its beauty for you and me, my boy. And I can tell you more, Curdie. I don't know much about ladies and gentlemen, but I am sure your inside mother must be a lady, as her hand tells you, and I will try to say how I know it. This is how: when I forget myself looking at her as she goes about her work – and that happens oftener as I grow older – I fancy for a moment or two that I am a gentleman; and when I wake up from my little dream, it is only to feel the more strongly that I must do everything as a gentleman should. I will try to tell you what I mean, Curdie. If a gentleman – I mean a real gentleman, not a pretended one, of which sort they say there are a many above ground – if a real gentleman were to lose all his money and come down to work in the mines to get bread for his family – do you think, Curdie, he would work like the lazy ones? Would he try to do as little as he could for his wages? I know the sort of the true gentleman – pretty near as well as he does himself. And my wife, that's your mother, Curdie, she's a true lady, you may take my word for it, for it's she that makes me want to be a true gentleman. Wife, the boy is in the right about your hand.'

'Now, father, let me feel yours,' said Curdie, daring a little more.

'No, no, my boy,' answered Peter. 'I don't want to hear anything about my hand or my head or my heart. I am what I am, and I hope growing better, and that's enough. No, you shan't feel my hand. You must go to bed, for you must start with the sun.'

It was not as if Curdie had been leaving them to go to prison, or to make a fortune, and although they were sorry enough to lose him, they were not in the least heart-broken or even troubled at his going.

As the princess had said he was to go like the poor man he was, Curdie came down in the morning from his little loft dressed in his working clothes. His mother, who was busy getting his breakfast for him, while his father sat reading to her out of an old book, would have had him put on his holiday garments, which, she said, would look poor enough amongst the fine ladies and gentlemen he was going to. But Curdie said he did not know that he was going amongst ladies and gentlemen, and that as work was better than play, his work-day clothes must on the whole be better than his play-day clothes; and as his father accepted the argument, his mother gave in.

When he had eaten his breakfast, she took a pouch made of goatskin, with the long hair on it, filled it with bread and cheese, and hung it over his shoulder. Then his father gave him a stick he had cut for him in the wood, and he bade them good-bye rather hurriedly, for he was afraid of breaking down. As he went out, he caught up his mattock and took it with him. It had on the one side a pointed curve of strong steel, for loosening the earth and the ore, and on the other a steel hammer for breaking the stones and rocks. Just as he crossed the threshold the sun showed the first segment of his disk above the horizon.

10   The Heath

He had to go to the bottom of the hill to get into a country he could cross, for the mountains to the north were full of precipices, and it would have been losing time to go that way. Not until he had reached the king's house was it any use to turn northwards. Many a look did he raise, as he passed it, to the dove-tower, and as long as it was in sight, but he saw nothing of the lady of the pigeons.

On and on he fared, and came in a few hours to a country where there were no mountains more – only hills, with great stretches of desolate heath. Here and there was a village, but that brought him little pleasure, for the people were rougher and worse mannered than those in the mountains, and as he passed through, the children came behind and mocked him.

'There's a monkey running away from the mines!' they cried.

Sometimes their parents came out and encouraged them.

'He don't want to find gold for the king any longer – the lazybones!' they would say. 'He'll be well taxed down here though, and he won't like that either.

But it was little to Curdie that men who did not know what he was about should not approve of his proceedings. He gave them a merry answer now and then, and held diligently on his way. When they got so rude as nearly to make him angry, he would treat them as he used to treat the goblins, and sing his own songs to keep out their foolish noises. Once a child fell as he turned to run away after throwing a stone at him. He picked him up, kissed him, and carried him to his mother. The woman had run out in terror when she saw the strange miner about, as she thought, to take vengeance on her boy. When he put him in her arms, she blessed him, and Curdie went on his way rejoicing.

And so the day went on, and the evening came, and in the middle of a great desolate heath he began to feel tired, and sat down under an ancient hawthorn, through which every now and then a lone wind that seemed to come from nowhere and to go nowhither sighed and hissed. It was very old and distorted. There was not another tree for miles all round. It seemed to have lived so long, and to have been so torn and tossed by the tempests on that moor, that it had at last gathered a wind of its own, which got up now and then, tumbled itself about, and lay down again.

Curdie had been so eager to get on that he had eaten nothing since his breakfast. But he had had plenty of water, for many little streams had crossed his path. He now opened the wallet his mother had given him, and began to eat his supper. The sun was setting. A few clouds had gathered about the west, but there was not a single cloud anywhere else to be seen.

Now Curdie did not know that this was a part of the country very hard to get through. Nobody lived there, though many had tried to build in it. Some died very soon. Some rushed out of it. Those who stayed longest went raving mad, and died a terrible death. Such as walked straight on, and did not spend a night there, got through well, and were nothing the worse. But those who slept even a single night in it were sure to meet with something they could never forget, and which often left a mark everybody could read. And that old hawthorn might have been enough for a warning – it looked so like a human being dried up and distorted with age and suffering, with cares instead of loves, and things instead of thoughts. Both it and the heath around it, which stretched on all sides as far as he could see, were so withered that it was impossible to say whether they were alive or not.

And while Curdie ate there came a change. Clouds had gathered over his head, and seemed drifting about in every direction, as if not 'shepherded by the slow, unwilling wind,' but hunted in all directions by wolfish flaws across the plains of the sky. The sun was going down in a storm of lurid crimson, and out of the west came a wind that felt red and hot the one moment, and cold and pale the other. And very strangely it sung in the dreary old hawthorn-tree, and very cheerily it blew about Curdie, now making him creep close up to the tree for shelter from its shivery cold, now fan himself with his cap, it was so sultry and stifling. It seemed to come from the death-bed of the sun, dying in fever and ague.

And as he gazed at the sun, now on the verge of the horizon, very large and very red and very dull – for though the clouds had broken away a dusty fog was spread all over him – Curdie saw something strange appear against him, moving about like a fly over his burning face. It looked as if it were coming out of his hot furnace-heart, and was a living creature of some kind surely; but its shape was very uncertain, because the dazzle of the light all around it melted its outlines. It was growing larger, it must be approaching! It grew so rapidly that by the time the sun was half down its head reached the top of his arch, and presently nothing but its legs were to be seen, crossing and recrossing the face of the vanishing disk. When the sun was down he could see nothing of it more, but in a moment he heard its feet galloping over the dry crackling heather, and seeming to come straight for him. He stood up, lifted his pickaxe, and threw the hammer end over his shoulder: he was going to have a fight for his life! And now it appeared again, vague, yet very awful, in the dim twilight the sun had left behind him. But just before it reached him, down from its four long legs it dropped flat on the ground, and came crawling towards him, wagging a huge tail as it came.

11   Lina

It was Lina. All at once Curdie recognized her – the frightful creature
he had seen at the princess's. He dropped his pickaxe, and held out his
hand. She crept nearer and nearer, and laid her chin in his palm, and
he patted her ugly head. Then she crept away behind the tree, and lay
down, panting hard. Curdie did not much like the idea of her being
behind him. Horrible as she was to look at, she seemed to his mind
more horrible when he was not looking at her. But he remembered the
child's hand, and never thought of driving her away. Now and then
he gave a glance behind him, and there she lay flat, with her eyes closed
and her terrible teeth gleaming between her two huge fore-paws.

After his supper and his long day's journey it was no wonder
Curdie should now be sleepy. Since the sun set the air had been warm
and pleasant. He lay down under the tree, closed his eyes, and thought
to sleep. He found himself mistaken, however. But although he could
not sleep, he was yet aware of resting delightfully. Presently he heard a
sweet sound of singing somewhere, such as he had never heard before
– a singing as of curious birds far off, which drew nearer and nearer. At
length he heard their wings, and, opening his eyes, saw a number of
very large birds, as it seemed, alighting around him, still singing. It
was strange to hear song from the throats of such big birds. And still
singing, with large and round but not the less bird-like voices, they
began to weave a strange dance about him, moving their wings in time
with their legs. But the dance seemed to be troubled and broken, and
to return upon itself in an eddy, in place of sweeping smoothly on. And
he soon learned, in the low short growls behind him, the cause of the
imperfection: they wanted to dance all round the tree, but Lina would
not permit them to come on her side.

Now Curdie liked the birds, and did not altogether *like* Lina. But neither, nor both together, made a *reason* for driving away the princess's creature. Doubtless she *had been* a goblins' creature, but the last time he saw her was in the king's house and the dove-tower, and at the old princess's feet. So he left her to do as she would, and the dance of the birds continued only a semicircle, troubled at the edges, and returning upon itself. But their song and their motions, nevertheless, and the waving of their wings, began at length to make him very sleepy. All the time he had kept doubting every now and then whether they could really be birds, and the sleepier he got the more he imagined them something else, but he suspected no harm. Suddenly, just as he was sinking beneath the waves of slumber, he awoke in fierce pain. The birds were upon him – all over him – and had begun to tear him with beaks and claws. He had but time, however, to feel that he could not move under their weight, when they set up a hideous screaming and scattered like a cloud. Lina was amongst them, snapping and striking with her paws while her tail knocked them over and over. But they flew up, gathered, and descended on her in a swarm, perching upon every part of her body, so that he could see only a huge misshapen mass, which seemed to go rolling away into the darkness. He got up and tried to follow, but could see nothing, and after wandering about hither and thither for some time, found himself again beside the hawthorn. He feared greatly that the birds had been too much for Lina, and had torn her to pieces. In a little while, however, she came limping back, and lay down in her old place. Curdie also lay down, but, from the pain of his wounds, there was no sleep for him. When the light came he found his clothes a good deal torn and his skin as well, but gladly wondered why the wicked birds had not at once attacked his eyes. Then he turned looking for Lina. She rose and crept to him. But she was in far worse plight than he – plucked and gashed and torn with the beaks and claws of the birds, especially about the bare part of her neck, so that she was pitiful to see. And those worst wounds she could not reach to lick.

'Poor Lina!' said Curdie; 'you got all those helping me.'

She wagged her tail, and made it clear she understood him. Then it flashed upon Curdie's mind that perhaps this was the companion the princess had promised him. For the princess did so many things differently from what anybody looked for! Lina was no beauty certainly, but already, the first night, she had saved his life.

'Come along, Lina,' he said; 'we want water.'

She put her nose to the earth, and after snuffing for a moment, darted off in a straight line. Curdie followed. The ground was so uneven, that after losing sight of her many times, at last he seemed to have lost her altogether. In a few minutes, however, he came upon her waiting for him. Instantly she darted off again. After he had lost and found her again many times, he found her the last time lying beside a great stone. As soon as he came up she began scratching at it with her paws. When he had raised it an inch or two, she shoved in first her nose and then her teeth, and lifted with all the might of her strong neck.

When at length between them they got it up, there was a beautiful little well. He filled his cap with the clearest and sweetest water, and drank. Then he gave to Lina, and she drank plentifully. Next he washed her wounds very carefully. And as he did so, he noted how much the bareness of her neck added to the strange repulsiveness of her appearance. Then he bethought him of the goat-skin wallet his mother had given him, and taking it from his shoulder, tried whether it would do to make a collar of for the poor animal. He found there was just enough, and the hair so similar in colour to Lina's, that no one could suspect it of having grown somewhere else. He took his knife, ripped up the seams of the wallet, and began trying the skin to her neck. It was plain she understood perfectly what he wished, for she endeavoured to hold her neck conveniently, turning it this way and that while he contrived, with his rather scanty material, to make the collar fit. As his mother had taken care to provide him with needles and thread, he soon had a nice gorget ready for her. He laced it on with one of his boot laces, which its long hair covered. Poor Lina looked much better in it. Nor could any one have called it a piece of finery. If ever green eyes with a yellow light in them looked grateful, hers did.

As they had no longer any bag to carry them in, Curdie and Lina now ate what was left of the provisions. Then they set out again upon their journey. For seven days it lasted. They met with various adventures, and in all of them Lina proved to helpful, and so ready to risk her life for the sake of her companion, that Curdie grew not merely very fond but very trustful of her, and her ugliness, which at first only moved his pity, now actually increased his affection for her. One day, looking at her stretched on the grass before him, he said:

'Oh, Lina! if the princess would but burn you in her fire of roses!'

She looked up at him, gave a mournful whine like a dog, and laid her head on his feet. What or how much he could not tell, but clearly she had gathered something from his words.

12 More Creatures

One day from morning till night they had been passing through a forest. As soon as the sun was down Curdie began to be aware that there were more in it than themselves. First he saw only the swift rush of a figure across the trees at some distance. Then he saw another and then another at shorter intervals. Then he saw others both farther off and nearer. At last, missing Lina and looking about after her, he saw an appearance almost as marvellous as herself steal up to her, and begin conversing with her after some beast fashion which evidently she understood.

Presently what seemed a quarrel arose between them, and stranger noises followed, mingled with growling. At length it came to a fight, which had not lasted long, however, before the creature of the wood threw itself upon its back, and held up its paws to Lina. She instantly walked on, and the creature got up and followed. They had not gone far before another strange animal appeared, approaching Lina, when precisely the same thing was repeated, the vanquished animal rising and following with the former. Again, and yet again and again, a fresh animal came up, seemed to be reasoned and certainly was fought with and overcome by Lina, until at last, before they were out of the wood, she was followed by forty-nine of the most grotesquely ugly, the most extravagantly abnormal animals imagination can conceive. To describe them were a hopeless task. I knew a boy who used to make animals out of heather roots. Wherever he could find four legs, he was pretty sure to find a head and a tail. His beasts were a most comic menagerie, and right fruitful of laughter. But they were not so grotesque and extravagant as Lina and her followers. One of them, for instance, was like a boa constrictor walking on four little stumpy legs near its tail. About the same distance from its head were two little wings, which it was for ever fluttering as if trying to fly with them.

Curdie thought it fancied it did fly with them, when it was merely plodding on busily with its four little stumps. How it managed to keep up he could not think, till once when he missed it from the group: the same moment he caught sight of something at a distance plunging at an awful serpentine rate through the trees, and presently, from behind a huge ash, this same creature fell again into the group, quietly waddling along on its four stumps. Watching it after this, he saw that, when it was not able to keep up any longer, and they had all got a little space ahead, it shot into the wood away from the route, made a great round, serpenting along in huge billows of motion, devouring the ground, undulating awfully, galloping as if it were all legs together, and its four stumps nowhere. In this mad fashion it shot ahead, and, a few minutes after, toddled in again amongst the rest, walking peacefully and somewhat painfully on its few fours.

From the time it takes to describe one of them it will be readily seen that it would hardly do to attempt a description of each of the forty-nine. They were not a goodly company, but well worth contemplating nevertheless; and Curdie had been too long used to the goblins' creatures in the mines and on the mountain to feel the least uncomfortable at being followed by such a herd. On the contrary the marvellous vagaries of shape they manifested amused him greatly, and shortened the journey much. Before they were all gathered, however, it had got so dark that he could see some of them only a part at a time, and every now and then, as the company wandered on, he would be startled by some extraordinary limb or feature, undreamed of by him before, thrusting itself out of the darkness into the range of his ken. Probably there were some of his old acquaintances among them, although such had been the conditions of semi-darkness in which alone he had ever seen any of them that it was not likely he would be able to identify any of them.

On they marched solemnly, almost in silence, for either with feet or voice the creatures seldom made any noise. By the time they reached the outside of the wood it was morning twilight. Into the open trooped the strange torrent of deformity, each one following Lina. Suddenly she stopped, turned towards them, and said something which they understood, although to Curdie's ear the sounds she made seemed to have no articulation. Instantly they all turned, and vanished in the forest, and Lina alone came trotting lithely and clumsily after her master.

13   The Baker's Wife

They were now passing through a lovely country of hill and dale and rushing stream. The hills were abrupt, with broken chasms for watercourses, and deep little valleys full of trees. But now and then they came to a larger valley, with a fine river, whose level banks and the adjacent meadows were dotted all over with red and white kine, while on the fields above, that sloped a little to the foot of the hills, grew oats and barley and wheat, and on the sides of the hills themselves vines hung and chestnuts rose. They came at last to a broad, beautiful river, up which they must go to arrive at the city of Gwyntystorm, where the king had his court. As they went the valley narrowed, and then the river, but still it was wide enough for large boats. After this, while the river kept its size, the banks narrowed, until was only room for a road between the river and the great cliffs that overhung it. At last river and road took a sudden turn, and lo! a great rock in the river, which dividing flowed around it, and on the top of the rock the city, with lofty walls and towers and battlements, and above the city the palace of the king, built like a strong castle. But the fortifications had long been neglected, for the whole country was now under one king, and all men said there was no more need for weapons or walls. No man pretended to love his neighbour, but every one said he knew that peace and quiet behaviour was the best thing for himself, and that, he said, was quite as useful, and a great more reasonable. The city was prosperous and rich, and if anybody was not comfortable, everybody else said he ought to be.

When Curdie got up opposite the mighty rock, which sparkled all over with crystals, he found a narrow bridge, defended by gates and portcullis and towers with loop-holes. But the gates stood wide open, and were dropping from their great hinges; the portcullis was eaten away with rust, and clung to the grooves evidently immovable; while the loop-holed towers had neither floor nor roof, and their tops were fast filling up their interiors. Curdie thought it a pity, if only for their old story, that they should be thus neglected. But everybody in the city regarded these signs of decay as the best proof of the prosperity of the place. Commerce and self-interest, they said, had got the better of violence, and the troubles of the past were whelmed in the riches that flowed in at their open gates. Indeed there was one sect of philosophers in it which taught that it would be better to forget all the past history of the city, were it not that its former imperfections taught its present inhabitants how superior they and their times were, and enabled them to glory over their ancestors. There were even certain quacks in the city who advertised pills for enabling people to think well of themselves, and some few bought of them, but most laughed, and said, with evident truth, that they did not require them. Indeed, the general theme of discourse when they met was, how much wiser they were than their fathers.

Curdie crossed the river, and began to ascend the winding road that led up to the city. They met a good many idlers, and all stared at them. It was no wonder they should stare, but there was an unfriendliness in their looks which Curdie did not like. No one, however, offered them any molestation: Lina did not invite liberties. After a long ascent, they reached the principal gate of the city and entered.

The street was very steep, ascending towards the palace, which rose in great strength above all the houses. Just as they entered, a baker, whose shop was a few doors inside the gate, came out in his white apron, and ran to the shop of his friend the barber on the opposite side of the way. But as he ran he stumbled and fell heavily. Curdie hastened to help him up, and found he had bruised his forehead badly. He swore grievously at the stone for tripping him up, declaring it was the third time he had fallen over it within the last month; and saying what was the king about that he allowed such a stone to stick up for ever on the main street of his royal residence of Gwyntystorm! What was a king for if he would not take care of his people's heads! And he stroked his forehead tenderly.

'Was it your head or your feet that ought to bear the blame of your fall?' asked Curdie.

'Why, you booby of a miner! my feet, of course,' answered the baker.

'Nay, then,' said Curdie, 'the king can't be to blame.'

'Oh, I see!' replied the baker. 'You're laying a trap for me. Of course, if you come to that, it was my head that ought to have looked after my feet. But it is the king's part to look after us all, and have his streets smooth.'

'Well, I don't see,' said Curdie, 'why the king should take care of the baker, when the baker's head won't take care of the baker's feet.'

'Who are you to make game of the king's baker?' cried the man in a rage.

But, instead of answering, Curdie went up to the bump on the street which had repeated itself on the baker's head, and turning the hammer end of his mattock, struck it such a blow that it flew wide in pieces. Blow after blow he struck, until he had levelled it with the street.

But out flew the barber upon him in a rage.

'What do you break my window for, you rascal, with your pickaxe?'

'I am very sorry,' said Curdie. 'It must have been a bit of stone that flew from my mattock. I couldn't help it, you know.'

'Couldn't help it! A fine story! What do you go breaking the rock for – the very rock upon which the city stands?'

'Look at your friend's forehead,' said Curdie. 'See what a lump he has got on it with falling over that same stone.'

'What's that to my window?' cried the barber.

'His forehead can mend itself; my poor window can't.'

'But he's the king's baker,' said Curdie, more and more surprised at the man's anger.

'What's that to me? This is a free city. Every man here takes care of himself, and the king takes care of us all. I'll have the price of my window out of you, or the exchequer shall pay for it.'

Something caught Curdie's eye. He stooped, picked up a piece of stone he had just broken, and put it in his pocket.

'I suppose you are going to break another of my windows with that stone!' said the barber.

'Oh, no,' said Curdie. 'I didn't mean to break your window, and I certainly won't break another.'

'Give me that stone,' said the barber.

Curdie gave it him, and the barber threw it over the city wall.

'I thought you wanted the stone,' said Curdie.

'No, you fool!' answered the barber. 'What should I want with a stone?'

Curdie stooped and picked up another.

'Give me that stone,' said the barber.

'No,' answered Curdie. 'You have just told me you don't want a stone, and I do.'

The barber took Curdie by the collar.

'Come, now! you pay me for that window.'

'How much?' asked Curdie.

The barber said: 'A crown.' But the baker, annoyed at the heartlessness of the barber, in thinking more of his broken window than the bump on his friend's forehead, interfered.

'No, no,' he said to Curdie; 'don't you pay any such sum. A little pane like that cost only a quarter.'

'Well, to be certain,' said Curdie, 'I'll give him a half.' For he doubted the baker as well as the barber. 'Perhaps one day, if he finds he has asked too much, he will bring me the difference.'

'Ha! ha!' laughed the barber. 'A fool and his money are soon parted.'

But as he took the coin from Curdie's hand he grasped it in affected reconciliation and real satisfaction. In Curdie's, his was the cold smooth leathery palm of a monkey. He looked up, almost expecting to see him pop the money in his cheek; but he had not yet got so far as that, though he was well on the road to it: then he would have no other pocket.

'I'm glad that stone is gone, anyhow,' said the baker. 'It was the bane of my life. I had no idea how easy it was to remove it. Give me your pickaxe, young miner, and I will show you how a baker can make the stones fly.'

He caught the tool out of Curdie's hand, and flew at one of the foundation stones of the gateway. But he jarred his arm terribly, scarcely chipped the stone, dropped the mattock with a cry of pain, and ran into his own shop. Curdie picked up his implement, and looking after the baker, saw bread in the window, and followed him in. But the baker, ashamed of himself, and thinking he was coming to laugh at him, popped out of the back door, and when Curdie entered, the baker's wife came from the bakehouse to serve him. Curdie requested to know the price of a certain good-sized loaf.

Now the baker's wife had been watching what had passed since first her husband ran out of the shop, and she liked the look of Curdie. Also she was more honest than her husband. Casting a glance to the back door, she replied:

'That is not the best bread. I will sell you a loaf of what we bake for ourselves.' And when she had spoken she laid a finger on her lips. 'Take care of yourself in this place, my son,' she added. 'They do not love strangers. I was once a stranger here, and I know what I say.' Then fancying she heard her husband, 'That is a strange animal you have,' she said, in a louder voice.

'Yes,' answered Curdie. 'She is no beauty, but she is very good, and we love each other. Don't we, Lina?'

Lina looked up and whined. Curdie threw her the half of his loaf, which she ate while her master and the baker's wife talked a little. Then the baker's wife gave them some water, and Curdie having paid for his loaf, he and Lina went up the street together.

14   The Dogs of Gwyntystorm

The steep street led them straight up to a large market-place, with butchers' shops, about which were many dogs. The moment they caught sight of Lina, one and all they came rushing down upon her, giving her no chance of explaining herself. When Curdie saw the dogs coming he heaved up his mattock over his shoulder, and was ready, if they would have it so. Seeing him thus prepared to defend his follower, a great ugly bull-dog flew at him. With the first blow Curdie struck him through the brain, and the brute fell dead at his feet. But he could not at once recover his weapon, which stuck in the skull of his foe, and a huge mastiff, seeing him thus hampered, flew at him next. Now Lina, who had shown herself so brave upon the road thither, had grown shy upon entering the city, and kept always at Curdie's heel. But it was her turn now. The moment she saw her master in danger she seemed to go mad with rage. As the mastiff jumped at Curdie's throat, Lina flew at his, seized him with her tremendous jaws, gave one roaring grind, and he lay beside the bull-dog with his neck broken. They were the best dogs in the market, after the judgment of the butchers of Gwyntystorm. Down came their masters, knife in hand.

Curdie drew himself up fearlessly, mattock on shoulder, and awaited their coming, while at his heel his awful attendant showed not only her outside fringe of icicle-teeth, but a double row of right serviceable fangs she wore inside her mouth, and her green eyes flashed yellow as gold. The butchers, not liking the look either of them or of the dogs at their feet, drew back, and began to remonstrate in the manner of outraged men.

'Stranger,' said the first, 'that bull-dog is mine.'

'Take him, then,' said Curdie, indignant.

'You've killed him!'

'Yes – else he would have killed me.'

'That's no business of mine.'

'No?'

'No.'

'That makes it the more mine, then.'

'This sort of thing won't do, you know,' said the other butcher.

'That's true,' said Curdie.

'That's my mastiff,' said the butcher.

'And as he ought to be,' said Curdie.

'Your brute shall be burnt alive for it,' said the butcher.

'Not yet,' answered Curdie. 'We have done no wrong. We were walking quietly up your street, when your dogs flew at us. If you don't teach your dogs how to treat strangers, you must take the consequences.'

'They treat them quite properly,' said the butcher. 'What right has any one to bring an abomination like that into our city? The horror is enough to make an idiot of every child in the place.'

'We are both subjects of the king, and my poor animal can't help her looks. How would you like to be served like that because you were ugly? She's not a bit fonder of her looks than you are – only what can she do to change them?'

'I'll do to change them,' said the fellow.

Thereupon the butchers brandished their long knives and advanced, keeping their eyes upon Lina.

'Don't be afraid, Lina,' cried Curdie. 'I'll kill one – you kill the other.'

Lina gave a howl that might have terrified an army and crouched ready to spring. The butchers turned and ran.

By this time a great crowd had gathered behind the butchers, and in it a number of boys returning from school, who began to stone the strangers. It was a way they had with man or beast they did not expect to make anything by. One of the stones struck Lina; she caught it in her teeth and crunched it that it fell in gravel from her mouth. Some of the foremost of the crowd saw this, and it terrified them. They drew back; the rest took fright from their retreat; the panic spread; and at last the crowd scattered in all directions. They ran, and cried out, and said the devil and his dam were come to Gwyntystorm. So Curdie and Lina were left standing unmolested in the market-place. But the terror of them spread throughout the city, and everybody began to shut and lock his door, so that by the time the setting sun shone down the street there was not a shop left open, for fear of the devil and his horrible dam. But all the upper windows within sight of them were crowded with heads watching them where they stood lonely in the deserted market-place.

Curdie looked carefully all round, but could not see one open door. He caught sight of the sign of an inn, however, and laying down his mattock, and telling Lina to take care of it, walked up to the door of it and knocked. But the people in the house, instead of opening the door, threw things at him from the windows. They would not listen to a word he said, but sent him back to Lina with the blood running down his face. When Lina saw that, she leaped up in a fury and was rushing at the house, into which she would certainly have broken; but Curdie called her, and made her lie down beside him while he bethought him what next he should do.

'Lina,' he said, 'the people keep their gates open, but their houses and their hearts shut.'

As if she knew it was her presence that had brought this trouble upon him, she rose, and went round and round him, purring like a tigress, and rubbing herself against his legs.

Now there was one little thatched house that stood squeezed in between two tall gables, and the sides of the two great houses shot out projecting windows that nearly met across the door of the little one, so that it lay in the street like a doll's house. In this house lived a poor old woman, with a grandchild. And because she never gossiped or quarrelled, or chaffered in the market, but went without what she could not afford, the people called her a witch, and would have done her many an ill turn if they had not been afraid of her. Now while Curdie was looking in another direction the door opened, and out came a little dark-haired, black-eyed, gipsy-looking child, and toddled across the market-place towards the outcasts. The moment they saw her coming, Lina lay down flat on the road, and with her two huge fore-paws covered her mouth, while Curdie went to meet her, holding out his arms. The little one came straight to him, and held up her mouth to be kissed. Then she took him by the hand, and drew him towards the house, and Curdie yielded to the silent invitation. But when Lina rose to follow, the child shrunk from her, frightened a little. Curdie took her up, and holding her on one arm, patted Lina with the other hand. Then the child wanted also to pat doggy, as she called her by a right bountiful stretch of courtesy, and having once patted her, nothing would serve but Curdie must let her have a ride on doggy. So he set her on Lina's back, holding her hand, and she rode home in merry triumph, all unconscious of the hundreds of eyes staring at her foolhardiness from the windows about the market-place, or the murmur of deep disapproval that rose from as many lips. At the door stood the grandmother to receive them. She caught the child to her bosom with delight at her courage, welcomed Curdie, and showed no dread of Lina. Many were the significant nods exchanged, and many a one said to another that the devil and the witch were old friends. But the woman was only a wise woman, who having seen how Curdie and Lina behaved to each other, judged from that what sort they were, and so bade them welcome to her house. She was not like her fellow townspeople, for that they were strangers recommended them to her.

The moment her door was shut, the other doors began to open, and soon there appeared little groups about here and there a threshold, while a few of the more courageous ventured out upon the square – all ready to make for their houses again, however, upon the least sign of movement in the little thatched one.

The baker and the barber had joined one of these groups, and were busily wagging their tongues against Curdie and his horrible beast.

'He can't be honest,' said the barber; 'for he paid me double the worth of the pane he broke in my window.'

And then he told them how Curdie broke his window by breaking a stone in the street with his hammer. There the baker struck in.

'Now that was the stone,' said he, 'over which I had fallen three times within the last month: could it be by fair means he broke that to pieces at the first blow? Just to make up my mind on that point I tried his own hammer against a stone in the gate; it nearly broke both my arms, and loosened half the teeth in my head!'

15　Derba and Barbara

Meantime the wanderers were hospitably entertained by the old woman and her grandchild, and they were all very comfortable and happy together. Little Barbara sat upon Curdie's knee, and he told her stories about the mines and his adventures in them. But he never mentioned the king or the princess, for all that story was hard to believe. And he told her about his mother and his father, and how good they were. And Derba sat and listened. At last little Barbara fell asleep in Curdie's arms, and her grandmother carried her to bed.

It was a poor little house, and Derba gave up her own room to Curdie, because he was honest and talked wisely. Curdie saw how it was, and begged her to allow him to lie on the floor, but she would not hear of it.

In the night he was waked by Lina pulling at him. As soon as he spoke to her she ceased, and Curdie listening, thought he heard someone trying to get in. He rose, took his mattock, and went about the house, listening and watching; but although he heard noises, now at one place, now at another, he could not think what they meant, for no one appeared. Certainly, considering how she had frightened them all in the day, it was not likely any one would attack Lina at night. By and by the noises ceased, and Curdie went back to his bed, and slept undisturbed.

In the morning, however, Derba came to him in great agitation, and said they had fastened up the door, so that she could not get out. Curdie rose immediately and went with her: they found that not only the door, but every window in the house was so secured on the outside that it was impossible to open one of them without using great force. Poor Derba looked anxiously in Curdie's face. He broke out laughing.

'They are much mistaken,' he said, 'if they fancy they could keep

Lina and a miner in any house in Gwyntystorm – even if they built up doors and windows.'

With that he shouldered his mattock. But Derba begged him not to make a hole in her house just yet. She had plenty for breakfast, she said, and before it was time for dinner they would know what the people meant by it.

And indeed they did. For within an hour appeared one of the chief magistrates of the city, accompanied by a score of soldiers with drawn swords, and followed by a great multitude of the people, requiring the miner and his brute to yield themselves, the one that he might be tried for the disturbance he had occasioned and the injury he had committed, the other that she might be roasted alive for her part in killing two valuable and harmless animals belonging to worthy citizens. The summons was preceded and followed by flourish of trumpet, and was read with every formality by the city marshal himself.

The moment he ended, Lina ran into the little passage, and stood opposite the door.

'I surrender,' cried Curdie.

'Then tie up your brute, and give her here.'

'No, no,' cried Curdie through the door. 'I surrender; but I'm not going to do your hangman's work. If you want my dog, you must take her.'

'Then we shall set the house on fire, and burn witch and all.'

'It will go hard with us, but we shall kill a few dozen of you first,' cried Curdie. 'We're not the least afraid of you.'

With that Curdie turned to Derba, and said:

'Don't be frightened. I have a strong feeling that all will be well. Surely no trouble will come to you for being good to strangers.'

'But the poor dog!' said Derba.

Now Curdie and Lina understood each more than a little by this time, and not only had he seen that she understood the proclamation, but when she looked up at him after it was read, it was with such a grin, and such a yellow flash, that he saw also she was determined to take care of herself.

'The dog will probably give you reason to think a little more of her ere long,' he answered. 'But now,' he went on, 'I fear I must hurt your house a little. I have great confidence, however, that I shall be able to make up to you for it one day.'

'Never mind the house, if only you can get safe off,' she answered. 'I don't think they will hurt this precious lamb,' she added, clasping little Barbara to her bosom. 'For myself, it is all one; I am ready for anything.'

'It is but a little hole for Lina I want to make,' said Curdie. 'She can creep through a much smaller one than you would think.'

Again he took his mattock, and went to the back wall.

'They won't burn the house,' he said to himself. 'There is too good a one on each side of it.'

The tumult had kept increasing every moment, and the city marshal had been shouting, but Curdie had not listened to him. When now they heard the blows of his mattock, there went up a great cry, and the people taunted the soldiers that they were afraid of a dog and his miner. The soldiers therefore made a rush at the door, and cut its fastenings.

The moment they opened it, out leaped Lina, with a roar so unnaturally horrible that the sword-arms of the soldiers dropped by their sides, paralysed with the terror of that cry; the crowd fled in every direction, shrieking and yelling with mortal dismay; and without even knocking down with her tail, not to say biting a man of them with her pulverizing jaws, Lina vanished – no one knew whither, for not one of the crowd had had courage to look upon her.

The moment she was gone Curdie advanced and gave himself up. The soldiers were so filled with fear, shame, and chagrin that they were ready to kill him on the spot. But he stook quietly facing them, with his mattock on his shoulder; and the magistrate wishing to examine him, and the people to see him made an example of, the soldiers had to content themselves with taking him. Partly for derision, partly to hurt him, they laid his mattock against his back, and tied his arms to it.

They led him up a very steep street, and up another still, all the crowd following. The king's palace-castle rose towering above them; but they stopped before they reached it, at a low-browed door in a great, dull, heavy-looking building.

The city marshal opened it with a key which hung at his girdle, and ordered Curdie to enter. The place within was dark as night, and while he was feeling his way with his feet, the marshal gave him a rough push. He fell, and rolled once or twice over, unable to help himself because his hands were tied behind him.

It was the hour of the magistrate's second and more important breakfast, and until that was over he never found himself capable of attending to a case with concentration sufficient to the distinguishing of the side upon which his own advantage lay; and hence was this respite for Curdie, with time to collect his thoughts. But indeed he had very few to collect, for all he had to do, so far as he could see, was to wait for what would come next. Neither had he much power to collect them, for he was a good deal shaken.

In a few minutes he discovered, to his great relief, that, from the projection of the pick-end of his mattock beyond his body, the fall had loosened the ropes tied round it. He got one hand disengaged, and then the other; and presently stood free, with his good mattock once more in right serviceable relation to his arms and legs.

16   The Mattock

While the magistrate reinvigorated his selfishness with a greedy breakfast, Curdie found doing nothing in the dark rather wearisome work. It was useless attempting to think what he should do next, seeing the circumstances in which he was presently to find himself were altogether unknown to him. So he began to think about his father and mother in their little cottage home, high in the clear air of the open mountain-side, and the thought, instead of making his dungeon gloomier by the contrast, made a light in his soul that destroyed the power of darkness and captivity. But he was at length startled from his waking dream by a swell in the noise outside. All the time there had been a few of the more idle of the inhabitants about the door, but they had been rather quiet. Now, however, the sounds of feet and voices began to grow, and grew so rapidly that it was plain a multitude was gathering. For the people of Gwyntystorm always gave themselves an hour of pleasure after their second breakfast, and what greater pleasure could they have than to see a stranger abused by the officers of justice? The noise grew till it was like the roaring of the sea, and that roaring went on a long time, for the magistrate, being a great man, liked to know that he was waited for: it added to the enjoyment of his breakfast, and, indeed, enabled him to eat a little more after he had thought his powers exhausted. But at length, in the waves of the human noises rose a bigger wave, and by the running and shouting and outcry, Curdie learned that the magistrate was approaching.

Presently came the sound of the great rusty key in the lock, which yielded with groaning reluctance; the door was thrown back, the light rushed in, and with it came the voice of the city marshal, calling upon Curdie, by many legal epithets opprobrious, to come forth and be tried for his life, inasmuch as he had raised a tumult in His Majesty's city of

Gwyntystorm, troubled the hearts of the king's baker and barber, and slain the faithful dogs of His Majesty's well-beloved butchers.

He was still reading, and Curdie was still seated in the brown twilight of the vault, not listening, but pondering with himself how this king the city marshal talked of could be the same with the majesty he had seen ride away on his grand white horse, with the Princess Irene on a cushion before him, when a scream of agonized terror arose on the farthest skirt of the crowd, and, swifter than flood or flame, the horror spread shrieking. In a moment the air was filled with hideous howling, cries of unspeakable dismay, and the multitudinous noise of running feet. The next moment, in at the door of the vault bounded Lina, her two green eyes flaming yellow as sunflowers, and seeming to light up the dungeon. With one spring she threw herself at Curdie's feet, and laid her head upon them panting. Then came a rush of two or three soldiers darkening the doorway, but it was only to lay hold of the key, pull the door to, and lock it; so that once more Curdie and Lina were prisoners together.

For a few moments Lina lay panting hard: it is breathless work leaping and roaring both at once, and that in a way to scatter thousands of people. Then she jumped up, and began snuffing about all over the place; and Curdie saw what he had never seen before – two faint spots of light cast from her eyes upon the ground, one on each side of her snuffing nose. He got out his tinder-box – a miner is never without one – and lighted a precious bit of candle he carried in a division of it – just for a moment, for he must not waste it.

The light revealed a vault without any window or other opening than the door. It was very old and much neglected. The mortar had vanished from between the stones, and it was half filled with a heap of all sorts of rubbish, beaten down in the middle, but looser at the sides; it sloped from the door to the foot of the opposite wall: evidently for a long time the vault had been left open, and every sort of refuse thrown into it. A single minute served for the survey, so little was there to note.

Meantime, down in the angle between the back wall and the base of the heap, Lina was scratching furiously with all the eighteen great strong claws of her mighty feet.

'Ah, ha!' said Curdie to himself, catching sight of her, 'if only they will leave us long enough to ourselves!'

With that he ran to the door, to see if there was any fastening on the inside. There was none: in all its long history it never had had one. But a few blows of the right sort, now from the one, now from the other end of his mattock, were as good as any bolt, for they so ruined the lock that no key could ever turn in it again. Those who heard them fancied he was trying to get out, and laughed spitefully. As soon as he had done, he extinguished his candle, and went down to Lina.

She had reached the hard rock which formed the floor of the dungeon, and was now clearing away the earth a little wider. Presently she looked up in his face and whined, as much as to say: 'My paws are not hard enough to get any farther.'

'Then get out of my way, Lina,' said Curdie, 'and mind you keep your eyes shining, for fear I should hit you.'

So saying, he heaved his mattock, and assailed with the hammer end of it the spot she had cleared.

The rock was very hard, but when it did break it broke in good-sized pieces. Now with hammer, now with pick, he worked till he was weary, then rested, and then set to again. He could not tell how the day went, as he had no light but the lamping of Lina's eyes. The darkness hampered him greatly, for he would not let Lina come close enough to give him all the light she could, lest he should strike her. So he had, every now and then, to feel with his hands to know how he was getting on, and to discover in what direction to strike: the exact spot was a mere imagination.

He was getting very tired and hungry, and beginning to lose heart a little, when out of the ground, as if he had struck a spring of it, burst a dull, gleamy, lead-coloured light, and the next moment he heard a hollow splash and echo. A piece of rock had fallen out of the floor, and dropped into water beneath. Already Lina, who had been lying a few yards off all the time he worked, was on her feet and peering through the hole. Curdie got down on his hands and knees, and looked. They were over what seemed a natural cave in the rock, to which apparently the river had access, for, at a great distance below, a faint light was gleaming upon water. If they could but reach it, they might get out; but even if it was deep enough, the height was very dangerous. The first thing, whatever might follow, was to make the hole larger. It was comparatively easy to break away the sides of it, and in the course of another hour he had it large enough to get through.

And now he must reconnoitre. He took the rope they had tied him with – for Curdie's hindrances were always his furtherance – and fastened one end of it by a slip-knot round the handle of his pickaxe, then dropped the other end through, and laid the pickaxe so that, when he was through himself, and hanging on to the edge, he could place it across the hole to support him on the rope. This done, he took the rope in his hands, and, beginning to descend, found himself in a narrow cleft widening into a cave. His rope was not very long, and would not do much to lessen the force of his fall – he thought with himself – if he should have to drop into the water; but he was not more than a couple of yards below the dungeon when he spied an opening in the opposite side of the cleft; it might be but a shallow hole, or it might lead them out. He dropped himself a little below its level, gave the rope a swing by pushing his feet against the side of the cleft, and so penduled himself into it. Then he laid a stone on the end of the rope that it should not forsake him, called to Lina, whose yellow eyes were gleaming over the mattock-grating above, to watch there till he returned, and went cautiously in.

It proved a passage, level for some distance, then sloping gently up. He advanced carefully, feeling his way as he went. At length he was stopped by a door – a small door, studded with iron. But the wood was in places so much decayed that some of the bolts had dropped out, and he felt sure of being able to open it. He returned, therefore, to fetch Lina and his mattock. Arrived at the cleft, his strong miner arms bore him swiftly up along the rope and through the hole into the dungeon. There he undid the rope from his mattock, and making Lina take the end of it in her teeth, and get through the hole, he lowered her – it was all he could do, she was so heavy. When she came opposite the passage, with a slight push of her tail she shot herself into it and let go the rope, which Curdie drew up. Then he lighted his candle, and searching the rubbish found a bit of iron to take the place of his pickaxe across the hole. Then he searched again in the rubbish, and found half an old shutter. This he propped up leaning a little over the hole, with a bit of stick, and heaped against the back of it a quantity of the loosened earth. Next he tied his mattock to the end of the rope, dropped it, and let it hang. Last, he got through the hole himself, and pulled away the propping stick, so that the shutter fell over the hole with a quantity of earth on the top of it. A few motions of hand over hand, and he swung himself and his mattock into the passage beside Lina. There he secured the end of the rope, and they went on together to the door.

17　The Wine-cellar

He lighted his candle and examined it. Decayed and broken as it was, it was strongly secured in its place by hinges on the one side, and either lock or bolt, he could not tell which, on the other. A brief use of his pocket-knife was enough to make room for his hand and arm to get through, and then he found a great iron bolt – but so rusty that he could not move it. Lina whimpered. He took his knife again, made the hole bigger, and stood back. In she shot her small head and long neck, seized the bolt with her teeth, and dragged it grating and complaining back. A push then opened the door. It was at the foot of a short flight of steps. They ascended, and at the top Curdie found himself in a space which, from the echo to his stamp, appeared of some size, though of what sort he could not at first tell, for his hands, feeling about, came upon nothing. Presently, however, they fell on a great thing: it was a wine-cask. He was just setting out to explore the place by a thorough palpation, when he heard steps coming down a stair. He stood still, not knowing whether the door would open an inch from his nose or twenty yards behind his back. It did neither. He heard the key turn in the lock, and a stream of light shot in, ruining the darkness, about fifteen yards away on his right.

A man carrying a candle in one hand and a large silver flagon in the other, entered, and came towards him. The light revealed a row of huge wine-casks, that stretched away into the darkness of the other end of the long vault. Curdie retreated into the recess of the stair, and peeping round the corner of it, watched him, thinking what he could do to prevent him from locking them in. He came on and on, until Curdie feared he would pass the recess and see them. He was just preparing to rush out, and master him before he should give alarm, not in the least knowing what he should do next, when, to his relief, the man stopped at the third cask from where he stood. He set down his light on the top of it, removed what seemed a large vent-peg, and poured into the cask a quantity of something from the flagon. Then he turned to the next cask, drew some wine, rinsed the flagon, threw the wine away, drew and rinsed and threw away again, then drew and drank, draining to the bottom. Last of all, he filled the flagon from the cask he had first visited, replaced then the vent-peg, took up his candle, and turned towards the door.

'There is something wrong here!' thought Curdie.

'Speak to him, Lina,' he whispered.

The sudden howl she gave made Curdie himself start and tremble for a moment. As to the man, he answered Lina's with another horrible howl, forced from him by the convulsive shudder of every muscle of his body, then reeled gasping to and fro, and dropped his candle. But just as Curdie expected to see him fall dead he recovered himself, and flew to the door, through which he darted, leaving it open behind him. The moment he ran, Curdie stepped out, picked up the candle still alight, sped after him to the door, drew out the key, and then returned to the stair and waited. In a few minutes he heard the sound of many feet and voices. Instantly he turned the tap of the cask from which the man had been drinking, set the candle beside it on the floor, went down the steps and out of the little door, followed by Lina, and closed it behind them.

Through the hole in it he could see a little, and hear all. He could see how the light of many candles filled the place, and could hear how some two dozen feet ran hither and thither through the echoing cellar; he could hear the clash of iron, probably spits and pokers, now and then; and at last heard how, finding nothing remarkable except the best wine running to waste, they all turned on the butler, and accused him of having fooled them with a drunken dream. He did his best to defend himself appealing to the evidence of their own senses that he was as sober as they were. They replied that a fright was no less a fright that the cause was imaginary, and a dream no less a dream that the fright had waked him from it. When he discovered, and triumphantly adduced as corroboration, that the key was gone from the door, they said it merely showed how drunk he had been – either that or how frightened, for he had certainly dropped it. In vain he protested that he had never taken it out of the lock – that he never did when he went in, and certainly had not this time stopped to do so when he came out;

Curdie was just setting out to explore the place
when he heard steps coming down a stair

they asked him why he had to go to the cellar at such a time of the day, and said it was because he had already drunk all the wine that was left from dinner. He said if he had dropped the key, the key was to be found, and they must help him to find it. They told him they wouldn't move a peg for him. He declared, with much language, he would have them all turned out of the king's service. They said they would swear he was drunk. And so positive were they about it, that at last the butler himself began to think whether it was possible they could be in the right. For he knew that sometimes when he had been drunk he fancied things had taken place which he found afterwards could not have happened. Certain of his fellow servants, however, had all the time a doubt whether the cellar goblin had not appeared to him, or at least roared at him, to protect the wine. In any case nobody wanted to find the key for him; nothing could please them better than that the door of the wine-cellar should never more be locked. By degrees the hubbub died away, and they departed, not even pulling to the door, for there was neither handle nor latch to it.

As soon as they were gone, Curdie returned, knowing now that they were in the wine-cellar of the palace, as, indeed, he had suspected. Finding a pool of wine in a hollow of the floor, Lina lapped it up eagerly: she had had no breakfast, and was now very thirsty as well as hungry. Her master was in a similar plight, for he had just begun to eat when the magistrate arrived with the soldiers. If only they were all in bed, he thought, that he might find his way to the larder! For he said to himself that, as he was sent there by the young princess's great-great-grandmother to serve her or her father in some way, surely he must have a right to his food in the palace, without which he could do nothing. He would go at once and reconnoitre.

So he crept up the stair that led from the cellar. At the top was a door, opening on a long passage, dimly lighted by a lamp. He told Lina to lie down upon the stair while he went on. At the end of the passage he found a door ajar, and, peeping through, saw right into a great stone hall, where a huge fire was blazing, and through which men in the king's livery were constantly coming and going. Some also in the same livery were lounging about the fire. He noted that their colours were the same with those he himself, as king's miner, wore; but from what he had seen and heard of the place, he could not hope they would treat him the better for that.

The one interesting thing at the moment, however, was the plentiful supper with which the table was spread. It was something at least to stand in sight of food, and he was unwilling to turn his back on the prospect so long as a share in it was not absolutely hopeless. Peeping thus, he soon made up his mind that if at any moment the hall should be empty, he would at that moment rush in and attempt to carry off a dish. That he might lose no time by indecision, he selected a large pie upon which to pounce instantaneously. But after he had watched for some minutes, it did not seem at all likely the chance would arrive before supper-time, and he was just about to turn away and rejoin Lina, when he saw that there was not a person in the place. Curdie never made up his mind and then hesitated. He darted in, seized the pie, and bore it, swiftly and noiselessly, to the cellar stair.

18 The King's Kitchen

Back to the cellar Curdie and Lina sped with their booty, where, seated on the steps, Curdie lighted his bit of candle for a moment. A very little bit it was now, but they did not waste much of it in examination of the pie; that they effected by a more summary process. Curdie thought it the nicest food he had ever tasted, and between them they soon ate it up. Then Curdie would have thrown the dish along with the bones into the water, that there might be no traces of them; but he thought of his mother, and hid it instead; and the very next minute they wanted it to draw some wine into. He was careful it should be from the cask of which he had seen the butler drink. Then they sat down again upon the steps, and waited until the house should be quiet. For he was there to do something, and if it did not come to him in the cellar, he must go to meet it in other places. Therefore, lest he should fall asleep, he set the end of the helve of his mattock on the ground, and seated himself on the cross part, leaning against the wall, so that as long as he kept awake he should rest, but the moment he began to fall asleep he must fall awake instead. He quite expected some of the servants would visit the cellar again that night, but whether it was that they were afraid of each other, or believed more of the butler's story than they had chosen to allow, not one of them appeared.

When at length he thought he might venture, he shouldered his mattock and crept up the stair. The lamp was out in the passage, but he could not miss his way to the servants' hall. Trusting to Lina's quickness in concealing herself, he took her with him.

When they reached the hall they found it quiet and nearly dark. The last of the great fire was glowing red, but giving little light. Curdie stood and warmed himself for a few moments: miner as he was, he had found the cellar cold to sit in doing nothing; and standing thus he thought of looking if there were any bits of candle about. There were many candlesticks on the supper-table, but to his disappointment and indignation their candles seemed to have been all left to burn out, and some of them, indeed, he found still hot in the neck.

Presently, one after another, he came upon seven men fast asleep, most of them upon tables, one in a chair, and one the floor. They seemed, from their shape and colour, to have eaten and drunk so much that they might be burned alive without waking. He grasped the hand of each in succession, and found two ox-hoofs, three pig-hoofs, one concerning which he could not be sure whether it was the hoof of a donkey or a pony, and one dog's paw. 'A nice set of people to be about a king!' thought Curdie to himself, and turned again to his candle hunt. He did at last find two or three little pieces, and stowed them away in his pockets.

They now left the hall by another door, and entered a short passage, which led them to the huge kitchen, vaulted, and black with smoke. There too the fire was still burning, so that he was able to see a little of the state of things in this quarter also. The place was dirty and disorderly. In a recess, on a heap of brushwood, lay a kitchenmaid, with a table-cover around her, and a skillet in her hand: evidently she too had been drinking. In another corner lay a page, and Curdie noted how like his dress was to his own. In the cinders before the hearth were huddled three dogs and five cats, all fast asleep, while the rats were running about the floor. Curdie's heart ached to think of the lovely child-princess living over such a sty. The mine was a paradise to a palace with such servants in it.

Leaving the kitchen, he got into the region of the sculleries. There horrible smells were wandering about, like evil spirits that come forth with the darkness. He lighted a candle – but only to see ugly sights. Everywhere was filth and disorder. Mangy turnspit dogs were lying about, and grey rats were gnawing at refuse in the sinks. It was like a hideous dream. He felt as if he should never get out of it, and longed for one glimpse of his mother's poor little kitchen, so clean and bright and airy. Turning from it at last in miserable disgust, he almost ran back through the kitchens, re-entered the hall, and crossed it to another door.

It opened upon a wider passage, leading to an arch in a stately corridor, all its length lighted by lamps in niches. At the end of it was a large and beautiful hall, with great pillars. There sat three men in the royal livery, fast asleep, each in a great arm-chair, with his feet on a huge footstool. They looked like fools dreaming themselves kings; and Lina looked as if she longed to throttle them. At one side of the hall was the grand staircase, and they went up.

Everything that now met Curdie's eyes was rich – not glorious like the splendours of the mountain cavern, but rich and soft – except where, now and then, some rough old rib of the ancient fortress came through, hard and discoloured. Now some dark bare arch of stone, now some rugged and blackened pillar, now some huge beam, brown with the smoke and dust of centuries, looked like a thistle in the midst of daisies, or a rock in a smooth lawn.

They wandered about a good while, again and again finding themselves where they had been before. Gradually, however, Curdie was gaining some idea of the place. By and by Lina began to look frightened, and as they went on Curdie saw that she looked more and more frightened. Now by this time he had come to understand that what made her look frightened was always the fear of frightening, and he therefore concluded they must be drawing nigh to somebody. At last, in a gorgeously painted gallery, he saw a curtain of crimson, and on the curtain a royal crown wrought in silks and stones. He felt sure this must be the king's chamber, and it was here he was wanted; or, if it was not the place he was bound for, something would meet him and turn him aside; for he had come to think that so long as a man wants to do right he may go where he can: when he can go no farther, then it is not the way. 'Only,' said his father, in assenting to the right theory, 'he must really want to do right, and not merely fancy he does. He must want it with his heart and will, and not with his rag of a tongue.'

So he gently lifted the corner of the curtain, and there behind it was a half-open door. He entered, and the moment he was in, Lina stretched herself along the threshold between the curtain and the door.

19   The King's Chamber

He found himself in a large room, dimly lighted by a silver lamp that hung from the ceiling. Far at the other end was a great bed, surrounded with dark heavy curtains. He went softly towards it, his heart beating fast. It was a dreadful thing to be alone in the king's chamber at the dead of night. To gain courage he had to remind himself of the beautiful princess who had sent him. But when he was about half-way to the bed, a figure appeared from the farther side of it, and came towards him, with a hand raised warningly. He stood still. The light was dim, and he could distinguish little more than the outline of a young girl. But though the form he saw was much taller than the princess he remembered, he never doubted it was she. For one thing, he knew that most girls would have been frightened to see him there in the dead of the night, but like a true princess, and the princess he used to know, she walked straight on to meet him. As she came she lowered the hand she had lifted, and laid the forefinger of it upon her lips. Nearer and nearer, quite near, close up to him she came, then stopped, and stood a moment looking at him.

'You are Curdie,' she said.

'And you are the Princess Irene,' he returned.

'Then we know each other still,' she said, with a smile of pleasure. 'You will help me.'

'That I will,' answered Curdie. He did not say, 'If I can'; for he knew that what he was sent to do, that he could do. 'May I kiss your hand, little princess?'

She was only between nine and ten, though indeed she looked several years older, and her eyes almost those of a grown woman, for she had had terrible trouble of late.

She held out her hand.

'I am not the *little* princess any more. I have grown up since I saw you last, Mr. Miner.'

The smile which accompanied the words had in it a strange mixture of playfulness and sadness.

'So I see, Miss Princess,' returned Curdie; 'and therefore, being more of a princess, you are the more my princess. Here I am, sent by your great-great-grandmother, to be your servant. May I ask why you are up so late, princess?'

'Because my father wakes *so* frightened, and I don't know what he *would* do if he didn't find me by his bed-side. There! he's waking now.'

She darted off to the side of the bed she had come from. Curdie stood where he was.

A voice altogether unlike what he remembered of the mighty, noble king on his white horse came from the bed, thin, feeble, hollow, and husky, and in tone like that of a petulant child:

'I will not, I will not. I am a king, and I *will* be a king. I hate you and despise you, and you shall not torture me!'

'Never mind them, father dear,' said the princess. 'I am here, and they shan't touch you. They dare not, you know, so long as you defy them.'

'They want my crown, darling; and I can't give them my crown, can I, for what is a king without his crown?'

'They shall never have your crown, my king,' said Irene. 'Here it is – all safe, you see. I am watching it for you.'

Curdie drew near the bed on the other side. There lay the grand old king – he looked grand still, and twenty years older. His body was pillowed high; his beard descended long and white over the crimson coverlid; and his crown, its diamonds and emeralds gleaming in the twilight of the curtains, lay in front of him, his long, thin old hands folded round the rigol, and the ends of his beard straying among the lovely stones. His face was like that of a man who died nobly; but one thing made it dreadful: his eyes, while they moved about as if searching in this direction and in that, looked more dead than his face. He saw neither his daughter nor his crown: it was the voice of the one and the touch of the other that comforted him. He kept murmuring what seemed words, but was unintelligible to Curdie, although, to judge from the look of Irene's face, she learned and concluded from it.

By degrees his voice sank away and the murmuring ceased,

although still his lips moved. Thus lay the old king on his bed, slumbering with his crown between his hands; on one side of him stood a lovely little maiden, with blue eyes, and brown hair going a little back from her temples, as if blown by a wind that no one felt but herself; and on the other a stalwart young miner, with his mattock over his shoulder. Stranger sight still was Lina lying along the threshold – only nobody saw her just then.

A moment more and the king's lips ceased to move. His breathing had grown regular and quiet. The princess gave a sigh of relief, and came round to Curdie.

'We can talk a little now,' she said, leading him towards the middle of the room. 'My father will sleep now till the doctor wakes him to give him his medicine. It is not really medicine, though, but wine. Nothing but that, the doctor says, could have kept him so long alive. He always comes in the middle of the night to give it him with his own hands. But it makes me cry to see him waked up when so nicely asleep.'

'What sort of man is your doctor?' asked Curdie.

'Oh, such a dear, good, kind gentleman!' replied the princess. 'He speaks so softly, and is so sorry for his dear king! He will be here presently, and you shall see for yourself. You will like him very much.'

'Has your king-father been long ill?' asked Curdie.

'A whole year now,' she replied. 'Did you not know? That's how your mother never got the red petticoat my father promised her. The lord chancellor told me that not only Gwyntystorm but the whole land was mourning over the illness of the good man.'

Now Curdie himself had not heard a word of His Majesty's illness, and had no ground for believing that a single soul in any place he had visited on his journey had heard of it. Moreover, although mention had been made of His Majesty again and again in his hearing since he came to Gwyntystorm, never once had he heard an allusion to the state of his health. And now it dawned upon him also that he had never heard the least expression of love to him. But just for the time he thought it better to say nothing on either point.

'Does the king wander like this every night?' he asked.

'Every night,' answered Irene, shaking her head mournfully. 'That is why I never go to bed at night. He is better during the day – a little, and then I sleep – in the dressing-room there, to be with him in a moment if he should call me. It is *so* sad he should have only me and not my mamma! A princess is nothing to a queen!'

'I wish he would like me,' said Curdie, 'for then I might watch by him at night, and let you go to bed, princess.'

'Don't you know then?' returned Irene in wonder. 'How was it you came? Ah! you said my grandmother sent you. But I thought you knew that he wanted you.'

And again she opened wide her blue stars.

'Not I,' said Curdie, also bewildered, but very glad.

'He used to be constantly saying – he was not so ill then as he is now – that he wished he had you about him.'

'And I never to know it!' said Curdie with displeasure.

'The master of the horse told papa's own secretary that he had written to the miner-general to find you and send you up; but the miner-general wrote back to the master of the horse, and he told the secretary, and the secretary told my father, that they had searched every mine in the kingdom and could hear nothing of you. My father gave a great sigh, and said he feared the goblins had got you after all, and your father and mother were dead of grief. And he has never mentioned you since, except when wandering. I cried very much. But one of my grandmother's pigeons with its white wing flashed a message to me through the window one day, and then I knew that my Curdie wasn't eaten by the goblins, for my grandmother wouldn't have taken care of him one time to let him be eaten the next. Where were you, Curdie, that they couldn't find you?'

'We will talk about that another time, when we are not expecting the doctor,' said Curdie.

As he spoke, his eyes fell upon something shining on the table under the lamp. His heart gave a great throb, and he went nearer. Yes, there could be no doubt – it was the same flagon that the butler had filled in the wine-cellar.

'It looks worse and worse!' he said to himself, and went back to Irene, where she stood half dreaming.

'When will the doctor be here?' he asked once more – this time hurriedly.

The question was answered – not by the princess, but by something which that instant tumbled heavily into the room. Curdie flew towards it in vague terror about Lina.

On the floor lay a little round man, puffing and blowing, and uttering incoherent language. Curdie thought of his mattock, and ran and laid it aside.

'Oh, dear Dr. Kelman!' cried the princess, running up and taking hold of his arm; 'I am *so* sorry!' She pulled and pulled, but might almost as well have tried to set up a cannon-ball. 'I hope you have not hurt yourself?'

'Not at all, not at all,' said the doctor, trying to smile and to rise both at once once, but finding it impossible to do either.

'If he slept on the floor he would be late for breakfast,' said Curdie to himself, and laid out his hand to help him.

But when he took hold of it, Curdie very nearly let him fall again, for what he held was not even a foot: it was the belly of a creepy thing. He managed, however, to hold his peace and his grasp, and pulled the doctor roughly on his legs – such as they were.

'Your Royal Highness has rather a thick mat at the door,' said the doctor, patting his palms together. 'I hope my awkwardness may not have startled His Majesty.'

While he talked Curdie went to the door: Lina was not there.

The doctor approached the bed.

'And how has my beloved king slept to-night?' he asked.

'No better,' answered Irene, with a mournful shake of her head.

'Ah, that is very well!' returned the doctor, his fall seeming to have muddled either his words or his meaning. 'We must give him his wine, and then he will be better still.'

Curdie darted at the flagon, and lifted it high, as if he had expected to find it full, but had found it empty.

'That stupid butler! I heard them say he was drunk!' he cried in a loud whisper, and was gliding from the room.

'Come here with that flagon, you! page!' cried the doctor.

Curdie came a few steps towards him with the flagon dangling from his hand, heedless of the gushes that fell noiseless on the thick carpet.

'Are you aware, young man,' said the doctor, 'that it is not every wine can do His Majesty the benefit I intend he should derive from my prescription?'

'Quite aware, sir,' answered Curdie. 'The wine for His Majesty's use is in the third cask from the corner.'

'Fly, then,' said the doctor, looking satisfied.

Curdie brings wine to the King

Curdie stopped outside the curtain and blew an audible breath – no more: up came Lina noiseless as a shadow. He showed her the flagon.

'The cellar, Lina: go,' he said.

She galloped away on her soft feet, and Curdie had indeed to fly to keep up with her. Not once did she make even a dubious turn. From the king's gorgeous chamber to the cold cellar they shot. Curdie dashed the wine down the back stair, rinsed the flagon out as he had seen the butler do, filled it from the cask of which he had seen the butler drink, and hastened with it up again to the king's room.

The little doctor took it, poured out a full glass, smelt, but did not taste it, and set it down. Then he leaned over the bed, shouted in the king's ear, blew upon his eyes, and pinched his arm: Curdie thought he saw him run something bright into it. At last the king half woke. The doctor seized the glass, raised his head, poured the wine down his throat, and let his head fall back on the pillow again. Tenderly wiping his beard, and bidding the princess good-night in paternal tones, he then took his leave. Curdie would gladly have driven his pick into his head, but that was not in his commission, and he let him go.

The little round man looked very carefully to his feet as he crossed the threshold.

'That attentive fellow of a page has removed the mat,' he said to himself, as he walked along the corridor. 'I must remember him.'

20 Counter-plotting

Curdie was already sufficiently enlightened as to how things were going to see that he must have the princess of one mind with him, and they must work together. It was clear that amongst those about the king there was a plot against him: for one thing, they had agreed in a lie concerning himself; and it was plain also that the doctor was working out a design against the health and reason of His Majesty, rendering the question of his life a matter of little moment. It was in itself sufficient to justify the worst fears, that the people outside the palace were ignorant of His Majesty's condition: he believed those inside it also – the butler excepted – were ignorant of it as well. Doubtless His Majesty's councillors desired to alienate the hearts of his subjects from their sovereign. Curdie's idea was that they intended to kill the king, marry the princess to one of themselves, and found a new dynasty; but whatever their purpose, there was treason in the palace of the worst sort: they were making and keeping the king incapable, in order to effect that purpose. The first thing to be seen to, therefore, was that His Majesty should neither eat morsel nor drink drop of anything prepared for him in the palace. Could this have been managed without the princess, Curdie would have preferred leaving her in ignorance of the horrors from which he sought to deliver her. He feared also the danger of her knowledge betraying itself to the evil eyes about her; but it must be risked – and she had always been a wise child.

Another thing was clear to him – that with such traitors no terms of honour were either binding or possible, and that, short of lying, he might use any means to foil them. And he could not doubt that the old princess had sent him expressly to frustrate their plans.

While he stood thinking thus with himself, the princess was earnestly watching the king, with looks of childish love and womanly tenderness that went to Curdie's heart. Now and then with a great fan of peacock feathers she would fan him very softly; now and then, seeing a cloud begin to gather upon the sky of his sleeping face, she would climb upon the bed, and bending to his ear whisper into it, then draw back and watch again – generally to see the cloud disperse. In his deepest slumber, the soul of the king lay open to the voice of his child, and that voice had power either to change the aspect of his visions, or, which was better still, to breathe hope into his heart, and courage to endure them.

Curdie came near, and softly called her.

'I can't leave papa just yet,' she returned, in a low voice.

'I will wait,' said Curdie; 'but I want very much to say something.'

In a few minutes she came to him where he stood under the lamp.

'Well, Curdie, what is it?' she said.

'Princess,' he replied, 'I want to tell you that I have found why your grandmother sent me.'

'Come this way, then,' she answered, 'where I can see the face of my king.'

Curdie placed a chair for her in the spot she chose, where she would be near enough to mark any slightest change on her father's countenance, yet where their low-voiced talk would not disturb him. There he sat down beside her and told her all the story – how her grandmother had sent her good pigeon for him, and how she had instructed him, and sent him there without telling him what he had to do. Then he told her what he had discovered of the state of things generally in Gwyntystorm, and specially what he had heard and seen in the palace that night.

'Things are in a bad state enough,' he said in conclusion – 'lying and selfishness and inhospitality and dishonesty everywhere; and to crown all, they speak with disrespect of the good king, and not a man of them knows he is ill.'

'You frighten me dreadfully,' said Irene, trembling.

'You must be brave for your king's sake,' said Curdie.

'Indeed I will,' she replied, and turned a long loving look upon the beautiful face of her father. 'But what *is* to be done? And how *am* I to believe such horrible things of Dr. Kelman?'

'My dear princess,' replied Curdie, 'you know nothing of him but his face and his tongue, and they are both false. Either you must beware of him, or you must doubt your grandmother and me; for I tell you, by the gift she gave me of testing hands, that this man is a snake. That round body he shows is but the case of a serpent. Perhaps the creature lies there, as in its nest, coiled round and round inside.'

'Horrible!' said Irene.

'Horrible indeed; but we must not try to get rid of horrible things by refusing to look at them, and saying they are not there. Is not your beautiful father sleeping better since he had the wine?'

'Yes.'

'Does he always sleep better after having it?'

She reflected an instant.

'No; always worse – till to-night,' she answered.

'Then remember that was the wine I got him – not what the butler drew. Nothing that passed through any hand in the house except yours or mine must henceforth, till he is well, reach His Majesty's lips.'

'But how, dear Curdie?' said the princess, almost crying.

'That we must contrive,' answered Curdie. 'I know how to take care of the wine; but for his food – now we must think.'

'He takes hardly any,' said the princess, with a pathetic shake of her little head which Curdie had almost learned to look for.

'The more need,' he replied, 'there should be no poison in it.' Irene shuddered. 'As soon as he has honest food he will begin to grow better. And you must be just as careful with yourself, princess,' Curdie went on, 'for you don't know when they may begin to poison you too.'

'There's no fear of me; don't talk about me,' said Irene. 'The good food! – how are we to get it, Curdie? That is the whole question.'

'I am thinking hard,' answered Curdie. 'The good food? Let me see – let me see! Such servants as I saw below are sure to have the best of everything for themselves: I will go and see what I can find on their supper-table.'

'The chancellor sleeps in the house, and he and the master of the king's horse always have their supper together in a room off the great hall, to the right as you go down the stair,' said Irene. 'I would go with you, but I dare not leave my father. Alas! he scarcely ever takes more than a mouthful. I can't think how he lives! And the very thing he would like, and often asks for – a bit of bread – I can hardly ever get for him: Dr. Kelman has forbidden it, and says it is nothing less than poison to him.'

'Bread at least he *shall* have,' said Curdie; 'and that, with the honest wine, will do as well as anything, I do believe. I will go at once and look for some. But I want you to see Lina first, and know her, lest, coming upon her by accident at any time, you should be frightened.'

'I should like much to see her,' said the princess.

Warning her not to be startled by her ugliness, he went to the door and called her.

She entered, creeping with downcast head, and dragging her tail over the floor behind her. Curdie watched the princess as the frightful creature came nearer and nearer. One shudder went from head to foot of her, and next instant she stepped to meet her. Lina dropped flat on the floor, and covered her face with her two big paws. It went to the heart of the princess: in a moment she was on her knees beside her, stroking her ugly head, and patting her all over.

'Good dog! Dear ugly dog!' she said.

Lina whimpered.

'I believe,' said Curdie, 'from what your grandmother told me, that Lina is a woman, and that she was naughty, but is now growing good.'

Lina had lifted her head while Irene was caressing her; now she dropped it again between her paws; but the princess took it in her hands, and kissed the forehead betwixt the gold-green eyes.

'Shall I take her with me or leave her?' asked Curdie.

'Leave her, poor dear,' said Irene, and Curdie, knowing the way now, went without her.

He took his way first to the room the princess had spoken of, and there also were the remains of supper; but neither there nor in the kitchen could he find a scrap of wholesome-looking bread. So he returned and told her that as soon as it was light he would go into the city for some, and asked her for a handkerchief to tie it in. If he could not bring it himself, he would send it by Lina, who could keep out of sight better than he, and as soon as all was quiet at night he would come to her again. He also asked her to tell the king that he was in the house.

His hope lay in the fact that bakers everywhere go to work early. But it was yet much too early. So he persuaded the princess to lie down, promising to call her if the king should stir.

21   The Loaf

His majesty slept very quietly. The dawn had grown almost day, and still Curdie lingered, unwilling to disturb the princess.

At last, however, he called her, and she was in the room in a moment. She had slept, she said, and felt quite fresh. Delighted to find her father still asleep, and so peacefully, she pushed her chair close to the bed, and sat down with her hands in her lap.

Curdie got his mattock from where he had hidden it behind a great mirror, and went to the cellar, followed by Lina. They took some breakfast with them as they passed through the hall, and as soon as they had eaten it went out the back way.

At the mouth of the passage Curdie seized the rope, drew himself up, pushed away the shutter, and entered the dungeon. Then he swung the end of the rope to Lina, and she caught it in her teeth. When her master said: 'Now, Lina!' she gave a great spring, and he ran away with the end of the rope as fast as ever he could. And such a spring had she made that by the time he had to bear her weight she was within a few feet of the hole. The instant she got a paw through, she was all through.

Apparently their enemies were waiting till hunger should have cowed them, for there was no sign of any attempt having been made to open the door. A blow or two of Curdie's mattock drove the shattered lock clean from it, and telling Lina to wait there till he came back, and let no one in, he walked out into the silent street, and drew the door to behind him. He could hardly believe it was not yet a whole day since he had been thrown in there with his hands tied at his back.

Down the town he went, walking in the middle of the street, that, if any one saw him, he might see he was not afraid, and hesitate to rouse an attack on him. As to the dogs, ever since the death of their two companions, a shadow that looked like a mattock was enough to make them scamper. As soon as he reached the archway of the city gate he turned to reconnoitre the baker's shop, and perceiving no sign of movement, waited there watching for the first.

After about an hour; the door opened, and the baker's man appeared with a pail in his hand. He went to a pump that stood in the street, and having filled his pail returned with it into the shop. Curdie stole after him, found the door on the latch, opened it very gently, peeped in, saw nobody, and entered. Remembering perfectly from what shelf the baker's wife had taken the loaf she said was the best, and seeing just one upon it, he seized it, laid the price of it on the counter, and sped softly out, and up the street. Once more in the dungeon beside Lina, his first thought was to fasten up the door again, which would have been easy, so many iron fragments of all sorts and sizes lay about; but he bethought himself that if he left it as it was, and they came to find him, they would conclude at once that they had made their escape by it, and would look no farther so as to discover the hole. He therefore merely pushed the door close and left it. Then once more carefully arranging the earth behind the shutter, so that it should again fall with it, he returned to the cellar.

And now he had to convey the loaf to the princess. If he could venture to take it himself, well; if not, he would send Lina. He crept to the door of the servants' hall, and found the sleepers beginning to stir. One said it was time to go to bed; another, that he would go to the cellar instead, and have a mug of wine to waken him up; while a third challenged a fourth to give him his revenge at some game or other.

'Oh, hang your losses!' answered his companion; 'you'll soon pick up twice as much about the house, if you but keep your eyes open.'

Perceiving there would be risk in attempting to pass through, and reflecting that the porters in the great hall would probably be awake also, Curdie went back to the cellar, took Irene's handkerchief with the loaf in it, tied it round Lina's neck, and told her to take it to the princess.

Using every shadow and every shelter, Lina slid through the servants like a shapeless terror through a guilty mind, and so, by corridor and great hall, up the stair to the king's chamber.

Irene trembled a little when she saw her glide soundless in across the silent dusk of the morning, that filtered through the heavy drapery of the windows, but she recovered herself at once when she saw the bundle about her neck, for it both assured of Curdie's safety, and gave her hope of her father's. She untied it with joy, and Lina stole away, silent as she had come. Her joy was the greater that the king had woke up a little while before, and expressed a desire for food – not that he felt exactly hungry, he said, and yet he wanted something. If only he might have a piece of nice fresh bread! Irene had no knife, but with eager hands she broke a great piece from the loaf, and poured out a full glass of wine. The king ate and drank, enjoyed the bread and the wine much, and instantly fell asleep again.

It was hours before the lazy people brought their breakfast. When it came, Irene crumbled a little about, threw some into the fire-place, and managed to make the tray look just as usual.

In the meantime, down below in the cellar, Curdie was lying in the hollow between the upper sides of two of the great casks, the warmest place he could find. Lina was watching. She lay at his feet, across the two casks, and did her best so to arrange her huge tail that it should be a warm coverlid for her master.

By and by Dr. Kelman called to see his patient; and now that Irene's eyes were opened, she saw clearly enough that he was both annoyed and puzzled at finding His Majesty rather better. He pretended, however, to congratulate him, saying he believed he was quite fit to see the lord chamberlain: he wanted his signature to something important; only he must not strain his mind to understand it, whatever it might be: if His Majesty did, he would not be answerable for the consequences. The king said he would see the lord chamberlain, and the doctor went. Then Irene gave him more bread and wine, and the king ate and drank, and smiled a feeble smile, the first real one she had seen for many a day. He said he felt much better, and would soon be able to take matters into his own hands again. He had a strange miserable feeling, he said, that things were going terribly wrong, although he could not tell how. Then the princess told him that Curdie was come, and that at night, when all was quiet, for nobody in the palace must know, he would pay His Majesty a visit. Her great-great-grandmother had sent him, she said. The king looked strangely upon her, but the strange look passed into a smile clearer than the first, and Irene's heart throbbed with delight.

22 The Lord Chamberlain

At noon the lord chamberlain appeared. With a long, low bow, and paper in hand, he stepped softly into the room. Greeting His Majesty with every appearance of the profoundest respect, and congratulating him on the evident progress he had made, he declared himself sorry to trouble him, but there were certain papers, he said, which required his signature – and therewith drew nearer to the king, who lay looking at him doubtfully. He was a lean, long, yellow man, with a small head, bald over the top, and tufted at the back and about the ears. He had a very thin, prominent, hooked nose, and a quantity of loose skin under his chin and about the throat, which came craning up out of his neckcloth. His eyes were very small, sharp, and glittering, and looked black as jet. He had hardly enough of a mouth to make a smile with. His left hand held the paper, and the long, skinny fingers of his right a pen just dipped in ink.

But the king, who for weeks had scarcely known what he did, was to-day so much himself as to be aware that he was not quite himself; and the moment he saw the paper, he resolved that he would not sign without understanding and approving of it. He requested the lord chamberlain therefore to read it. His lordship commenced at once, but the difficulties he seemed to encounter, and the fits of stammering that seized him, roused the king's suspicion tenfold. He called the princess.

'I trouble his lordship too much,' he said to her; 'you can read print well, my child – let me hear how you can read writing. Take that paper from his lordship's hand, and read it to me from beginning to end, while my lord drinks a glass of my favourite wine, and watches for your blunders.'

'Pardon me, Your Majesty,' said the lord chamberlain, with as much of a smile as he was able to extemporize, 'but it were a thousand pities to put the attainments of Her Royal Highness to a test altogether too severe. Your Majesty can scarcely with justice expect the very organs of her speech to prove capable of compassing words so long, and to her so unintelligible.'

'I think much of my little princess and her capabilities,' returned the king, more and more aroused. 'Pray, my lord, permit her to try.'

'Consider, Your Majesty: the thing would be altogether without precedent. It would be to make sport of statecraft,' said the lord chamberlain.

'Perhaps you are right, my lord,' answered the king, with more meaning than he intended should be manifest, while to his growing joy he felt new life and power throbbing in heart and brain. 'So this morning we shall read no farther. I am indeed ill able for business of such weight '

'Will Your Majesty please sign your royal name here?' said the lord chamberlain, preferring the request as a matter of course, and approaching with the feather end of the pen pointed to a spot where was a great red seal.

'Not to-day, my lord,' replied the king.

'It is of the greatest importance, Your Majesty,' softly insisted the other.

'I descried no such importance in it,' said the king.

'Your Majesty heard but a part.'

'And I can hear no more to-day.'

'I trust Your Majesty has ground enough, in a case of necessity like the present, to sign upon the representation of his loyal subject and chamberlain? Or shall I call the lord chancellor?' he added, rising.

'There is no need. I have the very highest opinion of your judgment, my lord,' answered the king: 'that is, with respect to means: we *might* differ as to ends.'

The lord chamberlain made yet further attempts at persuasion; but they grew feebler and feebler, and he was at last compelled to retire without having gained his object. And well might his annoyance be keen! For that paper was the king's will, drawn up by the attorney-general; nor until they had the king's signature to it was there much use in venturing farther. But his worst sense of discomfiture arose from finding the king with so much capacity left, for the doctor had pledged himself so to weaken his brain that he should be as a child in their hands, incapable of refusing anything requested of him: his lordship began to doubt the doctor's fidelity to the conspiracy.

The princess was in high delight. She had not for weeks heard so many words, not to say words of such strength and reason, from her father's lips: day by day he had been growing weaker and more lethargic. He was so much exhausted, however, after this effort, that he asked for another piece of bread and more wine, and fell fast asleep the moment he had taken them.

The lord chamberlain sent in a rage for Dr. Kelman. He came, and while professing himself unable to understand the symptoms described by his lordship, yet pledged himself again that on the morrow the king should do whatever was required of him.

The day went on. When His Majesty was awake the princess read to him – one story-book after another; and whatever she read, the king listened as if he had never heard anything so good before, making out in it the wisest meanings. Every now and then he asked for a piece of bread and a little wine, and every time he ate and drank he slept, and every time he woke he seemed better than the last time. The princess bearing her part, the loaf was eaten up and the flagon emptied before night. The butler took the flagon away, and brought it back filled to the brim, but both were thirsty as well as hungry when Curdie came again.

Meantime he and Lina, watching and waking alternately, had plenty of sleep. In the afternoon, peeping from the recess, they saw several of the servants enter hurriedly, one after the other, draw wine, drink it, and steal out; but their business was to take care of the king, not of his cellar, and they let them drink. Also, when the butler came to fill the flagon, they restrained themselves, for the villain's fate was not yet ready for him. He looked terribly frightened, and had brought with him a large candle and a small terrier – which latter indeed threatened to be troublesome, for he went roving and sniffing about until he came to the recess where they were. But as soon as he showed himself, Lina opened her jaws so wide, and glared at him so horribly, that, without even uttering a whimper, he tucked his tail between his legs and ran to his master. He was drawing the wicked wine at the moment, and did not see him, else he would doubtless have run too.

When supper-time approached, Curdie took his place at the door into the servants' hall, but after a long hour's vain watch, he began to fear he should get nothing: there was so much idling about, as well as coming and going. It was hard to bear – chiefly from the attractions of a splendid loaf, just fresh out of the oven, which he longed to secure for the king and princess. At length his chance did arrive: he pounced upon the loaf and carried away, and soon after got hold of a pie.

This time, however, both loaf and pie were missed. The cook was called. He declared he had provided both. One of themselves, he said, must have carried them away for some friend outside the palace. Then a housemaid, who had not long been one of them, said she had seen someone like a page running in the direction of the cellar with something in his hands. Instantly all turned upon the pages, accusing them, one after another. All denied, but nobody believed one of them: where there is no truth there can be no faith.

To the cellar they all set out to look for the missing pie and loaf. Lina heard them coming, as well she might, for they were talking and quarrelling loud, and gave her master warning. They snatched up everything, and got all signs of their presence out at the back door before the servants entered. When they found nothing, they all turned on the chambermaid, and accused her, not only of lying against the pages, but of having taken the things herself. Their language and behaviour so disgusted Curdie, who could hear a great part of what passed, and he saw the danger of discovery now so much increased, that he began to devise how best at once to rid the palace of the whole pack of them. That, however, would be small gain so long as the treacherous officers of state continued in it. They must be first dealt with. A thought came to him, and the longer he looked at it the better he liked it.

As soon as the servants were gone, quarrelling and accusing all the way, they returned and finished their supper. Then Curdie, who had long been satisfied that Lina understood almost every word he said, communicated his plan to her, and knew by the wagging of her tail and the flashing of her eyes that she comprehended it. Until they had the king safe through the worst part of the night, however, nothing could be done.

They had now merely to go on waiting where they were till the household should be asleep. This waiting and waiting was much the hardest thing Curdie had to do in the whole affair. He took his mattock, and going again into the long passage, lighted a candle-end, and proceeded to examine the rock on all sides. But this was not merely to pass the time: he had a reason for it. When he broke the stone in the street, over which the baker fell, its appearance led him to pocket a fragment for further examination; and since then he had satisfied himself that it was the kind of stone in which gold is found, and that the yellow particles in it were pure metal. If such stone existed here in any plenty, he could soon make the king rich, and independent of his ill-conditioned subjects. He was therefore now bent on an examination of the rock; nor had he been at it long before he was persuaded that there were large quantities of gold in the half-crystalline white stone, with its veins of opaque white and of green, of which the rock, so far as he had been able to inspect it, seemed almost entirely to consist. Every piece he broke was spotted with particles and little lumps of a lovely greenish yellow – and that was gold. Hitherto he had worked only in silver, but he had read, and heard talk, and knew therefore about gold. As soon as he had got the king free of rogues and villains, he would have all the best and most honest miners, with his father at the head of them, to work this rock for the king.

It was a great delight to him to use his mattock once more. The time went quickly, and when he left the passage to go to the king's chamber, he had already a good heap of fragments behind the broken door.

23   Dr. Kelman

As soon as he had reason to hope the way was clear, Curdie ventured softly into the hall, with Lina behind him. There was no one asleep on the bench or floor, but by the fading fire sat a girl weeping. It was the same who had seen him carrying off the food, and had been so hardly used for saying so. She opened her eyes when he appeared, but did not seem frightened at him.

'I know why you weep,' said Curdie; 'and I am sorry for you.'

'It *is* hard not to be believed just *because* one speaks the truth,' said the girl, 'but that seems reason enough with some people. My mother taught me to speak the truth, and took such pains with me that I should find it hard to tell a lie, though I could invent many a story these servants would believe at once; for the truth is a strange thing here, and they don't know it when they see it. Show it them, and they all stare as if it were a wicked lie, and that with the lie yet warm that has just left their own mouths! You are a stranger,' she said, and burst out weeping afresh, 'but the stranger you are to such a place and such people the better!'

'I am the person,' said Curdie, 'whom you saw carrying the things from the supper-table.' He showed her the loaf. 'If you can trust, as well as speak the truth, I will trust you. Can you trust me?'

She looked at him steadily for a moment.

'I can,' she answered.

'One thing more,' said Curdie: 'have you courage as well as faith?'

'I think so.'

'Look my dog in the face and don't cry out. Come here, Lina.'

Line obeyed. The girl looked at her, and laid her hand on her head.

'Now I know you are a true woman,' said Curdie. 'I am come to set things right in this house. Not one of the servants knows I am here. Will you tell them to-morrow morning, that, if they do not alter their ways, and give over drinking, and lying, and stealing, and unkindness, they shall every one of them be driven from the palace?'

'They will not believe me.'

'Most likely; but will you give them the chance?'

'I will.'

'Then I will be your friend. Wait here till I come again.'

She looked him once more in the face, and sat down.

When he reached the royal chamber, he found His Majesty awake, and very anxiously expecting him. He received him with the utmost kindness, and at once as it were put himself in his hands by telling him all he knew concerning the state he was in. His voice was feeble, but his eye was clear, and although now and then his words and thoughts seemed to wander, Curdie could not be certain that the cause of their not being intelligible to him did not lie in himself. The king told him that for some years, ever since his queen's death, he had been losing heart over the wickedness of his people. He had tried hard to make them good, but they got worse and worse. Evil teachers, unknown to him, had crept into the schools; there was a general decay of truth and right principle at least in the city; and as that set the example to the nation, it must spread. The main cause of his illness was the despondency with which the degeneration of his people affected him. He could not sleep, and had terrible dreams; while, to his unspeakable shame and distress, he doubted almost everybody. He had striven against his suspicion, but in vain, and his heart was sore, for his courtiers and councillors were really kind; only he could not think why none of their ladies came near his princess. The whole country was discontented he heard, and there were signs of gathering storm outside as well as inside his borders. The master of the horse gave him sad news of the insubordination of the army; and his great white horse was dead, they told him; and his sword has lost its temper: it bent double the last time he tried it! – only perhaps that was in a dream; and they could not find his shield; and one of his spurs had lost the rowel. Thus the poor king went wandering in a maze of sorrows, some of which were purely imaginary, while others were truer than he understood. He told how thieves came at night and tried to take his crown, so that he never dared let it out of his hands even when he slept; and how, every night, an evil demon in the shape of his physician came and poured poison down his throat. He knew it to be poison, he said, somehow, although it tasted like wine.

Here he stopped, faint with the unusual exertion of talking. Curdie seized the flagon, and ran to the wine-cellar.

In the servants' hall the girl still sat by the fire, waiting for him. As he returned he told her to follow him, and left her at the chamber door till he should rejoin her. When the king had had a little wine, he informed him that he had already discovered certain of His Majesty's enemies, and one of the worst of them was the doctor, for it was no other demon than the doctor himself who had been coming every night, and giving him a slow poison.

'So!' said the king. 'Then I have not been suspicious enough, for I thought it was but a dream! Is it possible Kelman can be such a wretch? Who then am I trust?'

'Not one in the house, except the princess and myself,' said Curdie.

'I will not go to sleep,' said the king.

'That would be as bad as taking the poison,' said Curdie. 'No, no, sire; you must show your confidence by leaving all the watching to me, and doing all the sleeping Your Majesty can.'

The king smiled a contented smile, turned on his side, and was presently fast asleep. Then Curdie persuaded the princess also to go to sleep, and telling Lina to watch, went to the housemaid, He asked her if she could inform him which of the council slept in the palace, and show him their rooms. She knew every one of them, she said, and took him the round of all their doors, telling him which slept in each room. He then dismissed her, and returning to the king's chamber, seated himself behind a curtain at the head of the bed, on the side farthest from the king. He told Lina to get under the bed, and make no noise.

About one o'clock the doctor came stealing in. He looked round for the princess, and seeing no one, smiled with satisfaction as he approached the wine where it stood under the lamp. Having partly filled a glass, he took from his pocket a small phial, and filled up the glass from it. The light fell upon his face from above, and Curdie saw the snake in it plainly visible. He had never beheld such an evil countenance: the man hated the king, and delighted in doing him wrong.

With the glass in his hand, he drew near the bed, set it down, and began his usual rude rousing of His Majesty. Not at once succeeding, he took a lancet from his pocket, and was parting its cover with an involuntary hiss of hate between his closed teeth, when Curdie stooped and whispered to Lina: 'Take him by the leg, Lina.' She darted noiselessly upon him. With a face of horrible consternation, he gave his leg one tug to free it; the next instant Curdie heard the one scrunch with which she crushed the bone like a stick of celery. He tumbled on the floor with a yell.

'Drag him out, Lina,' said Curdie.

Lina took him by the collar, and dragged him out. Her master followed to direct her, and they left him lying across the lord chamberlain's door, where he gave another horrible yell, and fainted.

The king had waked at his first cry, and by the time Curdie re-entered he had got at his sword where it hung from the centre of the tester, had drawn it, and was trying to get out of bed. But when Curdie told him all was well, he lay down again as quietly as a child comforted by his mother from a troubled dream. Curdie went to the door to watch.

The doctor's yells had roused many, but not one had yet ventured to appear. Bells were rung violently, but none were answered; and in a minute or two Curdie had what he was watching for. The door of the lord chamberlain's room opened, and, pale with hideous terror, his lordship peeped out. Seeing no one, he advanced to step into the corridor, and tumbled over the doctor. Curdie ran up, and held out his hand. He received in it the claw of bird of prey – vulture or eagle, he could not tell which.

His lordship, as soon as he was on his legs, taking him for one of the pages, abused him heartily for not coming sooner, and threatened him with dismissal from the king's service for cowardice and neglect. He began indeed what bade fair to be a sermon on the duties of a page, but catching sight of the man who lay at his door, and seeing it was the doctor, he fell out upon Curdie afresh for standing there doing nothing, and ordered him to fetch immediate assistance. Curdie left him, but slipped into the king's chamber, closed and locked the door, and left the rascals to look after each other. Ere long he heard hurrying footsteps, and for a few minutes there was a great muffled tumult of scuffling feet, low voices, and deep groanings; then all was still again.

Irene slept through the whole – so confidently did she rest, knowing Curdie was in her father's room watching over him.

24   The Prophecy

Curdie sat and watched every motion of the sleeping king. All the night, to his ear, the palace lay as quiet as a nursery of healthful children. At sunrise he called the princess.

'How has His Majesty slept?' were her first words as she entered the room.

'Quite quietly,' answered Curdie; 'that is, since the doctor was got rid of.'

'How did you manage that?' inquired Irene; and Curdie had to tell all about it.

'How terrible!' she said. 'Did it not startle the king dreadfully?'

'It did rather. I found him getting out of bed, sword in hand.'

'The brave old man!' cried the princess.

'Not so old!' said Curdie, 'as you will soon see. He went off again in a minute or so; but for a little while he was restless, and once when he lifted his hand it came down on the spikes of his crown, and he half waked.'

'But where *is* the crown?' cried Irene, in sudden terror.

'I stroked his hands,' answered Curdie, 'and took the crown from them; and ever since he has slept quietly, and again and again smiled in his sleep.'

'I have never seen him do that,' said the princess. 'But what have you done with the crown, Curdie?'

'Look,' said Curdie, moving away from the bedside.

Irene followed him – and there, in the middle of the floor, she saw a strange sight. Lina lay at full length, fast asleep, her tail stretched out straight behind her and her fore-legs before her: between the two paws meeting in front of it, her nose just touching it behind, glowed and flashed the crown, like a nest for the humming-birds of heaven.

Irene gazed, and looked up with a smile.

'But what if the thief were to come, and she not to wake?' she said. 'Shall I try her?' And as she spoke she stooped towards the crown.

'No, no, no!' cried Curdie, terrified. 'She would frighten you out of your wits. I would do it to show you, but she would wake your father. You have no conception with what a roar she would spring at my throat. But you shall see how lightly she wakes the moment I speak to her. Lina!'

She was on her feet the same instant, with her great tail sticking out straight behind her, just as it had been lying.

'Good dog!' said the princess, and patted her head. Lina wagged her tail solemnly, like the boom of an anchored sloop. Irene took the crown, and laid it where the king would see it when he woke.

'Now, princess,' said Curdie, 'I must leave you for a few minutes. You must bolt the door, please, and not open it to any one.'

Away to the cellar he went with Lina, taking care, as they passed through the servants' hall, to get her a good breakfast. In about one minute she had eaten what he gave her, and looked up in his face: it was not more she wanted, but work. So out of the cellar they went through the passage, and Curdie into the dungeon, where he pulled up Lina, opened the door, let her out, and shut it again behind her. As he reached the door of the king's chamber, Lina was flying out of the gate of Gwyntystorm as fast her mighty legs could carry her.

'What's come to the wench?' growled the menservants one to another, when the chambermaid appeared among them the next morning. There was something in her face which they could understand, and did not like.

'Are we all dirt?' they said. 'What are you thinking about? Have you seen yourself in the glass this morning, miss?'

She made no answer.

'Do you want to be treated as you deserve, or will you speak, you hussy?' said the first woman-cook. 'I would fain know what right *you* have to put on a face like that!'

'You won't believe me,' said the girl.

'Of course not. What is it?'

'I must tell you, whether you believe me or not,' she said.

'Of course you must.'

'It is this, then: if you do not repent of your bad ways, you are all going to be punished – all turned out of the palace together.'

'A mighty punishment!' said the butler. 'A good riddance, say I, of the trouble of keeping minxes like you in order! And why, pray, should we be turned out? What have I to repent of now, your holiness?'

'That you know best yourself,' said the girl.

'A pretty piece of insolence! How should *I* know, forsooth, what a menial like you has got against me! There *are* people in this house – oh! I'm not blind to their ways! but every one for himself, say I! Pray, Miss Judgment, who gave you such an impertinent message to His Majesty's household.'

'One who is come to set things right in the king's house.'

'Right, indeed!' cried the butler; but that moment the thought came back to him of the roar he had heard in the cellar, and he turned pale and was silent.

The steward took it up next.

'And pray, pretty prophetess,' he said, attempting to chuck her under the chin, 'what have *I* got to repent of?'

'That you know best yourself,' said the girl. 'You have but to look into your books or your heart.'

'Can you tell *me*, then, what I have to repent of?' said the groom of the chambers.

'That you know best yourself,' said the girl once more. 'The person who told me to tell you said the servants of this house had to repent of thieving, and lying, and unkindness, and drinking; and they will be made to repent of them one way, if they don't do it of themselves another.'

Then arose a great hubbub; for by this time all the servants in the house were gathered about her, and all talked together, in towering indignation.

'Thieving, indeed!' cried one. 'A pretty word in a house where everything is left lying about in a shameless way, tempting poor innocent girls! – a house where nobody cares for anything, or has the least respect to the value of property!'

'I suppose you envy me this brooch of mine,' said another. 'There was just a half-sheet of note-paper about it, not a scrap more, in drawer that's always open in the writing-table in the study! What sort of a place is that for a jewel? Can you call it stealing to take a thing from such a place as that? Nobody cared a straw about it. It might as well have been in the dust-hole! If it had been locked up – then, to be sure!'

'Drinking!' said the chief porter, with a husky laugh. 'And who wouldn't drink when he had a chance? Or would repent it, except that the drink was gone? Tell me that, Miss Innocence.'

'Lying!' said a great, coarse footman. 'I suppose you mean when I told you yesterday you were a pretty girl when you didn't pout? Lying, indeed! Tell us something worth repenting of! Lying is the way of Gwyntystorm. You should have heard Jabez lying to the cook last night! He wanted a sweetbread for his pup, and pretended it was for the princess! Ha! ha! ha!'

'Unkindness! I wonder who's unkind! Going and listening to any stranger against her fellow servants, and then bringing back his wicked words to trouble them!' said the oldest and worst of the housemaids. 'One of ourselves, too! Come, you hypocrite! this is all an invention of yours and your young man's, to take your revenge of us because we found you out in a lie last night. Tell true now – wasn't it the same that stole the loaf and the pie that sent you with the impudent message?'

As she said this, she stepped up to the housemaid and gave her, instead of time to answer, a box on the ear that almost threw her down; and whoever could get at her began to push and hustle and pinch and punch her.

'You invite your fate,' she said quietly.

They fell furiously upon her, drove her from the hall with kicks and blows, hustled her along the passage, and threw her down the stair to the wine-cellar, then locked the door at the top of it, and went back to their breakfast.

In the meantime the king and the princess had had their bread and wine, and the princess, with Curdie's help, had made the room as tidy as she could – they were terribly neglected by the servants. And now Curdie set himself to interest and amuse the king, and prevent him from thinking too much, in order that he might the sooner think the better. Presently, at His Majesty's request, he began from the beginning, and told everything he could recall of his life, about his father and mother their cottage on the mountain, of the inside of the mountain and the work there, about the goblins and his adventures with them. When he came to finding the princess and her nurse overtaken by the twilight on the mountain, Irene took up her share of the tale, and told all about herself to that point, and then Curdie took it up again; and so they went on, each fitting in the part that the other did not know, thus keeping the hoop of the story running straight; and the king listened with wondering and delighted ears, astonished to find what he could so ill comprehend, yet fitting so well together from the lips of two narrators. At last, with the mission given him by wonderful princess and his consequent adventures. Curdie brought up the whole tale the the present moment. Then a silence fell, and Irene and Curdie thought the king was asleep. But he was far from it; he was thinking about many things. After a long pause he said:

'Now at last, my children, I am compelled to believe many things I could not and do not yet understand – things I used to hear, and sometimes see, as often as I visited my mother's home. Once for instance, I heard my mother say to her father – speaking of me – "He is a good, honest boy, but he will be an old man before he understands"; and my grandfather answered: "Keep up your heart, child: my mother will look after him." I thought often of their words, and the many strange things besides I both heard and saw in that house; but by degrees, because I could not understand them, I gave up thinking of them. And indeed I had almost forgotten them, when you, my child, talking that day about the Queen Irene and her pigeons, and what you had seen in her garret, brought them all back to my mind in a vague mass. But now they keep coming back to me, one by one, every one for itself; and I shall just hold my peace, and lie here quite still, and think about them all till I get well again.'

What he meant they could not quite understand, but they saw plainly that already he was better.

'Put away my crown,' he said. 'I am tired of seeing it, and have no more any fear of its safety.'

They put it away together, withdrew from the bedside, and left him in peace.

25 The Avengers

There was nothing now to be dreaded from Dr. Kelman, but it made Curdie anxious, as the evening drew near, to think that not a soul belonging to the court had been to visit the king, or ask how he did, that day. He feared, in some shape or other, a more determined assault. He had provided himself a place in the room to which he might retreat upon approach, and whence he could watch; but not once had he had to betake himself to it.

Towards night the king fell asleep. Curdie thought more and more uneasily of the moment when he must again leave them for a little while. Deeper and deeper fell the shadows. No one came to light the lamp. The princess drew her chair close to Curdie: she would rather it were not so dark, she said. She was afraid of something – she could not tell what; nor could she give any reason for her fear but that all was so dreadfully still. When it had been dark about an hour, Curdie thought Lina might be returned; and reflected that the sooner he went the less danger was there of any assault while he was away. There was more risk of his own presence being discovered, no doubt, but things were now drawing to a crisis, and it must be run. So, telling the princess to lock all the doors of the bedchamber, and let no one in, he took his mattock, and with here a run and there a halt under cover, gained the door at the head of the cellar-stair in safety. To his surprise he found it locked, and the key was gone. There was no time for deliberation. He felt where the lock was, and dealt it a tremendous blow with his mattock. It needed but a second to dash the door open. Someone laid a hand on his arm.

'Who is it?' said Curdie.

'I told you they wouldn't believe me, sir,' said the housemaid. 'I have been here all day.'

He took her hand, and said: 'You are a good brave girl. Now come with me, lest your enemies imprison you again.'

He took her to the cellar, locked the door, lighted a bit of candle, gave her a little wine, told her to wait there till he came, and went out the back way.

Swiftly he swung himself up into the dungeon. Lina had done her part. The place was swarming with creatures – animal forms wilder and more grotesque than ever ramped in nightmare dream. Close by the hole, waiting his coming, her green eyes piercing the gulf below, Lina had just laid herself down when he appeared. All about the vault and up the slope of the rubbish-heap lay and stood and squatted the forty-nine whose friendship Lina had conquered in the wood. They all came crowding about Curdie.

He must get them into the cellar as quickly as ever he could. But when he looked at the size of some of them, he feared it would be a long business to enlarge the hole sufficiently to let them through. At it he rushed, hitting vigorously at its edge with his mattock. At the very first blow came a splash from the water beneath, but ere he could heave a third, a creature like a tapir, only that the grasping point of its probiscus was hard as the steel of Curdie's hammer, pushed him gently aside, making room for another creature, with a head like a great club, which it began banging upon the floor with terrible force and noise. After about a minute of this battery, the tapir came up again, shoved Clubhead aside, and putting its own head into the hole began gnawing at the sides of it with the fingers of its nose, in such a fashion that the fragments fell in a continuous gravelly shower into the water. In a few minutes the opening was large enough for the biggest creature amongst them to get through it.

Next came the difficulty of letting them down: some were quite light, but the half of them were too heavy for the rope, not to say for his arms. The creatures themselves seemed to be puzzling where or how they were to go. One after another of them came up, looked down through the hole, and drew back. Curdie thought if he let Lina down, perhaps that would suggest something; possibly they did not see the opening on the other side. He did so, and Lina stood lighting up the entrance of the passage with her gleaming eyes. One by one the creatures looked down again, and one by one they drew back, each standing aside to glance at the next, as if to say: 'Now you have a look.'

At last it came to the turn of the serpent with the long body, the four short legs behind, and the little wings before. No sooner had he poked his head through than he poked it farther through – and farther, and farther yet, until there was little more than his legs left in the dungeon. By that time he had got his head and neck well into the passage beside Lina. Then his legs gave a great waddle and spring, and he tumbled himself, far as there was betwixt them, heels over head into the passage.

'That is all very well for you, Mr. Legserpent!' thought Curdie to himself; 'but what is to be done with the rest?'

He had hardly time to think it, however, before the creature's head appeared again through the floor. He caught hold of the bar of iron to which Curdie's rope was tied, and settling it securely across the narrowest part of the irregular opening, held fast to it with his teeth. It was plain to Curdie, from the universal hardness amongst them, that they must all, at one time or another, have been creatures of the mines.

Curdie saw at once what this one was after. He had planted his feet firmly upon the floor of the passage, and stretched his long body up and across the chasm to serve as a bridge for the rest. Curdie mounted instantly upon his neck, threw his arms round him as far as they would go, and slid down in ease and safety, the bridge just bending a little as his weight glided over it. But he thought some of the creatures would try the serpent's teeth.

One by one the oddities followed, and slid down in safety. When they seemed to be all landed, he counted them: there were but forty-eight. Up the rope again he went, and found one which had been afraid to trust himself to the bridge, and no wonder! for he had neither legs nor head nor arms nor tail: he was just a round thing, about a foot in diameter, with a nose and mouth and eyes on one side of the ball. He had made his journey by rolling as swiftly as the fleetest of them could run. The back of the legserpent not being flat, he could not quite trust himself to roll straight and not drop into the gulf. Curdie took him in his arms, and the moment he looked down through the hole, the bridge made itself again, and he slid into the passage in safety, with Ballbody in his bosom.

He ran first to the cellar, to warn the girl not be frightened at the avengers of wickedness. Then he called to Lina to bring in her friends.

One after another they came trooping in, till the cellar seemed full of them. The housemaid regarded them without fear.

'Sir,' she said, 'there is one of the pages I don't take to be a bad fellow.'

'Then keep him near you,' said Curdie. 'And now can you show me a way to the king's chamber not through the servants' hall?'

'There is a way through the chamber of the colonel of the guard,' she answered, 'but he is ill, and in bed.'

'Take me that way,' said Curdie.

By many ups and downs and windings and turnings she brought him to a dimly lighted room, where lay an elderly man asleep. His arm was outside the coverlid, and Curdie gave his hand a hurried grasp as he went by. His heart beat for joy, for he had found a good, honest human hand.

'I suppose that is why he is ill,' he said to himself.

It was now close upon supper-time, and when the girl stopped at the door of the king's chamber, he told her to go and give the servants one warning more.

'Say the messenger sent you,' he said. 'I will be with you very soon.'

The king was still asleep. Curdie talked to the princess for a few minutes, told her not to be frightened whatever noises she heard, only to keep her door locked till he came, and left her.

26   The Vengeance

By the time the girl reached the servants' hall they were seated at supper. A loud, confused exclamation arose when she entered. No one made room for her; all stared with unfriendly eyes. A page, who entered the next minute by another door, came to her side.

'Where do *you* come from, hussy?' shouted the butler, and knocked his fist on the table with a loud clang.

He had gone to fetch wine, had found the stair door broken open and the cellar door locked, and had turned and fled. Amongst his fellows, however, he had now regained what courage could be called his.

'From the cellar,' she replied. 'The messenger broke open the door, and sent me to you again.'

'The messenger! Pooh! What messenger?'

'The same who sent me before to tell you to repent.'

'What! will you go fooling it still? Haven't you had enough of it?' cried the butler in a rage, and starting to his feet, drew near threateningly.

'I must do as I am told,' said the girl.

'Then why *don't* you do as *I* tell you, and hold your tongue?' said the butler. 'Who wants your preachments? If anybody here has anything to repent of, isn't that enough – and more than enough for him – but you must come bothering about, and stirring up, till not a drop of quiet will settle inside him? You come along with me, young woman; we'll see if we can't find a lock somewhere in the house that'll hold you in!'

'Hands off, Mr. Butler!' said the page, and stepped between.

'Oh, ho!' cried the butler, and pointed his fat finger at him. 'That's you, is it, my fine fellow? So it's you that's up to her tricks, is it?'

The youth did not answer, only stood with flashing eyes fixed on him, until, growing angrier and angrier, but not daring to step nearer, he burst out with rude but quavering authority:

'Leave the house, both of you! Be off, or I'll have Mr. Steward to talk to you. Threaten your masters, indeed! Out of the house with you, and show us the way you tell us of!'

Two or three of the footmen got up and ranged themselves behind the butler.

'Don't say *I* threaten you, Mr. Butler,' expostulated the girl from behind the page. 'The messenger said I was to tell you again, and give you one chance more.'

'Did the *messenger* mention me in particular?' asked the butler, looking the page unsteadily in the face.

'No, sir,' answered the girl.

'I thought not! I should like to hear him!'

'Then hear him now,' said Curdie, who that moment entered at the opposite corner of the hall. 'I speak of the butler in particular when I say that I know more evil of him than of any of the rest. He will not let either his own conscience or my messenger speak to him: I therefore now speak myself. I proclaim him a villain, and a traitor to His Majesty the king. But what better is any one of you who cares only for himself, eats, drinks, takes good money, and gives vile service in return, stealing and wasting the king's property, and making of the palace, which ought to be an example of order and sobriety, a disgrace to the country?'

For a moment all stood astonished into silence by this bold speech from a stranger. True, they saw by his mattock over his shoulder that he was nothing but a miner boy, yet for a moment the truth told notwithstanding. Then a great roaring laugh burst from the biggest of the footmen as he came shouldering his way through the crowd towards Curdie.

'Yes, I'm right,' he cried; 'I thought as much! This *messenger*, forsooth, is nothing but a gallows-bird – a fellow the city marshal was going to hang, but unfortunately put it off till he should be starved enough to save rope and be throttled with a pack-thread. He broke prison, and here he is preaching!'

As he spoke, he stretched out his great hand to lay hold of him. Curdie caught it in his left hand, and heaved his mattock with the other. Finding, however, nothing worse than an ox-hoof, he restrained himself, stepped back a pace or two, shifted his mattock to his left hand, and struck him a little smart blow on the shoulder. His arm dropped by his side, he gave a roar, and drew back.

His fellows came crowding upon Curdie. Some called to the dogs; others swore; the women screamed; the footmen and pages got round him in a half-circle, which he kept from closing by swinging his mattock, and here and there threatening a blow.

'Whoever confesses to having done anything wrong in this house, however small, however great, and means to do better, let him come to this corner of the room!' he cried.

None moved but the page, who went towards him skirting the wall. When they caught sight of him, the crowd broke into a hiss of derision.

'There! see! Look at the sinner! He confesses! actually confesses! Come, what is it you stole? The barefaced hypocrite. There's your sort to set up for reproving other people! Where's the other now?'

But the maid had left the room, and they let the page pass, for he looked dangerous to stop. Curdie had just put him betwixt him and the wall, behind the door, when in rushed the butler with the huge kitchen poker, the point of which he had blown red hot in the fire, followed by the cook with his longest spit. Through the crowd, which scattered right and left before them, they came down upon Curdie. Uttering a shrill whistle, he caught the poker a blow with his mattock, knocking the point to the ground, while the page behind him started forward, and seizing the point of the spit, held on to it with both hands, the cook kicking him furiously.

Ere the butler could raise the poker again, or the cook recover the spit, with a roar to terrify the dead, Lina dashed into the room, her eyes flaming like candles. She went straight at the butler. He was down in a moment, and she on the top of him, wagging her tail over him like a lioness.

'Don't kill him, Lina,' said Curdie.

'Oh, Mr. Miner!' cried the butler.

'Put your foot on his mouth, Lina,' said Curdie. 'The truth Fear tells is not much better than her lies.'

The rest of the creatures now came stalking, rolling, leaping, gliding, hobbling into the room, and each as he came took the next place along the wall, until, solemn and grotesque, all stood ranged, awaiting orders.

And now some of the culprits were stealing to the doors nearest them. Curdie whispered to the two creatures next him. Off went Ballbody, rolling and bounding through the crowd like a spent cannon shot, and when the foremost reached the door to the corridor, there he lay at the foot of it grinning; to the other door scuttled a scorpion, as big as a huge crab. The rest stood so still that some began to think they were only boys dressed up to look awful; they persuaded themselves they were only another part of the housemaid and page's vengeful contrivance, and their evil spirits began to rise again. Meantime Curdie had, with a second sharp blow from the hammer of his mattock, disabled the cook, so that he yielded the spit with a groan. He now turned to the avengers.

'Go at them,' he said.

The whole nine-and-forty obeyed at once, each for himself, and after his own fashion. A scene of confusion and terror followed. The crowd scattered like a dance of flies. The creatures had been instructed not to hurt much, but to hunt incessantly, until every one had rushed from the house. The women shrieked, and ran hither and thither through the hall, pursued each by her own horror, and snapped at by every other in passing. If one threw herself down in hysterical despair, she was instantly poked or clawed or nibbled up again. Though they were quite as frightened at first, the men did not run so fast; and by and by some of them, finding they were only glared at, and followed, and pushed, began to summon up courage once more, and with courage came impudence. The tapir had the big footman in charge: the fellow stood stock-still, and let the beast come up to him, then put out his finger and playfully patted his nose. The tapir gave the nose a little twist, and the finger lay on the floor. Then indeed the footman ran, and did more than run, but nobody heeded his cries. Gradually the avengers grew more severe, and the terrors of the imagination were fast yielding to those of sensuous experience, when a page, perceiving one of the doors no longer guarded, sprang at it, and ran out. Another and another followed. Not a beast went after, until, one by one, they were every one gone from the hall, and the whole menie in the kitchen. There they were beginning to congratulate themselves that all was over, when in came the creatures trooping after them, and the second act of their terror and pain began. They were flung about in all

A scene of confusion and terror followed.
The crowd scattered like a dance of flies

directions; their clothes were torn from them; they were pinched and scratched any and everywhere; Ballbody kept rolling up them and over them, confining his attentions to no one in particular; the scorpion kept grabbing at their legs with his huge pincers; a three-foot centipede kept screwing up their bodies, nipping as he went; varied as numerous were their woes. Nor was it long before the last of them had fled from the kitchen to the sculleries. But thither also they were followed, and there again they were hunted about. They were bespattered with the dirt of their own neglect; they were soused in the stinking water that had boiled greens; they were smeared with rancid dripping; their faces were rubbed in maggots: I dare not tell all that was done to them. At last they got to the door into a back yard open, and rushed out. Then first they knew that the wind was howling and the rain falling in sheets. But there was no rest for them even there. Thither also were they followed by the inexorable avengers, and the only door here was a door out of the palace: out every soul of them was driven, and left, some standing, some lying, some crawling, to the farther buffeting of the waterspouts and whirlwinds ranging every street of the city. The door was flung to behind them, and they heard it locked and bolted and barred against them.

27 More Vengeance

As soon as they were gone, Curdie brought the creatures back to the servants' hall and told them to eat up everything on the table. It *was* a sight to see them all standing round it – except such as had to get upon it – eating and drinking, each after its fashion, without a smile, or a word, or a glance of fellowship in the act. A very few moments served to make everything eatable vanish, and then Curdie requested them to clean the house, and the page who stood by to assist them.

Every one set about it except Ballbody: he could do nothing at cleaning, for the more he rolled the more he spread the dirt. Curdie was curious to know what he had been, and how he had come to be such as he was; but he could only conjecture that he was a gluttonous alderman whom nature had treated homoeopathically.

And now there was such a cleaning and clearing out of neglected places, such a burying and burning of refuse, such a rinsing of jugs, such a swilling of sinks, and such a flushing of drains, as would have delighted the eyes of all true housekeepers and lovers of cleanliness generally.

Curdie meantime was with the king, telling him all he had done. They heard a little noise, but not much, for he had told the avengers to repress outcry as much as possible; and they had seen to it that the more any one cried out the more he had to cry out upon, while the patient ones they scarcely hurt at all.

Having promised His Majesty and Her Royal Highness a good breakfast, Curdie now went to finish the business. The courtiers must be dealt with. A few who were the worst, and the leaders of the rest, must be made examples of; the others should be driven from their beds to the street.

He found the chiefs of the conspiracy holding a final consultation in the smaller room off the hall. These were the lord chamberlain, the attorney-general, the master of the horse, and the king's private secretary: the lord chancellor and the rest, as foolish as faithless, were but the tools of these.

The housemaid had shown him a little closet, opening from a passage behind, where he could overhear all that passed in that room; and now Curdie heard enough to understand that they had determined, in the dead of that night, rather in the deepest dark before the morning, to bring a certain company of soldiers into the palace, make away with the king, secure the princess, announce the sudden death of His Majesty, read as his the will they had drawn up, and proceed to govern the country at their ease, and with results: they would at once levy severer taxes, and pick a quarrel with the most powerful of their neighbours. Everything settled, they agreed to retire, and have a few hours' quiet sleep first – all but the secretary, who was to sit up and call them at the proper moment. Curdie stole away, allowed them half an hour to get to bed, and then set about completing his purgation of the palace.

First he called Lina, and opened the door of the room where the secretary sat. She crept in, and laid herself down against it. When the secretary, rising to stretch his legs, caught sight of her eyes, he stood frozen with terror. She made neither motion nor sound. Gathering courage, and taking the thing for a spectral illusion, he made a step forward. She showed her other teeth, with a growl neither more than audible nor less than horrible. The secretary sank fainting into a chair. He was not a brave man, and besides, his conscience had gone over to the enemy, and was sitting against the door by Lina.

To the lord chamberlain's door next, Curdie conducted the legserpent, and let him in.

Now his lordship had had a bedstead made for himself, sweetly fashioned of rods of silver gilt: upon it the legserpent found him asleep, and under it he crept. But out he came on the other side, and crept over it next, and again under it, and so over it, under it, over it, five or six times, every time leaving a coil of himself behind him, until he had softly folded all his length about the lord chamberlain and his bed. This done, he set up his head, looking down with curved neck right over his lordship's, and began to hiss in his face. He woke in terror unspeakable, and would have started up; but the moment he moved the legserpent drew his coils closer, and closer still, and drew and drew until the quaking traitor heard the joints of his bedstead grinding and gnarring. Presently he persuaded himself that it was only a horrid nightmare, and began to struggle with all his strength to throw it off. Thereupon the legservant gave his hooked nose such a bite that his teeth met through it – but it was hardly thicker than the bowl of a spoon; and then the vulture knew that he was in the grasp of his enemy the snake, and yielded. As soon as he was quiet the legserpent began to untwist and retwist, to uncoil and recoil himself, swinging and swaying, knotting and relaxing himself with strangest curves and convolutions, always, however, leaving at least one coil around his victim. At last he undid himself entirely, and crept from the bed. Then first the lord chamberlain discovered that his tormentor had bent and twisted the bedstead, legs and canopy and all, so about him, that he was shut in a silver cage out of which it was impossible for him to find a way. Once more, thinking his enemy was gone, he began to shout for help. But the instant he opened his mouth his keeper darted at him and bit him, and after three or four such essays, with like result, he lay still.

The master of the horse Curdie gave in charge to the tapir. When the soldier saw him enter – for he was not yet asleep – he sprang from his bed, and flew at him with his sword. But the creature's hide was invulnerable to his blows, and he pecked at his legs with his proboscis until he jumped into bed again, groaning, and covered himself up; after which the tapir contènted himself with now and then paying a visit to his toes.

For the attorney-general, Curdie led to his door a huge spider, about two feet long in the body, which, having made an excellent supper, was full of webbing. The attorney-general had not gone to bed, but sat in a chair asleep before a great mirror. He had been trying the effect of a diamond star which he had that morning taken from the jewel-room. When he woke he fancied himself paralysed; every limb, every finger even, was motionless: coils and coils of broad spider-ribbon bandaged his members to his body, and all to the chair. In the glass he saw himself wound about, under and over and around, with slavery infinite. On a footstool a yard off sat the spider glaring at him.

Clubhead had mounted guard over the butler, where he lay tied hand and foot under the third cask. From that cask he had seen the wine run into a great bath, and therein he expected to be drowned. The doctor, with his crushed leg, needed no one to guard him.

And now Curdie proceeded to the expulsion of the rest. Great men or underlings, he treated them all alike. From room to room over the house he went, and sleeping or waking took the man by the hand. Such was the state to which a year of wicked rule had reduced the moral condition of the court, that in it all he found but three with human hands. The possessors of these he allowed to dress themselves and depart in peace. When they perceived his mission, and how he was backed, they yielded without dispute.

Then commenced a general hunt, to clear the house of the vermin. Out of their beds in their night-clothing, out of their rooms, gorgeous chambers or garret nooks, the creatures hunted them. Not one was allowed to escape. Tumult and noise there was little, for the fear was too deadly for outcry. Ferreting them out everywhere, following them upstairs and downstairs, yielding no instant of repose except upon the way out, the avengers persecuted the miscreants, until the last of them was shivering outside the palace gates, with hardly sense enough left to know where to turn.

When they set out to look for shelter, they found every inn full of the servants expelled before them, and not one would yield his place to a superior suddenly levelled with himself. Most houses refused to admit them on the ground of the wickedness that must have drawn on them such a punishment; and not a few would have been left in the streets all night, had not Derba, roused by the vain entreaties at the doors on each side of her cottage, opened hers, and given up everything to them. The lord chancellor was only too glad to share a mattress with a stable-boy, and steal his bare feet under his jacket.

In the morning Curdie appeared, and the outcasts were in terror, thinking he had come after them again. But he took no notice of them: his object was to request Derba to go to the palace: the king required her services. She need take no trouble about her cottage, he said; the palace was henceforward her home: she was the king's chatelaine over men and maidens of his household. And this very morning she must cook His Majesty a nice breakfast.

28   The Preacher

Various reports went undulating through the city as to the nature of
what had taken place in the palace. The people gathered, and stared at
the house, eyeing it as if it had sprung up in the night. But it looked
sedate enough, remaining closed and silent, like a house that was dead.
They saw no one come out or go in. Smoke rose from a chimney or two;
there was hardly another sign of life. It was not for some little time
generally understood that the highest officers of the crown as well as
the lowest menials of the palace had been dismissed in disgrace: for
who was to recognize a lord chancellor in his night-shirt, and what lord
chancellor would, so attired in the street, proclaim his rank and office
aloud? Before it was day most of the courtiers crept down to the river,
hired boats, and betook themselves to their homes or their friends in
the country. It was assumed in the city that the domestics had been
discharged upon a sudden discovery of general and unpardonable
peculation; for, almost everybody being guilty of it himself, petty
dishonesty was the crime most easily credited and least easily passed
over in Gwyntystorm.

Now that same day was Religion day, and not a few of the clergy,
always glad to sieze on any passing event to give interest to the dull and
monotonic grind of their intellectual machines, made this remarkable
one the ground of discourse to their congregations. More especially
than the rest, the first priest of the great temple where was the royal
pew, judged himself, from his relation to the palace, called upon to
'improve the occasion' – for they talked ever about improvement at
Gwyntystorm, all the time they were going downhill with a rush.

The book which had, of late years, come to be considered the most
sacred, was called *The Book of Nations*, and consisted of proverbs, and
history traced through custom: from it the first priest chose his text;

and his text was 'Honesty is the best policy.' He was considered a very eloquent man, but I can offer only a few of the larger bones of his sermon. The main proof of the verity of their religion, he said, was, that things always went well with those who professed it; and its first fundamental principle, grounded in inborn invariable instinct, was, that every One should take care of that One. This was the first duty of Man. If every one would but obey this law, number one, then would every one be perfectly cared for – one being always equal to one. But the faculty of care was in excess of need, and all that overflowed, and would otherwise run to waste, ought to be gently turned in the direction of one's neighbour, seeing that this also wrought for the fulfilling of the law, inasmuch as the reaction of excess so directed was upon the director of the same, to the comfort, that is, and well-being of the original self. To be just and friendly was to build the warmest and safest of all nests, and to be kind and loving was to line it with the softest of all furs and feathers, for the one precious, comfort-loving self there to lie, revelling in downiest bliss. One of the laws therefore most binding upon men because of its relation to the first and greatest of all duties, was embodied in the proverb he had just read; and what stronger proof of its wisdom and truth could they desire than the sudden and complete vengeance which had fallen upon those worse than ordinary sinners who had offended against the king's majesty by forgetting that *Honesty is the best policy?*

At this point of the discourse the head of the legserpent rose from the floor of the temple, towering above the pulpit, above the priest, then curving downwards, with open mouth slowly descending upon him. Horror froze the sermon-pump. He stared upwards aghast. The great teeth of the animal closed upon a mouthful of the sacred vestments, and slowly lifted the preacher from the pulpit, like a handful of linen from a wash-tub, and, on his four solemn stumps, bore him out of the temple, dangling aloft from his jaws. At the back of it he dropped him into the dust-hole amongst the remnants of a library whose age had destroyed its value in the eyes of the chapter. They found him burrowing in it, a lunatic henceforth – whose madness presented the peculiar feature that in its paroxysms he jabbered sense.

Bone-freezing horror pervaded Gwyntystorm. If their best and wisest were treated with such contempt, what might not the rest of them look for? Alas for their city! their grandly respectable city! their loftily reasonable city! Where it was all to end, the Convenient alone could tell!

But something must be done. Hastily assembling, the priests chose a new first priest, and in full conclave unanimously declared and accepted that the king in his retirement had, through the practice of the blackest magic, turned the palace into a nest of demons in the midst of them. A grand exorcism was therefore indispensable.

In the meantime the fact came out that the greater part of the courtiers had been dismissed as well as the servants, and this fact swelled the hope of the Party of Decency, as they called themselves. Upon it they proceeded to act, and strengthened themselves on all sides.

The action of the king's bodyguard remained for a time uncertain. But when at length its officers were satisfied that both the master of the horse and their colonel were missing, they placed themselves under the orders of the first priest.

Every one dated the culmination of the evil from the visit of the miner and his mongrel; and the butchers vowed, if they could but get hold of them again, they would roast both of them alive. At once they formed themselves into a regiment, and put their dogs in training for attack.

Incessant was the talk, innumerable were the suggestions, and great was the deliberation. The general consent, however, was that as soon as the priests should have expelled the demons, they would depose the king, and, attired in all his regal insignia, shut him in a cage for public show; then choose governors, with the lord chancellor at their head, whose first duty should be to remit every possible tax; and the magistrates, by the mouth of the city marshal, required all able-bodied citizens, in order to do their part towards the carrying out of these and a multitude of other reforms, to be ready to take arms at the first summons.

Things needful were prepared as speedily as possible, and a mighty ceremony, in the temple, in the market-place, and in front of the palace, was performed for the expulsion of the demons. This over, the leaders retired to arrange an attack upon the palace.

But that night events occurred which, proving the failure of their first, induced the abandonment of their second intent. Certain of the prowling order of the community, whose numbers had of late been steadily on the increase, reported frightful things. Demons of indescribable ugliness had been espied careering through the midnight streets and courts. A citizen – some said in the very act of house-breaking, but no one cared to look into trifles at such a crisis – had been seized from behind, he could not see by what, and soused in the river. A well-known receiver of stolen goods had had his shop broken open, and when he came down in the morning had found everything in ruin on the pavement. The wooden image of justice over the door of the city marshal had had the arm that held the sword *bitten* off. The gluttonous magistrate had been pulled from his bed in the dark, by beings of which he could see nothing but the flaming eyes, and treated to a bath of the turtle soup that had been left simmering by the side of the kitchen fire. Having poured it over him, they put him again into his bed, where he soon learned how a mummy must feel in its cerements. Worst of all, in the market-place was fixed up a paper, with the king's own signature, to the effect that whoever henceforth should show inhospitality to strangers, and should be convicted of the same, should be instantly expelled the city; while a second, in the butchers' quarter, ordained that any dog which henceforward should attack a stranger should be immediately destroyed. It was plain, said the butchers, that the clergy were of no use; *they* could not exorcise demons! That afternoon, catching sight of a poor old fellow in rags and tatters, quietly walking up the street, they hounded their dogs upon him, and had it not been that the door of Derba's cottage was standing open, and was near enough for him to dart in and shut it ere they reached him, he would have been torn in pieces.

And thus things went on for some days.

29 Barbara

In the meantime, with Derba to minister to his wants, with Curdie to protect him, and Irene to nurse him, the king was getting rapidly stronger. Good food was what he most wanted, and of that, at least of certain kinds of it, there was plentiful store in the palace. Everywhere since the cleansing of the lower regions of it, the air was clean and sweet, and under the honest hands of the one housemaid the king's chamber became a pleasure to his eyes. With such changes it was no wonder if his heart grew lighter as well as his brain clearer.

But still evil dreams came and troubled him, the lingering result of the wicked medicines the doctor had given him. Every night, sometimes twice or thrice, he would wake up in terror, and it would be minutes ere he could come to himself. The consequence was that he was always worse in the morning, and had loss to make up during the day. This retarded his recovery greatly. While he slept, Irene or Curdie, one or the other, must still be always by his side.

One night, when it was Curdie's turn with the king, he heard a cry somewhere in the house, and as there was no other child, concluded, notwithstanding the distance of her grandmother's room, that it must be Barbara. Fearing something might be wrong, and noting the king's sleep more quiet than usual, he ran to see. He found the child in the middle of the floor, weeping bitterly, and Derba slumbering peacefully in bed. The instant she saw him the night-lost thing ceased her crying, smiled, and stretched out her arms to him. Unwilling to wake the old woman, who had been working hard all day, he took the child, and carried her with him. She clung to him so, pressing her tear-wet radiant face against his, that her little arms threatened to choke him. When he re-entered the chamber, he found the king sitting up in bed, fighting the phantoms of some hideous dream. Generally upon such occasions, although he saw his watcher, he could not dissociate him from the dream, and went raving on. But the moment his eyes fell upon little Barbara, whom he had never seen before, his soul came into them with a rush, and a smile like the dawn of an eternal day overspread his countenance: the dream was nowhere, and the child was in his heart. He stretched out his arms to her, the child stretched out hers to him, and in five minutes they were both asleep, each in the other's embrace. From that night Barbara had a crib in the king's chamber, and as often as he woke, Irene or Curdie, whichever was watching, took the sleeping child and laid her in his arms, upon which, invariably and instantly, the dream would vanish. A great part of the day too she would be playing on or about the king's bed; and it was a delight to the heart of the princess to see her amusing herself with the crown, now sitting upon it, now rolling it hither and thither about the room like a hoop. Her grandmother entering once while she was pretending to make porridge in it, held up her hands in horror-struck amazement; but the king would not allow her to interfere, for the king was now Barbara's playmate, and his crown their plaything.

The colonel of the guard also was growing better. Curdie went often to see him. They were soon friends, for the best people understand each other the easiest, and the grim old warrior loved the miner boy as if he were at once his son and his angel. He was very anxious about his regiment. He said the officers were mostly honest men, he believed, but how they might be doing without him, or what they might resolve, in ignorance of the real state of affairs, and exposed to every misrepresentation, who could tell? Curdie proposed that he should send for the major, offering to be the messenger. The colonel agreed, and Curdie went – not without his mattock, because of the dogs.

But the officers had been told by the master of the horse that their colonel was dead, and although they were amazed he should be buried without the attendance of his regiment, they never doubted the information. The handwriting itself of their colonel was insufficient, counteracted by the fresh reports daily current, to destroy the lie. The major regarded the letter as a trap for the next officer in command, and sent his orderly to arrest the messenger. But Curdie had had the wisdom not to wait for an answer.

The king's enemies said that he had first poisoned the good colonel of the guard, and then murdered the master of the horse, and other faithful councillors; and that his oldest and most attached domestics had but escaped from the palace with their lives – nor all of them, for the butler was missing. Mad or wicked, he was not only unfit to rule any longer, but worse than unfit to have in his power and under his influence the young princess, only hope of Gwyntystorm and the kingdom.

The moment the lord chancellor reached his house in the country and had got himself clothed, he began to devise how yet to destroy his master; and the very next morning set out for the neighbouring kingdom of Borsagrass, to invite invasion, and offer a compact with its monarch.

30 Peter

At the cottage on the mountain everything for a time went on just as before. It was indeed dull without Curdie, but as often as they looked at the emerald it was gloriously green, and with nothing to fear or regret, and everything to hope, they required little comforting. One morning, however, at last, Peter, who had been consulting the gem, rather now from habit than anxiety, as a farmer his barometer in undoubtful weather, turned suddenly to his wife, the stone in his hand, and held it up with a look of ghastly dismay.

'Why, that's never the emerald!' said Joan.

'It is,' answered Peter; 'but it were small blame to any one that took it for a bit of bottle glass!'

For, all save one spot right in the centre, of intensest and most brilliant green, it looked as if the colour had been burnt out of it.

'Run, run, Peter!' cried his wife. 'Run and tell the old princess. It may not be too late. The boy must be lying at death's door.'

Without a word Peter caught up his mattock, darted from the cottage, and was at the bottom of the hill in less time than he usually took to get half-way.

The door of the king's house stood open; he rushed in and up the stair. But after wandering about in vain for an hour, opening door after door, and finding no way farther up, the heart of the old man had wellnigh failed him. Empty rooms, empty rooms! – desertion and desolation everywhere.

At last he did come upon the door to the tower-stair. Up he darted. Arrived at the top, he found three doors, and, one after the other, knocked at them all. But there was neither voice nor hearing. Urged by his faith and his dread, slowly, hesitatingly, he opened one. It revealed a bare garret-room, nothing in it but one chair and one spinning-wheel. He closed it, and opened the next – to start back in terror, for he saw nothing but a great gulf, a moonless night, full of stars, and, for all the stars, dark, dark! – a fathomless abyss. He opened the third door, and a rush like the tide of a living sea invaded his ears. Multitudinous wings flapped and flashed in the sun, and, like the ascending column from a volcano, white birds innumerable shot into the air, darkening the day with the shadow of their cloud, and then, with a sharp sweep, as if bent sideways by a sudden wind, flew northward, swiftly away, and vanished. The place felt like a tomb. There seemed no breath of life left in it. Despair laid hold upon him; he rushed down thundering with heavy feet. Out upon him darted the housekeeper like an ogress-spider, and after her came her men; but Peter rushed past them, heedless and careless – for had not the princess mocked him? – and sped along the road to Gwyntystorm. What help lay in a miner's mattock, a man's arm, a father's heart, he would bear to his boy.

Joan sat up all night waiting his return, hoping and hoping. The mountain was very still, and the sky was clear; but all night long the miner sped northwards, and the heart of his wife was troubled.

31   The Sacrifice

Things in the palace were in a strange condition: the king playing with a child and dreaming wise dreams, waited upon by a little princess with the heart of a queen, and a youth from the mines, who went nowhere, not even into the king's chamber without his mattock on his shoulder and a horrible animal at his heels; in a room near by the colonel of his guard, also in bed, without a soldier to obey him; in six other rooms, far apart, six miscreants, each watched by a beast-jailer; ministers to them all, an old woman, a young woman, and a page; and in the wine-cellar, forty-three animals, creatures more grotesque than ever brain of man invented. None dared approach its gates, and seldom one issued from them.

All the dwellers in the city were united in enmity to the palace. It swarmed with evil spirits, they said; whereas the evil spirits were in the city, unsuspected. One consequence of their presence was that, when the rumour came that a great army was on the march against Gwyntystorm, instead of rushing to their defences, to make new gates, free portcullises and drawbridges, and bar the river, each and all flew to their treasures, burying them in their cellars and gardens, and hiding them behind stones in their chimneys; and, next to rebellion, signing an invitation to His Majesty of Borsagrass to enter at their open gates, destroy their king, and annex their country to his own.

The straits of isolation were soon found in the palace: its invalids were requiring stronger food, and what was to be done? for if the butchers sent meat to the palace, was it not like enough to be poisoned? Curdie said to Derba he would think of some plan before morning.

But that same night, as soon as it was dark, Lina came to her master, and let him understand she wanted to go out. He unlocked a little private postern for her, left it so that she could push it open when she returned, and told the crocodile to stretch himself across it inside. Before midnight she came back with a young deer.

Early the next morning the legserpent crept out of the wine-cellar, through the broken door behind, shot into the river, and soon appeared in the kitchen with a splendid sturgeon. Every night Lina went out hunting, and every morning Legserpent went out fishing, and both invalids and household had plenty to eat. As to news, the page, in plain clothes, would now and then venture out into the market-place, and gather some.

One night he came back with the report that the army of the King of Borsagrass had crossed the border. Two days after, he brought the news that the enemy was now but twenty miles from Gwyntystorm.

The colonel of the guard rose, and began furbishing his armour — but gave it over to the page, and staggered across to the barracks, which were in the next street. The sentry took him for a ghost or worse, ran into the guard-room, bolted the door, and stopped his ears. The poor colonel who was yet hardly able to stand, crawled back despairing.

For Curdie, he had already, as soon as the first rumour reached him, resolved, if no other instructions came, and the king continued unable to give orders, to call Lina and the creatures, and march to meet the enemy. If he died, he died for the right, and there was a right end of it. He had no preparations to make, except a good sleep.

He asked the king to let the housemaid take his place by His Majesty that night, and went and lay down on the floor of the corridor, no farther off than a whisper would reach from the door of the chamber. There, with an old mantle of the king's thrown over him, he was soon fast asleep.

Somewhere about the middle of the night, he woke suddenly, started to his feet, and rubbed his eyes. He could not tell what had waked him. But could he be awake, or was he not dreaming? The curtain of the king's door, a dull red ever before, was glowing a gorgeous, a radiant purple; and the crown wrought upon it in silks and gems was flashing as if it burned! What could it mean? Was the king's chamber on fire? He darted to the door and lifted the curtain. Glorious terrible sight!

A long and broad marble table, that stood at one end of the room, had been drawn into the middle of it, and thereon burned a great fire,

In the midst of the roses lay the King,
moaning, but motionless

of a sort that Curdie knew – a fire of glowing, flaming roses, red and white. In the midst of the roses lay the king, moaning, but motionless. Every rose that fell from the table to the floor, someone, whom Curdie could not plainly see for the brightness, lifted and laid burning upon the king's face, until at length his face was too covered with the live roses, and he lay all within the fire, moaning still, with now and then a shuddering sob. And the shape that Curdie saw and could not see wept over the king as he lay in the fire, and often she hid her face in handfuls of her shadowy hair, and from her hair the water of her weeping dropped like sunset rain in the light of the roses. At last she lifted a great armful of her hair, and shook it over the fire, and the drops fell from it in showers, and they did not hiss in the flames, but there arose instead as it were the sound of running brooks. And the glow of the red fire died away, and the glow of the white fire grew grey, and light was gone, and on the table all was black – except the face of the king, which shone from under the burnt roses like a diamond in the ashes of a furnace.

Then Curdie, no longer dazzled, saw and knew the old princess. The room was lighted with the splendour of her face, of her blue eyes, of her sapphire crown. Her golden hair went streaming out from her through the air till it went off in mist and light. She was large and strong as a Titaness. She stooped over the table-altar, put her mighty arms under the living sacrifice, lifted the king, as if he were but a little child, to her bosom, walked with him up the floor, and laid him in his bed. Then darkness fell.

The miner boy turned silent away, and laid himself down again in the corridor. An absolute joy filled his heart, his bosom, his head, his whole body. All was safe; all was well. With the helve of his mattock tight in his grasp, he sank into a dreamless sleep.

He woke like a giant refreshed with wine.

When he went into the king's chamber, the housemaid sat where he had left her, and everything in the room was as it had been the night before, save that a heavenly odour of roses filled the air of it. He went up to the bed. The king opened his eyes, and the soul of perfect health shone out of them. Nor was Curdie amazed in his delight.

'Is it not time to rise, Curdie?' said the king.

'It is, Your Majesty. To-day we must be doing,' answered Curdie.

'What must we be doing to-day, Curdie?'

'Fighting, sire.'

'Then fetch me my armour – that of plated steel, in the chest there. You will find the underclothing with it.'

As he spoke, he reached out his hand for his sword, which hung in the bed before him, drew it, and examined the blade.

'A little rusty!' he said, 'but the edge is there. We shall polish it ourselves to-day – not on the wheel. Curdie, my son, I wake from a troubled dream. A glorious torture has ended it, and I live. I know not well how things are, but thou shalt explain them to me as I get on my armour. No, I need no bath. I am clean. Call the colonel of the guard.'

In complete steel the old man stepped into the chamber. He knew it not, but the old princess had passed through his room in the night.

'Why, Sir Bronzebeard!' said the king, 'you are dressed before me! Thou needest no valet, old man, when there is battle in the wind!'

'Battle, sire!' returned the colonel. 'Where then are our soldiers?'

'Why, there, and here,' answered the king, pointing to the colonel first, and then to himself. 'Where else, man? The enemy will upon us ere sunset, if we be no upon him ere noon. What other thing was in thy brave brain when thou didst don thine armour, friend?'

'Your Majesty's orders, sire,' answered Sir Bronzebeard.

The king smiled and turned to Curdie.

'And what was in thine, Curdie – for thy first word was of battle?'

'See, Your Majesty,' answered Curdie; 'I have polished my mattock. If Your Majesty had not taken the command, I would have met the enemy at the head of my beasts, and died in comfort, or done better.'

'Brave boy!' said the king. 'He who takes his life in his hand is the only soldier. Thou shalt head thy beasts to-day. Sir Bronzebeard, wilt thou die with me if need be?'

'Seven times, my king,' said the colonel.

'Then shall we win this battle!' said the king. 'Curdie, go and bind securely the six, that we lose not their guards. Canst thou find us a horse, think'st thou, Sir Bronzebeard? Alas! they told us our white charger was dead.'

'I will go and fright the varletry with my presence, and secure, I trust, a horse for Your Majesty, and one for myself.'

'And look you, brother!' said the king; 'bring one for my miner boy too, and a sober old charger for the princess, for she too must go to the battle, and conquer with us.'

'Pardon me, sire,' said Curdie; 'a miner can fight best on foot. I might smite my horse dead under me with a missed blow. And besides, I must be near my beasts.'

'As you will,' said the king. 'Three horses then, Sir Brozebeard.'

The colonel departed, doubting sorely in his heart how to accoutre and lead from the barrack stables three horses, in the teeth of his revolted regiment.

In the hall he met the housemaid.

'Can you lead a horse?' he asked.

'Yes, sir.'

'Are you willing to die for the king?'

'Yes, sir.'

'Can you do as you are bid?'

'I can keep on trying, sir.'

'Come, then. Were I not a man I would be a woman such as thou.'

When they entered the barrack yard, the soldiers scattered like autumn leaves before a blast of winter. They went into the stable unchallenged – and lo! in a stall, before the colonel's eyes, stood the king's white charger, with the royal saddle and bridle hung high beside him!

'Traitorous thieves!' muttered the old man in his beard, and went along the stalls, looking for his own black charger. Having found him, he returned to saddle first the king's. But the maid had already the saddle upon him, and so girt that the colonel could thrust no finger-tip between girth and skin. He left her to finish what she had so well begun, and went and graithed his own. He then chose for the princess a great red horse, twenty years old, which he knew to possess every equine virtue. This and his own he led to the palace, and the maid led the king's.

The king and Curdie stood in the court, the king in full armour of silvered steel, with a circlet of rubies and diamonds round his helmet. He almost leaped for joy when he saw his great white charger come in, gentle as a child to the hand of the housemaid. But when the horse saw his master in his armour, he reared and bounded in jubilation, yet did not break from the hand that held him. Then out came the princess attired and ready, with a hunting-knife her father had given her by her side. They brought her mother's saddle, splendent with gems and gold, set it on the great red horse, and lifted her to it. But the saddle was so big, and the horse so tall, that the child found no comfort in them.

'Please, king papa,' she said, 'can I not have my white pony?'

'I did not think of him, little one,' said the king. 'Where is he?'

'In the stable,' answered the maid. 'I found him half starved, the only horse within the gates, the day after the servants were driven out. He has been well fed since.'

'Go and fetch him,' said the king.

As the maid appeared with the pony, from a side door came Lina and the forty-nine, following Curdie.

'I will go with Curdie and the Uglies!' cried the princess; and as soon as she was mounted she got into the middle of the pack.

So out they set, the strangest force that ever went against an enemy. The king in silver armour sat stately on his white steed, with the stones flashing on his helmet; beside him the grim old colonel, armed in steel, rode his black charger; behind the king, a little to the right, Curdie walked aloft, his mattock shining in the sun; Lina followed at his heel; behind her came the wonderful company of

Uglies; in the midst of them rode the gracious little Irene, dressed in blue, and mounted on the prettiest of white ponies; behind the colonel, a little to the left, walked the page, armed in a breastplate, headpiece, and trooper's sword he had found in the palace, all much too big for him, and carrying a huge brass trumpet which he did his best to blow; and the king smiled and seemed pleased with his music, although it was but the grunt of a brazen unrest. Alongside of the beasts walked Derba carrying Barbara – their refuge the mountains, should the cause of the king be lost; as soon as they were over the river they turned aside to ascend the cliff, and there awaited the forging of the day's history. Then first Curdie saw that the housemaid, whom they had all forgotten, was following, mounted on the great red horse, and seated in the royal saddle.

Many were the eyes unfriendly of women that had stared at them from door and window as they passed through the city; and low laughter and mockery and evil words from the lips of children had rippled about their ears; but the men were all gone to welcome the enemy, the butchers the first, the king's guard the last. And now on the heels of the king's army rushed out the women also, to gather flowers and branches, wherewith to welcome their conquerors.

About a mile down the river, Curdie, happening to look behind him, saw the maid, whom he had supposed gone with Derba, still following on the great red horse. The same moment the king, a few paces in front of him, caught sight of the enemy's tents, pitched where, the cliffs receding, the bank of the river widened to a little plain.

33   The Battle

He commanded the page to blow his trumpet; and, in the strength of the moment, the youth uttered a right warlike defiance.

But the butchers and the guard, who had gone over armed to the enemy, thinking that the king had come to make his peace also, and that it might thereafter go hard with them, rushed at once to make short work with him, and both secure and commend themselves. The butchers came on first – for the guards had slackened their saddle-girths – brandishing their knives, and talking to their dogs. Curdie and the page, with Lina and her pack, bounded to meet them. Curdie struck down the foremost with his mattock. The page, finding his sword too much for him, threw it away and seized the butcher's knife, which as he rose he plunged into the foremost dog. Lina rushed raging and gnashing amongst them. She would not look at a dog so long as there was a butcher on his legs, and she never stopped to kill a butcher, only with one grind of her jaws crushed a leg of him. When they were all down, then indeed she flashed amongst the dogs.

Meantime the king and the colonel had spurred towards the advancing guard. The king clove the major through skull and collar-bone, and the colonel stabbed the captain in the throat. Then a fierce combat commenced – two against many. But the butchers and their dogs quickly disposed of, up came Curdie and his beasts. The horses of the guard, struck with terror, turned in spite of the spur, and fled in confusion.

Thereupon the forces of Borsagrass, which could see little of the affair, but correctly imagined a small determined body in front of them, hastened to the attack. No sooner did their first advancing wave appear through the foam of the retreating one, than the king and the colonel and the page, Curdie and the beasts, went charging upon them.

The King and the Colonel and the page,
Curdie and the beasts went charging upon them

Their attack, especially the rush of the Uglies, threw the first line into great confusion, but the second came up quickly; the beasts could not be everywhere, there were thousands to one against them, and the king and his three companions were in the greatest possible danger.

A dense cloud came over the sun, and sank rapidly towards the earth. The cloud moved 'all together,' and yet the thousands of white flakes of which it was made up moved each for itself in ceaseless and rapid motion: those flakes were the wings of pigeons. Down swooped the birds upon the invaders; right in the face of man and horse they flew with swift-beating wings, blinding eyes and confounding brain. Horses reared and plunged and wheeled. All was at once in confusion. The men made frantic efforts to seize their tormentors, but not one could they touch; and they outdoubled them in numbers. Between every wild clutch came a peck of beak and a buffet of pinion in the face. Generally the bird would, with sharp-clapping wings, dart its whole body, with the swiftness of an arrow, against its single mark, yet so as to glance aloft the same instant, and descend skimming; much as the thin stone, shot with horizontal cast of arm, having touched and torn the surface of the lake, ascends to skim, touch, and tear again. So mingled the feathered multitude in the grim game of war. It was a storm in which the wind was birds, and the sea men. And ever as each bird arrived at the rear of the enemy, it turned, ascended, and sped to the front to charge again.

The moment the battle began, the princess's pony took fright, and turned and fled. But the maid wheeled her horse across the road and stopped him; and they waited together the result of the battle.

And as they waited, it seemed to the princess right strange that the pigeons, every one as it came to the rear, and fetched a compass to gather force for the re-attack, should make the head of her attendant on the red horse the goal around which it turned; so that about them was an unitermittent flapping and flashing of wings, and curving, sweeping torrent of the side-poised wheeling bodies of birds. Strange also it seemed that the maid should be constantly waving her arm towards the battle. And the time of the motion of her arm so fitted with the rushes of birds, that it looked as if the birds obeyed her gesture, and she were casting living javelins by the thousand against the enemy. The moment a pigeon had rounded her head, it went off straight as bolt from bow, and with trebled velocity.

But of these strange things others besides the princess had taken note. From a rising ground whence they watched the battle in growing dismay, the leaders of the enemy saw the maid and her motions, and, concluding her an enchantress, whose were the airy legions humiliating them, set spurs to their horses, made a circuit, outflanked the king, and came down upon her. But suddenly by her side stood a stalwart old man in the garb of a miner, who, as the general rode at her, sword in hand, heaved his swift mattock, and brought it down with such force on the forehead of his charger that he fell to the ground like a log. His rider shot over his head and lay stunned. Had not the great red horse reared and wheeled, he would have fallen beneath that of the general.

With lifted sabre, one of his attendant officers rode at the miner. But a mass of pigeons darted in the faces of him and his horse, and the next moment he lay beside his commander. The rest of them turned and fled, pursued by the birds.

'Ah, friend Peter!' said the maid; 'thou hast come as I told thee! Welcome and thanks!'

By this time the battle was over. The rout was general. The enemy stormed back upon their own camp, with the beasts roaring in the midst of them, and the king and his army, now reinforced by one, pusuing. But presently the king drew rein.

'Call off your hounds, Curdie, and let the pigeons do the rest!' he shouted, and turned to see what had become of the princess.

In full panic fled the invaders, sweeping down their tents, stumbling over their baggage, trampling on their dead and wounded, ceaselessly pursued and buffeted by the white-winged army of heaven. Homeward they rushed the road they had come, straight for the borders, many dropping from pure fatigue, and lying where they fell. And still the pigeons were in their necks as they ran. At length to the eyes of the king and his army nothing was visible save a dust-cloud below, and a bird-cloud above.

Before night the bird-cloud came back, flying high over Gwyntystorm. Sinking swiftly, it disappeared among the ancient roofs of the palace.

34   Judgment

The king and his army returned, bringing with them one prisoner only, the lord chancellor. Curdie had dragged him from under a fallen tent, not by the hand of a man, but by the foot of a mule.

When they entered the city, it was still as the grave. The citizens had fled home. 'We must submit,' they cried, 'or the king and his demons will destroy us.' The king rode through the streets in silence, ill-pleased with his people. But he stopped his horse in the midst of the market-place, and called, in a voice loud and clear as the cry of a silver trumpet: 'Go and find your own. Bury your dead, and bring home your wounded.' Then he turned him gloomily to the palace.

Just as they reached the gates, Peter, who, as they went, had been telling his tale to Curdie, ended it with the words:

'And so there I was, in the nick of time to save the two princesses!'

'The *two* princesses, father! The one on the great horse was the housemaid,' said Curdie, and ran to open the gates for the king.

They found Derba returned before them, and already busy preparing them food. The king put up his charger with his own hands, rubbed him down, and fed him.

When they had washed, and eaten and drunk, he called the colonel, and told Curdie and the page to bring out the traitors and the beasts, and attend him to the market-place.

By this time the people were crowding back into the city, bearing their dead and wounded. And there was lamentation in Gwyntystorm, for no one could comfort himself, and no one had any to comfort him. The nation was victorious, but the people were conquered.

The king stood in the centre of the market-place, upon the steps of the ancient cross. He had laid aside his helmet and put on his crown, but he stood all armed beside, with his sword in his hand. He called the people to him, and, for all the terror of the beasts, they dared not disobey him. Those even who were carrying their wounded laid them down, and drew near trembling.

Then the king said to Curdie and the page:

'Set the evil men before me.'

He looked upon them for a moment in mingled anger and pity, then turned to the people and said:

'Behold your trust! Ye slaves, behold your leaders! I would have freed you, but ye would not be free. Now shall ye be ruled with a rod of iron, that ye may learn what freedom is, and love it and seek it. These wretches I will send where they shall mislead you no longer.'

He made a sign to Curdie, who immediately brought up the legserpent. To the body of the animal they bound the lord chamberlain, speechless with horror. The butler began to shriek and pray, but they bound him on the back of Clubhead. One after another, upon the largest of the creatures they bound the whole seven, each through the unveiling terror looking the villain he was. Then said the king:

'I thank you, my good beasts; and I hope to visit you ere long. Take these evil men with you, and go to your place.'

Like a whirlwind they were in the crowd, scattering it like dust. Like hounds they rushed from the city, their burdens howling and raving.

What became of them I have never heard.

Then the king turned once more to the people and said: 'Go to your houses'; nor vouchsafed them another word. They crept home like chidden hounds.

The king returned to the palace. He made the colonel a duke, and the page a knight, and Peter he appointed general of all his mines. But to Curdie he said:

'You are my own boy, Curdie. My child cannot choose but love you, and when you are both grown up – if you both will – you shall marry each other, and be king and queen when I am gone. Till then be the king's Curdie.'

Irene held out her arms to Curdie. He raised her in his, and she kissed him.

'And my Curdie too!' she said.

Thereafter the people called him Prince Conrad; but the king always called him either just *Curdie*, or *My miner boy*.

They sat down to supper, and Derba and the knight and the housemaid waited, and Barbara sat on the king's left hand. The housemaid poured out the wine; and as she poured out for Curdie red wine that foamed in the cup, as if glad to see the light whence it had been banished so long, she looked him in the eyes. And Curdie started, and sprang from his seat, and dropped on his knee, and burst into tears. And the maid said with a smile, such as none but one could smile:

'Did I not tell you, Curdie, that it might be you would not know me when next you saw me?'

Then she went from the room, and in a moment returned in royal purple, with a crown of diamonds and rubies, from under which her hair went flowing to the floor, all about her ruby-slippered feet. Her face was radiant with joy, the joy overshadowed by a faint mist as of unfulfilment. The king rose and kneeled on one knee before her. All kneeled in like homage. Then the king would have yielded her his royal chair. But she made them all sit down, and with her own hands placed at the table seats for Derba and the page. Then in ruby crown and royal purple she served them all.

35 The End

The king sent Curdie out into his dominions to search for men and women that had human hands. And many such he found, honest and true, and brought them to his master. So a new and upright government, a new and upright court, was formed, and strength returned to the nation.

But the exchequer was almost empty, for the evil men had squandered everything, and the king hated taxes unwillingly paid. Then came Curdie and said to the king that the city stood upon gold. And the king sent for men wise in the ways of the earth, and they built smelting furnaces, and Peter brought miners, and they mined the gold, and smelted it, and the king coined it into money, and therewith established things well in the land.

The same day on which he found his boy, Peter set out to go home. When he told the good news to Joan, his wife, she rose from her chair and said: 'Let us go.' And they left the cottage, and repaired to Gwntystorm. And on a mountain above the city they built themselves a warm house for their old age, high in the clear air.

As Peter mined one day by himself, at the back of the king's wine-cellar, he broke into a cavern all crusted with gems, and much wealth flowed therefrom, and the king used it wisely.

Queen Irene – that was the right name of the old princess – was thereafter seldom long absent from the palace. Once or twice when she was missing, Barbara, who seemed to know of her sometimes when nobody else had a notion whither she had gone, said she was with the dear old Uglies in the wood. Curdie thought that perhaps her business might be with others there as well. All the uppermost rooms in the palace were left to her use, and when any one was in need of her help, up thither he must go. But even when she was there, he did not always succeed in finding her. She, however, always knew that such a one had been looking for her.

Curdie went to find her one day. As he ascended the last stair, to meet him came the well-known scent of her roses; and when he opened her door, lo! there was the same gorgeous room in which his touch had been glorified by her fire! And there burned the fire – a huge heap of red and white roses. Before the hearth stood the princess, an old grey-haired woman, with Lina a little behind her, slowly wagging her tail, and looking like a beast of prey that can hardly so long restrain itself from springing as to be sure of its victim. The queen was casting roses, more and more roses, upon the fire. At last she turned and said: 'Now, Lina!' and Lina dashed burrowing into the fire. There went up a black smoke and a dust, and Lina was never more seen in the palace.

Irene and Curdie were married. The old king died, and they were king and queen. As long as they lived Gwyntystorm was a better city, and good people grew in it. But they had no children, and when they died the people chose a king. And the new king went mining and mining in the rock under the city, and grew more and more eager after the gold, and paid less and less heed to his people. Rapidly they sunk towards their old wickedness. But still the king went on mining, and coining gold by the pailful, until the people were worse even than in the old time. And so greedy was the king after gold, that when at last the ore began to fail, he caused the miners to reduce the pillars which Peter and they that followed him had left standing to bear the city. And from the girth of an oak of a thousand years, they chipped them down to that of a fir-tree of fifty.

One day at noon, when life was at its highest, the whole city fell with a roaring crash. The cries of men and the shrieks of women went up with its dust, and then there was a great silence.

Where the mighty rock once towered, crowded with homes and crowned with a palace, now rushes and raves a stone-obstructed rapid of the river. All around spreads a wilderness of wild deer, and the very name of Gwyntystorm has ceased from the lips of men.